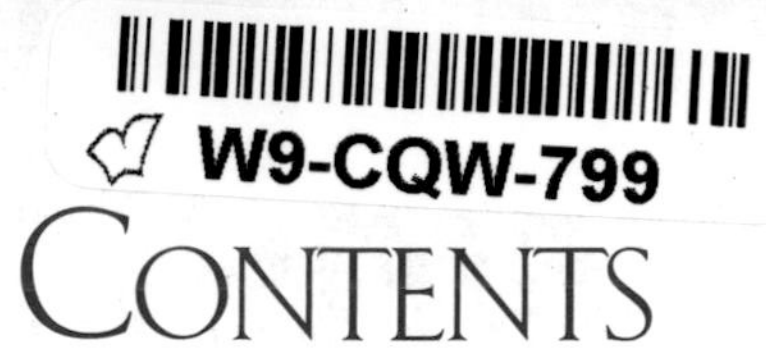

Contents

SELECTIONS

Preface

This is a collection of translations of ancient Greek and Roman sources that we have found suitable for teaching classical mythology at the undergraduate level. In that sense, the title is misleading, but *Anthology of Stuff That Is Connected in One Way or Another with Mythology in the Ancient World* seemed a tad unwieldy to us. It must be stated at the outset that there are literally thousands of pages of such material; we had to choose some five hundred. We have learned from numerous conversations with other instructors that no two are in complete agreement as to what would be most useful. Some colleagues who saw early versions said they would like to have more of the mythographers. Others wanted less of them—although some wanted to replace them with more literary pieces, while still others preferred more ancient interpretations of myth. One commented that the emphasis should lie in the archaic and classical material written in Greek; two days later, an e-mail arrived from another wondering whether there really shouldn't be more of the interesting later material, especially from authors writing in Latin. Even we three editors often disagreed, and there is much material that one of us would have liked to see included, as well as texts that were included over objections.

In the end our goal became an affordable book that would offer a wide variety of sources set around a core of indispensable texts. First and foremost is Hesiod's *Theogony*, which is a mainstay of every syllabus. Next are the *Homeric Hymns*, also central texts. For about the same price as our students were spending to get translations of one of these fundamental books, they now get both, with a bonus of hundreds of pages of additional primary material, some of it rarely seen on syllabi.

Most of the translations in this volume are our own. We aimed at accuracy and clarity above all, though we also tried to ensure that more literary authors retained some of their original style intact. Lucian and Ovid, for instance, should not sound much like each other and nothing like Hyginus or a scholiast's crabbed summary of a mythographer. Wherever the Greek or Latin original depends upon particular language, we have tried to make this obvious in one fashion or another. This has, we trust, helped to keep etymology and wordplay as central to the texts in translation as they were to the ancients reading them. As for translations not our own, it was to our good fortune that Hackett Publishing has an excellent catalog, from which we were able to reprint fine versions of several pieces here.

We decided early on that primary sources deserved pride of place in this book. Our introductions are short but, we hope, useful without limiting the options of instructors. Our brevity here was designed to allow us to include as much primary material as possible, but there are other factors too. In our experience, for instance, students often become wedded to interpretations they take from introductions or modern summaries rather than those gotten from a close reading of the texts themselves or from individual instructors. Notes too have been kept to a minimum, particularly in the case of cross-references (the Index/Glossary usually serves usefully in place of these).

We hope that this volume will fill a long-standing need and that its virtues will come through in day-to-day usage. While it will never satisfy everyone in every way, we think that this collection of texts offers teachers of classical myth more options, flexibility, and variety for their classrooms.

Preface to the Second Edition

The preparation of a second edition of the *Anthology of Classical Myth* allows us the welcome opportunity to introduce a new appendix that includes major excerpts of important and frequently requested comparative material from the ancient Near East. We are pleased to offer major excerpts of the *Epic of Gilgamesh, Atrahasis, Epic of Creation,* and *Genesis*, as well as a brand-new translation of the Hittite *Song of Emergence* by Scott Smith and our colleague, Gregory McMahon, a specialist in the civilization of the Hittites. In order to make room for these texts without substantially increasing the size of the book, we made the difficult decision to remove a number of Hyginus' *Stories* (*Fabulae*). We wanted to minimize the changes that instructors would need to make to their syllabi, so we thought it best to remove a large portion of a single author rather than make numerous deletions from the works of many. Another consideration was that all of Hyginus is readily available in *Apollodorus'* Library *and Hyginus'* Fabulae: *Two Handbooks of Greek Mythology* (Hackett 2007).

We are thankful to Ben Foster, and his publishers CDL Press and W. W. Norton & Company, for allowing us to reprint selections of his translations of *Gilgamesh*, *Atrahasis*, and the Babylonian *Epic of Creation*. We have adapted his scholarly introductions and notes to fit a more general audience. We encourage interested readers to consult the original publications for further insights and bibliography. We are also thankful to our colleague, Gregory McMahon, not only for producing the translation of the Hittite *Song of Emergence*, but also for sharing his expertise with the other Near Eastern materials.

Acknowledgments

We have many people to thank for their support and input, not least Brian Rak and Rick Todhunter, our editors at Hackett, who not only saw the potential in this project but also helped bring it to fruition. Their design and production team handled a complex project with aplomb. The press' proofreader saved us from many a potential error. Many colleagues at other universities read parts of the anthology and commented upon selections. We are grateful in particular to William M. Calder III, Debbie Felton, William Hansen, Gregory Hays, Stanley Lombardo, S. Douglas Olson, and Joel Relihan. Their insight helped us immensely, although we accept full responsibility for our inability to accommodate all of their suggestions, which were often at odds.

The Dean's Office of the College of Liberal Arts here at the University of New Hampshire (UNH) provided funding to each of us in conjunction with this project, as did the University's Center for Humanities. Three weeks for Smith and Trzaskoma in the idyllic setting and excellent library of the Fondation Hardt pour l'étude de l'antiquité classique in Geneva, Switzerland, were vital for completion of the translations. Their visit was made possible partly by financial support from the William A. Oldfather Research Fund at the University of Illinois at Urbana–Champaign.

We also extend our thanks to Richard Clairmont, our colleague in classics at UNH. We and our readers must be grateful to Margaret Russell, who worked many hours helping to compile the raw data behind the index/glossary. And without the goodwill and efficiency of the Interlibrary Loan Office of the Dimond Library this project would have been far more difficult.

The excellent work of other translators also lies between these covers: J. G. Frazer (Pausanias), G. M. A. Grube (Plato, *Republic*, revised by C. D. C. Reeve), A. Lang (*Homeric Hymns*), S. Lombardo (Hesiod), A. Miller (Lyric Poetry), A. Nehamas and P. Woodruff (Plato, *Symposium*), S. Shirley (Herodotus), P. Woodruff (Thucydides), and N. Zeiner (Statius). We were happy to be able to take advantage of the products of the expertise of all these scholars.

Finally, thanks are also due to Laurel Trzaskoma and Kathy Brunet, who perforce were much more a part of this project than they wanted to be.

This volume is dedicated to Richard V. Desrosiers and John C. Rouman, who began the Classics Program at UNH, which we were lucky to inherit. From the 1960s to the late 1990s they educated thousands of students and passed along their love of the classics to every one. We hold Dick and John in the highest esteem and hope that this book goes some way toward showing how grateful we are for all they have done and continue to do for New Hampshire classics.

A Note to Students

WHAT'S IN THIS BOOK?

In ancient Greece and Rome evidence of myth was literally everywhere. It was portrayed in art of all kinds, from the friezes and statues that adorned temples to paintings on decorated vases. Myths were also recounted, discussed, and alluded to in writing of all sorts, from inscriptions engraved in stone recording gifts made to the gods, to songs sung in honor of gods and heroes, tragedies, comedies, philosophical discussions, historical accounts, stories about the constellations in the sky, and even classroom exercises. This book is an attempt to give you some idea of that universal presence of myth in ancient literature and life. To that end we present translations of more than fifty authors who wrote at different times, for different reasons, in both Greek and Latin, from the Greek poet Hesiod in the 7th century BC to the Latin mythographer Fulgentius in the 6th century AD. Although this book contains some famous authors, it also contains many who are unfamiliar to most people today. What it specifically does not do is provide a continuous modern retelling or give you a "complete" picture of what classical mythology was—it should be clear after just a bit of reading in this book that such a task is essentially impossible.

Because of the variety of texts here, it is important to keep some things in mind when using this book. First and foremost, because the Romans adopted and adapted Greek myths to their own purposes, you will sometimes encounter different names for the same character (Greek: Zeus/Latin: Jupiter) or a slightly different spelling of the same name (Medeia/Medea; Heracles/Hercules), depending on whether the particular author wrote in Greek or Latin. You should read the section on Names and Transliteration at the back of the book to familiarize yourself with why there are different spellings for the same person. The Index/Glossary at the back of this book should also easily clear up any questions you have.

Second, you will encounter works written in many styles. While readability and clarity have been our primary goals, we have tried as much as possible to capture the tone and style of a particular work. By nature, then, some texts will be elevated. For instance, the *Homeric Hymns*, all sung in honor of gods, are for the most part lofty and solemn. By contrast, Ovid's poetic letters from mythical women to their lovers are livelier in tone, and Lucian's prose parodies of famous mythical episodes are conversational and humorous. Different again are Hyginus' *Stories*, which, while informative, are straightforward and plain. One of the most basic differences is that between poetic texts (following rules that governed how a line of poetry was formed in Latin or Greek) and works written in prose. Most poetic texts in this book retain the original formats of the originals. Exceptions are the *Homeric Hymns* and the excerpts from Vergil's poems, which, because of their length, have been printed continuously to save space.

Additionally, the authors represented here approached myth very differently and for different purposes. Some were interested in telling a myth in an interesting and often unusual fashion, while some sought to summarize the content of the myths told by authors who had preceded them. Others only mentioned select details of a well-known myth to make a point in a larger context. Some authors were concerned with the search for deeper meanings beyond the literal sense, or for an original truth behind the myths. Many of the texts here do not retell a story, but are instead concerned with the interpretation of myth or engage with myth from a nonmythical perspective.

What this means for you is that using this volume is not like reading a book written by one author. You should expect that the tone, style, and character of your readings will vary greatly. Sometimes you might need to reread part of a passage to catch every nuance. The advantage is that you get to read what the Greeks and Romans wrote about their myths in their own words—or as close as you can get until you learn Greek and Latin (and you know you should!).

Here are some general categories of readings included in this book. This list is meant as a general guide, and the categories are fluid and inexact. For instance, Lucretius, who is listed with the philosophers, conveyed his philosophy through the medium of epic poetry. The *Homeric Hymns* naturally fit into the category of "Early Greek Poetry," but we have put them here under "Hymns" because it is useful to look at them in relation to the work of later poets who were working within the same genre.

Poetry

Early Greek Poetry: Archilochus, Bacchylides, Hesiod, Pindar, Sappho, Semonides, Simonides, Xenophanes, the Epic Cycle (as summarized in Proclus)

—Poetry written from the 7th to the 5th century BC is our earliest source for Greek myth. Hesiod's poems were composed in the meter of epic (dactylic hexameter), which is also found in Homer's *Iliad* and *Odyssey*. Other such epics are now lost to us, but their contents were summarized and preserved by Proclus. The other poets listed here are known as lyric poets because their poems were originally sung to the accompaniment of the lyre. These poets often use myth as inspiration and material for their poems.

Hymns: Callimachus, Cleanthes, *Homeric Hymns*

—Throughout their literary history, the Greeks composed poetic prayers to gods. These give us great insight into the religious life of antiquity and very often include extended mythological narrative. Most were composed in dactylic hexameter, the meter of the great epic poet Homer.

Tragedians: Aeschylus, Critias, Euripides, Sophocles

—The tragic poets of 5th-century Athens based nearly all their dramas on myth. Since the tragedies that survive whole are readily available in English translation, we have included only some fragments of the lost works, including one by Critias, one of the many tragedians of whom we do not have even one complete play.

Other Greek Poets: Babrius, Bion, Theocritus

—These poets are later than the early Greek poets and tragedians, and their poetry is vastly different, but all look to earlier myth for their material. Bion and Theocritus belong to the Hellenistic period (as does Callimachus), which began after the death of

Alexander in 323 BC and was marked by experimentation and a love of novelty. Babrius, who turned Aesop's fables into verse, is much later and only occasionally touches upon myth and religion in his fables.

Latin Poets: Horace, Ovid, Statius, Vergil

—Inspired by the great poetic masterpieces of Greek literature, Roman poets turned their own genius in many directions. The poets Statius and Vergil wrote in epic meter about the exploits of the heroes from past Greek literature, but their sensibilities and purposes were entirely Roman. Although Ovid's mythological masterpiece, the *Metamorphoses*, is not included here (it is readily available in many good translations), his interest in mythology is also apparent in much of his other poetry, particularly the *Heroides*, several of which are in this book. Horace took much of his inspiration and technique from the Greek lyric poets. Like them, he touched upon and incorporated myth into his work.

Prose

Early Greek Mythographers: Acusilaus, Andron, Hellanicus, Herodorus, Pherecydes

—Among the earliest nonpoetic texts in Greece are those of the mythographers, who attempted to synthesize and comment upon earlier mythical traditions. Only fragments of the works of these early mythographers are preserved, mainly in quotations by later authors.

Later Mythical Handbooks: Apollodorus, Antoninus Liberalis, Conon, Hyginus, Parthenius

—Later authors, using earlier literature and the works of the early Greek mythographers, either attempted to synthesize myth into one cohesive account, as Apollodorus did, or collected separate stories into a single work, sometimes dealing with a particular theme, such as Parthenius' collection of love stories or Antoninus Liberalis' summaries of myths about metamorphosis.

Historians and Biographers: Arrian, Diodorus of Sicily, Herodotus, Plutarch, Thucydides

—When the Greeks began to think critically about their past, their historians and biographers had to take into consideration myth, which offered the only evidence of events from the remote past. And because of myth's importance in all aspects of Greek life, historians also used it to interpret and explain events closer to their own time.

Philosophers: Cleanthes, Lucretius, Plato, Prodicus (as paraphrased in Xenophon)

—Myth often arises in philosophical works because myths dealt with some of the same issues with which philosophers were concerned, such as explaining how the world worked, how the cosmos was organized, and how mankind was supposed to act. Some philosophers, such as Plato, even went so far as to create their own myths.

Rationalists and Allegorists: Cornutus, Fulgentius, Heraclitus, Palaephatus, Sallustius

—Many philosophical thinkers believed that myths were not literally true. Instead, they attempted to explain them as normal events that had been distorted or misunderstood (called rationalization) or as stories with different or deeper meanings (called allegory).

Other Greek Prose: Aelian, Eratosthenes, Longus, Lucian, Pausanias, Theophrastus

—Of course, some authors do not easily fit into any category. Each of these incorporates myth and religion into his works differently, depending on topic and purpose, which will be briefly explained in their individual introductions.

SOURCES AND PROBLEMS

So, how do we know about classical myth, given that we are some 2,700 years removed from the earliest full Greek texts? Apart from the artistic representations of myths found on vases, temples, statues, and the like, the primary sources are the various Greek and Latin literary, historical, and philosophic accounts that have survived from antiquity. These literary accounts and discussions of myth are supplemented by additional written evidence discovered by archaeologists. This includes inscriptions that survived because they were written on stone or other durable material, and records written on papyrus (an ancient form of paper) preserved in the dry climate of Egypt. Some archaeological material related to myth is included and discussed in the appendices.

The fact is that we are fortunate to know as much as we do. While this volume may seem to include an immense amount of material (and that does not represent everything that we could have included!), we actually possess only a small fraction of the ancient works that dealt with mythology. The works we are lucky enough to possess were copied by hand repeatedly from the time of the Greeks and Romans through the Middle Ages until the invention of the printing press in the 15th century. In this process of copying, errors occasionally crept in. More important, many works were lost when scribes thought they were not worth copying—especially as the changeover was made in late antiquity from writing on scrolls to producing what we would recognize as books with separate pages (the technical term is a codex)—or when libraries burned or books suffered other disasters.

How much we have lost can be seen by looking at the details surrounding the death of Achilles, the great hero of the Trojan War. You probably know the story that Achilles was invulnerable except on his heel (hence the term Achilles' heel) because his mother had dipped him in the river Styx. What most people do not know, however, is that the Roman epic poet Statius is the first ancient author to mention this story, and he was writing in the 1st century AD, nearly a thousand years after the time of Homer. The Homeric poems do not treat the death of Achilles nor do they give any indication of a special invulnerability. So, although we have several early vase paintings that show Achilles struck in the ankle with an arrow, we do not actually know when the story of his invulnerability arose or what author or authors created it.

So you can see why the reconstruction of a "myth" (as if one and only one version existed!) is so difficult, especially when the sources present so many problems. While some authors or texts survive complete or almost complete, many are lost or only survive in fragments. A fragment is part of a lost work—sometimes as short as one word, sometimes quite lengthy—that has survived through indirect channels. It is worth a few words to discuss how these fragments are passed down to us.

Some survive only because a later writer decided that earlier literature was worth quoting verbatim. If the work was short, an author might quote all of it. For instance, Cleanthes' *Hymn to Zeus*, a hymn making the king of the gods the supreme controller of the cosmos of Stoic philosophy, would have been completely lost if a scholar had not thought it worthwhile to quote the entire poem in the 5th century AD. More typical is the case of the Greek tragedians, where later writers record a speech, a few lines or (all too often) a single word from an otherwise lost play, leaving us to make guesses about the context or where the fragments fit into the plot.

The contents of other works survived, but not in their original form, when ancient scholars summarized or paraphrased works they found interesting. Take, for example, the series of early epic poems that treated the entirety of the Trojan War from its inception to the death of Odysseus at the hands of his son Telegonos. While we have the two complete epics of this cycle, the *Iliad* and *Odyssey*, the many other epics would have been entirely lost if Proclus had not summarized them in the 5th century AD. Similarly, we would have lost the *Stories* of Conon (1st century BC/AD) if the Byzantine scholar Photius had not summarized them in the 9th century AD. Many authors in this volume are only preserved in these condensed summaries termed *epitomes*.

Another way that mythological material has survived is through the ancient equivalent of the footnote. In antiquity, scholars often added notes called *scholia* (singular *scholion*) to texts, but they did so in the margins of texts rather than at the bottom. Often these marginal notes were designed to explain elements of a story that were hard to understand, or to mention interesting or alternate versions of that story. The commentators who wrote these *scholia* had access to texts that are now lost, and so often the quotes and paraphrases in the *scholia* are all we have of certain authors. A case in point is Pherecydes, an early and important Greek mythographer. A commentator on the *Argonautica* of Apollonius of Rhodes (itself a very important work for mythology) sought to elucidate features of the Perseus story by providing extensive quotes from Pherecydes' second book. Without these *scholia* we would know virtually nothing about Pherecydes' discussion of Perseus.

FINAL ADVICE

As you can see, the study of classical myth is a complex task. When you think in terms of "a myth," you must always keep in mind that ancient sources will differ in the manner in which they deal with that myth, and that this situation is made even more difficult by loss or transformation of sources. Versions of a myth found in different authors may also simply contradict one another, often in fundamental ways, as is to be expected from sources that were produced over many centuries, in many places, and by writers from different cultural settings. One more thing to remember at all times is that the ancients were writing for each other, not for modern audiences. That goes regardless of whether the authors in question are writing to give an overview of a myth, to provide a "fleshed out" literary account, to make a philosophical point, to use the mythical tradition to support an argument about historical or contemporary events, or even to discuss what the nature and uses of myth are in a basic way. What was clear and familiar to that ancient audience may not be so clear to you, so slow down, reread when necessary, and be sure to make use of the tools available to you: the introductions, the glossary in the back, the notes, and your readings outside of this book. Above all, pay attention to the context that your instructor has created. Some readings are pretty transparent, but others are clear only when viewed within a larger framework of material or when set against other readings.

ORGANIZATION AND LAYOUT

You should pay close attention to how this book is organized. Authors are arranged alphabetically. The layout for each follows a standard pattern (refer to diagram below). Following the author's name are the date and whether the selection was written in Latin or Greek. Paying attention to the language will allow you to anticipate whether the names will be spelled according to Latin or Greek practice. Next, we provide an introduction to the author and sometimes separate ones to individual works.

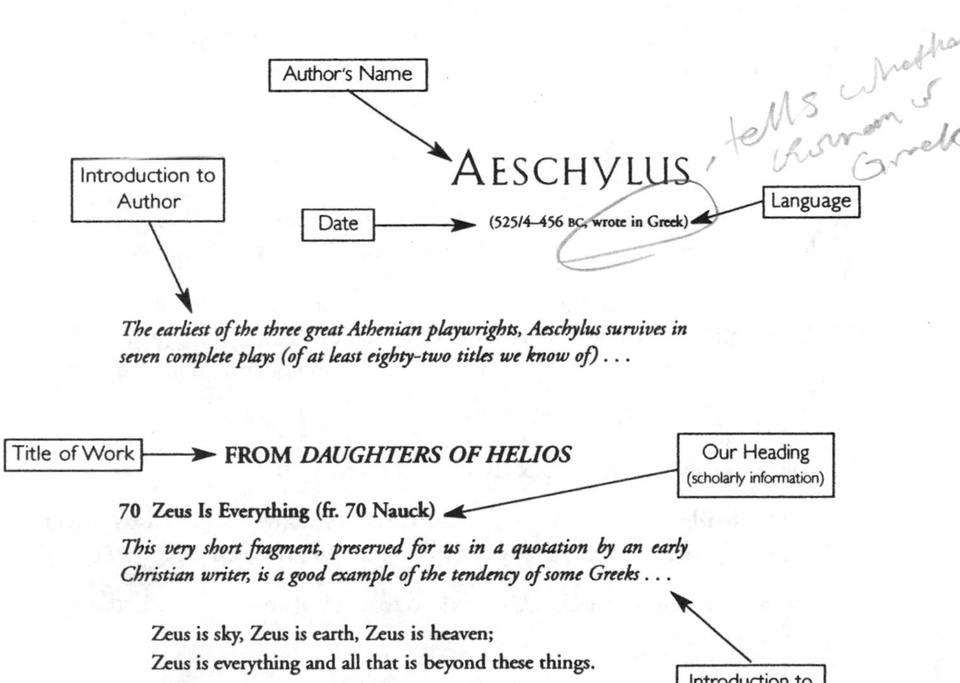

An important feature to note is how the selections are numbered. In the example above, the translation is of what is known to scholars as "fragment 70," and this passage can be referred to as Aeschylus 70 or Aeschylus fr. 70. This system allows your instructor to locate the passage in the original Latin or Greek, and references in other books usually use this format as well. For Apollodorus, the longer *Homeric Hymns,* Pausanias, and Vergil we have used a system of letters to make referring to specific passages easier. These letters are for convenience only and are *not* used outside of this book, though we also give the standard references. You will find gaps in the numbers because we have often not included all the possible selections from an author. So here, for instance, we have not included the fragments numbered 1 through 69.

After the individual authors are four appendices devoted to ancient texts discovered by archaeologists: 1) texts in Linear B, an early Greek writing system found in Bronze Age Mycenaean sites; 2) inscriptional evidence related to myth; 3) papyri of mythological and magical significance; 4) a selection of mythological texts from the Near East, many of which predate the earliest Greek texts and may have inspired Greek myth to some extent.

At the end of the book there is a combined glossary and index of mythological figures. Each entry gives the Latin spelling of a name when it is very different from the Greek, the original Greek spelling, and basic information, and indicates those passages where that character is mentioned. The Index/Glossary is the best place to look if you run across an unfamiliar name in your reading or are trying to find all the authors who mention a particular character.

SYMBOLS FOUND IN TEXTS

You will see different kinds of brackets to signify different types of information added to the translations. Here is a list of them and what they mean:

{ } This marks the addition of etymological and other information (such as the meaning of a name, a translation of a Greek or Latin word, or the original Greek or Latin word), when it is necessary for a full understanding of a passage.

His name was Tauros {"Bull"}.

The name/word Tauros means "Bull" in Greek.

Shepherds raised the boys as their own and named one Zethus because their mother sought {Greek *zetein*} a place to give birth . . .

The author here connects the Greek verb *zetein* ("to seek") with the name *Zethus.*

[ ] This marks material that is thought not to be by the original author.

[Now I recall not only what I am about to endure,
but what any deserted woman could endure.]

Many scholars think this material was added later.

[*italics*] Stage directions and the like (which are our additions and are *not* found in the original texts) are also put into square brackets.

Well, your referee is right here, so let's talk to him. ***[to Paris]*** **Hello to you, cowherd!**

< > Text is missing or scholars have used guesswork to fill in the missing portion. These gaps are due to mistakes made in the copying process or to physical damage to surviving copies. We sometimes comment briefly to give some idea of the damage or problem.

Yes, better to tell how (so that one may not transgress),
< . . . > to see.

Something is clearly missing before "to see" but we cannot guess what.

Will the pointless criticism by men < . . . ***uncertain text*** **. . . >**
never stop criticizing all women . . . ?

Some letters remain but no sense can be made of them.

Ta<ke> them
into the house and lo<ck them in a dung>eon . . .

Words here are partially or completely restored based on what is preserved, context, similar works, and guesswork. When you are reading a passage that is partially reconstructed *it is important that you should not regard such material as absolutely certain. You must use it with caution, particularly when making it the basis of a thesis or argument.*

A Note to Instructors

This book grew from our attempts to assemble a wide variety of primary sources for our own classical mythology courses. We wanted our students to be exposed to sources of different genres, dates, and purposes, and we wanted them to experience those texts with a minimal amount of modern commentary (not least because the three of us often differ in interpretation of or approaches to the texts). Although there is a wealth of material here, this book is not designed to provide the complete readings for such a class, but rather to complement either a selection of major primary sources (essentially our own method now) or one of the major textbooks on classical myth that rely heavily on excerpts of such primary sources (an approach we have used in the past).

The nature of this volume means that some instructors will have questions about how we have used this material ourselves. This is especially true because there is far more here than could ever be used in any single mythology course. Below we try to give some sense of what the volume covers and suggest ways, based on our own experiences, that this material might be used in both large lecture courses and smaller classes. These suggestions do not come close to exhausting all the possibilities, but we hope that this makes obvious one of the benefits we ourselves have observed in using earlier versions: flexibility.

One of our major goals was to put together a set of translations that we ourselves could use to teach from primary sources without making our courses prohibitively expensive. To accomplish this we joined together in one inexpensive volume texts that also appear on many other instructors' syllabi: the *Homeric Hymns* (in our heavily modernized reworking of A. Lang's stately prose translations), S. Lombardo's version of the complete *Theogony* and the opening section of the *Works and Days*, and large excerpts of Apollodorus' *Library*. We decided early on that it would not be productive to excerpt the *Iliad* and *Odyssey*, any of the extant Greek tragedies, Apollonius Rhodius' *Argonautica*, or Ovid's *Metamorphoses*, because of their length and because there are many inexpensive and good translations available. To this core we added dozens of texts of various sorts and dates, from numerous *Stories* of Hyginus to selected *Heroides* of Ovid, all of which we found useful as our own courses evolved. The good folks at Hackett Publishing shared our goal of keeping the price of this book down, so that even instructors who make relatively limited use of more obscure pieces will, we think, find it a bargain.

Of course this volume can also be profitably employed as a supplement to the textbooks commonly used in mythology classes. While there is some overlap in terms of coverage, many of the sources here either complement or fill gaps in the standard textbooks. One quick example: while textbooks often summarize ancient approaches to interpreting myth (euhemerism, rationalism, allegory, philosophical critiques, etc.), passages from our volume, such as Plato's criticism of Homer or Diodorus Siculus' discussion of the origin of the gods, directly illustrate such techniques in practice.

MATERIAL FOR BACKGROUND AND COMPARISON

Many entries were chosen because they provide an overview or important details about major myths or mythical figures. Sometimes these readings can obviate the need to provide a synthetic summary or can help emphasize the ways that a particular author chose to treat a story. Even the addition of a few sources to an existing reading list can go a long way. For example, readings offering differing views of the origin of the Trojan War can help students contextualize the *Iliad*, while those about the myths of Thebes quickly give the background to more literary texts like Sophocles' *Oedipus the King* or Euripides' *Bacchae*. We also found that the selection of material is wide enough to encompass our various and quite different teaching styles and has allowed us to add and subtract readings as our courses change over time.

For example, for some classes Apollodorus' account might represent the bulk of the reading assigned for Heracles. It is comprehensive and is in fact the basis of many modern summaries of his life and exploits.[1] After reading it, a class is well equipped to explore the depiction of Heracles in Greek art and deal with questions such as which labors were more popular with artists, or how the canonical picture of Heracles with club and lion skin developed.[2] On the other hand, other sources used in conjunction with Apollodorus give a broader picture of Heracles, from Hesiod's early view of his labors and immortality to his position as object of divine worship in the *Homeric Hymn to Heracles*, Babrius' *Fable* 20, and an inscription (Appendix Two) detailing regulations for his cult (one may also compare Arrian's report of the Greeks' unwillingness to treat Alexander as a god, which employs Heracles as a precedent). Herodorus and Palaephatus show rationalized accounts of his exploits; Xenophon's paraphrase of Prodicus' *Choice of Heracles* uses the hero as the basis for allegory; Andron's story about the origin of cremation shows him as a culture-bearer.

The *Theogony* is another case where students' comprehension of a text can be enhanced if students read it alongside Apollodorus and other texts. Students can explore the differences between an early poetic work and a late handbook, such as 1) how the creation of Earth and Eros, a central event for Hesiod, is missing from Apollodorus' account, or 2) why their accounts of Aphrodite's birth are so radically different. Students also quickly sense that the issues of justice and of Zeus' unique position among the gods are central concerns for Hesiod but not for the later mythographer. Other authors add new dimensions. Hesiod's treatment of Zeus' primacy is worth

[1] Other mythological figures are similarly well served by Apollodorus, e.g., Jason and Theseus, for whom the accounts in Apollonius Rhodius' *Argonautica* and Plutarch's *Life of Theseus* are too complex to serve as basic readings (although we have included Plutarch's account of the *synoikismos*).

[2] The availability of online resources, notably the Beazley archive and Perseus (which has its own mini–Web site on Heracles that uses images to illustrate what is essentially Apollodorus' account), make Heracles a good choice for projects in which students assess the popularity of particular labors and *parerga*. Other possible art projects that tie in with readings in this volume include having students look for Renaissance images of the judgment of Paris to see if these share Lucian's humorous interpretation, vases that justify Apollodorus' view that giants and other gods born of the earth tend to be snakelike or that Prometheus or, in other traditions, Hephaistos was responsible for freeing Athena from Zeus' head, and Palaephatus' observation (found in Daidalos 21) that statues became more lifelike as Greek art progressed.

comparing with the views of at least five other authors: Aeschylus (fr. 70), Archilochus (fr. 122 and fr. 177), Babrius (*Fable* 68), Cleanthes, and Cornutus.

One short passage that is helpful in teaching tragedy is Aelian's report that Euripides was bribed to portray Medeia as responsible for the death of her children (one may also add Pausanias' account of the tomb of Medeia's children in Corinth). Students can easily grasp how Aelian's testimony relates to our assessment of Euripides' originality as a playwright and how myth may be fundamentally changed by a highly successful dramatic performance—not to mention how it sharpens issues regarding Medeia's moral culpability. We have also included some fragments of the lost plays of Aeschylus, Critias, Euripides, and Sophocles. Useful for those teaching the *Prometheus Bound* is a fragment from the *Prometheus Freed*, while Bellerophontes' indictment of the gods in a Euripidean fragment is illustrative when compared with Euripides' treatment of the gods in his extant works.

The Trojan War represents another good example of how this volume can contribute to students' understanding of the ways that various authors, including but not limited to Homer, reacted and added to the mythic tradition. Proclus' summaries of the poems of the epic cycle and many of Hyginus' *Stories* make clear where the *Iliad* and *Odyssey* fit into the complete story of the war; Vergil's second book gives a detailed account of the Trojan Horse; and Lucian's *Judgment of the Goddesses* trivializes the cause of the war unforgettably. Herodotus' argument that the Trojans would have never kept Helen can be used as a parallel to *Iliad* 3 and 6, raising the issue of whether Homer adequately explained or, at this point in the war, even needed to explain the relationship of Helen and the Trojans. That Helen's culpability was an issue for relatively early commentators on the *Iliad*, as it often is for students, is also apparent from Acusilaus' claim that Aphrodite made Paris fall in love with Helen in order to destroy Priam's family and allow Aineias to become king of the Trojans.

Other selections elucidate myths of the heroes. Statius describes Thetis' attempts to protect Achilles in spite of his own heroic nature (Hyginus 96 provides the background). This contrasts sharply with the Achilles of *Iliad* 9, who questions the value of being a hero and agonizes over whether to continue fighting or to leave Troy. For students reading the *Odyssey* or Sophocles' *Ajax* (or the *Philoctetes* for that matter), a variety of sources reveals a strongly anti-Odyssean tradition. Sophocles (fr. 432) has Nauplios imply that Odysseus destroyed Palamedes because he surpassed him in cleverness (the full story of Palamedes is given in Hyginus 95, 105, and 116). Later sources follow the negative traditions about the hero, notably Conon's description of Odysseus' attempt to kill Diomedes for the Palladion and the selections from Parthenius on Odysseus' seduction of his hosts' daughters. Vergil in his vivid portrayal of a deceitful Ulysses became probably the most influential proponent of the view that Odysseus was a malicious, self-serving schemer.

A feature of the second edition of this book is the addition of several texts from the Ancient Near East (Appendix Four), many of which show interesting parallels with Greek myth. Instructors interested in the wider Mediterranean context can assign these texts on own or may pair them with Greek versions of myth. For instance, the short Hittite *Song of Emergence* could be read alongside Hesiod's *Theogony*, which has numerous points of contact with the Near Eastern text (e.g., the overthrow of a god by castration, the emergence of a supreme Sky God, and perhaps the birth of a god from another god's head). Likewise, the flood myths in the *Epic of Gilgamesh*, *Atrahasis* and *Genesis* could serve as comparanda to the account of the deluge in Apollodorus (E2) or Ovid. Further information can be found in the extensive introduction to Appendix Four, which also includes helpful historical context and a list of important Near Eastern gods.

ANCIENT APPROACHES TO MYTH

Our own teaching has not only concentrated on introducing students to the details of myths, but also to how the Greeks consciously reacted to, commented on, rejected, or sought to explain them. We have found that many readings in this collection are useful in addressing more general questions students have, such as whether the Greeks believed their myths, and in helping students to understand ancient interest in etymology and etiology. These readings also provide excellent opportunities to discuss the similarities between modern and ancient theoretical approaches to interpreting myth.

MYTH AND HISTORY

Since the stories told by poets and other early writers represented the major evidence for the events for which the Greeks had no written records, historians could not escape considering the role of myth in history. One approach—represented here by Herodotus' and Thucydides' analyses of the Trojan, Persian, and Peloponnesian Wars—was to seek to distinguish where myth left off and history began. Other approaches are exemplified by Diodorus' complete historicizing of myth (including one of the finest examples of euhemerism) and Plutarch's consideration of Theseus' role as the historical figure responsible for the unification of Attica. A parallel to the issues faced by ancient historians can be found in the modern debate over the historicity of the *Iliad*. A central question—and one often raised by students—is whether (or to what degree) Homer reflected events centuries before his time; in Appendix 1, Thomas G. Palaima has collected and commented on samples of Linear B texts that record sacrifices to many of the gods mentioned by Homer (a complete list of all gods mentioned in Linear B is also included) and individuals who bore names familiar from Greek epic.

PHILOSOPHICAL, RATIONALIZING, AND ALLEGORICAL APPROACHES TO MYTH

Doubt about whether the stories told by the poets about the gods should be trusted can be traced in a wide variety of authors in this volume, ranging from Xenophanes' complaints about Homer and Hesiod to Plato's attacks on the poets in the *Republic* (as well as the distinction Plato makes, in Protagoras' speech, between *mythos* and *logos*). Yet, we felt it was important to show that such skepticism was not limited to philosophers, but that their concerns resonated with many other writers and had a long history continuing well into the Roman Empire. So early on, Pindar expressed his doubts about the truth that Pelops was served to the gods. Fragments from Euripides and Critias respectively doubt the existence of the gods because they do not punish injustice, and posit that the idea of divine retribution was a human creation required for the growth of civilization. The philosophical rejection of myth can also be seen in Lucretius' Epicurean position that, contrary to what stories like Iphigenia's sacrifice might suggest, the gods did not have a role in human life, as well as in Lucian's relentless ridicule of sacrifice.

The strong trend of rationalizing (both generally and in the specific form of euhemerism), which essentially granted that ordinary events underlay mythological stories but that over time they had been misunderstood or distorted, can also be traced with readings from this volume. Instead of merely learning about these theories, students can read Palaephatus' pointed attack on the credulity of poets, or Diodorus Siculus' account of how the gods were mythologized mortals.

Another major form of interpretation in antiquity, and one that remained influential long after the end of the ancient world, was allegory, which rejected the literal meaning of myths but sought to find in them deeper and greater value. Early examples include interpretation of Heracles' struggles as an allegory of the pursuit of virtue (Prodicus in Xenophon; Herodorus). Later attempts to explain important myths either as moral or physical allegories can be found in Cornutus, Fulgentius, Heraclitus, and Sallustius.

RELIGION AND MYTH

It is beyond the scope of this work—probably of any work—to demonstrate all the connections between religion and myth. We did, however, want to make it clear to students that the gods were very much part of the daily world of the Greeks, not just something the Greeks encountered in literary works. For instance, the selections from Pausanias give students a sense of the degree to which the Greeks were surrounded by statues, wall paintings, engravings, and even features of the natural landscape that recalled the gods and heroes, especially in what we would consider nonreligious contexts. Additional testimony to the role of religion comes from *inter alia*, Aelian's description of the Bouphonia and from Theophrastus' effective description of the superstitious man's fear of pollution. This can inform readings of countless myths, including those in which an individual is forced to leave his home because of an accidental killing (e.g., Bellerophontes [Apollodorus I], Patroclos [Hellanicus 145], Heracles [Apollodorus K2, K15]), and the stories of Apollo's period of enslavement to Admetos.

Furthermore, the rationale for several other rituals and religious customs is given in mythological terms by Andron, Hellanicus 125, Hyginus 130, and, of course, in the *Homeric Hymn to Demeter*. Callimachus and Bion both demonstrate how ritual could be the source of artistic inspiration. Actual religious (and magical) practices can also be illustrated by the inscriptions and papyri in the appendices. Several inscriptions involving dedications can be used to show the practical expression of the *do ut des* principle in Greek religion. Asclepios' relatively minor role in myth can be compared to his central importance in Epidauros (as inscriptions and Pausanias G show). The spells recorded in papyri sometimes invoke the power of the gods in ways that explicitly recall stories that will be familiar to students from their other readings. Also interesting is the documentary evidence of the Linear B tablets in Appendix One, which shows among other things that Dionysos definitely was not a late arrival to the Greek pantheon, despite the impression given by many myths.

GENDER AND SEXUALITY

Mythology provides one of the best avenues for examining ancient attitudes toward women and, more broadly, gender in antiquity, and we have tried to make it possible to explore this subject in several different ways. A wide range of sources—Sappho on the power of Aphrodite, a fragment from Aeschylus in which Europa tells her story, Procne's complaints about the life of women from Sophocles, Pasiphae's and Melanippe's defense of themselves in fragments from Euripides, a Hellenistic papyrus giving a lament from Helen to Menelaus, and the letters Ovid composed from Penelope, Briseis, Phaedra, Ariadne, and Medea to the men they love (*Heroides* 1, 3, 4, 10, 12)—give women a voice and allow them to tell their side of the story. Except for Sappho's poem, these passages, of course, represent the feminine voice as imagined by male authors. This feature naturally leads to interesting discussions as to whether male authors could adequately capture women's views and why they would even have been interested in putting such views forward in the first place.

There are also those myths in which characters violate the traditional gender roles. The prime example are the Amazons, whose assumption of the roles of warrior and leader was considered such an aberration by Diodorus Siculus and Palaephatus that they tried to explain the Amazons away as either having lived long in the past or never at all. On the other hand, Apollodorus is more accepting of the existence of Amazons in his account of Heracles and Hippolyte. Procris and Leucippe are two examples of women who do not so much take on men's roles but simply pretend to be men, with the implication that they could not live their lives as freely as they wanted as women (Antoninus Liberalis 41). The most obvious case of a man who breaks gender barriers by dressing and living as a woman is Statius' account of Achilles in drag.

Negative views of women are also represented here. Attacks on the female gender in Greek literature date back to Hesiod's two versions of the Pandora story, both of which are included in this volume, as is Semonides' poem on the different types of women. A contrasting example can be found in a fragment of Euripides in which Melanippe argues that the longstanding primacy of women should not be forgotten, especially in religious matters. Students will find support for this claim in the inscriptions in the appendices that document women's religious activities.

Some passages in this book also can be used to explore Greek attitudes toward sexuality. Heracles' love of Hylas (Antoninus Liberalis 26), Apollo's pursuit of Hyacinthos (Lucian *Dialogue of the Gods* 16), Zeus' rape of Ganymedes (*Homeric Hymn 5 to Aphrodite*), Laius' rape of Chrysippus (Hyginus 85), Aristophanes' tale in the *Symposium* about the creation of the sexes, and a papyrus listing the boys loved by the gods (Appendix Three)—all can be used to discuss homosexuality. One can also discuss the violence inherent in the sexual relationships between gods and mortals depicted in myth, e.g., whether the Io story (Apollodorus H) reflects in some way the experience of young girls on their marriage night. Students then would not be surprised that some girls in the world of myth avoid growing up and losing their virginity: prime examples are Atalante (Aelian 13.1), Echo (Longus 3.23), and Daphne (Parthenius 15). The common assumption among Greek literary authors (medical writers did not necessarily agree) that women were more interested in sex than men is testified to by the story of Teiresias' judgment (Hyginus 75, Apollodorus M8) and indirectly by the two cases of the Potiphar's Wife motif, in which older women cannot control their lust for younger men: Stheneboia for Bellerophontes (Apollodorus I; Hyginus 57), and Phaedra for Hippolytus (Ovid 4).

MYTH AS A SOURCE OF INSPIRATION

Many selections testify to the continuing inspiration that artists found in well-known stories. Parthenius' introduction clearly reveals that the mining of mythology for subject matter was a deliberate and accepted process among poets. Lucian's take on tales such as Hera's problems with Ixion reveals that many stories can be quite humorous, an approach to which students relate well and one that is familiar to them if they have read the *Homeric Hymn to Hermes*, Aristophanes' speech about the nature of Eros from the *Symposium*, or Theocritus' depiction of Polyphemos as a country hick besotted with love. There are many opportunities to explore mythological works that exhibit great poetic skill and charm, such as Horace's *Ode to Mercury*. Students who have studied Hermes may be asked to evaluate what Horace was trying to do, thereby gaining a greater appreciation of Horace's achievement as a poet and not merely as a conveyer of a myth. A project that drives home the challenge faced by poets who treat a well-worn story in a novel way is to ask students to write their own poem on a mythological subject.[3] Having students analyze modern poems that draw their subject matter from ancient myth—e.g., Ronald Bottrall's *Hermes*, which seeks, like Horace's poem, to capture Hermes' various roles, or Jorge Luis Borges' *The Labyrinth*, which gives voice to the Minotaur as Ovid did for the heroines of myth—can also serve to heighten students' sense of the enduring interest in myth.[4]

MATERIAL FOR MODERN INTERPRETATION AND CLASSIFICATION OF MYTH

The sheer amount of raw material here (and the variety of genres, approaches, and

[3] One of our colleagues here at UNH has had good success with having students write their own poems modeled on the *Heroides* (in English, of course). They respond well to Ovid's ironic tone, and through this project he is able to teach them some of the fundamentals of English versification.

[4] For collections of modern poetry on themes drawn from Greek mythology, see N. Kossman (ed.), *Modern Poems on Classical Myths,* Oxford Univ. Press 2001 (includes the two poems cited here); D. DeNicola (ed.), *Orpheus & Company: Contemporary Poems on Greek Mythology,* Univ. of New England Press 1999.

dates) will be helpful for instructors who have their students employ modern theoretical tools to analyze or classify myths. Extended portions of Apollodorus and Hyginus, as well as selections from other ancient mythographers, can be particularly useful both in dealing with the general concept of mutability and transmission of myths, and in establishing the details of specific variations. Students can also associate particular myths with terminology, rather than learning such things in the abstract.

Likewise, there is much here for instructors who like to emphasize recurrent elements in myth, whether because such elements may reflect constants of human psychology or because they can be used to introduce students to the theories of Propp and others. The following list is *exempli gratia* and does not seek to be comprehensive:

Incest, intentional or not: Smyrna and Cinyras (Antoninus Liberalis 34); Harpalyce and Clymenus (Parthenius 13); Thyestes and Pelopia (Hyginus 88); Oidipous and Iocaste (Apollodorus M6); Lucian on Zeus and Hera (*Sacrifices* 5).

Bride won in tournament: Iole (Apollodorus K15); Deianeira (Apollodorus K19, Sophocles fr. 1130 [perhaps Atalante]); Hippodameia (Pindar *Olympian* 1, Hyginus 84).

Exposed children: Telephos (Apollodorus K18); Oidipous (Apollodorus M6, Hyginus 66); Atalante (Aelian 13.1); Amphion and Zethos (Apollodorus M5); Paris (Hyginus 91), Asclepius (Pausanias G); Perseus (Apollodorus J1, Pherecydes 10, Simonides); Aegisthus (Hyginus 88); Leucippos (Antoninus Liberalis 17).

Mortals rejecting Dionysos: Lycourgos (Apollodorus M4); Pentheus (Apollodorus M4); the Minyades (Antoninus Liberalis 10); the Athenians (Hyginus 130); Tyrrhenian pirates (*Homeric Hymn* 7).

PRACTICAL CONSIDERATIONS

On a more practical note, we attempted to make it easy for instructors on their syllabi to refer to the readings in this book. Except in rare occasions they can be cited by author and number, e.g., Hyginus 120. If possible the numbering for authors corresponds to the numbering of the standard text, e.g., the fragments of Aeschylus are numbered according to Nauck. For some authors, as in the case of Apollodorus, the standard numbering system did not divide passages into manageable sections, and we have added letters and occasionally section titles (the standard numbering is also always given). Finally, we have tried to make the entries comprehensible to students by providing brief introductions that place the readings in context and by adding explanations of Greek terms and the like in the text. We have tried to keep interpretation to the minimum since the significance of many of the readings is subject to debate and any analysis we might give would stand in the way of students discovering the meaning of particular myths for themselves. The exception is the archaeological material contained in the appendices. We felt that the Linear B tablets, inscriptions, and papyri included there require more commentary than the literary texts if they are to be readily comprehensible.

To help students make the best use of this volume we have included a separate introduction explaining how this volume is laid out, along with giving some information about how the texts of ancient authors were transmitted. It will probably be helpful to point out the Index/Glossary to which students can refer if they encounter an unfamiliar name since the index includes a brief glossary for important characters and terms in the volume. The Index/Glossary also lists the passages in which these are mentioned, making it a useful tool for students to locate parallel passages when writing papers and doing class projects. The index can also be very helpful when one is planning assignments and is trying to ensure a particular hero or myth is covered properly. For the same reason the Contents is quite full and often gives an indication of which myth a particular source covers.

FINAL REMARKS

Our hope, a hope borne of our own experience, is that this volume will be a great aid to instructors who have felt, as we long did, that they could provide their students with a much better picture of classical mythology if they had access to a wider range of sources in an accessible and inexpensive format. Moreover, we anticipate that this volume will make it much easier to show students that the study of classical mythology is much more complex, yet much more fruitful, than they may have thought. And, in the end they may appreciate that a full understanding of the role of myth in ancient society depends very much on harnessing the results of the many disciplines—literary, historical, and archaeological—that make up the field of classics.

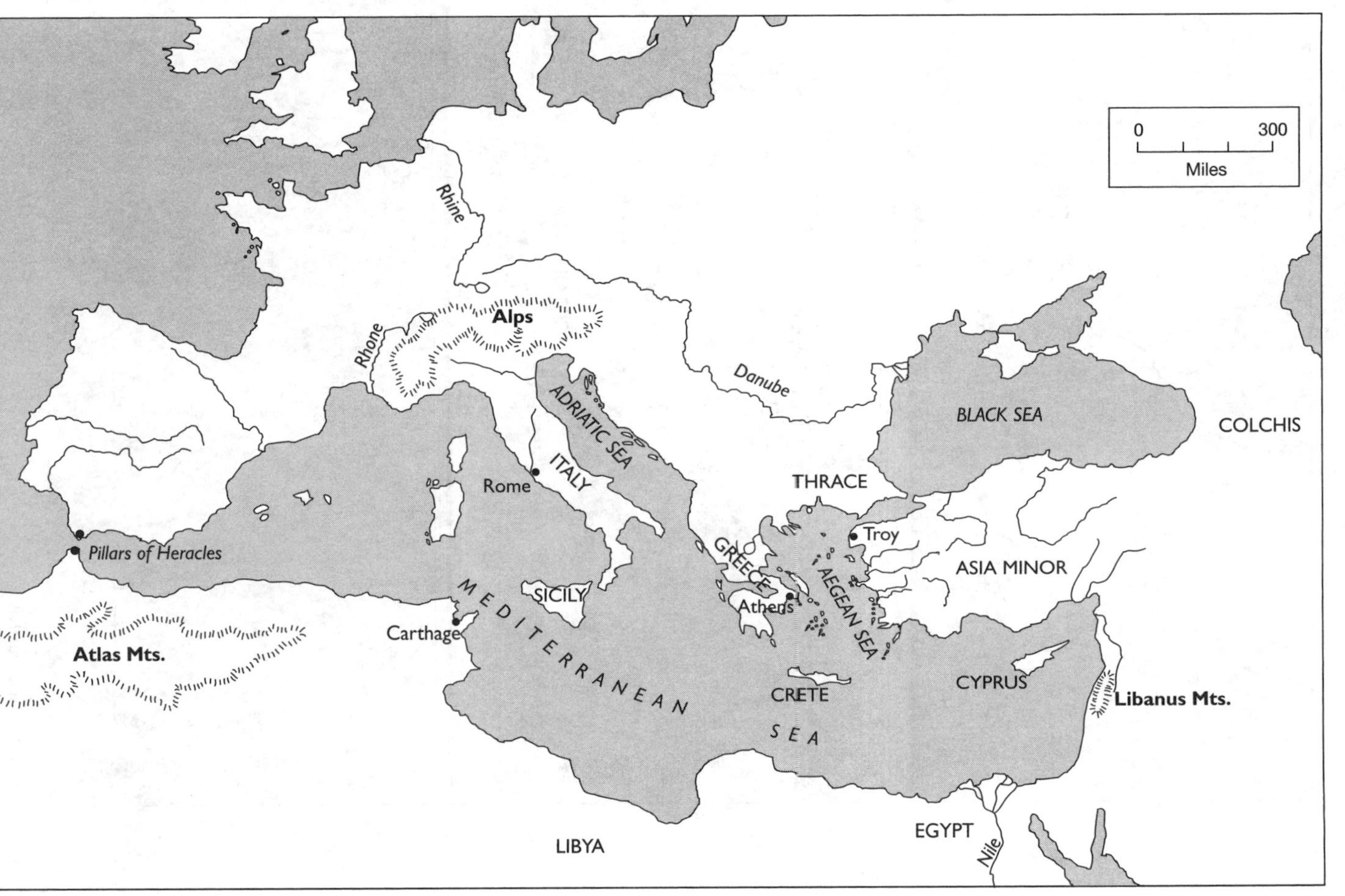

The Mediterranean World

Homeric Geography

CICONIA
THRACE
BOSPOROS
PAPHLAGONIA
THRACE
HELLESPONT
Abydos
Troy
PHRYGIA
TENEDOS
CILICIA
MYSIA
LESBOS
MAEONIA
CHIOS
SAMOS
DELOS
CARIA
Xanthus R.
COS
SYME
LYCIA
RHODES
Sestos
Percote
Arisbe
Abydos
Simois R.
Troy
Scamander R.
Mt. Ida
Lyrnessus
Thebe
Larissa
Chryse
0 5 10 15 20 25 30
miles

Mainland Greece and Its Environs

BLACK SEA
THRACE
BOSPOROS
PROPONTIS
THASOS
SAMOTHRACE
HELLESPONT
PHRYGIA
Troy
LEMNOS
TENEDOS
MYSIA
AEOLIS
LESBOS
AEGEAN SEA
SCYROS
LYDIA
CHIOS
IONIA
Ephesos
SAMOS
Miletos
CARIA
DELOS
NAXOS
RHODES
CRETE
Cnossos

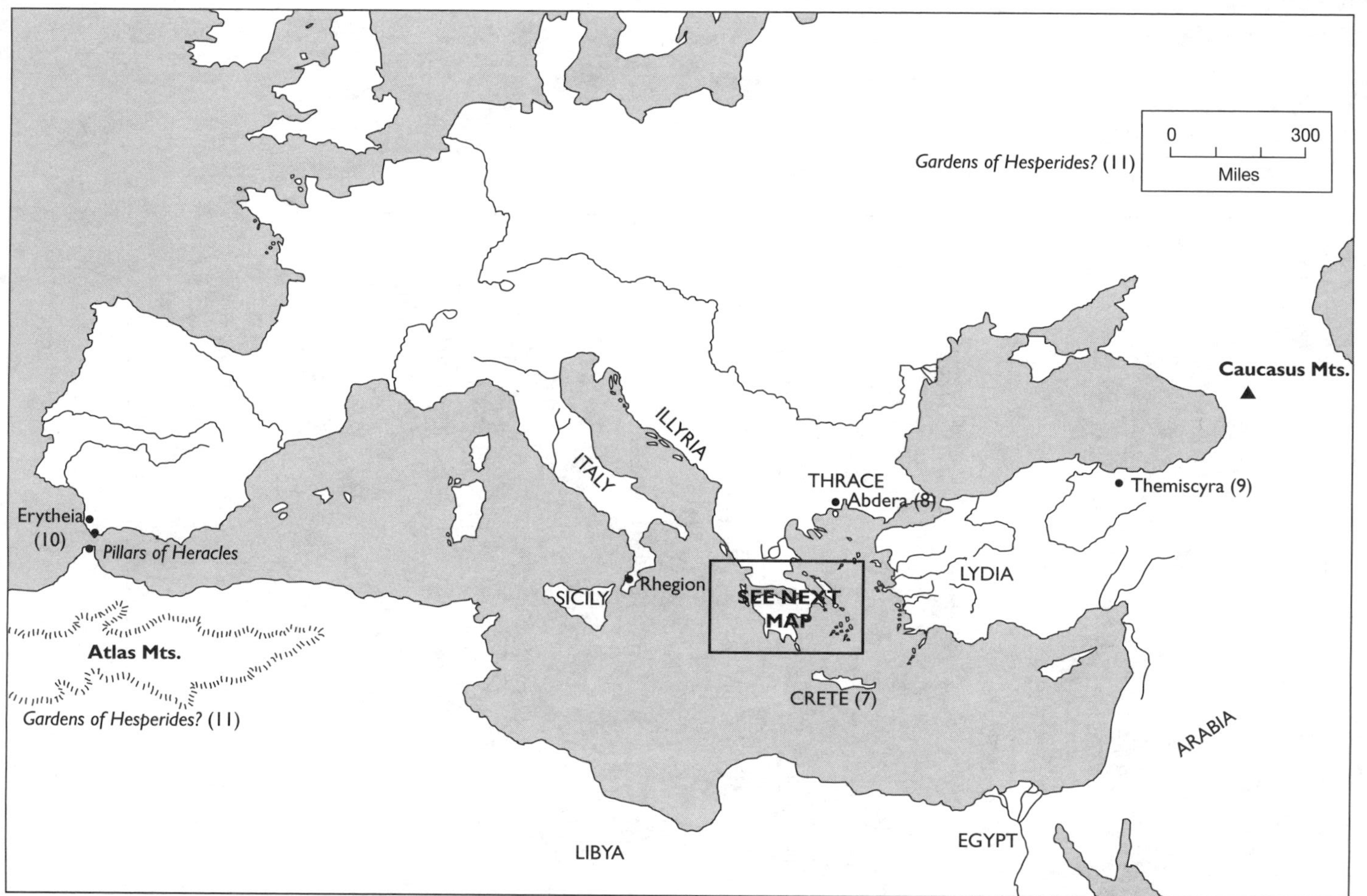

Heracles (numbers in this map and the next correspond to the Labors of Heracles)

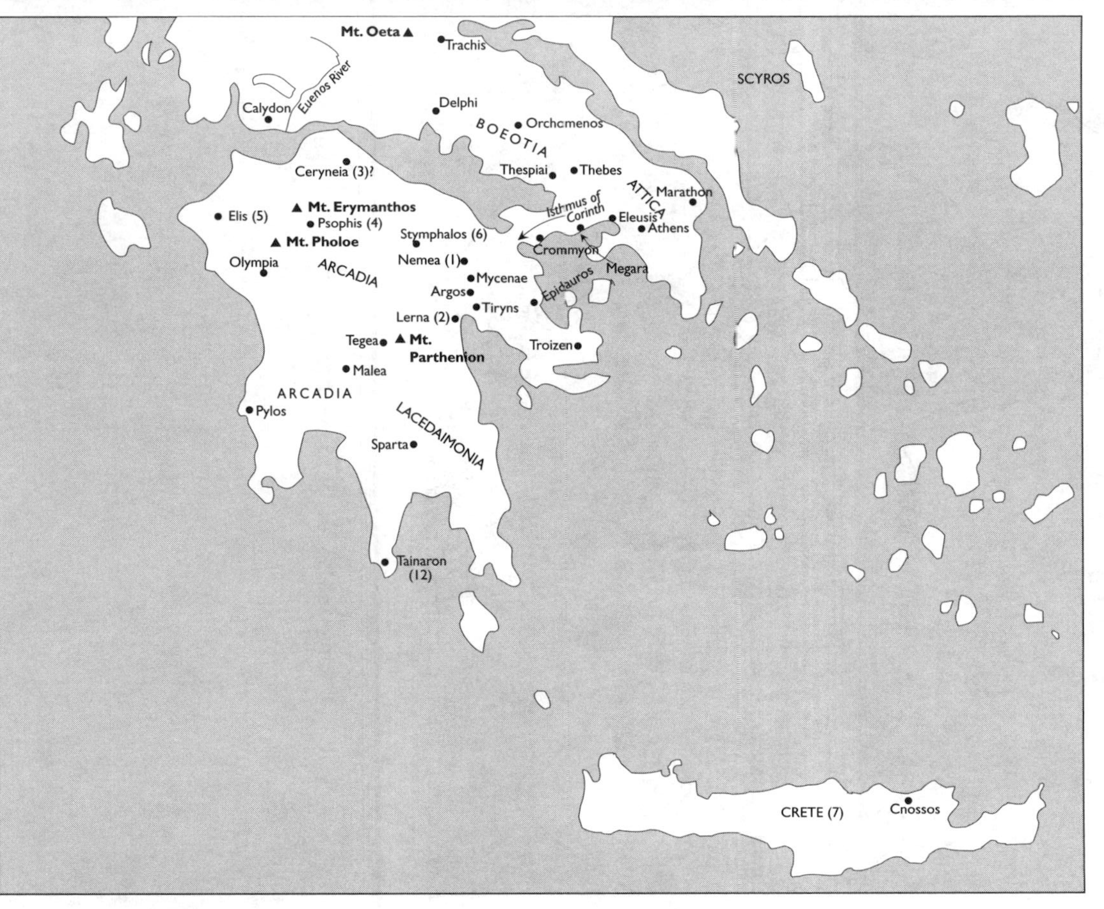

Heracles and Theseus

Early Greek View of the World

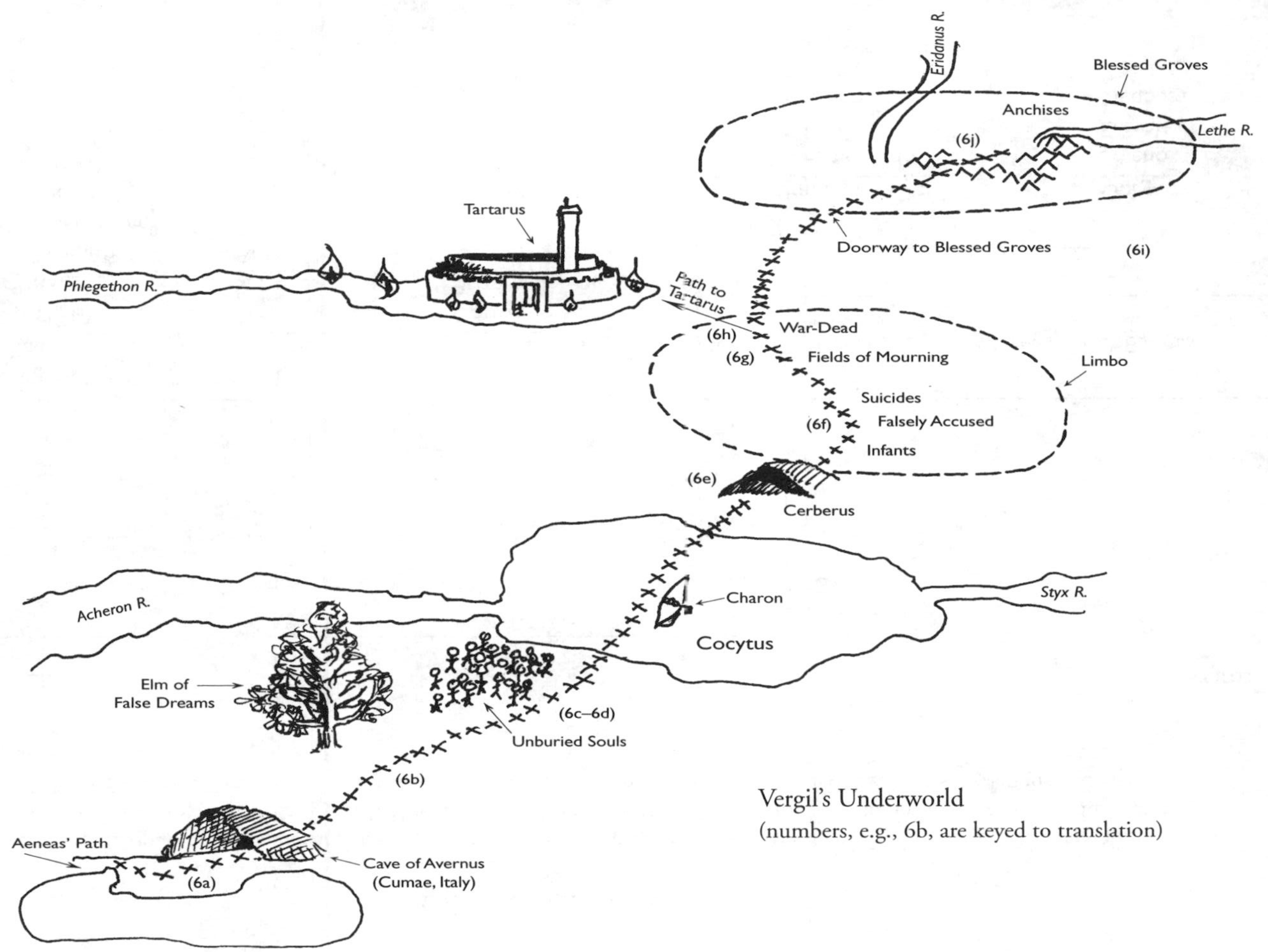

Vergil's Underworld
(numbers, e.g., 6b, are keyed to translation)

GENEALOGICAL CHARTS

The superscript numerals following different character names represent crossreferences to other charts. Appearances of Zeus in these charts (see 2, 4, 5, 8a–f, 9, 12, 15–18, 20, 21, 22) are so frequent that they have not been noted. Apollodorus and Hesiod have been favored over other sources but absolute consistency cannot be achieved given the variations and gaps in ancient sources.

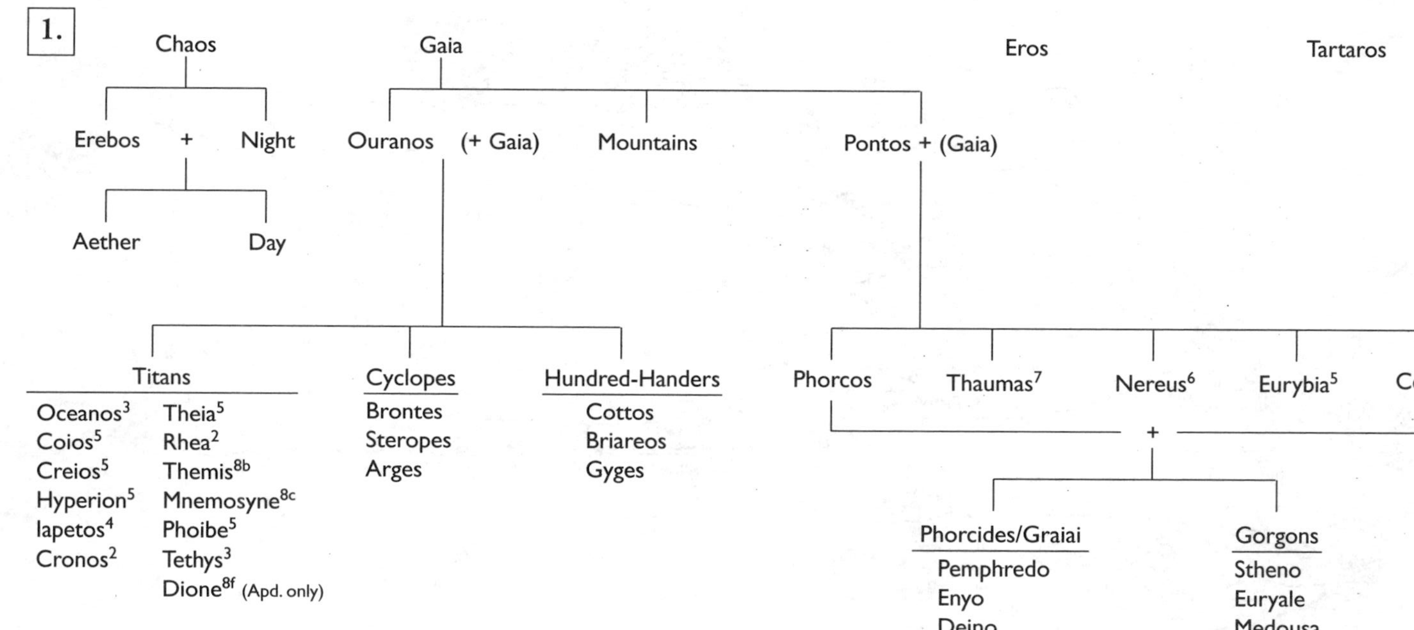

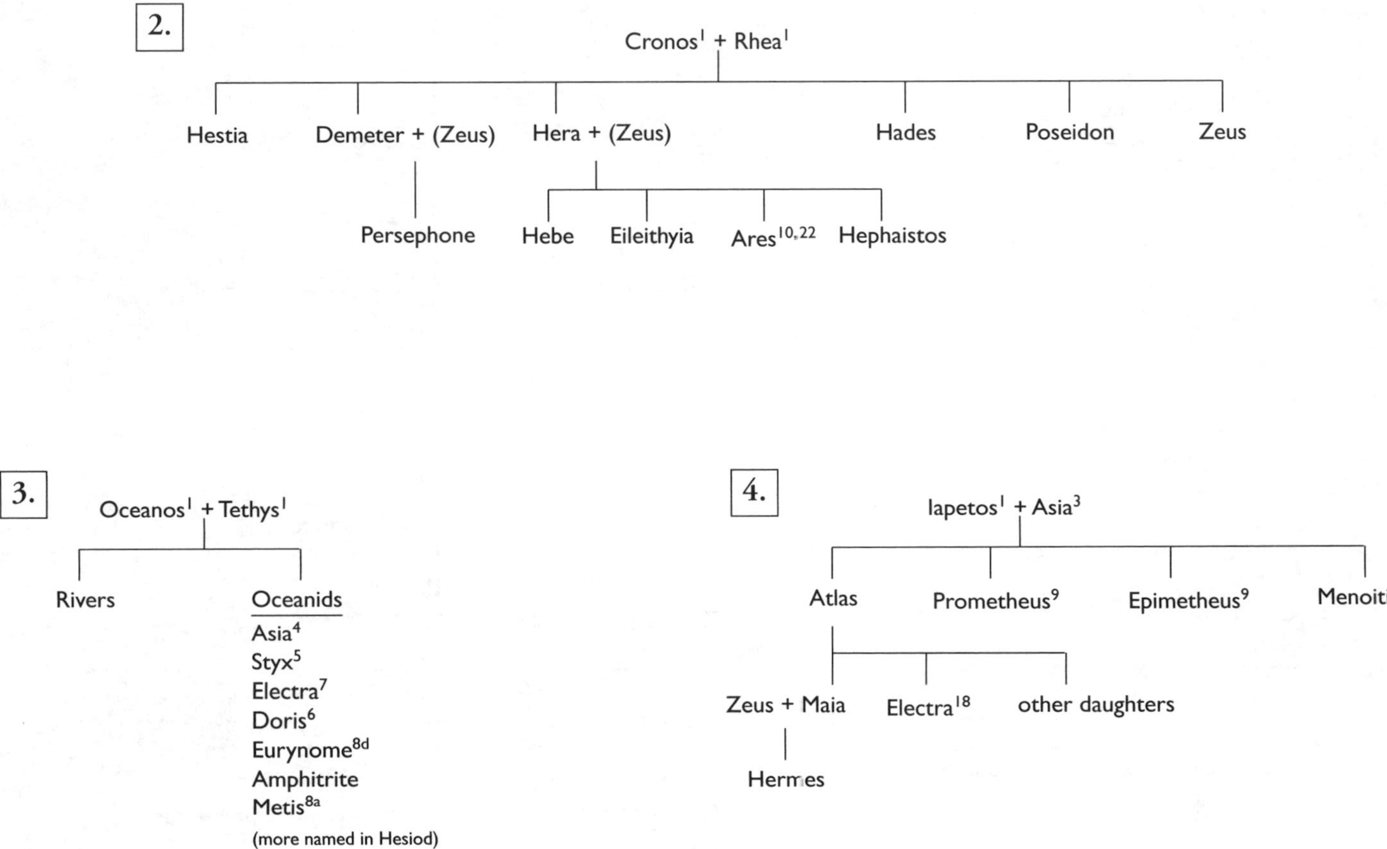

2.
Cronos[1] + Rhea[1]
Hestia
Demeter + (Zeus)
Hera + (Zeus)
Hades
Poseidon
Zeus
Persephone
Hebe
Eileithyia
Ares[10, 22]
Hephaistos
3.
Oceanos[1] + Tethys[1]
Rivers
Oceanids
Asia[4]
Styx[5]
Electra[7]
Doris[6]
Eurynome[8d]
Amphitrite
Metis[8a]
(more named in Hesiod)
4.
Iapetos[1] + Asia[3]
Atlas
Prometheus[9]
Epimetheus[9]
Menoitios
Zeus + Maia
Electra[18]
other daughters
Hermes

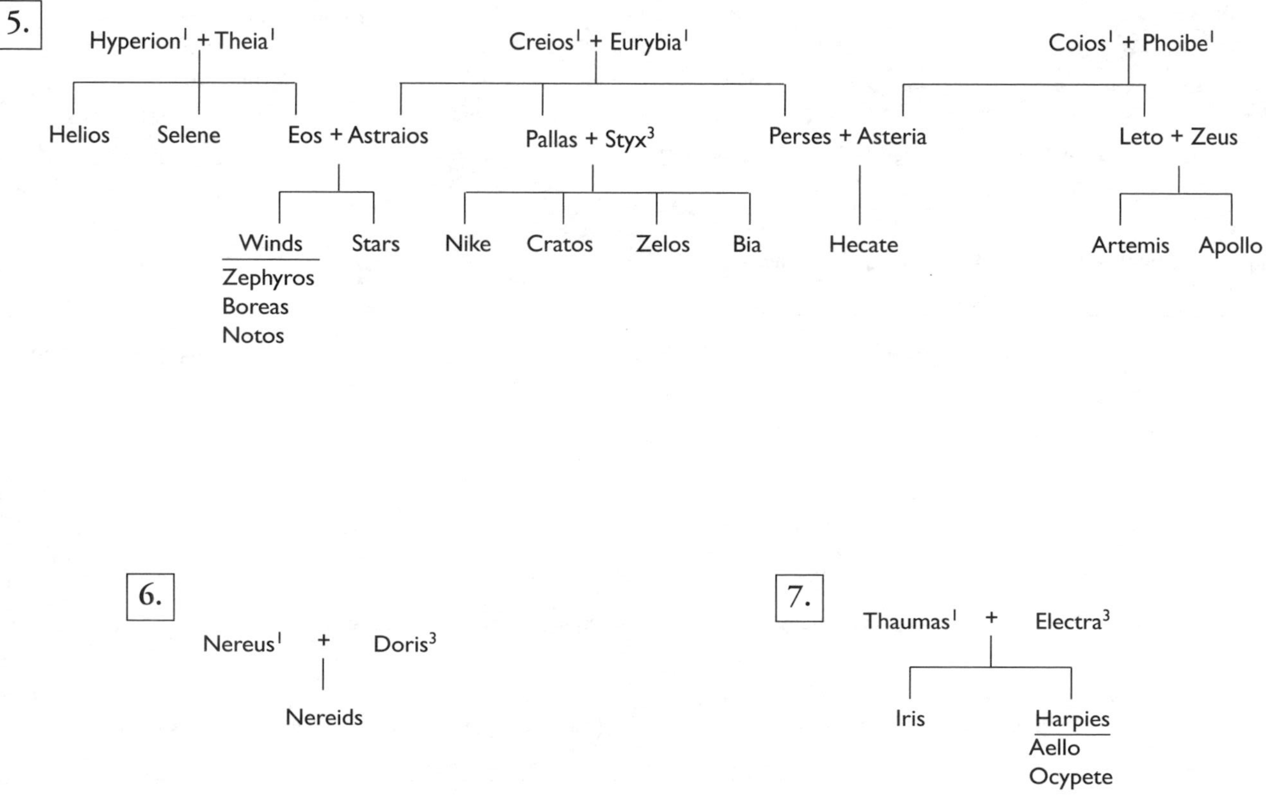
5.
Hyperion[1] + Theia[1]
Helios
Selene
Eos + Astraios
Winds
Zephyros
Boreas
Notos
Stars
Creios[1] + Eurybia[1]
Pallas + Styx[3]
Nike
Cratos
Zelos
Bia
Perses + Asteria
Hecate
Coios[1] + Phoibe[1]
Leto + Zeus
Artemis
Apollo
6.
Nereus[1] + Doris[3]
Nereids
7.
Thaumas[1] + Electra[3]
Iris
Harpies
Aello
Ocypete

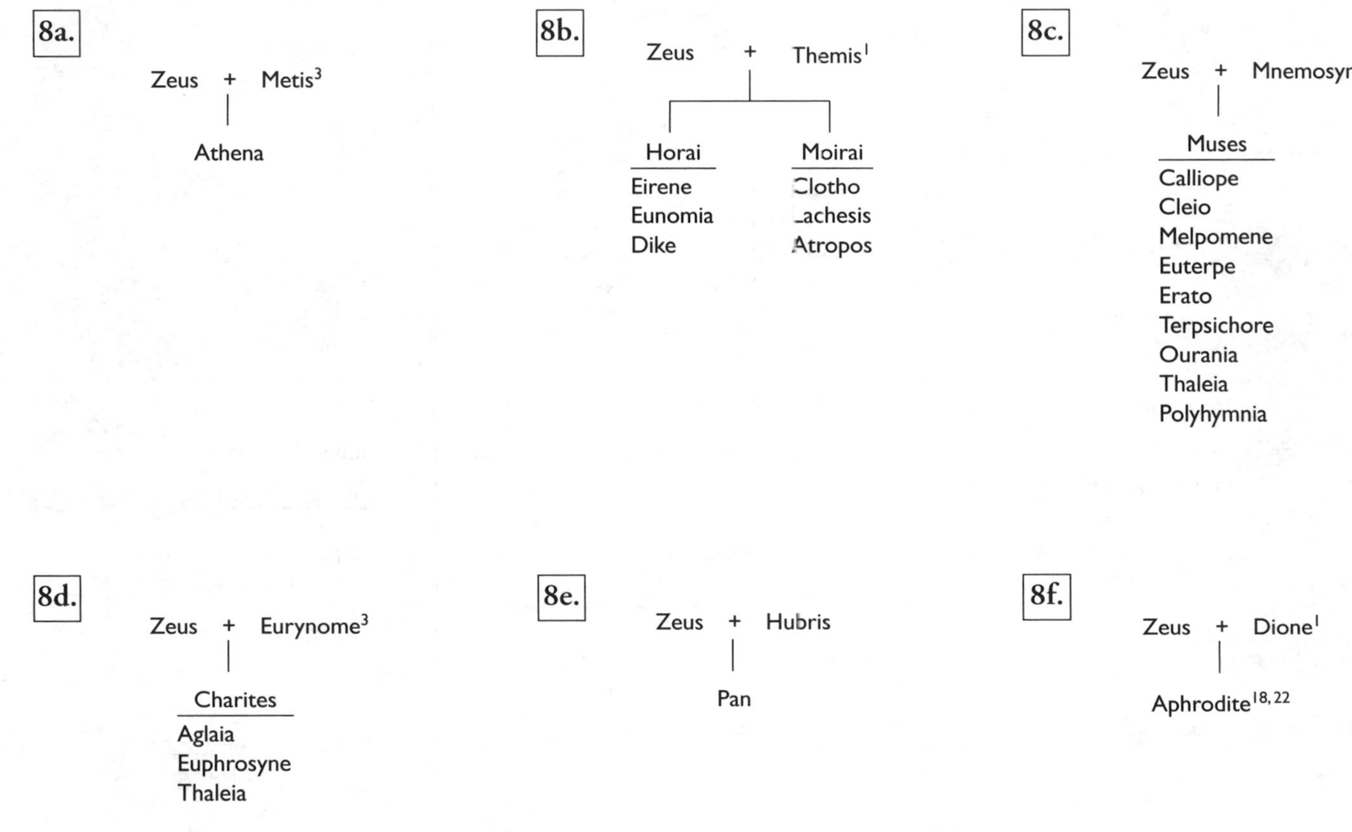
8a.
Zeus + Metis[3]
Athena
8b.
Zeus + Themis[1]
Horai
Eirene
Eunomia
Dike
Moirai
Clotho
Lachesis
Atropos
8c.
Zeus + Mnemosyne[1]
Muses
Calliope
Cleio
Melpomene
Euterpe
Erato
Terpsichore
Ourania
Thaleia
Polyhymnia
8d.
Zeus + Eurynome[3]
Charites
Aglaia
Euphrosyne
Thaleia
8e.
Zeus + Hubris
Pan
8f.
Zeus + Dione[1]
Aphrodite[18, 22]

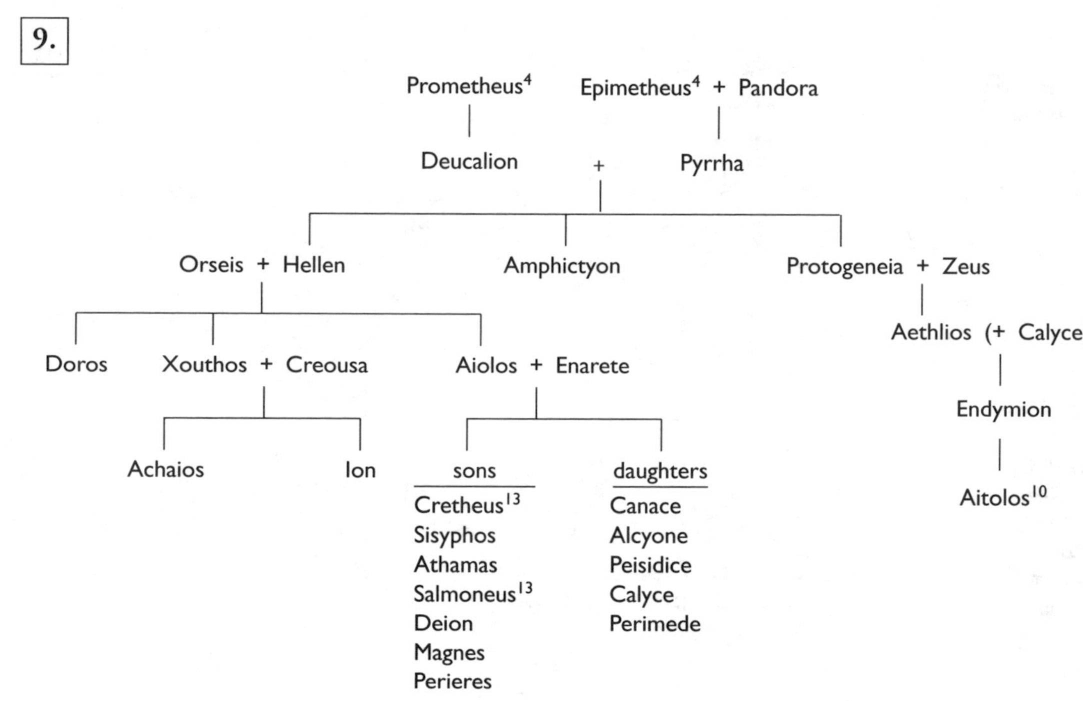
9.
Prometheus[4]
Epimetheus[4] + Pandora
Deucalion + Pyrrha
Orseis + Hellen
Amphictyon
Protogeneia + Zeus
Doros
Xouthos + Creousa
Aiolos + Enarete
Aethlios (+ Calyce)
Achaios
Ion
sons
Cretheus[13]
Sisyphos
Athamas
Salmoneus[13]
Deion
Magnes
Perieres
daughters
Canace
Alcyone
Peisidice
Calyce
Perimede
Endymion
Aitolos[10]

10.

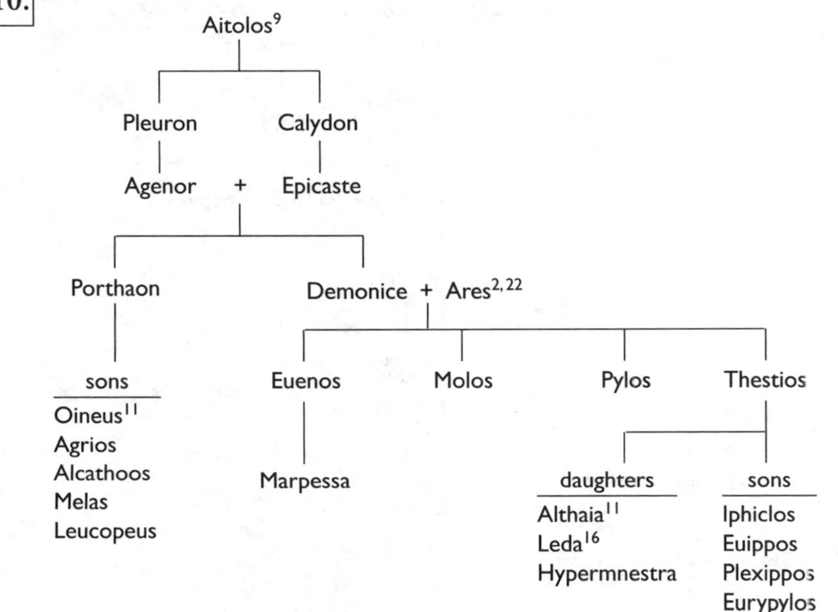
Aitolos9
Pleuron
Calydon
Agenor + Epicaste
Porthaon
Demonice + Ares2, 22
sons
Oineus11
Agrios
Alcathoos
Melas
Leucopeus
Euenos
Molos
Pylos
Thestios
Marpessa
daughters
Althaia11
Leda16
Hypermnestra
sons
Iphiclos
Euippos
Plexippos
Eurypylos

11.

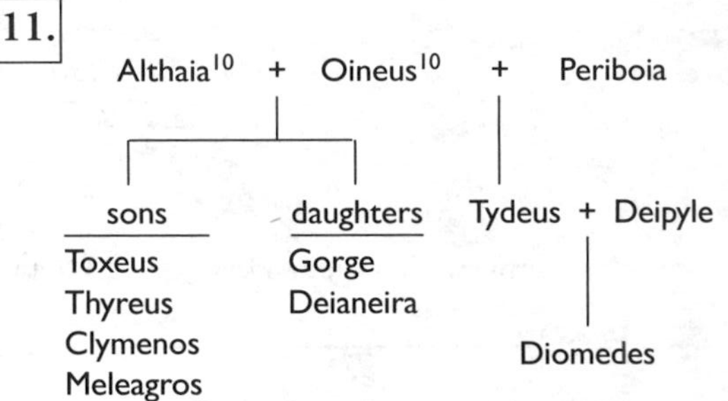
Althaia10 + Oineus10 + Periboia
sons
Toxeus
Thyreus
Clymenos
Meleagros
daughters
Gorge
Deianeira
Tydeus + Deipyle
Diomedes

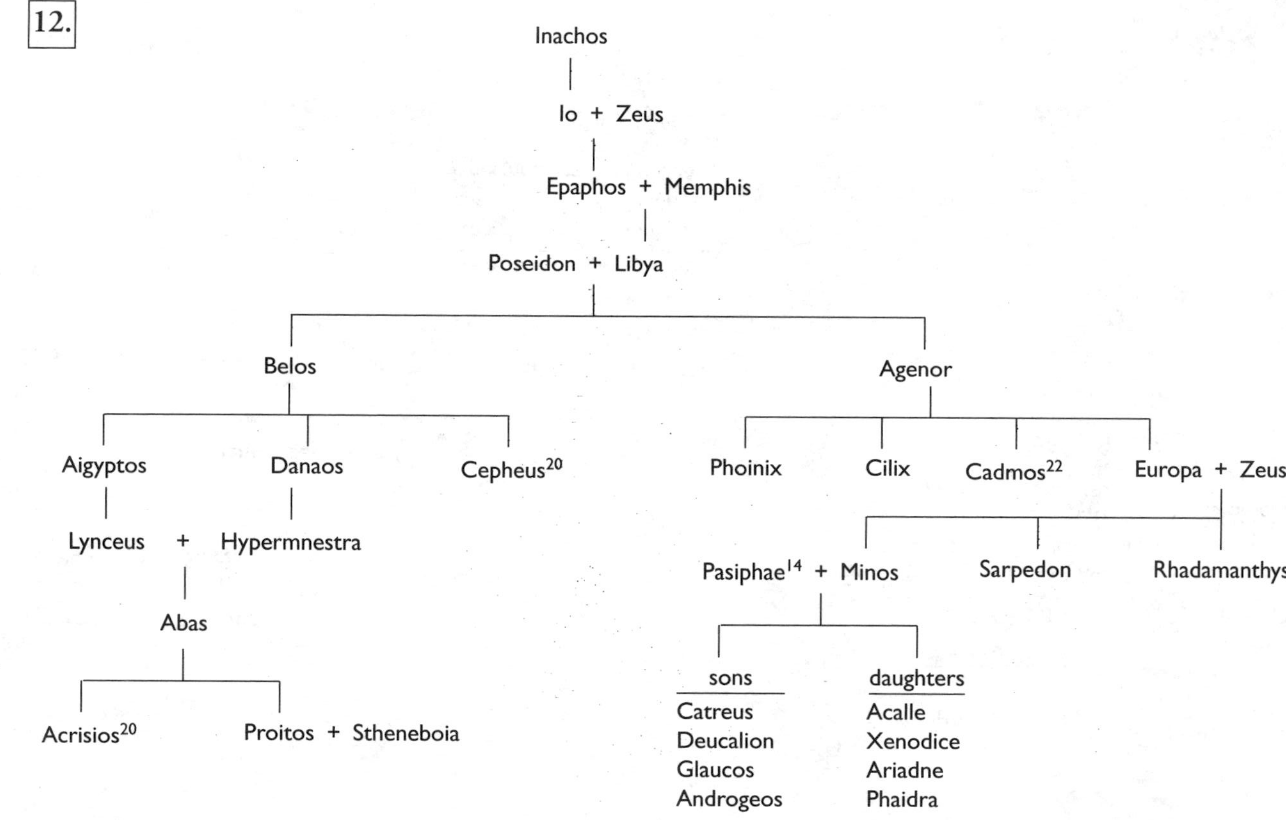
12.
Inachos
Io + Zeus
Epaphos + Memphis
Poseidon + Libya
Belos
Agenor
Aigyptos
Danaos
Cepheus[20]
Phoinix
Cilix
Cadmos[22]
Europa + Zeus
Lynceus + Hypermnestra
Pasiphae[14] + Minos
Sarpedon
Rhadamanthys
Abas
sons
Catreus
Deucalion
Glaucos
Androgeos
daughters
Acalle
Xenodice
Ariadne
Phaidra
Acrisios[20]
Proitos + Stheneboia

13.

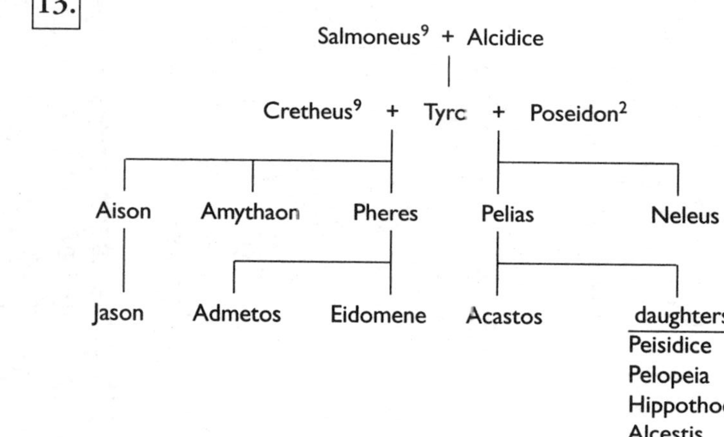
Salmoneus9 + Alcidice
Cretheus9 + Tyrc + Poseidon2
Aison
Amythaon
Pheres
Pelias
Neleus
Jason
Admetos
Eidomene
Acastos
daughters
Peisidice
Pelopeia
Hippothoe
Alcestis

14.

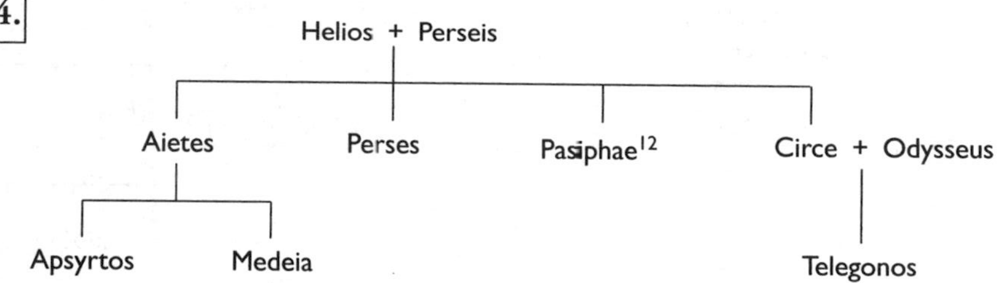
Helios + Perseis
Aietes
Perses
Pasiphae12
Circe + Odysseus
Apsyrtos
Medeia
Telegonos

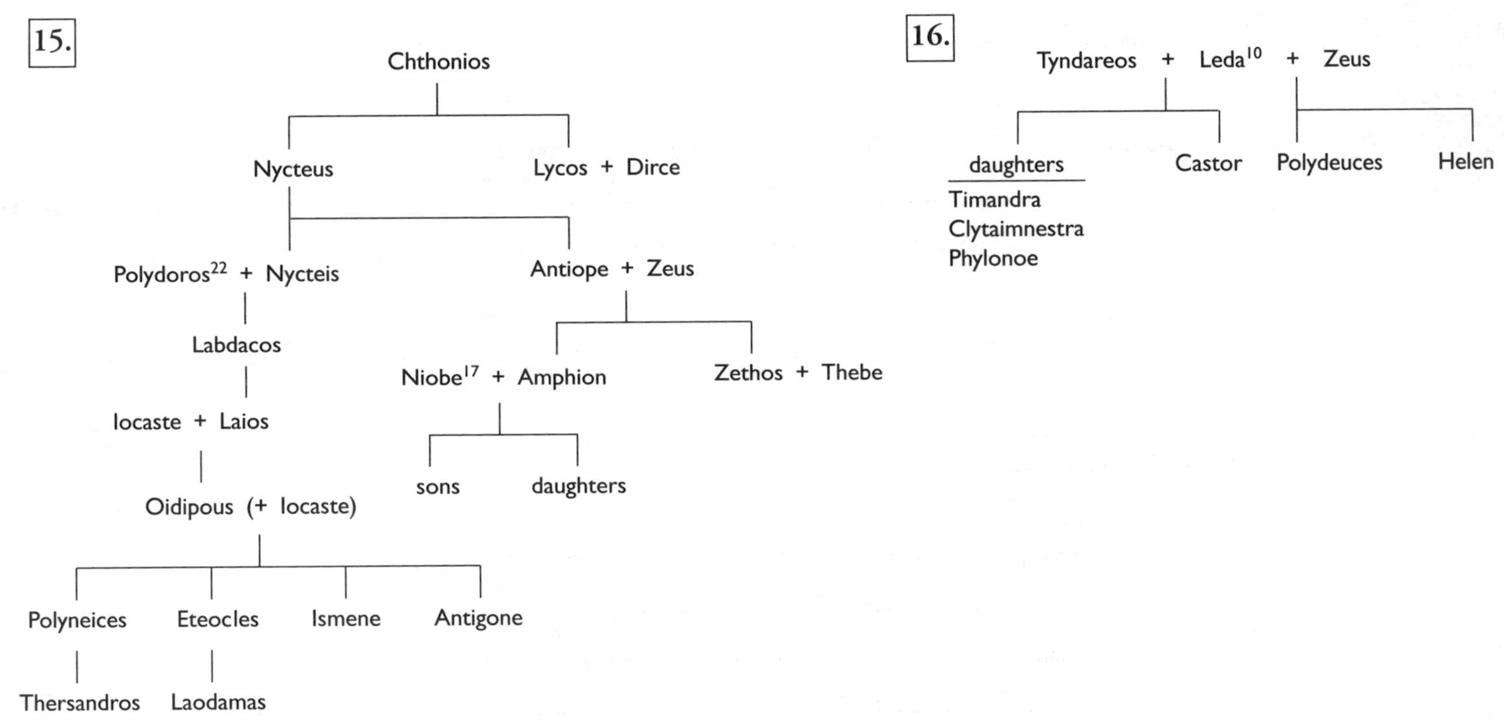
15.
Chthonios
Nycteus
Lycos + Dirce
Polydoros22 + Nycteis
Antiope + Zeus
Labdacos
Niobe17 + Amphion
Zethos + Thebe
Iocaste + Laios
sons
daughters
Oidipous (+ Iocaste)
Polyneices
Eteocles
Ismene
Antigone
Thersandros
Laodamas
16.
Tyndareos + Leda10 + Zeus
daughters
Timandra
Clytaimnestra
Phylonoe
Castor
Polydeuces
Helen

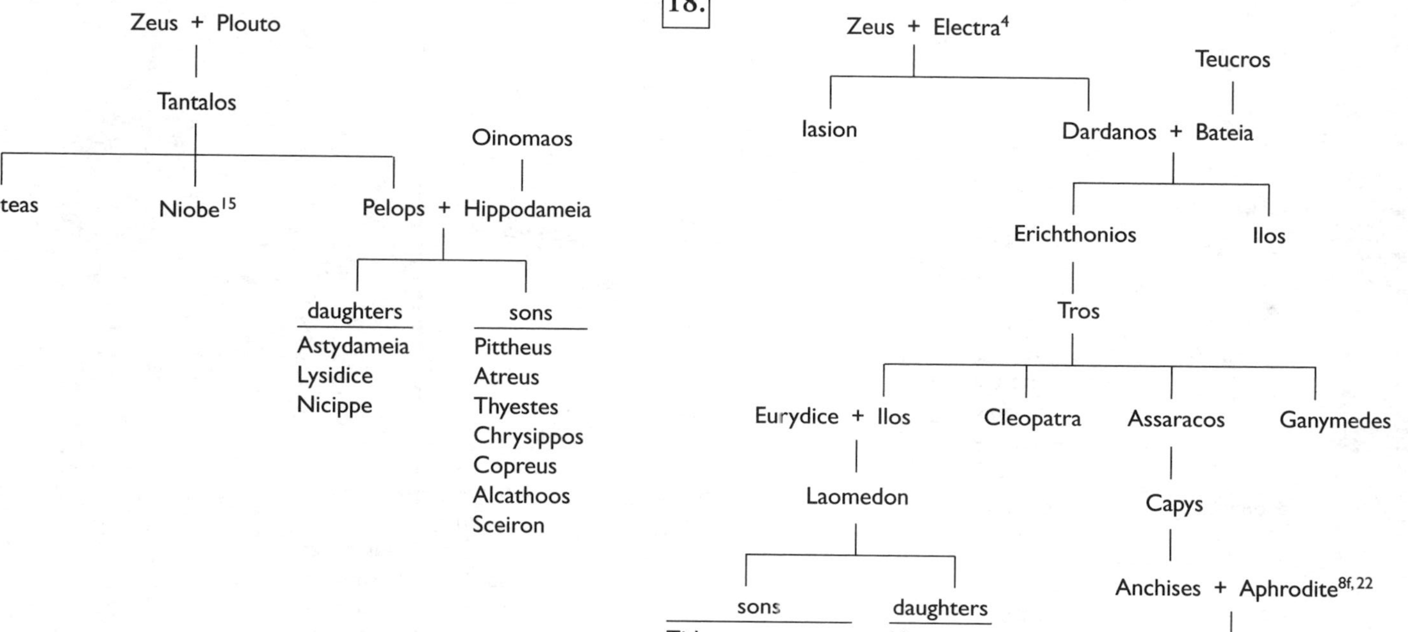
17.
Zeus + Plouto
Tantalos
Broteas
Niobe[15]
Pelops + Hippodameia
Oinomaos
daughters
Astydameia
Lysidice
Nicippe
sons
Pittheus
Atreus
Thyestes
Chrysippos
Copreus
Alcathoos
Sceiron
18.
Zeus + Electra[4]
Teucros
Iasion
Dardanos + Bateia
Erichthonios
Ilos
Tros
Eurydice + Ilos
Cleopatra
Assaracos
Ganymedes
Laomedon
Capys
Anchises + Aphrodite[8f,22]
Aineias
sons
Tithonos
Lampos
Clytios
Hicetaon
Podarces (= Priam)[19]
daughters
Hesione
Cilla
Astyoche

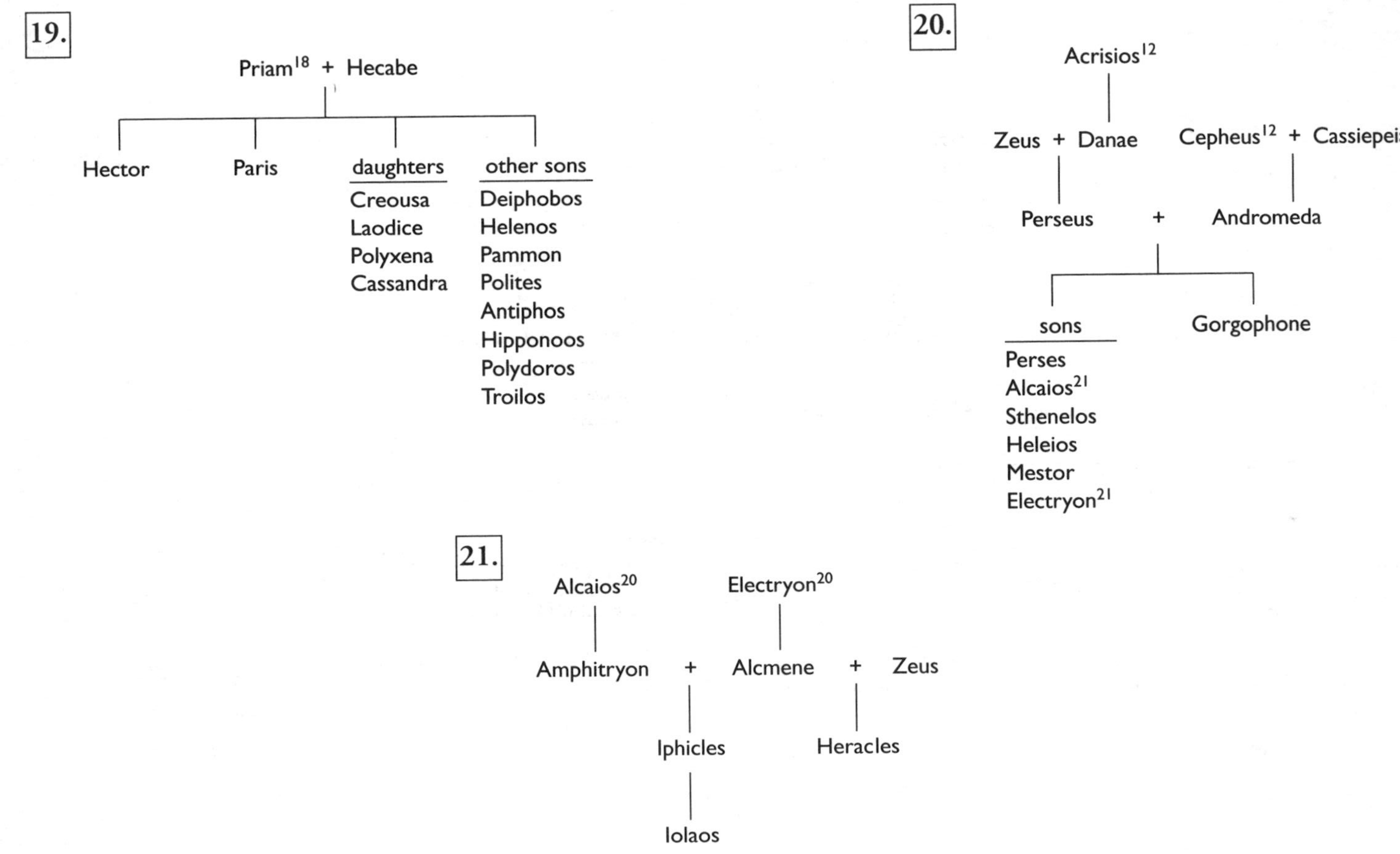
19.
Priam[18] + Hecabe
Hector
Paris
daughters
Creousa
Laodice
Polyxena
Cassandra
other sons
Deiphobos
Helenos
Pammon
Polites
Antiphos
Hipponoos
Polydoros
Troilos
20.
Acrisios[12]
Zeus + Danae
Cepheus[12] + Cassiepeia
Perseus + Andromeda
sons
Perses
Alcaios[21]
Sthenelos
Heleios
Mestor
Electryon[21]
Gorgophone
21.
Alcaios[20]
Electryon[20]
Amphitryon + Alcmene + Zeus
Iphicles
Heracles
Iolaos

22.

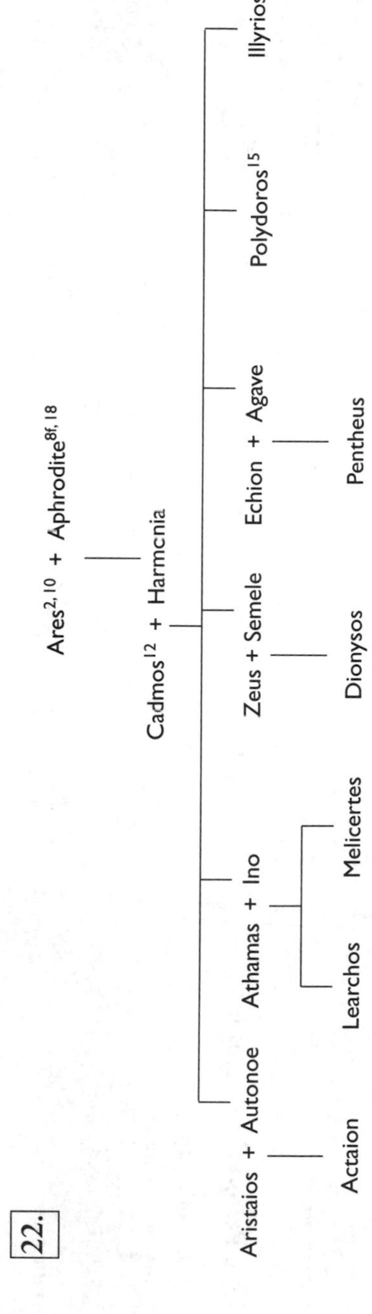

Ares[2,10] + Aphrodite[8f,18]
Cadmos[12] + Harmonia
Aristaios + Autonoe
Actaion
Athamas + Ino
Learchos
Melicertes
Zeus + Semele
Dionysos
Echion + Agave
Pentheus
Polydoros[15]
Illyrios

TIMELINES

All dates are BC unless otherwise noted

Overview of Periods

Mycenaean Bronze Age	Dark Age	Archaic Period	Classical Period	Hellenistic Period	Roman Period
1550–1050 (Linear B 1400–1200)	1050–750	750–479 (Introduction of alphabetic writing)	479–323	323–31	31 BC–5th c. AD

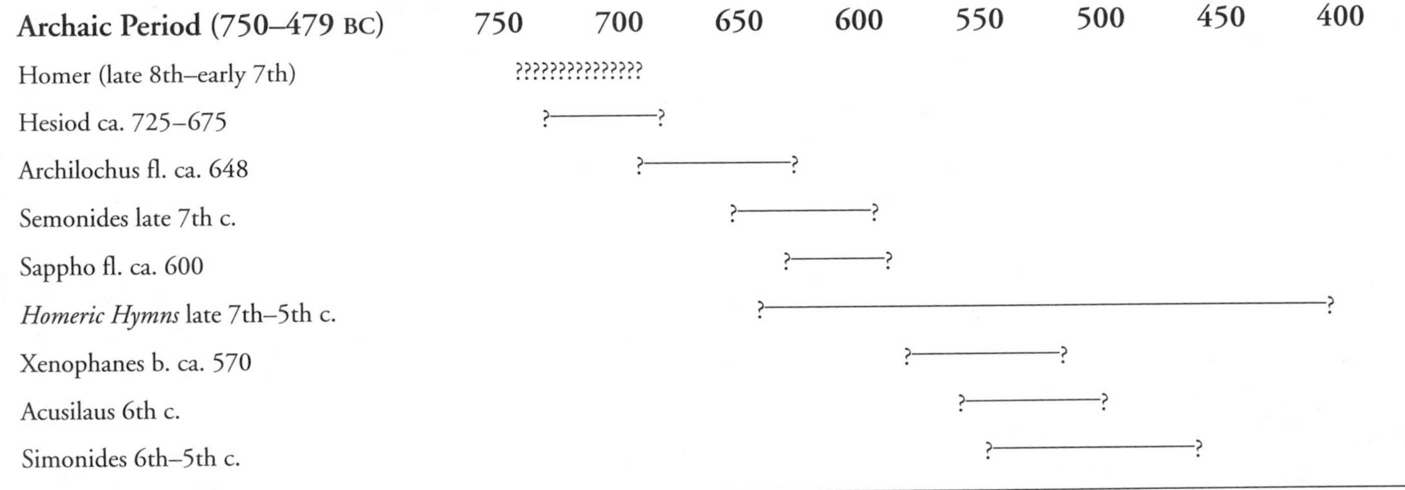

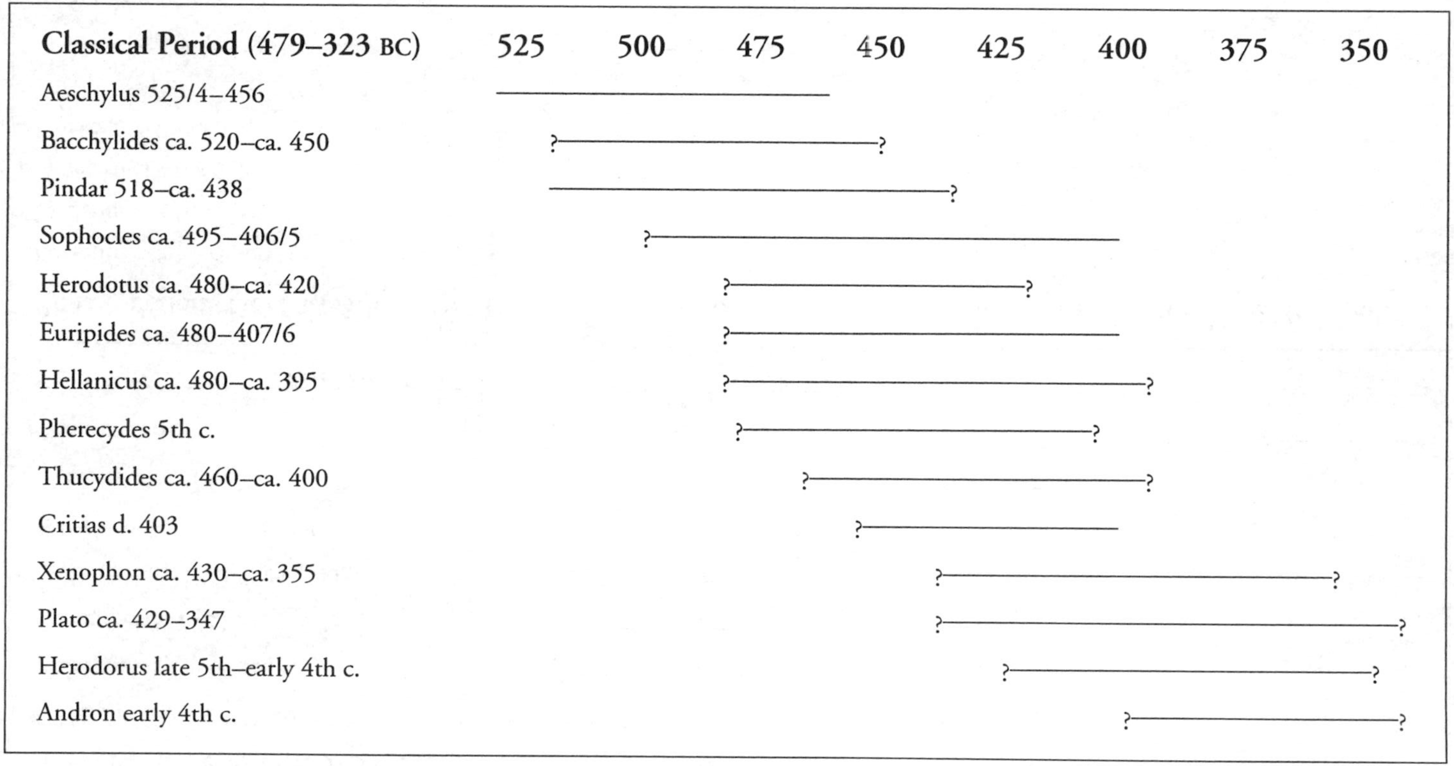

Classical Period (479–323 BC)	525	500	475	450	425	400	375	350
Aeschylus 525/4–456								
Bacchylides ca. 520–ca. 450								
Pindar 518–ca. 438								
Sophocles ca. 495–406/5								
Herodotus ca. 480–ca. 420								
Euripides ca. 480–407/6								
Hellanicus ca. 480–ca. 395								
Pherecydes 5th c.								
Thucydides ca. 460–ca. 400								
Critias d. 403								
Xenophon ca. 430–ca. 355								
Plato ca. 429–347								
Herodorus late 5th–early 4th c.								
Andron early 4th c.								

Hellenistic Period (323–31 BC) 350 300 250 200 150 100

Theophrastus ca. 371–ca. 287

Palaephatus 4th or 3rd c.

Cleanthes 331–232

Callimachus ca. 305–ca. 240

Theocritus ca. 300–ca. 260

Eratosthenes 3rd c.

Bion fl. 100

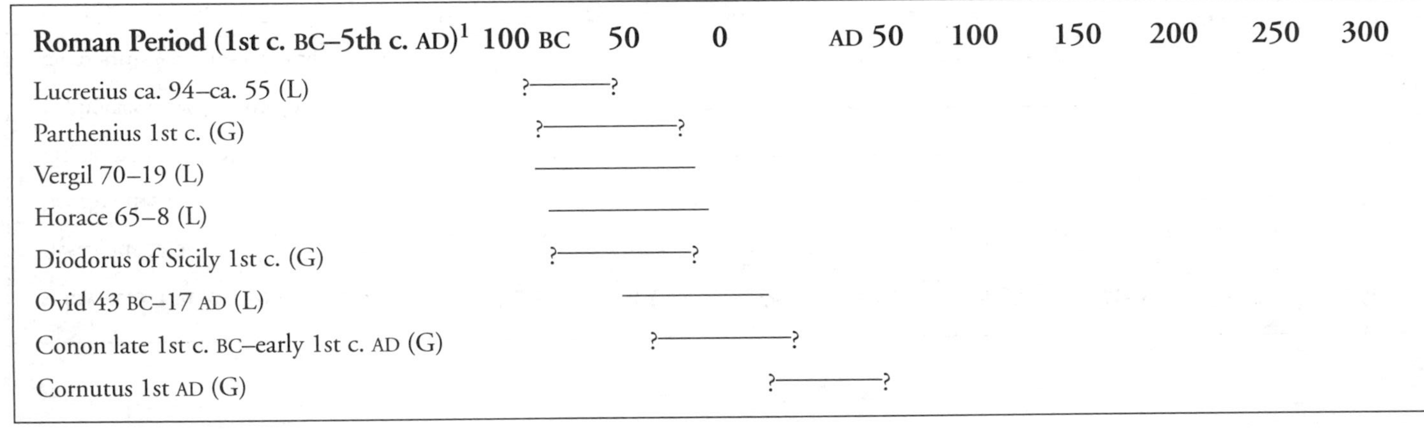

Roman Period (1st c. BC–5th c. AD)[1]	**100 BC**	**50**	**0**	**AD 50**	**100**	**150**	**200**	**250**	**300**
Heraclitus 1st c. (G)									
Statius 48–96 AD (L)									
Plutarch ca. 50–ca. 120 AD (G)									
Apollodorus 1st or 2nd c. (G)									
Babrius 1st or 2nd c. (G)									
Arrian ca. 86–160 AD (G)									
Antoninus Liberalis 2nd c. (G)									
Longus 2nd c. (G)									
Pausanias 2nd c. (G)									
Lucian ca. 120–ca. 185 AD (G)									
Aelian ca. 165–ca. 230 AD (G)									
Late Authors									
Sallustius 4th c. (G)									
Hyginus 4th or 5th c. (L)									
Proclus 410–485 AD (G)									
Fulgentius 5th or 6th c. (L)									

[1] We have included Latin authors under Roman period although the Roman period traditionally begins in 31 BC. G = wrote in Greek. L = wrote in Latin.

ACUSILAUS

(6th c. BC, wrote in Greek)

Acusilaus was an early mythographer whose work was organized genealogically. Although he seems to have covered everything from creation to the fall of Troy, we have only about forty-five short fragments including the following two: the first derived from a commentary by an early Christian writer about a tradition derived from Acusilaus; the second a scholion *(ancient footnote) summarizing Acusilaus' intriguing notion of the cause of the Trojan War.*

23 Phoroneus, the First Mortal (fr. 23a Fowler)

The flood of Ogyges[1] occurred in Greece in the time of Phoroneus, who succeeded Inachos, while the kingdom in Sicyon existed (first it was Aigialeus', then Europs', then Telchis'), as did Cres' kingdom in Crete. For Acusilaus says that Phoroneus was the first mortal, and so the poet of the *Phoronis* says he was the "father of mortal men." Then Plato in his *Timaios*, following Acusilaus, writes: "And once, wishing to get them to discuss antiquity, Solon tried to tell them the most ancient of the tales in this city {Athens}, about Phoroneus, who is called the first man, and Niobe and about the events after the flood."[2]

39 Aphrodite and the Trojan War (fr. 39a Fowler)

An oracle was issued that when the rule of the family of Priam was ended, the descendants of Anchises would be kings of the Trojans. So Aphrodite slept with Anchises though he was already past his prime. She gave birth to Aineias and, wanting to create a pretext to depose the family of Priam, she filled Alexander with desire for Helen. After he stole Helen away, Aphrodite, though she was really pressing for the Trojans' defeat, pretended to fight on their side so that they would not completely lose hope and give Helen back. The account is in Acusilaus.

[1] In one tradition the first king of Thebes, in another the father of Eleusis, the eponymous hero of the Attic city of Eleusis.

[2] The story in the *Timaios* involves the visit of the Athenian statesman and philosopher Solon to Egypt. In response to this "most ancient" of Greek myths, an Egyptian priest is made to utter the famous words asserting the great antiquity of Egyptian tradition as opposed to Greek: "O Solon, Solon, you Greeks are forever children; there is no old Greek."

AELIAN

(ca. 165–ca. 230 AD, wrote in Greek)

Although he was a native speaker of Latin, Aelian produced his Historical Miscellany (Poikile Historia) *in Greek. Living up to its name, the work presents a collection of miscellaneous anecdotes running the gamut from the mating habits of sea turtles to the feats of famous figures of history and legend. Not explicitly a mythological work, it nevertheless touches upon numerous matters related to religion and myth. Many of the anecdotes are short, but Aelian also can be expansive, as in 13.1 following, where in the myth of Atalante he describes her home with great rhetorical elaboration.*

FROM *HISTORICAL MISCELLANY*

3.22 Aineias and the Fall of Troy

When Ilion was captured, the Greeks pitied the fate of the conquered and made this very Greek decree: each of the free men was to pick up and take whichever single possession he wanted. Aineias picked up and started to carry off his ancestral gods, ignoring everything else. Taking delight in the man's piety, the Greeks allowed him to take also a second item. Aineias picked up his very aged father and carried him on his shoulders. No less astonished at this, they gave him all of his possessions, evidence that even natural enemies become gentle toward those people who treat the gods and their parents with reverence.

5.21 Medeia's Children

One account says that the report concerning Medeia is false, that she did not kill her children, but the Corinthians did. They say that Euripides made up this myth about the Colchian woman and his play because the Corinthians asked him to, and the lie prevailed over the truth because of the poet's excellence. To atone for the outrage against the children, they say, up to the present day the Corinthians offer sacrifice to the children as if paying them tribute.

8.3 Sacrifices at Athens

This is an Attic custom: when the ox is sacrificed, after trying each person individually for murder, they acquit the rest of them but condemn the knife and say that it did the killing. And they call the festival when they do these things the Dipolieia {"Festival of Zeus Guardian of the City"} and Bouphonia {"Festival of Ox-killing"}.

13.1 Atalante

This is an Arcadian story about Atalante daughter of Iasion. Her father exposed her at birth; he said he wanted not female, but male children. But the man who took her to be exposed did not kill her. Instead, he went to Mount Parthenion and put her near a spring. There was an overhanging ledge there, and a thick forest covered it. And while death was decreed for the infant, still she was not forsaken by fate, for a little later a she-bear, deprived of her own cubs by hunters, came by with her teats swollen and weighed down by milk. Then, according to some divine guidance, she took a liking to the infant and suckled it, and simultaneously the beast was relieved of its discomfort and provided food for the infant. So, full once more of milk and directing it into a new mouth (since she was no longer the mother of her own young), she provided nourishment to one who was in no way related to her. The very hunters who had originally snared her young now watched the beast. They monitored her every movement, and when the she-bear went out to hunt and feed as she regularly did, they spirited away Atalante, who was not yet named that. These very hunters gave her her name, and she was raised among them in the way mountain dwellers are normally raised. Little by little her body began to develop as she got older, but she loved her virginity and avoided the company of men. She longed for solitude and made her home on the highest peak in the Arcadian mountains in a place where there was a well-watered valley, tall oaks, as well as pine trees and the deep shadows they cast.

What does it hurt for us to hear of Atalante's cave, so like Calypso's in Homer? There was in the hollow ravine a large, very deep cave, shielded in front by a high cliff. Ivy twined around it, weaving itself loosely among the trees and climbing through them. There were crocuses growing around the place in the soft, deep grass. Rising up with them were hyacinths and a profusion of many other colors of flowers, and it was not just that they each contributed to a feast for the eyes, but the scents they gave off pervaded the encircling air. It was just like a festival, and the perfume was the main course of the feast. There were many laurels, and the foliage of the ever-flourishing plant was sweet to look upon. In front of the cave, vines loaded with spectacularly flourishing grape clusters demonstrated Atalante's industriousness. Streams flowed abundantly and unstintingly, constantly flowing in, clear to the eye and cold (as a man touching it would judge and a man drinking it would conclude). These streams served to irrigate the aforementioned trees with their continuous flow, allies in their struggle to grow. The spot, then, was full of charms and gave the impression of a most holy and chaste home for a virgin.

The skins of the animals she caught were Atalante's bed; their meat was her food; water was her drink. She was clad in a simple dress exactly like Artemis'. For she said that she was emulating the goddess, both in this matter and in her desire to be a virgin forever. She was very swift-footed, and no beast could escape her, nor could any man who plotted treachery against her. And when she wanted to escape, no one could have caught her. Those who saw her were not the only ones to love her—no, she was even loved by those who had only heard reports of her.

Come, let us describe her appearance since it does no harm, and it is not at all harmful because we might derive experience and skill with words by doing so. When she was still a child, she was taller than grown women, and she blossomed with beauty like no other young woman who lived in the Peloponnese at that time. Her expression was fierce, like a man's, first because she had been nursed by a wild animal, but also because of her exertions in the mountains. Because she was spirited, she was not at all girlish or delicate. She did not come from the women's quarters, nor was she one of those raised by mothers and nurses. And she was not overweight either, as is to be expected, given that she toned her whole body in hunting and working out. Her hair was blond, though not through any womanly fiddling, dyes, or concoctions; the color was nature's work. Her face was tanned by the sun, like a constant blush. What flower could be as beautiful as the face of a young woman brought up with a sense of shame? She had two striking features: irresistible beauty and, along with it, the ability to be frightening. No lazy man looking at her would have fallen in love with her, and in fact would not have dared to meet her eye at all, so great was the radiance that shone with her beauty upon those who saw her. It was unnerving to meet her, all the more because it seldom happened. For no one could see her in a normal setting; but unexpectedly, with no warning, she showed up, chasing a beast or fighting one off, and, shining like a star, she streaked like a flash of lightning. Racing off, she would then hide herself in woods or a thicket or some other thick growth on the mountain.

Once, in the middle of the night, those who lived in the territory near her, two Centaurs, Hylaios and Rhoicos, bold lovers and violent revelers, came to her on a wild revel. But their revel had no flute girls nor any of the other things one sees with young men in a city. No, they carried pinewood torches. And when they lit these and made them blaze, at the first sight of the fire they would have terrified even city folk, much less a young woman all by herself. They broke fresh branches off of pine trees, then wove them together and made garlands for themselves. The racing clatter of hooves resounded incessantly through the mountains. Burning the trees, they hastened after the girl, evil suitors seeking before the wedding to pay the bride-price with violence and madness. But their design did not go unnoticed by her. When she saw the fire from her cave and recognized just who the revelers were, she did not hesitate at all or cower from the sight. She stretched her bow back and sent a shaft, hitting the first with a very well placed shot. He lay there, but the second one kept coming, no longer a reveler, but now an enemy, wishing to defend his friend and to satisfy his rage. But the girl's next arrow—payback—met him too. That is the story of Atalante daughter of Iasion.

Aeschylus

(525/4–456 BC, wrote in Greek)

The earliest of the three great Athenian playwrights, Aeschylus survives in seven complete plays (of at least eighty-two titles we know of), the most famous being the Oresteia *trilogy and the* Prometheus Bound *(though some question whether Aeschylus wrote this play). In addition, some 400 fragments are preserved in many different sources.*

FROM *DAUGHTERS OF HELIOS*

70 Zeus Is Everything (fr. 70 Nauck)

This very short fragment, preserved for us in a quotation by an early Christian writer, is a good example of the tendency of some Greeks to view their gods as a single divine force. One can see the same impulse in Sophocles fr. 941 on Aphrodite, and philosophical elaborations of this idea in Cleanthes' Hymn to Zeus *and Xenophanes fr. 23.*

Zeus is sky, Zeus is earth, Zeus is heaven;
Zeus is everything and all that is beyond these things.

FROM *THE CARIANS* (OR *EUROPA*)

99 Europa Tells Her Story (fr. 99 Nauck)

This portion of the play was recovered from a papyrus and is missing some material, which has been reconstructed in various ways, so material in < brackets > must not be considered certain. The speaker is Europa, who was carried off by a bull from her father's palace in Phoenicia to Crete, where she bore Zeus three sons. At the time of her speech, her last surviving son, Sarpedon, was off fighting in the Trojan War, and her speech alludes to his ultimate demise at the hands of Patroclos (Iliad *16).*

. . . and the all-bountiful meadow served as lodging for the bull.
That is how Zeus, not moving from his place, accomplished
his theft from my aged father without any effort.
Let me tell the whole long tale in but a few words:
I, a woman, united with a god, and in return for the purity
of virginity I was yoked to him, my partner in children.
I endured the pangs of a woman's labor for three

offspring; he found no fault with the field
for not bearing the seeds of a noble father.
From these mighty implantations I first
gave birth to Minos < . . . >
< . . . I next gave birth to>
Rhadamanthys, the child of mine who cannot perish.
But he does not live his life before these eyes of mine,[1]
and his absence brings no joy to those who love him dear.
Third-born was he for whom a storm now rages in my thoughts,
Sarpedon, since war-lust sent from Ares has come over him.
For <Lord Agamemnon has come to the land> of the Carians,
<leading forth the whole> flower of all of
<Greece>, preeminent in their valiant might,
and he boasts that he will sack the city of Troy in violence.
It is for Sarpedon that I fear, that raging with his spear
he might go too far and suffer horribly.
For this hope of mine is slim and balanced upon a razor's edge—
I might see everything slip away at the bloody death of my son.

FROM *NIOBE*

161 Thanatos {Death} (fr. 161 Nauck)

This short fragment is preserved only in a collection of quotations compiled in late antiquity. It adds vivid personification of Death (Thanatos) and Persuasion (Peitho) to the commonly made observation among the Greeks that death was an inevitable part of human existence, particularly fitting in a play about Niobe, whose children were killed by the gods because of her foolish boast.

Alone of the gods Death does not love gifts;
sacrifices and libations will do you no good at all.
He has no altar; men do not sing him songs of praise.
Of all the gods Persuasion stays away only from him.

FROM *PROMETHEUS FREED*

193 Prometheus Describes His Punishment (fr. 193 Nauck)

Aeschylus is credited with a trilogy about Prometheus' theft of fire and his subsequent punishment. The Prometheus Bound, *the only play of the trilogy surviving, ends with the*

[1] Because he lives in the underworld, where he presides as one of the judges of the dead.

beginning of Prometheus' torture. In this fragment from the Prometheus Freed, *the next play, in which Heracles frees him, the Titan speaks after many years of torment. This is a good example of how fickle the preservation of ancient texts can be. This play was translated into Latin by an unknown playwright of the 2nd century* BC *(which explains the Latin names for the gods here). Even this Latin play does not survive, but the Roman author Cicero (1st c.* BC*) quoted this passage in a philosophical text on pain and suffering.*

O race of Titans, kinsmen of mine by blood,
begotten by Heaven, look upon me bound and fettered
on jagged rocks. Just as a ship is anchored by frightened sailors
in the dread of night upon the stormy, raging seas,
just so has Saturnian Jupiter bound me,
and Mulciber's[2] hand carried out Jupiter's will.
That one bored through my body, driving in these wedges
with cruel skill. By his ingenuity transfixed,
I reside here, a wretched tenant of the Furies' outpost.
And now, every third day, a grievous day,
Jupiter's attendant makes its grim swoop and tears at me,
rending me with hooked talons in a frenzied feeding.
Then when on rich liver it is glutted, stuffed and sated,
it emits an awesome screech, and, skying aloft,
it fans my blood with its feathered tail.
But when my devoured liver has swollen back to size,
then it returns again, ravenous, for its foul feeding.
Thus I nourish this sentinel of my grim torture,
who mutilates me, still living, with everlasting woe.
For as you can see, constrained by Jupiter's chains,
I cannot ward off this dread bird from my chest.
Thus I, helpless and alone, face the plague that brings me anguish,
yearning for death in search of an end to my affliction.
But by the will of Jupiter I am kept far away from death.
And this now ancient misfortune, accumulating over
dreadful generations, has taken root inside my body,
from which blood, warmed by the sun's heat,
falls and drips constantly upon the crags of Caucasus.

[2] Vulcan.

ANDRON

(possibly early 4th c. BC, wrote in Greek)

We know essentially nothing about Andron the mythographer other than his birthplace, Halicarnassos in Asia Minor. Even his date is difficult to determine. We have only two short quotations from his works on myth, along with several summaries of his ideas. The following fragment is of this latter category, consisting of Andron's etiology of cremation found in an ancient scholion *(footnote).*

10 Origins of the Custom of Cremation (fr. 10 Fowler)

This is the reason that the Greeks cremate corpses: Argeios son of Licymnios was the first to be buried in this fashion out of necessity by Heracles. They say that Heracles was gathering an army for an expedition to Ilion because Laomedon broke the agreement he made with Heracles, who had saved his daughter Hesione from the sea monster, by not giving him the horses that he had promised him in exchange for this good service. Heracles sought out Argeios because of their family connection. They say that Argeios' father, Licymnios, was afraid because he had lost his older son (named Oionos) when he sent him to Lacedaimonia with Heracles. So he was unwilling to let Argeios go until Heracles swore to bring him back home. When Argeios met with the end of his life, Heracles had no idea how he could fulfill his oath. So he burned the body,[1] and they say that Argeios was the first to receive this treatment. The story is in Andron.

[1] Which would allow him to transport the remains over so great a distance without their rotting.

ANTONINUS LIBERALIS

(probably 2nd c. AD, wrote in Greek)

Antoninus Liberalis' Collection of Metamorphoses (Metamorphoseon Synagoge) *presents short prose summaries of transformation myths found in earlier writers, particularly the poets of the Hellenistic era. He is thus a treasure trove of information that would otherwise be lost to us, including local myths (1, 17, and 26, for instance) and many variations from what we think of as standard versions of myths (see, for example, the unusual account of Iphigeneia's birth in 27).*

FROM *COLLECTION OF METAMORPHOSES*

1 Ctesylla

Ctesylla, a Ceian by birth from the village of Ioulis, was the daughter of Alcidamas. When Hermochares the Athenian saw her dance at the Pythian festival around the altar of Apollo in Carthaia, he desired her. Writing a message on an apple, he threw it into the temple of Artemis, and she picked it up and read it aloud. He had written an oath on it, "By Artemis, I swear that I will marry Hermochares the Athenian." Horrified, Ctesylla threw the apple away and was miserable—exactly like when Acontios deceived Cydippe.[1]

Hermochares asked Ctesylla's father for his blessing, and her father agreed to the marriage and swore an oath by Apollo to that effect while grasping a laurel tree. When the time of the Pythian festival had elapsed, Alcidamas forgot the oath he had sworn and gave his daughter in marriage to another man. The girl was starting to make her prewedding sacrifice in the temple of Artemis when Hermochares, miserable at his failure to marry her, ran into Artemis' temple. The girl saw him and, in accordance with divine will, fell in love. Making arrangements through her nurse without her father's knowledge, she sailed off at night to Athens and married Hermochares.

When Ctesylla was giving birth and having a hard time of it, she died in accordance with the will of the gods because her father had broken his oath. They took her body and carried it out for burial, but out from the bier flew a dove, and the body of Ctesylla disappeared. Hermochares consulted an oracle, and the god proclaimed that a temple named after Ctesylla should be established in Ioulis. The god made this pronouncement also to the rest of the people of Ceios, and they to this day make

[1] In a more famous myth than the present one, Acontios played the same trick on Cydippe, who eventually married him.

sacrifices to her. The people of Ioulis call her Aphrodite Ctesylla; the others call her Ctesylla Hecaerges.[2]

2 The Meleagrides

Oineus, who was the son of Ares' son Portheus, was king in Calydon. By Althaia daughter of Thestios he had sons, Meleagros, Phereus, Ageleos, Toxeus, Clymenos, and Periphas, and daughters, Gorge, Eurymede, Deianeira, and Melanippe. When he was sacrificing the firstfruits on behalf of his kingdom, he left out Artemis. In anger she sent a wild boar to attack, and it devastated the land and killed many people. When Meleagros and the sons of Thestios roused the heroes of Greece against the boar, they came and killed it. But Meleagros, in dividing its flesh among the heroes, reserved the head and skin for himself as a prize. Artemis, after they killed her sacred boar, was angered even more and caused them to quarrel. The sons of Thestios and the rest of the Couretes grabbed the skin and said that half of the prize belonged to them. Meleagros forcibly took it from them and killed the sons of Thestios, and with this as pretext, war broke out between the Couretes and the Calydonians. Meleagros did not go out to fight in the war, disgruntled because his mother had cursed him for her brothers' deaths.

As the Couretes were just about to capture the city, Meleagros' wife Cleopatra convinced him to defend the Calydonians. When he went out against the army of the Couretes, he died after his mother burned the log that had been given to her by the Moirai. For they spun out the thread of his destiny for as long a time as the log might exist. The other sons of Oineus also died fighting. The Calydonians greatly mourned the loss of Meleagros. His sisters stayed by his body and lamented incessantly until Artemis touched them with a wand and transformed them into birds. She moved them to the island of Leros and gave them the name *meleagrides* {"guinea fowls" and "sisters of Meleagros"}. To this day they still say that at the right time of year they call out their grief for Meleagros.

They say that two of Althaia's daughters, Gorge and Deianeira, were not changed because Dionysos was well disposed toward them, and Artemis did him this favor.

4 Cragaleus

Cragaleus son of Dryops dwelled in the land of Dryopis by the springs known as the Baths of Heracles, which, according to the myth, Heracles caused to start flowing when he struck the plateau of the mountain with his club. This Cragaleus was already an old man and had a reputation among the locals for being just and wise. While he was pasturing his cattle, Apollo, Artemis, and Heracles approached him so that he could decide which of them would be the patron god of Ambracia, the city in Epeiros.

Apollo said that the city was his because his son Melaneus was the king of the Dryopes and had captured the whole of Epeiros in war. His children were Eurytos and Ambracia, and the city had been named Ambracia after his daughter. Besides, he himself had shown the greatest favor to the city in question, for he had commanded

[2] Hecaerges {"Who works from afar"} is a cult name associated with Artemis.

the descendants of Sisyphos to come and help the Ambracians win the war they were having with the Epirotes. And it had also been in accordance with his oracles that Gorgos, the son of Cypselos, led a colony of settlers from Corinth to Ambracia. Because of his prophecies the Ambracians had revolted against Phalaicos when he was tyrant of the city, and that is why Phalaicos and so many of his men had been killed. He had put a stop once and for all to the frequent internecine war, quarrels, and dissent in the city and replaced them with order, the rule of law, and justice. For this he was honored among the Ambracians with hymns addressed to Pythian Soter {"Savior"} at festivals and banquets.

Artemis, for her part, although she was trying to settle the quarrel with her brother, thought that he should willingly give her Ambracia, for she claimed the city for the following reason: When Phalaicos was tyrant of the city and no one was able to kill him because they were afraid, she herself showed him a lion cub while he was out hunting. When he picked it up, the mother lioness ran out from the woods, attacked Phalaicos, and ripped open his chest. The Ambracians, freed from their slavery, made propitiatory sacrifices to Artemis Hegemone {"Leader of the Way"}. They also made a likeness of her as Agrotere {"Huntress"} and put a bronze statue of the lioness next to it.

Heracles argued that Ambracia and all of Epeiros were his, for all those who fought against him—the Celts, the Chaonians, the Thesprotians, and all the Epirotes—had been defeated by him when they joined together and planned to take the cattle of Geryones from him. And some time later a group of colonists came from Corinth, uprooted the previous inhabitants, and founded the city of Ambracia—and all Corinthians are descendants of Heracles.

When Cragaleus heard these statements, he decided that the city was Heracles'. Apollo in his anger touched Cragaleus with his hand and turned him to stone right where he had been standing. The Ambracians sacrifice to Apollo Soter, but they believe that the city is Heracles' and his descendants', and to this day they sacrifice victims to Cragaleus following the festival of Heracles.

6 Periphas

Periphas was a man born of the earth in Attica before Cecrops son of Ge appeared. He was king of the ancient people and was just, wealthy, and pious. He made very many offerings to Apollo and decided very many court cases, and no mortal found fault with him. On the contrary, everyone was willing to be led by him. In exchange for his superlative deeds the people withdrew the honors they paid to Zeus and decided they belonged to Periphas. They built temples and shrines to him and addressed him as Zeus Soter {"Savior"}, Epopsios {"All-seeing"}, and Meilichios {"Gracious"}. Enraged, Zeus wished to incinerate Periphas' entire household with a thunderbolt, but Apollo begged Zeus not to destroy him utterly since Periphas had honored him to an extraordinary degree. Zeus granted Apollo this favor and went to Periphas' palace, where he found him having sex with his wife. Zeus squeezed him with both hands and turned him into an eagle. After Periphas' wife begged him to turn her into a companion bird for her husband, he turned her into a vulture. Zeus also granted Periphas honors in return for the piety he had displayed among mankind. He made him king of all the birds and gave him the right both to guard his holy scepter and to approach his throne. He granted that Periphas' wife, whom he had made a vulture, appear as a good omen to humanity in every matter.

10 The Minyades

Minyas son of Orchomenos had daughters, namely Leucippe, Arsippe, and Alcathoe, who proved to be amazingly industrious. Because the rest of the women abandoned the city and were now Bacchai in the mountains, the daughters were extremely critical of them until Dionysos disguised himself as a girl and advised them not to neglect the rites or mysteries of the god. But they would not listen, so Dionysos grew angry at their behavior and changed from a girl into a bull, a lion, and then a leopard. He made nectar and milk flow from the daughters' looms. Fear gripped the girls at the sight of the miracles. Right away the three put lots into a pitcher and shook them. Since Leucippe's lot fell out, she vowed to give the god a sacrificial victim and, along with her sisters, ripped apart her own son Hippasos.

After leaving behind their father's palace, they became Bacchai in the mountains; they grazed on ivy, holm-oak, and laurel until Hermes touched them with his rod and transformed them into birds. The first of them became a bat, the second a little owl, and the third an eagle owl. The three avoided the rays of the sun.

17 Leucippos

Galateia daughter of Eurytios (son of Sparton) married Lampros son of Pandion in Phaistos, a city in Crete. Lampros was well off in family heritage, but he lacked means. So when Galateia became pregnant, he prayed that he would have a son and told his wife to expose the child if she had a girl. He went off to herd his flocks, and Galateia had a daughter. Pitying the baby and taking into consideration how isolated their house was—the dreams and seers that told her to raise the girl as a boy also played a role—she lied to Lampros and said that she had had a male child. She raised her as a boy and named her Leucippos.

When the girl grew up and became an indescribable beauty, Galateia, afraid of Lampros since she could no longer hide it from him, fled to the temple of Leto. She supplicated the goddess over and over again in the hope that somehow the girl might change from a daughter into a son, just as when, by the will of Poseidon, Cainis, who was the daughter of Atrax, became Caineus the Lapith. Teiresias changed from a man to a woman because he killed the snakes he encountered as they coupled at the crossroads; he changed back from a woman to a man because he later killed another snake. Also, Hypermestra received proceeds by selling herself over and over again in the form of a woman, but then was able to take food back to her father Aithon by changing into a man. Siproites the Cretan was transformed because he saw Artemis bathing while he was out hunting.

As Galateia lamented and supplicated constantly, Leto pitied her and transformed her daughter's sex into that of a boy. The people of Phaistos still remember her transformation and sacrifice to Leto Phytia {"Productive"}, because she was the one who produced male genitals for the girl. They call the festival the Ecdysia because the girl took off {*ekduo*} her dress. And it is a custom at their weddings first to lie down by the statue of Leucippos.

26 Hylas

When Heracles was sailing with the Argonauts after being appointed by them as leader, he also brought along with him Hylas, Ceyx's son, who was <*unintelligible word*>, young, and handsome. When they reached the strait of Pontos and were sailing past the edge of Mount Arganthone, there was a storm and rough seas, so they let down their anchors there and stopped the ship. While Heracles was preparing the meal for the heroes, the boy Hylas went with a bucket to the Ascanios River to fetch water for the champions. Some Nymphs, the daughters of the river, fell in love with him at first sight and dragged him down into the spring as he drew water. After Hylas' disappearance, Heracles, when he realized he was not returning to him, left the heroes behind and searched everywhere in the woods and called out "Hylas!" again and again. The Nymphs, afraid that Heracles would find him hidden with them, changed Hylas and made him into an echo, and he responded over and over to Heracles' shout. When Heracles was extremely worn out and unable to find Hylas, he went to the ship and set sail with the champions. He left Polyphemos behind in that place in the hope that somehow he would be able to search and find Hylas for him. But Polyphemos died before finding him, and even now the locals sacrifice to Hylas by the spring. The priest calls him three times by name, and three times an echo answers him.

27 Iphigeneia

Theseus and Helen daughter of Zeus had a daughter, Iphigeneia. Clytaimnestra, Helen's sister, raised her and told Agamemnon that she had given birth to her; for when their brothers asked, Helen said that she was still a virgin when she had left Theseus. When the army of the Achaians was held back in Aulis by its inability to sail, the seers foretold that they would sail if they sacrificed Iphigeneia to Artemis. When the Achaians demanded her as a sacrificial victim, Agamemnon gave her to them. As she was led to the altar, the leaders did not look at her, but all turned their eyes elsewhere. But Artemis made a calf appear at the altar in place of Iphigeneia and took the girl very far from Greece to the so-called Euxine Sea to be with Thoas, Borysthenes' son. The goddess called the nomadic tribe there the Tauroi (because she made a bull {*tauros*} appear at the altar in Iphigeneia's place) and appointed Iphigeneia priestess of Artemis Tauropolos {perhaps "Worshiped at Tauros"}.

When the appointed time came, Artemis settled Iphigeneia on the so-called White Isle with Achilles. She changed her into an unaging and immortal divinity and named her Orsilochia instead of Iphigeneia. She became Achilles' mate.

28 Typhon

Typhon was Ge's son, a divinity prodigious in strength and bizarre in appearance, for a lot of heads, hands, and wings grew on him, and from his thighs grew huge serpent coils. He emitted all sorts of sounds, and nothing could stand against his power. He desired to have Zeus' rule, and none of the gods could stand up to him as he attacked. They all fled to Egypt out of fear, and only Athena and Zeus stayed behind. Typhon followed the gods' tracks. They escaped through foresight by changing their appearances into animals. Apollo became a hawk; Hermes an ibis; Ares the lepidotus fish; Artemis a cat; Dionysos changed into a goat; Heracles into a fawn; Hephaistos a bull; and Leto a field mouse. Each of the other gods changed his appearance as he could. When Zeus hit Typhon with a thunderbolt, Typhon, burning, hid himself in the sea and put out the flame. But Zeus did not relent; no, he threw Aitna, the biggest mountain, on top of Typhon and set Hephaistos on its peaks to guard him. Hephaistos installed his anvils on Typhon's neck and on them works red-hot molten metal.

34 Smyrna

Theias, the son of Belos and Oreithyia (one of the Nymphs), had on Mount Lebanon a daughter, Smyrna. Because of her beauty, numerous men from numerous cities came to ask for her hand, but she came up with many ways to deceive her parents and create delay; for a terrible passion for her father held her in its mad grip. In the beginning she hid her malady out of shame. But when her passion goaded her on, she revealed her story to her nurse, Hippolyte. The nurse promised to provide her a cure for her deviant passion and brought word to Theias that the daughter of a rich family desired to come to his bed secretly. Theias, who did not know what sort of deception was being played on him, accepted the proposition. In his room, on his bed, in the dark, he awaited the girl; the nurse brought in Smyrna after dressing the girl in a disguise. For a long time this odious and sinful act went on without being discovered. When Smyrna became pregnant, a desire came over Theias to find out whom he had impregnated. He concealed a light in his room, and when Smyrna came to him, the light was suddenly uncovered and she was exposed. She gave birth to the child prematurely, raised her hands into the air, and prayed to appear no more among the living or the dead. Zeus transformed her, making her into a tree and calling it *smyrna* {"myrrh"} after her. This tree is said each year to weep its fruit from its wood. Theias, Smyrna's father, killed himself because of his sinful act. As for their baby, he was by Zeus' will raised. They called him Adonis, and Aphrodite loved him very much because of his beauty.

36 Pandareos

When Rhea was afraid of Cronos and concealed Zeus in his Cretan hiding place, a goat offered her teat and nursed him. By Rhea's will a golden dog guarded the goat. When Zeus drove out the Titans and took power from Cronos, he transformed the goat and made her immortal. Even now her image is in the stars.[3] He appointed the golden dog to guard his sanctuary in Crete. Pandareos son of Merops stole the dog

[3] The constellation Aiga (Latin Capella).

and brought it to Mount Sipylos, where Tantalos, the son of Zeus and Plouto, received it from Pandareos for safekeeping. When after some time Pandareos came back to Sipylos and asked for the dog, Tantalos swore that he never got it in the first place. In return for the theft Zeus turned Pandareos into a rock right where he stood. As for Tantalos, because he swore a false oath, Zeus struck him down with a thunderbolt and placed Mount Sipylos over his head.

41 The Fox

In Thoricos in Attica, Cephalos son of Deion married Procris, the daughter of Erechtheus. Cephalos was young, handsome, and brave. Because of his beauty, Eos fell in love with him, abducted him, and made him her mate. < . . . >[4] So then, Cephalos tested Procris to see if she wanted to remain faithful to him. On some pretext or other he pretended to go hunting, but he sent to her a male slave she did not know with a great deal of gold. Cephalos instructed the slave to tell Procris that a foreigner was in love with her and offered her this gold if she would sleep with him. Procris at first refused the gold, but when Cephalos sent twice the amount, she agreed and accepted the proposition. When Cephalos saw her coming to the chamber and lying down to sleep with the foreigner, he brought out a burning torch and caught her.

Disgraced, Procris left Cephalos and made her way as an exile to the court of Minos, the king of the Cretans. She found him unable to have children and promised a cure. She taught him the way in which he would have children. For Minos was ejaculating snakes, scorpions, and millipedes, killing all the women he slept with. But Pasiphae was the immortal daughter of Helios, so Procris devised the following means for Minos to have children. She inserted a goat's bladder into a woman's vagina; Minos would first discharge the snakes into the bladder, then he would go to Pasiphae and sleep with her. After Minos and Pasiphae had children, Minos gave Procris his javelin and his dog. No beast could escape them; they brought down every one. Procris took them and went to Thoricos in Attica, where Cephalos lived. She changed her clothes and her feminine hairstyle to those of a man and hunted with him. No one who saw her recognized her. When Cephalos saw that he was bagging none of the prey, but that it was all going to Procris, he desired to get the javelin for himself. She promised to give him the dog too, if he was willing to favor her with his youthful beauty. Cephalos accepted the proposition, and when they lay down, Procris revealed herself and reproached him for committing an act far more disgraceful than her own.

Cephalos got the dog and the javelin, but Amphitryon, who needed the dog, came to Cephalos in the hope that he would be willing to bring his dog and go after the fox with him. In return Amphitryon promised to give Cephalos his share of the booty that he got from the Teleboans. At that time a fox, a prodigious beast, had appeared in the land of the Cadmeians. It continuously came down off Teumessos and snatched the Cadmeians again and again. Every thirty days they put out for it a little

[4] Cephalos at first refused Eos, but she convinced him that Procris may have been unfaithful.

child, which it would take and devour. When Amphitryon asked Creon and the Cadmeians to march with him against the Teleboans, they said they would not unless he aided them in killing the fox. So Amphitryon agreed to the Cadmeians' condition. He went to Cephalos, told him of the agreement, and urged him to come to Thebes with his dog. Cephalos accepted the proposition and came to hunt the fox. It was fated that the fox would not be caught by anything that pursued it, and that nothing that the dog pursued would escape. So when they reached the plain of the Thebans, Zeus saw them and turned both the dog and fox to stone.

APOLLODORUS

(probably 1st or 2nd c. AD, wrote in Greek)

The Library (Bibliotheke) *is a mythological work attributed to Apollodorus (sometimes he is called Pseudo-Apollodorus because our author is certainly not the famous scholar Apollodorus, who had written a work on the gods in the 2nd century* BC*). The work is essentially a basic handbook of Greek myth that was probably compiled sometime during the first two centuries* AD*. It is organized by lineage: the first book covers the gods and the family of Deucalion; the second the lineage of Inachos; the third the lineage of Agenor. The last section of the work is missing (it breaks off in the middle of the accounts of Theseus), but we have an epitome (an abridged version), which covers the remainder of the tale of Theseus and the events surrounding the Trojan War. The* Library *is a valuable source for modern students of myth both for its usually clear narration and for the amount of material in it that is derived from earlier writers, including such important mythographers as Acusilaus and Pherecydes. One difficulty caused by this is the presence of sometimes conflicting pieces of information where Apollodorus follows or reports different authorities. Included here are extended excerpts of the* Library, *mostly centered on creation and the major heroes.*

FROM *LIBRARY*

A1 The Early Gods, the Rise of Zeus, and the Titanomachy (1.1.1–1.2.6)

[1.1] Ouranos was the first to rule the entire cosmos. Having married Ge, he first fathered the ones called "Hundred-Handers," namely Briareos, Gyes, and Cottos, who stood unsurpassed in size and power, each with a hundred hands and each with fifty heads. After them Ge bore him the Cyclopes, namely Arges, Steropes, and Brontes, and each of them had a single eye on his forehead. But Ouranos bound them and threw them into Tartaros (this is a gloomy place in the house of Hades that is as far away from Ge as Ge is from Ouranos). Then he had more children with Ge—sons who were called the Titans, namely Oceanos, Coios, Hyperion, Creios, Iapetos, and, youngest of them all, Cronos; and also daughters, called the Titanesses, namely Tethys, Rhea, Themis, Mnemosyne, Phoibe, Dione, and Theia.

Ge grew angry at the destruction of her children who had been thrown into Tartaros. She persuaded the Titans to attack their father and gave an adamantine sickle to Cronos. And, except for Oceanos, they attacked him, and Cronos cut off his father's genitals and threw them into the sea. From the drops of flowing blood the Erinyes were born, Alecto, Tisiphone, and Megaira. Having removed Ouranos from power, the Titans brought up their brothers who had been thrown down into Tartaros and entrusted the kingship to Cronos.

But he again bound the Hundred-Handers and Cyclopes and shut them up in Tartaros. He married his sister Rhea, and since Ge and Ouranos told him in a prophecy that he would be deposed from power by his own child, he swallowed his children as they were born. He swallowed the firstborn Hestia, then Demeter and Hera, and after them Plouton and Poseidon. Rhea grew angry at what he had done, and when it happened that her belly was swollen with Zeus, she went to Crete. She gave birth to Zeus in a cave on Mount Dicte. And she gave him to the Couretes and to the daughters of Melisseus, the Nymphs Adrasteia and Ida, to raise. These same Nymphs raised the child on the milk of Amaltheia, and the Couretes, wearing armor, stood guard over the infant in the cave and banged their shields with their spears so that Cronos would not hear the sound of his child. Rhea wrapped a stone in swaddling clothes and gave it to Cronos to swallow as if it were their newborn child.

A2 The Titanomachy

[1.2] When Zeus became an adult, he took Metis daughter of Oceanos as his accomplice, and she gave Cronos a drug to swallow. Under its influence he was forced first to vomit up the stone, then the children that he had swallowed. Along with them Zeus fought the war against Cronos and the Titans. They had been fighting for ten years when Ge foretold that Zeus would be victorious if he took as allies those who had been thrown into Tartaros. He killed Campe, who guarded them, and loosed their bindings. And then the Cyclopes gave Zeus thunder, lightning, and the thunderbolt; they gave Hades a helmet; and they gave Poseidon a trident. Armed with these weapons, they defeated the Titans, threw them into Tartaros and set the Hundred-Handers to guard them. As for themselves, they cast lots for dominion, and Zeus received power in the sky, Poseidon power in the sea, and Plouton power in the house of Hades.

The Titans had offspring. Oceanos and Tethys had the Oceanids: Asia, Styx, Electra, Doris, Eurynome, Amphitrite, and Metis. Coios and Phoibe had Asteria and Leto. Hyperion and Theia had Eos, Helios, and Selene. Creios and Eurybia daughter of Pontos had Astraios, Pallas, and Perses. Iapetos and Asia had Atlas, who holds the sky on his shoulders, Prometheus, Epimetheus, and Menoitios, whom Zeus threw down into Tartaros after striking him with a thunderbolt during the Titanomachy. Cronos and Philyra had Cheiron, a Centaur of double form. Eos and Astraios had the Winds and Stars. Perses and Asteria had Hecate. Pallas and Styx had Nike, Cratos, Zelos, and Bia. And Zeus gave the water of Styx, which flows from a rock in Hades, the power to bind oaths. He gave her this honor as a reward for her joining, along with her children, his fight against the Titans.

Pontos and Ge had Phorcos, Thaumas, Nereus, Eurybia, and Ceto. Thaumas and Electra then had Iris and the Harpies (named Aello and Ocypete). Phorcos and Ceto had the Phorcides and the Gorgons, whom we will discuss when we tell the story of Perseus. Nereus and Doris had the Nereids, whose names are Cymothoe, Speio, Glauconome, Nausithoe, Halie, Erato, Sao, Amphitrite, Eunice, Thetis, Eulimene, Agaue, Eudora, Doto, Pherousa, Galateia, Actaia, Pontomedousa, Hippothoe, Lysianassa, Cymo, Eione, Halimede, Plexaure, Eucrante, Proto, Calypso, Panope, Cranto, Neomeris, Hipponoe, Ianeira, Polynome, Autonoe, Melite, Dione, Nesaia, Dero, Euagore, Psamathe, Eumolpe, Ione, Dynamene, Ceto, and Limnoreia.

B1 The Children of Zeus, Other Genealogies and Tales (1.3.1–1.4.5)

[1.3] Zeus married Hera and fathered Hebe, Eileithyia, and Ares, but he had intercourse with many mortal and immortal women. Now, by Themis daughter of Ouranos he had daughters, first the Horai, namely Eirene, Eunomia, and Dike, then the Moirai, namely Clotho, Lachesis, and Atropos. By Dione he had Aphrodite. By Eurynome daughter of Oceanos he had the Charites, namely Aglaia, Euphrosyne, and Thaleia. By Styx he had Persephone. By Mnemosyne he had the Muses, first Calliope, then Cleio, Melpomene, Euterpe, Erato, Terpsichore, Ourania, Thaleia, and Polymnia.

B2 Orpheus

Calliope and Oiagros (though supposedly Apollo) had Linos, whom Heracles killed, and Orpheus, who was trained to sing to the cithara and moved stones and trees by his singing. When his wife Eurydice died after being bitten by a snake, he went down to the house of Hades, wishing to bring her back, and persuaded Plouton to send her up. Plouton promised to do this if Orpheus would not turn around as he made his way until he arrived at his own house. But Orpheus, in doubt, turned around and looked at his wife, and she returned to the underworld. Orpheus also discovered the mysteries of Dionysos, and he was buried near Pieria after he was torn apart by Mainads.

B3 Hyacinthos, Thamyris, and Others

Cleio fell in love with Pieros son of Magnes because of Aphrodite's anger (Cleio had reproached her for loving Adonis). She shared his bed and had a son by him, Hyacinthos. Thamyris, the son of Philammon and the Nymph Argiope, came to desire Hyacinthos and was the first to love other men. But Apollo later accidentally killed Hyacinthos, who was his boyfriend, by hitting him with a discus. Thamyris, on the other hand, who excelled in beauty and singing to the cithara, had a musical contest with the Muses and agreed that if he were found better, he would get to sleep with all of them, but if he lost, he would be deprived of whatever they wished. When the Muses bested him, they deprived him of his sight and his skill at the cithara.

Euterpe and the river Strymon had Rhesos, whom Diomedes killed at Troy. According to some he was Calliope's son. Thaleia and Apollo had the Corybantes. Melpomene and Acheloos had the Sirens, of whom we shall speak when we tell the story of Odysseus.

B4 Hephaistos and Athena

Hera bore Hephaistos without sexual intercourse. According to Homer, however, she had him with Zeus, and Zeus threw him out of heaven for helping Hera when she was in chains. Zeus hung her from Olympos for sending a storm against Heracles when he was sailing away after taking Troy. Thetis saved Hephaistos after he fell on Lemnos and became crippled in his legs.

Zeus slept with Metis, who changed into many forms in order not to have sex with him, and when she became pregnant, he swallowed her down quickly because Ge had said that after having the daughter she was pregnant with she would have a son who would become ruler of heaven. Zeus was afraid of this and swallowed her. When it was time for the birth, Prometheus (although others say it was Hephaistos) struck Zeus' head with an ax, and Athena, dressed for battle, sprang up out of the top of his head near the river Triton.

B5 Artemis and Apollo

[1.4] As for the daughters of Coios, Asteria changed herself into a quail and threw herself into the sea to avoid intercourse with Zeus, and a city was called Asteria after her in former times, though later it was called Delos. Leto, after sleeping with Zeus, was driven over the whole earth by Hera until she came to Delos. She gave birth first to Artemis. Then, with her daughter acting as midwife, she bore Apollo.

Artemis spent her time engaged in hunting and remained a virgin. Apollo learned to prophesy from Pan, the son of Zeus and Hubris, and came to Delphi. At that time Themis gave the oracles. But when the serpent Python, the guardian of the oracle, tried to keep him from passing near the chasm, Apollo killed it and took possession of the oracle. Not much later he also killed Tityos, who was the son of Zeus and Orchomenos' daughter Elare. Out of fear of Hera, Zeus had hidden this woman underground after sleeping with her, though he did bring up into the light her gargantuan son Tityos, with whom she was pregnant. When Leto was coming to Pytho, Tityos saw Leto and, being filled with desire, tried to drag her off with him. But she called her children, and they shot him down with their bows. Even after death he is punished; vultures eat his heart in the house of Hades.

Apollo also killed Marsyas, the son of Olympos, who found the flutes that Athena had thrown away because they made her face ugly and who entered into a musical contest with Apollo. They agreed that the winner would do whatever he wanted to the loser. When the contest started, Apollo flipped his cithara upside down and competed. He told Marsyas to do the same thing. When he could not, Apollo was declared the winner and, suspending Marsyas from an overhanging pine tree, sliced off his skin and thus killed him.

Artemis killed Orion in Delos. They say he was born of the earth and had a gigantic body. Pherecydes says he was the son of Poseidon and Euryale. Poseidon gave him the ability to walk on the sea. He first married Side, whom Hera tossed into the house of Hades because she rivaled her in beauty. Then he went to Chios and sued for the hand of Merope daughter of Oinopion. But Oinopion got him drunk, blinded him after he passed out, and then had him dumped by the shore. Orion went to Hephaistos' forge and picked up a boy. Placing the child on his shoulders, Orion ordered him to guide him to where the sun rises. When he arrived there, he recovered his sight after being completely healed by the solar brightness and set off quickly after Oinopion. But Poseidon had Hephaistos build a house for Oinopion under the earth, and Eos, who had fallen in love with Orion (Aphrodite made Eos fall in love constantly because she had shared Ares' bed), kidnapped him and brought him to Delos. But Orion, according to others, was killed because he challenged Artemis to a discus contest; according to some he was shot by Artemis for trying to rape Opis, one of the virgins who had come from the Hyperboreans. Poseidon married Amphitrite and fathered Triton and Rhode, the latter of whom Helios married.

C The Rape of Persephone (1.5.1–1.5.3)

[1.5] Plouton fell in love with Persephone and secretly kidnapped her with Zeus' help. Demeter wandered over the whole earth in search of her by day and night with torches. When she learned from the people of Hermion that Plouton had kidnapped her, she was angry with the gods and left heaven. She made herself look like a mortal woman and came to Eleusis. First she sat down upon the rock called Agelastos {"Laughless"} after her, which is located near the well known as Callichoros. Then she went to Celeos, who was at that time ruling the Eleusinians. There were women in his house, and they told her to sit with them. An old woman named Iambe joked with the goddess and made her smile. This is why they say women make jokes at the festival of the Thesmophoria.

When Celeos' wife Metaneira had a child, Demeter took it and nursed it. Wishing to make it immortal, she placed the infant in the fire during the night and stripped away its mortal flesh. By day Demophon (for this was the child's name) grew astoundingly, and so Praxithea kept watch, and when she found him hidden in the fire, she cried out. For this reason the infant was destroyed by the fire, and the goddess revealed herself. She prepared a chariot with winged dragons and gave wheat to Triptolemos, the eldest of Metaneira's children. Drawn through the sky in the chariot, he scattered seed over the whole inhabited world. But Panyasis says that Triptolemos was Eleusis' son, for he says that it was to Eleusis[1] that Demeter came. Pherecydes says that he was the son of Oceanos and Ge.

When Zeus ordered Plouton to send Kore back up, Plouton gave her a pomegranate seed to eat so that she would not remain for a long time by her mother's side. Not foreseeing what would result, she ate it. Ascalaphos, the son of Acheron and Gorgyra, testified against Persephone, and so Demeter placed a heavy rock on top of him in the house of Hades. Persephone was forced to remain for a third of each year with Plouton and the rest of the year with the gods. That is what is told about Demeter.

D1 The Gigantomachy and Typhon (1.6.1–1.6.3)

[1.6] But Ge, angry about what happened to the Titans, produced the Giants by Ouranos, unsurpassed in bodily size, in power unconquerable. They looked frightful in countenance, with thick hair hanging from their heads and chins, and they had serpent coils for legs. According to some they were born in Phlegrai, but according to others in Pallene. They hurled rocks and flaming trees into heaven. Greatest of them all were Porphyrion and Alcyoneus. Alcyoneus was immortal as long as he fought in the same land where he was born, and he even drove the cattle of Helios out of Erytheia. It had been prophesied to the gods that none of the Giants could be killed by gods, but that if a mortal fought as their ally, the Giants would die. When Ge learned of this, she sought a magic plant to prevent them from being killed even by a mortal, but Zeus forbade Eos, Selene, and Helios to shine. Then he himself cut the plant before Ge could and had Athena call Heracles to help them as an ally. Heracles first shot Alcyoneus, but when he fell onto the earth, he was reinvigorated. At Athena's direction, Heracles dragged him outside of Pallene. That, then, is how he died; but Porphyrion moved against Heracles and Hera in the battle. Zeus put desire for Hera into him. She called for help when the Giant was tearing her clothes in his desire to rape her, and after Zeus hit him with a thunderbolt, Heracles shot and

[1] King Eleusis, eponymous ruler of the city.

killed him with his bow. As for the other Giants, Apollo shot Ephialtes' left eye out; Heracles shot out the right. Dionysos killed Eurytos with his thyrsos. Hecate killed Clytios with torches. Hephaistos killed Mimas by hitting him with molten metal. Athena threw the island of Sicily onto Encelados as he fled, and she cut the skin off of Pallas and covered her own body with it during the battle. Polybotes was pursued by Poseidon across the sea and came to Cos. Poseidon broke off a piece of the island (called Nisyron) and threw it on him. Hermes, wearing Hades' cap, killed Hippolytos in the fight, while Artemis killed Gration. The Moirai, fighting with bronze clubs, killed Agrios and Thoas. Zeus destroyed the rest by hurling his thunderbolts. Heracles shot all of them as they died.

D2 Typhon

When the gods had defeated the Giants, Ge became more angry, copulated with Tartaros, and bore Typhon in Cilicia. He had a form that was a mix of man and beast. He bested in size and strength everything that Ge had produced. As far as the thighs he was man-shaped and of such immense size that he was taller than all the mountains, and his head often touched the stars. One of his hands stretched out to the west and one to the east, and from them stood out a hundred dragon heads. From the thighs down he had gigantic viper coils that, when stretched out, reached as far as the very top of his head and produced a great hissing. His whole body was covered in wings, his coarse hair was whipped away from his head and chin by the wind, and fire flashed from his eyes. [Such was Typhon, so great was Typhon when he threw flaming rocks as he moved against heaven itself with hissing noises and shouting, and he belched a great blast of fire from his mouth.]

When the gods saw him attacking heaven, they took refuge in Egypt and, being pursued, changed their forms into animals. But Zeus threw thunderbolts when Typhon was far off and cut him down with an adamantine sickle when he came close. He doggedly pursued him as he fled to Mount Casios, which looks over Syria. There Zeus saw that Typhon was seriously wounded and engaged him hand-to-hand. But Typhon wrapped his coils around Zeus and got him in a hold. He stripped away the sickle and cut out the sinews of his hands and feet. Lifting Zeus onto his shoulders, he carried him across the sea to Cilicia, and when he arrived, he put him into the Corycian cave. Likewise, hiding the sinews in a bearskin, he stowed them there. He set the dragoness Delphyne to guard him. This girl was half-beast. But Hermes and Aigipan stole the sinews and put them back in Zeus without being caught. Zeus, having gotten his strength back, suddenly flew down from heaven in a chariot pulled by winged horses and threw thunderbolts at Typhon as he pursued him to the mountain called Nysa, where the Moirai deceived him as he fled, and, persuaded that he would be reinvigorated, he tasted the ephemeral fruits. When the pursuit began again, he came to Thrace and, fighting around Mount Haimos, hurled whole mountains. But these were forced back on him by the thunderbolt, and blood {*haima*} gushed out onto the mountain, and they say that it is from this that the mountain is called Haimos. As Typhon tried to flee across the Sicilian sea, Zeus threw Mount Aitna in Sicily on him. This mountain is enormous, and down to this day they say that the eruptions of fire from it come from the thunderbolts that were hurled. But enough about that.

E1 Prometheus and Humanity (1.7.1–1.7.3)

[1.7] Prometheus fashioned humans from water and earth. He also gave them fire without Zeus' knowledge by hiding it in a fennel stalk. When Zeus discovered this, he ordered Hephaistos to nail his body to Mount Caucasus (this is a mountain in Scythia). Prometheus was nailed to it and bound for many years. Each day an eagle flew down to him and would eat the lobes of his liver, which grew back at night. Prometheus paid this penalty for the stolen fire until Heracles later freed him, as I will explain in the section on Heracles.

E2 Deucalion and Pyrrha

Prometheus had a son, Deucalion. He was king of the area around Phthia and married Pyrrha, the daughter of Epimetheus and Pandora, whom the gods made as the first woman. When Zeus wished to wipe out the bronze race, Deucalion built an ark at Prometheus' direction. He put into it supplies and boarded it with Pyrrha. Zeus poured a great rain from heaven and flooded most of Greece so that all the people were destroyed except a few who escaped to the nearby high mountains. At that time the mountains in Thessaly split, and everything outside of the Isthmos and the Peloponnese was flooded. Deucalion was carried in the ark across the sea for nine days and an equal number of nights and landed on Mount Parnassos. There, when the rains stopped, he disembarked and sacrificed to Zeus Phyxios {"God of Escape"}. Zeus sent Hermes to him and bade him choose whatever he wanted. Deucalion chose to have people. At Zeus' direction he picked up rocks and threw them over his head; the ones Deucalion threw became men and the ones Pyrrha threw became women. From this they were also metaphorically called people {*laos*} from the word for stone {*laas*}.

E3 Children of Deucalion

Deucalion had children by Pyrrha: first Hellen, whom some say Zeus fathered; second Amphictyon, who ruled Attica after Cranaos; then a daughter, Protogeneia, by whom Zeus fathered Aethlios. Hellen with the Nymph Orseis had Doros, Xouthos, and Aiolos. The people called Greeks he named Hellenes after himself and divided the land among his children. Xouthos got the Peloponnese, and by Creousa daughter of Erechtheus he fathered Achaios and Ion. The Achaians and the Ionians are named after them. Doros got the land outside the Peloponnese and named the inhabitants Dorians after himself. Aiolos ruled over the places in Thessaly and called those who dwelled there Aiolians. He married Enarete daughter of Deimachos and fathered seven sons, Cretheus, Sisyphos, Athamas, Salmoneus, Deion, Magnes, and Perieres, and five daughters, Canace, Alcyone, Peisidice, Calyce, and Perimede. Perimede and Acheloos had Hippodamas and Orestes. Peisidice and Myrmidon had Antiphos and Actor.

F Oineus, Meleagros, and the Calydonian Boar Hunt (1.8.1–1.8.3)

[1.8] Oineus was king of Calydon and was the first to get a vine plant from Dionysos. He married Althaia daughter of Thestios and fathered Toxeus. When Toxeus jumped over the ditch around the city, Oineus himself killed him. In addition to him, Oineus had Thyreus, Clymenos, a daughter named Gorge, whom Andraimon married, and another daughter, Deianeira, whom they say Althaia had with Dionysos. This daughter drove chariots and trained for war; Heracles wrestled with Acheloos to see who would marry her. Althaia had a son, Meleagros, with Oineus, though they say that he was fathered by Ares. The story goes that when he was seven days old, the Moirai arrived and said that Meleagros would die when the log burning in the fireplace was burned up. When she heard this, Althaia picked up the log and put it into a chest. Although Meleagros grew to be an invulnerable and strong man, he died in the following way. When the annual crop had come to the countryside, Oineus sacrificed the firstfruits to all the gods but completely forgot about Artemis. She grew wroth and sent a boar, greater than any other in size and strength, which caused the land to remain fallow and destroyed the livestock and any people who met with it. Oineus called together all the heroes of Greece to go after this boar and promised to give the hide as a prize of valor to the man who killed the beast.

Those who came to hunt the boar were: from Calydon, Meleagros son of Oineus, and Dryas son of Ares; from Messene, Idas and Lynceus, the sons of Aphareus; from Lacedaimon, Castor and Polydeuces, the sons of Zeus and Leda; from Athens, Theseus son of Aigeus; from Pherai, Admetos son of Pheres; from Arcadia, Ancaios and Cepheus, the sons of Lycourgos; from Iolcos, Jason son of Aison; from Thebes, Iphicles son of Amphitryon; from Larissa, Peirithous son of Ixion; from Phthia, Peleus son of Aiacos; from Salamis, Telamon son of Aiacos; from Phthia, Eurytion son of Actor; from Arcadia, Atalante daughter of Schoineus; and from Argos, Amphiaraos son of Oicles. The sons of Thestios also joined them.

After they had assembled, Oineus entertained them as his guests for nine days, but on the tenth, Cepheus, Ancaios, and some of the others decided it was beneath them to go out hunting with a woman. Although Meleagros had a wife (Cleopatra, the daughter of Idas and Marpessa), he also wanted to have a child by Atalante. So he forced them to go out hunting with her. When they had surrounded the boar, Hyleus and Ancaios were killed by the beast, and Peleus accidentally killed Eurytion with a javelin. Atalante was the first to shoot the boar with her bow, hitting it in the back. Amphiaraos was the second, hitting it in the eye. But Meleagros killed it with a blow to the flank. When he received the hide, he gave it to Atalante. The sons of Thestios thought it disgraceful that a woman would get the prize for valor when there were men around and took it from her, saying that if Meleagros preferred not to take it, it belonged to them because they were his uncles. Meleagros grew angry, killed the sons of Thestios, and gave the hide to Atalante. Althaia grieved over the death of her brothers and set fire to the log. Meleagros died immediately.

But some say that Meleagros did not die in this way, but that when the sons of Thestios laid claim to the skin, alleging that Iphiclos had struck the first blow, war erupted between the Couretes and the Calydonians. When Meleagros went out and killed some of the sons of Thestios, Althaia called down a curse upon him. He was angry and would not leave his house. But then when the enemy came near the walls of the city and when his fellow citizens, with the olive branches of suppliants in their hands, prayed for him to help, he was with difficulty persuaded by his wife to go out. After he killed the remaining sons of Thestios, he died while fighting. After Meleagros died, Althaia and Cleopatra hanged themselves, and the women who mourned for his corpse were turned into birds.

G1 Jason and the Argonauts; Medeia (1.9.16–1.9.28)

Jason was the son of Aison (who was the son of Cretheus) and Polymede daughter of Autolycos. He lived in Iolcos, where Pelias became king after Cretheus. When Pelias consulted an oracle about his kingdom, the god declared, "Beware the one-sandaled man." At first he did not understand the oracle, but later it became clear to him. When he was performing a sacrifice to Poseidon on the shore, he invited many people to it, including Jason. Jason, who lived in the country out of a desire to farm, hurried to the sacrifice. In crossing the Anauros River, he lost a sandal in the stream and so came out the other side "one-sandaled." When Pelias caught sight of him, he connected him with the oracle, approached him, and asked what he would do if he were the ruler and received an oracle saying that he would be killed by one of his citizens. Jason, either because it happened to occur to him or because of the wrath of Hera (so that Medeia would turn out to be Pelias' undoing since he dishonored Hera), said, "I would command him to bring the Golden Fleece." When Pelias heard this, he immediately ordered him to go after the Fleece, which was in a grove of Ares in Colchis, hanging from an oak tree and guarded by a serpent that never slept.

Sent in quest of it, Jason summoned Argos son of Phrixos. At Athena's direction Argos built the fifty-oared ship named the *Argo* after its builder. Athena affixed to the prow a piece of wood that could speak from the oak at Dodona.[2] When the ship was built, Jason consulted an oracle, and the god commanded him to set sail after gathering the heroes of Greece. The ones he gathered were: Tiphys son of Hagnias, who was the ship's helmsman; Orpheus son of Oiagros; Zetes and Calais, the sons of Boreas; Castor and Polydeuces, the sons of Zeus; Telamon and Peleus, the sons of Aiacos; Heracles son of Zeus; Theseus son of Aigeus; Idas and Lynceus, the sons of Aphareus; Amphiaraos son of Oicles; Caineus son of Coronos; Palaimon son of Hephaistos or Aitolos; Cepheus son of Aleos; Laertes son of Arceisios; Autolycos son of Hermes; Atalante daughter of Schoineus; Menoitios son of Actor; Actor son of Hippasos; Admetos son of Pheres; Acastos son of Pelias; Eurytos son of Hermes; Meleagros son of Oineus; Ancaios son of Lycourgos; Euphemos son of Poseidon; Poias son of Thaumacos; Boutes son of Teleon; Phanos and Staphylos, the sons of Dionysos; Erginos son of Poseidon; Periclymenos son of Neleus; Augeas son of Helios; Iphiclos son of Thestios; Argos son of Phrixos; Euryalos son of Mecisteus; Peneleos son of Hippalmos; Leitos son of Alector; Iphitos son of Naubolos; Ascalaphos and Ialmenos, the sons of Ares; Asterios son of Cometes; and Polyphemos son of Elatos.

G2 The Voyage to Colchis

With Jason as captain these men put to sea and landed on the island of Lemnos. It happened that Lemnos at that time was empty of men and ruled by Hypsipyle daughter of Thoas for the following reason. The Lemnian women did not honor Aphrodite, so she afflicted them with an awful smell. For this reason their husbands took female captives from nearby Thrace and brought them into their beds. Because they were dishonored, the Lemnian women killed their fathers and husbands. Hypsipyle alone hid her father Thoas and saved him. Having landed on Lemnos at that time when it

[2] The sacred oak of Zeus in Dodona had oracular powers.

was ruled by women, the Argonauts slept with the women. Hypsipyle took Jason into her bed and had sons, Euneos and Nebrophonos.

After Lemnos they landed in the land of the Doliones, whose king was Cyzicos. He received them in a very friendly fashion. But when they put to sea from there at night and encountered adverse winds, they landed again among the Doliones without realizing it. The Doliones thought they were a Pelasgian army (they happened to be under constant attack by the Pelasgians) and engaged them in a night battle, the unrealizing attacking the unrealizing. The Argonauts killed many, including Cyzicos. When day came and they realized what had happened, they bitterly lamented, cut off their hair, and gave Cyzicos a lavish burial. After the funeral they sailed off and landed in Mysia.

There they left behind Heracles and Polyphemos. Hylas son of Theiodamas, was Heracles' boyfriend. He had been sent off to get water when he was abducted by a Nymph because of his beauty. Polyphemos heard him shouting, drew his sword, and chased after him in the belief that the boy was being abducted by pirates. When Heracles met him, he told him about it. While the two of them searched for Hylas, the ship put to sea. Polyphemos founded the city of Cios in Mysia and became its king, while Heracles returned to Argos. But Herodorus says that Heracles at that time did not sail at all, but that he was a slave at the court of Omphale. Pherecydes says that he was left behind at Aphetai in Thessaly after the *Argo* said that it was unable to bear his weight. Demaratos hands down the story that he had sailed all the way to Colchis, for Dionysios says that he was the leader of the Argonauts.

From Mysia they went off to the land of the Bebryces, ruled by Amycos, the son of Poseidon and a Bithynian Nymph. Because he was strong, he forced strangers who landed there to box and in that way killed them. Approaching the *Argo* in his usual way, he challenged the best of them to box. Polydeuces took it upon himself to box against him, struck him on the elbow, and killed him. When the Bebryces attacked him, the heroes snatched up their weapons and killed many of them as they tried to flee.

Setting sail from there, they arrived at Salmydessos in Thrace, where Phineus, a prophet who had lost his sight, lived. Some say he was the son of Agenor; some say he was the son of Poseidon. Some say he was blinded by the gods because he foretold the future to mortals; some say he was blinded by Boreas and the Argonauts because he was persuaded to blind his own children by their stepmother; and some say he was blinded by Poseidon because he told the sons of Phrixos how to sail from Colchis to Greece. The gods also sent the Harpies to him. They had wings, and when a meal was set out for Phineus, they flew down from the sky. They would snatch up most of it, and what little they left behind was all tainted with a bad odor so that no one could eat it. When the Argonauts wanted to learn what would happen on their voyage, he said that he would give them advice about it if they would rid him of the Harpies. They set out a table of food for him. The Harpies flew down suddenly with a cry and snatched the food. When Zetes and Calais, the sons of Boreas, saw them, they drew their swords and, being themselves winged, pursued them through the air. It was fated that the Harpies would die at the hands of the sons of Boreas and that the sons of Boreas would die at the time when they would pursue something they could not catch. As the Harpies were pursued, in the Peloponnese one of them fell into the river Tigres, which is now called the Harpys after her. This one some call

Nicothoe, others Aellopous. The other was called Ocypete (or according to some, Ocythoe; Hesiod says she is called Ocypode). She fled across the Propontis until she came to the Echinadian Islands, which are now called the Strophades after her, for she turned around {*strepho*} as she approached them and, coming to the shore, fell from exhaustion, as did the one pursuing her. Apollonios says in his *Argonautica* that they were pursued as far as the Strophades and did not suffer at all after swearing an oath that they would no longer harm Phineus.

Rid of the Harpies, Phineus gave the Argonauts information about their voyage and advised them about the Symplegades in the sea. These were enormous rocks that closed off the passage by sea when they were smashed together by the force of the winds. The fog over them was dense and the clashing loud. It was impossible even for birds to get through them. So Phineus told them to send a pigeon between the rocks. If they saw that it survived, they were to sail through and not worry. But if they saw it die, they were not to try to press on with sailing. After hearing this they set sail. When they were near the rocks, they released a pigeon from the prow. As it flew, the collision of the rocks cut off the tip of its tail. So they watched for the rocks to retract and then, with earnest rowing and the help of Hera, they passed through, the tip of the ship's stern being clipped off. The Symplegades have stood still since that time, for it was fated that they would stop completely when a ship passed through them.

The Argonauts came to the Mariandynoi, and their king Lycos received them in very friendly fashion. There Idmon the prophet died after a boar wounded him. Tiphys also died, and Ancaios took over the job of steering the ship.

G3 Events in Colchis

They sailed past the Thermodon River and Mount Caucasus and then came to the river Phasis, which is in Colchis. When the ship came to port, Jason went to Aietes. Explaining what he had been ordered to do by Pelias, he asked Aietes to give him the Fleece. Aietes promised to give it to him if Jason would yoke his bronze-footed bulls by himself. These were two wild bulls of exceptional size that he had received as gifts from Hephaistos. They had bronze feet and breathed fire from their mouths. He ordered Jason to yoke them and then plant teeth from a serpent; he had gotten from Athena the other half of the teeth that Cadmos had planted at Thebes.[3] While Jason was at a loss as to how he might be able to yoke the bulls, Medeia fell in love with him. She was the daughter of Aietes and Eidyia daughter of Oceanos. She was also a sorceress. Afraid that he would be destroyed by the bulls, she, unbeknownst to her father, promised to help Jason with yoking the bulls and to get the Fleece into his hands if he would swear to take her as his wife to Greece as his companion on the voyage. After Jason swore that he would, she gave him a potion and ordered him to smear it on his shield, spear, and body when he was getting ready to yoke the bulls. She said that when he was smeared with it, he could not be hurt by fire or iron for the space of one day. She explained to him that once the teeth were planted, men were going to rise up fully armed out of the earth and attack him. She told him that when he saw them crowded together, he was to throw some rocks into the middle of them while keeping his distance. When they fought amongst themselves over this, then he was to kill them.

[3] Apollodorus gives the account of Cadmos and the teeth in M1.

Jason listened to these instructions and smeared himself with the potion. Going to the temple grove, he searched out the bulls. Though they attacked him with a great deal of fire, he succeeded in yoking them. Jason planted the teeth, and armed men grew up out of the ground. Hidden from view, he threw stones where he saw the majority had gathered. Then he approached them while they fought each other and destroyed them. Although the bulls were yoked, Aietes did not give up the Fleece. He wished to destroy the *Argo* by burning it and to kill its sailors. Medeia anticipated him by leading Jason to the Fleece during the night. She put the guardian serpent to sleep with her potions and then, with the Fleece in hand, went to the *Argo* with Jason. Her brother Apsyrtos also went with her. With them the men set sail at night.

G4 The Homeward Voyage

When Aietes found out what Medeia had dared to do, he set out to pursue the ship. When Medeia saw that he was close, she murdered her brother, dismembered him, and cast the pieces into the sea. Aietes gathered up the pieces of his son, and in doing so, fell behind in the pursuit. For that reason he turned back, buried the recovered pieces of his son, and named the place Tomoi {"Cuts"}. He sent out many Colchians to search for the *Argo*, threatening that they would suffer the punishments he intended for Medeia if they did not bring her to him. They divided themselves up and made the search, each in a different place.

Angry over the murder of Apsyrtos, Zeus sent a violent storm against the Argonauts when they were just sailing past the Eridanos River and threw them off course. As they sailed past the Apsyrtides Islands, the ship spoke and said that the anger of Zeus would not come to an end unless they went to Ausonia and had the pollution of Apsyrtos' murder cleansed by Circe. After they sailed past the Ligurian and Celtic peoples, crossed the Sardinian Sea, and coasted along Tyrrhenia, they came to Aiaia, where they supplicated Circe and were cleansed.

When they sailed past the Sirens, Orpheus sang music to counteract their song and so restrained the Argonauts. Boutes alone swam out to them, but Aphrodite snatched him up and settled him in Lilybaion. After the Sirens, Charybdis was next, then Scylla, and the Wandering Rocks, over which a huge flame and thick smoke were seen rising. But Thetis and the Nereids brought the ship through these obstacles at the request of Hera.

They sailed past the island of Thrinacia (which held the cattle of Helios) and came to Corcyra, the island of the Phaiacians ruled by Alcinoos. When the Colchians were unable to find the ship, some of them made new homes in the Ceraunian Mountains, and some went to Illyria and colonized the Apsyrtides Islands. Still others came to the Phaiacians, caught up with the *Argo,* and demanded Medeia from Alcinoos. He said that if she had already had intercourse with Jason he would give her to him. But if she were still a virgin, he said that he would send her back to her father. Arete, the wife of Alcinoos, anticipated him by having Medeia sleep with Jason. As a result, the Colchians decided to live with the Phaiacians, and the Argonauts set sail with Medeia.

While they were sailing at night, they ran into a strong storm. But Apollo stood on the ridges of Melas and used his bow to shoot a bolt of lightning down into the sea. They saw that an island was nearby and, having anchored near it, called it

Anaphe because it had appeared {*anaphaino*} unexpectedly. They dedicated an altar to Apollo Aigletos {"Radiant"}, made sacrifice, and turned their attention to feasting. Twelve female servants given to Medeia by Arete mocked the heroes playfully. As a result, even to this day it is customary for women to make jokes at this sacrifice.

Setting sail from there, they were prevented from landing on Crete by Talos. Some say that he was one of the men of the Bronze Age, but others say he was given to Minos by Hephaistos and was actually a man made of bronze, though others say he was a bull. He had a single vein stretching down from his neck to his ankles. A bronze nail was set firmly into the end of the vein. This Talos guarded the island by running around it three times a day. Therefore, when he saw the *Argo* sailing in, he threw stones at it in his usual manner. He died after being tricked by Medeia. According to some, Medeia threw him into a fit of madness with magic. According to others, she promised to make him immortal but pulled out the nail instead, and he died when all the ichor flowed out. Still others say that he died after being shot in the ankle with an arrow by Poias.

After remaining there for one night, they landed on Aigina because they wanted to get water. A contest arose among them over fetching it. From there they sailed between Euboia and Locris and reached Iolcos. It took them four months to complete the whole voyage.

G5 The Death of Pelias and Exile in Corinth

Pelias, who had decided that there was no possibility of the Argonauts' returning, wanted to kill Aison. Aison, however, asked to be allowed to kill himself. While making a sacrifice, he intentionally drank the bull's blood and died. Jason's mother put a curse on Pelias and hanged herself, leaving behind an infant son named Promachos. Pelias killed even the son she left behind. When Jason returned, he handed over the Fleece and waited for the right moment, wanting to get revenge for the injustices done to him. He sailed then with the heroes to the Isthmos and dedicated the ship to Poseidon. Later, he asked Medeia to look for a way that Pelias might be punished for his crimes against him. She went into the palace of Pelias and by promising to make him young again through her magic, persuaded his daughters to chop him up and boil him. To make them believe, she butchered a ram and, after boiling it, turned it into a lamb. Believing her, they cut their father up and boiled him. Acastos, with the help of the inhabitants of Iolcos, buried his father and kicked Jason out of Iolcos along with Medeia.

They went to Corinth and lived there prosperously for ten years. Later, when Creon, the king of Corinth, betrothed his daughter Glauce to Jason, Jason decided to marry her and divorce Medeia. But Medeia called upon the gods by whom Jason had sworn his oaths and strongly criticized Jason's ingratitude. Then she sent to the bride a dress that had magical potions worked into it. When the girl put it on, she was burned up by vicious fire, as was her father too when he tried to help her. Medeia killed Mermeros and Pheres, the sons she had with Jason. From Helios she got a chariot that was pulled by winged serpents and made her escape to Athens on it. It is also said that when she fled, she left behind her sons, who were still infants, setting them on the altar of Hera Acraia as suppliants. The Corinthians took them out of the sanctuary and wounded them fatally.

Medeia made it to Athens. There she married Aigeus and bore him a son, Medos. Later, she plotted against Theseus and was driven into exile from Athens with her son. But her son conquered many barbarians and called the whole area under his control Media. He died while campaigning against the Indians. Medeia returned unrecognized to Colchis and discovered that Aietes had been deprived of his kingdom by his brother Perses. She killed Perses and restored the kingdom to her father.

H Io (2.1.3)

Iasos, who they say was the father of Io, was the son of Argos and Ismene daughter of Asopos. But the chronicler Castor and many of the tragedians say that Io was the daughter of Inachos. Hesiod and Acusilaus say that she was the daughter of Peiren. Zeus seduced her while she was serving as priestess of Hera. When he was caught by Hera, he touched the girl and turned her into a white cow, swearing that he had not had intercourse with her. Therefore, Hesiod says that oaths made in matters of love do not draw the ire of the gods. Hera asked Zeus for the cow and set all-seeing Argos to guard her. Pherecydes says that Argos was the son of Arestor, Asclepiades that he was the son of Inachos, and Cercops that he was the son of Argos and Ismene daughter of Asopos. But Acusilaus says that he was earth-born. Argos tied her to an olive tree that was in the grove of the Mycenaeans. Zeus ordered Hermes to steal the cow. But since Hierax revealed the plan and Hermes could not do so undetected, he killed Argos by throwing a stone at him (and from that he was called Argeiphontes {"Killer of Argos"}). Hera sent a gadfly against the cow. First, the cow came to the Ionian Gulf (so-called after her), then traveled across Illyria, went over Mount Haimos, and then crossed what at the time was called the Thracian Strait but is now called the Bosporos {"Cow's Crossing"} after her. Going to Scythia and the land of the Cimmerians, she wandered over a great deal of dry land and swam across a lot of sea in both Europe and Asia. Finally, she came to Egypt, where she recovered her old form, and by the river Nile she bore a son, Epaphos. Hera asked the Couretes to kidnap him, and kidnap him they did. But when Zeus learned of it, he killed the Couretes, and Io went in search of her son. She wandered through all of Syria (it was revealed to her there that the wife of the king of Byblos was nursing her son) and found Epaphos. Coming to Egypt, she married Telegonos, who was then king of the Egyptians. She dedicated a statue of Demeter, whom the Egyptians call Isis. In the same way they also called Io Isis.

I Bellerophontes (2.3.1–2.3.2)

[2.3] Bellerophontes son of Glaucos (Sisyphos' son) came to Proitos and was purified after accidentally killing his brother Deliades (or, according to some, Peiren, or, according to others, Alcimenes). Stheneboia fell in love with him and sent him a message about getting together. He rejected her advances, so she told Proitos that Bellerophontes had sent her a message to seduce her. Proitos believed her and gave Bellerophontes a letter to take to Iobates. In the letter he had written, "Kill Bellerophontes."

When Iobates read the letter, he ordered Bellerophontes to kill the Chimaira in the belief that he would be destroyed by the beast, for she could not easily be taken by many men, much less by one, since she had the forepart of a lion and the tail of a serpent, and her third head in the middle was that of a goat. She breathed fire through the last. She was ravaging the land and devastating the livestock, for her body had the power of three beasts. It is said that this Chimaira had been raised by Amisodaros (Homer also says this) and that she was the offspring of Typhon and Echidna (which is Hesiod's account). Bellerophontes got onto Pegasos (this was his winged horse, the child of Medousa and Poseidon) and, carried aloft, shot down Chimaira from Pegasos' back.

After this task Iobates ordered him to battle the Solymoi. When he had accomplished that too, he ordered him to fight the Amazons. When Bellerophontes had killed them too, Iobates selected those with a reputation among the Lycians for excellence in might and ordered them to ambush and kill him. But when he killed all these men too, Iobates was astounded at his power, showed him the letter, and asked him to remain at his court. He gave him his daughter Philonoe to marry, and when he lay on his deathbed, he passed the kingdom on to him.

J1 Acrisios, Danae, and Perseus (2.4.1–2.4.5)

[2.4] When Acrisios consulted an oracle about fathering male children, the god told him that from his daughter a male child would be born who would kill him. In fear of this, he had a bronze chamber constructed under the earth and put Danae under guard. According to some, Proitos seduced her, and that is how the wrangling started between Proitos and Acrisios, but others say that Zeus transformed himself into gold, flowed down through the ceiling into Danae's lap, and had intercourse with her. When Acrisios later learned that she had given birth to Perseus, he refused to believe that she had been seduced by Zeus and so put his daughter and her child into a chest and cast it into the sea. When the chest landed on the island of Seriphos, Dictys took Perseus and raised him.

Dictys' brother Polydectes, who was king of Seriphos, fell in love with Danae, but since Perseus had in the meantime grown to manhood, he was unable to sleep with her. So he called his friends together—and Perseus too—and told them that he was trying to collect contributions so that he could marry Hippodameia daughter of Oinomaos. Perseus said that he would not refuse even to give the head of the Gorgon, so Polydectes asked for horses from everybody else, and when he did not get horses from Perseus, he ordered him to bring the Gorgon's head. With Hermes and Athena guiding him on his way, he came to the daughters of Phorcos, namely Enyo, Pephredo, and Deino (they were the children of Ceto and Phorcos and so the sisters of the Gorgons). They had been old women from birth. These three had a single eye and a single tooth that they took turns passing between them. Perseus gained possession of the eye and tooth, and when they asked for them back, he said that he would hand them over if they told him the way that led to the Nymphs. These Nymphs had winged sandals and the *kibisis*, which they say was a pouch. They also had Hades' cap.

After the Phorcides told him the way, he gave them back their tooth and eye, went to the Nymphs, and got what he was searching so earnestly for. He put on the *kibisis*, tied the sandals to his ankles, and put the cap on his head. While he was wearing the cap, he could see whom he wanted, but he could not be seen by others. He got an adamantine sickle from Hermes, flew all the way to Oceanos, and caught the Gorgons while they slept. Their names were Stheno, Euryale, and Medousa. Only Medousa was mortal, and this was the reason that Perseus had been sent for her head. The Gorgons had heads with serpents' coils spiraling around them, large tusks like boars, bronze arms, and gold wings with which they could fly. They turned those who saw them into stone, so Perseus came to them while they slept. While Athena guided his hand, he turned away, looked into a bronze shield by which he could see the Gorgon's image, and decapitated her. When her head was cut off, the winged horse Pegasos leapt out of the Gorgon, as did Chrysaor, the father of Geryones. Poseidon was the father of both of them. Then Perseus put the head of Medousa into the *kibisis* and went back the way he came. The Gorgons stirred from their bed and set off in pursuit of Perseus, but they were unable to see him because of the cap, for he was concealed by it.

J2 Events After the Gorgons

Arriving in Ethiopia, where Cepheus was king, he found the king's daughter Andromeda set out as food for a sea monster. Cassiepeia, the wife of Cepheus, had vied with the Nereids over beauty, boasting that she was superior to all of them. Because of this the Nereids were enraged. Since Poseidon shared their anger, he sent a flood and a sea monster against the land. The oracle of Ammon said that the disaster would end if Cassiepeia's daughter Andromeda were set out as food for the monster. Forced by the Ethiopians, Cepheus did just that, chaining his daughter to a rock. When Perseus saw her, he fell in love. He promised Cepheus that he would destroy the monster if he would give him the girl to marry after she had been rescued. Oaths were sworn on these terms, and then Perseus faced the monster, killed it, and freed Andromeda.

Phineus, who was Cepheus' brother and had been Andromeda's original fiancé, began to plot against Perseus. When Perseus discovered the plot, he showed him the Gorgon and instantly turned him and his fellow conspirators to stone.

When he came to Seriphos and found that his mother had taken refuge with Dictys at the altars because of Polydectes' violence, he went into the palace. After Polydectes had summoned his friends, Perseus turned away and showed them the Gorgon's head. When they looked upon it, each was turned to stone in the position he happened to be in. After installing Dictys as king of Seriphos, Perseus returned the sandals, *kibisis,* and cap to Hermes and gave the Gorgon's head to Athena. Hermes then gave the aforementioned items back to the Nymphs, and Athena put the Gorgon's head in the middle of her shield. Some say that Medousa had her head cut off because of Athena; they say that the Gorgon wanted to compare her own beauty to the goddess'.

Perseus hurried with Danae and Andromeda to Argos to see Acrisios. When Acrisios learned of this, he grew fearful of the oracle, left Argos, and went to the land of the Pelasgians. King Teutamides of Larissa was holding athletic games in honor of his father, who had passed away, and Perseus came because he wanted to compete. While competing in the pentathlon, he killed Acrisios instantly by hitting him on the foot with the discus. Understanding that the prophecy had been fulfilled, he buried Acrisios outside the city. But he was ashamed to return to Argos to inherit the kingdom of the man who had died because of him, so he went to Tiryns, traded kingdoms with Proitos' son Megapenthes, and handed Argos over to him. Megapenthes became king of the Argives and Perseus became king of Tiryns, fortifying Mideia and Mycenae as well.

Perseus had children with Andromeda. Before returning to Greece, he had Perses, whom he left behind with Cepheus (it is said that the kings of the Persians are his descendants). In Mycenae he had Alcaios, Sthenelos, Heleios, Mestor, and Electryon. He also had a daughter, Gorgophone, whom Perieres married.

K1 Heracles (2.4.8–2.7.7)

Before Amphitryon reached Thebes,[4] Zeus came during the night and made the one night as long as three. He made himself look like Amphitryon, slept with Alcmene, and told her what had happened with the Teleboans. When Amphitryon arrived and saw that his wife did not welcome him home, he asked the reason. After she said that he had arrived the night before and slept with her, he learned from Teiresias of the encounter she had had with Zeus. Alcmene bore two sons, Heracles, the older by a day, to Zeus, and Iphicles to Amphitryon. When Heracles was eight months old, Hera sent two enormous serpents into his bed because she wanted to destroy the infant. Alcmene called to Amphitryon for help, but Heracles stood up, throttled them, one in each hand, and killed them. Pherecydes says that Amphitryon, wishing to know which of the boys was his son, put the serpents into the bed. When Iphicles fled and Heracles confronted them, Amphitryon knew that Iphicles was his.

K2 Heracles' Youth

Heracles was taught to drive chariots by Amphitryon, to wrestle by Autolycos, to shoot a bow by Eurytos, to fight in armor by Castor, and to play the lyre by Linos, who was Orpheus' brother. After Linos had come to Thebes and become a Theban, he was slain by Heracles, who hit him with his lyre (Heracles killed him in a fit of rage because Linos had struck him). When some men prosecuted him for murder, he read out a law of Rhadamanthys that said that any man who defends himself against an instigator of unjust violence is innocent. In this way he was acquitted. Afraid that Heracles would do something like that again, Amphitryon sent him out to tend his herd of cattle. Growing up there, Heracles surpassed everyone in size and strength. It was obvious from his appearance that he was Zeus' son, for his body was four cubits tall, and a fiery radiance shone from his eyes. He also did not miss when he shot a bow or threw a javelin. When he was eighteen years old and out with the herd, he killed the Cithaironian lion, which used to rush from Mount Cithairon and ravage the cattle of Amphitryon, as well as those of Thespios.

Thespios was king of Thespiai, and when Heracles wanted to kill the lion, he went to this man. Thespios entertained him as a guest for fifty days and had one of his daughters (he had fifty of them by Megamede daughter of Arneos) sleep with him every night before Heracles went out to hunt, for he was eager for all of them to have children with Heracles. Though Heracles thought that he was always sleeping with the same one, he slept with all of them. After overpowering the lion, he wore its skin and used its gaping jaws as a helmet.

When he was returning from the hunt, he ran into some heralds sent by Erginos to collect the tribute from the Thebans. The Thebans paid tribute to Erginos for the

[4] Amphitryon, Alcmene's husband, was away fighting a war against the Teleboans.

following reason: One of Menoiceus' charioteers, named Perieres, hit Clymenos, king of the Minyans, with a stone and wounded him in the precinct of Poseidon in Onchestos. When Clymenos was brought to Orchomenos, he was barely alive. As he was dying, he directed his son Erginos to avenge his death. Erginos marched against Thebes, and after inflicting many casualties, he made an oath-bound treaty that the Thebans would send him a hundred cows as tribute each year for twenty years. As the heralds were going to Thebes to get this tribute, Heracles met up with them and mutilated them. He cut off their ears, noses, and hands, tied them around their necks, and told them to take that back to Erginos and the Minyans as tribute. Enraged by this, Erginos marched against Thebes. After Heracles got armor and weapons from Athena and became the commander, he killed Erginos, routed the Minyans, and forced them to pay double the tribute to the Thebans. It happened that Amphitryon died fighting bravely in the battle. Heracles received from Creon his oldest daughter Megara as a prize for bravery. He had three sons with her, Therimachos, Creontiades, and Deicoon. Creon gave his youngest daughter to Iphicles, who had already had a son, Iolaos, with Automedousa daughter of Alcathos. After the death of Amphitryon, Rhadamanthys, the son of Zeus, married Alcmene and, exiled from his country, settled in Ocaleai in Boiotia.

Heracles had already been taught archery by Eurytos. Now he got a sword from Hermes, a bow from Apollo, a golden breastplate from Hephaistos, and a robe from Athena; he cut his own club at Nemea.

After his battle against the Minyans it happened that Heracles was driven mad because of the jealously of Hera. He threw his own children by Megara into a fire, along with two of Iphicles' sons. For this he condemned himself to exile. He was purified by Thespios, and going to Delphi, he asked the god where he should settle. The Pythia then for the first time called him by the name Heracles; up until then he had been called Alceides. She told him to settle in Tiryns and serve Eurystheus for twelve years. She also told him to accomplish the ten labors imposed upon him and said that when the labors were finished, he would become immortal.

K3 First Labor: The Nemean Lion

[2.5] After Heracles heard this, he went to Tiryns and did Eurystheus' bidding. First, he commanded him to bring back the skin of the Nemean Lion. This animal, Typhon's offspring, was invulnerable. When he was going after the lion, he came to Cleonai and was put up as a guest by Molorchos, a poor man. When Molorchos wanted to sacrifice a victim, Heracles told him to hold off for thirty days: if he returned from his hunt safe and sound, he told Molorchos to make a sacrifice fit for a god to Zeus Soter {"Savior"}; if he died, he told Molorchos to make a sacrifice to himself fit for a hero. When he got to Nemea and tracked down the lion, he first shot it with his bow. When he found that it was invulnerable, he brandished his club and pursued it. When it fled into a cave with two entrances, Heracles blocked up one entrance and went after the beast through the other. Getting it in a headlock, he held on, squeezing until he choked it. He put it across his shoulders and brought it back to Cleonai. He found Molorchos on the last of the thirty days about to offer the victim to Heracles in the belief that he was dead. Instead, Heracles sacrificed it to Zeus Soter and then took the lion to Mycenae. Terrified by Heracles' demonstration of manly courage, Eurystheus forbade Heracles from entering the city in the future and ordered him to display his labors before the gates of the city. They say that out of fear Eurystheus also had a bronze storage jar installed under the ground for him to hide in, and he sent a herald, Copreus, the son of Pelops the Eleian, to command Heracles to do his labors. This Copreus had killed Iphitos, gone into exile in Mycenae, and settled there after receiving purification from Eurystheus.

K4 Second Labor: The Lernaian Hydra

The second labor Eurystheus commanded Heracles to perform was to kill the Lernaian Hydra, which had been raised in the swamp of Lerna and was making forays onto the plain and wreaking havoc on both the livestock and the land. The Hydra had an enormous body with nine heads, eight of them mortal, and the one in the middle immortal. Heracles mounted a chariot driven by Iolaos and traveled to Lerna. He brought his horses to a halt and found the Hydra on a hill by the Springs of Amymone, where she had her lair. He shot flaming arrows at her and forced her to come out. As she did so, he seized her and put her in a hold, but she wrapped herself around one of his legs and held on tight. Heracles got nowhere by smashing her heads with his club, for when one was smashed, two heads grew back. An enormous crab came to assist the Hydra and pinched Heracles' foot. Because of this, after he killed the crab, he called for Iolaos to help. Iolaos set fire to a portion of the nearby forest and with the burning pieces of wood he scorched the stumps of the heads, preventing them from coming back. Having overcome the regenerating heads in this way, Heracles then cut off the immortal one, buried it, and placed a heavy rock over it by the road that leads through Lerna to Elaious. As for the Hydra's body, he ripped it open and dipped his arrows in her bile. Eurystheus told Heracles that he should not have to count this labor as one of the ten, for Heracles had not overcome the Hydra by himself, but with the help of Iolaos.

K5 Third Labor: The Cerynitian Deer

The third labor Eurystheus commanded Heracles to perform was to bring the Cerynitian Deer alive to Mycenae. This deer was in Oinoe. It had golden horns and was sacred to Artemis. Because of this Heracles did not want to kill or wound it, so he pursued it for an entire year. When the beast was wearied by the chase, it fled to a mountain known as Artemisios and then to the Ladon River. When it was about to cross this river, Heracles shot the deer with his bow and captured it. Putting it on his shoulders, he hurried through Arcadia. But Artemis, with Apollo, met up with him and was ready to take the deer away. She reproached him because he was killing her sacred animal, but he made the excuse that he was being forced to do it and said that the guilty party was Eurystheus. This soothed the goddess' anger, and Heracles brought the beast alive to Mycenae.

K6 Fourth Labor: The Erymanthian Boar

The fourth labor Eurystheus commanded Heracles to perform was to bring the Erymanthian Boar alive. This beast was causing destruction in Psophis by making attacks from a mountain they call Erymanthos. Traveling through Pholoe, Heracles stayed as a guest with the Centaur Pholos, the son of Seilenos and an ash-tree Nymph. This Centaur offered Heracles meat that was roasted, but he himself ate his raw. When Heracles asked for wine, Pholos said that he was afraid to open the Centaurs' communal storage jar. Heracles told him not to worry and opened the jar. Not much later the Centaurs scented the odor and came armed with rocks and fir trees to Pholos' cave. Heracles repelled Anchios and Agrios, the first to grow bold enough to enter, by hitting them with burning firewood, and he shot the rest with his bow, pursuing them all the way to Malea. From there they fled to the home of Cheiron, who had settled at Malea after being driven from Mount Pelion by the Lapiths. Heracles shot an arrow from his bow at the Centaurs, who had surrounded Cheiron. The arrow went through Elatos' arm and lodged in Cheiron's knee. Distressed by this, Heracles ran, pulled out the arrow, and applied a drug that Cheiron gave him. Cheiron, with his wound unable to be cured, left to return to his cave. He wanted to die there but was unable to do so because he was immortal. Prometheus offered himself to Zeus to become immortal in Cheiron's place, and that is how Cheiron died. The rest of the Centaurs fled, each to a different place: some came to Mount Malea; Eurytion went to Pholoe; and Nessos went to the river Euenos. Poseidon took in the rest at Eleusis and concealed them with a mountain. As for Pholos, he pulled an arrow out of a corpse and marveled that such a small thing could kill such large foes. The arrow slipped from his hand and fell onto his foot, killing him instantly. When Heracles returned to Pholoe and saw that Pholos was dead, he buried him and went to hunt the boar. He chased it from a thicket by shouting, and when it was tired out, he forced it into deep snow, lassoed it, and brought it to Mycenae.

K7 Fifth Labor: The Cattle of Augeias

The fifth labor Eurystheus commanded Heracles to perform was to clear out the dung of the Cattle of Augeias in only a single day. Augeias was king of Elis. According to some, he was the son of Helios, according to others, of Poseidon, and according to still others, of Phorbas. He had many herds of cattle. Heracles came to him and, without revealing Eurystheus' command, told him he would clear out the dung in a single day if Augeias would give him one-tenth of the cattle. Augeias promised he would, but did not believe that it was possible. Heracles called upon Augeias' son Phyleus to act as witness. Then he made a hole in the foundation of the stable and diverted the rivers Alpheios and Peneios, which flowed near one another, and caused them to flow in after he made an outlet through another opening. When Augeias learned that this had been accomplished at Eurystheus' command, he would not render payment and went so far as to deny ever having promised to do so in the first place, saying that he was ready to be brought to trial over the issue. When the judges had taken their seats, Phyleus was called by Heracles as a witness against his father and said that he had agreed to make a payment. Augeias, enraged, ordered both Phyleus and Heracles to depart from Elis before the vote was cast. So Phyleus went to Doulichion and settled there, and Heracles came to Olenos to the house of Dexamenos and found him on the point of being forced to engage his daughter Mnesimache to the Centaur Eurytion. When Heracles was asked by Dexamenos to help, he killed Eurytion when he came for his bride. Eurystheus did not count this labor among the ten either, because he said that it was done for payment.

K8 Sixth Labor: The Stymphalian Birds

The sixth labor Eurystheus commanded Heracles to perform was to chase away the Stymphalian Birds. There was in the city of Stymphalos in Arcadia a marsh called the Stymphalian Marsh, which was covered by thick woods. Countless birds took refuge in it out of fear of being eaten by the wolves. When Heracles was at a loss how to drive the birds from the woods, Athena got bronze castanets from Hephaistos and gave them to him. By rattling these on a mountain situated near the marsh, he startled the birds. They could not stand the racket and took to wing in fright. In this way Heracles shot them.

K9 Seventh Labor: The Cretan Bull

The seventh labor Eurystheus commanded Heracles to perform was to bring the Cretan Bull. Acusilaus says that this was the bull that carried Europa across the sea for Zeus, but some say that it was the one sent forth from the sea by Poseidon when Minos said that he would sacrifice to Poseidon whatever appeared from the sea. But they say that when he caught sight of the beauty of the bull, he sent it off to his herds and sacrificed another to Poseidon, and that the god, angered by this, made the bull go wild. Heracles went to Crete after this bull, and when he asked for help capturing it, Minos told him to take it himself if he could subdue it. He captured it, carried it back, and showed it to Eurystheus. Afterward, he let it go free, and it wandered to Sparta and all of Arcadia, and, crossing the Isthmos, it came to Marathon in Attica, where it plagued the locals.

K10 Eighth Labor: The Mares of Diomedes

The eighth labor Eurystheus commanded Heracles to perform was to bring the Mares of Diomedes the Thracian to Mycenae. Diomedes was the son of Ares and Cyrene. He was king of the Bistones, a very warlike Thracian tribe, and owned man-eating mares. So Heracles sailed with his willing followers, overpowered the men in charge of the mares' mangers, and drove them to the sea. When the Bistones came out under arms to rescue them, Heracles handed the mares over to Abderos to guard. Abderos, a son of Hermes, was a Locrian from Opous and Heracles' boyfriend. The mares dragged him to death. Heracles fought the Bistones, and by killing Diomedes he forced the rest to flee. He founded a city, Abdera, by the tomb of the slain Abderos, and then took the mares and gave them to Eurystheus. Eurystheus released them, and they went to the mountain called Olympos, where they were destroyed by the beasts.

K11 Ninth Labor: The War-Belt of Hippolyte

The ninth labor Eurystheus commanded Heracles to perform was to bring the war-belt of Hippolyte. She was the queen of the Amazons, who used to dwell near the river Thermodon, a tribe great in war. For they cultivated a manly spirit; whenever they had sex and gave birth, they raised the female children. They would constrict their right breasts so that these would not interfere with throwing a javelin, but allowed their left breasts to grow so that they could breastfeed. Hippolyte had Ares' war-belt, a symbol of her preeminence over all the Amazons. Heracles was sent to get this belt because Admete, Eurystheus' daughter, wanted to have it. Assembling some willing allies, he sailed with one ship and landed on the island of Paros, where the sons of Minos dwelled, Eurymedon, Chryses, Nephalion, and Philolaos. It happened that those on the ship disembarked, and two of them were killed by the sons of Minos. Angry over their deaths, Heracles killed the sons of Minos on the spot, blockaded the rest of the population, and besieged them until they sent ambassadors and appealed to him to take whichever two men he wanted in place of those who were killed.

So he ended the siege and took with him Alcaios and Sthenelos, the sons of Androgeos son of Minos. He came to Lycos son of Dascylos in Mysia and was his guest. When Lycos and the king of the Bebryces fought, Heracles aided Lycos and killed many Bebryces, including their king, Mygdon, a brother of Amycos. He took away a large portion of the Bebryces' territory and gave it to Lycos, who called the whole territory Heracleia.

Heracles sailed to the harbor in Themiscyra, and Hippolyte came to him. After she asked why he had come and promised to give him the war-belt, Hera made herself look like one of the Amazons and went among the populace saying that the strangers who had come were abducting the queen. Under arms they rode down on horseback to the ship. When Heracles saw that they were armed, he thought that this was the result of some treachery. He killed Hippolyte and took the war-belt, and then he fought the rest, sailed away, and landed at Troy.

It happened at that time that the city was in difficulties because of the wrath of Apollo and Poseidon. For Apollo and Poseidon, desiring to test the insolence of Laomedon, made themselves look like mortals and promised to build walls around Pergamon for a fee. But after they built the walls, Laomedon would not pay them. For this reason Apollo sent a plague, and Poseidon sent a sea monster that was carried up on shore by a tidal wave and made off with the people in the plain. The oracles said that there would be an end to the misfortunes if Laomedon set out his daughter Hesione as food for the sea monster, so he set her out and fastened her to the cliffs near the sea. When Heracles saw that she had been set out, he promised to save her if he would get from Laomedon the mares that Zeus had given as compensation for the kidnapping of Ganymedes. After Laomedon said that he would give them, Heracles killed the sea monster and saved Hesione. But Laomedon refused to pay up, so Heracles set sail threatening that he would make war against Troy.

He landed at Ainos, where he was the guest of Poltys. On the Ainian shore, when he was about to sail off, he shot and killed Sarpedon, Poseidon's son and Poltys' brother, because he was insolent. Coming to Thasos and conquering the Thracians who lived there, he gave the island to the sons of Androgeos to live in. He set out from Thasos to Torone, and after being challenged to wrestle by Polygonos and Telegonos, sons of Proteus son of Poseidon, he killed them in the course of the match. He brought the war-belt to Mycenae and gave it to Eurystheus.

K12 Tenth Labor: The Cattle of Geryones

The tenth labor Eurystheus commanded Heracles to perform was to bring back the Cattle of Geryones from Erytheia. Erytheia (now called Gadeira) was an island lying near Oceanos. Geryones, the son of Chrysaor and Callirrhoe daughter of Oceanos, lived here. He had a body that was three men grown together, joined into one at the belly but separated into three from the waist down. He had red cattle, which were herded by Eurytion and guarded by Orthos, the two-headed dog that was the offspring of Echidna and Typhon. So traveling across Europe in quest of the cattle of Geryones, he killed many wild beasts before arriving in Libya. Going to Tartessos, he set up as tokens of his journey two facing pillars at the limits of Europe and Libya. When he was made hot by Helios during his journey, he pulled his bow back and took aim at the god. Helios marveled at his courage and gave him a golden cup in which he traveled across Oceanos. Arriving in Erytheia, he camped on Mount Abas. The dog sensed his presence and charged him, but Heracles hit it with his club and killed the cowherd Eurytion when he tried to help the dog. Menoites, who was there pasturing Hades' cattle, reported what had happened to Geryones, who caught up with Heracles as he was driving the cattle along the Anthemous River. He joined battle with Heracles, was shot by an arrow, and died. Heracles put the cattle into the cup and sailed over to Tartessos, where he gave the cup back to Helios.

He went through Abderia and arrived at Ligystine, where Ialebion and Dercynos, the sons of Poseidon, stole the cows. But Heracles killed them and went through Tyrrhenia. One of the bulls broke loose {*rhegnumi*} at Rhegion, swiftly plunged into the sea, and swam across to Sicily. Traveling through the nearby territory, the bull came to the plain of Eryx, who was king of the Elymoi. Eryx, the son of Poseidon, incorporated the bull into his own herds. So Heracles handed the cattle over to Hephaistos and hurried off in search of the bull. He discovered it among the herds of Eryx, who said that he would not give it back unless Heracles wrestled and beat him. Heracles beat him three times and killed him during the match. He took the bull and drove it along with the others to the Ionian Sea. When he reached the top of the Adriatic Sea, Hera sent a gadfly against the cattle, and they were scattered throughout the foothills of Thrace. Heracles chased after them; he captured some and took them to the Hellespont, but others were left behind and afterward were wild. Because he had such a hard time collecting the cows, he blamed the Strymon River and, whereas in the old days its stream used to be navigable, he filled it with rocks and rendered it unnavigable. He brought the cows and gave them to Eurystheus, who sacrificed them to Hera.

K13 Eleventh Labor: The Apples of the Hesperides

Although the labors were finished in eight years and one month, Eurystheus, who would not count the Cattle of Augeias or the Hydra, ordered Heracles as an eleventh labor to bring back the Golden Apples from the Hesperides. These apples were not in Libya, as some have said, but on Mount Atlas in the land of the Hyperboreans. Ge had given them as a gift to Zeus when he married Hera. They were guarded by an immortal serpent, the offspring of Typhon and Echidna, which had a hundred heads and used to talk with all sorts of various voices. Alongside the serpent the Hesperides, named Aigle, Erytheia, Hesperia, and Arethousa, stood guard. So Heracles traveled to the Echedoros River. Cycnos, the son of Ares and Pyrene, challenged him to single combat. When Ares tried to avenge Cycnos and met Heracles in a duel, a thunderbolt was thrown in between the two and broke up the fight. Traveling through Illyria and hurrying to the Eridanos River, Heracles came to some Nymphs, daughters of Zeus and Themis. These Nymphs pointed out Nereus to him. Taking hold of him as he slept, Heracles tied Nereus up though he turned into all sorts of shapes. He did not release him until he learned where the apples and the Hesperides were. After he got this information, he passed through Libya. Poseidon's son Antaios, who used to kill strangers by forcing them to wrestle, was king of this land. When Heracles was forced to wrestle with him, he lifted him off the ground in a bear hug, broke his back, and killed him. He did this because it happened that Antaios grew stronger when he touched the earth. This is why some said that he was a son of Ge.

He passed through Egypt after Libya. Bousiris, the son of Poseidon and Lysianassa daughter of Epaphos, was king there. He used to sacrifice foreigners on an altar of Zeus in accordance with a prophecy. For nine years barrenness befell Egypt when Phrasios, a seer by profession, arrived from Cyprus and said that the barrenness would end if a foreigner were sacrificed every year to Zeus. Bousiris sacrificed the seer first and then went on to sacrifice those foreigners who landed on his shores. Heracles too was seized and brought to the altars. He broke the chains and killed both Bousiris and his son, Amphidamas.

Passing through Asia, he came to Thermydrai, the harbor of the Lindians. He loosed one of the bulls from a cart-driver's wagon, sacrificed it, and feasted. The driver was unable to protect himself, so he stood on a certain mountain and called down curses. For this reason even today when they sacrifice to Heracles, they do so with curses.

Skirting Arabia, he killed Tithonos' son Emathion, and, traveling across Libya to the outer sea, he received the cup from Helios. Crossing over to the continent on the other side, on Mount Caucasus he shot down the eagle that ate Prometheus' liver and that was the offspring of Echidna and Typhon. He freed Prometheus after taking the bond of the olive for himself, and to Zeus he offered up Cheiron, who was willing to die in Prometheus' place despite being immortal.[5]

Prometheus told Heracles not to go after the apples himself, but to take over holding up the sky from Atlas and send him instead. So when he came to Atlas in the land of the Hyperboreans, Heracles followed this advice and took over holding up the sky. After getting three apples from the Hesperides, Atlas came back to Heracles. Atlas, not wanting to hold the sky, <said that he would himself carry the apples to Eurystheus and bade Heracles hold up the sky in his stead. Heracles promised to do so, but succeeded by craft in putting it on Atlas instead. For at the advice of Prometheus he begged Atlas to hold up the sky because he>[6] wanted to put a pad on his head. When he heard this, Atlas put the apples down on the ground and took over holding up the sky, so Heracles picked them up and left. But some say that he did not get them from Atlas, but that he himself picked the apples after killing the guardian serpent. He brought the apples and gave them to Eurystheus. After he got them, he gave them to Heracles as a gift. Athena received them from him and took them back, for it was not holy for them to be put just anywhere.

K14 Twelfth Labor: Cerberos

The bringing back of Cerberos from the house of Hades was ordered as a twelfth labor. Cerberos had three dog heads, the tail of a serpent, and along his back, the heads of all sorts of snakes. When Heracles was about to go off to get him, he went to Eumolpos in Eleusis because he wanted to be initiated into the mysteries. Since he was unable to see the mysteries because he had not been purified of the killing of the Centaurs, Eumolpos purified him and then initiated him. He came to Tainaron in Laconia, where the cave that leads down to the house of Hades is located. He made

[5] Heracles wears a wreath of olive as a substitute for the real bonds of Prometheus. For the trading of immortality between Prometheus and Cheiron, see K6.

[6] The words in brackets are a modern editor's reconstruction based on an ancient commentator (translation is from Frazer, modified).

his descent through it. When the souls saw him, they all fled except for Meleagros and Medousa the Gorgon. He drew his sword against the Gorgon in the belief that she was still alive, but he learned from Hermes that she was just an empty phantom. When he went near the gates of Hades' realm, he found Theseus together with Peirithous, the man who tried to win Persephone's hand in marriage and for that reason was in bonds. When they caught sight of Heracles, they stretched forth their arms so that they could rise up by means of Heracles' might. He did take hold of Theseus by the hand and lift him up, but when he wanted to raise up Peirithous, the earth shook and he let go. He also rolled Ascalaphos' rock off.[7] He wanted to provide some blood for the souls, so he slaughtered one of the cows of Hades. Their herder, Menoites son of Ceuthonymos, challenged Heracles to wrestle. Heracles grabbed him around the middle and broke his ribs. Menoites was saved when Persephone begged for mercy for him. When Heracles asked Plouton for Cerberos, Plouton told him to take him if he could defeat him without any of the weapons he carried. Heracles found Cerberos by the gates of Acheron, and, encased by his breastplate and covered entirely by the lion's skin, he threw his arms around Cerberos' head and did not stop holding on and choking the beast until he prevailed, even though he was being bitten by the serpent that served as his tail. So he took Cerberos and returned, making his ascent through Troizen. Demeter turned Ascalaphos into an owl; Heracles showed Cerberos to Eurystheus and then brought him back to the house of Hades.

K15 After the Labors

[2.6] After the labors Heracles came to Thebes and gave Megara to Iolaos. When he himself wanted to get married, he learned that Eurytos, ruler of Oichalia, had made marriage to his daughter Iole the prize for whoever beat him and his sons in an archery contest. So Heracles went to Oichalia and beat them in archery, but he was not allowed the marriage. Although Iphitos, the eldest of Eurytos' sons, said that Iole ought to be given to Heracles, Eurytos and the rest went back on their word and said that they were afraid that Heracles might once again kill any children he might happen to father.

Not long afterward, some cattle were stolen from Euboia by Autolycos. Eurytos thought that this had been done by Heracles, but Iphitos did not believe it and went to Heracles. He met him leaving Pherai, where Heracles had saved the dying Alcestis for Admetos, and invited him to join in the search for the cattle. Heracles promised that he would and treated Iphitos as his guest, but he went crazy once more and threw him from the walls of Tiryns. Wishing to be purified of the killing, he went to Neleus, who was the ruler of the Pylians. After Neleus turned him down because of his friendship with Eurytos, Heracles went to Amyclai and was purified by Deiphobos son of Hippolytos. But he was afflicted with an awful disease because of the killing of Iphitos and so went to Delphi to find out how to stop the disease. When the Pythia would not chant a prophecy for him, he wanted to rob the temple, carry off the tripod, and establish his own oracle. When Apollo fought Heracles, Zeus sent a thunderbolt between them, and when they had been separated in that

[7] A rock was placed on top of him by Demeter for informing against Persephone when she ate the pomegranate seed (see Apollodorus C).

way, Heracles received a prophecy that said there would be an end to his disease when he had been sold, served three years, and given compensation to Eurytos for the killing.

After the oracle was given, Hermes put Heracles up for sale, and Omphale daughter of Iardanes bought him. She was the queen of the Lydians, for her husband Tmolos had bequeathed her the rulership on his death. Eurytos did not accept the compensation when it was brought to him. While Heracles was serving Omphale, he captured and bound the Cercopes near Ephesos, and he killed Syleus at Aulis. Syleus used to force passing strangers to dig, but Heracles burned his vines, roots and all, and killed him along with his daughter Xenodoce. Landing on the island of Doliche, he saw the body of Icaros being washed up by the waves, buried it, and named the island Icaria instead of Doliche. In return for this Daidalos made a statue in Pisa in the likeness of Heracles. One night Heracles, not recognizing what it was, threw a stone at it and hit it in the belief that it was alive. During the time he served at Omphale's court, it is said that the voyage to Colchis took place, as did the hunt for the Calydonian boar, and that Theseus cleared out the Isthmos as he came from Troizen.

K16 Expedition Against Troy

After his period of servitude he was rid of his disease and sailed against Ilion with eighteen fifty-oared ships after gathering an army of heroes who volunteered to fight of their own accord. When he landed at Ilion, he left the security of the ships in Oicles' hands and set out for the city with the other heroes. But although Laomedon came against the ships with the main part of his army and killed Oicles in the battle, he was driven off by the troops that were with Heracles and was besieged. Once the siege was under way, Telamon broke through the wall and was the first to enter the city with Heracles behind him. When Heracles saw that Telamon had been the first to enter, he drew his sword and charged him because he did not want anyone else to be considered greater than himself. When Telamon realized this, he started gathering together stones that were lying nearby. Heracles asked him what he was doing, and he said that he was building an altar to Heracles Callinicos {"Noble Victor"}. Heracles commended him, and when he took the city and shot and killed Laomedon and all of his sons except Podarces, he gave Laomedon's daughter Hesione to Telamon as the prize for bravery and agreed to allow her to take with her whichever of the prisoners she wanted. When she chose her brother Podarces, Heracles said that Podarces had to become a slave first, and then Hesione could get him, but only after giving something—anything—in exchange. So when he was being sold, she took the veil from her head and paid for him with it. This is why Podarces was called Priam.[8]

[2.7] As Heracles sailed from Troy, Hera sent harsh storms. Zeus grew angry at this and hung her from Olympos. Heracles tried to sail to Cos, but the Coans thought he was leading a fleet of pirates and threw stones to stop him from sailing in. But Heracles forced his way in at night, took the island, and killed King Eurypylos, the son of Astypalaia and Poseidon. Heracles was wounded by Chalcodon during the fight, but he suffered no real injury because Zeus whisked him away. After plundering Cos, he came to Phlegra with Athena's help and alongside the gods defeated the Giants.

[8] Apollodorus follows a common etymology of Priam's name from "to buy" {*priamai*}.

K17 Wars in the Peloponnese

Not long afterward, he gathered an army from Arcadia, took on some willing heroes from Greece, and set out on campaign against Augeias. When Augeias heard about the war being prepared by Heracles, he appointed as generals of the Eleians Eurytos and Cteatos, conjoined twins who surpassed in might all other mortals of the time. They were the sons of Molione and Actor, but they were said to be Poseidon's sons. Actor was Augeias' brother. It happened that Heracles grew ill during the campaign, and for this reason he actually made a treaty with the Molionidai. But when they later discovered that he was ill, they made an attack on his army and killed many. So at that time Heracles withdrew; afterward, when the third Isthmian festival was being held and the Eleians sent the Molionidai to take part in the sacrifice as their representatives, Heracles ambushed and killed them in Cleonai, then marched against Elis and took the city. After he killed Augeias and his sons, he brought Phyleus back from exile and gave him the kingdom. He also founded the Olympic Games, established an altar to Pelops, and built six altars to twelve gods.[9]

After the sack of Elis, he marched against Pylos, and after capturing the city, he killed Periclymenos, the mightiest of Neleus' sons, who changed shapes as he fought. Heracles killed Neleus and all his sons except Nestor, for he was young and was being raised in the land of the Gerenians. During the battle, Heracles also wounded Hades, who was helping the Pylians.

After capturing Pylos, he marched against Lacedaimon out of a desire to punish Hippocoon's sons. He was angry with them because they had fought alongside Neleus, but he was even more angry because they had killed the son of Licymnios. While this man was admiring the palace of Hippocoon, one of the Molossian hounds ran out and made for him. So he threw a rock and hit the dog, and the Hippocoontidai sallied forth and beat him to death with their clubs. To avenge this man's death Heracles had gathered an army against the Lacedaimonians. When he came to Arcadia, he asked Cepheus to join him as an ally along with his sons (he had twenty). But Cepheus was afraid that if he left Tegea, the Argives would attack, so he declined to go on the campaign. But Heracles received from Athena a lock of hair from the Gorgon in a bronze urn, and he gave it to Cepheus' daughter Sterope, telling her that if an army attacked, she should stand on the walls and raise the lock into the air three times, and—so long as she did not look at it—the enemy would be routed. After this Cepheus went on the campaign with his sons. He and his sons all died in the battle, as did Heracles' brother Iphicles. After Heracles killed Hippocoon and his sons and conquered the city, he brought Tyndareos back from exile and handed the kingdom over to him.

K18 Auge and Telephos

As he passed by Tegea, Heracles raped Auge without realizing that she was Aleos' daughter. She gave birth to the baby in secret and set him down in the sanctuary of Athena. But Aleos entered the sanctuary because the land was being devastated by a plague and discovered after a search that his daughter had had a child. So he exposed the baby on Mount Parthenios, but by the gods' providence it was saved. For a deer {*elaphos*} that had just given birth offered her teat {*thele*} to the baby, and some shep-

[9] See Herodorus 34 for these six altars.

herds took him up and named him Telephos {as if somehow from *thele* + *elaphos*}. Aleos gave Auge to Nauplios son of Poseidon to sell into slavery in a foreign land. Nauplios gave her to Teuthras, the ruler of Teuthrania, and he made her his wife.

K19 Deianeira

When Heracles came to Calydon, he became a suitor for Deianeira, Oineus' daughter. For her hand in marriage he wrestled with Acheloos, and when he changed himself into a bull, Heracles broke off one of his horns. He married Deianeira, and Acheloos got his horn back by trading it for the horn of Amaltheia. Amaltheia was Haimonios' daughter, and she had a bull's horn. This horn, according to Pherecydes, had such great power that it could provide meat or drink aplenty—whatever one might ask for.

Heracles marched alongside the Calydonians against the Thesprotians. After capturing the city of Ephyra, where King Phylas ruled, he slept with the king's daughter Astyoche and became the father of Tlepolemos. While he was living with them, he sent a message to Thespios and told him to keep seven of his sons, to send three off to Thebes, and to send the remaining forty to the island of Sardinia to found a colony. After this happened, during a feast at Oineus' house, with a blow from his fist he killed Architeles' son Eunomos while the boy was pouring water over Heracles' hands. (The boy was related to Oineus.) But since the event had been an accident, the boy's father pardoned Heracles. Heracles, however, wanted to undergo exile in accordance with the law and decided to leave for the house of Ceyx in Trachis. Taking Deianeira, he came to the Euenos River, where Nessos the Centaur stationed himself and used to ferry passersby across for a fee, saying that he had been set up as ferryman by the gods because of his righteousness. Now, Heracles crossed the river by himself, but he was asked for the fee and entrusted Deianeira to Nessos to carry across. But while Nessos was ferrying her across, he tried to rape her. When Heracles heard her crying out, he shot Nessos through the heart as he was coming out of the river. Just before he died, Nessos called Deianeira over and told her that if she ever wanted a love potion to use on Heracles, she should mix the seed that he had discharged onto the ground with the blood that was flowing from the arrow wound. She did this and always kept it nearby.

K20 Other Deeds

As Heracles passed through the land of the Dryopes and ran out of food, he encountered Theiodamas, who was driving a cart. He unhitched one of the bulls, slaughtered it, and feasted. When he came to Ceyx's house in Trachis, he was hosted by him and defeated the Dryopes.

Later, when he set out from there, he fought as an ally of Aigimios, the king of the Dorians. The Lapiths, with Coronos as their general, were fighting with him over territorial boundaries. He was under siege when he called Heracles to help him in exchange for a portion of the territory. Heracles helped him and killed Coronos and others, but he handed the entire piece of territory over to Aigimios with no strings attached. He also killed Laogoras, the king of the Dryopes, along with his children, as he feasted in the sanctuary of Apollo, for he was insolent and an ally of the Lapiths. As Heracles was passing Itonos, Cycnos, the son of Ares and Pelopia, challenged him to single combat. Heracles fought and killed him. When he came to Ormenion, King Amyntor took up arms and would not allow him to go through his territory. Heracles killed him too when he tried to prevent his passing.

K21 Iole and Heracles' Death

Arriving in Trachis, he raised an army against Oichalia out of a desire to punish Eurytos. With the Arcadians, the Melians from Trachis, and the Epicnemidian Locrians as his allies, he killed Eurytos and his sons and took the city. He buried those who had fallen while fighting on his side, Hippasos son of Ceyx, and Argeios and Melas, the sons of Licymnios. He then sacked the city and took Iole captive. When he anchored his ships at Cenaion, a promontory in Euboia, he built an altar to Cenaian Zeus. Intending to make a sacrifice, he sent his herald Lichas to Trachis to get some splendid clothes. From this man Deianeira learned of the situation with Iole, and, afraid that Heracles might love Iole more than her and thinking that Nessos' spilled blood really was a love potion, she anointed the tunic with it. Heracles put it on and began to make sacrifice, but when the tunic grew warm, the Hydra's poison ate away his flesh. He picked up Lichas by the feet and hurled him off the promontory. Then he tried to tear off the tunic, but his flesh was torn off with it because it was sticking to his body. Afflicted by such a terrible misfortune, he was brought to Trachis on a ship. When Deianeira learned what had happened, she hanged herself. Heracles ordered Hyllos, who was his oldest child by Deianeira, to marry Iole when he grew to manhood, and then went to Mount Oita (this is in Trachis). He built a pyre there, climbed atop, and gave the command to light it. No one was willing to do this, but Poias, who was passing by looking for his sheep, did light it, and Heracles gave him his bow as a gift. As the pyre burned, they say that a cloud settled under Heracles and with a clap of thunder sent him up to heaven. There he received immortality, was reconciled with Hera, and married her daughter Hebe. He had sons by her, Alexiares and Anicetos.

L1 Europa and Her Cretan Children (3.1.1–3.1.4)

[3.1] Now that we have gone through the lineage of Inachos and explained it from Belos down to the Heracleidai, let us tell the story of Agenor next. As we have said, Libya had two sons with Poseidon, namely Belos and Agenor. Now Belos was king of the Egyptians and had the sons discussed before.[10] Agenor went to Phoenicia and married Telephassa. They had a daughter, Europa, and sons, Cadmos, Phoinix, and Cilix. Some say that Europa was not Agenor's daughter, but Phoinix's. Zeus fell in love with her, turned himself into a tame bull, got her to climb up on his back, and brought her across the sea to Crete. Zeus shared her bed there, and she gave birth to Minos, Sarpedon, and Rhadamanthys. According to Homer, however, Sarpedon was the son of Zeus and Laodameia daughter of Bellerophontes. After Europa's disappearance her father Agenor sent out his sons in search of her, telling them not to return until they had discovered Europa's whereabouts. Her mother Telephassa and Thasos son of Poseidon (or son of Cilix, according to Pherecydes) joined them in the search. When they had made a thorough search, they were unable to find her and gave up hope of returning home. They each settled in different places: Phoinix settled in Phoenicia; Cilix settled near Phoenicia, and the whole territory that was subject to

[10] The sons of Belos are Danaos and Aigyptos.

him adjacent to the Pyramos River he called Cilicia; Cadmos and Telephassa settled in Thrace. Likewise, Thasos founded the city of Thasos in Thrace and settled there.

Asterios, the ruler of the Cretans, married Europa and raised her sons. But when they came of age, they quarreled with each other because they all loved a boy named Miletos, who was the son of Apollo and Areia daughter of Cleochos. Since the boy showed greater affection for Sarpedon, Minos went to war against them and prevailed. They fled; Miletos landed in Caria and founded the city of Miletos (named for himself), and Sarpedon became an ally of Cilix, who was at war with the Lycians, in exchange for a part of the territory and became king of Lycia. Zeus granted that he live for three generations. But some say that they were in love with Atymnios, the son of Zeus and Cassiepeia, and their quarrel was over him. As for Rhadamanthys, he was a lawgiver to the islanders and later went into exile in Boiotia, where he married Alcmene. Since his death he has been acting as a judge with Minos in the realm of Hades. Minos lived in Crete and wrote laws. He married Pasiphae, the daughter of Helios and Perseis, though according to Asclepiades he married Asterios' daughter Crete. He had sons, namely Catreus, Deucalion, Glaucos, and Androgeos, and daughters, namely Acalle, Xenodice, Ariadne, and Phaidra. With the Nymph Pareia he had Eurymedon, Nephalion, Chryses, and Philolaos. With Dexithea he had Euxanthios.

L2 Minos

After Asterios died childless, Minos wanted to be king of Crete, but was opposed. He claimed that he had received the right to rule the kingdom from the gods, and to prove it he said that whatever he prayed for would happen. He made a sacrifice to Poseidon and prayed for a bull to appear from the depths, promising to sacrifice it when it appeared. Poseidon sent a magnificent bull up for him, and he received the kingdom, but he sent the bull to his herds and sacrificed another.

Poseidon grew angry at Minos because he did not sacrifice the bull. So he made it savage and brought it about that Pasiphae came to desire it. When she had fallen in love with the bull, she took as her accomplice Daidalos, who was an architect exiled from Athens for murder. He constructed a wooden cow on wheels, then took and hollowed it out. Stripping the skin from a cow, he sewed it around the wooden one. He placed it in the meadow where the bull usually grazed and put Pasiphae inside. The bull came and mated with it as if it were a real cow. Pasiphae gave birth to Asterios, who is known as the Minotaur. He had the face of a bull {*tauros*}, but the rest of his body was that of a man. Minos shut him in the labyrinth in accordance with certain prophecies and kept him under guard. The labyrinth, which Daidalos built, was a cell "that confused its exit with tangled twistings."[11] I will give the account of the Minotaur, Androgeos, Phaidra, and Ariadne later in the section on Theseus.

M1 Cadmos and Thebes (3.4.1–3.7.7)

[3.4] After Telephassa died and Cadmos buried her, he was treated as a guest by the Thracians and went to Delphi to inquire about Europa. The god told him not to

[11] Apparently Apollodorus quotes from a lost Greek tragedy.

pursue the matter of Europa, but to make a cow his guide and found a city wherever she collapsed in exhaustion. After receiving this oracle, he traveled through Phocis and then came across a cow among the herds of Pelagon and followed behind her. While she was passing through Boiotia, she lay down where the city of Thebes is now. Wishing to sacrifice the cow to Athena, Cadmos sent some of his companions to get water from Ares' Spring. Guarding the spring was a serpent (some say it was Ares' offspring), and it destroyed most of those who had been sent. Cadmos became angry and killed the serpent. On the advice of Athena he sowed the dragon's teeth like seeds. When these were sown {*sparentes*}, there grew up from the earth some armed men whom they call the Spartoi {"Sown Men"}. They killed each other, some coming to fight on purpose, some by mistake. Pherecydes says that when Cadmos saw armed men sprouting up from the earth, he threw rocks at them, and they thought they were being hit by each other and fell to fighting. Five of them survived: Echion, Oudaios, Chthonios, Hyperenor, and Peloros.

In return for those he killed, Cadmos was in Ares' service for an "eternal" year—in those days a year was eight years long. After his service Athena arranged for him to have the kingdom, and Zeus gave him as wife Harmonia, the daughter of Aphrodite and Ares. All the gods left heaven and celebrated the marriage feast in the Cadmeia with much singing. Cadmos gave Harmonia a dress and the Hephaistos-made necklace, which some say was given as a gift to Cadmos by Hephaistos, but Pherecydes says it was given by Europa, who had gotten it from Zeus.

M2 The Daughters of Cadmos

Cadmos had daughters, Autonoe, Ino, Semele, and Agaue, and a son, Polydoros. Athamas married Ino, Aristaios married Autonoe, and Echion married Agaue. Zeus fell in love with Semele and shared her bed without Hera's knowledge. But Semele was tricked by Hera. Zeus had agreed to do what she asked, and Semele asked him to come to her as he had come to Hera when he courted her. Zeus was unable to refuse and came to her chamber on a chariot with lightning and thunder and hurled a thunderbolt. Semele died from the fright, but Zeus snatched from the fire their child, who was miscarried at six months of age, and stitched him into his thigh.

After Semele's death, the remaining daughters of Cadmos spread a story that Semele had been sleeping with some mortal man and had faked her affair with Zeus, and that that was why she was struck by a thunderbolt. When the proper time came, Zeus gave birth to Dionysos by undoing the stitches. He gave him to Hermes, who brought him to Ino and Athamas and convinced them to raise him as a girl. Hera was enraged and cast madness upon them. Athamas hunted down and killed their oldest son, Learchos, thinking that he was a deer. Ino threw Melicertes into a boiling cauldron, then took him and jumped into the deep with her son's corpse. She is called Leucothea, and her son is called Palaimon, having been given these names by sailors, for the two of them help those caught in storms. The Isthmian Games were founded in Melicertes' honor, and Sisyphos is the one who founded them. Zeus changed Dionysos into a baby goat and thwarted Hera's anger. Hermes took and carried him to some Nymphs who lived in Nysa in Asia. Later, Zeus turned them into stars and named them the Hyades.

M3 Actaion

Autonoe and Aristaios had a son, Actaion, who was raised by Cheiron and trained to be a hunter, and then later was devoured by his own dogs on Mount Cithairon. He died in this way, according to Acusilaus, because Zeus grew wrathful because Actaion courted Semele. But most say it was because Actaion saw Artemis as she bathed. They say that the goddess changed his shape instantly into that of a deer and sent madness upon the fifty dogs who followed him. As a consequence they did not recognize him and so devoured him. After Actaion's death his dogs searched for their master and howled terribly. When they came in their search to Cheiron's cave, he made a statue of Actaion, and this put an end to their grieving.[12]

M4 Dionysos

[3.5] Dionysos was the one who discovered the grapevine. When Hera cast madness upon him, he wandered through Egypt and Syria. At first Proteus, the king of the Egyptians, was his host, but later he went to Cybela in Phrygia and there was purified by Rhea, learned her rites, and adopted her accoutrements. He pushed on through Thrace against the Indians. Dryas' son Lycourgos, the king of the Edonoi, who dwell along the Strymon River, was the first to treat Dionysos insolently and cast him out. Dionysos fled for protection to the sea to Thetis daughter of Nereus, but his Bacchai and the throng of Satyrs that accompanied him were taken captive. Then the Bacchai were suddenly set free, and Dionysos made Lycourgos go mad. In his raving he struck his son Dryas with an ax and killed him, thinking that he was chopping the branch of a vine. After dismembering him, he regained his senses. When the land remained infertile, the god gave a prophecy that it would bear crops if Lycourgos were put to death. When the Edonoi heard this, they led him to Mount Pangaion and tied him up. There, in accordance with the will of Dionysos, Lycourgos was destroyed by horses and died.

After going through Thrace and all of India (where he set up pillars), he came to Thebes and made the women leave their houses and celebrate Bacchic rites on Mount Cithairon. Pentheus, whom Agaue bore to Echion, had inherited the kingdom from Cadmos and tried to keep this from happening. When he came to Cithairon to spy on the Bacchai, he was dismembered by his mother Agaue in a fit of madness, for she thought he was a beast. Having proven to the Thebans that he was a god, he came to Argos, where once again they did not honor him, so he drove the women out of their minds. In the mountains they ate the flesh of the still-nursing children they had with them. Then Dionysos wanted to cross from Icaria to Naxos, so he hired a pirate ship manned by Tyrrhenians. They took him aboard, but they sailed past Naxos and made for Asia to sell him into slavery. He turned the mast and the oars into snakes and filled the ship with ivy and the sound of flutes. The pirates went mad, escaped by jumping into the sea, and were turned into dolphins. In this way mortals learned that he was a god and honored him. He brought his mother up from the realm of Hades, gave her the name Thyone, and went with her up to heaven.

[12] The manuscripts of Apollodorus include here a passage, almost certainly added later, naming some of Actaion's dogs.

Cadmos left Thebes with Harmonia and went to the Encheleans. These people were being attacked by the Illyrians, and the god had delivered an oracle that they would defeat the Illyrians if they took Cadmos and Harmonia as their leaders. So they followed the oracle by making these two their leaders against the Illyrians and were victorious. Cadmos ruled as king of the Illyrians and had a son Illyrios. Later Cadmos and Harmonia were changed into serpents and were sent off to the Elysian Fields by Zeus.

M5 Amphion and Zethos

When Polydoros became king of Thebes, he married Nycteis, the daughter of Nycteus son of Chthonios, and had a son, Labdacos, who was killed after Pentheus for holding similar beliefs. Labdacos left behind a one-year-old son, Laios, and while he was still a child, Nycteus' brother Lycos took power for himself. Both Lycos and Nycteus had gone into exile from Euboia after killing Phlegyas, the son of Ares and Dotis the Boiotian. There they settled in Hyria, and <after going from there to Thebes,> they were made citizens because of their relationship with Pentheus. Lycos was chosen by the Thebans as war-leader and exercised the power of a ruler. After he was king for twenty years, he died at the hands of Zethos and Amphion for the following reason. Antiope was Nycteus' daughter, and Zeus slept with her. When she became pregnant, her father threatened her, so she escaped to Epopeus in Sikyon and became his wife. In despair Nycteus killed himself after giving instructions to Lycos to punish both Epopeus and Antiope. Lycos went on a campaign against Sicyon and conquered it. He killed Epopeus, but he brought Antiope back as a prisoner. As she was being brought back, she gave birth to two sons at Eleutherai in Boiotia. They were exposed, but a cowherd discovered them, raised them, and named them Zethos and Amphion. Now Zethos took care of herds of cattle, and Amphion practiced playing the lyre (Hermes had given him a lyre). Lycos and his wife, Dirce, locked Antiope up and tormented her. But once, without it being noticed, her bonds came off of their own accord, and she came to the cottage of her sons, wanting to be taken in by them. They recognized their mother, killed Lycos, and after tying Dirce to a bull, they threw her dead body into the spring that is now named Dirce after her. Succeeding to the rule, they built walls around the city (the stones followed Amphion's lyre) and banished Laios. He lived in the Peloponnese as the guest of Pelops, and when he was teaching his host's son Chrysippos to drive a chariot, he fell in love with him and kidnapped him.

Zethos married Thebe, after whom the city is called Thebes, and Amphion married Niobe daughter of Tantalos, who bore seven sons, Sipylos, Eupinytos, Ismenos, Damasichthon, Agenor, Phaidimos, and Tantalos, and the same number of daughters, Ethodaia (or Neaira according to some), Cleodoxa, Astyoche, Phthia, Pelopia, Astycrateia, and Ogygia. But Hesiod says that she had ten sons and ten daughters, Herodorus that she had two male and three female children, and Homer that she had six sons and six daughters. Because she was so blessed with children, Niobe said that she was more blessed with children than Leto. Leto was enraged and provoked Artemis and Apollo against Niobe's children. Artemis shot down the females in their house, and Apollo killed all the males together on Mount Cithairon while they were out hunting. But of the males Amphion was saved, and of the females so was Chloris, the eldest, whom Neleus married. But according to Telesilla, Amyclas and Meliboia were the ones saved, and Amphion was shot down by Artemis and Apollo. Niobe herself left Thebes and came to her father Tantalos in Sipylos. There she made prayer to Zeus and turned into stone, and tears flow from the stone both night and day.

M6 Laios and Oidipous

After the death of Amphion, Laios succeeded to the kingdom. He married Menoiceus' daughter, whom some call Iocaste and others Epicaste. They received an oracle not to have children (for their offspring would be a patricide), but Laios got drunk and slept with his wife. After boring through its ankles with pins, Laios gave the child to a shepherd to expose. But although the shepherd exposed it on Mount Cithairon, some herders of Polybos, the king of the Corinthians, found the infant and brought it to his wife, Periboia. She adopted it and passed it off as her own child. After treating its ankles, she called it Oidipous, giving this name because its feet {*pous*} had swollen {*oideo*}. When the boy grew up, he surpassed his peers in strength. Out of jealousy they mocked him for not really being his parents' son. He asked Periboia, but was not able to find out the truth. So he went to Delphi and inquired about his own parents. The god told him not to travel to his country, for he would kill his father and have sex with his mother. When he heard this, he left Corinth behind, believing that he had been born from those who were said to be his parents. Riding in a chariot through Phocis on a certain narrow stretch of road, he ran into Laios driving in a chariot. Polyphontes, who was Laios' herald, ordered Oidipous to get out of the way and killed one of his horses because of the holdup caused by his refusal to do so. So Oidipous became enraged and killed both Polyphontes and Laios. Then he arrived in Thebes.

Now Damasistratos, king of the Plataians, buried Laios, and Creon son of Menoiceus succeeded to the throne of Thebes. While he was king, a great misfortune befell the city; Hera sent the Sphinx, whose mother was Echidna and whose father was Typhon. She had the face of a woman, the chest, feet, and tail of a lion, and the wings of a bird. She had learned a riddle from the Muses, set herself up on Mount Phicion, and proposed it to the Thebans. This was the riddle: What is four-footed and two-footed and three-footed though it has but one voice? The Thebans had at that time an oracle that they would be rid of the Sphinx when they solved her riddle. So they gathered together often to search for what the answer was. And when they did not find it, she would snatch and devour one of them. After many had died, and last of all Creon's son Haimon, Creon proclaimed that he would give both the kingdom and Laios' wife to the man who solved the riddle. When Oidipous heard this, he solved it, saying that the answer to the riddle spoken by the Sphinx was a human being, four-footed as an infant carried on four limbs, two-footed when grown up, and in old age taking a staff as a third foot. Then the Sphinx threw herself off of the acropolis. Oidipous received the kingdom and unwittingly married his mother. With her he had sons, Polyneices and Eteocles, and daughters, Ismene and Antigone, though there are some who say that the children's mother was Euryganeia daughter of Hyperphas.

When what was hidden was later revealed, Iocaste hanged herself in a noose, and Oidipous put out his eyes and was driven out of Thebes. He laid curses on his sons because they watched him being banished from the city and did not come to his aid.

He came with Antigone to Colonos in Attica, where the sanctuary of the Eumenides is, and sat down as a suppliant. He was received as a guest by Theseus and died not long afterward.

M7 Eteocles and Polyneices; The Seven Against Thebes

[3.6] Eteocles and Polyneices came to an agreement with each other concerning the kingdom, resolving that they would each rule for one year at a time. Some say that Polyneices ruled first and handed the kingdom over to Eteocles after a year, but others say that Eteocles ruled first and refused to hand over the kingdom. So Polyneices went into exile from Thebes and came to Argos, taking the necklace and dress.[13] Adrastos son of Talaos was king of Argos, and Polyneices approached his palace at night and fell to fighting with Tydeus son of Oineus, who was an exile from Calydon. At the sudden noise Adrastos appeared and separated them. Recalling a certain seer telling him to yoke his daughters to a boar and a lion, he chose them both as husbands, for one had on his shield the forequarters of a boar and the other had those of a lion. Tydeus married Deipyle, and Polyneices married Argeia, and Adrastos promised to restore them both to their homelands. He was eager to march against Thebes first and assembled the nobles.

Amphiaraos son of Oicles was a seer and foresaw that all those who undertook the campaign were bound to die except Adrastos. So he himself shrank from campaigning and tried to dissuade the others. But Polyneices came to Iphis son of Alector and asked to learn how Amphiaraos could be forced to go to war. Iphis said that he could be forced if Eriphyle got the necklace. Now, Amphiaraos had forbidden Eriphyle to accept any gifts from Polyneices, but Polyneices gave her the necklace and asked her to persuade Amphiaraos to undertake the campaign. It was in her power, for Amphiaraos had once quarreled with Adrastos, and after settling it swore to let Eriphyle settle any further dispute he might have with Adrastos. So when it was time to march against Thebes and Adrastos encouraged it and Amphiaraos discouraged it, Eriphyle took the necklace and persuaded him to campaign with Adrastos. Amphiaraos was compelled to go to war, but he gave his sons instructions to kill their mother and go to war against Thebes when they grew up.

After Adrastos assembled an army with seven leaders, he hurried to make war on Thebes. The leaders were the following: Adrastos son of Talaos, Amphiaraos son of Oicles, Capaneus son of Hipponoos, and Hippomedon son of Aristomachos (some say he was son of Talaos), all from Argos; and Polyneices son of Oidipous from Thebes, Tydeus son of Oineus from Aitolia, and Parthenopaios son of Melanion from Arcadia. But some do not count Tydeus and Polyneices and include in the seven Eteoclos son of Iphis, and Mecisteus.

When they arrived in Nemea, where Lycourgos was king, they went looking for water. Hypsipyle guided them to the spring, leaving behind the infant Opheltes, the son of Eurydice and Lycourgos, whom she was nursing. She was doing so because when the Lemnian women found out later that she had saved Thoas, they killed him and sold Hypsipyle into slavery. So she was bought and served in the home of Lycourgos. While she was showing them the spring, the child she left behind was killed by a serpent.

[13] The gifts given to Harmonia at her marriage to Cadmos (see M1).

Adrastos and his men showed up, killed the serpent, and buried the boy. But Amphiaraos told them that it was a sign that foretold the future, and they called the boy Archemoros {"Beginner of Doom"}. They held in his honor the Nemean Games. Adrastos was the victor in the horse race, Eteoclos in running, Tydeus in boxing, Amphiaraos in jumping and discus, Laodocos in the javelin toss, Polyneices in wrestling, and Parthenopaios in archery.

When they came to Mount Cithairon, they sent Tydeus ahead to tell Eteocles to yield the kingdom to Polyneices, as they had agreed. Eteocles paid no attention, so Tydeus made a test of the Thebans by challenging them one at a time and defeating them all. The Thebans armed fifty men and had them ambush Tydeus as he departed, but he killed all of them except Maion and then returned to his camp.

The Argives took up arms and advanced to the walls. There were seven sets of gates. Adrastos stood at the Homoloidian Gates, Capaneus at the Ogygian, Amphiaraos at the Proitidian, Hippomedon at the Oncaidian, Polyneices at the Hypsistan, Parthenopaios at the Electran, and Tydeus at the Crenidian. Eteocles also armed the Thebans and appointed commanders equal in number to those on the other side. He then consulted seers as to how they might defeat their enemies.

M8 Teiresias

There was in Thebes a seer, Teiresias, the son of Eueres and the Nymph Chariclo, a descendant of Oudaios, one of the Spartoi, who was blind. They tell varying accounts of his blindness and his prophetic art. Some say that he was blinded by the gods because he used to reveal to mortals what the gods wished to hide. But Pherecydes says that he was blinded by Athena, for although Chariclo was dearly loved by Athena, < . . . > Teiresias saw Athena completely naked, and she covered his eyes with her hands and made him blind. Although Chariclo asked her to restore his sight, Athena was unable to do so, but she cleaned out his ears and rendered him capable of understanding every utterance of the birds, and she gave him a cornel-wood staff as a gift, and when he carried this, he could walk around like those who can see. But Hesiod says that near Mount Cyllene he once saw some snakes mating, and when he injured them, he changed from a man to a woman. Then, when he observed the same snakes mating a second time, he changed back into a man. Because of this experience, Hera and Zeus asked him to settle their dispute when they were arguing whether it happens that women or men take more pleasure in the sexual act. Teiresias said that if you divide sexual pleasure into ten portions, men enjoy one of these and women nine. So Hera blinded him, but Zeus granted him the power of prophecy. He also lived to an advanced age.

The Thebans consulted Teiresias, and he told them they would be victorious if Menoiceus son of Creon gave himself freely to Ares as a sacrificial offering. When Menoiceus son of Creon heard this, he cut his own throat before the gates. When the battle occurred, the Cadmeians were pushed back all the way to the walls, and Capaneus put a ladder against the wall and began to climb it, but Zeus struck him with a thunderbolt.

M9 End of the Seven's Expedition

After this happened, the Argives were routed. Since many died, both armies made a decision, and Eteocles and Polyneices fought a duel for the kingdom, killing each other.

There was another mighty battle, and the sons of Astacos displayed great bravery: Ismaros killed Hippomedon, Leades killed Eteoclos, and Amphidicos killed Parthenopaios (though according to Euripides, Poseidon's son Periclymenos killed Parthenopaios). Melanippos, the last of Astacos' sons, wounded Tydeus in the stomach. As he lay half-dead, Athena begged Zeus for a drug and brought it with the intention of making him immortal with it. But when Amphiaraos perceived this, in his hatred for Tydeus because he had persuaded the Argives to go on campaign against Amphiaraos' judgment, he cut off Melanippos' head and gave it to Tydeus. He broke the head open and gulped down the brain. When Athena saw this, she was revolted and withheld the bounty, denying it to Tydeus. As for Amphiaraos, as he was fleeing along the Ismenos River, before he could be wounded in the back by Periclymenos, Zeus split open the earth by casting a thunderbolt. Amphiaraos disappeared along with his chariot and his charioteer Baton (Elaton according to some), and Zeus made him immortal. Adrastos alone was saved by his horse Areion. Demeter bore this horse after having sex in the guise of an Erinys with Poseidon.

[3.7] Creon, after taking over the kingdom of the Thebans, cast the Argives' corpses out unburied, made a proclamation that no one was to bury them, and set guards. But Antigone, one of Oidipous' daughters, secretly stole the body of Polyneices and buried it. Caught by Creon, she was buried alive in his tomb. Adrastos came to Athens and fled to the altar of Pity for refuge. After placing an olive branch on it, he asked that they bury the bodies. The Athenians marched with Theseus, captured Thebes, and gave the bodies to their relatives for burial. When the pyre of Capaneus was burning, Euadne, Capaneus' wife and Iphis' daughter, threw herself onto it and was cremated with him.

M10 The Epigonoi

Ten years later the dead men's sons, known as the Epigonoi {"The Next Generation"}, proposed to march on Thebes, desiring to avenge the deaths of their fathers. When they sought oracles, the god prophesied victory, provided Alcmaion was their leader. Alcmaion did not want to lead the army until he punished his mother, but he went on the campaign anyway, for Eriphyle got the dress[14] from Thersandros son of Polyneices and helped him convince her sons to go on the campaign also. The Epigonoi chose Alcmaion leader and made war on Thebes. Those who went on the campaign were: Amphiaraos' sons Alcmaion and Amphilochos, Aigialeus son of Adrastos, Diomedes son of Tydeus, Promachos son of Parthenopaios, Sthenelos son of Capaneus, Thersandros son of Polyneices, and Euryalos son of Mecisteus. They first plundered the surrounding villages, then when the Thebans, led by Laodamas son of Eteocles, attacked them, they fought mightily. Laodamas killed Aigialeus, but Alcmaion killed Laodamas. After his death the Thebans fled within the walls *en masse*. Teiresias told them to send a herald to the Argives to discuss ending the war while the rest of them fled. So they sent a herald to the enemy while they themselves loaded the women and children onto their wagons and fled from the city. Arriving by night at the spring known as Tilphoussa, Teiresias drank from it and brought his life to a close. After traveling for a long time, the Thebans founded the city of Hestiaia and settled there.

Later, when the Argives discovered the Thebans' getaway, they entered the city of

[14] The dress given to Harmonia at her marriage to Cadmos (see M1).

Thebes, collected the plunder, and took down the walls. They sent a portion of the plunder to Apollo in Delphi, as well as Teiresias' daughter Manto; for they had vowed to dedicate to the god the finest of the plunder if they captured Thebes.

N1 Theseus (3.15.6–E.1.19)

Aigeus' first wife was Meta daughter of Hoples, and his second was Chalciope daughter of Rhexenor. Since he had no children and was afraid of his brothers, he went to Pytho and consulted the oracle about having children. The god prophesied to him:

> The projecting mouth of the wineskin, O best of men,
> Loose not until you come to the Athenians' peak.[15]

At a loss about the oracle, he set off to return to Athens. As he traveled through Troizen, he stayed with Pittheus son of Pelops, who understood the oracle, got Aigeus drunk, and put him into bed with his daughter Aithra. During the same night Poseidon also had intercourse with her. Aigeus instructed Aithra to raise the child if it were a boy, but not to tell anyone who the father was. He left under a certain rock a sword and a pair of sandals and told her to send their son to him with the objects when he could roll aside the rock and retrieve them.

N2 Minos' War on Athens

Aigeus returned to Athens and held the Panathenaic Games, where Minos' son Androgeos defeated everyone. Aigeus sent him against the Marathonian bull, and he was killed by it. But some say that while he was traveling to Thebes to attend the funeral games of Laios, he was ambushed and killed by his competitors out of jealousy. When his death was reported to Minos as he was sacrificing to the Charites on Paros, he threw his garland from his head and stopped the flute, but he still finished the sacrifice. For this reason even to the present day they sacrifice to the Charites without flutes or garlands on Paros. Soon thereafter, he attacked Athens with a fleet (he controlled the sea) and captured Megara, a city then ruled by Nisos son of Pandion. He killed Megareus son of Hippomenes, who had come from Onchestos to help Nisos. Through the treachery of his daughter, Nisos also died. He had a purple hair in the middle of his head, and an oracle said that he would die when this was plucked out. His daughter Scylla fell in love with Minos and pulled out the hair. After Minos conquered Megara, he tied the girl by the feet to the stern of his ship and drowned her.

The war dragged on as he was unable to capture Athens, so he prayed to Zeus to punish the Athenians. When a famine and epidemic broke out in the city, the Athenians, following an ancient oracle, first sacrificed the daughters of Hyacinthos, namely Antheis, Aigleis, Lytaia, and Orthaia, on the tomb of Geraistos the Cyclops. (Their father Hyacinthos had come from Lacedaimon and settled in Athens.) When this accomplished nothing, they consulted an oracle about how to rid themselves of

[15] The riddling oracle means that he will father a child during his next sexual encounter ("the projecting mouth of the wineskin" is a veiled reference to his genitals) and should wait until he returns to Athens if he wishes to produce a legitimate heir.

their trouble. The god ordained that they pay Minos whatever penalty he might choose. So they sent to Minos and left it up to him to name the penalty. Minos ordered them to send seven young men and the same number of young women, all unarmed, as food for the Minotaur, who had been shut up in a labyrinth, which was impossible for someone who entered to get out of, for it closed off its secret exit with complex twists and turns.

N3 Daidalos

Daidalos son of Eupalamos (who was the son of Metion) and Alcippe, built the labyrinth. He was the finest architect and the first sculptor of statues. He had gone into exile from Athens for throwing his sister's son Talos, who was his student, off the acropolis because he was afraid of being surpassed by him in talent—Talos found the jawbone of a snake and sawed through a thin piece of wood with it. But Talos' body was discovered, and after Daidalos stood trial in the Areopagos and was condemned, he went to Minos' court in exile.

N4 Theseus' Journey to Athens

[3.16] Theseus was Aigeus' son by Aithra, and when he grew up, he pushed aside the rock, picked up the sandals and sword, and hurried to Athens on foot. He cleared the road of the evildoers who had taken control of it. First, in Epidauros he killed Periphetes, the son of Hephaistos and Anticleia, also known as Corynetes {"Clubber"} because of the club he carried; since he had weak legs, he used to carry an iron club, and with it he would kill passing travelers. Theseus took the club away from him and carried it around. Second, he killed Sinis, the son of Polypemon and Sylea (daughter of Corinthos). Sinis was also known as Pityocamptes {"Pine-bender"} because he lived on the Isthmos of Corinth and forced passing travelers to bend down pine trees and hold them. Since they were not strong enough, they could not do so, and when they were catapulted by the trees, they would be utterly destroyed. This is how Theseus also killed Sinis.

[E.1[16]] Third, he killed in Crommyon the sow known as Phaia after the old woman who raised it. Some say it was the offspring of Echidna and Typhon. Fourth, he killed Sceiron the Corinthian, who was the son of Pelops or, according to some, Poseidon. He occupied the cliffs in the Megarid called the Sceironian Cliffs after him and used to force passing travelers to wash his feet. As they washed them, he would cast them into the deep as food for an enormous turtle. But Theseus grabbed him by the feet and cast him into the sea. Fifth, in Eleusis he killed Cercyon, the son of Branchos and the Nymph Argiope. He used to force passing travelers to wrestle and would kill them when they did. Theseus lifted him up high and then slammed him to the ground. Sixth, he killed Damastes, whom some call Polypemon. He had his house by the side of the road and had two beds, one short, the other long, and would invite passing travelers to be his guests. He would make short travelers lie in the large bed and beat them with hammers so that they would be the same size as the bed. He would put tall travelers into the short bed and then saw off the parts of the body that hung over the ends.

After clearing the road, Theseus arrived in Athens. But Medeia, who at that time

[16] From this point on the text of Apollodorus survives only in an epitomized form.

was married to Aigeus, plotted against him. She persuaded Aigeus to be on guard, alleging that Theseus was plotting against him. Aigeus did not recognize his own son and in fear sent him against the Marathonian bull. When he destroyed it, Aigeus got a poison from Medeia that same day and gave it to him. When Theseus was about to drink the poison, he presented his sword to his father as a gift. When Aigeus recognized it, he knocked the cup from his hands. After being recognized by his father and learning of the plot against him, Theseus drove Medeia out of the country.

N5 Crete, the Minotaur, and Ariadne

Theseus was chosen for the third group sent as tribute to the Minotaur, though some say he volunteered to go. The ship had a black sail, but Aigeus instructed his son that if he came back alive he should rig the ship with white sails. When he arrived in Crete, Minos' daughter Ariadne fell in love with him and offered to help him if he promised to take her back to Athens and make her his wife. After Theseus promised and swore oaths on it, she asked Daidalos to reveal the way out of the labyrinth, and at his suggestion she gave a thread to Theseus as he entered. Theseus tied this to the door and went in dragging it behind. He found the Minotaur in the innermost part of the labyrinth and beat him to death with his fists. He got out by following the thread back. During the night he arrived on Naxos with Ariadne and the children.[17] There Dionysos fell in love with Ariadne and carried her off. He brought her to Lemnos and slept with her, fathering Thoas, Staphylos, Oinopion, and Peparethos.

Grieving for Ariadne, Theseus forgot to rig the ship with white sails as he put into port. From the Acropolis Aigeus saw that the ship had black sails and thought that Theseus was dead, so he jumped off and died. Theseus succeeded to the rule of the Athenians and killed the sons of Pallas, fifty in all. Likewise any who thought to oppose him were killed by him, and so he alone came to hold all the power.

N6 Daidalos, Icaros, and the Death of Minos

Minos, learning of the escape of Theseus and his companions, held Daidalos responsible and put him into the labyrinth along with his son Icaros, whom he had with Naucrate, one of Minos' slaves. But Daidalos made wings for himself and his son, and told his son not to fly too high when he was aloft, or else the glue would be melted by the sun and the wings would fall apart, and not to fly near the sea, or else the wings would fall apart from the moisture. But Icaros, lost in delight, paid no attention to his father's instructions and went ever higher. When the glue melted, he plunged into the sea that is named the Icarian Sea after him and died. Daidalos made it safely to Camicos in Sicily. But Minos pursued Daidalos, and as he searched each land, he brought with him a murex shell, promising to give a great reward to anyone who could pass a thread through the spiral shell. He was sure that he would find Daidalos by this means. When he came to the court of Cocalos in Camicos in Sicily, where Daidalos was being hidden, he showed the shell. Cocalos took it, promised to thread it, and gave it to Daidalos, who attached a thread to an ant, bored a hole in the shell, and let the ant go through it. When Minos found out that a thread had been passed through the shell, he understood that Daidalos was with Cocalos and

[17] The young Athenians sent as tribute.

demanded him back immediately. Cocalos promised to give him back and invited Minos to be his guest. But after Minos took a bath, he was killed by Cocalos' daughters, though others say that he died when he had boiling water poured over him.

N7 The Amazons, Phaidra, and Hippolytos

Theseus joined Heracles' campaign against the Amazons and carried off Antiope, though others say Melanippe, and Simonides says Hippolyte. So the Amazons marched against Athens. They set up their camp around the Areopagos, but Theseus and the Athenians defeated them. He had a son Hippolytos with the Amazon woman, but from Deucalion[18] he later got Minos' daughter Phaidra, and when his wedding to her was being celebrated, his Amazon ex-wife showed up dressed for battle with her Amazonian companions and intended to kill the guests. But they quickly shut the doors and killed her. But some say that she was killed by Theseus in battle. After Phaidra bore two sons for Theseus, namely Acamas and Demophon, she fell in love with the son he had with the Amazon and begged him to sleep with her. He hated all women and shrank from sleeping with her. Phaidra, afraid that he would tell his father, broke open the doors to her bedroom, ripped open her clothes, and made up a story that Hippolytos raped her. Theseus believed her and prayed to Poseidon that Hippolytos be destroyed. As Hippolytos rode on his chariot and was driving along the sea, Poseidon sent forth a bull from the waves. The horses were spooked and the chariot was smashed to pieces. Hippolytos, tangled in the reins, was dragged to death. Phaidra hanged herself when her love became public knowledge.

[18] Minos' son, who succeeded him as king.

ARCHILOCHUS

(7th c. BC, wrote in Greek)

Archilochus was a lyric poet from the island of Paros in the Aegean Sea and was active in the middle of the 7th century BC (the eclipse mentioned in fragment 122 below is likely dated to 648 BC). Although he was known in subsequent generations primarily for the poetry he wrote that contained insults and scandalous charges against individuals, his output also contained poems on other topics, including political and military events of his time. The three fragments below, found in a collection of quotations from late antiquity, dwell on the power of the gods.

122 Zeus and the Eclipse (fr. 122 West)

Nothing is unexpected, nothing can be sworn as impossible
or marveled at, since Zeus, the father of the Olympians,
made night out of noonday, keeping back the light
of the beaming sun; and upon mankind came fear.
Henceforth all things are to be believed, all things expected
by men. None of you should in future be amazed, not even to see
the beasts change place with dolphins and go grazing
in the deep, holding the sea's resounding billows
dearer than land, while dolphins love the wooded hills.

130 All Things Are Easy for the Gods (fr. 130 West)

All things are easy for the gods. Often out of misfortunes
they set men upright who have been laid low on the black earth;
often they trip even those who are standing firm and roll them
onto their backs, and then many troubles come to them,
and a man wanders in want of livelihood, unhinged in mind.

177 Zeus and Justice (fr. 177 West)

O Zeus, father Zeus, yours is the rulership of heaven;
   you oversee the deeds of men,
villainous and lawful; you care about
   the outrage and right-doing of beasts.

ARRIAN

(ca. 86–160 AD, wrote in Greek)

Arrian's Anabasis *is a history of the life, reign, and death of Alexander the Great. The following passage reveals the attitudes of the Greeks toward the institution of divine kingship, using the mythological examples of Dionysos and Heracles as precedents. Although some peoples in the Near East considered kings to be gods (e.g., the Egyptian pharaohs), the Persians felt their monarch was merely the chosen representative of the gods. In Greek eyes the difference was slight and the only real contrast was between Greek ways and barbarian ways; the treatment of Persian monarchs, including the practice of making obeisance (ritually demonstrating one's inferiority to the king), was repulsive—such behavior was appropriate only toward the gods, not mortals. So, when Alexander conquered Persia and began to appropriate some of the characteristics of a Persian king, many Greeks were disturbed.*

FROM *ANABASIS*

4.10.5–4.11.8 Worship of Alexander the Great

Also widespread is the following account of how Callisthenes of Olynthos, a former student of Aristotle, opposed Alexander in the matter of obeisance. Alexander concocted a plan with the sophists[1] and the most important Persians and Medes in his retinue that they would bring up this issue at a drinking party. Anaxarchos started the conversation by saying that it would be far more just to consider Alexander a god than Dionysos and Heracles. This was not just because Alexander had accomplished many great deeds, but also because Dionysos was a Theban and in no way related to the Macedonians, and Heracles was from Argos and also not related—except through Alexander's lineage, since Alexander was a descendant of Heracles. The Macedonians would be more just in giving their own king divine honors. After all, there was no question about it: they would certainly honor Alexander as a god after he had departed this life, so it would be that much more just for them to honor him while he was still alive instead of when he was dead, when it would do him no good to be honored.

After Anaxarchos made these and similar arguments, his fellow schemers applauded his speech and wanted to begin making obeisance there and then. But the Macedonians, most of whom were upset by his words, kept quiet. Then Callisthenes took up the argument and said, "Anaxarchos, I declare that Alexander is worthy of

[1] Greek professional intellectuals, teachers, and scholars. Several accompanied Alexander on his expedition.

every single honor that is fitting for a mortal. But mortal honors and divine honors have been separated by people in many different ways, for instance in the building of shrines and the erection of holy images. Sacred areas are given to the gods. We sacrifice and pour libations to them. Hymns are sung for the gods, but simple praise for mortals. But most important, the distinction is made regarding the custom of obeisance. Mortals welcome each other with a kiss, but the divine, because I suppose it is on a higher level and it is wrong even to touch it, is therefore honored with obeisance. There are also dances for the gods and paeans are sung to them.

"There is nothing surprising here, not when different honors are paid even to different gods, and, yes by Zeus, different ones are paid to heroes, and these are distinguished from divine honors. So it is not fair to mix them up by making mortals larger than life with extravagant honors and by bringing the gods down (as much as they can, anyway) to an unseemly low level by honoring them with the same honors that mortals get. Likewise, Alexander would not put up with it if some ordinary person were to usurp the royal honors by an election or vote that was unjust. The gods would be that much more justified in being displeased with any mortals who usurped divine honors—or who let others put them in a situation where they were usurping them. Alexander not only seems to be, but actually *is* by far the bravest of the brave, the most royal of royals, and the most strategic of strategists.

"Anaxarchos, you of all people should have been the one to bring these things up and stop those on the other side. You are with Alexander to instruct him in wisdom, so it was inappropriate for you to start this discussion. You ought to have remembered that you are not here to instruct Cambyses or Xerxes.[2] No, you are the instructor of the son of Philip, one from the lineage of Heracles and Aiacos, one whose ancestors came from Argos to Macedon and have continued to rule the Macedonians by law, not force. The Greeks did not even pay Heracles divine honors while he was still alive. In fact, even after he died they did not do so until the god at Delphi told them in an oracle to honor Heracles as a god.

"But if we have to think like barbarians because we are talking in a barbarian land, even so I demand that you remember Greece, Alexander. Your entire expedition is about adding Asia to Greece. So think about this: When you return there, are you also going to force the Greeks, who are the freest men, to give obeisance? Or will you not force the Greeks but just subject the Macedonians to this dishonor? Or will you settle the matter of your honors once and for all by deciding that you are to be honored as a mortal by the Greeks and Macedonians in the Greek way, and that you will be honored by the barbarians alone in the barbarian way?"

[2] Famous Persian kings.

Babrius

(1st or 2nd c. AD, wrote in Greek)

Babrius was a poet who rendered Aesopic fables into short poems. We have two books of these, containing 144 poems. Though these fables are closer to folktales than mythical texts, such as Homer's epics or Greek tragedy, a few of them are nonetheless quite revealing about popular attitudes toward religious and mythical matters.

FROM *FABLES*

20 The Gods Help Those Who Help Themselves

A cattle driver was driving his cart out of town.
When it fell down into a deep gully,
something needed to be done, but he stood idly by
and prayed to Heracles, who was the only one
of all the gods he truly worshiped and honored.
The god appeared next to him and said, "Grab the wheels
and whip your oxen. Pray to the gods
when you are doing something or you'll pray in vain."

68 The Preeminence of Zeus

Apollo used to say to the gods when he made a long shot,
"No one could shoot farther than I, not even Zeus."
So as a joke, Zeus challenged Phoibos to a contest.
Hermes shook the lots in Ares' helmet.
Phoibos won and, having bent his golden bowstring
into a circle, he quickly took the first shot
and sent his arrow all the way inside the gardens of Hesperos.
Zeus took a step across the same distance, stopped
and said, "Son, where do I shoot? I don't have any room!"
He took the prize for archery without even taking a shot.

70 The Marriage of Polemos {"War"} and Hubris

The gods were getting married, and when each was paired off,
War drew the last lot and came after everyone.

He married Hubris, who was the only one left.
He loved her excessively, they say,
and he still follows her everywhere she goes.
So may Hubris never come upon nations or
cities of men, smiling upon the people,
since War will come immediately after her.

117 We Are Ants to the Gods

Once upon a time a ship sank with its crew.
Someone watching said that the gods made unjust decisions.
For, because a single impious man had been aboard,
many who had done no wrong died along with him.
At the same time he was saying this, as it happens,
a great swarm of ants came up to him,
hurrying to make a meal of the chaff of some wheat.
When he was bitten by one, he stomped on lots of them.
Hermes appeared next to him and, hitting him with his rod,
said, "And so you won't suffer the gods to be
the same sort of judges of mortals as you are of ants?"

BACCHYLIDES

(ca. 520–450 BC, wrote in Greek)

Bacchylides, like his contemporary Pindar, was a celebrated lyric poet who wrote epinicia *(victory odes) and* dithyrambs *(choral poems in honor of Dionysos). Although we know that his poems were collected into nine books in the Hellenistic period, it was not until the end of the 19th century AD that we possessed more than mere fragments of his poems, when a papyrus containing nearly all of his victory odes and parts of his* dithyrambs *was found in Egypt. As for many early lyric poets, myth is a central feature in the structure of Bacchylides' poems, and the two provided here are no exceptions. The first, an* epinicion *(victory ode) in honor of Hieron's success in the horse race at the Olympic Games, dramatizes the encounter between Heracles and Meleagros in the underworld. The second depicts the dispute between Theseus and Minos on the ship taking the Athenian youths as food for the Minotaur on Crete.*

ODE 5

Like Pindar's Olympian 1 (in this volume), this poem begins (1–55) and ends (176–200) with praise for Hieron of Syracuse (and his horse, Pherenicos) who won the horse race at the Olympic Games in 476 BC. The extended mythical narrative that occupies the central portion of the ode (56–175) brings together two great figures of Greek legend: Heracles, who has descended into the realm of the dead while performing one of his famous labors, and the Aitolian warrior Meleagros, whose ghost or shade Heracles encounters there. At Heracles' prompting, Meleagros tells the story of his own untimely death, which was brought upon him by fate and the burning anger of his mother Althaia. The narrative as a whole ends with an allusion to Meleagros' sister, Deianeira (172–175), whom Heracles will later marry and at whose hands he in turn is destined to die. In this way Bacchylides contrives to suggest a parallel between the two heroes that underscores the truth of the maxim that the myth is introduced to illustrate: "No mortal on earth is born in all ways fortunate."

For Hieron son of Deinomenes, from Syracuse,
victor in the horserace at the Olympic games

Fortunate leader of the Syracusans [Str. 1]
renowned for their whirling chariots,
you will know how to judge the violet-crowned
Muses' sweet gift and ornament, if any can

of those now living on the earth,
correctly. Let your thought, intent on justice,
relax a while in peace, cares laid aside,
and turn your mind's gaze hither:
this hymn, woven with the aid
of the deep-girded Charites,
is being sent from the holy isle
to your illustrious city by a guest-friend,
the celebrated servant of
gold-banded Ourania.[1] He is ready
to pour forth from his breast loud song

in praise of Hieron. Quickly [Ant. 1]
cutting the depth of air
on high with tawny wings,
the eagle, messenger of Zeus
who thunders in wide lordship,
is bold, relying on his mighty
strength, while other birds
cower, shrill-voiced, in fear.
The great earth's mountain peaks do not hold him back,
nor the tireless sea's
rough-tossing waves, but in
the limitless expanse
he guides his fine sleek plumage
along the West Wind's breezes,
manifest to men's sight.

So now for me too countless paths extend in all directions [Ep. 1]
by which to praise your prowess
in song, by the grace of dark-haired Nike
and Ares of the brazen breastplate,
O lordly sons of Deinomenes!
May god not tire in his beneficence.
When Pherenicos with his auburn mane
ran like the wind
beside the eddies of broad Alpheios,[2]
Eos, with her arms all golden, saw his victory;

[1] One of the Muses.

[2] The river at Olympia.

and so too at most holy Pytho. [Str. 2]
Calling the earth to witness, I declare
that never yet has any horse outstripped him
in competition, sprinkling him with dust
as he rushed forward to the goal.
For like the North Wind's blast,
keeping the man who steers him safe,
he hurtles onward, bringing to Hieron,
that generous host, victory with its fresh applause.
Blessed is he on whom the gods
bestow a share of noble things
and, along with enviable success,
a life passed amid wealth. For no
mortal on earth is born
to be in all ways fortunate.

Once, they say, that ruiner of gates,[3] [Ant. 2]
the unconquerable son of Zeus
whose thunderbolt is bright, went down
into the halls of slender-ankled Persephone,
seeking to fetch the saw-toothed hound[4]
from Hades up into the light,
the offspring of the terrible Echidna.
There he observed the souls
of wretched mortals by Cocytos' streams,
like leaves tossed by the wind
up and down the clear-edged heights
of Ida where sheep graze.
Conspicuous among them was the shade
of Porthaon's grandson,[5]
bold-hearted shaker of the spear.

Seeing him in his shining armor, [Ep. 2]
Alcmene's son, the wondrous hero,
stretched a clear-sounding sinew on his bow;
then, lifting up the lid
of his quiver, he took out
a brazen-headed arrow. But right there before him

[3] Heracles.
[4] Cerberos.
[5] Meleagros.

the soul of Meleagros loomed
and with full knowledge spoke to him:
"Great Zeus' son,
stand where you are, and, making your heart calm,

do not launch from your hands [Str. 3]
a rough-edged arrow to no purpose
against the souls of those who have perished.
You have no cause to fear." He spoke thus, and amazement seized
Amphitryon's lordly son.
He said, "Who is it of immortals
or mortals that has nurtured such
a sapling, and in what great land?
Who killed him? Truly, Hera of the lovely belt
will soon send such a one
against me, to my hurt—but then perhaps
the fair-haired Pallas has the matter already in mind."
Then Meleagros said to him
in tears: "To turn aside
the gods' intent is difficult

for men who live upon the earth. [Ant. 3]
For otherwise my father, horse-driving Oineus, would
have put an end to the wrath of Artemis,[6]
august, white-armed, with rosebuds in her hair,
by means of prayers and
the sacrifice of many goats
and cattle, ruddy-backed.
But not to be conquered was the wrath
which the goddess had conceived. And so the Maiden sent a boar
wide-ranging in violence, a ruthless fighter,
into the lovely fields of Calydon,
and there, strength overflowing,
it ravaged vineyards with its tusks
and slaughtered flocks, and any man
who met it face to face.

Against it we waged hateful battle—we, the best [Ep. 3]
among the Greeks—with force and fury,
six days on end; but when some power

[6] Meleagros' father, Oineus, omitted Artemis in his sacrifices. She sent the Calydonian boar, which began a series of events ending with the death of Meleagros (Apollodorus F).

had handed victory to the Aitolians,
we buried those who had been killed
by the boar's impetuous, bellowing charge:
Ancaios and Agelaos, bravest
of my dear brothers,
whom in Oineus' celebrated halls
< . . . > Althaia bore.

< . . . > destroyed by baleful destiny < . . . > [Str. 4]
< . . . > for not yet had Leto's wild
and fiery-hearted daughter brought
her wrath to an end. Contesting for the gleaming hide,
we fought with force and fury
against the Couretes[7] staunch in war.
And then I killed, along
with many others, Iphiclos
and noble Aphares, my mother's quick-limbed brothers; for in truth
strong-hearted Ares
does not distinguish friends in war:
blindly do weapons leave the hand,
aimed against the lives
of enemies but bringing death
to those whom heaven chooses.

Of these things Thestios' fiery-hearted [Ant. 4]
daughter took no thought,
although she was my mother—and my evil fate.
Plotting my death, that woman whom no fear could shake
took from a chest of intricate workmanship
the log that spelled my speedy doom
and set it burning: destiny
had so spun out its thread that then
and thus would be the limit of my life.[8] It happened
that I was stripping Clymenos
of armor, Deipylos' valiant son
whose body was without flaw;
before the ramparts I had overtaken him,

[7] The war over the hide pitted the Aitolians, led by Meleagros, against the Couretes, led by his mother's uncles.

[8] Meleagros was destined to live so long as a certain log existed. This was guarded by his mother, Althaia (Apollodorus F).

as they fled toward the stout
walls of that ancient city,

Pleuron. But the sweet breath of life began to fail me [Ep. 4]
and I felt my strength grow less.
Alas! With one last gasp, I burst out weeping, grieved
to leave behind the radiance of youth."
They say that Amphitryon's son,
whom cries of battle did not daunt, at that time and no other
shed tears, in pity for
the man's calamitous fate;
and answering him
he said, "For mortals, not to be born is best,

nor to gaze upon the sun's [Str. 5]
bright light. And yet no good
can come of such lamentation:
a man should speak of what he really means to accomplish.
Tell me, is there within the halls
of Oineus, dear to Ares,
one of his daughters still unwedded,
bearing your likeness in her form?
Her I would gladly make my lustrous wife."
To him the shade
of Meleagros staunch in war
replied: "I left one with youth's bloom about her neck
there in the house, Deianeira,
as yet without experience of golden
Cypris who casts her spells on mortal men."

White-armed Calliope, [Ant. 5]
halt the well-wrought chariot
right here! Make Zeus the son of Cronos
your theme of song, the Olympian ruler of the gods,
and the untiring current
of Alpheos, and Pelops' might,
and Pisa, where famed Pherenicos
won victory on the race course
by speed of feet, and came then to the towers of Syracuse,
bearing for Hieron
the leaves of happiness.
One must for the sake of truth

give praise, with both hands thrusting
envy aside,
if anyone among mortals is successful.

A man from Boiotia said this, [Ep. 5]
Hesiod, servant of the sweet
Muses: he whom immortals honor
has men's report attending him as well.
I readily am persuaded
to see that glorious speech, not straying from the path of justice,
be sent to Hieron, for from that source
the roots of all nobility draw strength and flourish.
May Zeus, the greatest of all fathers,
preserve them in unshaken peace.

DITHYRAMB 17

The narrative setting for this poem is the ship carrying Theseus and the other Athenian youths sent as tribute for the Minotaur in Crete. In this version, King Minos himself captains the ship and provokes a dispute with Theseus by attempting to take advantage of Eriboia, one of the young Athenian girls on board. Theseus rebukes Minos, who proves his own divine heritage and challenges Theseus to do the same. Although in antiquity this poem was identified as a dithyramb, *like many* dithyrambs *it shows no obvious connection to the worship of Dionysos, the original purpose of this type of poetry.*

With darkly gleaming prow the ship [Str. 1]
was cutting through the Cretan sea,
carrying Theseus, staunch in the battle din,
and twice seven splendid young Ionian folk;
for into the far-shining sail
a breeze from the north was falling,
thanks to glorious Athena, shaker of the aegis.
And Minos' heart was pricked
by lust, the holy gift
of Aphrodite, goddess diademed with desire.
No longer did he keep his hand
away from the girl, but touched
her white cheeks.
And Eriboia[9] shouted to

[9] One of the maidens being taken to the Minotaur.

Pandion's grandson in his bronze
breastplate. When Theseus saw it,
his dark eyes rolled
under his brows, and cruel pain
tore at his heart,
and he said, "Son of mightiest Zeus,
no longer are your passions steered
in righteousness within the compass of
your wits. Hero that you are, restrain your vaunting violence.

Whatever thing all-mastering destiny [Ant. 1]
has stipulated for us from the gods, and Dike swings her scales
in confirmation, that apportionment
we shall fulfill as fated when
it comes. But as for you, hold back
from the grave wrong that you are planning. Even if it is true
that Phoinix's cherished daughter,[10] famed
for beauty, lay with Zeus beneath the crest of Ida
and bore you to be foremost
of mortals, still I too
am son of a god,
born to Poseidon of the sea
from his union with opulent
Pittheus' daughter,[11] who received
a golden veil from the dark-haired Nereids.
Therefore I urge you, warlord of the Cnossians,
to curb your arrogance, which will otherwise
be cause of many groans. I would not wish
to see the immortal loveliness
of Eos' light after you had forced
any of these young people to your will;
before that comes to pass, the power of our hands
will be shown forth, and what ensues will be as heaven determines."

So much the hero said, that valiant spearman. [Ep. 1]
Amazement gripped the sailors
at the man's inordinate
boldness, but it enraged the Sun-god's son-in-law.[12]

[10] Europa.

[11] Aithra.

[12] Minos was married to Pasiphae, the daughter of Helios.

Beginning to weave a new and cunning
plan, he said: "O you whose strength is mighty,
Zeus, father, listen: if indeed your white-armed
bride from Phoenicia bore me as your son,
now send forth from the sky a swift
lightning flash with fiery tresses
as a sign easy to recognize. And if
in turn Troizenian Aithra
engendered *you* by earth-shaking
Poseidon, fetch this ring of gold,
my hand's splendid
ornament, out of the sea's depths,
hurling yourself with boldness into your father's home.
You will learn whether my prayer
is heeded by the son of Cronos,
the lord of thunder who rules all things."

Then Zeus, whose strength is mighty, heeded [Str. 2]
the unimpeachable prayer. Engendering honor unsurpassed
for Minos his beloved son, and wishing
to make it visible to all,
he sent a flash of lightning. At the sight
of a portent that so fitted his desires, the hero staunch in war
stretched up his hands toward the glorious sky
and said, "Theseus, here you see
the clear gifts given to me
by Zeus. Now you in turn must leap into
the sea's loud turbulence, and Cronos' son,
your father, lord Poseidon, will
bring your fame to unequaled heights
throughout the earth with its fair trees."
Thus he spoke, and the other's spirit
did not give way. Upon
the well-built sterndeck
he took his stand and leapt, and the precinct of the sea
welcomed him willingly.
Amazement filled the heart
of Zeus' son, and he commanded that
the ship, so intricately crafted, should keep on before
the wind; but Destiny was readying a different course.

The vessel under swift escort rushed along, being driven [Ant. 2]

by a gale that blew behind it from the north.
The crowd of young
Athenians had trembled when
the hero leapt into the sea, and from
their lily-lustrous eyes they shed
tears, expecting compulsion's heavy grip.
Dolphins, meanwhile, those salt-sea dwellers,
quickly carried the great
Theseus to the home of his
father, the god of horses; and he came
to the sea gods' hall. There, at the sight
of blessed Nereus' glorious daughters,
fear seized on him, for from their radiant limbs
brightness shone forth
like that of fire, and about their hair
bands plaited out of gold
were twisting, as they took delight
in dancing on supple feet.
He also saw the dear wife of his father
there in the lovely house, august
ox-eyed Amphitrite,
who clothed him in a mantle of sea-purple

and set upon his thick-curled locks [Ep. 2]
a plaited garland without flaws,
which earlier, at her marriage,
deceitful Aphrodite had given her, dark with roses.
Nothing willed to be so by higher powers
is unbelievable to mortals of sound mind.
By the ship's slender stern he rose to view, and ah!
amid what thoughts did he cut short
the Cnossian commander, when
he came unwetted from the sea,
a wonder to all, and round his limbs
the gods' gifts shimmered, and the bright-
throned maidens, settled
anew in joyousness,
cried aloud, and the sea
resounded, and nearby the youths
sang a paean with lovely voice.
O god of Delos, warmed at heart
by the dances of the Ceans,
grant that heaven may send good fortune.

Bion

(probably late 2nd c. BC, wrote in Greek)

One of the finest poets of the Hellenistic period, Bion of Smyrna was most famous as a writer of bucolic (pastoral) poetry. The longest of his surviving pieces is this poem describing the expressive lamentation of Aphrodite for her dead lover Adonis. The poem builds upon ritual laments of the sort that would have been used at the Adoneia, *a festival in many cities that celebrated the young man, transferring the lament from female worshipers at a ceremony to the goddess herself at the moment of Adonis' death from a wound delivered by a boar's tusk.*

LAMENT FOR ADONIS

I lament for Adonis, "Beautiful Adonis is dead."
"Beautiful Adonis is dead," the Erotes lament back.
Cypris, sleep no more in your scarlet-dyed coverlets.
Awaken, poor woman, and dressed in black beat
your breast and tell everyone, "Beautiful Adonis is dead."
   I lament for Adonis; the Erotes lament back.
Beautiful Adonis lies in the mountains, his thigh by a white tusk
gored, white thigh by white tusk, bringing Cypris pain
with his last feeble breaths. The dark blood oozes down
his snow-white flesh, the eyes beneath his brows glaze over,
and the rose deserts his lips, on which
dies the kiss that Cypris will never be able to collect.
Cypris is grateful for his kiss though he no longer lives,
but Adonis is not aware that she has kissed him after he died.
   I lament for Adonis; the Erotes lament back.
Vicious—Adonis has a vicious wound in his thigh,
but Cythereia bears a worse one in her heart.
His beloved hounds howl around that boy,
and mountain Nymphs mourn, but Aphrodite,
her hair let down, wanders through the woods
grief-stricken, her braids undone, no shoes on. The brambles,
as she moves, tear at her, plucking drops of her divine blood.
Wailing shrilly, she roams through the long mountain valleys,
wailing an Assyrian lament, calling for her boy-husband.

Around her, pulled down to her waist, hung her black robe.
Her chest was reddened by her hands, her breasts
just below, once snow-white, were dyed scarlet for Adonis.
"*Aiai,* Cythereia!" the Erotes lament back.
She lost her beautiful husband, lost her divine beauty with him.
Cypris' beauty was fair when Adonis lived,
but her loveliness perished with Adonis. "Cypris, *aiai*!"
say all the mountains, and the trees say, "*Ai,* Adonis!"
The rivers mourn for Aphrodite's griefs.
The springs in the mountains weep for Adonis.
The flowers blush red from sorrow. Cythera,
over every foothill, over every wooded vale, pitiably sings,
"*Aiai,* Cythereia! Beautiful Adonis is dead."
Echo calls back, "Beautiful Adonis is dead."
Who would not have cried "*Aiai*!" for Cypris' terrible love?
When she saw, discerned the unstaunchable wound of Adonis,
when she saw the red blood on his withering thigh,
opening her arms wide, she wailed, "Hold on, Adonis,
hold on, ill-starred Adonis, so that I can come to you for the last time,
so that I can embrace you and unite my lips with yours.
Awaken a bit, Adonis, and then kiss me your last kiss.
Kiss me for as long as your kiss lives,
until you breathe out your life into my mouth, and your breath
flows into my heart, and I drink your sweet love,
and I drain your love. I will keep this kiss
as if it were Adonis himself, since you, ill-fated, are leaving me.
You leave me far behind, Adonis, and go to Acheron,
to the court of a dread and cruel king. I, in misery,
live on. I am a goddess and cannot chase you.
Persephone, receive my husband, for you yourself
are far greater than me, for all beauty flows down to you.
I am completely hapless and have unquenchable sorrow.
I mourn my Adonis because he died, and stand in awe of you.
You are dead, much-desired one; my desire has flown off like a dream.
I, Cythereia, am a widow, the Erotes around my house are orphaned,
and my magic belt died with you. Why, daring one, did you hunt?
Despite your beauty, were you crazed enough to wrestle with a beast?"
Cypris mourned in this way; the Erotes lament back,
"*Aiai,* Cythereia! Beautiful Adonis is dead."
The goddess of Paphos pours forth as many tears as Adonis
pours blood, and all of it turns to flowers on the earth:
the blood produces the rose, the tears the anemone.

I lament for Adonis, "Beautiful Adonis is dead."
Bewail your husband no more in the woodlands, Cypris.
A lonely heap of leaves is not a good bed for Adonis.
Let Adonis have a bed, Cythereia, let him, now a corpse, have yours.
Though a corpse, he is beautiful, a beautiful corpse, as if only sleeping.
Place him in the soft coverlets among which he used to sleep,
where with you he used to toil at holy sleep through the night.
Lay out Adonis on your all-golden couch though he is dreadful.
Throw garlands and flowers over him. All flowers have,
since he is dead, withered along with him too.
Sprinkle him with Syrian oils, sprinkle him with perfumes.
Let all the perfumes perish; your perfume—Adonis—has perished.
Delicate Adonis has been laid on the purple-dyed bedclothes.
Around him, weeping, the Erotes groan in lamentation and
shear their hair for Adonis. One put his arrows on the bed,
another his bow, and one brought his well-feathered quiver.
One untied Adonis' sandal, others bring water
in a golden bowl, another washes his thighs,
and one stands behind Adonis and dries him with his wings.
"*Aiai,* Cythereia!" the Erotes lament back.
The torches at the doorposts, Hymenaios put them all out,
and he undid the wedding wreath. He sang "Hymen,
Hymen!" no longer, no longer his own song, but "*Aiai,*
aiai!" and "Adonis!" even louder than the hymenaeal.
The Charites weep for the son of Cinyras,
"Beautiful Adonis is dead," they say to one another;
"*Aiai*!" they say, far more shrilly than you do, Dione.
And the Moirai summon Adonis back from the dead, "Adonis!"
and sing spells over him, but he does not obey them.
It is not that he is unwilling, but Kore does not release him.
Cease lamenting for today, Cythereia, refrain from beating your breast.
You must weep again, again shed tears in another year.

CALLIMACHUS

(ca. 305–240 BC, wrote in Greek)

Callimachus was a poet of extraordinary talent, originality, and industry, but the majority of his works have been lost. Six of his hymns survive; the two below are "mimetic" hymns, that is, poems that attempt to recreate the feeling of a real ritual as if it were taking place. He accomplishes this both by including a great deal of detail appropriate to such occasions and by imitating earlier hymns (such as the ones we know as the Homeric Hymns*), which really were performed. These poems are, therefore, literary exercises, but literary exercises executed by a poet thoroughly familiar with both Greek ritual and hymnic literature.*

5 *Hymn to Athena*

The Hymn to Athena *may reflect an actual ritual in Argos, in which the icon of Athena was transported to the river Inachos for its yearly bathing. But apart from this hymn, we have no other evidence for this festival. What we do have are parallels in other cities, most notably the Athenian Plynteria {"Washing"}, which only women could attend. There, the sacred statue of the goddess was carried by wagon down to the river. It was then washed, anointed, dressed, and carried back up to the Acropolis. Callimachus' hymn is also notable for the myth of Teiresias' blindness as punishment for viewing Athena as she bathed, an account that we know from Apollodorus'* Library *3.6 goes all the way back to Pherecydes in the 5th century BC.*

All you attendants of Pallas' bath, come forth, one and all,
    come forth. Her mares, her sacred mares just
neighed—I heard them: the goddess is ready to come.
    Quickly now, my fair-haired Pelasgian maidens, quickly.
Never has Athena washed off her mighty arms
    before scouring off the dust from her horses' flanks,
not even when she returned from the unjust Earth-born ones[1]
    wearing armor all splattered with their gore.
No, first she unyoked her horses' necks from the chariot
    and in the streams of Oceanos rinsed off
the sweat and grime and cleansed all the encrusted
    foam from their bit-chomping mouths.

[1] The Giants.

O come, Achaian maidens, and bring no jars of scented oil,
(I hear the creak of the axle in the wheel-well),
no jars of scented oils for Pallas, bath attendants,
(for oils mixed with perfume are not dear to Athena)
and bring no mirror—always lovely is her appearance.
Not even when the Phrygian[2] judged the dispute on Ida
did the mighty goddess look into orichalc[3]
or the clear currents of the river Simoeis,
nor did Hera. But Cypris took the reflective bronze
and repeatedly adjusted the same lock of hair twice.
But twice did Athena run sixty circuits of the racetrack,
as on the banks of the river Eurotas ran the Lacedaimonian
stars.[4] She then took up oils and skillfully rubbed them in,
plain oils, her own tree's progeny.
O girls, the flush suffused her skin, the color
of an early spring rose or a pomegranate seed.
So now too bring something manly, only olive oil,
with which Castor and Heracles anoint themselves.
Also bring her a comb of solid gold, so she can brush out her
flowing hair after she washes her luxurious locks.
Come forth, Athena, here for you is a troop after your own heart,
maiden daughters of Arestor's mighty line.
O Athena, the shield of Diomedes too is being carried,
just as this custom was taught to the Argives of old
by Eumedes, your beloved priest.
He once learned that the people were plotting
his death, so he fled into exile with your sacred icon,
and he settled on the Creian mountain,
the Creian mountain, where he set you, goddess, on the sheer
crags which now bear the name "Pallas' Cliffs."
Come, Athena, you sacker of cities, golden-helmed,
who revel in the clash of horses and shields.
Today, water-bearers, do not draw river water—today, Argos,
you are to drink from the springs and not the river.
Today, slaves, bring your pitchers to Physadeia,
or to Amymone[5] daughter of Danaos.
For Inachos, mixing his waters with gold and flowers,

[2] Paris.

[3] *Oreichalkos* ("mountain-bronze") is a legendary metal of great beauty, fitting for a goddess' mirror.

[4] Castor and Polydeuces.

[5] That is, to the spring named after her.

will come down from the mountains that feed his stream,
bringing Athena her beautiful bath. But you, Pelasgian man,
mind that you do not look, even unwitting, upon the queen.
Whoever looks upon Pallas, protector of this city, unclothed,
will behold this city of Argos for the very last time.
Mistress Athena, come forth. Meanwhile, I will tell a tale
to these maidens—the tale is not mine, but others'.
Children, once upon a time in Thebes, Athena loved one Nymph
very much, far more than all her other companions.
She was Teiresias' mother, and at no time were they apart.
Never: even when to ancient Thespiai
< . . . > or she drove her horses
to Haliartos, crossing Boiotia's farmland,
or to Coroneia where lay her grove, fragrant with incense,
and her altars beside the river Couralios,
the goddess always placed her upon her chariot,
and neither dalliances of the Nymphs nor joyful
choral dances did arise without Chariclo in the lead.
But many tears were yet in store even for her
although she was a companion dear to Athena's heart.
Once upon a time the two unfastened the pins from their dresses
beside the fair-flowing Horse's Fountain on Helicon
and were taking a bath. Midday stillness gripped the mountain.
Both were bathing, and the time was midday,
and total stillness gripped that hill.
Only Teiresias with just his pack of dogs, his cheeks just
darkening with a beard, was roaming about the sacred place.
Thirsting unspeakably, he came to the fountain's stream,
poor fool, and unwittingly he looked upon what was not allowed,
and though Athena grew wroth, she addressed him nonetheless,
"What god led you, who will never leave here with your sight,
O son of Eueres, down this grim path?"
She spoke, and Night took away the boy's eyes.
He stood speechless, for distress froze
his limbs and helplessness took hold of his voice.
But the Nymph cried out, "What have you done to my boy,
mistress? Are these the kind of friends you goddesses are?
You took my son's *eyes*! O son, my wretched child,
you looked upon Athena's breast and loins,
but never again will you look upon the sun. Oh, poor me!
O mountain! O Helicon never to be trod by me again!
Great indeed was the price you exacted for so little: you lost
a few does, a few roe-deer, but you have my son's eyes."

At once the mother, putting both arms around her dear son,
joined in the lamentation of mournful nightingales,
keening heavily, and the goddess pitied her companion.
Athena addressed her with the following words,
"Blessed woman, reconsider everything you said in anger.
I am not the one who made your son blind;
Athena finds no joy in robbing children of their eyes.
No, Cronos' laws decree that this is how it is:
whoever gazes upon a deathless god, when the god himself
wishes it not, sees him at a price that is great.
Blessed woman, the deed may never hereafter be taken back
since this is what the threads of the Moirai spun out
at the moment you bore him. So, son of Eueres,
take you now the balance that is due you.
How many offerings Cadmos' daughter[6] will burn,
how many will Aristaios, praying to see
their youthful son, their only son, Actaion, blind.
He too will hunt alongside mighty Artemis,
and yet neither hunting nor shooting bows
side by side in the mountains will avail him at all then,
when he unwittingly looks upon the graceful baths
of the goddess. No, his very own hounds will feast upon
their former master, and his mother will collect her son's
bones as she roams through every thicket.
Most blessed she will say you are, and fortunate in life,
since you welcomed home a son, though blind, from the mountains.
Friend, do not mourn for him, since many other gifts
from my hand await him for your sake:
I will make him a prophet celebrated in the songs of posterity,
and one greatly surpassing all the rest.
He will understand birds, which are holy, which take wing
without meaning, and those whose flights bode ill.
Many oracles will he deliver to the Boiotians, many to Cadmos
and later to the mighty descendants of Labdacos.
I will grant him a great staff that will direct his step as he needs
and a life that shall end in the distant future.
And when he dies, he alone will move about the dead
with awareness, honored by mighty Hagesilas."[7]
She spoke and nodded her head, and whatever Pallas nods assent to

[6] Autonoe.

[7] Hades.

is fulfilled, since Zeus granted to Athena alone of his daughters
that she inherit all of her father's powers.
Bath attendants, no mother gave birth to the goddess,
but the head of Zeus did. The head of Zeus does not nod
at lies < . . . > the daughter.
Now Athena is coming! Welcome the goddess,
O maidens—for this is your task—
with words of praise, prayers, and ritual cries.
Hail, goddess, watch over Argos, Inachos' land!
Hail, as you drive off and as you drive your horses back again,
and may you preserve the entire kingdom of the Danaans!

6 *Hymn to Demeter*

The opening and closing portions of the Hymn to Demeter *seem to emulate the* Thesmophoria, *a festival of the goddess celebrated throughout the Greek world in autumn for the purpose of promoting fertility. The fasting mentioned (line 6) is paralleled in the Athenian* Thesmophoria, *where on the second day the participants fasted while sitting on the ground. Unlike the* Hymn to Athena, *there is no indication in the poem where the festival is supposed to be taking place, and perhaps Callimachus is less interested in specifying the location than in capturing a moment. The poem is set in the evening, just before the fall of night when the basket carrying the sacred objects is brought back and the participants can finally break their fast. The centerpiece of the poem is the cautionary tale of Erysichthon (lines 24–117), which simultaneously emphasizes Demeter's fertility and the importance of revering the gods.*

As the basket returns, women, sing the refrain,
"Great welcome, Demeter, feeder of many, giver of much grain."
Uninitiated women, view the returning basket from the ground!
Let neither girl nor woman look down from the rooftop
or from above, not even if she has let down her hair,
nor even when we spit from mouths that are dry from our fasting.
Hesperos has shone down through the clouds (when will he come?),
Hesperos, who alone persuaded Demeter to take drink
while searching for her stolen daughter's tracks that left no trace.
Mistress, how did your feet carry you as far as the setting sun,
to the Melanes,[8] to where the golden apples grow?
You did not drink or eat during that time, nor even bathe.
Three times you forded the silver-swirling Acheloos,
and as many times you crossed every ever-flowing river,
and three times you rested on the ground beside the Callichoros Well.

[8] "Dark-skinned men" said to live near the setting sun, hence their dark skin.

Parched with thirst, you did not eat nor even bathe.
But no! Let us not speak of these events that brought a tear to Deo—
better to tell how she gave pleasing laws to cities,
better, how she was the first to reap the wheat stalk and sacred
sheaves of grain, and the first to send in oxen to thresh it
when Triptolemos was taught the noble skill.
Yes, better to tell how (so that one may not transgress),
< . . . > to see.
Pelasgians did not yet dwell in the Cnidian land, but were still
in sacred Dotion, where they established a beautiful grove for you,
so thickly wooded an arrow could hardly have passed through it.
In it were pines and mighty elms, pear trees
and fine sweet-apple trees, and glimmering water
gushed up from hollows. The goddess loved the place passionately,
as much as Eleusis, and she loved Triopas as much as Enna.[9]
But when their favorable *daimon*[10] grew angry at the Triopidai,
then the vile idea took hold of Erysichthon.
He hastened with twenty servants, all in their prime,
all giant men with brawn enough to lift up an entire city,
men he had outfitted with axes and hatchets.
They all ran recklessly into the grove of Demeter.
There was a poplar, a mighty tree reaching up to the sky,
around which Nymphs used to dally in the noontime.
This, struck first, gave forth an awful shriek to the others.
Demeter perceived that her sacred wood was pained,
and, mightily angry, asked, "Who fells my beautiful trees?"
Immediately she took the form of Nicippe, whom the city had
appointed as her official priestess; in her hand were
garlands and a poppy, and over her shoulder hung a key.
She spoke, attempting to calm the evil, reckless man,
"Child, you who fell the trees consecrated to the gods,
child, cease! Child, much longed for by your parents,
stop and stay your servants' hands, lest Mistress Demeter
grow enraged—for you are ravaging her sacred place."
Then he scowled at her more savagely than a lioness
in the mountains of Tmaros scowls at a hunter
just after giving birth (when her look, they say, is most menacing).
"Give way," he said, "or I'll plant this great ax in your flesh.
These trees will put a roof over my halls, where I will

[9] Enna is a city in Sicily; perhaps here the name refers to the eponymous Nymph of the city.

[10] The guardian spirit that controls the destiny of a family or individual.

forever set delightful feasts before my friends in abundance."
The boy spoke, and Nemesis wrote down his ill-spoken words.
Demeter was unspeakably wroth and turned back into a goddess.
Her feet touched the ground, but her head touched Olympos.
The men, scared half to death when they saw the Mistress,
scurried away at once, leaving their bronze axes in the trees.
She let the others be (they were following him out of necessity,
subject to his authority), but to their violent lord she responded,
"Yes, yes, build a home, you dog, where you will hold
your feasts. For many, many banquets await you in the future."
Thus she spoke as she wrought pains for Erysichthon:
at once she implanted in him an intractable, insatiable hunger,
burning and intense, and he was stricken with a great disease.
No matter what the wretch ate, a desire for just as much seized him.
Twenty slaved over his meals; twelve poured his wine
(for alongside Demeter, Dionysos grew angry
since all that angers Demeter angers Dionysos too).
His embarrassed parents would not send him to feasts
or dinner parties. They concocted every kind of excuse.
The Ormenidai came to invite him to the games
in honor of Itonian Athena; his mother declined:
"He's not at home. He went off to Crannon yesterday
to demand the hundred cows owed to him." When Polyxo,
Actorion's mother, was arranging her son's wedding,
she came to invite both Triopas and his son.
But the heavy-hearted woman answered with tears in her eyes,
"Triopas is coming, but Erysichthon was gored by a boar
on green-forested Pindos and has been laid up for nine days now."
What lie did you not tell, wretched mother, to protect your dear son?
Someone gave a banquet: "Erysichthon is out of town."
Someone got married: "Erysichthon was hit by a discus"
or "fell off his chariot" or "is doing inventory on his flocks on Othrys."
And all the while he, holed up in his house, feasting all day long,
kept eating everything possible. His foul belly spasmed with hunger
though he ate ever more, and all the food he ate sank down
to absolutely no effect as if to the bottom of the deep sea.
Just as snow on Cape Mimas or a wax doll in the sun's heat,
still more quickly than these did he melt away to his sinews;
all that was left of the poor creature were skin and bones.
His mother cried, and many times his two sisters groaned deeply,
as did the breast he nursed on and his ten servant girls.
Triopas himself put his hands upon his graying hair,

calling upon Poseidon, who did not hearken,
"You sham father—look at this third generation of yours (if I am
the offspring of you and Aiolos' daughter Canace, and if
this pitiful child is mine). How I wish that he had been
struck by Apollo and buried by my own hands!
But as it stands, an evil hungering sits before my eyes.
Either cure him of this intractable disease, or take him and
feed him yourself! My tables have given up!
My pens are vacant and my cattle stalls are already
empty since the cooks never refused him anything.
No, they even unhitched the mules from the big carts!
He ate the cow his mother was raising for Hestia
and the prize-winning racehorse and the warhorse
and the white-tailed creature that used to scare off small vermin."
While wealth still lay within Triopas' household,
the evil was only known to the halls of the house.
But once the son's teeth consumed the affluent estate,
then the king's son sat where three roads met
and begged for crumbs and scraps left over from a feast.
Demeter, let the man who is hostile to you be neither my friend
nor my nextdoor neighbor. Evil neighbors are my enemies.
< . . . > maidens and mothers, sing the refrain:
"Great welcome, Demeter, feeder of many, giver of much grain."
As the four white mares bring the basket,
so too will the mighty, wide-ruling goddess come to us
bringing a white spring, a white summer, winter
and autumn, and will watch over us for another year.
As we walk through the city with our feet and heads uncovered,
so will we forever have feet and heads uninjured.
And as the basket carriers bear baskets full of gold,
so will we possess gold in abundance.
The uninitiated are to advance only to the city hall.
The initiates shall go all the way to the goddess,
those under sixty. All women who are heavy with age
or who stretch out their hands to Eileithyia or are in pain shall go
as far as their knees can easily carry them. Deo will give to these
all things in full measure just as to those who reach her temple.
Welcome, goddess, and keep this city both in harmony
and prosperity, and produce all things in abundance.
Nourish our cattle. Produce fruit, produce crops, produce a harvest.
Nourish peace too, so that he who sows may reap.
Be gracious to me, thrice-prayed-for one, mighty queen of goddesses!

Cleanthes

(331–232 BC, wrote in Greek)

Cleanthes, like other early Stoic philosophers, is only preserved in fragmentary form. The Hymn to Zeus, *the longest and most famous of these fragments, shows how Cleanthes unites philosophical material with traditional Greek theology and myth by equating Zeus with* logos *("reason"), the divine power that, according to Stoic cosmology, permeates the whole universe and orders and controls all things. Also important for this poem is the Stoic idea of divine providence, whereby all things in the world are predetermined. Even morally base actions (and their punishments) have a part in the divine plan. Thus, to Cleanthes' mind, Zeus is nothing other than this* logos, *the supreme divine force guiding our world, put into mythical form. Cleanthes does not reject traditional myth, as an Epicurean would have (compare Lucretius' attitude), because for the Stoics even myth reflects* logos *and the reality of the universe to some degree.*

HYMN TO ZEUS

Most honored of immortals, many-named, all-powerful always,
Zeus! Source of all things, directing all things according to law,
hail! It is right for all mortals to address you
since you provided the power of speech to them
alone of all things that live and crawl along the earth.
For this I will hymn you without end and sing of your power.
   This whole universe spinning about the earth
obeys you, wherever you lead it, and meekly accepts your mastery.
Such is the servant you hold in your unconquerable hands,
the double-edged, fiery, everlasting thunderbolt.
Everything is brought to pass beneath its threat.
With it you guide the universal force that pervades everything,
intermixed with both great and small lights.
With it you have become the supreme king for time eternal.
   Nothing happens apart from you, God,
on earth or in the divine vault of heaven or the sea,
save for what wicked men do in their folly.
But yours is the skill to make the uneven even,
the disorderly orderly and the unpleasing pleasing to you.

Thus you have harmonized all goodness and wickedness into one,
so that there is for all things a single, everlasting force,
which every wicked mortal flees and rejects.
Doomed fools! They in their unending hunger for wealth
neither see nor give ear to God's universal law.
If only they heeded it, they might have a life of worth and good sense.
But they mindlessly rush headlong, each to his own evil:
some have an antagonistic drive for fame;
others have turned to ill-gotten gain;
still others incline to indulgence and the pleasures of the body.
These will indeed meet their sorrow, some now, some later,
however ardently they wish for the opposite.
But Zeus, all-giving, shrouded in clouds, master of bright lightning,
protect mankind from their baneful ignorance!
Dispel it, Father, from our souls and grant that we find
judgment, on which you rely when you steer the universe justly,
so long as we, when honored, repay you with honor,
celebrating your deeds eternally, as is seemly for a
mortal, since there is no greater boon for either mortals
or gods than due celebration of everlasting universal law.

Conon

(late 1st c. BC–early 1st c. AD, wrote in Greek)

It is sheer chance that anything survives of Conon's Stories, *prose retellings of myths from earlier writers. In the 9th century AD a Byzantine scholar named Photios summarized them for his brother, and the originals were subsequently lost. These fifty summaries nevertheless show that Conon was interested in local myths, love stories, foundation myths, and aetiological myths, and they reveal interesting details found nowhere else.*

FROM *STORIES*

24 Narcissos

The twenty-fourth story: In Thespeia in Boiotia (the city is not far from Mount Helicon), the boy Narcissos was born. He was very beautiful and scorned both Eros and lovers. His other lovers gave up loving him, but Ameinias kept right on begging. When the boy not only did not let him in, but went so far as to send him a sword, Ameinias slew himself in front of Narcissos' door after a very heartfelt prayer that the god become his avenger. When at a fountain Narcissos caught sight of his own face and figure as they appeared in the water, he was the first and only person to become his own lover contrary to nature. Finally, with no idea what to do and supposing that he had gotten his just desserts for insolently rejecting Ameinias' love, he killed himself. Ever since then the people of Thespeia resolved to pay greater respect and honor to Eros and to make private sacrifices to him in addition to the public ones. The local people believe that the narcissus flower first sprang up from that ground onto which Narcissos' blood poured out.

27 Deucalion

The twenty-seventh story relates the tale of Deucalion, the king of Phthiotis, of the inundation of Greece that took place in his reign, and of his son Hellen (some say he was Zeus' son), who inherited the kingship upon Deucalion's death and had three sons. Hellen ordained that Aiolos, the first of his sons, would become king of the territory he ruled, setting the boundaries of his kingdom between two rivers, the Asopos and the Enipeus. From Aiolos are descended the Aiolian people. The second son, Doros, received a portion of the populace from his father and left to form a colony. At the foot of Mount Parnassos he founded cities, Boion, Cytinion, and Erineos. The Dorians are descended from him. The youngest, Xouthos, came to Athens and founded the so-called Tetrapolis {"Four Cities"} of Attica. He married Creousa daughter of Erechtheus, and with her had Achaios and Ion. After Achaios accidentally killed someone, he was banished, went to the Peloponnese, and founded the Dodecapolis {"Twelve Cities"}. The Achaians are descended from him. Ion, when his mother's father died, ruled the Athenians, chosen on account of his courage and general worthiness. The Athenians and all the rest of the Ionic people began to be called Ionians after him.

34 Diomedean Necessity

The thirty-fourth story tells how after Alexander Paris' death, Priam's sons, Helenos and Deiphobos, quarreled over marrying Helen. Deiphobos, though he was younger than Helenos, prevailed by force and by providing his services to the powerful. Unable to bear the insult, Helenos withdrew to Ida, where he lay low. On the advice of Calchas, the Greeks besieging Troy captured Helenos in an ambush. In response to a combination of threats and bribes (though more because of his own anger against the Trojans), Helenos revealed to them that Ilion was destined to be captured by a wooden horse and that this would only happen when the Achaians took the Palladion of Athena that fell from Zeus, the smallest one of the many there were. So Diomedes and Odysseus were sent on a mission to steal the Palladion. Diomedes got on top of the wall by standing on Odysseus' shoulders, but then, although Odysseus was stretching out his hands, he did not pull him up after him. He went after the Palladion, took it, and returned with it to Odysseus. As they made their way across the plain, Diomedes (knowing the man's deceitfulness) said in response to all of Odysseus' questions that he had not taken the exact Palladion that Helenos had described, but another instead. But the Palladion moved by the will of some god, and Odysseus recognized that it was the right one. So getting behind Diomedes, he drew his sword, intending to kill him and to bring the Palladion to the Achaians himself. As he was about to strike, Diomedes saw the glint off the sword (the moon was out), and when he also drew a sword, Odysseus held off from killing him. Diomedes reproached him for his cowardice and drove the unwilling Odysseus forward by beating him on the back with the flat of his sword. From this the proverbial expression "Diomedean necessity" is applied to everything one is forced to do.

37 Cadmos

The thirty-seventh story tells how the island of Thasos was named after Cadmos' brother Thasos since his brother left him there with a part of his army; also how Cadmos was sent by the king of the Phoenicians to Europe, being himself a very important man among the Phoenicians. The Phoenicians at that time were (so the story goes) very powerful, had conquered much of Asia, and had the seat of their empire in Thebes in Egypt. Cadmos was not sent, as the Greeks say, to search for Europa (she was Phoinix's daughter whom Zeus abducted in the shape of a bull), but in trying to establish his own kingdom in Europe he made up the fiction that he was making a search for his abducted sister. From that the myth of Europa has come down to the Greeks.

As he sailed along the coast of Europe, he left his brother Thasos, as was mentioned, on the island; he himself sailed to Boiotia and went inland to what is now called Thebes. He used his troops to build a wall around the place and named it Thebes after his homeland. When the Boiotians fought them hand-to-hand, the Phoenicians were defeated. So they used ambushes, traps, and the unfamiliar sight of their armor to win; for the helmet and shield were previously unknown to the Greeks. Cadmos conquered the land of the Boiotians, and when the surviving Boiotians fled to their own cities, he settled the Phoenicians in Thebes and married Harmonia, the daughter of Ares and Aphrodite. The Thebans, because of their shock at the arms, traps, and ambush, came to believe that the earth had sprouted the men with their armor and called them Spartoi {"Sown Men"} as if they had grown on the spot. This is the true account of Cadmos and the settling of Thebes; the rest is myth and the magic of hearsay.

40 Andromeda

The fortieth account gives the story of Andromeda differently than the myth of the Greeks: Cepheus and Phineus were two brothers, and Cepheus' kingdom was then in what would later be known as Phoenicia, but in those days was called Ioppa, taking its name from the coastal city of Ioppa. The frontiers of his realm were from our sea {the Mediterranean} all the way to the Arabs who live on the Red Sea.

Cepheus also had a very beautiful daughter, Andromeda; both Phoinix and Cepheus' brother, Phineus, asked for her hand in marriage. After much careful calculation about them both, Cepheus decided to give her to Phoinix, but to hide the fact that he willingly gave her by having her suitor abduct her. Andromeda was abducted from an uninhabited little island where she was accustomed to visit and make sacrifices to Aphrodite. When Phoinix abducted her with his ship (this was called the *Cetos* {"Sea-monster"} either by happenstance or because of its resemblance to the animal), Andromeda, thinking that she was being kidnapped without her father's knowledge, screamed and piteously called for someone to help her.

Perseus son of Danae was by a stroke of luck sailing past. He landed his ship and, gripped by pity and love for the girl at first sight, destroyed the ship *Cetos* and killed those aboard, who were practically petrified by shock. This became, for the Greeks, the sea-monster of the myth and the people who were turned into stone by the Gorgon's head. So Perseus made Andromeda his wife, and she sailed off together with him to Greece. When he was king, Argos was settled.

Cornutus

(1st c. AD, wrote in Greek)

From Cornutus, a Stoic philosopher of the 1st century AD, we have the Compendium of the Traditions of Greek Theology. *This work extensively employs allegory and etymology to analyze myths in an attempt to make them understandable in terms of the doctrines of the Stoics, particularly their detailed theories about the nature of the universe. For a modern linguist his etymologies are almost always falsely derived, but etymology was central to many aspects of ancient thought, particularly the interpretation of myth.*

FROM *COMPENDIUM OF THE TRADITIONS OF GREEK THEOLOGY*

2–3 The Real Natures of Zeus and Hera

Cornutus' analysis of Zeus combines two major ideas: first, the identification of Zeus with the governing principle of the cosmos (compare Cleanthes' Hymn to Zeus*); second, the identification of the gods with the elements outlined in Stoic theories of physics. Here, for instance, the marriage of the siblings Zeus and Hera is viewed as an allegory of the relationship between aether (pure, unmixed fire) and air. In this system the four elements—fire, air, water, and earth—are in constant flux as matter changes from heaviest to lightest (earth to fire) and lightest to heaviest in a continuous circular flow.*

[2] Just as we are governed by a soul, so too the cosmos has a soul that holds it together, and it is called Zeus. Being alive from the very beginning and for all time, it is the reason that everything that lives is alive {*zen*}. And so Zeus is also said to rule everything, just as the soul and nature within us might be said to rule us. We call him Dia because it is through {*dia*} him that everything is born and kept alive. He is called Deus by some, perhaps from the fact that he moistens {*deuein*} the earth or shares the moisture that gives life with what is alive. He is said to dwell in heaven because the supreme portion of the cosmos' soul is there; for our souls are fire.

[3] His wife and sister is traditionally Hera, who is in fact air {*aer*}. For she is connected and united with him, rising up from the earth as he has settled over her. And they arise from the flow {*rheo*} in the same direction, for as substance flows toward fineness it gives rise to fire and air. For this reason in the myths their mother is said to be Rhea.

20 Athena

In this excerpt from Cornutus' discussion of Athena, the goddess is seen as the embodiment of pronoia, *the Stoic idea that divine* logos *(reason) determines and orders everything. The close connection between* pronoia *and* logos *is for Cornutus reflected by the closeness of Athena to Zeus in myth and her birth from his head. Her name and other parts of her myth are interpreted accordingly.*

[20] Athena is Zeus' intelligence since she is the same as his providence {*pronoia*}, and that is why temples are dedicated to "Pronoia Athena." She is said to have been born from Zeus' head, perhaps because the ancients understood that the governing part of our soul is there (just as others later on believed too), or perhaps because the head is the highest portion of the human body, just as in the cosmos the highest portion is aether, where its governing part and the very substance of thought are located. As Euripides says, "the bright aether around the earth is the summit of the gods." So Zeus gave birth to Athena by swallowing Metis, since he, being wise {*metietes*} and intelligent, got the capacity for thought from no source other than his internal deliberation. The name of Athena is hard to explain etymologically because of its great antiquity. Some say that she is Ath*r*ena, as it were, because she perceives {*athrein*} everything; others say that she is Athena {as if from *a* "not" + *thelus* "female"} because, though a female, she has no share of femininity or feebleness. Perhaps, if it is Athenaia (as the ancients used to say Athena), she is Aitheronaia {"Aether-dweller"}, and her virginity is a symbol of aether's purity and clarity. She is portrayed as wearing armor, and they tell the story that she was born that way, suggesting that thought is in and of itself ready to face the most serious and grievous situations; for the situations of war are seen as the most serious.

30 Dionysos

In this excerpt from Cornutus' discussion of Dionysos, he turns to an allegorical analysis of the myth, iconography, and ritual surrounding this god, particularly in his connection with wine. One can compare this with the allegory of Dionysos as given in Fulgentius 2.12.

[30] The thyrsos indicates that those who have drunk a lot of wine cannot function with their own two feet, but need thyrsoi for support. Some of the thyrsoi have spear tips concealed under their leaves, just as sometimes when something painful is concealed by the cheerfulness of hard drinking, some people break into violent frenzies, which is why Dionysos is called Mainoles {"Frenzied"} and the women around him are called Mainads. He is portrayed both as a young and an old man because of his suitability for any age; young men drink him boisterously, while old men drink him merrily. With him are shown the Satyrs having intercourse with the Nymphs—making attempts on some, playfully trying to force others—so that one can see that the mixing of wine with water is useful.[1] Artists yoke leopards to Dionysos' chariot

[1] Because Nymphs are water spirits. The ancients normally diluted their wine before drinking it.

and show them following him either because of the spots on their coats (just like the fawnskin he himself and his Bacchai wear) or because moderate intoxication tames even the wildest character. People sacrifice a goat to him because this animal has the reputation of being destructive to vines and figs. And so in the villages of Attica the young farmers skin the goat and jump on its hide. But perhaps Dionysos would take delight in such a sacrificial victim because the goat is randy, which is also the reason the ass takes part in his processions, votive phalluses are dedicated to him, and the phallus parades are celebrated. For since wine is a stimulant to intercourse, some people sacrifice to Dionysos and Aphrodite jointly. The narthex indicates by the crookedness of its segments the staggering of drunk people this way and that. But some say that it represents the inarticulateness of their speech. The Bacchai wander the mountains and love the wilderness because wine is not produced in cities, but in the countryside.

Critias

(late 5th c. BC, wrote in Greek)

Several ancient authors quote this fragment, in which the trickster Sisyphos makes the remarkable claim that the gods were merely the invention of another clever human being in the distant past, as a prime example of atheism. Some of those writers attribute the lines to Euripides (because his characters sometimes express similar sentiments, as in Euripides fr. 286), but in fact they were most likely written by Critias, who is named as the author by other sources. Critias was an uncle of the philosopher Plato and an important politician in Athens. In later antiquity he developed a reputation for atheism, but that reputation probably derives from this fragment, and it is difficult, if not impossible, to determine what Critias' true views on religion were.

Two matters complicate interpretation: first, these are lines in a drama and a character in a play is rarely simply a spokesperson for the views of the playwright; second, we are missing the context of the speech, and it is quite likely (though not certain) that the passage is from a Satyr play, not a tragedy, meaning that in its original setting it was meant to evoke in part a humorous response.

FROM *SISYPHOS*

SISYPHOS: There was a time when human life was without order
and bestial and subject to brute force,
when there was neither any reward for the noble
nor any punishment for the base.
And then, I think, men established
punitive laws, so that Justice would be sovereign
< . . . > and have Hubris as her subject.
Whoever did wrong was punished.
Next, now that the laws kept people from
openly committing violent deeds
but they still did them secretly, at that time I think
< . . . > some man of shrewd and clever intelligence
hit upon the idea of inventing the gods for mortals, so
the base would have something to fear even when
they acted or spoke or thought secretly.
So, building on this, he taught that the Divine

was a supernatural being thriving with unending life,
with the power of intellect listening, watching, contemplating,
and attending to these acts and possessing a divine nature,
one who would hear everything said among mortals
and be able to see everything that was done.
If you plan something base, even without breathing a word of it,
it will not escape the notice of the gods; for understanding
< . . . > is theirs. Giving these explanations,
he taught a most agreeable lesson,
confounding the truth with a false story.
He said that the gods dwelled in the place
that would most astonish men when talked about,
the place he realized mortals derive their fears from,
and their life of suffering draws its delights—
from the circling firmament above, where he discerned
there were the flashes of lightning and terrible crashes
of thunder and the starry brightness of heaven,
a beautiful tapestry of the wise creator Time.
From there the gleaming falling star blazes,
and the wet rainstorm pours out onto the earth.
He hedged men in with such terrible
fears, and with his story he neatly gave
the divinity a home in a fitting location
and doused lawlessness with these fears of his.
< . . . >
In this way, I think, someone first convinced
mortals to believe that a race of gods existed.

Diodorus of Sicily

(1st c. BC, wrote in Greek)

Diodorus of Sicily attempted to compose a "universal history," that is, one encompassing all events from the beginning of time until his own day. In doing so, he was forced to reconstruct the earliest events from mythical accounts and other authors' discussions of such material (sometimes resulting in conflicting accounts). One common feature of his method of utilizing such earlier material is his impulse toward the interpretive strategy of rationalization, the view that myths are elaborations around kernels of truth and that that truth can be reconstructed. One particular method of rationalization that Diodorus employs (below in 3.56 and 5.66–5.73) is what we call euhemerism (named for Euhemeros, who first employed it), that is, the attempt to see gods as the distorted reflections of real men whose deeds merited immortalization.

FROM *HISTORICAL LIBRARY*

2.45–2.46 The Amazons

[2.45] Near the Thermodon River they say that the predominant race was one ruled by women, and that the women, like the men, had a hand in the business of war. They say that one of these women, who held royal power, excelled in courage and strength. She raised an army of women and trained it, and then subdued some of the neighboring peoples in war. As her reputation for valor increased, she made continual war upon the people near her borders. As she continued to enjoy good fortune, she was filled with arrogance and called herself "the daughter of Ares." She also assigned to the men the task of spinning wool and the other domestic work of women. She introduced laws by which she led the women forth to the struggles of war, while she imposed on the men a life of degradation and servitude. They maimed the arms and legs of their male offspring, rendering them useless for military purposes. They cauterized the right breast of their female offspring so that it would not increase in size and be an annoyance when their bodies reached puberty. For this reason it came to pass that the tribe of Amazons received their name {from *a* "without" + *mazos* "breast"}. On the whole, excelling in intelligence and generalship, she founded a great city, Themiscyra by name, where the Thermodon River meets the sea, and built a renowned palace; and paying close attention to discipline on her expeditions, she first conquered all of her neighbors as far as the Tanais River. They say that after she accomplished these deeds, she fought brilliantly in a battle, in which she died heroically.

[2.46] Her daughter inherited the realm, emulating her mother's excellence and outdoing her in particular achievements. She trained the girls from the earliest age in hunting, and every day she drilled them in military exercises. She introduced magnificent sacrifices to Ares and to Artemis, the one called Tauropolos. She carried her campaign into the territory beyond the Tanais River and conquered each tribe in succession all the way to Thrace. Having returned with many spoils to her own country, she built magnificent temples to the aforementioned gods, and she received the greatest acclaim for ruling her subjects equitably. She campaigned also in the other direction, annexed much of Asia, and extended her power all the way to Syria.

After the death of this woman, female members of her line continuously inherited control and ruled with distinction, and the nation of the Amazons increased in both power and repute. Many generations later, when their reputation had spread through the whole of the inhabited world, they say that Heracles, the son of Alcmene and Zeus, had the war belt of the Amazon Hippolyte assigned to him by Eurystheus as one of his labors. And so he marched out and, in winning a great battle, cut down the army of the Amazons, captured Hippolyte with her war belt, and completely wiped out this tribe. And so the surrounding barbarian peoples, despising the Amazons' weakness and remembering how they had mistreated them in the past, made continuous war upon the tribe to the point that they did not leave so much as the name of the Amazonian race behind.

They say that a few years after Heracles' expedition, during the Trojan War, Penthesileia, Ares' daughter and the queen of the remaining Amazons, killed one of her kin and for this abominable act went into exile from her native land. Fighting as an ally of the Trojans after Hector's death, she killed many Greeks, and after displaying great prowess in the battle, her life came to a heroic end when she was killed by Achilles. They say that she was the last of the Amazons to excel in courage, and after her death the tribe declined continually until it was completely enfeebled. For this reason in more recent times, when anyone gives an account of their courage, the ancient legends of the Amazons are thought to be fictional myths.

3.56 Ouranos

[3.56] Now that I have mentioned the Atlantians,[1] I do not think it out of place to go into detail about their mythical account of the origin of the gods because of its similarity to the myths of the Greeks. Because the Atlantians inhabit the districts near Oceanos and live in a fertile country, they are thought to surpass by far their neighbors both in piety and in the humane treatment of strangers, and they say that the origin of the gods lies with them. They also assert that the most illustrious of the poets in Greece, Homer, agrees with what they say in the verses in which he has Hera say,

> For I go to the ends of the bounteous earth to see
> Oceanos, who is the source of the gods, and Mother Tethys.

[1] Diodorus took them to be an ancient civilization at the edges of the world that had neighbored the Amazons and Gorgons.

They tell this myth: Ouranos was the first to rule as king among them and gathered together the people, who lived scattered, into the compass of a city. He put an end to his subjects' lawlessness and their brutish existence by discovering the cultivation and storage of domesticated crops, as well as many other useful things. He gained possession of most of the inhabited world, particularly the districts to the west and north. By making careful observations of the stars, he predicted many things that would happen in the heavens. He introduced to the populace the year based on the movement of the sun and the months based on that of the moon, and he taught them about the seasons that come each year. As a result the common people, who were ignorant of the stars' eternal regularity and were amazed at the events that matched his predictions, supposed that the man who explained these things had a divine nature. After he left the world of the living, they imparted divine honors to him on account of his good services and his astronomical expertise. They also transferred his name to the heavens, partly because he seemed to have been familiar with the risings and settings of the stars and the other events in the heavens, and partly because they wished to outdo his good services by the magnitude of their honors and by proclaiming him the king of the universe for all time.

4.25 Orpheus

[4.25] Orpheus, the son of Oiagros, was a Thracian. He was by far the most preeminent man in learning, music, and poetry of those whom we know from history. For he composed marvelous poetry that was musically remarkable when sung. He advanced so far in repute that he was thought to charm the beasts and trees with his music. After occupying himself with learning and gaining knowledge of the mythical accounts concerning theological matters, he traveled to Egypt. There he learned many additional things and became the greatest of the Greeks in theology, initiatory rites, poems, and songs. He campaigned with the Argonauts, and because of his love for his wife, he dared—incredibly—to descend to the underworld. By winning Persephone over with his music, he persuaded her to help him achieve his desires and to allow him to lead his wife up from the underworld though she was dead, along the lines of what Dionysos had done. For they tell the myth that Dionysos led up his mother, Semele, from the underworld, gave her a share of immortality, and changed her name to Thyone.

5.66–5.73 A Euhemerizing Account of the Origin of the Gods

[5.66] The Cretans tell the following myth: when the Couretes were young men, the so-called Titans were born. They resided in the land around Cnossos, where even now the foundations of Rhea's house are shown, along with a cypress grove that has been dedicated to her since antiquity. They numbered six men and five women. Some tell the myth that they were the children of Ouranos and Ge, but according to others they were the children of one of the Couretes and Titaia, and it is from their mother that they got the name Titans. Now the males were Cronos, Hyperion, Coios, Iapetos, Crios, and finally, Oceanos. Their sisters were Rhea, Themis, Mnemosyne, Phoibe, and Tethys. Each of them made certain discoveries for humanity, and because of their benefits toward all mankind they received honors and everlasting renown.

Because Cronos was the eldest, he became king; he made all the people he ruled change from a primitive to a civilized lifestyle. Because of this he received widespread approval and visited many places in the inhabited world. He introduced to all the notions of justice and genuineness of spirit, and so the idea has been handed down to posterity that the people of Cronos' era were honest, entirely without vice, and blessedly happy. His power was strongest, and he received the greatest honor in places in the west, so even down to more recent times among the Romans, Carthaginians (while their city existed), and other nearby peoples, there have been noteworthy festivals and sacrifices for this god, and there have been many places named after him as well. Because of the extraordinary lawfulness of his reign, no unjust act at all was ever accomplished by anyone. All those who were subject to his leadership lived a blessed life and enjoyed every pleasure without hindrance. The poet Hesiod also provides evidence about this in the following verses:

> They actually lived when Cronos was king of the sky
> And they lived like gods, not a care in their hearts,
> Nothing to do with troubles or hard toil
> Or painful illnesses, they had no cares,
> And miserable old age didn't come on their limbs,
> But from fingers to toes they never changed,
> And the good times rolled. And when they died
> It was like sleep just raveled them up.
> They had many other things. The land bore them fruit
> All on its own, and plenty of it too. Cheerful folk,
> They worked their land in prosperity,
> With plenty of flocks, and they were dear to the gods.[2]

That is the myth they tell about Cronos.

[5.67] They say that Hyperion was the first to understand by study and careful observation the motion of the sun, moon, and the other stars, as well as the seasons that are brought about by these heavenly bodies, and he passed along this knowledge to others. For this reason he is known as the father of these heavenly bodies since he had, as it were, given birth to the systematic contemplation of them. Coios and Phoibe were the parents of Leto, and Iapetos had Prometheus, who traditionally is said by some mythographers to have stolen fire from the gods and given it to mortals. The truth is that he was the discoverer of the firesticks with which fire is kindled.

Now for the female Titans: they say that Mnemosyne discovered logical thinking and assigned words to everything that exists, and with these words we also explain everything and communicate with each other (though some say that Hermes

[2] These verses are from Hesiod's *Works and Days*, but they differ in some ways from the received text of that poem. The translation is based on lines 131–41 of S. Lombardo's translation (reprinted in this volume), but it has been modified to reflect those differences.

introduced these ideas). They attribute to this goddess the means people have for recollecting and memorizing {*mneme*} information, and it is from this that she got this name of hers. They tell the myth that Themis was the first to introduce divination, sacrifice, and the regulations {*thesmoi*} concerning the gods, and that she formulated and taught the principles of lawfulness and peace. And so those who maintain the laws about what is holy regarding the gods and the laws about human behavior are called "guardians of the law" {*thesmophylakes*} and "law-givers" {*thesmothetai*}. And we say that Apollo is "issuing pronouncements" {*themisteuein*} during the time that he is getting ready to give oracles, because of Themis' discovery of oracles. So because these gods benefited human existence greatly, they were not only deemed worthy of immortal honors, but they were also the first to be thought to dwell on Mount Olympos after their departure from the world of men.

[5.68] Cronos and Rhea are said to have had Hestia, Demeter, and Hera, as well as Zeus, Poseidon, and Hades. Of these, it is said that Hestia discovered how to construct dwellings, and for this benefit she has a consecrated place in every home among practically all peoples and receives honors and sacrifices. Demeter was the first to gather grain, to find methods for its preparation and storage, and to teach how to cultivate it. Earlier, it had grown randomly among the other vegetation and was unknown to humanity. She discovered grain before she gave birth to her daughter Persephone, but after she was born and Plouton abducted her, Demeter burned the entire crop because of her hostility toward Zeus and her grief over her daughter. But after Persephone was found, Demeter reconciled with Zeus and gave the seed-grain to Triptolemos. She instructed him to share the gift with all men and teach them about the production of grain. And some say that she also introduced laws by which people have become accustomed to deal justly with one another, and they call the goddess that imparted these laws to them Thesmophoros {"Law-bringer"}. Since she has been the source of the greatest good for humanity, she received the most distinguished honors and sacrifices, as well as magnificent festivals and holy days, not only among the Greeks, but also among practically all the barbarians who have shared in this food.

[5.69] Many people wrangle over the discovery of this crop, all claiming that the goddess appeared among them first and instructed them about grain's nature and use. The Egyptians, for instance, say that Demeter and Isis are the same and that she first brought the seed to Egypt because the Nile river floods the plain at the right time and this country enjoys the best seasons. And although the Athenians declare that the discovery of this crop took place among them, they nevertheless provide evidence that it was brought into Attica from elsewhere; for they call the place that originally received this gift Eleusis {"Arrival"} after the fact that the seed of the grain was imported and arrived from others. But the Greeks in Sicily, who live on an island sacred to Demeter and Kore, say that it is likely that this gift was given first to those who inhabit the land dearest to the goddess; for it would be odd for her to make Sicily so very fertile because it is her own, but to share her benefit with the island last of all, as though it did not belong to her. And what is more, her home is on the island since it has been agreed that the abduction of Persephone took place there. The land is also the most suited for these crops, and the poet says that on the island

> everything grows without sowing or tilling,
> both wheat and barley.[3]

That is the myth they tell about Demeter.

Now onto the other gods born from Cronos and Rhea: The Cretans say that Poseidon was the first to involve himself in the work of seafaring and the construction of fleets because Cronos granted him authority over these things. So it has been passed down to later generations that he is the master of what happens on the sea and he is honored by sailors with sacrifices. They also give him credit for being the first to tame horses {*hippoi*} and teach the knowledge of horsemanship, from which he is called Hippios. Hades is said to have taught the customs that surround the burial, funeral, and honors accorded to the dead, there having been no special attention paid to them in the time before Hades. So this god, because in antiquity he was assigned authority over and responsibility for the deceased, has been traditionally accepted as lord of the dead.

[5.70] There is disagreement about the birth and kingship of Zeus. Now, some say that after Cronos was removed from the world of men to that of the gods, Zeus received the kingship not by overcoming his father with force, but by lawfully and justly being deemed worthy of this honor. But others tell a myth that Cronos received an oracle that concerned Zeus' birth, namely that the child Cronos fathered would dethrone him by force. Accordingly, Cronos again and again did away with the children he fathered; but Rhea was enraged, and although she could not change her husband's plan, she did hide Zeus on the mountain called Ida when she gave birth to him. She gave him secretly to the Couretes, who lived near Mount Ida, to be raised. They took him to a certain cave and handed him over to the Nymphs there, telling them to care for him in every way. These Nymphs mixed honey and milk and raised him on it. They also provided the udder of the she-goat named Amaltheia for him to feed from. Many signs of this god's birth and rearing remain on the island down to the present day. They say that when he was being carried by the Couretes as an infant, his umbilical cord {*omphalos*} fell off near the river called the Triton. Because of what happened at that time this spot was consecrated and called Omphalos, and the surrounding plain likewise became known as Omphaleion. On Mount Ida, where it happened that the god grew up, the cave in which he lived has been consecrated, and the meadows around it, which are on the mountain ridge, are likewise hallowed ground. But the most incredible part of the myth—the part about the bees—should not be passed over. They say that the god, wishing to preserve an immortal record of his relationship with the bees, changed their color and made it like golden copper. And because the place was very high in altitude and the winds there were strong and a lot of snow fell, he made them impervious to and unaffected by the climate though they inhabited places with the most brutal cold. To the she-goat who raised him he dispensed other honors, including taking an epithet from her, inasmuch as he is called Aigiochos {"Aegis-holder"; *aigis:* "goatskin"}. And when he grew

[3] This is Homer's description (*Odyssey* 9.109–10) of the land of the Cyclopes, which was identified in antiquity with Sicily.

to manhood, they say, he was the first to found a city in the area of Dicte, exactly where their myth says that his birth took place. In later times this city was abandoned, but even now some of the footings for the foundations remain.

[5.71] This god excelled everyone in courage, intelligence, justice, and every other virtue. For this reason he succeeded to the kingdom after Cronos and provided the greatest and most numerous benefits for human life. He was the very first one to teach people to deal justly with one another where injustice is concerned, to shrink from committing violent acts, and to settle their disputes by trial and courtroom. Basically, he provided a full system concerning lawfulness and peace by persuading the good people and cowing the bad into submission with punishment and fear. He went around almost the entire inhabited world destroying pirates and iniquitous men and introducing equality and democracy, and this was when, they say, he destroyed the Giants, both those who were followers of Mylinos in Crete and those who followed Typhon in Phrygia. Before the battle against the Cretan Giants, Zeus is said to have sacrificed one ox each to Helios, Ouranos, and Ge. During each of the sacrifices the outcome of the war was made apparent, and those predictions indicated victory and a defection from the enemy to Zeus' side. The outcome of the war matched these predictions. First, Mousaios deserted from the enemy and received agreed-upon honors. Second, all those who met Zeus in battle were cut down by the gods.

Zeus also fought other wars against the Giants, one in Macedonia near Pallene and one in Italy on the plain that in antiquity was named the Phlegraion {"Fiery"} Plain because the place was thoroughly burned, but which in later times was called the Cumaian Plain. The Giants were punished by Zeus because of their lawless behavior toward other people, and also because they, relying on their physical superiority and strength, enslaved the people of neighboring lands; because they were not following the laws that he had established about justice; and because they were initiating a war against those who were universally considered gods because of the general benefits they had conferred. So Zeus, they say, not only completely removed the godless and wicked from among humanity, but also assigned fitting honors to the best gods and heroes, and men as well. Because of the enormity of the benefits he brought and the superiority of his power he has been unanimously and universally granted both his kingship for all eternity and his dwelling on Olympos.

[5.72] The practice was instituted of offering him sacrifices beyond all the other gods, and after his departure from earth to heaven there arose in the souls of men that had received benefits from him perfectly reasonable ideas that he was lord of heavenly phenomena, by which I mean rain, thunder, lightning, and all other such things. It is for this reason that he is called Zen from the belief among people that he causes things to live {*zen*} by bringing crops to ripeness through the moderate temperatures of the environment. He is called Father because of the care and kindness he shows toward all, and also because of the belief that he is in a way the originator of the human race. And he is called Hypatos {"Highest"} and Basileus {"King"} because of the superiority of his rule, and Euboules {"Good-counselor"} and Metietes {"Deviser"} because of his wisdom in giving excellent counsel.

They also tell the myth that Zeus gave birth to Athena in Crete at the springs of the Triton River, and so she was called Tritogeneia {"Triton-born"}. There is even now near these springs a temple sacred to this goddess at the place where, according to the myth, her birth occurred. They also say that the wedding of Zeus and Hera happened in the land of the Cnossians in a place near the Theren River where now there is a temple in which sacred offerings are made annually by the locals, and the wedding is reenacted just as it is traditionally said to have originally happened.

They say that Zeus had goddesses as children: Aphrodite and the Charites, and in addition to them Eileithyia and her helper Artemis, and the so-called Horai, namely Eunomia, Dike, and Eirene, as well as Athena and the Muses. He also had gods: Hephaistos, Ares, and Apollo, and in addition to them Hermes, Dionysos, and Heracles.

[5.73] Their myth relates that Zeus distributed to each of these the knowledge of the things he discovered and was perfecting, as well as the honors for their discovery. He did so out of a desire to preserve for them an everlasting memory among all mankind. To Aphrodite was entrusted the prime of virgins' lives (the time when they should marry) and responsibility for taking care of the other wedding customs that are still observed even today, as well as sacrifices and libations that mortals make to this goddess. But everyone sacrifices first to Zeus Teleios and Hera Teleia[4] because they are the originators and discoverers of everything, as was said earlier. To the Charites was given the beautifying of one's appearance and the adornment of the parts of the body to make them attractive and enticing to the viewer, and, in addition to these things, they were made the source of good deeds and of paying back with appropriate favors {*charites*} those who have treated one well. Eileithyia took charge of women giving birth and the care of those who are faring badly in childbirth. This is why women in such dangers call upon this goddess above all others. They say that Artemis discovered both the method of caring for infant children and certain foods that are suitable for them. For this reason she is also called Kourotrophos {"Child-rearer"}. Each of those known as the Horai was given a responsibility named after her for the ordering and arranging of life for the greatest benefit of mankind. For there is nothing more capable of furnishing a prosperous life than lawfulness {*eunomia*}, justice {*dike*}, and peace {*eirene*}.

They credit Athena for handing down to mankind the domestication and planting of olive trees, along with the preparation of this fruit. For before this goddess was born, this species of tree grew with the other wild trees, but even down to the present the responsibility for and expertise of these trees belong to her. In addition to this, she introduced to humanity the making of clothes and the art of building, as well as many things involved with the other professions. She discovered how to make flutes and the music produced in their use, and, to sum up, many artistic products, which is why she is called Ergane {"Producer"}.

[4] The epithets Teleios and Teleia convey the sense of having become fully adult, a state reached only after marriage.

ERATOSTHENES

(3rd c. BC, wrote in Greek; epitomized perhaps 1st c. AD)

The extant text Constellation Myths (Katasterismoi) *is an epitome (abridged version) of a longer work of the same name by one of the most famous scientists of antiquity, Eratosthenes (so this is often referred to as the work of pseudo-Eratosthenes). The work as we have it consists of forty-two short accounts of the constellations and the myths behind them, as well as three others on the five planets and the Milky Way. Below are the accounts of the Zodiac (Greek for "Circle of Animals"), a series of twelve signs used to indicate time, each zone equivalent to one month. The Greeks originally inherited these signs from the older civilizations of the Near East, but ultimately attached their own myths to them. The traditional order, not followed by Eratosthenes (who treats the heavens by quadrant), is: Aries, Taurus, Gemini, Cancer, Leo, Virgo, Libra, Scorpio, Sagittarius, Capricorn, Aquarius, and Pisces.*

FROM *CONSTELLATION MYTHS*

7 Scorpios (Scorpio the Scorpion)

Because of its size this constellation is divided into two zodiac signs.[1] One consists of the claws, the other the body and the stinger. They say that Artemis had a scorpion issue forth from its hill on the island of Chios and sting Orion, and thus Orion died when he improperly assaulted Artemis while hunting. Zeus placed the scorpion among the bright stars, so that future generations could see its power and might.

Scorpios has two stars on each of its claws (the front ones are of great magnitude, while the second pair are faint), three bright stars on its brow (of which the middle is the brightest), three bright stars on its spine, two on its belly, five on its tail, and two on its stinger. The leading star[2] in this constellation, shining more brightly than all the others, is the bright star on the northern claw. Nineteen stars in all.

9 Parthenos (Virgo the Virgin)

Hesiod has said in the *Theogony* that she is the daughter of Zeus and Themis and is named Dike {"Justice"}. Aratos, taking the story from him, says that she, though

[1] The Greek says "two-twelfth parts," meaning that it occupies two zones of the Zodiac. Libra was not a Greek but a Roman creation. Both our author and Ptolemy speak of the claws of Scorpio; the Roman Hyginus (*De Astronomia* 2.26) says "one of these parts our people say looks like scales (*libra*)."

[2] I.e., the westernmost, as the heavenly bodies move westward.

immortal, also once lived on the earth among mankind and that they called her Dike. But when mankind took a turn for the worse and no longer observed justice, she did not stay with them, but withdrew to the mountains. Then, when dissent and wars broke out among them, she grew to hate their complete lack of justice and returned to heaven. A great many other accounts are told about her: some say she is Demeter because she is holding a stalk of wheat; others say she is Isis, Artagatis, or even Tyche and thus configure her without a head.[3]

Parthenos has one faint star on her head, one star on each of her shoulders, two on each of her wings (the one on the right wing between her shoulder and the top of her wing is called Protrygeter {"Harbinger of the Harvest"}), one on each of her elbows, and one at the tip of each hand (the bright star on the left hand is called Stachys {"Wheat Stalk"}). At the bottom of her dress six faint stars, < . . . > one faint star, and one on each foot. Twenty stars in all.

10 Didymoi (Gemini the Twins)

These are said to be the Dioscouroi. When they were growing up in Laconia, they had great fame and surpassed all others in their brotherly love, for they did not fight over the throne or over anything else. Zeus wanted to create a memorial of their partnership, so he named them the Didymoi and set them together in the same spot among the stars.

The twin that is positioned over the Crab has one bright star on its head, one bright star on each of its shoulders, one on his right elbow, one on his right hand, one on each knee, and one on each foot, for a total of nine. The other twin has one bright star on his head, a bright one on his left shoulder, one on each of his pectorals, one on his left elbow, one at the tip of his hand, one on his left knee, one on each of his feet, and one under his left foot, which is called Propous {"Leading the foot"}, for a total of ten.

11 Carcinos (Cancer the Crab)

This constellation was thought to have been set in the stars because of Hera, since it alone, when everything else was on Heracles' side when he was trying to kill the Hydra, sallied forth from the marsh and pinched his foot, as Panyasis says in the *Heracleia*. Heracles was enraged and, it is believed, squashed him with his foot. Because of this the Crab has enjoyed great glory by being numbered among the twelve signs of the zodiac.

Some of the stars in this constellation are called the Asses, which Dionysos elevated to the stars. They also have an attribute, the Manger. The following is their story. When the gods were campaigning against the Giants, they say that Dionysos, Hephaistos, and the Satyrs were riding on asses. When they were close to but not yet seen by the Giants, the asses brayed. When the Giants heard the sound, they fled. For this reason they were honored by being set in the western zone of Carcinos.

[3] That is, without eyes because Tyche {Fortune} is blind.

Carcinos has on its shell two bright stars—these are the Asses, and the nebulous area that is seen between the two is the Manger, beside which they appear to stand. On each of the right legs there is a single faint star; as for the left legs, there are two faint stars on the first, two stars on the second, one on the third, and likewise one on the tip of the fourth. On the mouth there is one. On the right claw there are three, all uniformly not of great magnitude, and likewise two on the left claw. Eighteen stars in all.

12 Leon (Leo the Lion)

This is one of the conspicuous constellations. It is believed that this sign was honored by Zeus because the lion is king of the four-footed animals. But some say that it was to memorialize Heracles' first labor. For this is the only beast that Heracles in his quest for glory killed without weapons, instead putting it in a stranglehold and choking it. Peisandros the Rhodian tells the story about him. Heracles took his skin from it since he had performed a glorious feat. This is the one that was killed by him in Nemea.

Leon has three stars on its head, one on its chest, two beneath its chest, one bright one on the right foot, one in the middle of the belly, one beneath the belly, one on his haunch, one on the hind knee, a bright one at the tip of the foot, two along the neck, three on the spine, one in the middle of the tail, and a bright one at the end. Nineteen stars in all.

Above it, along its tail, there are visible seven faint stars in a triangle; these are called the "Lock of Berenice Euergetis."

14 Tauros (Taurus the Bull)

It is said that Tauros was placed among the stars for having carried Europa over the sea from Phoenicia to Crete, as Euripides says in his play *Phrixos*. In return for this it was honored by Zeus among the most conspicuous constellations. Others say that it is a cow, the image of Io, and that it is for her sake that it was honored by Zeus.

Comprising the brow and face of Tauros are the so-called Hyades. Where the spine breaks off,[4] there is the constellation of the Pleiades with its seven stars; hence, it is called "Seven-Starred." Only six are visible; the seventh is extremely faint.

Tauros has seven stars.[5] It moves backward, turning its head toward itself. At the point where each horn sprouts from the head there is one star, of which the left one is brighter; there is one on each of the eyes, one on the snout, and one on each of the shoulders. These are called the Hyades. There is one star on his left front knee, one on each of the hooves, one on the right knee, two on its neck, three on its spine (the one on the end is the brightest), one beneath the belly, and one bright one on its chest. Eighteen stars in all.

[4] Tauros represents only the front half of the bull, so the spine "breaks off."

[5] That is, the head of Tauros.

19 Crios (Aries the Ram)

This is the ram that transported Phrixos and Helle. This immortal creature was given to them by their mother, Nephele. It had a golden fleece, as Hesiod and Pherecydes have said. The ram threw Helle off as it was carrying them over the narrowest part of the sea, the part that is named Hellespont after her. Poseidon saved her, slept with her, and fathered by her a son named Paion. However, it carried Phrixos safely to the Euxine Sea and King Aietes. The ram shed its golden fleece and gave it to him so that he could have a reminder. As for the ram itself, it ascended into the stars, where it shines rather faintly.

Crios has one star on its head, three at the end of its snout, two along the neck, a bright one at the tip of the front foot, four along the spine, one on the tail, three beneath the belly, one on its haunch, and one at the tip of its back foot. Seventeen stars in all.

21 Ichthyes (Pisces the Fish)

These are the offspring of the Great Fish, the story of which we will treat in more detail when we come to it.[6] Each of these lies in a different direction, separated from the other; one is called the northern, the other the southern. The Knot {in the line connecting them} reaches the front foot of Crios.

The northern Fish has twelve stars; the southern, fifteen. The fishing line by which they are tied together has three to the north, three to the south, three to the east, and three at the Knot, for a total of twelve. The total number of stars in the two fish and the line is thirty-nine.

26 Hydrochoos (Aquarius the Water Pourer)

He, it seems, was named Hydrochoos because of what he is doing. For he stands holding a wine pitcher and is pouring out a large volume of water. Some say that he is Ganymedes, supposing it sufficient proof that the constellation has a shape like a cupbearer in the act of pouring. They bring in Homer as a witness, because he says that Ganymedes was deemed worthy by the gods, carried up to Zeus to be his cupbearer on account of his unrivalled beauty, and achieved immortality, which is unknown to mankind. Some believe that what is pouring out is a representation of nectar, the drink of the gods, on the assumption that it is testimony to the aforementioned drink.

Hydrochoos has two faint stars on his head, one on each shoulder (both of great magnitude), one on each elbow, a bright one at the tip of his right hand, one on each pectoral, one beneath each pectoral, one on his left hip, one on each knee, one on his right shin, and one on each foot. Seventeen stars in all. The outpouring of water is made up of thirty-one stars, with two of them being bright.

[6] A nearby constellation that Eratosthenes says was placed among the stars for saving Derceto, a Near Eastern fertility goddess identified by some Greeks as Aphrodite's daughter.

27 Aigoceros (Capricorn the Goat-Horned)

He looks like Aigipan and was begotten by him. He has the lower parts of a beast and horns on his head. He was honored, according to Epimenides, the historian of the *Cretica*, because he was with Zeus on Ida when he was warring against the Titans (Zeus and he nursed together). He is believed to have discovered the conch shell trumpet when he provided his allies with the weapon of "Panic" (as it is called), caused by the instrument's sound, which the Titans fled. When Zeus took power, he set both him and his mother Aega {"She-goat"} in the stars. Because of his discovery of the conch shell in the sea, he has the tail of a fish as an attribute.

Aigoceros has one star on each horn, a bright one on the snout, two on his head, one at the base of his neck, two on his chest, one on the front foot, one on the tip of the foot, seven along the spine, five along the stomach, and two bright ones on the tail. Twenty-four stars in all.

28 Toxotes (Sagittarius the Archer)

This is Toxotes, whom most say is a Centaur; others deny this because he does not appear to be four-footed, but rather standing and shooting, and none of the Centaurs uses a bow. Toxotes, though a man, has the legs and tail of a horse like the Satyrs. Therefore, they did not think that a Centaur was a credible choice and thought him rather to be Crotos, the son of the Muses' nurse Eupheme {"Acclaim"}. He dwelled and spent all his time on Mount Helicon. The Muses brought it about that he invented the bow and arrow and gained his food from wild animals, according to Sositheos. When he was visiting with the Muses and listening to their song, he showed his approval with acclamations by clapping {*krotos*}. When everyone else saw that the Muses' amorphous melody was being set to time by Crotos all by himself, they too began to do the same. Therefore, since the Muses gained glorious fame from his idea, they asked Zeus to make him famous since he was devout. Thus he was placed among the stars because of the use of his hands, taking his bow and arrow with him as an attribute. And among men his innovation remains. His Ship[7] is testament that his innovation is to be heard not only on land but also on sea.[8] This is why those who write that he is a Centaur are completely mistaken.

Toxotes has two stars on his head, two on his bow, two on the arrow, one on his right elbow, one on the tip of his hand, a bright one on his abdomen, two on his spine, one on his tail, one on the front knee, one on his hoof, and one on the back knee. Fifteen stars in all. The remaining seven stars are below his leg. They are similar to those behind him that are not completely visible.

[7] The Argo, which rises along with Sagittarius.

[8] The Greeks set time for their rowers either by the rhythm of a voice or flute.

EURIPIDES

(ca. 480–407/6 BC, wrote in Greek)

From Euripides, the youngest of the three great Athenian playwrights, nineteen of around ninety plays survive in full (if the Rhesos *is authentic). Furthermore, over one thousand fragments are preserved in quotations and on papyrus scraps, some of them extensive, giving us a more complete picture of his work. These reveal a playwright who continually returned to the exploration on stage of many of the most compelling intellectual and social issues of his day through the vehicle of heroic myth.*

FROM *BELLEROPHONTES*

286 Bellerophontes on the Gods (fr. 286 Nauck)

Ancient accounts of Bellerophontes speak of him riding Pegasos up to heaven. Sometimes he does so from a hubristic desire to elevate himself to the status of a god, but in many versions he is angry with the gods (either because of the death of his children through divine action or because of his depression over the life he leads after his heroic deeds) and wishes to confront them. The following speech is likely early in Euripides' tragedy on the subject, at a moment when Bellerophontes is laying out the reasons for the flight he is to undertake. The hero's sense that life is unjust leads him here to the hyperbolic claim that the gods, supposedly the source of justice, must not exist. Euripides often put controversial opinions into the mouths of his characters, and speeches such as this garnered the playwright a reputation among some ancient critics as an atheist, but in this he was not unique (compare the fragment from Critias' Sisyphos*).*

BELLEROPHONTES: Does anyone say there are really gods in heaven?
There are not! There are not, if any mortal is willing
not to employ foolishly the old way of thinking.
Think about it yourselves and do not base your
opinion on my words. I say that tyranny
kills many men, deprives many of their property,
and that tyrants break their oaths and plunder cities.
By doing these things they prosper more
than those who live in quiet piety day in and day out.
I also know that some small cities have honored the gods,
but they submit to larger, more ungodly ones

because they are beaten, outnumbered in spearmen.
I think that if one of you were idle and prayed
to the gods without collecting his livelihood with his own hand,
< . . . >
they build up religion. And the evil misfortunes
< . . . >.

FROM *THE CRETANS*

473 Pasiphae Defends Herself (fr. 472e Kannicht)

Pasiphae has given birth to the Minotaur after sleeping with the bull sent to her husband Minos by Poseidon. Although she has tried to keep it a secret, the outraged Minos publicly demands her death. Here Pasiphae strongly defends her innocence by firmly casting the blame upon Minos himself for disobeying the will of the gods. The ideas of shame and impropriety surrounding female sexuality are also explored in his extant play, Hippolytus, *where Pasiphae's daughter is also destroyed by illicit passion.*

MINOS: I say that no other woman has dared to do these things.

CHORUS: Lord, you must find a good way
to conceal these great evils.

PASIPHAE: I will no longer mislead you by denying it,
for the situation is now altogether obvious.
Now, if I threw my body at a man,
trying to buy a clandestine affair,
I would rightly now appear to be a degenerate.
As it stands now, because I was crazed by a god's assault,
I suffer though my misdeed was not intentional.
Otherwise it makes no sense. What in a bull did I see
that my heart was stung with a most shameful ailment?
Was he that handsome to look at in his robes?
Did a blaze shine forth from his long red hair and
his eyes, < . . . > cheeks?
No, his body was not graceful like a groom's.
For such a marriage bed < . . . > animal
hide < . . . > did he < . . . >?
But not even < . . . > children < . . . > to make him
my husband. So why was I crazed by this ailment?
This man's ill-fortune <has filled> me also with troubles,
but *he* most of all < . . . >.
For he did not slaughter the bull <though he pr>omised that he
would sacrifice it to the god of the sea when it came, a prodigy.

Because of this, you know, Poseidon trapped and
punished you, though he had <the ailment> fall on me.
And now you shout and try to shame me
when it was *you* who did this and brought shame on me?
But I, the mother, though not at all guilty,
hid this heaven-sent blow of fortune,
while you, the most ill-minded of husbands, proclaim your wife's
affairs—yes, those are proper, fine things to tell the world—
to all as though you have played no part in them.
You are the one destroying me. The transgression was yours.
I am ailing because of you. If for this you have decided
to drown me in the sea, then kill me. You are certainly
capable of bloodstained deeds and murderous slaughters.
Or if you are desirous of feasting on my raw flesh,
it is right here. Do not go without your feasting,
for, free and completely unstained by guilt,
we will die for the sake of your punishment.

CHORUS: It is clear to many <that> this evil is
<heaven-sent>. My lord, < . . . > anger < . . . >.

MINOS: Hasn't she been muzzled yet? < . . . > shouts.
Go! < . . . > spear < . . . >.
Seize the villai<ness so that> she may die terribly,
and her accomplice < . . . >. Ta<ke> them
into the house and lo<ck them in a dung>eon
<so n>o longer will <they> look on the or<b of the sun.>

CHORUS: Lord, hold off. The matter demands
some thought. < . . . > no mortal < . . . > well advised.

MINOS: <I have decided.> Punishment will not be put off.

FROM *THE CAPTIVE MELANIPPE*

660 Melanippe in Defense of Women (fr. 660M)

As in the Medea, *Euripides took the opportunity in this play to have one of his female characters voice a defense of women. Melanippe, who was ravished by the god Poseidon, has given birth to twins and been imprisoned by her father as punishment.*

MELANIPPE: In vain the criticism of men against women
shoots a pointless arrow and speaks ill.
3 They are better than men and I will prove it.
< . . . *5 damaged lines* . . . >

They manage households and preserve what is brought by sea
within their houses. And without a woman
a house is neither neat nor prosperous.
With respect to divine matters (for I think them most important),
we have the greatest share. In the house
of Phoibos women prophesy the thought
of Loxias. Around the sacred foundations of Dodona
by the holy oak it is the female sex that conveys
the will of Zeus to those from Greece who wish it.
The rites done for the Moirai and the Unnamed Goddesses[1]—
it is not holy for them to be performed
in the presence of men. But all rites benefit from the presence
of women. *That* is the proper status of women with respect
to divine matters. Why then must the womanly sex be spoken of
badly? Will the pointless criticism by men < . . . *uncertain text* . . . >
never stop criticizing all women alike if one wicked woman
is found? I will distinguish them in my argument.
There is nothing more wicked than a wicked
woman, but there is nothing better in preeminence
than a noble one. Their natures are different.

[1] The Erinyes.

FULGENTIUS

(5th or 6th c. AD, wrote in Latin)

Fulgentius was an early Christian writer who was active in North Africa. His work, Myths (Mitologiae), *consists of mini-essays that give allegorical interpretations of pagan myth in both physical and abstract terms. So, in the two excerpts below, Vulcan, often allegorized as fire, represents for Fulgentius the fire of passion, Minerva is wisdom and chastity, and Dionysus is intoxication in all its forms. He is also notable for his use of etymologies to explain myths. While these ancient etymologies are often entirely incorrect from the viewpoint of modern linguistic science, Fulgentius' concern with such matters as they pertain both to the Greek of the original stories and his own language, Latin, shows the continued vigor of the etymological method in late antiquity.*

FROM *MYTHS*

2.11 The Story of Vulcan and Minerva

When Vulcan made thunderbolts for Jupiter, he received a promise from him that he could have whatever he wanted. He asked to have Minerva as his wife; Jupiter ordered Minerva to protect her virginity through force of arms. When they entered the bedroom, a struggle ensued, and Vulcan ejaculated his semen onto the floor. From this Erichthonius was born: *eris* is the Greek word for "struggle" and *chthonus* for "earth." Minerva hid him in a chest, set a snake as guard, and entrusted it to the two sisters Aglaurus and Pandora; he was the first to invent the chariot.

They intended Vulcan to mean, as it were, the fire of passion, and this is why he is called Vulcan, as if he was the heat of desire.[1] Finally, he also makes thunderbolts for Jupiter, which is to say he incites madness. Moreover, they decided to have him assault Minerva because sometimes madness insinuates itself even into the wise. She defends her virginity through force of arms, meaning that wisdom always protects the integrity of its own conduct from desire by using the strength of the mind. This is also the reason for Erichthonius' birth. For *eris* is Greek for "struggle," and *thonos* can not only indicate "earth" {Greek *chthon*} but also "envy" {Greek *phthonos*}. This is also behind Thales the Milesian's comment, "Envy of earthly glory is destruction." And what else could desire insinuating itself into wisdom have given birth to but the struggle of envy? This is precisely what Wisdom (i.e., Minerva) hid in the chest, that

[1] "Desire" here is *voluntatis*, perhaps etymologizing *Volcanus*.

is to say, what she concealed in her heart. For every wise man conceals his desire in his heart.

So Minerva set a snake as a guard, that is to say ruin. And him she entrusted to the two young women, i.e., Aglaurus and Pandora. Pandora means universal gift; Aglaurus, as it were, *aconleron*,[2] i.e., the forgetting of sadness, since the wise man entrusts his pain either to kindness, which is the gift of all mankind, or to forgetting, as was said of Caesar, "You who were accustomed to forget nothing except affronts."[3] Moreover, when Erichthonius grew up, what was he said to have invented? Why, what else but the racetrack, where there is always the struggle of envy. This is behind Vergil's line, "Erichthonius was the first to dare joining a chariot and four horses together."[4] Behold the power of chastity joined with wisdom, over which the god of fire has no power!

2.12 The Story of Dionysus

Jupiter slept with Semele, and from her Father Liber was born. When Jupiter came to her with his thunderbolt, she was burned to a crisp. He, the father, took the boy from her, put him in his thigh, and later handed him over to Maro to be raised. Liber warred against India and was assigned a place among the gods. And the four sisters (including Semele) were called Ino, Autonoe, Semele, and Agave.

Now, let us examine what this story's secret meaning is. There are four kinds of intoxication: the first is drunkenness; the second, loss of awareness; the third, sexual appetite; and the fourth, madness. This is why four Bacchae received these names (they are called Bacchae because they are, so to speak, frenzied {*bacchantes*} with wine): first Ino, because we call wine *inos* in Greek;[5] second Autonoe as if from *autenunoe*, meaning "not aware of herself"; third Semele as if from *somalion*, which translates to "loose body" in Latin (this is also the reason why she was also made to give birth to Father Liber, that is to say, intoxication is born from sexual appetite); and the fourth, Agave, who is linked to madness because she violently ripped off her son's head.

He is called Father Liber because the effect of wine liberates men's minds. He conquered the Indians because this nation is particularly fond of wine in two obvious ways: either because the sun's intense heat makes them drink it or because they have Falernian or Mareotic wine there, which is so strong that even a drunkard could scarcely drink a pint over the course of a month. This is behind Lucan's line, "Meroe forcing the untamed Falernian to ferment;"[6] for it cannot be tamed at all with water. Dionysus is handed over to Maro to be nourished as if to *mero*; for all drunkenness is nourished by undiluted wine {*merum*}.

[2] The word is obscure though the first part is probably a form of *achos*, Greek for "pain, distress."

[3] Cicero, *Pro Ligario* 12.35.

[4] Vergil, *Georgics* 3.113.

[5] Representing the late pronunciation of *oinos*, the Greek word for wine.

[6] Lucan, *Bellum Civile* 10.163.

Dionysus is also said to ride tigers, because drunkenness always represses wildness, or perhaps it is also because unbridled minds are soothed by wine. This is why he is also called *lieus* {Greek "The Relaxer"} since he, as it were, provides relaxation. Dionysus is depicted as a young man, because intoxication is never mature. He is also naked either because every inebriated man is inclined to squander his resources or because an inebriated man lays bare the secrets of his mind.

HELLANICUS

(ca. 480–ca. 395 BC, wrote in Greek)

Hellanicus of Lesbos wrote numerous works of mythography that were of extreme importance. Unfortunately, we only have him in some two hundred fragments, most of them quite small. It seems he had an interest in integrating myth and history and in providing chronologies and genealogies that connected the present with the myths of the past (see 125 Melanthos and Codros*). The excerpts below are all summaries of material from Hellanicus preserved in* scholia *(ancient footnotes).*

88 The Three Kinds of Cyclopes (fr. 88 Fowler)

Hellanicus says that the Cyclopes are named after Cyclops, a son of Ouranos. He is not speaking of the Cyclopes in Homer. No, there are three kinds of Cyclopes: the Cyclopes who built the walls around Mycenae, Polyphemos and those who lived around him, and the ones who were gods.

125 Melanthos and Codros (fr. 125 Fowler)

According to Hellanicus, Codros was a descendant of Deucalion, for Deucalion and Pyrrha (some say Zeus and Pyrrha) had Hellen. Hellen and Othreis had Xouthos, Aiolos, Doros, and Xenopatra. Aiolos and Iphis daughter of Peneios had Salmoneus. Salmoneus and Alcidice had Tyro, who with Poseidon had Neleus. Neleus and Chloris had Periclymenos. Periclymenos and Peisidice had Boros. Boros and Lysidice had Penthilos. Penthilos and Anchiroe had Andropompos. Andropompos and Henioche daughter of Armenios (son of Zeuxippos, son of Eumelos, son of Admetos), had Melanthos. When the Heracleidai came, he left Messene for Athens. He had a son, Codros.

Sometime later the Boiotians had a quarrel with the Athenians over Oinoe and Panacton (according to some; others say it was over Melainai). The Boiotians demanded that the kings put their lives on the line for the territory by meeting in single combat. While King Xanthios of the Boiotians accepted, King Thymoites of the Athenians refused, saying that he would hand over his kingdom to whoever was willing to fight the duel. Melanthos undertook the danger on the condition that he become king of the Athenians and that his descendants rule after him. He armed himself and went forth. When he drew near to Xanthios, he said, "Xanthios, you have acted unjustly by coming with a companion to meet me instead of coming by yourself as was agreed." Xanthios turned around when he heard this because he wanted to see if someone was following him. When he turned around, Melanthos struck and killed him, and he became king of Attica. The Athenians decided to hold a festival because they retained control of the territory. The festival was in olden times called the Apatenoria (later it was called the Apatouria) since it started because of the trick {*apate*} that had occurred.

Since Codros was Melanthos' son, he succeeded him in the kingship. He died for his country in the following way. When the Dorians were waging war against the Athenians, the god delivered an oracle to the Dorians that they would capture Athens so long as they did not kill King Codros. When Codros learned of this, he dressed himself in shabby clothes like a woodsman, took up a pruning knife, and went out to the enemy camp. Two enemy soldiers came upon him. He struck and killed the first, but he was hit and killed by the other, who did not recognize him. He left the kingdom to his eldest son, Medon; his youngest son, Neleus, was the founder of the twelve Ionian cities. They say that because of this the nobility of Codros' family became proverbial among the Athenians, who say, "Nobler than Codros" about the very noble.

145 The Story of Patroclos (fr. 145 Fowler)

Patroclos son of Menoitios grew up in Opous in Locris and fell into an unintentional error: angry over a game of dice, he killed one of his peers, Cleisonymos (or, according to some, Aianes), a son of an important man named Amphidamas. As a result he went into exile in Phthia and there lived with Peleus' son, Achilles, because of their kinship. They sustained an extraordinary friendship with each other and marched against Troy together. The story is in Hellanicus.

157 The Murder of Chrysippos Son of Pelops (fr. 157 Fowler)

Pelops already had a son, Chrysippos, by another woman when he married Hippodameia daughter of Oinomaos, with whom he had a large number of children. Pelops was exceedingly fond of Chrysippos, so his stepmother and her children, envious that the royal scepter might be bequeathed to him, plotted his death and chose the eldest sons, Atreus and Thyestes, to be the leaders in this affair. So they killed Chrysippos. When Pelops found out, he banished the murderers though they were his own children, and cursed them and their offspring to destruction. So they were driven from Pisa, each going his own way. When Pelops died, Atreus, as the oldest, came with a large army and conquered the place. Hellanicus gives the account.

HERACLITUS

(probably 1st c. AD, wrote in Greek)

Heraclitus (not to be confused with the pre-Socratic philosopher of the same name) is known to us only through his work Homeric Problems. *In it Heraclitus defends Homer against those who, like the philosophers Plato (in the second book of his* Republic*) and Epicurus, regularly denounced Homer for his immoral portrayals of the gods; one can compare the similar criticisms leveled by Xenophanes. Heraclitus bases his defense of Homer on allegorical interpretation, a method he defines straightforwardly early in his work (see 5 below). After this he goes on to give interpretations of major episodes from the* Iliad *and the* Odyssey, *particularly those that received the greatest criticism, for example, the battles between the gods (*Iliad *20 and 21) and the love affair of Aphrodite and Ares (*Odyssey *8).*

FROM *HOMERIC PROBLEMS*

5 The Nature of Allegory[1]

[5] Perhaps now it is necessary to give a brief and concise systematic treatment of allegory, for the word itself, when spoken in a strictly literal sense, practically gives proof of its meaning: the method of saying {*agoreuein*} different things {*alla*} but meaning something other than what is said is called allegory. Just as Archilochus, feeling threatened amidst the dangers posed by the Thracians, likens the war to the sea surge when he says the following:

> Look, Glaucos! The sea is now troubled, its waves
> high. Around Cape Gyrai there's a vertical cloud,
> sign of the storm. Fear's gotten to me, and I didn't expect it.

We will also find the lyric poet from Mytilene {Alcaios} engaging in allegory in a considerable number of poems. Following the same method, he compares the political troubles of the tyranny to the condition of a storm-tossed sea:

> I cannot figure out the winds' direction.
> A wave rolls in on this side,
> then on that. And here we are in the middle,

[1] In this piece Heraclitus quotes the Greek lyric poets Archilochus (fr. 105 West), Alcaios (fr. 326LP and fr. 6LP), and Anacreon (fr. 417PMG).

tossed about on our dark ship,
hard-pressed by the great storm.
The bilge-water is up over the mast-hole;
the sail is now all tattered
and there are huge holes in it;
the anchors are coming loose.

Who would not immediately think from the foregoing description of the sea that the fear of the sea was being felt by men on a ship? But it is not so. It is Myrsilos who is being alluded to, as is the tyrannical faction he was stirring up against the Mytileneans.

Secretly referring to this man's actions in the same way, he elsewhere says:

That next wave is on its way, higher than
the last ones. It'll give us lots of trouble
to bail once it's come aboard.

As an islander he uses nautical language excessively in his allegories, and most of the time he likens the evils that spread on account of the tyrants to storms at sea.

Anacreon the Teian, in reproaching the meretricious attitude and haughtiness of a capricious woman, speaks allegorically of her skittish mind as a horse, putting it this way:

Thracian filly, why do you look askance at me,
obstinately fleeing, thinking that I lack expertise?
You should know I could bridle you neatly, and,
holding your reins, turn you round the track's posts.
But for now you graze the meadows and sport, nimbly skittish.
You just don't have a skillful rider to handle your reins.

In general, it would take me a long time to detail each of the allegories to be found in the poets and prose writers. But a few examples are enough to demonstrate the entire workings of the technique. Now, isn't Homer himself found to make use of allegories that are sometimes ambiguous and even still unexplained? He has taught us this method of interpretation clearly when Odysseus, detailing the evils of war and battle, says:

When the bronze heaps the most straw on the ground,
but the crop is smallest, when Zeus tips his
scale.[2]

[2] *Iliad* 19.222–19.224.

The words are about farming, but the message is about battle. The upshot is that we have spoken of what we are referring to by talking about something completely different.

54 Athena versus Ares

[54] Homer sets virtues against vices and the corresponding elements against their opposites. Right from the start the pairing up of the gods in the battle has been philosophically devised as follows: Athena and Ares, i.e., thought and thoughtlessness. For he is, as I said, "raving, a total evil, unpredictable."[3] But she is "famous among the gods for wisdom and shrewdness."[4] There is an irreconcilable enmity between reason that leads to the best judgments and thoughtlessness that sees nothing. And just as reason must have been of the greatest benefit in life, so too it made good judgments in the battle. For raging and deranged insensibility is not stronger than intelligence. Athena beat Ares and sent him sprawling on the ground, inasmuch as every vice, crashing to the ground, has been cast in the lowest pits, an illness that is downtrodden and lies beneath all hubris. Of course, Homer lays Aphrodite (i.e., licentiousness) down next to Ares: "So the two lay on the much-nourishing earth."[5] Illnesses of the mind are kin and neighbors to the emotions.

56 Poseidon versus Apollo

[56] The battle of the rest of the gods is more a matter of physics, "for against Lord Poseidon stood Phoibos Apollo."[6] Homer matches fire against water, calling the sun Apollo and the element of water Poseidon. Why is it even necessary to say that each of these has an opposite force? Each continually destroys and prevails over the other. And furthermore, Homer breaks up the battle between the two because of a subtle observance of the truth—inasmuch as I have demonstrated that the watery substances, especially seawater, are what nourish the sun. For the sun, invisibly drawing up the moisture of vapor from the earth, uses it above all to increase its fiery element. It was difficult for the one taking nourishment to withstand the one providing it, and for this reason they withdrew from one another.

69 The Love of Ares and Aphrodite

[69] So now let us leave aside everything else and turn to the accusation made regularly and with painful repetition by Homer's false accusers. For they embellish the story of Ares and Aphrodite every which way and say that it is an impious fiction. For Homer has given to those in heaven the right to licentiousness and was not ashamed to tell a story set among the gods about something that, when it happens among

[3] *Iliad* 5.831.

[4] *Odyssey* 13.298–13.299.

[5] *Iliad* 21.426.

[6] *Iliad* 20.67–20.68.

men, is punishable by death (I mean adultery). He tells "about the love of Ares and fair-crowned Aphrodite, how they first made love in Hephaistos' house."[7] And after that, there are chains, the laughter of the gods, and Poseidon's beseeching of Hephaistos. As the gods can be subject to the illnesses of passion, it followed that those mortals who commit crimes should no longer be punished.

But I think that although this was sung among the Phaiacians (people who were slaves to pleasure), it relates to some philosophical knowledge. For Homer seems to confirm the dogmas of the Sicilian school and the doctrine of Empedocles by calling strife {*neikos*} Ares and love {*philia*} Aphrodite. And he brings them into his poem, though they were originally at variance, united together after their ancient rivalry {*philoneikia*} in one accord. So with good reason Harmonia was born from these two since everything was joined together {*harmosthenai*} tranquilly and harmoniously. It was reasonable for all the gods to laugh and rejoice together at this because their individual inclinations were not at variance over immoral acts, but were enjoying peaceful accord.

It is also possible that he is giving an allegory about the art of metalworking. For Ares can reasonably be called iron, which Hephaistos easily masters. For when iron is placed in fire, the fire—since, I think, it has a power greater than iron—easily softens[8] the metal's hardness. But the craftsman also requires Aphrodite for what he is making, that is to say, that after he softens the iron with fire, I think, he successfully completes his work with loving {*epaphroditos*} skill. And, plausibly, Poseidon is the one who frees Ares from Hephaistos, inasmuch as the mass of iron, red-hot from the forge, is taken and plunged into water. Its fieriness is quenched and stopped by water's own power.

70 Odysseus' Adventures

[70] One will find the wanderings of Odysseus to be completely allegorical if one is willing to examine them meticulously. For Homer has provided himself with Odysseus as a kind of instrument of every virtue, and through this instrument he has set out philosophy, since he hated the vices that feed on human life. The land of the Lotos-eaters, where exotic enjoyment grows, is pleasure, which Odysseus sails past. With the exhortation of his words he blinded the savagery in each man's heart as if with a brand. And the savagery has been called Cyclops because it is what steals away[9] {*hypoklopon*} rational thoughts.

What else? Was he not thought to have controlled winds because, thanks to his astronomical knowledge, he was the first to recognize when a voyage could be made in fair weather? And he was stronger than Circe's magical drugs, i.e., he was the one who discovered through his great wisdom how to cure ailments caused by foreign foods.

[7] *Odyssey* 8.267–8.268.

[8] Lit. "feminizes."

[9] The exact sense of the word is in doubt.

His wisdom has descended all the way to the realm of Hades to show that nothing is beyond scrutiny, not even what is inferior. Who listens to the Sirens, i.e., learns the many lessons of historical knowledge from every age? And while decadence that is wasteful and insatiable for drink has been given the well-chosen name Charybdis {"Whirlpool"}, Homer allegorizes shamelessness that takes many forms as Scylla, which is why she is with good reason girdled with dogs, their heads showing greed, audacity, and avarice. The cattle of Helios are mastery over the belly since he did not even consider hunger to be something that should compel injustice.

These things are put in the form of myths for the audience, but if they have led to wisdom through allegory, they will be most profitable to those who imitate them.

HERODORUS

(late 5th–early 4th c. BC, wrote in Greek)

Herodorus of Heraclea, easily confused with the more famous historian Herodotus, is an important early mythographer who has survived only in scattered quotations and references in many different sources (the first two excerpts below are summaries by early Christian writers and the last two are scholia *[ancient footnotes], the second of which seems to preserve the exact wording of Herodorus). We have parts of his work on Heracles, the Argonauts, the family of Pelops, and the legendary musicians Orpheus and Mousaios. Apparently Herodorus made heavy use of rationalization and allegory to explain the true meanings of myth, a tendency displayed in the fragments below on Heracles.*

FROM *ON HERACLES*

13 A Reinterpretation of Heracles' Holding Up the Sky (fr. 13 Fowler)

Herodorus records that Heracles, after becoming a seer and a natural philosopher, received from the barbarian Atlas the Phrygian the pillars of the cosmos—the meaning of the story is that he received the knowledge of heavenly phenomena through instruction.

14 The Myth of Heracles as Philosophical Allegory (fr. 14 Fowler)

Zeus also fathered another son by the name of Heracles (referred to as Triesperos {"Conceived in a triple night"}), this one with Alcmene of Thebes. This Heracles was the man who introduced the practice of philosophy in the Hesperian regions (where the sun sets). After his death his people deified him and called a constellation in heaven "Heracles" after him. They write that he wore a lion's skin instead of a tunic, carried a club, and got hold of three apples. These are the apples the myth says he took away after killing the serpent with his club, that is to say, after overcoming the worthless and difficult argument inspired by his keen desire, using the club of philosophy while wearing noble purpose wrapped around him like a lion's skin. Thus he took possession of the three apples, i.e., three virtues: to not grow angry, to not love money, and to not love pleasure. Through the club of his enduring spirit and the skin of his very bold and prudent argument he prevailed in his earthly struggle with petty desire, philosophizing until he died, as Herodorus, that very wise author, writes, who also records that there were seven other men named Heracles.

30 A Rationalized Account of the Punishment of Prometheus (fr. 30 Fowler)

Herodorus has a different account about the chains of Prometheus. He says that Prometheus was a king of the Scythians. When he was unable to provide for his subjects because of the river called the Aetos {"Eagle"}, he was chained up by the Scythians. Heracles showed up, diverted the river into the sea (which is why Heracles in the myth is said to have "done away with the eagle"), and released Prometheus from his chains. In his second book Pherecydes says that the eagle sent against Prometheus was the offspring of Typhon and Echidna (the daughter of Phorcys).

34 The Six Altars at Olympia (fr. 34a Fowler)

Herodorus the scholar gives the following account of the six altars: "Coming to Elis, Heracles founded the temple of Olympian Zeus at Olympia and named the place Olympia after the god. On that spot he set up altars to Zeus and other gods, six in number for the twelve gods who share them. The first he set up for Olympian Zeus and made Poseidon his altar-mate. The second for Hera and Athena. The third for Hermes and Apollo. The fourth for the Charites and Dionysos. The fifth for Artemis and Alpheios. The sixth for Cronos and Rhea."

Herodotus

(ca. 480–ca. 420 BC, wrote in Greek)

Herodotus lived some 300 years after Homer and was the first Greek historian whose works survive. Hence he is often termed "the Father of History." His Histories *treated the Persian Wars (end of 6th century–479 BC), first investigating the reasons the Persians and the Greeks were brought into conflict and then providing an account of the war itself. Herodotus is one of the first Greek authors to have attempted a cohesive historical treatment of a past event (and the earliest one to survive), and because myth was so central to the Greeks' concept of the past, he was forced to take these traditional myths into account. In many instances one can see Herodotus' critical reasoning at work; a prime example of this is the coda at the end of the Helen account given below (2.120), where Herodotus rationalizes the myth according to what is plausible. This does not mean, however, that Herodotus scrutinized every myth to ensure its plausibility; he often includes fabulous and fantastic stories without comment for the delight of his audience or is content merely to provide conflicting accounts, allowing the reader to judge. Herodotus' impulse to treat myth critically is taken to its natural conclusion in Thucydides, who criticizes Herodotus for not going far enough.*

FROM *HISTORIES*

1.1–1.5 An Historical Interpretation of the Conflict Between Asia and Greece

Herodotus of Halicarnassos here gives the results of his researches,[1] so that the events of human history may not fade with time and the notable achievements both of Greeks and foreigners may not lack their due fame; and, among other things, to show why these peoples came to make war on one another.

[1.1] Persian storytellers place the responsibility for the quarrel on the Phoenicians, a people who came to the Mediterranean from the so-called Red Sea region and settled in the country where they now dwell. They at once began to make long trading voyages with cargoes of Egyptian and Assyrian goods, and one of the places they called at was Argos, at that time the most eminent of the places in what is now called Hellas. Here on one occasion they were displaying their goods, and five or six days after their arrival, when they had sold almost all their goods, there came down to the shore a considerable number of women. Among these was the king's daughter, whose name was Io daughter of Inachos (and on this point the Greeks are

[1] The word here translated as "researches" is *historie*, literally "inquiry," which later evolved (largely due to Herodotus' prominent use of it here) into our word *history*.

in agreement). These women were standing about the vessel's stern, buying what they most fancied, when the Phoenicians, at a signal, made a rush at them. The greater number of the women escaped, but Io was seized along with some others. They were thrust on board, after which the ship made off for Egypt.

[1.2] This is the Persian account of how Io came to Egypt—the Greeks have a different account—and how the series of wrongs began.

Some time later, they say that certain Greeks—their name is not given, but they were probably Cretans—put into the Phoenician port of Tyre and carried off the king's daughter, Europa. So far it had been a case of an eye for an eye, but the Persians say that the Greeks were responsible for the next outrage. They sailed in a warship to Aia in Colchis on the river Phasis, and then, when they had finished the business for which they had come, they seized the king's daughter, Medeia. The king sent an envoy to Greece to demand reparation for the abduction and to request the return of his daughter. The Greeks replied that, since they had received no reparation for the abduction of Io from Argos, they in turn refused to give one.

[1.3] The Persians say that it was two generations later when Paris son of Priam, influenced by these stories, resolved to use abduction to get a wife from Greece, being confident that he would get away with this unpunished, just as the Greeks had done; so he carried off Helen. The Greeks decided to send messengers to demand the return of Helen, together with reparations for her abduction. But they were answered with a rebuke about the seizure of Medeia, for which the Greeks had made no reparations, nor had they returned the woman. So how could they now expect reparations from others?

[1.4] Up to this point there had been nothing worse than the abduction of women on both sides, but thereafter, say the Persians, the Greeks were much to blame; for before the Persians had made any assault on Europe, the Greeks mounted a military expedition against Asia. The abduction of women is, of course, quite wrong, but only fools make a great fuss about it, while wise men pay little heed; for it's obvious that women would not be carried off unless they themselves were willing. The Persians say that the peoples of Asia paid little regard to the seizure of their women, whereas the Greeks, merely for the sake of a Spartan woman, gathered a great army, invaded Asia, and destroyed the kingdom of Priam. Thereafter they have always regarded Greece as an enemy, for the Persians consider Asia, and the peoples dwelling there, as their concern, while Europe and the Greeks are something apart.

[1.5] Such, then, is the Persian account; the destruction of Troy, they say, was the origin of their hostility to Greece. As to Io, the Phoenicians disagree with the Persian account, and they deny that it was by abduction that they brought her to Egypt. They say that while in Argos she had an affair with the ship's captain, and finding herself pregnant, she voluntarily accompanied the Phoenicians to escape the shame of exposure.

Well, believe what you please; I will pass no judgment. Rather, by indicating the man whom I myself know to have begun the outrages against the Greeks,[2] I shall

[2] Croisos, king of Lydia starting about 560 BC, is meant. Herodotus chooses to begin his narrative with events that preceded him by about a century; these, he suggests, are subject to investigation and confirmation ("I myself know"), whereas the earlier episodes of the mythic tradition are not, and are therefore summarily dismissed.

proceed with my history, which will be no less concerned with unimportant cities than with the great. For those that were formerly great are now diminished, while those that are now great were once small. Being well aware that human prosperity never long endures, I shall deal with both alike.

1.23–1.24 Arion and the Dolphin

[1.23] This Periandros, the one who gave information about the oracle to Thrasyboulos, was the son of Cypselos, and ruler over Corinth. During his lifetime there occurred a very great wonder, as the Corinthians say (and the Lesbians agree with them): Arion of Methymna, by far the foremost lyre player of his period—the man who first, as far as we know, composed the dithyramb, gave it its name, and taught it at Corinth[3]—was carried on a dolphin's back to Tainaron.

[1.24] Arion, they say, after spending a great part of his life at Periandros' court, felt an urge to sail to Italy and Sicily. There he amassed a great fortune and eventually decided to return to Corinth. Having faith in Corinthians above all others, he hired a Corinthian vessel to sail from Tarentum. But when they were at sea, the crew formed a conspiracy to throw Arion overboard and seize his wealth. Realizing what they were about, he gave them his money and begged for his life. But the sailors, unmoved, ordered him to take his own life if he wished to be buried on land, or else to leap overboard forthwith. Faced with this painful dilemma, Arion asked the crew to allow him to stand on the quarterdeck, dressed in his full musician's robes, and to sing for the last time, after which he undertook to do away with himself. The sailors, pleased at the prospect of hearing a performance by the best musician in the world, gathered amidships, and Arion, donning his full attire, took up his lyre, stood on the quarterdeck, sang a stirring air, and then flung himself into the sea, fully robed just as he was.

The sailors continued their voyage to Corinth, but the story goes that a dolphin swam up, took Arion on his back, and carried him to Tainaron. Arion reached land, made his way to Corinth in his musician's attire, and related what had befallen him. The incredulous Periandros would not release him but kept him under strict guard while he watched for the crew's arrival. When at last they did arrive, he summoned them and asked them if they had any news of Arion. "Yes," they replied, "he is in Italy; we left him safe and well at Tarentum." Thereupon Arion made his appearance, attired just as he had been when he leapt overboard. The sailors were dumbfounded and could make no further denial. This is the story as told by the people of Corinth and Lesbos, and there is at Tainaron an offering made by Arion, a small bronze figure of a man riding a dolphin.

2.113–2.120 The Egyptians on Whether Helen Ever Went to Troy

[2.113] When I was conducting my investigations, the priests told me that the following was the story of Helen. When Alexander had carried Helen off, he sailed from Sparta to his own land. When he reached the Aegean Sea, adverse winds drove him

[3] The dithyramb is a kind of choral poetry especially used for hymns in honor of the god Dionysos.

into the Egyptian Sea, and then (for the winds did not let up) into the mouth of the Nile (which is now called Canopic) and into the salted fish factories. There was, and still is, on that shore a shrine of Heracles. If a slave flees to that temple and has the sacred mark put on him that signifies he has given himself to the god, it is forbidden to lay hands upon him. This custom has remained the same from the beginning up to my own time.

Learning of the custom involving the shrine, some of Alexander's servants deserted him and sat down in the shrine as suppliants of the god. They made accusations against Alexander, wanting to harm him, and they reported the whole story about Helen and the injustice Alexander had done to Menelaos. They made these accusations to the priests and to Thonis, the overseer of this mouth of the Nile.

[114] After he had heard their accusations, Thonis with all haste sent a message to King Proteus in Memphis reporting the following: "A foreigner has arrived, who is of the race of Teucros and who has committed an impious deed in Greece. He seduced his host's wife and has come here with her and a great deal of wealth, driven to your land by the winds. Should we allow him to sail away unharmed or should we confiscate the things he brought with him?" Proteus sent a message back, saying: "Whoever this man is who acted so impiously against his host, arrest him and bring him to me so that I may learn what he has to say."

[115] After he heard this message, Thonis arrested Alexander, seized his ships, and brought Alexander with him to Memphis, along with Helen, the wealth, and the suppliants as well. When all of them had arrived, Proteus asked Alexander who he was and where he was sailing from. Alexander told him his lineage and the name of his country. He also explained where he was sailing from. Then Proteus asked him where he had gotten hold of Helen. Since Alexander was not being very forthright about his story and was not telling the truth, the suppliants refuted his testimony and told the whole tale of his crime.

In the end Proteus made clear his position, saying: "If I were not against killing foreigners who have come here to my land driven by the winds, I would punish you on behalf of your Greek host, you, most evil man, who committed such an impious deed after having been his guest. You slept with your host's wife! But that was not enough for you: you picked her up and ran off with her! And not even that was enough, but you have come here after plundering your host's home! Now, I am against killing foreigners, but I will not let you take this woman and her husband's wealth away with you. I myself will look after it for your Greek host until such time as he comes to take it back. Now as for you and your fellow sailors, I declare that you have three days to sail away from my land to another. If you do not, I will treat you as enemies."

[116] The priests report that this was how Helen arrived at Proteus' kingdom. I think that Homer also knew this version, but since it was not as suitable for poetry as the one he used, he disregarded it, although he made it clear that he was aware of this one as well. This is evident from the way in which he describes the episode of Alexander's wandering in the *Iliad* (and nowhere else does he correct himself), telling how he was driven off course with Helen, wandered to many places, and came to Sidon in Phoenicia. He mentions this during his account of the great deeds of Diomedes, and the verses are:

Here there were well-worked robes, the product
of Sidonian women, whom god-like Alexander himself
had brought from Sidon, as he sailed the wide sea,
the voyage he took when carrying off noble-born Helen.[4]

In these lines it is clear that he knew about Alexander's wandering off course to Egypt. For Syria lies next to Egypt, and the Phoenicians, who control Sidon, live in Syria.

[117] Based on these lines in this passage, it is particularly clear that the *Cypria* is not the work of Homer but of some other poet.[5] For in the *Cypria* it is said that on the third day after leaving Sparta Alexander arrived in Ilion with Helen after enjoying good winds and a smooth sea. In the *Iliad* Homer says that he went off course with her. But enough about Homer and the *Cypria.*

[118] When I asked the priests whether the story the Greeks tell about the events at Ilion had any truth to it or was just silly, they responded as follows, saying that they had inquired about it and gotten this information from Menelaos himself: After Helen had been abducted, a large Greek army came to Teucros' land {Troy} to help Menelaos. They landed, set up camp, and sent messengers to Ilion; Menelaos himself went with these messengers. When they had entered the city walls, they demanded that Helen and the wealth that Alexander had stolen and carried off be restored to them, and that the Trojans pay restitution for the wrongs Alexander had committed. On this occasion the descendants of Teucros gave the same response that they did later, both under oath and not: they did not have Helen or the wealth under dispute; everything was in Egypt, and they would not be held responsible for what the Egyptian Proteus possessed. The Greeks thought that they were being mocked and so besieged the city until they captured it. When they had taken the city, Helen was nowhere to be found. They were told the same story as before, so they came to believe that it was true. So they sent Menelaos himself to Proteus.

[119] When Menelaos arrived in Egypt and had sailed up to Memphis, he told the truth of what had happened. He was well treated as a guest and recovered Helen, who had not been harmed, along with all his wealth. But after he had received these things, he proved himself to be unjust toward the Egyptians. For when he was setting sail, the weather held him back. When this situation went on for a while, he devised an impious plan. He seized two children belonging to men of that country and he offered them up as sacrifices. After the Egyptians discovered what he had done, although he was hated and pursued, he got away with his ships straight to Libya. Where he went from there the Egyptians could not say. While they say that they know some of these events because of their own investigations, the events that happened in their country they were able to speak about with certainty.

[120] So this is what the Egyptian priests said. I myself agree with what has been said about Helen, with the following addendum. If Helen had been in Ilion, they

[4] After this quotation (*Iliad* 6.289–6.292) a later writer added two other examples from the *Odyssey*, which have been omitted here.

[5] Of the six epics of the Trojan cycle summarized by Proclus, the *Cypria* is the only one that is anonymous, but some ancients thought it the work of Homer.

would have given her back to the Greeks whether Alexander agreed or not. For neither Priam nor any of his relatives were so crazy that they would have put themselves, their children, and the city at risk so that Alexander could stay married to Helen. And even if at first they put up with this, after not only many other Trojans had been killed in battle with the Greeks, but also two, three, or even more of Priam's sons were killed in each battle, if we are to follow what the epic poets say—after all this transpired, I expect that even if Priam himself had been the one married to Helen, he would have given her back to the Achaians if by doing so he would have relieved their present troubles. And the kingship was not going to pass into Alexander's hands, which would have made him the one in charge since Priam was elderly. No, since Hector was older and more of a man than Alexander, he was in line to assume the kingship upon Priam's death. Furthermore, it was not right for Hector to yield to his brother, who was the one at fault since he was responsible for great harm to Hector personally and to all the other Trojans as well. But the Trojans did not in fact have Helen to give back, and the Greeks did not believe them although they were telling the truth. To give my own opinion, some divine spirit was arranging it that when the Trojans had been destroyed, their complete destruction would make it clear to men that in return for great injustices committed there are also great retributions from the gods. This is my opinion of these matters.

HESIOD

(8th or 7th c. BC, composed in Greek)

The Homeric epics, the Iliad *and the* Odyssey, *are probably slightly earlier than Hesiod's two surviving poems, the* Works and Days *and the* Theogony. *Yet in many ways Hesiod is the more important author for the study of Greek mythology. While Homer treats certain aspects of the saga of the Trojan War, he makes no attempt at treating myth more generally. He often includes short digressions and tantalizes us with hints of a broader tradition, but much of this remains obscure. Hesiod, by contrast, sought in his* Theogony *to give a connected account of the creation of the universe. For the study of myth he is important precisely because his is the oldest surviving attempt to treat systematically the mythical tradition from the first gods down to the great heroes.*

Also unlike the legendary Homer, Hesiod is for us an historical figure and a real personality. His Works and Days *contains a great deal of autobiographical information, including his birthplace (Ascra in Boiotia), where his father had come from (Cyme in Asia Minor), and the name of his brother (Perses), with whom he had a dispute that was the inspiration for composing the* Works and Days. *His exact date cannot be determined with precision, but there is general agreement that he lived in the 8th century or perhaps the early 7th century BC.*

His life, therefore, was approximately contemporaneous with the beginning of alphabetic writing in the Greek world. Although we do not know whether Hesiod himself employed this new invention in composing his poems, we can be certain that it was soon used to record and pass them on. Since the Homeric epics and Hesiod's works both came into form at this important time, they stood for the later Greeks at the very beginnings of their literary traditions. Because of this early and authoritative position in Greek literature, later authors looked to these two poets time and time again, quoting them as authorities, commenting on their views (both positively and negatively), and looking to them for inspiration.

THEOGONY

Although the Theogony *is our earliest surviving account of the origins of the gods from the Greek world, it must always be remembered that there were other contemporary accounts, and every indication suggests that they sometimes differed radically from Hesiod's version. Thus, the* Theogony *is merely the most important Greek poem on the subject, but it is not possible to say that it straightforwardly represents "what the Greeks believed" or even "what the Greeks of Hesiod's time believed." Despite the poem's status as a classic with special authority that derived from its early date and the greatness of its poet, the Greeks did not approach it with the same degree of reverence that modern revelation religions such as*

Judaism, Christianity, and Islam approach their sacred books. The Greeks always kept in mind that Hesiod as poet had the choice to follow one tradition or another, or even to depart from all previous traditions, just as his audience had the choice to favor his account or not as the circumstances demanded.

In Hesiod's case we also have to concern ourselves with the question of influence from the civilizations of the Near East, which had older, elaborate creation myths of their own. To what degree these influences had been incorporated into Greek mythical thought before Hesiod is difficult to determine, but there is no doubt that many of the features that stand out in the Theogony derive from or are parallel to myths from the Near East. Because the poem is the sole surviving example of such Greek literature of this date, however, it is impossible to make categorical assertions.

Hesiod's Theogony (literally, "Birth of the Gods") is also a cosmogony ("birth of the cosmos"), because for Hesiod the physical universe was itself made up of gods. His poem, then, is a description of how the universe came to exist in the form his audience recognized; that process of evolution takes place through the birth of gods. First, there is simply Chaos, the space in which the creation takes place. Then Gaia (Earth) is formed, along with Tartaros, which is conceived of as a sort of underworld. Gaia will, in turn, produce Ouranos (Sky), then the mountains and the sea. Thus, one can trace the development of the physical features of the universe as successive gods come into being. For the Greeks, however, the universe is not only filled with places, but also with ideas and unseen forces, and Hesiod's account is concerned with these too. So Eros, the power of desire, comes into being along with Gaia and Tartaros, and Hesiod's audience learns of the creation of everything from night and day to justice and pain, each a divine figure.

The central figure in the Theogony is Zeus, and the whole poem can be read as an elaboration of the greatness of this god. Not only do the early gods ultimately give way to his rule, but he is also either the progenitor of the gods that come after him or the one who dispenses to them their privileges and functions. Although most of the physical creation in the universe occurs before Zeus' birth, he stamps the final impression onto the world as the Greeks knew it, and he fends off challenges to his authority (in the form of the monster Typhoios) to emphasize the permanence of his rule and to show that this eternal just rule and this particular ordering of the cosmos is the proper culmination of cosmogonic evolution.

The transition from the old order to the rule of Zeus is told in the stories where the kingship passes from Ouranos to Cronos and finally to Zeus. The basic structure of this succession myth is certainly derived from older theogonies of the Near East; the clearest parallels are found in the texts from the Hittites, a people of Anatolia (today central Turkey) whose civilization had thrived during the last centuries of the 2nd millennium BC. There we read about Anush (Sky) having his genitals bitten off by his son Kumarbi. Kumarbi, in turn, produces Teshub, a storm god, who eventually overthrows his father. This coincides so closely with the story of Cronos' castration of Ouranos and Zeus' subsequent rise to power that there is no doubt the Greek story is derivative. Still, we cannot know whether the early Greeks borrowed the story directly from the Hittites or whether the two traditions had a common ancestor in the myths of some other people. Nonetheless, as important as this insight is for the study of the history of myth, Hesiod's account is completely understandable in purely Greek terms.

Despite the central importance of the succession myth, Hesiod's poem is not solely concerned with the transmission of heavenly power from generation to generation. Because *the poet is interested in showing the overall evolution of the cosmos from the beginning of time to something recognizable to his audience, much has to be accounted for. To that end, long lists of the offspring of various divinities are given, most notably the list of the progeny of Night, Pontos, and other gods in lines 211–455. Hesiod also begins a list of mortal heroes born from goddesses at line 970, and the last two lines of the poem show that it was followed by the* Catalog of Women, *Hesiod's now mostly lost poem on the mortal women who produced children by gods. Since many aristocratic families and even entire cities traced their lineages back to these heroes, this extensive list acts as a bridge between the* Theogony *and the world of Hesiod's audience.*

The poem begins with an invocation to the Muses (1–115). The first primordial gods (116–136) follow, along with the tale of the castration of Ouranos (137–187) and its outcome, including the birth of Aphrodite (188–210). After the lengthy genealogical digression (211–455), which includes an excursus on the nature of the goddess Hecate (413–455) that is difficult to account for (various theories have been proposed, but they need not concern us here), the birth of the older Olympians from Cronos and Rhea comes next (456–508). The story of Prometheus and the trick he played on Zeus at Mecone (509–572) is, at heart, an explanation for the ritual of sacrifice, but it also explains mankind's technical skills (the gift of fire), as well as the origin of women told in the story of Pandora (573–620). But Hesiod has gotten ahead of himself, for in the grand sweep of the poem Zeus is not yet king of the cosmos. The poet then returns (621–725) to that theme with the Titanomachy ("Battle with the Titans"), in which Zeus finally defeats Cronos. The defeated are thrown into Tartaros, which is described at some length (726–825). Zeus' power is challenged by the monster Typhoios (826–885). After his victory, Zeus begins a series of divine marriages, which, along with the matings of other gods, shows the continuing evolution of the universe (886–969). The poem ends with the list of goddesses who slept with mortal men (970–1028) and the transition to the Catalog of Women *(1029–1030).*

Invocation to the Muses

Begin our singing with the Heliconian Muses,
Who possess Mount Helicon, high and holy,
And near its violet-stained spring on petal-soft feet
Dance circling the altar of almighty Cronion,[1]

And having bathed their silken skin in Permessos
Or in Horse Spring or the sacred creek Olmeios,
They begin their choral dance on Helicon's summit
So lovely it pangs, and with power in their steps
Ascend veiled and misted in palpable air
Treading the night, and in a voice beyond beauty
They chant:

[1] "Son of Cronos," i.e., Zeus.

Zeus Aegisholder and his lady Hera
Of Argos, in gold sandals striding,
And the Aegisholder's girl, owl-eyed Athena,
And Phoibos Apollo and arrowy Artemis,
Poseidon earth-holder, earthquaking god,
Modest Themis and Aphrodite, eyelashes curling,
And Hebe gold-crowned and lovely Dione,
Leto and Iapetos and Cronos, his mind bent,
Eos and Helios and glowing Selene,
Gaia, Oceanos, and the black one, Night,[2]

And the whole eerie brood of the eternal Immortals.

And they once taught Hesiod the art of singing verse,
While he pastured his lambs on holy Helicon's slopes.
And this was the very first thing they told me,
The Olympian Muses daughters of Zeus Aegisholder:

"Hillbillies and bellies, poor excuses for shepherds:
We know how to tell many believable lies,
But also, when we want to, how to speak the plain truth."
So spoke the daughters of great Zeus, mincing their words.
And they gave me a staff, a branch of good sappy laurel,[3]
Plucking it off, spectacular. And they breathed into me
A voice divine, so I might celebrate past and future.
And they told me to hymn the generation of the eternal gods,

But always to sing of themselves, the Muses, first and last.

But why all this about oak tree or stone?[4]

Start from the Muses: when they sing for Zeus Father
They thrill the great mind deep in Olympos,
Telling what is, what will be, and what has been,
Blending their voices, and weariless the sound
Flows sweet from their lips and spreads like lilies,
And Zeus' thundering halls shine with laughter,

[2] Nyx.

[3] The laurel is associated with Apollo and so with poets.

[4] This apparently proverbial line seems to be a way of saying "Enough about that."

And Olympos' snowy peaks and the halls of the gods
Echo the strains as their immortal chanting
Honors first the primordial generation of gods
Whom in the beginning Earth[5] and Sky[6] bore,
And the divine benefactors born from them;
And, second, Zeus, the Father of gods and men,
Mightiest of the gods and strongest by far;
And then the race of humans and of powerful Giants.
And Zeus' mind in Olympos is thrilled by the song
Of the Olympian Muses, the Storm King's daughters.

They were born on Pieria after our Father Cronion
Mingled with Memory,[7] who rules Eleutherai's hills.
She bore them to be a forgetting of troubles,
A pause in sorrow. For nine nights wise Zeus
Mingled with her in love, ascending her sacred bed
In isolation from the other Immortals,
But when the time drew near, and the seasons turned,
And the moons had waned, and the many days were done,
She bore nine daughters, all of one mind, with song
In their breasts, with hearts that never failed,
Near the topmost peak of snowcapped Olympos.

There are their polished dancing grounds, their fine halls,
And the Graces[8] and Desire[9] have their houses close by,
And all is in bloom. And they move in the dance, intoning
The careful ways of the gods, celebrating the customs
Of all the Immortals in a voice enchanting and sweet.
Then they process to Olympos, a glory of pure
Sound and dance, and the black earth shrieks with delight
As they sing, and the drum of their footfalls rises like love
As they go to their father. He is king in the sky,
He holds the thunder and flashing lightning.
He defeated his father Cronos by force, and he ordained
Laws for the gods and assigned them their rights.

[5] Gaia.

[6] Ouranos.

[7] Mnemosyne.

[8] Charites.

[9] Himeros.

Thus, sing the Muses who have their homes on Olympos,

The nine daughters born of great Zeus,

Cleio, Euterpe, Thaleia, Melpomene,
Terpsichore, Erato, Polyhymnia, Ourania,

And Calliope, the most important of all,

For she keeps the company of reverend kings.
When the daughters of great Zeus will honor a lord
Whose lineage is divine, and look upon his birth,
They distill a sweet dew upon his tongue,
And from his mouth words flow like honey. The people
All look to him as he arbitrates settlements
With judgments straight. He speaks out in sure tones
And soon puts an end even to bitter disputes.
A sound-minded ruler, when someone is wronged,
Sets things to rights in the public assembly,
Conciliating both sides with ease.
He comes to the meeting place propitiated as a god,
Treated with respect, preeminent in the crowd.
Such is the Muses' sacred gift to men.
For though it is singers and lyre players
That come from the Muses and far-shooting Apollo
And kings come from Zeus, happy is the man
Whom the Muses love. Sweet flows the voice from his mouth.
For if anyone is grieved, if his heart is sore
With fresh sorrow, if he is troubled, and a singer
Who serves the Muses chants the deeds of past men
Or the blessed gods who have their homes on Olympos,
He soon forgets his heartache, and of all his cares
He remembers none: the goddesses' gifts turn them aside.

Farewell Zeus' daughters, and bestow song that beguiles.
Make known the eerie brood of the eternal Immortals
Who were born of Earth and starry Sky,
And of dusky Night, and whom the salt Sea[10] bore.
Tell how first the gods and earth came into being
And the rivers and the sea, endless and surging,

[10] Pontos.

And the stars shining and the wide sky above;
How they divided wealth and allotted honors,
And first possessed deep-ridged Olympos.

Tell me these things, Olympian Muses,
From the beginning, and tell which of them came first.

The First Gods

In the beginning there was only Chaos, the Abyss,
But then Gaia, the Earth, came into being,
Her broad bosom the ever-firm foundation of all,
And Tartaros, dim in the underground depths,
And Eros, loveliest of all the Immortals, who
Makes their bodies (and men's bodies) go limp,
Mastering their minds and subduing their wills.

From the Abyss were born Erebos and dark Night.
And Night, pregnant after sweet intercourse
With Erebos, gave birth to Aether and Day.

Earth's first child was Ouranos, starry Heaven,
Just her size, a perfect fit on all sides,
And a firm foundation for the blessed gods.
And she bore the Mountains in long ranges, haunted
By the Nymphs who live in the deep mountain dells.
Then she gave birth to the barren, raging Sea
Without any sexual love. But later she slept with
Ouranos and bore Ocean with its deep currents,
And also: Coios, Crios, Hyperion, Iapetos,
   Theia, Rheia, Themis, Mnemosyne,
   Gold-crowned Phoibe, and lovely Tethys.

The Castration of Ouranos

After them she bore a most terrible child,
Cronos, her youngest, an arch-deceiver,
And this boy hated his lecherous father.

She bore the Cyclopes too, with hearts of stone,
Brontes, Steropes, and ponderous Arges,
Who gave Zeus thunder and made the thunderbolt.
In every other respect they were just like gods,

But a lone eye lay in their foreheads' middle.
They were nicknamed Cyclopes because they had
A single goggle eye in their foreheads' middle.
Strong as the dickens, and they knew their craft.

And three other sons were born to Gaia and Ouranos,
Strong, hulking creatures that beggar description,
Cottos, Briareos, and Gyges, outrageous children.
A hundred hands[11] stuck out of their shoulders,
Grotesque, and fifty heads grew on each stumpy neck.
These monsters exuded irresistible strength.
They were Gaia's most dreaded offspring,
And from the start their father feared and loathed them.
Ouranos used to stuff all of his children
Back into a hollow of Earth soon as they were born,
Keeping them from the light, an awful thing to do,
But Heaven did it, and was very pleased with himself.

Vast Earth groaned under the pressure inside,
And then she came up with a plan, a really wicked trick.
She created a new mineral, gray flint, and formed
A huge sickle from it and showed it to her dear boys.
And she rallied them with this bitter speech:

"Listen to me, children, and we might yet get even
With your criminal father for what he has done to us.
After all, he started this whole ugly business."

They were tongue-tied with fear when they heard this.
But Cronos, whose mind worked in strange ways,
Got his pluck up and found the words to answer her:

"I think I might be able to bring it off, Mother.
I can't stand Father; he doesn't even deserve the name.
And after all, he started this whole ugly business."

This response warmed the heart of vast Earth.
She hid young Cronos in an ambush and placed in his hands
The jagged sickle. Then she went over the whole plan with him.

[11] So they are called the Hundred-handers.

And now on came great Ouranos, bringing Night with him.
And, longing for love, he settled himself all over Earth.
From his dark hiding-place, the son reached out
With his left hand, while with his right he swung
The fiendishly long and jagged sickle, pruning the genitals
Of his own father with one swoop and tossing them
Behind him, where they fell to no small effect.
Earth soaked up all the bloody drops that spurted out,
And as the seasons went by she gave birth to the Furies[12]
And to great Giants gleaming in full armor, spears in hand,
And to the Meliai, as ash-tree Nymphs are generally called.

The Birth of Aphrodite

The genitalia themselves, freshly cut with flint, were thrown
Clear of the mainland into the restless, white-capped sea,
Where they floated a long time. A white foam from the god-flesh
Collected around them, and in that foam a maiden developed
And grew. Her first approach to land was near holy Cythera,
And from there she floated on to the island of Cypros.
There she came ashore, an awesome, beautiful divinity.
Tender grass sprouted up under her slender feet.
Aphrodite
Is her name in speech human and divine, since it was in foam[13]
She was nourished. But she is also called Cythereia since
She reached Cythera, and Cyprogenes because she was born
On the surf-line of Cypros, and Philommedes because she loves
The organs of sex,[14] from which she made her epiphany.
Eros became her companion, and ravishing Desire waited on her
At her birth and when she made her debut among the Immortals.
From that moment on, among both gods and humans,
She has fulfilled the honored function that includes
Virginal sweet-talk, lovers' smiles and deceits,
And all of the gentle pleasures of sex.

But great Ouranos used to call the sons he begot
Titans, a reproachful nickname, because he thought

[12] Erinyes.

[13] The Greek word is *aphros*.

[14] *Philommedes* means "fond of genitals." Aphrodite is elsewhere called *Philommeides*, "fond of smiles." The latter may have arisen as a polite alternative for the former. But the latter may be the original, and Hesiod may have altered it here to fit the context.

They had over-reached[15] themselves and done a monstrous deed
For which vengeance later would surely be exacted.

Other Early Gods

And Night bore hateful Doom and black Fate
And Death, and Sleep and the brood of Dreams.
And sleeping with no one, the ebony goddess Night
Gave birth to Blame and agonizing Grief,
And to the Hesperides who guard the golden apples
And the fruit-bearing trees beyond glorious Ocean.
And she generated the Destinies and the merciless,
Avenging Fates, Clotho, Lachesis, and Atropos,
Who give mortals at birth good and evil to have,
And prosecute transgressions of mortals and gods.
These goddesses never let up their dread anger
Until the sinner has paid a severe penalty.
And deadly Night bore Nemesis too, more misery
For mortals; and after her, Deception and Friendship
And ruinous Old Age, and hard-hearted Eris.
And hateful Eris bore agonizing Toil,
Forgetfulness, Famine, and tearful Pains,
Battles and Fights, Murders and Manslaughters,
Quarrels, Lying Words, and Words Disputatious,
Lawlessness and Recklessness, who share one nature,
And Oath, who most troubles men upon Earth
When anyone willfully swears a false oath.

And Pontos, the Sea, begot his eldest, Nereus,
True and no liar. And they call him Old Man
Because he is unerring and mild, remembers
What is right, and his mind is gentle and just.
Then Sea mated with Earth and begat great Thaumas,
And arrogant Phorcys, Ceto, her cheeks lovely,
And Eurybia, a stubborn heart in her breast.

To Nereus and Doris, her rich hair flowing,
Daughter of the perfect river, Ocean,
Children were born in the barren sea,
Divinely beautiful:

[15] Etymologizing the name from the verb *titaino* "to stretch."

Ploto, Eucrante, Amphitrite, and Sao,
Eudora, Thetis, Galene, and Glauce,
Cymothoe, Speio, lovely Halie, and Thoe,
Pasithea, Erato, and rose-armed Eunice,
Melite gracious, Eulimene, Agaue,
Doto, Proto, Dynamene, Pherousa,
Nesaia, Actaia, and Protomedeia,
Doris, Panope, and fair Galateia,
Hippothoe lovely and rose-armed Hipponoe,
Cymodoce who with Cymatolege
And Amphitrite (fine-sculpted ankles)
Calms winds and waves on the misty sea—
Cymo, Eione, and Alimede in wreaths,
Laughing Glauconome and Pontoporeia,
Leagora, Euagora, and Laomedeia,
Poulynoe, Autonoe, and Lysianassa,
Lovely Euarne, features perfectly formed,
Psamathe, graceful, and shining Menippe,
Neso, Eupompe, Themisto, Pronoe,
And Nemertes, who has her father's mind:

Fifty girls born to faultless Nereus,
And faultless all of their skills and crafts.

And Thaumas married deep-flowing Ocean's
Daughter, Electra, who bore swift Iris and
The rich-haired Harpies, Aello and Ocypete,
Who keep pace with storm winds and birds
Flying their missions on wings swift as time.
And Ceto bore to Phorcys the fair-cheeked Graiai,
Gray from their birth. Both the immortal gods
And men who go on the ground call them Graiai—
Pemphredo in robes and saffron-robed Enyo—
And the Gorgons, who live beyond glorious Ocean
On Night's frontier near the shrill Hesperides,
Stheno, Euryale, and Medousa, who suffered,
Being mortal, while her two sisters were deathless
And ageless too. The Dark-maned One[16] bedded her
In a meadow soft with springtime flowers.
When Perseus cut the head from her neck,

[16] Poseidon.

Great Chrysaor leaped out, and Pegasos the horse,
So-called from the springs[17] of Ocean nearby.
Chrysaor is named from the gold sword[18] he holds.
Pegasos left earth, the mother of flocks, and flew
Off to the gods, and there he lives, in the house
Of wise Zeus, and brings him thunder and lightning.

And Chrysaor begot Geryones, with a triple head,
After mingling with Callirhoe, Ocean's daughter.
Mighty Heracles stripped him of life and limb
By his shambling cattle on sea-circled Erytheia
The day he drove those broad-faced cattle away
To holy Tiryns, crossing the ford of Ocean
And killing Orthos and the herdsman Eurytion
In that hazy stead beyond glorious Ocean.

And she[19] bore another monster, irresistible,
Not like mortal men at all, or immortal gods,
Bore it in a hollow cave, divine brutal Echidna:
Half dancing-eyed Nymph with pretty cheeks,
Half horrible serpent, an iridescent monster
Eating raw flesh in sacred earth's dark crypts.
Her cave is deep underground in the hollow rock
Far from mortal men and from immortal gods,
Her glorious home, and there she keeps guard
In underground Arima, grim Echidna,
A Nymph immortal and all her days ageless.

This Nymph with dancing eyes mated, they say,
With dreadnaught Typhaon, willful and wild,
Got pregnant and bore him a brutal brood.
First she bore Orthos, Geryones' hound.
Second, a monster that beggars description,
The carnivore Cerberos, Hades' bronze-baying hound,
Fifty-headed and an irresistible force.
And third, a Hydra, malicious and grisly,
The Lernaian Hydra that the white-armed goddess
Hera nourished, infinitely peeved with Heracles,

[17] The Greek word is *pegai*.

[18] In Greek *chryseion aor*.

[19] Presumably Ceto.

The son of Zeus (but of the house of Amphitryon)
Who used merciless bronze to despoil the monster
With Iolaos' help and Athena's strategy.

And she[20] bore Chimaira, who breathed raging fire,
And she was dreadful and huge and fast and strong
And she had three heads: one of a green-eyed lion,
One of a goat, and one of a serpent, a gnarly dragon
(Lion in front, dragon in the rear, goat in the middle)
And every exhalation was a breath of pure flame.
Pegasos did her in, and noble Bellerophon.

She[21] was the mother of Sphinx, the deadly destroyer
Of Cadmos' descendants, after mating with Orthos,
And of the Nemean Lion, that Zeus' dutiful wife
Hera raised, to roam and ravage Nemea's hills,
A spectral killer that destroyed whole villages,
Master of Nemean Tretos and Apesas.
But Heracles muscled him down in the end.

And Ceto mingled in love with Phorcys
And bore her youngest, the dreaded serpent
Who guards the apples of solid gold
In the dark earth's crypts at its vast outer limits,
And is last of the offspring of Ceto and Phorcys.

And Tethys bore to Ocean eddying rivers:

Nilos, Alpheios, and Eridanos swirling,
Strymon, Maiandros, and Istros streaming,
Phasis, Rhesos, and Acheloos silvery,
Nessos, Rhodios, Haliacmon, Heptaporon,
Granicos, Aisepos, and holy Simois,
Peneios, Hermos, and lovely Caicos,
Sangarios the great, Parthenios and Ladon,
Euenos, Ardescos, and divine Scamandros.

And she bore as well a holy brood of daughters

[20] Echidna.

[21] Chimaira, or perhaps Echidna.

Who work with Apollo and with the Rivers
To make boys into men. Zeus gave them this charge.

Peitho, Admete, Ianthe, Electra,
Doris, Prymno, and godlike Ourania,
Hippo, Clymene, Rhodeia, Callirhoe,
Zeuxo, Clytie, Idyia, Pasithoe,
Plexaure, Galaxuare, lovely Dione,
Melobosis, Thoe, and fair Polydore,
Shapely Cerceis, and cow-eyed Plouto,
Perseis, Ianeira, Acaste, and Xanthe,
Beautiful Petraia, Menestho, Europa,
Metis, Eurynome, and Telesto in saffron,
Chryseis, Asia, desirable Calypso,
Eudora and Tyche, Amphiro and Ocyrhoe,
And Styx, who is most important of all.

These are Ocean's and Tethys' eldest daughters,
But there are many more besides, three thousand
Slender-ankled Ocean Nymphs scattered everywhere
Haunting earth and deep waters, offspring divine.
And as many other rivers, chattering as they flow,
Sons of Ocean that Lady Tethys bore,
But it is hard for a mortal to tell all their names.
People know the rivers near which they dwell.

And Theia bore great Helios and glowing Selene
And Eos, Dawn, who shines for all upon earth
And for the immortals who possess the wide sky,
After Theia was mastered by Hyperion in love.

And Eurybia mingled in love with Crios,
And the bright goddess bore great Astraios and Pallas,
And Perses, who was preeminent in wisdom.
And Dawn bore to Astraios the mighty Winds,
Silver-white Zephyros and onrushing Boreas,
And Notos, after the goddess slept with the god.
Then the early-born Goddess[22] bore the Dawnstar
And the other shining stars that crown the sky.

[22] Eos.

And Styx, Ocean's daughter, made love with Pallas
And bore Vying[23] in her house and beautiful Victory,[24]
And Strength[25] and Force[26]—notable children she bore,
And they have no house apart from Zeus, no dwelling
Or path except where the god leads them,
And they dwell forever with deep-thundering Zeus.
For this was how Styx, Ocean's undying daughter,
Made her decision on that fateful day
When the Lord of Lightning summoned the gods
To the slopes of Olympos, and told them whoever
Fought along with him against the Titans
He would not deprive of any rights and honors
Among the deathless gods, or if they had none
Under Cronos before, he would promote them
To rights and honors, as was only just.
And Styx undying was first to come to Olympos
Along with her children, her beloved father's idea.
And Zeus honored her and gave her extraordinary gifts,
Made her what the gods swear their great oaths by,
And decreed her children would live forever with him.
And what he promised to all of them he absolutely
Accomplished, but he himself has the power and rules.

And Phoibe came to Coios, and in the sensual embrace
Of the god she loved, the goddess became pregnant
And bore Leto, robed in midnight blue, gentle always,
Mild to mortal men and to immortal gods,
Gentle from the beginning, the kindest being on Olympos.
And she bore auspicious Asteria, whom Perses once
Led to his house to be called his dear wife.

Hecate

And she bore Hecate, whom Zeus son of Cronos
Has esteemed above all and given splendid gifts,
A share of the earth as her own, and of the barren sea.
She has received a province of starry heaven as well,
And is most highly esteemed by the deathless gods.

[23] Zelos.

[24] Nike.

[25] Cratos.

[26] Bia.

For even now when any man upon earth
Sacrifices and prays according to ancestral rites,
He calls upon Hecate and is greatly blessed
If the goddess propitiously receives his prayers,
And riches come to him, for she has the power.
She has a share of the privileges of all the gods
That were ever born of Earth and Heaven.
Nor did Cronos' Son violate or reduce
What she had from the earlier gods, the Titans.
She keeps what she had in the primeval allotment.
Nor does the goddess, since she is an only child,
Have any less privilege on earth, sea, or heaven,
But all the more, since Zeus privileges her.
Whom she will, she greatly aids and advances,
And makes preeminent in the assembly,
And she sits beside reverend kings in judgment.
And when men arm themselves for devastating war,
The goddess is at their sides, ready to give victory
And bestow glory upon whomever she will,
Good at standing by horsemen she wishes to help.
When men compete in athletic contests,
The goddess stands by them too, knows how to help,
And the triumphant victor wins a beautiful prize
For his prowess and strength, and praise for his parents.
And those who work the surly gray sea
Pray to Hecate and the booming Earthshaker,
And the goddess easily sends a big catch their way,
Or removes one in sight, as she wills in her heart.
She is good, with Hermes, at increasing stock in a pen,
Droves of cattle, herds of goats on a plain,
Flocks of wooly sheep—if she wills in her heart
She can multiply them or make them diminish.
And so although she is her mother's only child,
She is a privileged goddess among the Immortals.
And the Son of Cronos made her a nurse of the young
Who from that day on saw with their eyes
The light of Dawn that sees all. So from the beginning
She is a nurse of the young. These are Hecate's honors.

The Birth of the Olympians

Later, Cronos forced himself upon Rheia,

And she gave birth to a splendid brood:

Hestia and Demeter and gold-sandaled Hera,
Strong, pitiless Hades, the underworld lord,
The booming Earthshaker, Poseidon, and finally
Zeus, a wise god, our Father in heaven
Under whose thunder the wide world trembles.

And Cronos swallowed them all down as soon as each
Issued from Rheia's holy womb onto her knees,
With the intent that only he among the proud Ouranians
Should hold the title of King among the Immortals.
For he had learned from Earth and starry Heaven
That it was fated for him, powerful though he was,
To be overthrown by his child, through the scheming of Zeus.
Well, Cronos wasn't blind. He kept a sharp watch
And swallowed his children.
Rheia's grief was unbearable.
When she was about to give birth to Zeus our Father,
She petitioned her parents, Earth and starry Heaven,
To put together some plan so that the birth of her child
Might go unnoticed, and she would make devious Cronos
Pay the Avengers of her father and children.
They listened to their daughter and were moved by her words,
And the two of them told her all that was fated
For Cronos the King and his stout-hearted son.
They sent her to Lyctos, to the rich land of Crete,
When she was ready to bear the youngest of her sons,
Mighty Zeus. Vast Earth received him when he was born
To be nursed and brought up in the wide land of Crete.
She came first to Lyctos, traveling quickly by night,
And took the baby in her hands and hid him in a cave,
An eerie hollow in the woods of dark Mount Aigaion.
Then she wrapped up a great stone in swaddling clothes
And gave it to Cronos, Ouranos' son, the great lord and king
Of the earlier gods. He took it in his hands and rammed it
Down into his belly, the poor fool! He had no idea
That a stone had been substituted for his son, who,
Unscathed and content as a babe, would soon wrest
His honors from him by main force and rule the Immortals.
It wasn't long before the young lord was flexing
His glorious muscles. The seasons followed each other,

And great devious Cronos, gulled by Earth's
Clever suggestions, vomited up his offspring,
[Overcome by the wiles and power of his son]
The stone first, which he'd swallowed last.
Zeus took the stone and set it in the ground at Pytho
Under Parnassos' hollows, a sign and wonder for men to come.
And he freed his uncles,[27] other sons of Ouranos
Whom their father in a fit of idiocy had bound.
They remembered his charity and in gratitude
Gave him thunder and the flashing thunderbolt
And lightning, which enormous Earth had hidden before.
Trusting in these he rules mortals and Immortals.

Prometheus

Then Iapetos led away a daughter of Ocean,
Clymene, pretty ankles, and went to bed with her.
And she bore him a child, Atlas, stout heart,
And begat ultraglorious Menoitios, and Prometheus,
Complex, his mind a shimmer, and witless Epimetheus,
Who was trouble from the start for enterprising men,
First to accept from Zeus the fabricated woman,
The Maiden. Outrageous Menoitios broad-browed Zeus
Blasted into Erebos with a sulphurous thunderbolt
On account of his foolishness and excessive violence.
Atlas, crimped hard, holds up the wide sky
At earth's limits, in front of the shrill-voiced Hesperides,
Standing with indefatigable head and hands,
For this is the part wise Zeus assigned him.
And he bound Prometheus with ineluctable fetters,
Painful bonds, and drove a shaft through his middle,
And set a long-winged eagle on him that kept gnawing
His undying liver, but whatever the long-winged bird
Ate the whole day through, would all grow back by night.
That bird the mighty son of pretty-ankled Alcmene,
Heracles, killed, drove off the evil affliction
From Iapetos' son and freed him from his misery—
Not without the will of Zeus, high lord of Olympos,
So that the glory of Theban-born Heracles
Might be greater than before on the plentiful earth.
He valued that and honored his celebrated son.

[27] The Cyclopes.

And he ceased from the anger that he had before
Because Prometheus matched wits with mighty Cronion.

That happened when the gods and mortal men were negotiating
At Mecone. Prometheus cheerfully butchered a great ox
And served it up, trying to befuddle Zeus' wits.
For Zeus he set out flesh and innards rich with fat
Laid out on the oxhide and covered with its paunch.
But for the others he set out the animal's white bones
Artfully dressed out and covered with shining fat.
And then the Father of gods and men said to him:

"Son of Iapetos, my celebrated lord,
How unevenly you have divided the portions."

Thus Zeus, sneering, with imperishable wisdom.
And Prometheus, whose mind was devious,
Smiled softly and remembered his trickery:

"Zeus most glorious, greatest of the everlasting gods,
Choose whichever of these your heart desires."

This was Prometheus' trick. But Zeus, eternally wise,
Recognized the fraud and began to rumble in his heart
Trouble for mortals, and it would be fulfilled.
With both his hands he picked up the gleaming fat.
Anger seethed in his lungs and bile rose to his heart
When he saw the ox's white bones artfully tricked out.
And that is why the tribes of men on earth
Burn white bones to the immortals upon smoking altars.
But cloud-herding Zeus was terribly put out, and said:

"Iapetos' boy, if you're not the smartest of them all.
So you still haven't forgotten your tricks, have you?"

Thus Zeus, angry, whose wisdom never wears out.
From then on he always remembered this trick
And wouldn't give the power of weariless fire
To the ashwood mortals who live on the earth.
But that fine son of Iapetos outwitted him
And stole the far-seen gleam of weariless fire
In a hollow fennel stalk, and so bit deeply the heart

Of Zeus, the high lord of thunder, who was angry
When he saw the distant gleam of fire among men,
And straight off he gave them trouble to pay for the fire.

Pandora

The famous Lame God[28] plastered up some clay
To look like a shy virgin, just like Zeus wanted,
And Athena, the owl-eyed goddess,
Got her all dressed up in silvery clothes
And with her hands draped a veil from her head,
An intricate thing, wonderful to look at.
And Pallas Athena circled her head
With a wreath of luscious springtime flowers
And crowned her with a golden tiara
That the famous Lame God had made himself,
Shaped it by hand to please father Zeus,
Intricately designed and a wonder to look at.
Sea monsters and other fabulous beasts
Crowded the surface, and it sighed with beauty,
And you could almost hear the animals' voices.

He made this lovely evil to balance the good,
Then led her off to the other gods and men
Gorgeous in the finery of the owl-eyed daughter
Sired in power. And they were stunned,
Immortal gods and mortal men, when they saw
The sheer deception, irresistible to men.
From her is the race of female women,
The deadly race and population of women,
A great infestation among mortal men,
At home with Wealth but not with Poverty.
It's the same as with bees in their overhung hives
Feeding the drones, evil conspirators.
The bees work every day until the sun goes down,
Busy all day long making pale honeycombs,
While the drones stay inside, in the hollow hives,
Stuffing their stomachs with the work of others.
That's just how Zeus, the high lord of thunder,
Made women as a curse for mortal men,

[28] Hephaistos.

Evil conspirators. And he added another evil
To offset the good. Whoever escapes marriage
And women's harm, comes to deadly old age
Without any son to support him. He has no lack
While he lives, but when he dies, distant relatives
Divide up his estate. Then again, whoever marries
As fated, and gets a good wife, compatible,
Has a life that is balanced between evil and good,
A constant struggle. But if he marries the abusive kind,
He lives with pain in his heart all down the line,
Pain in spirit and mind, incurable evil.
There's no way to get around the mind of Zeus.
Not even Prometheus, that fine son of Iapetos,
Escaped his heavy anger. He knows many things,
But he is caught in the crimp of ineluctable bonds.

The Titanomachy

When their father Ouranos first grew angry
With Obriareos,[29] and with his brothers,
Cottos and Gyges, he clamped down on them hard.
Indignant because of their arrogant maleness,
Their looks and bulk, he made them live underground.
So there they lived in subterranean pain,
Settled at the outermost limits of earth,
Suffering long and hard, grief in their hearts.
But the Son of Cronos, and the other Immortals
Born of Rheia and Cronos, took Earth's advice
And led them up back into the light, for she
Told them the whole story of how with their help
They would win glorious honor and victory.

For a long time they fought, hearts bitter with toil,
Going against each other in the shock of battle,
The Titans and the gods who were born from Cronos.
The proud Titans fought from towering Othrys,
And from Olympos the gods, the givers of good
Born of rich-haired Rheia after lying with Cronos.
They battled each other with pain in their hearts
Continuously for ten full years, never a truce,

[29] Elsewhere the name of this Hundred-hander is given as Briareos.

No respite from the hostilities on either side,
The war's outcome balanced between them.
Then Zeus gave those three all that they needed
Of ambrosia and nectar, food the gods themselves eat,
And the fighting spirit grew in their breasts
When they fed on the sweet ambrosia and nectar.
Then the father of gods and men addressed them:

"Hear me, glorious children of Earth and Heaven,
While I speak my mind. For a long time now
The Titans and those of us born from Cronos
Have been fighting daily for victory and dominance.
Show the Titans your strength, the invincible might
Of your hands, oppose them in this grisly conflict
Remembering our kindness. After suffering so much
You have come back to the light from your cruel dungeon,
Returned by my will from the moldering gloom."

Thus Zeus, and the blameless Cottos replied:

"Divine One, what a thing to say. We already realize
That your thoughts are supreme, your mind surpassing,
That you saved the Immortals from war's cold light.
We have come from under the moldering gloom
By your counsel, free at last from bonds none too gentle,
O Lord, Son of Cronos, and from suffering unlooked for.
Our minds are bent therefore, and our wills fixed
On preserving your power through the horror of war.
We will fight the Titans in the crush of battle."

He spoke, and the gods who are givers of good
Heard him and cheered, and their hearts yearned for war
Even more than before. They joined grim battle again
That very day, all of them, male and female alike,
The Titans and the gods who were born from Cronos,
And the three Zeus sent from the underworld to light,
Dread and strong, and arrogant with might.
A hundred hands stuck out of their shoulders,
Grotesque, and fifty heads grew on each stumpy neck.
They stood against the Titans on the line of battle
Holding chunks of cliffs in their rugged hands.
Opposite them, the Titans tightened their ranks

Expectantly. Then both sides' hands flashed with power,
And the unfathomable sea shrieked eerily,
The earth crashed and rumbled, the vast sky groaned
And quavered, and massive Olympos shook from its roots
Under the Immortals' onslaught. A deep tremor of feet
Reached misty Tartaros, and a high whistling noise
Of insuppressible tumult and heavy missiles
That groaned and whined in flight. And the sound
Of each side shouting rose to starry heaven,
As they collided with a magnificent battle cry.

And now Zeus no longer held back his strength.
His lungs seethed with anger and he revealed
All his power. He charged from the sky, hurtling
Down from Olympos in a flurry of lightning,
Hurling thunderbolts one after another, right on target,
From his massive hand, a whirlwind of holy flame.
And the earth that bears life roared as it burned,
And the endless forests crackled in fire,
The continents melted and the Ocean streams boiled,
And the barren sea. The blast of heat enveloped
The chthonian Titans, and the flame reached
The bright stratosphere, and the incandescent rays
Of the thunderbolts and lightning flashes
Blinded their eyes, mighty as they were,
Heat so terrible it engulfed deep Chaos.
The sight of it all
And its sound to the ears was just as if broad Heaven
Had fallen on Earth: the noise of it crashing
And of Earth being crushed would be like the noise
That arose from the strife of the clashing gods.
Winds hissed through the earth, starting off tremors,
And swept dust and thunder and flashing bolts of lightning,
The weapons of Zeus, along with the shouting and din,
Into both sides. Reverberation from the terrible strife
Hung in the air, and sheer Power shone through it.

And the battle turned. Before they had fought
Shoulder to shoulder in the crush of battle,
But then Cottos, Briareos, and Gyges rallied,
Hungry for war, in the front lines of combat,
Firing three hundred stones one after the other

From their massive hands, and the stones they shot
Overshadowed the Titans, and they sent them under
The wide-pathed earth and bound them with cruel bonds—
Having beaten them down despite their daring—
As far under earth as the sky is above,
For it is that far from earth down to misty Tartaros.

Tartaros

A bronze anvil falling down from the sky
Would fall nine days and nights and on the tenth hit earth.
It is just as far from earth down to misty Tartaros.
A bronze anvil falling down from earth
Would fall nine days and nights and on the tenth hit Tartaros.
There is a bronze wall beaten round it, and Night
In a triple row flows round its neck, while above it grow
The roots of earth and the unharvested sea.

There the Titans are concealed in the misty gloom
By the will of Zeus who gathers the clouds,
In a moldering place, the vast earth's limits.
There is no way out for them. Poseidon set doors
Of bronze in a wall that surrounds it.
There Gyges and Cottos and stouthearted Briareos
Have their homes, the trusted guards of the Storm King, Zeus.

There dark Earth and misty Tartaros
And the barren Sea and the starry Sky
All have their sources and limits in a row,
Grim and dank, which even the gods abhor.
The gaping hole is immense. A man could not reach bottom
In a year's time—if he ever got through the gates—
But wind after fell wind would blow him about.
It is terrible even for the immortal gods,
Eerie and monstrous. And the house of black Night
Stands forbidding and shrouded in dark blue clouds.

In front the son of Iapetos supports the wide sky
With his head and indefatigable hands, standing
Immobile, where Night and Day greet each other
As they pass over the great threshold of bronze.
One goes down inside while the other goes out,
And the house never holds both inside together,

But one of them is always outside the house
And traverses the earth while the other remains
Inside the house until her journey's hour has come.
One holds for earthlings the far-seeing light;
The other holds Death's[30] brother, Sleep,[31] in her arms:
Night the destroyer, shrouded in fog and mist.

There the children of black Night have their house,
Sleep and Death, awesome gods. Never does Helios
Glowing in his rays look upon these two
When he ascends the sky or from the sky descends.
One roams the earth and the wide back of the sea,
A quiet spirit, and is gentle to humans;
The other's heart is iron, unfeeling bronze,
And when he catches a man, he holds on to him.
He is hateful even to the immortal gods.

In front of that stand the echoing halls
Of mighty Hades and dread Persephone,
Underworld gods, and a frightful, pitiless
Hound[32] stands guard, and he has a mean trick:
When someone comes in, he fawns upon him,
Wagging his tail and dropping his ears,
But he will not allow anyone to leave—
He runs down and eats anyone he catches
Leaving Persephone's and Hades' gates.

And there dwells a goddess loathed by the Immortals,
Awesome Styx, eldest daughter of back-flowing Ocean.
She lives in a glorious house apart from the gods,
Roofed in towering stone, surrounded on all sides
With silver columns that reach up to the sky.
Seldom does Iris, Thaumas' swift-footed daughter,
Come bearing a message over the sea's wide back.
Whenever discord and strife arise among the gods,
Or any who have homes on Olympos should lie,
Zeus sends Iris to bring the gods' great oath
Back from afar in a golden pitcher, the celebrated water

[30] Thanatos'.

[31] Hypnos.

[32] Cerberos.

That trickles down cold from precipitous stone.
Far underneath the wide-pathed earth it flows
From the holy river through midnight black,
A branch of Ocean, allotted a tenth of its waters.
Nine parts circle earth and the sea's broad back
In silvery currents returning to Ocean's brine.
But one part flows from stone, woe to the gods.
If ever a god who lives on snowcapped Olympos
Pours a libation of this and breaks his oath,
He lies a full year without any breath,
Not a taste of ambrosia, not a sip of nectar
Comes to his lips, but he lies breathless and speechless
On a blanketed bed, an evil coma upon him.
But when the long year brings this disease to its end,
Another more difficult trial is in store,
Nine years of exile from the everlasting gods,
No converse in council or at their feasts
For nine full years. In the tenth year finally
He rejoins the Immortals in their homes on Olympos.
Upon this the gods swear, the primordial, imperishable
Water of Styx, and it issues from a forbidding place.

There dark Earth and misty Tartaros
And the barren Sea and the starry Sky
All have their sources and limits in a row,
Grim and dank, which even the gods abhor.
There are shining gates and a bronze threshold,
Deeply rooted and firmly fixed, a natural
Outgrowth. Beyond and far from all the gods
The Titans dwell, past the gloom of Chaos.
But the famous helpers of thunderous Zeus
Inhabit houses on Ocean's deep fundaments,
Cottos and Gyges. And Briareos for his bravery
Deep-booming Poseidon made his son-in-law,
And gave him Cymopoleia in marriage.

Typhoios

When Zeus had driven the Titans from heaven,
Earth,
Pregnant by Tartaros thanks to golden Aphrodite,
Delivered her last-born child, Typhoios,
A god whose hands were like engines of war,

Whose feet never gave out, from whose shoulders grew
The hundred heads of a frightful dragon
Flickering dusky tongues, and the hollow eye sockets
In the eerie heads sent out fiery rays,
And each head burned with flame as it glared.
And there were voices in each of these frightful heads,
A phantasmagoria of unspeakable sound,
Sometimes sounds that the gods understood, sometimes
The sound of a spirited bull, bellowing and snorting,
Or the uninhibited, shameless roar of a lion,
Or just like puppies yapping, an uncanny noise,
Or a whistle hissing through long ridges and hills.
And that day would have been beyond hope of help,
And Typhoios would have ruled over Immortals and men,
Had the father of both not been quick to notice.
He thundered hard, and the Earth all around
Rumbled horribly, and wide Heaven above,
The Sea, the Ocean, and underground Tartaros.
Great Olympos trembled under the deathless feet
Of the Lord as he rose, and Gaia groaned.
The heat generated by these two beings—
Scorching winds from Zeus' lightning bolts
And the monster's fire—enveloped the violet sea.
Earth, sea, and sky were a seething mass,
And long tidal waves from the immortals' impact
Pounded the beaches, and a quaking arose that would not stop.
Hades, lord of the dead below, trembled,
And the Titans under Tartaros huddled around Cronos,
At the unquenchable clamor and fearsome strife.
When Zeus' temper had peaked, he seized his weapons,
Searing bolts of thunder and lightning,
And as he leaped from Olympos, struck. He burned
All the eerie heads of the frightful monster,
And when he had beaten it down, he whipped it until
It reeled off maimed, and vast Earth groaned.
And a firestorm from the thunder-stricken lord
Spread through the dark rugged glens of the mountain,
And a blast of hot vapor melted the earth like tin
When smiths use bellows to heat it in crucibles,
Or like iron, the hardest substance there is,
When it is softened by fire in mountain glens
And melts in bright earth under Hephaistos' hands.

So the earth melted in the incandescent flame.
And in anger Zeus hurled him into Tartaros' pit.

And from Typhoios come the damp monsoons,
But not Notos, Boreas, or silver-white Zephyros.
These winds are god-sent blessings to men,
But the others blow fitfully over the water,
Evil gusts falling on the sea's misty face,
A great curse for mortals, raging this way and that,
Scattering ships and destroying sailors—no defense
Against those winds when men meet them at sea.
And others blow over endless, flowering earth
Ruining beautiful farmlands of sod-born humans,
Filling them with dust and howling rubble.

Zeus in Power

So the blessed gods had done a hard piece of work,
Settled by force the question of rights with the Titans.
Then at Gaia's suggestion they pressed broad-browed Zeus,
The Olympian, to be their king and rule the Immortals.
And so Zeus dealt out their privileges and rights.

Now king of the gods, Zeus made Metis[33] his first wife,
Wiser than any other god, or any mortal man.
But when she was about to deliver the owl-eyed goddess
Athena, Zeus tricked her, gulled her with crafty words,
And stuffed her in his stomach, taking the advice
Of Earth and starry Heaven. They told him to do this
So that no one but Zeus would hold the title of King
Among the eternal gods, for it was predestined
That very wise children would be born from Metis,
First the gray-eyed girl, Tritogeneia,[34]
Equal to her father in strength and wisdom,
But then a son with an arrogant heart
Who would one day be king of gods and men.
But Zeus stuffed the goddess into his stomach first
So she would devise with him good and evil both.

[33] "Cunning Intelligence."

[34] Athena.

Next he married gleaming Themis,[35] who bore the Seasons,[36]
Eunomia,[37] Dike,[38] and blooming Eirene,[39]
Who attend to mortal men's works for them,
And the Moirai, whom wise Zeus gave honor supreme:
Clotho, Lachesis, and Atropos, who assign
To mortal men the good and evil they have.

And Ocean's beautiful daughter Eurynome
Bore to him the three rose-cheeked Graces,
Aglaia, Euphrosyne, and lovely Thalia.
The light from their eyes melts limbs with desire,
One beautiful glance from under their brows.

And he came to the bed of bountiful Demeter,
Who bore white-armed Persephone, stolen by Hades
From her mother's side. But wise Zeus gave her away.

And he made love to Mnemosyne with beautiful hair,
From whom nine Muses with golden diadems were born,
And their delight is in festivals and the pleasures of song.

And Leto bore Apollo and arrowy Artemis,
The loveliest brood of all the Ouranians
After mingling in love with Zeus Aegisholder.

Last of all Zeus made Hera his blossoming wife,
And she gave birth to Hebe, Eileithyia, and Ares,
After mingling in love with the lord of gods and men.

From his own head he gave birth to owl-eyed Athena,
The awesome, battle-rousing, army-leading, untiring
Lady, whose pleasure is fighting and the metallic din of war.
And Hera, furious at her husband, bore a child
Without making love, glorious Hephaistos,
The finest artisan of all the Ouranians.

[35] "Established Custom."

[36] Horai.

[37] "Lawfulness."

[38] "Justice."

[39] "Peace."

From Amphitrite and the booming Earthshaker
Mighty Triton was born, who with his dear mother
And kingly father lives in a golden palace
In the depths of the sea, an awesome divinity.

And Aphrodite bore to shield-piercing Ares
Phobos and Deimos, awesome gods who rout
Massed ranks of soldiers with pillaging Ares
In icy war. And she bore Harmonia also,
Whom high-spirited Cadmos made his wife.

The Atlantid Maia climbed into Zeus' sacred bed
And bore glorious Hermes, the Immortals' herald.

And Cadmos' daughter Semele bore to Zeus
A splendid son after they mingled in love,
Laughing Dionysos, a mortal woman
Giving birth to a god. But they are both divine now.

And Alcmene gave birth to the might of Heracles
After mingling in love with cloud-herding Zeus.

And Hephaistos the glorious Lame God married
Blossoming Aglaia, youngest of the Graces.

Gold-haired Dionysos made blond Ariadne,
Minos' daughter, his blossoming wife,
And Cronion made her deathless and ageless.

And Heracles, Alcmene's mighty son,
Finished with all his agonizing labors,
Made Hebe his bride on snowy Olympos,
Daughter of Zeus and gold-sandaled Hera.
Happy at last, his great work done, he lives
Agelessly and at ease among the Immortals.

To tireless Helios the glorious Oceanid,
Perseis, bore Circe and Aietes the king.
Aietes son of Helios who shines on mortals,
Wed fair-cheeked Idyia by the gods' designs,
Daughter of Ocean, the perfect river,
And she bore Medeia with her well-turned ankles
After she was mastered in love, thanks to golden Aphrodite.

Goddesses and Heroes

And now farewell, all you Olympians,
You islands and mainlands and salt sea between.
Now sing of the goddesses, Olympian Muses,
Word-sweet daughters of Zeus Aegisholder—
The goddesses who slept with mortal men,
And immortal themselves bore children like gods.

Demeter bore Ploutos after the shining goddess
Had made sweet love to the hero Iasion
In a thrice-ploughed field in the rich land of Crete.
Her good son travels all over land and sea,
And into whosoever's hands he falls, whoever he meets,
He makes that man rich and bestows great wealth upon him.

And Harmonia, daughter of golden Aphrodite,
Bore to Cadmos Ino and Semele
And fair-cheeked Agaue and Autonoe,
Whom deep-haired Aristaios wed,
And Polydoros in Thebes crowned with towers.

And Ocean's daughter Callirhoe mingled in love
Of Aphrodite golden with stout-hearted Chrysaor
And bore him a son, of all mortals the strongest,
Geryones, whom the might of Heracles killed
For his shambling cattle on wave-washed Erytheia.

And Dawn bore to Tithonos bronze-helmeted Memnon,
The Ethiopian king, and the Lord Emathion.
And for Cephalos she produced a splendid son,
Powerful Phaethon, a man in the gods' image.
When he was a boy in the tender bloom of youth,
Still childish in mind, Aphrodite rose smiling
And snatched him away and made him a keeper
Of her holy shrine by night, a spirit divine.

And Jason son of Aison led off from Aietes,
A king fostered by Zeus, Aietes' daughter,
By the eternal gods' will, after he completed
The many hard labors the outrageously arrogant,
Presumptuous bully, King Pelias, set for him.
The son of Aison suffered through the labors

And sailed to Iolcos with the dancing-eyed girl
And made her his wife, and in her bloom
She was mastered by Jason, shepherd of his people,
And bore a child, Medeios, whom the centaur Cheiron
Phillyrides raised in the hills. And Zeus' will was done.

Of the daughters of Nereus, the Old Man of the Sea,
The bright goddess Psamathe bore Phocos to Aiacos,
Out of love for him through golden Aphrodite.
And silver-footed Thetis was mastered by Peleus
And bore Achilles, the lion-hearted killer of men.

And Cythereia, beautifully crowned, bore Aineias,
After mingling in sweet love with the hero Anchises
On the peaks above Ida's many wooded glens.

And Circe, daughter of Hyperion's son Helios,
Loved enduring Odysseus and bore to him
Agrios and Latinos, faultless and strong,
And bore Telegonos through golden Aphrodite.
In a far off corner of the holy islands
They ruled over all the famous Tyrsenians.
And the bright goddess Calypso bore to Odysseus
Nausithoos and Nausinoos after making sweet love.

These are the goddesses who slept with mortal men,
And immortal themselves bore children like gods.

Now sing of the women, Olympian Muses,
Word-sweet daughters of Zeus Aegisholder. . . .

FROM *WORKS AND DAYS*

The ostensible subject of this poem is the dispute Hesiod had with his brother Perses over the unequal division of their inheritance. While Hesiod's outward motivation is to turn his brother from a life of injustice to that of a hard-working farmer, he takes the opportunity to delve deeply into many aspects of the laborious way of life in rural Greece. Though the Works and Days *is not primarily a mythological text, the opening section of the poem excerpted below uses myths centered on the rift that developed between humankind and gods to explore the reasons why man must toil and struggle to make ends meet. Two major myths are treated here. First is the tale of Pandora, the first mortal woman, created as punishment for Prometheus' theft of fire, a story he tells somewhat differently in the*

Theogony *(573–620). Second he gives the famous account of the Five Ages of Mankind, developing a theme found in several Near Eastern traditions of a decline in human life tied to a scheme of metals of declining value (gold-silver-bronze-iron). Hesiod has, however, adapted this motif to a Greek context and innovated a fifth age, the Age of Heroes, to account for the great heroes who lived in the generations just preceding and during the Trojan War.*

Muses of the sacred spring Pieria
Who give glory in song,
Come sing Zeus' praises, hymn your great Father
Through whom mortals are either
Renowned or unknown, famous or unfamed
As goes the will of great Zeus.
Easy for Him to build up the strong
And tear the strong down.
Easy for Him to diminish the mighty
And magnify the obscure.
Easy for Him to straighten the crooked
And wither the proud,

Zeus the Thunderer
Whose house is most high.

Bend hither your mind,
Hand down just judgments,
O Thou!

And as for me,
Well, brother Perses,
I'd like to state a few facts.

Two Kinds of Strife

It looks like there's not just one kind of Strife—
That's Eris—after all, but two on the Earth.
You'd praise one of them once you got to know her,
But the other's plain blameworthy. They've just got
Completely opposite temperaments.
One of them favors war and fighting. She's a mean cuss
And nobody likes her, but everybody honors her,
This ornery Eris. They have to; it's the gods' will.
The other was born first though. Ebony Night
Bore her, and Cronos' son who sits high in thin air

Set her in Earth's roots, and she's a lot better for humans.
Even shiftless folks she gets stirred up to work.

When a person's lazing about and sees his neighbor
Getting rich, because he hurries to plow and plant
And put his homestead in order, he tends to compete
With that neighbor in a race to get rich.

Strife like this does people good.

So potter feuds with potter
And carpenter with carpenter,
Beggar is jealous of beggar
And poet of poet.

Now, Perses, you lay these things up in your heart
And don't let the mischief-loving Eris keep you from work,
Spending all your time in the market eyeballing quarrels
And listening to lawsuits. A person hasn't any business
Wasting time at the market unless he's got a year's supply
Of food put by, grain from Demeter out of the ground.
When you've got plenty of that, you can start squabbling
Over other people's money.
Not that you're going to get
Another chance with me. Let's settle this feud right now
With the best kind of judgment, a straight one from Zeus.
We had our inheritance all divided up, then you
Made off with most of it, playing up to those
Bribe-eating lords who love cases like this.
Damn fools. Don't know the half from the whole,
Or the real goodness in mallows and asphodel.[40]

Why Life Is Hard

You know, the gods never have let on
How humans might make a living. Else,
You might get enough done in one day
To keep you fixed for a year without working.
You might just hang your plowshare up in the smoke,
And all the fieldwork done by your oxen

[40] Plants considered food for poor people.

And hard-working mules would soon run to ruin.
But Zeus got his spleen up, and went and hid
How to make a living, all because shifty Prometheus
Tricked him.[41] That's why Zeus made life hard for humans.
He hid fire. But that fine son of Iapetos stole it
Right back out from under Zeus' nose, hiding
The flame in a fennel stalk. And thundering Zeus
Who rides herd on the clouds got angry and said:

"Iapetos' boy, if you're not the smartest of them all!
I bet you're glad you stole fire and outfoxed me.
But things will go hard for you and for humans after this.
I'm going to give them Evil in exchange for fire,
Their very own Evil to love and embrace."

That's what he said, the Father of gods and men,
And he laughed out loud. Then he called Hephaistos
And told him to hurry and knead some earth and water
And put a human voice in it, and some strength,
And to make the face like an immortal goddess' face
And the figure like a beautiful, desirable virgin's.
Then he told Athena to teach her embroidery and weaving,
And Aphrodite golden to spill grace on her head
And painful desire and knee-weakening anguish.
And he ordered the quicksilver messenger, Hermes,
To give her a bitchy mind and a cheating heart.
That's what he told them, and they listened to Lord Zeus,
Cronos' son. And right away famous old Gimpy
Plastered up some clay to look like a shy virgin
Just like Zeus wanted, and the owl-eyed goddess
Got her all dressed up, and the Graces divine
And Lady Persuasion put some gold necklaces
On her skin, and the Seasons (with their long, fine hair)
Put on her head a crown of springtime flowers.
Pallas Athena put on the finishing touches,
And the quicksilver messenger put in her breast
Lies and wheedling words and a cheating heart,
Just like rumbling Zeus wanted. And the gods' own herald
Put a voice in her, and he named that woman

[41] For the trick see the *Theogony* 537–572.

Pandora,[42] because all the Olympians donated something,
And she was a real pain for human beings.

When this piece of irresistible bait was finished,
Zeus sent Hermes to take her to Epimetheus
As a present, and the speedy messenger-god did it.
Epimetheus didn't think on what Prometheus had told him,
Not to accept presents from Olympian Zeus but to send any
Right back, in case trouble should come of it to mortals.
No, Epimetheus took it, and after he had the trouble
Then he thought on it.
Because before that the human race
Had lived off the land without any trouble, no hard work,
No sickness or pain that the Fates give to men
(And when men are in misery they show their age quickly).
But the woman took the lid off the big jar with her hands
And scattered all the miseries that spell sorrow for men.
Only Hope was left there in the unbreakable container,
Stuck under the lip of the jar, and couldn't fly out:
The woman clamped the lid back on the jar first,
All by the plan of the Aegisholder, cloud-herding Zeus.
But ten thousand or so other horrors spread out among men,
The earth is full of evil things, and so's the sea.
Diseases wander around just as they please, by day and by night,
Soundlessly, since Zeus in his wisdom deprived them of voice.
There's just no way you can get around the mind of Zeus.

If you want, I can sum up another tale for you,
Neat as you please. The main point to remember
Is that gods and humans go back a long way together.

The Five Ages

Golden was the first race of articulate folk
Created by the immortals who live on Olympos.
They actually lived when Cronos was king of the sky,
And they lived like gods, not a care in their hearts,
Nothing to do with hard work or grief,
And miserable old age didn't exist for them.
From fingers to toes they never grew old,

[42] From *pan* "all" + *dora* "gifts."

And the good times rolled. And when they died
It was like sleep just raveled them up.
They had everything good. The land bore them fruit
All on its own, and plenty of it too. Cheerful folk,
They did their work peaceably and in prosperity,
With plenty of flocks, and they were dear to the gods.
And sure when Earth covered over that generation,
They turned into holy spirits, powers above ground,
Invisible wardens for the whole human race.
They roam all over the land, shrouded in mist,
Tending to justice, repaying criminal acts
And dispensing wealth. This is their royal honor.

Later, the Olympians made a second generation,
Silver this time, not nearly so fine as the first,
Not at all like the gold in either body or mind.
A child would be reared at his mother's side
A hundred years, just a big baby, playing at home.
And when they finally did grow up and come of age,
They didn't live very long, and in pain at that,
Because of their lack of wits. They just could not stop
Hurting each other and could not bring themselves
To serve the Immortals, nor sacrifice at their altars
The way men ought to, wherever and whenever. So Zeus,
Cronos' son, got angry and did away with them
Because they weren't giving the Blessed Gods their honors.

And when Earth had covered over that generation—
Blessed underground mortals is what they are called,
Second in status, but still they have their honor—
Father Zeus created a third generation
Of articulate folk, Bronze this time, not like
The silver at all, made them out of ash trees,[43]
Kind of monstrous and heavy, and all they cared about
Was fighting and war. They didn't eat any food at all.[44]
They had this kind of hard, untamable spirit.
Shapeless hulks. Terrifically strong. Grapplehook hands
Grew out of their shoulders on thick stumps of arms,

[43] The wood of this tree was used to make spears.

[44] The Greek word means specifically food made from grain. The point is that the people of the Bronze Age do not practice agriculture.

And they had bronze weapons, bronze houses,
And their tools were bronze. No black iron back then.
Finally they killed each other off with their own hands
And went down into the bone-chilling halls of Hades
And left no names behind. Astounding as they were,
Black Death took them anyway, and they left the sun's light.

So Earth buried that generation too,
And Zeus fashioned a fourth race
To live off the land, juster and nobler,
The divine race of Heroes, also called
Demigods, the race before the present one.
They all died fighting in the great wars,
Some at seven-gated Thebes, Cadmos' land,
In the struggle for Oidipous' cattle,
And some, crossing the water in ships,
Died at Troy, for the sake of beautiful Helen.
And when Death's veil had covered them over,
Zeus granted them a life apart from other men,
Settling them at the ends of the Earth.
And there they live, free from all care,
In the Isles of the Blest, by Ocean's deep stream,
Blessed heroes for whom the life-giving Earth
Bears sweet fruit ripening three times a year.

[Far from the Immortals, and Cronos is their king,
For the Father of gods and men has released him
And he still has among them the honor he deserves.
Then the fifth generation: Broad-browed Zeus
Made still another race of articulate folk
To people the plentiful Earth.]
I wish
I had nothing to do with this fifth generation,
Wish I had died before or been born after,

Because this is the Iron Age.
Not a day goes by
A man doesn't have some kind of trouble.
Nights too, just wearing him down. I mean
The gods send us terrible pain and vexation.
Still, there'll be some good mixed in with the evil,
And then Zeus will destroy this generation too,

Soon as they start being born gray around the temples.
Then fathers won't get along with their kids anymore,
Nor guests with hosts, nor partner with partner,
And brothers won't be friends, the way they used to be.
Nobody'll honor their parents when they get old
But they'll curse them and give them a hard time,
Godless rascals, and never think about paying them back
For all the trouble it was to raise them.
They'll start taking justice into their own hands,
Sacking each other's cities, no respect at all
For the man who keeps his oaths, the good man,
The just man. No, they'll keep all their praise
For the wrongdoer, the man who is violence incarnate,
And shame and justice will lie in their hands.
Some good-for-nothing will hurt a decent man,
Slander him, and swear an oath on top of it.
Envy will be everybody's constant companion,
With her foul mouth and hateful face, relishing evil.
And then
    up to Olympos from the wide-pathed Earth,
    lovely apparitions wrapped in white veils,
    off to join the Immortals, abandoning humans
There go Shame and Nemesis. And horrible suffering
Will be left for mortal men, and no defense against evil.

HOMERIC HYMNS

(various dates, composed in Greek)

The Homeric Hymns, *so-called because in antiquity they were attributed to Homer (they recall his language and are written in dactylic hexameter, the meter of epic poetry), are in fact a collection of anonymous hymns that were composed at different times. Most are thought to have been composed between the 7th and 5th centuries* BC, *though the* Hymn to Ares *(8) is almost certainly much later. The collection as we have it (aside from* Hymn *8) was perhaps assembled as early as the 1st century* BC *and contains thirty-two hymns that can be divided according to the simple criterion of length into long* Hymns *(1–5, though most of 1 is missing) and short* Hymns *(6–33). We have included separate introductions for the long* Hymns *and* Hymn *8.*

The purpose of the Homeric Hymns *seems originally to have been to serve as preludes to other, longer poems. A parallel can be found in the eighth book of the* Odyssey, *where the bard Demodicos sings a prelude to the god before setting on a formal piece about the Trojan horse. The* Hymns *themselves often conclude with words suggesting this function, for instance the common "I will be mindful of you and of another song." But while the short* Hymns *do seem perfectly suited to being preludes or invocations to gods before a longer piece, it is more difficult to say the same of the long* Hymns, *which reach several hundred lines and can stand on their own as complete pieces. These were perhaps composed for performance at religious festivals. Later hymns by Callimachus (3rd c.* BC*), for example, who was imitating the poems in the present collection for purely literary reasons, were explicitly meant to stand on their own.*

The most striking difference between the long and short Hymns *is the amount of narrative material. The long* Hymns *include extended narration of important aspects of the god's myth: in the* Hymn to Demeter *(2), for instance, we have the extended story of Persephone's abduction and the establishment of the Eleusinian mysteries. In the* Hymn to Hermes, *there is the delightful exposition of Hermes' essential nature as a clever, thieving god and his relationship to another young god, Apollo. By contrast, the short* Hymns *contain little or no story, but invoke and describe the gods in short compass.*

1 To Dionysos

This Hymn, *originally among the longest in the collection, has been heavily damaged and is preserved only in fragments found in later authors and on some papyrus remains. Translated below are the two sections of the* Hymn *that are mostly whole and not heavily reconstructed. These two parts contain 1) the controversy over the god's birthplace and 2) his acceptance on Mount Olympos by Zeus. Papyrus fragments suggest that between these two parts there was the story of Dionysos' role in reconciling Hephaistos with his mother Hera, who had cast him from Olympos. In revenge, he built a throne that held her fast and suspended her in midair. Dionysos then got Hephaistos drunk and triumphantly led him back to Olympos, where he freed his mother. Dionysos was rewarded by Hera with admission into the company of the Olympian gods.*

< . . . >[1] For some say that in Dracanos Semele conceived and bore you to Zeus, who delights in thunder, and some in windy Icaros, and some in Naxos, you seed of Zeus, Eiraphiotes; and others by the deep-swelling river Alpheios, and others, O Prince, say that you were born in Thebes. Falsely they all speak: for the father of gods and men begat you far away from men, while white-armed Hera did not know it. There is a hill called Nysa, a lofty hill, flowering into woodland, in a distant part of Phoenicia, near the streams of Egypt < . . . >.[2]

< . . . >[3]

"And they will raise many statues to you in the temples: as these your deeds are three, so men will sacrifice to you hecatombs every three years." So spoke Cronion and nodded with his dark brows, and the ambrosial hair moved lightly on the lord's immortal head as he made great Olympos tremble. So spoke Zeus the counselor and nodded approval with his head. Be gracious, Eiraphiotes, you who drive women mad. From you, beginning and ending with you, we singers sing: in no way is it possible for him who forgets you to be mindful of sacred song. Hail to you, Dionysos Eiraphiotes, with your mother, Semele, whom they call Thyone.

2 To Demeter

This Hymn *consists of two seemingly separate stories that are interrelated and center on Demeter and her daughter Persephone's role in the Eleusinian mysteries. The first story, comprising the beginning and end of the* Hymn, *is an aetiological myth that explains the creation of the seasons: Demeter's daughter is abducted, with Zeus' consent, by Hades, and in mourning over her Demeter refuses to let things grow: "Then the most dread and terrible of years did the goddess bring for mortals upon the fruitful earth, nor did the earth send up the seed, for Demeter of the fine garland concealed it." As the gods apparently need sacrifice from men, they finally relent and allow Persephone to return to her mother. But Persephone has eaten food in the underworld, and thus she is forced to remain there for one-third of the year.*

The second part concerns another aetiological story, that of the foundation of the worship of Demeter and Persephone (also called Kore) in the city of Eleusis, some 22 kilometers west of Athens. This is the earliest literary account of their cult there, and since there is no mention of Athens in the poem, it was probably composed for the Eleusinian celebration in the early part of the 6th century BC *before the Athenians took control of the mysteries and instituted the annual procession from Athens to Eleusis.*

The mysteries at Eleusis, held annually in autumn, were among the most celebrated in antiquity, and many from all parts of Greece traveled to take part in them. We know very

[1] It is uncertain how many lines are lost from the beginning.

[2] A papyrus contains 14 more lines, most of them heavily damaged.

[3] The bulk of the poem is missing.

little about them, however, because they were shrouded in secrecy and only those who were initiated into them could participate in the most important aspects of the ritual. The secrecy of the rituals is hinted at at the end of the Hymn, *where Demeter "showed the care of her rites . . . and taught Triptolemos, Polyxeinos, and Diocles her fine mysteries, holy mysteries that none may violate or search into or noise abroad, for the great curse from the gods restrains the voice." Mystery religions offered initiates a more pleasant existence after death, and those at Eleusis were no exception: "and he who is uninitiated and has no lot in them never has an equal lot in death beneath the murky gloom." The Mysteries at Eleusis survived until the site was destroyed in the late 4th century AD.*

2a The Rape of Persephone (1–89)

Of fair-haired Demeter, Demeter holy goddess, I begin to sing, of her and her slim-ankled daughter whom Aidoneus snatched away, the gift of far-seeing, loud-thundering Zeus. But Demeter knew it not, lady of the golden sword, the giver of fine crops. For her daughter was playing with the deep-bosomed maidens of Oceanos and was gathering flowers—roses and crocuses and fair violets in the soft meadow and lilies and hyacinths and the narcissus that the earth brought forth as a snare for the fair-faced maiden by the counsel of Zeus and to please the lord of many guests. Wondrously bloomed the flower, a marvel for all to see, whether deathless gods or mortal men. From its root grew forth a hundred blossoms, and with its fragrant odor the wide heaven above and the whole earth laughed, as did the salt wave of the sea. Then the maiden marveled and stretched forth both her hands to seize the fair plaything, but the wide-wayed earth gaped in the Nysian plain, and up rushed the prince, the host of many guests, the many-named son of Cronos, with his immortal horses. Against her will he seized her and drove her off weeping in his golden chariot, but she screamed aloud, calling on Father Cronides, the highest of gods and the best.

But no immortal god or mortal man heard her voice (in fact, not even the rich-fruited olive trees heard her), none except the daughter of Persaios, Hecate of the fair veil, as she was thinking delicate thoughts. She, along with Prince Helios, the glorious son of Hyperion, heard the cry from her cave, heard the maiden calling on Father Cronides. But he sat far off apart from the gods in his prayer-filled temple, receiving fine victims from mortal men. By the design of Zeus the brother of Zeus led the maiden away against her will, the lord of many, the host of many guests, with his deathless horses, he of many names, the son of Cronos. Now, so long as the goddess beheld the earth and the starry heaven and the tide of the teeming sea and the rays of the sun, so long as she still hoped to behold her dear mother and the tribes of the eternal gods, just so long, despite her sorrow, hope warmed her high heart. But then rang the mountain peaks and the depths of the sea to her immortal voice, and her lady mother heard her. Then sharp pain caught at her heart, and with her hands she tore the veil about her ambrosial hair and cast a dark mantle about her shoulders, and then she sped like a bird over land and sea, searching. But there was none who would tell the truth to her; neither god nor mortal man, not even a bird, a soothsaying messenger, came near her. Thereafter for nine days Lady Deo roamed the earth with torches burning in her hands, nor ever in her sorrow did she taste ambrosia and sweet nectar, nor bathe her body. But when at last the tenth morning came to her with the light, Hecate met her, a torch in her hands, and spoke a word of tidings, saying:

> Lady Demeter, you who bring the seasons, you giver of glad gifts, which of the heavenly gods or mortal men has ravished away Persephone and brought sorrow to your heart? For I heard a voice, but I saw not with my eyes who the ravisher was. All this I say to you truly.

So spoke Hecate, and the daughter of fair-haired Rhea did not answer, but swiftly rushed on with her, bearing burning torches in her hands. So they came to Helios, who watches both gods and men, and stood before his horses, and the lady goddess questioned him:

> Helios, have pity on me who am a goddess, if ever by word or deed I gladdened your heart. My daughter, whom I bore, a sweet plant and fair to see—it was her clear voice I heard through the air that bears no crops, like the voice of a woman being forced, but I saw her not with my eyes. But you who look down with your rays from the bright sky upon all the land and sea, tell me truly concerning my dear child, if you did behold her. Who it is that has gone off and ravished her away from me against her will? Who is it of gods or mortal men?

So spoke she, and Hyperion's son answered her:

> Daughter of fair-haired Rhea, Queen Demeter, you shall know it, for I greatly pity and revere you in your sorrow for your slim-ankled child. There is none other responsible of the immortals but Zeus himself, the gatherer of clouds, who gave your daughter to Hades, his own brother, to be called his lovely wife. And Hades has ravished her away in his chariot, loudly wailing, beneath the dusky gloom. But, Goddess, cease from your long lamenting. It is not fitting for you vainly to hold onto anger unassuaged like this. No unseemly son-in-law among the immortals is Aidoneus, the lord of many, your own brother and of one seed with you. For his share he won, when the threefold division was first made, sovereignty among those with whom he dwells.

So spoke he, and he called upon his horses, and at his call they swiftly bore the fleet chariot away like long-winged birds.

2b Demeter Withdraws from the Gods and Travels in Disguise to Eleusis (90–168)

But grief more dread and bitter fell upon her, and thereafter she was wroth with Cronion, who has dark clouds for his dwelling. She kept apart from the gathering of the gods and from tall Olympos, and, disfiguring her form, she went among the cities and rich fields of men for many days. Now no man that looked on her knew her, nor any deep-girdled woman, till she came to the dwelling of Celeos, who then was king of fragrant Eleusis. There sat she at the wayside with sorrow in her heart by the Maiden's Well from which the townsfolk were wont to draw water. In the shade she sat; above her grew a thick olive tree, and in appearance she was like an ancient crone who knows no more of childbearing and the gifts of Aphrodite, the lover of garlands. She was like the nurses of the children of verdict-pronouncing kings, like the housekeepers in their echoing halls.

Now the daughters of Celeos of Eleusis' line beheld her as they came to fetch the fair-flowing water, to carry it in bronze vessels to their father's home. There were four of them, like goddesses, all in the bloom of youth, Callidice, Cleisidice, charming

Demo, and Callithoe, the eldest of them all. Nor did they recognize her, for it is hard for mortals to know gods, but they stood near her and spoke winged words:

> Who are you, old woman, and of what ancient folk? And why were you wandering apart from the town, not drawing near to the houses where in the shadowy halls there are women of your own age, and younger too, who may treat you kindly in word and deed?

So spoke they, and the lady goddess answered:

> Dear children, whoever you are of womankind, I bid you hail, and I will tell you my story. It is proper to answer your questions truly. Deo is my name, for my lady mother gave it to me. But now I have come here from Crete over the wide ridges of the sea by no will of my own; no, by violence pirates brought me here under duress and thereafter touched with their swift ship at Thoricos, where the women and they themselves disembarked onto land. Then they were busy about supper beside the hawsers of the ship, but my heart did not desire pleasing food. No, stealthily setting forth through the dark land, I fled from these arrogant masters, so that they might not sell me, whom they had never bought, and gain my price. Thus have I come here in my wandering, and I do not know at all what land is this nor who dwells here. But to you may all those who have houses in Olympos give husbands and lords, and such children to bear as parents desire. But pity me, maidens, in your kindness <tell me> to the house of what husband and wife am I to go, where I might work zealously for them in such tasks as befit a woman of my years? I could carry in my arms a newborn babe, nurse it well, keep the house, make my master's bed within the well-built chambers, and teach the maids their tasks.

So spoke the goddess, and straightway answered her the unwed maiden, Callidice, the fairest of the daughters of Celeos:

> Mother, men must endure whatever things the gods give, though they are sorrowing, for the gods are far stronger than we; but I will tell you clearly and truly what men here have most honor, who lead the people and by their counsels and just verdicts safeguard the bulwarks of the city. Such are wise Triptolemos, Diocles, Polyxenos, noble Eumolpos, and Dolichos, and our lordly father. All their wives keep their houses, and not one of them would at first sight scorn your appearance and bar you from their halls, but gladly will they receive you, for your aspect is divine. So, if you will, abide here, so that we may go to the house of my father and tell out all this tale to my mother, the deep-girdled Metaneira, if perhaps she will bid you come to our house and not seek the homes of others. A dear son born in her later years is nurtured in the well-built hall, a welcome child of many prayers. If you would nurse him till he comes to the measure of youth, then whatever woman saw you would envy you. Such gifts would my mother give you in return for raising him.

2c In the House of Celeos and Metaneira (169–301)

So spoke she, and the goddess nodded assent. So rejoicing, they filled their shining pitchers with water and bore them away. Swiftly they came to the high hall of their father, and quickly they told their mother what they had heard and seen, and speedily she bade them run and call the stranger, offering a fine wage. Then as deer or calves in the season of spring leap along the meadow when they have had their fill of pasture, so lightly they lifted up the folds of their lovely dresses and ran along the rutted chariot-way, while their hair danced on their shoulders, in color like the crocus flower. They found the glorious goddess at the wayside, just where they had left her, and immediately they led her to their father's house. But she paced behind in heaviness of heart, her head veiled, and the dark robe floating about her slender feet divine. Speedily they came to the house of Celeos, the fosterling of Zeus, and they went through the corridor where their lady mother was sitting by the doorpost of the well-wrought hall with her child in her lap, a young blossom. And the girls ran up to her, but the goddess stood on the threshold, her head touching the roof beam, and she filled the doorway with her light divine. Then wonder and awe and pale fear seized the mother, and she gave place from her high seat and bade the goddess be seated. But Demeter, the bearer of the seasons, the giver of fine gifts, would not sit down upon the shining high seat. No, in silence she waited, casting down her lovely eyes, till the wise Iambe set for her a well-made stool and cast over it a glittering fleece. There she sat down and held the veil before her face; long in sorrow and silence she sat like this and spoke to no man nor made any sign, but she sat unsmiling, tasting neither meat nor drink, wasting with long desire for her deep-girdled daughter.

So she remained till wise Iambe with jests and many mockeries distracted the lady, the holy one, and made her smile and laugh and hold a happier heart, and ever pleased her moods thereafter. Then Metaneira filled a cup of sweet wine and offered it to her, but she refused it, saying that it was not permitted for her to drink red wine. But she bade them mix barley meal and water with the tender herb of mint and give it to her to drink. Then Metaneira made *kykeon*[4] and gave it to the goddess as she bade, and Lady Deo took it and made libation. < . . . > And to her fair-girdled Metaneira said:

> Hail, lady, for I think that you are not of mean parentage, but nobly born, for modesty and grace shine in your eyes as in the eyes of verdict-pronouncing kings. But the gifts of the gods, even in sorrow, we men of necessity endure, for the yoke is laid upon our necks; yet now that you have come here, such things as I have shall be yours. Rear for me this child that the gods have given in my later years and beyond my hope; and he is to me a child of many prayers. If you rear him, and he comes to the measure of youth, truly each woman that sees you will envy you, such shall be my gifts in return for raising him.

Then Demeter of the fair garland answered her again:

> And may you too, Lady, fare well, and the gods give you all things good. Gladly will I receive your child as you bid me. I will raise him and never, I think, by the folly of his nurse shall charm or sorcery harm him, for I know an antidote stronger than the wild wood herb and a fine salve for poisoned spells.

[4] A drink made from barley that had an important part in the mysteries of Demeter at Eleusis.

So spoke she, and with her immortal hands she placed the child on her fragrant breast, and the mother was glad at heart. So in the halls she nursed the fine son of wise Celeos, Demophon, whom fair-girdled Metaneira bore, and he grew like a god, upon no mortal food nor <on mother's milk. For during the day fair-garlanded> Demeter anointed him with ambrosia as though he had been a son of a god, breathing sweetness over him and keeping him on her lap. So wrought she by day, but at night she was wont to hide him in the force of fire like a brand, his dear parents knowing it not. No, to them it was a great marvel how he flourished and grew like the gods to look upon. And truly she would have made him exempt from old age and death forever, had not fair-girdled Metaneira in her witlessness spied on her in the night from her fragrant chamber. Then she wailed and smote both her thighs in terror for her child and in folly of heart, and lamenting she spoke winged words: "My child Demophon, the stranger is concealing you in the heart of the fire, causing bitter sorrow for me and lamentation."

So spoke she, wailing, and the lady goddess heard her. Then in wrath did fair-garlanded Demeter snatch out of the fire with her immortal hands and set upon the ground that woman's dear son, whom beyond all hope she had borne in the halls. Dread was the wrath of Demeter, and soon she spoke to fair-girdled Metaneira:

> O helpless and uncounseled race of men, who know not beforehand the fate of coming good or coming evil. For, behold, you have wrought upon yourself a bane incurable by your own witlessness. For by the oath of the gods, the relentless water of Styx, I would have made your dear child deathless and exempt from age forever and would have given him glory imperishable. But now in no way may he escape the Moirai and death, yet glory imperishable will ever be his, since he has lain on my knees and slept within my arms. But as the years go round, the sons of the Eleusinians will ever wage war and dreadful strife, one upon the other. I am the honored Demeter, the greatest good and gain to the immortals and mortal men. But, come now, let all the people build me a great temple and an altar beside, below the town and the steep wall, above Callichoros on the jutting rock. But I myself will prescribe the rites, so that in time to come you may duly perform them and appease my power.

With that the goddess changed her shape and height and cast off old age, and beauty breathed about her. Sweet scent breathed from her fragrant robes, and afar shone the light from the deathless body of the goddess, the yellow hair flowing about her shoulders, so that the fine house was filled with a splendor like that of lightning-fire, and forth from the halls went she.

But now the knees of the woman were loosened, and for a long time she was speechless, nor did she even pay heed to the child, her best beloved, to lift him from the floor. But the sisters of the child heard his pitiful cry and leapt from their fair-strewn beds. One of them, lifting the child in her hands, laid it in her bosom, another lit fire, and the third ran with smooth feet to take her mother forth from the fragrant chamber. Then they gathered about the child, hugged him, and gave him a bath as he squirmed, yet his mood was not softened, for lesser nurses and handmaidens held him now.

They the long night through were adoring the renowned goddess, trembling with fear, but at the dawning they told truly to mighty Celeos all that the goddess, Demeter of the fine garland, had commanded. Then he called into the marketplace the many people and bade them make a rich temple and an altar to fair-haired Demeter upon the jutting rock. Immediately they heard and obeyed his voice, and they built as he bade, and it increased by the goddess' will.

2d The Sorrowing Demeter Withdraws Fertility from the Earth (302–333)
Now when they had done their work and rested from their labors, each man started for his home, but yellow-haired Demeter remained, sitting there apart from all the blessed gods, wasting away with desire for her deep-girdled daughter. Then the most dread and terrible of years did the goddess bring for mortals upon the fruitful earth, nor did the earth send up the seed, for Demeter of the fine garland concealed it. Many crooked ploughs did the oxen drag through the furrows in vain, and much white barley fell fruitless upon the land. Now the whole race of mortal men would have perished utterly from the stress of famine, and the gods who hold mansions in Olympos would have lost the share and renown of gift and sacrifice, if Zeus had not taken note and conceived a counsel within his heart.

First, he roused Iris of the golden wings to speed forth and call fair-haired Demeter, whose form is beautiful. So spoke Zeus, and Iris obeyed him, the son of Cronos, he of the dark clouds, and swiftly she sped down through the space between heaven and earth. Then came she to the citadel of fragrant Eleusis, and in the temple she found Demeter clothed in dark raiment, and speaking winged words addressed her, "Demeter, Father Zeus, whose counsels are imperishable, bids you back unto the tribes of the eternal gods. Come then, lest the word of Zeus be of no avail." So spoke she in her prayer, but the goddess yielded not. Thereafter the Father sent forth all the blessed gods, all of the immortals, and coming one by one they bade Demeter return and offered her many splendid gifts and all honors that she might choose among the immortal gods. But none was able to persuade her by turning her mind and her angry heart, so stubbornly she refused their appeals. For she thought no more forever to enter fragrant Olympos, and no more to allow the earth to bear her fruit, until her eyes should behold her fair-faced daughter.

2e Zeus Relents; Persephone Is Returned (334–389)
But when far-seeing Zeus, the loud thunderer, had heard this, he sent the slayer of Argos, the god of the golden wand, to Erebos to win over Hades with soft words and to persuade him to bring up holy Persephone from the murky gloom into the light and among the gods, so that her mother might behold her and relent from her anger. And Hermes disobeyed not, but straightway and speedily went forth beneath the hollow places of the earth, leaving the home of Olympos. That king he found within his dwelling, sitting on a couch with his modest consort, who sorely grieved for desire of her mother, who still was cherishing a design against the ill deeds of the gods. Then the strong slayer of Argos drew near and spoke:

> Hades of the dark locks, you prince of worn-out men, Father Zeus bade me bring the glorious Persephone forth from Erebos among the gods, so that her mother may behold her and relent from her anger and terrible wrath against

> the immortals. For now she contrives a mighty deed, to destroy the feeble tribes of earth-born men by hiding the seed under the earth. Thereby the honors of the gods are diminished, and fierce is her wrath, and she does not mingle with the gods, but sits apart within the fragrant temple in the steep citadel of Eleusis.

So spoke he, and smiling were the brows of Aidoneus, prince of the dead, and he did not disobey the commands of King Zeus, as speedily he bade the wise Persephone:

> Go, Persephone, to your dark-mantled mother, go with a gentle spirit in your breast and do not be disconsolate beyond all others. Truly I shall be no unseemly lord of yours among the immortals, I that am the brother of Father Zeus. And while you are here, you shall be mistress over all that lives and moves, but among the immortals you shall have the greatest renown. Upon them that wrong you shall be vengeance unceasing, upon them that do not solicit your power with sacrifice and pious deeds and every acceptable gift.

So spoke he, and wise Persephone was glad. Joyously and swiftly she arose, but the god himself, stealthily looking around him, gave her a sweet pomegranate seed to eat, and this he did so that she might not abide forever beside revered Demeter of the dark mantle. Then openly did Aidoneus, the prince of all, get ready the steeds beneath the golden chariot, and she climbed up into the golden chariot, and beside her the strong slayer of Argos took the reins and whip in hand and drove forth from the halls, and gladly sped the two horses. Speedily they devoured the long way. Neither sea nor rivers nor grassy glades nor cliffs could stay the rush of the deathless horses; no, far above them they cleft the deep air in their course. Before the fragrant temple he drove them and checked them where Demeter of the fine garland dwelled, who, when she beheld them, rushed forth like a Mainad down a dark mountain woodland.

2f Persephone Reveals That She Has Eaten the Pomegranate Seed (390–469)[5] But Persephone on the other side rejoiced to see her mother dear, and leapt to meet her. But her mother said,

> Child, have you eaten any food in Hades? For if you have not, then with me and your father, the son of Cronos, who has dark clouds for his dwelling, shall you ever dwell honored among all the immortals. But if you have tasted food, you must return again and beneath the hollows of the earth dwell in Hades a third portion of the year. Yet two parts of the year you shall abide with me and the other immortals. When the earth blossoms with all manner of fragrant spring flowers, then from beneath the murky gloom shall you come again, a mighty marvel to gods and to mortal men. <Now tell me how he stole you down to the misty darkness, and> by what wile the strong host of many guests deceived you.

Then fair Persephone answered:

[5] The text of what follows down to the words "... fragrant spring flowers" in Demeter's speech is heavily reconstructed.

> Well, Mother, I shall tell you all the truth without fail. I leapt up for joy when good Hermes, the swift messenger, came from my father Cronides and the other heavenly gods with the message that I was to return out of Erebos, so that you might behold me and cease from your anger and dread wrath against the immortals. Then Hades himself stealthily compelled me to taste a sweet pomegranate seed against my will. And now I will tell you how, through the crafty device of Cronides my father, he ravished me and bore me away beneath the hollows of the earth. All that you ask I will tell you. We were all playing in the lovely meadow, Leucippe and Phaino and Electra and Ianthe and Melite and Iache and Rhodeia and Callirhoe and Melobosis and Tyche and flower-faced Ocyrhoe and Chryseis and Ianeira and Acaste and Admete and Rhodope and Plouto and charming Calypso and Styx and Ourania and beautiful Galaxaure and battle-rousing Pallas and the archer Artemis. There we were playing and plucking beautiful blossoms with our hands: mingled crocuses and iris and hyacinth and roses and lilies, a marvel to behold, and the narcissus, which the wide earth grew forth like a crocus. Gladly was I gathering them when the earth gaped beneath, and from it leapt the mighty prince, the host of many guests, and he bore me very much against my will beneath the earth in his golden chariot, and greatly did I cry. This all is true that I tell you.

So the whole day in oneness of heart they cheered each other with love, and their minds ceased from sorrow, and great gladness did either win from one another. Then came to them Hecate of the fair veil, and often did she kiss the holy daughter of Demeter, and from that day was her queenly comrade and handmaiden. But to them as a messenger did far-seeing Zeus of the loud thunder send fair-haired Rhea to bring dark-mantled Demeter among the gods, with pledge of what honor she might choose among the immortals. He vowed that her daughter for the third part of the revolving year should dwell beneath the murky gloom, but for the other two parts she should abide with her mother and the other gods.

Thus he spoke, and the goddess disobeyed not the commands of Zeus. Swiftly she sped down from the peaks of Olympos and came to fertile Rarion, fertile of old, but now no longer fruitful; for fallow and leafless it lay, and hidden was the white barley grain by the device of fair-ankled Demeter. Nonetheless, with the growing of the spring the land was to teem with tall ears of wheat, and the rich furrows were to be heavy with wheat and the wheat to be bound in sheaves. There first did she land from the unharvested aether, and gladly the goddesses looked on each other, and they rejoiced in heart, and thus first did Rhea of the fair veil speak to Demeter:

> Come here, child; for he calls you, far-seeing Zeus, the loud thunderer, to come among the gods, and has promised you such honors as you desire and has decreed that your child for a third of the rolling year shall dwell beneath the murky gloom, but the other two parts with her mother and the rest of the immortals. He promises that it shall be so and nods his head in agreement. But come, my child, obey, and be not too unrelenting against the son of Cronos, the lord of the dark cloud. And quickly make grow the grain that brings life to men.[6]

[6] The preceding section is heavily reconstructed.

2g Demeter Restores Fertility and Introduces the Mysteries to the Eleusinians (470–495)

So spoke she, and Demeter of the fair garland obeyed. Speedily she sent up the grain from the rich soil, and the wide earth was heavy with leaves and flowers. She hastened and showed the care of her rites to the verdict-pronouncing kings, Triptolemos and Diocles, the charioteer, and mighty Eumolpos and Celeos, the leader of the people. She taught Triptolemos, Polyxeinos, and Diocles her fine mysteries, holy mysteries that none may violate or search into or noise abroad, for the great curse from the gods restrains the voice. Happy is he among mortal men who has beheld these things! And he who is uninitiated and has no lot in them never has an equal lot in death beneath the murky gloom.

Now when the goddess had given instruction in all her rites, they went to Olympos, to the gathering of the other gods. There the goddesses dwell beside Zeus who delights in the thunderbolt; holy and revered are they. Right blessed is he among mortal men whom they dearly love; speedily do they send as a guest to his lofty hall Ploutos, who gives wealth to mortal men. But come you who hold the land of fragrant Eleusis and sea-girt Paros and rocky Antron. Come, Lady Deo, Queen, giver of fine gifts, bringer of the seasons! Come with your daughter, beautiful Persephone, and of your grace grant me fine substance in requital of my song. But I will be mindful of you and of another song.

3 To Apollo

It is very likely that this Hymn *was originally two separate hymns that were later joined together into a single poem, perhaps in 523 BC when Polycrates of Samos decided to celebrate a combined Delian and Pythian festival to the god. We know from an ancient commentator on the poet Pindar that one Cynaithos of Chios (where the* Homeridai, *"Descendants of Homer," were located) composed this poem and recited it in Syracuse at the end of the 6th century BC. The two parts, or rather two hymns, celebrate Apollo's association with his two major centers of worship, Delos and Delphi.*

The first "Delian" part (1–181) details his birth on Delos and the difficulty that his mother Leto had in finding a place to deliver the great god. It is an aetiological myth that explains the origin of Apollo's cult on the island of Delos, which was a small, barren island. The myth explains how Leto wandered in search of a place to give birth to her son because Hera, in anger over her husband's affair with Leto, drove her over the earth until she reached Delos (see Apollodorus B5 and Lucian, Dialogues of the Sea Gods *9). The long geographical list (lines 30–50) emphasizes the suffering Leto was to endure.*

The second "Pythian" part (182–end) documents his arrival in Delphi and the establishment of his cult there. This account is the earliest literary evidence about Apollo's oracular seat there. Again, we have aetiological myths explaining the establishment of his temple (the earliest archaeological evidence for a temple is the second half of the 7th century, the temple that still stands is from the 4th century) and the two names for the city, Pytho ("Rot") and Delphi ("Dolphin").

3a Preface (1–29)

Mindful, ever mindful, will I be of Apollo the Far-darter. Before him, as he goes through the hall of Zeus, the gods tremble and indeed rise up all from their thrones as he approaches and draws his shining bow. But Leto alone abides by Zeus, who delights in the thunderbolt, and she unstrings Apollo's bow and closes his quiver. Then taking with her hands from his mighty shoulders the bow, she hangs it on the pillar beside his father's seat from a peg of gold and leads him to his throne and seats him there, while the father welcomes his dear son and gives him nectar in a golden cup. Then do the other gods welcome him from where they sit, and Lady Leto rejoices, in that she bore the lord of the bow, her mighty son.

Hail! O blessed Leto, mother of glorious children, Prince Apollo and Artemis the Archer! Her in Ortygia, him in rocky Delos did you bear, leaning against the long sweep of the Cynthian Hill, beside a palm tree by the streams of Inopos.

How shall I hymn you, though you are, in truth, not hard to hymn? For, Phoibos, everywhere there are pastures for your song, both on the mainland, nurse of young cows, and among the isles; to you all the cliffs are dear, as are the steep mountain crests and rivers running onward to the sea and beaches sloping to the foam and havens of the deep. Shall I tell how Leto bore you first, a delight of men, leaning against the Cynthian Hill on the rocky island in sea-girt Delos—on either hand the black wave drives landward at the word of the whistling winds—where you arose to be lord over all mortals?

3b Leto Wanders to Delos Looking for a Land to Be Apollo's Birthplace (30–114)

Among the nations that dwell in Crete, and the people of Athens, and isle Aigina, and Euboia, famed for fleets, and Aigai and Eiresiai and Peparethos by the sea-strand, and Thracian Athos, and the tall crests of Pelion and Samothrace, and the shadowy mountains of Ida, and settled Imbros and inhospitable Lemnos, and fine Lesbos, the seat of Macar son of Aiolos, and Scyros and Phocaia, and the mountain wall of Autocane, and Chios, brightest of all islands of the deep, and craggy Mimas, and the steep crests of Corycos, and gleaming Claros, and the high hills of Aisagea and watery Samos, and the tall ridges of Mycale and Miletos, and Cos, a city of Meropian men, and steep Cnidos, and windy Carpathos, and Naxos and Paros and rocky Rhenaia—so far in labor with the Archer god went Leto, seeking if perchance any land would build a house for her son.

But the lands trembled sore and were afraid, and none, not even the richest, dared to welcome Phoibos, not till Lady Leto set foot on Delos and, speaking winged words, implored her:

> Delos, would that you were minded to be the seat of my son, Phoibos Apollo, and to let him build here a rich temple! No other god will touch you, nor will any honor you, for I think you will not be rich in cattle or in sheep, in fruit or grain, nor will you grow plants unnumbered. But were you to possess a temple of Apollo the Far-darter, then would all men bring you hecatombs, gathering to you, and ever will the savor of sacrifice waft up in full measure, and you will feed those who possess you from others' hands, though your soil is poor.

Thus spoke she, and Delos was glad and answered her, saying:

> Leto, daughter most renowned of mighty Coios, gladly would I welcome the birth of the archer prince, for truly about me there goes an evil report among men, and thus would I gain greatest renown. But at this word, Leto, I tremble,

> nor will I hide it from you, for the saying is that Apollo will be mighty of mood and mightily will lord it over mortals and immortals far and wide over the earth, the grain-giver. Therefore, I deeply dread in heart and soul lest, when first he looks upon the sunlight, he disdain my island, for rocky of soil am I, and spurn me with his feet and drive me down in the gulfs of the sea. Then a great sea-wave would wash mightily above my head forever. But he will go to another land, whichever pleases him, to fashion himself a temple and groves of trees. Yet in me would many-footed sea beasts and black seals make their chambers securely, no men dwelling by me. Nay, still, if you have the heart, Goddess, to swear a great oath that here first he will build a beautiful temple, to be an oracular shine of men—thereafter among all men let him raise his shrines, since his renown shall be the widest.

So spoke she, and Leto swore the great oath of the gods:

> Bear witness, Gaia, and wide Ouranos above, and trickling water of Styx—the greatest oath and the most dread among the blessed gods—that truly here shall ever be the fragrant altar and the sanctuary of Apollo, and he will honor you above all.

When she had sworn and made that oath, then Delos was glad in the birth of the archer prince. But Leto for nine days and nine nights continually was pierced with pangs of childbirth beyond all hope. With her were all the goddesses, the noblest, Dione, and Rhea, Ichnaian Themis, and Amphitrite of the moaning sea, and the other deathless ones—save white-armed Hera, for she sat in the halls of cloud-gathering Zeus. Only Eileithyia, the helper in difficult labor, knew not of it, for she sat on the crest of Olympos beneath the golden clouds by the wile of white-armed Hera, who held her afar in jealous grudge, because even then fair-tressed Leto was about to give birth to a strong and noble son.

But the goddesses sent forth Iris from the well-settled isle to bring Eileithyia, promising her a great necklace, strung with golden threads, nine cubits long. Iris they bade to call Eileithyia apart from white-armed Hera, lest even then the words of Hera might turn her from going. But wind-footed swift Iris heard and sped forth, and swiftly she devoured the space between. As soon as she came to steep Olympos, the dwelling of the gods, she called forth Eileithyia from hall to door and spoke winged words, all that the goddesses of Olympian mansions had bidden her. Thereby she won the heart in Eileithyia's breast, and forth they went like timid wild doves in their going.

3c Apollo's Birth and His Cult on Delos (115–181)

As soon as Eileithyia, the helper in difficult labor, set foot in Delos, labor took hold on Leto, and mad was she to give birth. Around a palm tree she cast her arms and set her knees on the soft meadow, while earth beneath smiled, and forth leapt the babe to light, and all the goddesses raised a cry. Then, great Phoibos, the goddesses washed you in fair water, holy and pure, and wound you in a white swaddling cloth, delicate, new woven, with a golden band around you. Nor did his mother suckle Apollo the golden-sworded, but Themis with immortal hands first touched his lips with nectar and sweet ambrosia, while Leto rejoiced, in that she had given birth to a strong son, the bearer of the bow.

Then Phoibos, as soon as you tasted the immortal food, the golden band was not proof against your squirming, nor could the knots hold you, but all their ends were loosened. Straightway among the goddesses spoke Phoibos Apollo: "Mine be the dear lyre and bended bow, and I will utter to men the unerring counsel of Zeus."

So speaking, he began to make his way over the wide ways of earth, Phoibos of the locks unshorn, Phoibos the Far-darter. And then all the goddesses were amazed, and all Delos blossomed with gold, as when a hilltop is heavy with woodland flowers, beholding the child of Zeus and Leto, and was glad because the god had chosen her to set his home, beyond mainland and isles, and loved her most at heart.

But you, O Prince of the silver bow, far-darting Apollo, now passed over rocky Cynthos, now wandered among islands and men. Many are your shrines and groves, and dear are all the headlands, and high peaks of lofty hills, and rivers flowing onward to the sea. But with Delos, Phoibos, you are most delighted at heart, where the long-robed Ionians gather in your honor with their children and wives. Mindful of you they delight you with boxing and dances and music. Whoever encountered them at the gathering of the Ionians would say that they are exempt from old age and death, beholding them so gracious, and would be glad at heart, looking on the men and fair-girdled women, their swift ships and great wealth. Moreover, there is this great marvel of renown imperishable, the Delian maidens, servants of the Far-darter. They, when first they have hymned Apollo and next Leto and Artemis the archer, then sing in memory of the men and women of old time, enchanting the tribes of mortals. And they know how to mimic the voices and chattering of all men, so that each would say he himself were singing, so well woven is their fair chant.

But now come, be gracious, Apollo, be gracious, Artemis! And all you maidens, farewell, but remember me even in time to come, when any of earthly men, yea, any stranger who has seen much and endured much, comes here and asks: "Maidens, who is the sweetest to you of singers here, and in whose song are you most glad?"

Then do you all with one voice make answer: "A blind man is he, and he dwells in rocky Chios; his songs will ever have the mastery for all time to come."

But I shall bear my renown of you as far as I wander over earth to the fairest cities of men, and they will believe my report, for my word is true. But, for me, never shall I cease singing of Apollo of the silver bow, the Far-darter, whom fair-tressed Leto bore.

O Prince, Lycia is yours, as is pleasant Maionia and Miletos, a pleasant city by the sea, and you are also the mighty lord of sea-washed Delos.

3d Apollo on Olympos (182–206)

The son of glorious Leto made his way harping on his hollow harp to rocky Pytho, clad in his divine raiment that is fragrant, and beneath the golden plectrum pleasantly sounds his lyre. Thence from earth to Olympos, fleet as thought, he goes to the house of Zeus, into the assembly of the other gods, and soon the immortals turn their thoughts to lyre and song. And all the Muses, responding in unison with sweet voice, sing of the imperishable gifts of the gods and the sufferings of men, all that they endure from the hands of the undying gods, lives witless and helpless, men unable to find remedy for death or shield against old age. Then the fair-tressed Charites, and merry Horai, and Harmonia and Hebe, and Aphrodite daughter of Zeus dance holding hands, while among them sings one neither unlovely nor of body contemptible, but divinely tall and fair, Artemis the archer, nurtured with Apollo. Among them sport Ares and the keen-eyed slayer of Argos, while Phoibos Apollo steps with high and fine strides, playing the lyre, and the light issues around him from twinkling feet and fair-woven raiment. But they are glad, seeing him so high of heart, Leto of the golden tresses and Zeus the counselor, beholding their dear son as he takes his pastime among the deathless gods.

3e Apollo's Search for a Place to Build His Temple Begins (207–245)

How shall I hymn you, though you are, in truth, not hard to hymn? Shall I sing of you in love and dalliance, how you went forth to woo the Azanian maiden,[7] competing with Ischys, peer of gods, Elation's son of the fine steeds, or with Phorbas son of Triopas, or Ereutheus? Or how with Leucippos and Leucippos' wife, you on foot, he in the chariot <*unintelligible Greek*>? Or how first, seeking a place of oracle for men, you came down to earth, far-darting Apollo?[8]

On Pieria first did you descend from Olympos and pass by sandy Lectos and the Ainianes and the Perrhaibians, and speedily you came to Iolcos and alighted on Cenaion in Euboia, renowned for ships. On the Lelantian plain you stood, but it did not please you to establish there a temple and a grove. Then you crossed the Euripos, far-darting Apollo, and went up the holy Green Mountain and came speedily to Mycalessos and grassy Teumessos and then to the place of wooded Thebe, for as yet no mortals dwelled in holy Thebe, and there were not yet paths nor ways along Thebe's wheat-bearing plain, but all was wild wood.

Thence journeying onward, Apollo, you came to Onchestos, the bright grove of Poseidon. There the new-broken colt takes breath again, weary from its labor of dragging the fine chariot. And the charioteer, though he is skilled, leaps down to earth and goes on foot, while the horses for a while rattle along the empty car without their driver. But if the car is broken in the grove of trees, their masters tend to the horses there but tilt the car and let it lie. Such is the rite from of old, and they pray to the prince, while the chariot is the god's portion to keep.[9] Going forward, far-darting Apollo, you reached Cephisos of the fair streams, which from Lilaia pours down its beautiful waters. This you crossed, Far-darter, and passed Ocalea, rich in grain, and came to grassy Haliartos. Then did you come to Telphousa, and to you the land seemed an exceedingly good one in which to establish a temple and a grove.

3f Telphousa Tricks Apollo (246–276)

Beside Telphousa, you stood and spoke to her:

> Telphousa, here I think to establish a very fair temple, an oracle for men, who, ever seeking for the word of truth, will bring to me here perfect hecatombs, even those that dwell in the rich Peloponnese, and all those on the mainland and sea-girt islands. To them all shall I speak a decree unerring, rendering oracles within my rich temple.

[7] Coronis.

[8] The preceding paragraph presents many difficulties in text and content.

[9] The ritual dedication of these chariots to Poseidon is otherwise unknown, but this god is often connected with horses.

So spoke Phoibos, and he thoroughly marked out the foundations, very long and wide. But at the sight the heart of Telphousa grew wroth, and she spoke her word:

> Phoibos, far-darting Prince, a word shall I set in your heart. Here you think to establish a fine temple, to be a place of oracle for men, who will ever bring to you here perfect hecatombs—but I will tell you this, and do you lay it up in your heart. The never-ending din of swift steeds will be a weariness to you, as will the watering of mules from my sacred springs. There men will choose to regard the well-wrought chariots and the stamping of the swift-footed steeds rather than your great temple and much wealth therein. But if you—who are greater and better than I, O Prince, and your strength is most mighty—if you will listen to me, in Crisa build your temple beneath a glade of Parnassos. There neither will fine chariots ring, nor will you be vexed with stamping of swift steeds about your well-built altar, but nonetheless shall the renowned tribes of men bring their gifts to Iepaieon,[10] and delighted you shall gather the sacrifices of them who dwell around.

At that she won over the heart of the Far-darter, so that Telphousa herself would be honored in that land and not the Far-darter.

3g Apollo Moves on to the Future Site of Delphi (277–374)

Then forward did you go, far-darting Apollo, and come to the city of the overweening Phlegyai, who, reckless of Zeus, dwelled there in a fine glade by the Cephisian lake. Then fleetly you sped to the ridge of the hills and came to Crisa beneath snowy Parnassos, to a knoll that faced westward. Above it hangs a cliff, and a hollow dell runs under, rough with wood, and right there Prince Phoibos Apollo deemed it well to build a fine temple and spoke, saying:

> Here I think to establish a very fair temple, to be an oracle to men, who will always bring to me here fine hecatombs, both those that dwell in the rich Peloponnese and those on the mainland and sea-girt isles, seeking here the word of truth. To them all shall I speak a decree unerring, rendering oracles within my rich temple.

So speaking, Phoibos Apollo marked out the foundations right long and wide, and on these Trophonios and Agamedes laid the threshold of stone, the sons of Erginos, dear to the deathless gods. But around the foundations, all the countless tribes of men built a temple with wrought stones to be famous forever in song.

Close by is a fair-flowing spring, and there with an arrow from his strong bow did the prince, the son of Zeus, slay the dragoness, mighty and huge, a wild monster, who was wont to wreak many woes on earthly men, on them and their straight-stepping flocks, so dread a bane was she.

It was this dragoness that took from golden-throned Hera and reared the dread Typhaon, not to be dealt with, a bane to mortals. Hera bore him, once upon a time, in wrath with father Zeus at the time when Cronides brought forth from his head renowned Athena. Straightway lady Hera was angered and spoke among the assembled gods:

[10] The word refers to a ritual song sung by worshipers of Apollo, and here is used as a title for the god.

> Listen to me, you gods and goddesses all, how cloud-gathering Zeus is first to begin the dishonoring of me, though he made me his wife in honor. And now, apart from me, he has brought forth gray-eyed Athena who excels among all the blessed immortals. But my son Hephaistos was feeble from birth among all the gods, lame and withered of foot, whom I myself bore. Him I myself lifted in my hands and cast into the wide sea. But the daughter of Nereus, Thetis of the silver feet, received him and nurtured him among her sisters. Would that she had done some other grace to the blessed immortals!
>
> You evil one of many wiles, what other wile are you devising? How did you have the heart now alone to bear gray-eyed Athena? Could I not have borne her? She still would have been called yours among the immortals who hold the wide heaven. Take heed now that I do not devise for you some evil to come. Yes, now I shall use arts whereby a child of mine shall be born, excelling among the immortal gods, without dishonoring your sacred bed or mine, for in truth to your bed I will not come, but far from you will I nurse my grudge against the immortal gods.

So spoke she and withdrew from the gods with angered heart. Immediately she made her prayer, the ox-eyed lady Hera, striking the earth with her palms, and spoke her word:

> Listen to me now, Gaia, and wide Ouranos above, and you gods called Titans, dwelling beneath earth in great Tartaros, you from whom spring gods and men! Listen to me now, all of you, and give me a child apart from Zeus, yet nothing inferior to him in might, no, stronger than he, as much as far-seeing Zeus is mightier than Cronos!

So spoke she and struck the ground with her firm hand. Then Gaia, the nurse of life, was stirred, and Hera, beholding it, was glad at heart, for she deemed that her prayer would be accomplished. From that hour for a full year she never came to the bed of wise Zeus, nor to her adorned throne, where she used to sit, planning deep counsel. But dwelling in her prayer-filled temples, she took joy in her sacrifices, the ox-eyed lady Hera.

Now when her months and days were fulfilled, the year revolving and the seasons in their course coming round, she bore a birth like neither gods nor mortals, the dread Typhaon, not to be dealt with, a bane of gods. Him now she took, the ox-eyed lady Hera, and carried and gave one evil to another, and the dragoness received him.

The dragoness always wrought many wrongs among the renowned tribes of men. Whoever met the dragoness, on him would she bring the day of destiny, until the Prince, far-darting Apollo, loosed at her the destroying shaft. Then, writhing in strong anguish and mightily heaving she lay, rolling about the land. Dread and dire was the din as she writhed this way and that through the wood and gave up the ghost, breathing out blood, and Phoibos spoke his curse:

> Rot[11] there upon the fruitful earth. No longer shall you, at least, live to be the evil bane of mortals who eat the fruit of the fertile soil and who shall bring perfect hecatombs here. Surely from you neither shall Typhoios nor accursed

[11] The Greek for "rot" is *pythe*, explaining one name of the place Pytho.

> Chimaira shield you from grisly death, but here shall black earth and bright Hyperion make you rot.

So spoke he in curse, and darkness veiled her eyes, and there the sacred strength of the sun did waste her quite away. From this the place is now named Pytho, and men call the Prince "Pythian" for that deed, for even there the might of the swift sun made the monster rot away.

3h Apollo Punishes Telphousa and Acquires His Priests (375–437)

Then Phoibos Apollo was aware in his heart that the fair-flowing spring Telphousa had beguiled him, and in wrath he went to her. He swiftly came, and standing close by her spoke his word:

> Telphousa, you were not destined to beguile my mind nor keep the pleasant lands and pour forth your fair waters. Nay, here shall my honor also dwell, not yours alone.

So spoke he and overturned the peak in a shower of stones and hid her streams, the prince, far-darting Apollo. And he made an altar in a grove of trees close by the fair-flowing spring, where all men name him in prayer as Telphousios because he shamed the streams of sacred Telphousa. Then Phoibos Apollo considered in his heart what men he should bring in to be his ministers and serve him in rocky Pytho. While he was pondering on this, he beheld a swift ship on the wine-dark sea, and aboard her many men and good, Cretans from Minoan Cnossos who make sacrifice to the god and speak the pronouncements of Phoibos Apollo of the golden sword, whatever word of truth he utters from the laurel in the dells of Parnassos. For barter and wealth they were sailing in the black ship to sandy Pylos and the Pylian men. Soon Phoibos Apollo set forth to meet them, and at sea he leapt upon the swift ship in the guise of a dolphin, and there he lay, a portent great and terrible.

Of the crew, whosoever sought in heart to <*unintelligible Greek*>, on all sides he would shake them off and shiver the timbers of the ship. So they all sat silent and in fear aboard the ship. They neither loosed the sheets nor the sail of the black-prowed ship, no, just as they had first set the sails, so they voyaged onward, the strong south wind speeding on the vessel from behind. First, they rounded Cape Malea and passed the Laconian land and came to a citadel by the sea, Tainaros, the land sacred to Helios, who is the joy of mortals, where the deep-fleeced flocks of Prince Helios always feed and he has his glad domain. There the crew thought to stay the ship, land, and consider the marvel, and see whether that strange thing would abide on the deck of the hollow ship or leap again into the swell of the fishes' home. But the well-wrought ship did not obey the rudder but kept ever on its way beyond the rich Peloponnese, Prince Apollo lightly guiding it by the gale.

So accomplishing its course, it came to Arene, and pleasant Argyphea, and Thryon, the ford of Alpheios, and well-built Aipy and sandy Pylos and the Pylian men, and it ran by Crounoi, and Chalcis, and Dyme, and holy Elis, where the Epeians hold sway. Then rejoicing in the breeze of Zeus, it was making for Pheia when to them out of the clouds appeared the steep ridge of Ithaca and Doulichion and Same and wooded Zacynthos. Soon when it had passed beyond all the Peloponnese, there straightway off Crisa appeared the wide sound that bounds the rich Peloponnese. Then the west wind came on, clear and strong, by the counsel of Zeus, blowing hard out of heaven, so that the running ship might most swiftly accomplish its course over the salt water of the sea. Backward then they sailed toward the dawn and the sun, and the prince was their guide, Apollo, the son of Zeus.

3i The Ship of Cretans Reaches Crisa (438–546)

Then came they to sunny Crisa, the land of vines, into the haven, and the seafaring ship beached itself on the sand. Then from the ship leapt the prince, far-darting Apollo, like a star at high noon, and many were the sparks that flew from him, and the splendor flashed to the heavens. Into his inmost holy place he went through the precious tripods, and in the midst he kindled a flame by showering forth his shafts, and the splendor filled all Crisa, and the wives of the Crisaians and their fair-girdled daughters raised a wail at the onrush of Phoibos, for great fear fell upon all. Thence again to the ship he set forth and flew, fleet as a thought, in shape of a man lusty and strong, in his first youth, his locks swathing his wide shoulders. Presently he spoke to the sailors winged words:

> Strangers, who are you? Where did you set sail over the wet ways? Is it after merchandise, or do you wander at adventure, over the sea, as pirates do, who roam staking their own lives and bringing woe to men of strange speech? Why do you sit thus afraid, not faring forth on the land, nor slackening the gear of your black ship? Surely this is the usual practice of enterprising seafarers when they come from the deep to the land in their black ship, done with labor, and soon a longing for sweet food seizes their hearts.

So spoke he and put courage in their breasts, and the leader of the Cretans answered him, saying:

> Stranger, behold, you are in no way like unto mortal men in shape or stature, but are a peer of the immortals, wherefore all hail, and may grace and all good things be yours at the hands of the gods. Tell me then truly so that I may indeed know: What people is this, what land, what mortals dwell here? Surely with our thoughts set on another goal we sailed the great sea to Pylos from Crete, where we claim our lineage hails; but now it is here that we have come, against our wills, with our ship—another path and other ways—we, longing to return, but some god has led us all unwilling to this place.

Then far-darting Apollo answered them:

> Strangers, who formerly dwelled around wooded Cnossos, never again shall you return, each to his own pleasant city, his house, and wife, but here shall you hold my rich temple, honored by multitudes of men. I am the son of Zeus and proclaim myself Apollo, and here have I brought you over the great gulf of the sea with no evil intent. Nay, here shall you possess my rich temple, held high in honor among all men, and you shall know the counsels of the immortals, by whose will you shall ever be held in renown. But now come and instantly obey my word. First lower the sails and loose the sheets and then beach the black ship on the land, taking forth the wares and gear of the trim ship, and build an altar on the shore of the sea. Kindle fire on it and sprinkle above in sacrifice the white barley-flour, and thereafter pray standing around the altar. And because I first, in the misty sea, sprang aboard the swift ship in the guise of a dolphin,

> therefore pray to me as Apollo Delphinios, while my altar shall ever be the Delphian and seen from afar. Then take supper beside the swift black ship and pour libations to the blessed gods who hold Olympos. But when you have dismissed the desire of sweet food, then with me come, singing the *Iepaieon*, till you reach that place where you shall possess the rich temple.

So spoke he, and they heard and obeyed eagerly. First they lowered the sails, loosing the sheets, and, lowering the mast by the forestays, they laid it in the maststead, and themselves went forth on the shore of the sea. Then forth from the sea to the mainland they dragged the fleet ship high up on the sands, laying long sleepers under it, and they built an altar on the sea-strand and lit a fire on it, scattering above white barley-flour in sacrifice, and standing around the altar they prayed as the god commanded. Soon they took supper beside the fleet black ship and poured forth libations to the blessed gods who hold Olympos. But when they had dismissed the desire of meat and drink, they set forth on their way, and Prince Apollo guided them, lyre in hand, and sweetly he harped, treading with high and fine strides. Dancing in his train the Cretans followed him to Pytho, and they were chanting *Iepaieon*, the paeans of the Cretans in whose breasts the Muse has put honey-sweet song. All unwearied they strode to the hill and swiftly came to Parnassos and a charming land, where he was to dwell, honored by many men.

Apollo guided them and showed his holy shrine and rich temple, and the spirit was moved in their breasts, and the captain of the Cretans spoke and questioned the god, saying:

> Prince, since you have led us far from friends and our own country—for so it pleases you—how now shall we live, we pray you tell us. This fair land does not bear harvests nor is it rich in meadows, from which we might live well and minister to men.

Then, smiling, Apollo, the son of Zeus, spoke to them:

> Foolish ones, enduring hearts who desire cares and sore toil and all straits! A light word will I speak to you; you consider it. Let each one of you, knife in right hand, be always slaughtering sheep that in abundance shall ever be yours, all the flocks that the renowned tribes of men bring to me here. Yours it is to guard my temple and receive the tribes of men that gather here, doing, above all, as my will enjoins < . . . >. But if any foolish word is spoken or foolish deed done or violence after the manner of mortal men, then shall others be your masters and hold you in servitude forever. I have spoken all; you keep it in your heart.

So, fare you well, son of Zeus and Leto, but I shall remember both you and another song.

4 To Hermes

The Hymn to Hermes *is remarkable because of its amusing and lighthearted tone, which is perfectly suited to the clever, adventurous nature of the god. Immediately after being born, Hermes escapes from his crib, and the poet announces his activities on the very first day of his life: "Born in the dawn, by midday he played the lyre and in the evening stole the cattle of Apollo the Far-darter, on that fourth day of the month when Lady Maia bore him." During his first day, Hermes invents the lyre, sandals, firesticks, a form of sacrifice, and reed pipes.*

Hermes' precocity may be compared to the other god who figures prominently in the Hymn, *Apollo, who (in the third* Hymn*) immediately upon birth announces "Mine be the dear lyre and bended bow, and I will utter to men the unerring counsel of Zeus." These two gods, both offspring of Zeus, have a special relationship in myth, particularly in Olympia, where they share an altar (see Herodorus 34). That Hermes divides the sacrifice into twelve portions also may reflect practice at Olympia. It seems probable, then, that this* Hymn *was recited in Olympia and, based upon linguistic peculiarities, sometime in the late 6th or early 5th century BC.*

4a Hermes' Birth (1–19)

Of Hermes sing, O Muse, the son of Zeus and Maia, lord of Cyllene and Arcadia rich in sheep, the fortune-bearing herald of the gods, him whom Maia bore, the fair-tressed Nymph that lay in the arms of Zeus. A modest Nymph was she, shunning the assembly of the blessed gods, dwelling within a shadowy cave. There Cronion was wont to embrace the fair-tressed Nymph in the deep of night, when sweet sleep held white-armed Hera, the immortal gods knowing it not, nor mortal men.

But when the mind of great Zeus was fulfilled, and over her the tenth moon stood in the sky, the babe was born to light, and remarkable deeds occurred: she bore a child of many a wile and cunning counsel, a robber, a driver of cattle, a bringer of dreams, a watcher of the night, a thief of the gates, who soon would show forth deeds renowned among the deathless gods. Born in the dawn, by midday he played the lyre and in the evening stole the cattle of Apollo the Far-darter, on that fourth day of the month when Lady Maia bore him.

4b Hermes Invents the Lyre (20–67)

When he leapt from the immortal legs of his mother, he did not long stay in the sacred cradle but sped forth to seek the cattle of Apollo, crossing the threshold of the high-roofed cave. There he found a tortoise and won endless delight, for it was Hermes who first made of the tortoise a singer. The creature met him at the outer door as she fed on the rich grass in front of the dwelling, waddling along, at which sight the luck-bringing son of Zeus laughed and spoke straightway, saying:

> Look, a lucky omen for me! I do not regard it lightly! Hail, companion of the feast who keeps time for the dance, you are welcome! Where did you get your fine garment, a speckled shell, you, a mountain-dwelling tortoise? I am going to carry you within, and you will be a boon to me, not to be scorned by me. No, you will first serve my turn. "Best it is to abide at home, since danger is abroad."[12] Living you will be a spell against ill witchery, and dead a very sweet music maker.

So spoke he, and raising in both hands the tortoise, he went back within the dwelling bearing the glad treasure. Then he probed with a gouge of gray iron and scooped out

[12] A quotation of Hesiod, *Works and Days* 365.

the marrow of the hill tortoise. And as a swift thought wings through the breast of one that crowding cares are haunting, or as bright glances fly from the eyes, so swiftly renowned Hermes devised both deed and word. He cut to measure stalks of reed and fixed them in through holes bored in the stony shell of the tortoise, and cunningly stretched round it the hide of an ox and put in the horns of the lyre, and to both he fitted the bridge and stretched seven harmonious strings of sheep-gut.

Then he took his treasure when he had fashioned it and touched the strings in turn with the plectrum, and wondrously it sounded under his hand, and the god sang sweetly to the notes, improvising his chant as he played like lads exchanging taunts at festivals. Of Zeus Cronides and fair-sandaled Maia he sang, how they had lived in loving dalliance, and he spun out the tale of his begetting and sang of the handmaidens and the fine halls of the Nymph and the tripods in the house and the store of cauldrons. So then he sang, but dreamed of other deeds. He took the hollow lyre and laid it in the sacred cradle; then, in longing for flesh of cows he sped from the fragrant hall to a place of outlook with such a design in his heart as robbing men pursue in the dark of night.

4c Hermes Steals Apollo's Cows (68–104)

Helios had sunk down beneath earth toward Oceanos with his horses and chariot when Hermes came running to the shadowy hills of Pieria, where the deathless cows of the blessed gods ever had their haunt. There they fed on the fair unshorn meadows. From their number did the keen-sighted Slayer of Argos, the son of Maia, cut off fifty loud-lowing cows and drive them here and there over the sandy land, reversing their tracks, and mindful of his cunning, confused the hoof-marks, the front behind, the hind in front, and himself went backward. Straightway he wove sandals on the sea-sand (things undreamed he wrought, works wonderful, unspeakable), mingling myrtle twigs and tamarisk; then binding together a bundle of the fresh young wood, he shrewdly fastened it for light sandals beneath his feet, leaves and all—brushwood that the renowned Slayer of Argos had plucked on his way from Pieria, inventing as he hastened on a long journey.

Then an old man who was working a fruitful vineyard marked the god racing down to the plain through grassy Onchestos, and the son of renowned Maia spoke to him first:

> Old man bowing your shoulders over your hoeing, truly you will have wine enough when all these vines are bearing fruit <provided that you>[13] see but do not see and hear but do not hear. Keep quiet, so long as nothing of yours is harmed.

With that he drove on the sturdy heads of cattle. And over many a shadowy hill and through echoing hollows and flowering plains drove renowned Hermes. Then his darkling ally, sacred Night, was mostly passed, and morning was swiftly approaching when men can work, and sacred Selene, the daughter of Megamedes' son Pallas, climbed to a new place of outlook, and then the strong son of Zeus drove the

[13] A line is missing. The supplement here gives only the general sense.

broad-browed cows of Phoibos Apollo to the river Alpheios. Unwearied they came to the high-roofed stall and the watering places in front of the fair meadow.

4d Hermes Invents Sacrifice (105–183)

There, when he had foddered the deep-voiced cows, he herded them huddled together into the byre, munching lotus and dewy marsh marigold. Next, he brought much wood and set himself to the craft of kindling fire. Taking a fine shoot of laurel, he peeled it with the knife < . . . > fitting it to his hand, and the hot vapor of smoke arose. For it was Hermes first who gave fire and the firesticks. Then he took much dry firewood, great plenty, and piled it in the trench, and flame began to glow, sending far the breath of burning fire. And when the force of renowned Hephaistos kept the fire aflame, then downward he dragged, so mighty his strength, two bellowing cows of twisted horn. Close up to the fire he dragged them and cast them both snorting upon their backs to the ground. Then bending over them he turned them upward and cut their throats. He performed task upon task: he sliced off the fat meat, pierced it with spits of wood and broiled it—flesh and chine, the joint of honor, and blood in the bowels all together. Then he laid all there in its place. The hides he stretched out on a broken rock, as even now they remain, enduring long, long after that ancient day. Soon glad Hermes dragged the fat portions onto a smooth ledge and cut twelve portions sorted out by lot, and he put in each the perfect amount.

Then a longing for the rite of the sacrifice of flesh came on renowned Hermes, for the sweet savor inflamed him, immortal as he was, but not even so did his stout heart allow the flesh to slip down his sacred throat, but rather he placed both fat and flesh in the high-roofed stall and swiftly raised it aloft, a trophy of his robbing. Then, gathering dry firewood, he burned heads and feet entire within the vapor of flame. Soon, when the god had duly finished all, he cast his sandals into the deep swirling pool of Alpheios, quenched the embers, and spent the rest of the night spreading smooth the black dust, Selene lighting him with her lovely light. Back to the crests of Cyllene came the god at dawn, and on that long way neither a blessed god nor mortal man encountered him, and no dog barked. Then Hermes son of Zeus bearer of boon, bowed his head and entered the hall through the hole of the bolt, like mist on the breath of autumn. Then, standing erect, he sped to the rich inmost chamber of the cave, lightly treading noiseless on the floor. Quickly to his cradle came glorious Hermes and wrapped the swaddling bands about his shoulders, like a witless babe, playing with the blanket about his knees. So lay he, guarding his dear lyre at his left hand. But the god did not deceive his goddess mother. She spoke, saying:

> Why, cunning one, and from where have you been in the night, clad in shamelessness? Soon, I think, you will go forth at the hands of Leto's son with bonds about your sides that may not be broken, or else you will elude him as he carries you through the glens. Be gone, wretch! Your father begat you as a trouble to deathless gods and mortal men.

But Hermes answered her with words of guile:

> Mother mine, why would you scare me so, as though I were a silly child with little craft in his heart, a trembling babe who dreads his mother's chidings? No, but I will try the wiliest craft to feed you and me forever. We two are not to suffer remaining here, to be alone of all the deathless gods to be unapproached

with sacrifice and prayer, as you command. It is better to spend time with immortals day in and day out, richly, nobly, well fed, than to be homekeepers in a dismal cave. And for honor, I too will have my dues of sacrifice, just like Apollo. Even if my father does not give it to me, I will endeavor—for I am capable—to be a captain of robbers. And if the son of renowned Leto tracks me down, I think some worse thing will befall him. For to Pytho I will go to break into his great house, from where I will steal fine tripods and cauldrons enough and gold and gleaming iron and much clothing. If you care to, you yourself will see it.

So they conversed with one another, the son of Zeus of the aegis, and Lady Maia.

4e Apollo Sets Out in Search of His Cattle (184–234)

Then early-born Eos was arising from the deep stream of Oceanos, bearing light to mortals, when Apollo came to Onchestos in his journeying, the gracious grove, a holy place of the loud girdler of the earth. There he found a slow-moving old man hoeing his vineyard by the side of the road. The son of renowned Leto spoke to him first:

Old man, pruner of grassy Onchestos, I have come here seeking cattle from Pieria, all the crook-horned cows out of my herd. My black bull was wont to graze apart from the rest, and my four bright-eyed hounds followed, four of them, wise as men and all of one mind. These were left, the hounds and the bull, a marvel, but the cows wandered away from their soft meadow and sweet pasture at the going down of the sun. Tell me, old man of ancient days, if you have seen any man faring after these cattle.

Then the old man spoke to him and answered:

My friend, hard it were to tell all that a man may see, for many wayfarers go by, some full of ill intent, and some of good, and it is difficult to be certain regarding each. Nevertheless, the whole day long till sunset I was digging about my vineyard plot, and I thought I marked—but I do not know for sure—a child that went after the horned cows. Right young he was and held a staff, and kept going from side to side, and backward he drove the cows, their heads facing him.

So the old man spoke, and Apollo heard and went faster on his path. Then he marked a bird long of wing, and soon he knew that the thief had been the son of Zeus Cronion. Prince Apollo, the son of Zeus, sped swiftly to fine Pylos, seeking the shambling cows, while his broad shoulders were swathed in purple cloud. Then the Far-darter marked the tracks and spoke:

Truly, my eyes behold a great marvel! These are the tracks of high-horned cows, but all are turned back to the meadow of asphodel. But these are not the footsteps of a man, nay, nor of a woman nor of gray wolves nor bears nor lions nor, I think, of a shaggy-maned Centaur, whoever makes such mighty strides with fleet feet. Uncanny are the tracks on this side of the path, still more uncanny are those on that.

So speaking, the Prince sped on, Apollo, the son of Zeus. He came to the Cyllenian hill, which is clad in forests, to the deep shadow of the hollow rock where the deathless Nymph brought forth the child of Zeus Cronion. A sweet fragrance was spread about the fine hill, and many tall sheep were grazing the grass. Thence he went fleetly over the stone threshold into the dusky cave, Apollo the Far-darter.

4f Apollo Confronts Hermes (235–312)

Now when the son of Zeus and Maia beheld Apollo the Far-darter thus in wrath for his cows, he sank down within his fragrant swaddling bands. Covered as piled embers of burnt tree roots are covered by thick ashes, so Hermes curled himself up when he saw the Far-darter and squeezed himself, feet, head, and hands, into small space, as a freshly bathed babe summoning sweet sleep, though really wide awake, and his tortoiseshell he kept beneath his armpit. But the son of Zeus and Leto marked them well, the lovely mountain Nymph and her dear son, a little babe, all wrapped in cunning wiles. Gazing round all the chamber of the vast dwelling, Apollo opened three closets with the shining key; they were full of nectar and glad ambrosia, and much gold and silver lay within, and much raiment of the Nymph, purple and glittering, such as are within the dwellings of the mighty gods. Soon, when he had searched out the chambers of the great hall, the son of Leto spoke to renowned Hermes:

> Child, you who are lying in the cradle, tell me straightway of my cows, or speedily between us two there will be unseemly strife. For I will seize you and cast you into murky Tartaros, into the darkness of doom where none is of avail. Nor shall your father or mother redeem you to the light. No, you will perish and go beneath the earth to be leader of the children.

Then Hermes answered with words of craft:

> Apollo, what ungentle word have you spoken? And is it your cattle of the homestead that you come here to seek? I did not see them or ask of them or give ear to any word of them. Of them I can tell no tidings nor win reward for telling. Not like a rustler of cattle, a stalwart man, am I. I have nothing to do with this. But other cares have I: sleep and mother's milk and about my shoulders swaddling bands and warmed baths. Let none know whence this feud arose! And a truly great marvel among the immortals it would be that a newborn child should cross the threshold after cows of the homestead; a silly story of yours. Yesterday I was born, my feet are tender, and rough is the earth below. But if you want, I will swear the great oath by my father's head that neither I myself am to blame, nor have I seen any other thief of your cows—whatever these cows are, for this is the first I've heard of them.

So spoke he with twinkling eyes and twisted brows, glancing here and there, with long-drawn whistling, hearing Apollo's word as a vain thing. Then, lightly laughing, Apollo the Far-darter spoke:

> Oh, you rogue! You crafty one! Truly I think that many a time you will break into well-built homes and by night leave many a man sitting on the floor, as you plunder his house in silence, such is your speech today! And you will vex many herdsmen of the steadings, when in lust for flesh you come on the herds and thick-fleeced sheep. No, come, lest you sleep the last and longest slumber, come forth from your cradle, you companion of black night! For surely this honor hereafter you will have among the immortals, to be called forever the captain of robbers.

So spoke Phoibos Apollo, and he lifted the child, but just then the strong slayer of Argos conceived a plan, and in the hands of the god let forth an omen, an evil belly-tenant, with tidings of worse,[14] and a speedy sneeze after that. Apollo heard and dropped renowned Hermes on the ground and then sat down before him, eager as he was to be gone, chiding Hermes, and thus he spoke:

> Do not worry, swaddling one, child of Zeus and Maia. By these omens of yours I will soon find the sturdy cows, and you will lead the way.

So spoke he, but Cyllenian Hermes swiftly arose and quickly went, pulling about his ears his swaddling bands that were his shoulder wrapping. Then he spoke:

> Where are you carrying me, Far-darter, most vehement of gods? Is it for wrath about your cows that you provoke me in this way? Would that the race of cows might perish, for I have not stolen your cattle, nor have I seen another steal them—whatever these cows are, for this is the first I've heard of them. But let our suit be judged before Zeus Cronion.

4g The Quarrel Between Hermes and Apollo Is Judged By Zeus (313–396)
Now lone Hermes and the splendid son of Leto were point by point disputing their case. Apollo with sure knowledge was righteously seeking to convict renowned Hermes for the sake of his cattle, but the Cyllenian sought to beguile with craft and cunning words the god of the silver bow. But when the wily one found one as wily, then speedily he strode forward through the sand in front, while behind came the son of Zeus and Leto. Swiftly they came to the crests of fragrant Olympos, to father Cronion they came, these fine sons of Zeus, for the balances of doom were set for them there. Quiet was snowy Olympos, but they who know not decay or death were gathering after gold-throned Eos. Then Hermes and Apollo of the silver bow stood before the knees of Zeus the thunderer, who inquired of his glorious son, saying:

> Phoibos, from where do you bring such mighty spoil, a newborn babe with the look of a herald? A mighty matter, this, to come before the gathering of the gods!

Then answered him the prince, Apollo the Far-darter:

> Father, soon you will hear no empty tale. Do you tease me as though I were the only lover of booty? I have found this boy, an accomplished robber, in the hills of Cyllene, a long way to wander, so fine a knave as I know not among gods or men of all robbers on earth. He stole my cattle from the meadows and went driving them at evening along the loud seashores straight to Pylos. Wondrous were the tracks, a thing to marvel on, work of a glorious god. For the black dust showed the tracks of the cows making backward to the meadow of asphodel. But this intractable child moved neither on hands nor feet through the sandy land, but he had this other strange craft, to tread the paths as if with oaken shoots instead of feet. While he drove the cows through a land of sand, all the tracks in the dust were very easy to see, but when he had crossed the great tract of sand, straightway on hard ground his traces and those of the cows were hard to

[14] Hermes farted.

> see. But a mortal man beheld him, driving the broad-browed cattle straight to Pylos. Now, when he had stalled the cows in quiet and confused his tracks on either side of the road, he lay dark as night in his cradle, in the dusk of a shadowy cave. The keenest eagle could not have spied him, and much he rubbed his eyes with crafty purpose and bluntly spoke his word: "I saw nothing, I heard nothing, nor learned it from another; I could give neither news nor win reward for telling."

With that Phoibos Apollo sat down, but Hermes told another tale among the immortals, addressing Cronion, the master of all gods:

> Father Zeus, I will tell you the real truth. For I am truthful and do not know the way of falsehood. Today at sunrise Apollo came to our house, seeking his shambling cows. He brought no witnesses of the gods, no god who had seen the deed. But he bade me declare the thing under duress, often threatening to cast me into wide Tartaros, for he wears the tender flower of glorious youth. But I was born but yesterday, as he himself well knows, and I am in no way like a stalwart cattle rustler. You give yourself out to be my father, so believe that I may never be well if I drove home the cows, no, or even crossed the threshold. This I say in truth! I greatly revere Helios, and the other gods too, and I love you, but I dread him. No, you yourself know that I am not to blame. And I will add a great oath to that: by these fair-wrought porches of the gods I am guiltless, and one day I shall repay him with interest for his cruel accusation, mighty though he be. But you, aid the younger!

So spoke the Cyllenian, the Slayer of Argos, and he winked, keeping his blanket on his arm, not casting it down. But Zeus laughed aloud at the sight of his evil-witted child, so well and wittily he pled denial about the cows. Then he bade them both be of one mind and so seek the cattle, with Hermes as guide to lead the way and show without guile where he had hidden the sturdy cows. The son of Cronos nodded, and glorious Hermes obeyed, for the counsel of Zeus of the aegis persuades easily.

4h Hermes and Apollo Exchange Gifts (397–580)

Then both of them sped, the fair children of Zeus, to sandy Pylos, at the ford of Alpheios, and to the fields they came and the lofty-roofed stall, where the booty was tended in the season of darkness. There soon Hermes went to the side of the rocky cave and began driving the sturdy cattle into the light. But the son of Leto, glancing aside, saw the flayed skins on the high rock and quickly asked renowned Hermes:

> How were you able, O crafty one, to flay two cows, newborn and childish as you are? For time to come I dread your might—no need for you to be growing long, Cyllenian son of Maia!

So spoke he, and with his hands he twisted strong bands of withes, but they were soon intertwined with each other at his feet, and lightly they were woven over all the cattle of the field by the counsel of thievish Hermes, and Apollo marveled at what he saw.

Then the strong Slayer of Argos glanced down at the ground with twinkling glances, wishing to hide his purpose. But he did lightly soothe to his will the harsh son of renowned Leto, the Far-darter. Taking his lyre in his left hand he tuned it with the plectrum, and wondrously it rang beneath his hand. At that Phoibos Apollo laughed and was glad, and the pleasant note passed through to his very soul as he heard. Then Maia's son took courage, and sweetly harping with his harp he stood at Apollo's left side, playing his prelude, and his delightful voice followed upon it. He sang the renown of the deathless gods and dark Gaia, how all things were in the beginning and how each god got his portion.

To Mnemosyne, first of gods, he gave the reward of his song, the mother of the Muses, for the Muse came upon the son of Maia. Then the splendid son of Zeus honored all the rest of the immortals, in order of rank and birth, telling duly the entire tale as he struck the lyre on his arm. But into Apollo's heart in his breast came uncontrollable desire, and he spoke to him winged words:

> Crafty slayer of cattle, comrade of the feast, your song is worth the price of fifty oxen! Henceforth, I think, we will be peacefully reconciled. But, come now, tell me this, you wily son of Maia, have these marvels been with you ever since your birth, or is it that some immortal or some mortal man has given you the glorious gift and shown you divine song? For marvelous in my ears is this new song, such as, I think, no one, either of men or of the immortals who have mansions in Olympos, has known except you, robber, son of Zeus and Maia! What art is this? What charm against the stress of cares? What is the technique? For truly here is choice of all three things, joy and love and sweet sleep. For truly though I am conversant with the Olympian Muses, to whom dances are a charge, and the bright strain of music and rich song and the lovesome sound of flutes, never yet has anything else been so dear to my heart, dear as the skill in the festivals of the gods. I marvel, son of Zeus, at this, the music of your song. But now since, despite your youth, you have such glorious skill, to you and your mother I speak this word of sooth: in truth, by this shaft of cornel wood, I shall lead you renowned and fortunate among the immortals and give you glorious gifts and in the end not deceive you.

Then Hermes answered him with cunning words:

> You question me shrewdly, Far-darter, and I do not grudge you to enter into my art. This day you will know it, and to you I would rather be kind in word and will. But within yourself you well know all things, for first among the immortals, son of Zeus, is your place. You are mighty and strong, and Zeus of wise counsels loves you well with due reverence and has given you honor and fine gifts. They say that you know soothsaying, Far-darter, by the voice of Zeus, for from Zeus are all oracles, in which I myself now know you to be all-wise. It is your province to know whatever you want. Since, then, your heart bids you to play the lyre, then play and sing and let joys be your care, taking this gift from me, and to me, friend, give glory. Sweetly sing with my clear-voiced comrade in your hands, which knows speech good and fair and in order due. Bear it freely hereafter into the glad feast and the lovely dance and the glorious revel, a joy by night and day. Whatsoever skilled hand will inquire of it artfully and wisely, surely its voice will teach him all things joyous, being easily played by gentle practice, fleeing dull toil. But if an unskilled hand first impetuously inquires of it, vain and discordant will the false notes sound. But

> it is yours of nature to know what things you wish, so to you I will give this lyre, glorious son of Zeus. But we for our part will let your cattle of the field graze on the pastures of hill and the horse-rearing plain, Far-darter. So will the cows, consorting with the bulls, bring forth calves male and female aplenty, and there is no need for you, wise as you are, to be vehement in anger.

So spoke he and held forth the lyre that Phoibos Apollo took, and in return he pledged his shining whip in the hands of Hermes and set him over the herds. Gladly the son of Maia received it, while the glorious son of Leto, Apollo, the prince, the Far-darter, held the lyre in his left hand and tuned it orderly with the plectrum. Sweetly it sounded to his hand, and fair was the song of the god to accompany it.

Soon the pair turned the cows from there to the rich meadow, but themselves, the glorious children of Zeus, hastened back to snow-clad Olympos, rejoicing in the lyre. And Zeus the counselor was glad of it. Both did he make one in friendship, and Hermes loved Leto's son constantly, as he does now, since in recognition of his love he pledged to the Far-darter the delightful lyre, who held it on his arm and played on it. But Hermes invented the skill of a new art, the far-heard music of the reed pipes.

Then spoke the son of Leto to Hermes thus:

> I fear, son of Maia, leader, crafty one, lest you steal from me both my lyre and my bent bow. For you have this gift from Zeus, to establish the exchange of property[15] among men on the fruitful earth. Therefore swear to me the great oath of the gods, with a nod of the head or by the trickling waters of Styx, that your doings will ever be kind and dear to my heart.

Then, with a nod of his head, Maia's son vowed that he would never steal the possessions of the Far-darter nor draw near his strong dwelling. And Leto's son Apollo made a vow and bond of friendship and alliance, that no other god would be a better friend, no god nor any man of descent from Zeus:

> And I shall make with you a perfect token of a covenant of all gods and all men, loyal to my heart and honored.[16] Thereafter I will give you a fair wand of wealth and fortune, a golden wand, three-pointed, which shall guard you harmless, accomplishing all things good of word and deed that it is mine to learn from the voice of Zeus. But concerning the prophetic art, O best fosterling of Zeus, concerning which you inquire, for you it is not fated to learn that art, no, nor for any other immortal. That lies in the mind of Zeus alone. I myself made pledge and promise and strong oath that, save me, none other of the eternal gods should know the secret counsel of Zeus. And you, my brother of the golden wand, do not bid me tell you what awful purposes the far-seeing Zeus is planning.
>
> One mortal I will harm, and another I will bless, with many a turn of fortune among hapless men. Whoever comes following the voice or flight of birds of omen will have profit. He shall have profit of my oracle, and him I will not deceive. But whoever, trusting birds not ominous, approaches my oracle to

[15] The phrase is a euphemism for "theft."

[16] The text is very uncertain here.

inquire beyond my will and know more than the eternal gods, he will come, I say, on a pointless journey, but I will take his gifts anyway. I will tell you another thing, son of renowned Maia and of Zeus of the aegis, you bringer of boon: There are certain Thriai,[17] sisters born, three maidens rejoicing in swift wings. Their heads are sprinkled with white barley flour, and they dwell beneath a glade of Parnassos, teachers of another sort of soothsaying. This art I learned while yet a boy I tended the cows, and my father heeded not. From there they flit continually here and there, feeding on honeycombs and bringing all things to fulfillment. They, when they are full of the spirit of soothsaying, having eaten of the pale honey, delight to speak forth the truth. But if they are bereft of the sweet divine food, then they lie all confusedly. I bestow these on you, and you, inquiring clearly, delight your own heart, and if you instruct any man, he will often hearken to your oracle, if he has the good fortune. These are yours, O son of Maia, and tend the cattle of the field with twisted horn and horses and toilsome mules < . . . > and be lord over the burning eyes of lions and white-tusked swine and dogs and sheep that wide earth nourishes, and be glorious Lord Hermes over all flocks. And let him alone be the herald appointed to Hades, who, though he is giftless, will give him highest gift of honor.

With such love did Apollo kindly pledge the son of Maia, and Cronion added grace to it. With all mortals and immortals he consorts. He blesses somewhat, but ever through the dark night he beguiles the tribes of mortal men.

Hail to you, son of Zeus and Maia, I will be mindful of you and of another song.

5 To Aphrodite

This Hymn *is closely related to the epic cycle about Troy and is likely the oldest of the* Hymns *since it is closest to Homer's language and because of its connection to the* Iliad. *The* Hymn *is an account of how Aphrodite was forced to sleep with a mortal man, the Trojan Anchises. But the* Hymn *is also a celebration of their child, the hero Aineias, who in* Iliad *20 is destined to survive the war. Comparison with Poseidon's words there is instructive (20.302–308): "For it is destined that Aineias escape / And the line of Dardanos not be destroyed / And disappear without seed—Dardanos, / Whom Zeus loved more than any of the sons / Born from his union with mortal women. / The son of Cronos has come to hate Priam's line, / And now Aineias will rule the Trojans with might, / And the sons born to his sons in the future" (trans. Lombardo).*

5a The Power of Aphrodite and Its Limits (1–44)

Tell me, Muse, of the deeds of golden Aphrodite, the Cyprian, who rouses sweet desire among the immortals and subdues the tribes of deathly men and birds that sport in the air and all beasts and even all the clans that the earth nurtures and all in the sea. To all are dear the deeds of fair-garlanded Cytherea.

Yet three hearts there are that she cannot persuade or beguile. The daughter of Zeus of the aegis, gray-eyed Athena; not to her are dear the deeds of golden Aphrodite, but

[17] The personification of the pebbles used in a minor form of divination.

war and the work of Ares, battle and combat and the mastery of noble arts. First was she to teach earthly men the fashioning of chariots and cars fair-wrought with bronze, and she teaches to tender maidens in the halls all fine arts, breathing skill into their minds. Nor ever does laughter-loving Aphrodite conquer in desire Artemis of the golden arrow, rejoicing in the sound of the chase; for the bow and arrow are her delight, and the slaughter of wild beasts on the hills, the lyre, the dance, the clear hunting call, the shadowy glens, and cities of righteous men. Nor to the revered maiden Hestia are the feats of Aphrodite a joy, eldest daughter of crooked-counseled Cronos—youngest, too,[18] by the design of Zeus of the aegis—that lady whom both Poseidon and Apollo sought to win. But she would not. Nay, stubbornly she refused, and she swore a great oath fulfilled, with her hand on the head of Father Zeus of the aegis, to be a maiden forever, that lady goddess. And to her, Father Zeus gave a good share of honor in lieu of wedlock; and in the middle of the hall she sat herself down choosing the best portion. And in all temples of the gods is she honored and among all mortals is chief of gods.

The hearts of these goddesses she cannot win or beguile. But of all others there is none, of blessed gods or mortal men, who has escaped Aphrodite. Yea, even the heart of Zeus who delights in the thunderbolt she led astray, of him that is greatest of all and has the highest lot of honor. Even his wise wit she has beguiled at her will, and easily she united him with mortal women, without Hera being aware of it, his sister and his wife, the fairest in goodliness of beauty among the deathless goddesses. To highest honor did they beget her, crooked-counseled Cronos and Mother Rhea, and Zeus of imperishable counsel made her his modest and dutiful wife.

5b Zeus Causes Aphrodite to Fall in Love with a Mortal (45–83)

But into Aphrodite herself Zeus sent sweet desire to sleep with a mortal man. This he did so that without delay not even she might be unfamiliar with a mortal bed and might not some day with sweet laughter make her boast among all the gods, the smiling Aphrodite, that she had united the gods to mortal lovers, that they had borne for deathless gods mortal sons, and that she united goddesses with mortal men. Therefore, Zeus sent into her heart sweet desire for Anchises, who as then was pasturing his cattle on the steep hills of many-fountained Ida, a man in appearance like the immortals. Him thereafter did smiling Aphrodite see and love, and measureless desire took hold of her heart.

To Cyprus went she, within her fragrant shrine, to Paphos, where is her sacred sanctuary and fragrant altar. There she went in and shut the shining doors, and there the Charites bathed and anointed her with ambrosial oil, such as is on the bodies of the eternal gods, sweet fragrant oil that she had with her. Then she clad her body in fine raiment and decked herself out with gold, the smiling Aphrodite. She sped to Troy, leaving fragrant Cyprus, and high among the clouds she swiftly made her way. She came to many-fountained Ida, mother of wild beasts, and made straight for the steading on the mountain, while behind her came fawning the beasts, gray wolves and lions fiery-eyed and bears and swift leopards, insatiate pursuers of deer. Glad was

[18] Having been born first she was swallowed by her father first. Then when she was vomited up, i.e., born again, she was the last one out and hence the youngest.

she at the sight of them and sent desire into their breasts, and they went coupling two by two in the shadowy dells. But she came to the well-built huts, and him she found left alone in the steading with no company, the hero Anchises, graced with beauty from the gods. All the rest were following the cattle through the grassy pastures, but he was left alone at the steading, walking up and down, playing the lyre sweet and pure. In front of him stood the daughter of Zeus, Aphrodite, in appearance and stature like an unwedded maiden, lest he should be frightened when he beheld her.

5c Aphrodite, in Disguise, Speaks to Anchises (84–167)

And Anchises marveled when he beheld her at her height and beauty and glittering raiment. For she was clad in a dress more shining than the flame of fire, and with twisted armlets and glittering earrings shaped like flowers. About her delicate neck were beautiful necklaces of gold and intricate design. Like the moon's was the light on her fair breasts, a wonder to behold, and love came upon Anchises, and he spoke unto her:

> Hail, Queen, whosoever of the immortals you are that come to this house, whether Artemis or Leto or golden Aphrodite or high-born Themis or gray-eyed Athena. Or perchance you are one of the Charites come hither, who dwell friendly with the gods and are called immortal; or one of the Nymphs that dwell in fair glades and in the well-heads of rivers and in grassy dells. But to you on some point of outlook, in a place far seen, will I make an altar and offer to you fine victims in every season. But for your part be kindly and grant me to be a man preeminent among the Trojans, and give fine seed of children to follow me. But as for me, let me live long and well, see the sunlight and come to the limit of old age, being ever in all things fortunate among men.

Then Aphrodite the daughter of Zeus answered him:

> Anchises, most renowned of men on earth, behold! No goddess am I. Why do you liken me to the immortals? Nay, mortal am I, and a mortal mother bore me, and my father is famous Otreus, if you perchance have heard of him, who reigns over strong-walled Phrygia. But I well know both your tongue and our own, for a Trojan nurse reared me in the hall and nurtured me ever from the day when she took me from my mother's hands and while I was but a little child. Thus it is, you see, that I know your tongue as well as my own. But even now Hermes, the Argos-slayer of the golden wand has stolen me away from the choir of Artemis, the goddess of the golden arrow, who loves the noise of the chase. Many Nymphs and much-courted maidens were we there at play, and a great circle of people was about us. But thence did he bear me away, the Argos-slayer, he of the golden wand, and bore me over much tilled land of mortal men and much wasteland untilled and uninhabited, where wild beasts roam through the shadowy dells. So fleet we passed that I seemed not to touch the fertile earth with my feet. Now Hermes said that I was bidden to be the bride of Anchises and mother of your fine children. But when he had pointed you out and spoken, instantly he went back among the immortal gods, the renowned Slayer of Argos. But I come to you, strong necessity being laid upon me, and by Zeus I beseech you and your good parents—for no lowly people

would have a child such as you—by them I implore you to take me, a maiden as I am and untried in love, and show me to your father and your dutiful mother and to your brothers of one lineage with you. No unseemly daughter to these, and sister to those will I be, but well worthy; but send a messenger swiftly to the Phrygians of the dappled steeds to tell my father and my sorrowing mother of my fortunes. Gold enough and woven raiment will they send, and many and fine gifts shall be your reward. Do all this and then prepare the delightful wedding feast, which brings honor to both men and immortal gods.

So speaking, the goddess brought sweet desire into his heart, and love came upon Anchises, and he spoke and said:

If indeed you are mortal and a mortal mother bore you, and if renowned Otreus is your father, and if you have come here by the will of Hermes, the immortal guide and are to be called my wife forever, then neither mortal man nor immortal god shall hold me from my desire before I lie with you in love, now and soon. No, not even if Apollo the Far-shooter himself were to send the shafts of sorrow from the silver bow. No, you lady like the goddesses, I would be willing to go down within the house of Hades if but first I climbed into bed with you.

So spoke he and took her hand, while laughter-loving Aphrodite turned and moved with fair downcast eyes toward the bed. It was strewn for the prince as usual with soft garments, and above it lay skins of bears and deep-voiced lions that he had slain in the lofty hills. When the two had gone up into the well-wrought bed, first Anchises took from her body her shining jewels, brooches and twisted armlets, earrings and chains. And he loosed her girdle and took off her glittering raiment, which he laid on a silver-studded chair. Then through the gods' will and design the mortal man lay by the immortal goddess, not knowing who she was.

5d Aphrodite Reveals Herself to Anchises (168–293)

Now in the hour when herdsmen drive back the cows and sturdy sheep to the steading from the flowery pastures, then the goddess poured sweet sleep into Anchises and clad herself in her fine raiment. Now when she was wholly clad, the lady goddess, her head touched the beam of the lofty roof, and from her cheeks shone forth immortal beauty—such was the beauty of fair-garlanded Cytherea. Then she roused him from sleep and spoke and said:

Rise, son of Dardanos, why now do you slumber so deeply? Consider, do I appear in aspect such as I was when first your eyes beheld me?

So spoke she, and straightway when he heard, he started up out of slumber. When he beheld the neck and the fair eyes of Aphrodite, he was terrified and he averted his eyes. His fine face he veiled again in a cloak, and imploring her, he spoke winged words:

Even so soon as my eyes first beheld you, Goddess, I knew you for divine, but you did not speak the truth to me. But by Zeus of the aegis I implore you, suffer me not to live a strengthless shadow among men, but pity me, for no man lives in strength that has couched with immortal goddesses.

Then answered him Aphrodite, the daughter of Zeus:

Anchises, most renowned of mortal men, take courage, nor fear overmuch. For no fear is there that you shall suffer harm from me nor from others of the blessed gods, for dear to the gods are you. And to you shall a dear son be born and hold sway among the Trojans, and his children's children shall arise after him continually. Aineias shall his name be, since dread[19] sorrow held me when I came into the bed of a mortal man. And of all mortal men those who spring from your race are always nearest to the immortal gods in beauty and stature.

Witness how wise-counseling Zeus carried away golden-haired Ganymedes because of his beauty so that he might abide with the immortals and be the cupbearer of the gods in the house of Zeus, a marvelous thing to behold, honored among all the immortals as he draws the red nectar from the golden mixing bowl. But grief incurable possessed the heart of Tros, who knew not where the wild wind had blown his dear son away. Therefore, day by day he lamented him continually till Zeus took pity upon him and gave him as a ransom for his son high-stepping horses that bear the immortal gods. These he gave him for a gift, and the guide, the Slayer of Argos, told all these things by the command of Zeus, how Ganymedes should be forever exempt from old age and death just like the gods. Now when his father heard this message of Zeus, he rejoiced in his heart and lamented no longer, but was gladly charioted by the wind-fleet horses.

So too did Eos of the golden throne carry off Tithonos, a man of your lineage, one like unto the immortals. Then she went to pray to Cronion of the dark cloud, that her lover might be immortal and exempt from death forever. Zeus consented to this and granted her desire, but foolish of heart was Lady Eos, nor did she think of asking for eternal youth for her lover to keep him unwrinkled by grievous old age. Now so long as pleasant youth was his, in joy did he dwell with golden-throned Eos, who is born early at the world's end beside the streams of Oceanos. But as soon as gray hairs began to flow from his fair head and fine chin, Lady Eos held aloof from his bed, but kept and cherished him in her halls, giving him food and ambrosia and beautiful raiment. But when hateful old age had utterly overcome him, and he could not move or lift his limbs, to her this seemed the wisest counsel: she laid him in a chamber and shut the shining doors, and his voice flows on endlessly, and no strength now is his such as once there was in his limbs.

Therefore I would not have you be immortal and live forever in such fashion among the deathless gods. But if, being such as you are in beauty and form, you could live on and be called my lord, then this grief would not overshadow my heart. But it may not be, for swiftly will pitiless old age come upon you, old age that stands close by mortal men, wretched and weary and detested by the gods; but among the immortal gods shall great blame be mine forever, and all for love of you. For the gods used to dread my words and wiles with which

[19] The poet is etymologizing Aineias from *ainos,* "dread."

I had subdued all the immortals to mortal women in love, my purpose overcoming them all. For now my mouth will no longer suffice to speak forth this boast among the immortals, for deep and sore has been my folly, wretched and not to be named. And distraught have I been who carry a child beneath my girdle, the child of a mortal. Now as soon as he sees the light of the sun, the deep-bosomed mountain Nymphs will rear him, the Nymphs who haunt this great and holy mountain, being of the clan neither of mortals nor of immortal gods. Long is their life, and immortal food do they eat, and they join in the fine dance with the immortal gods. With them the Seilenoi and the keen-sighted Slayer of Argos join in love in the recesses of the dark caves. At their birth there sprang up pine trees or tall-crested oaks on the fruitful earth, flourishing and fair, and on the lofty mountain they stand and are called the groves of the immortal gods, which in no way does man cut down with steel. But when the fate of death approaches, first do the fair trees wither on the ground, and the bark about them molders, and the twigs fall down, and as the tree perishes so too does the soul of the Nymph leave the light of the sun.

These Nymphs will keep my child with them and rear him; and him when first he enters on lovely youth shall these goddesses bring hither to you and show you. But I, to go through all this in my mind, will come back to you in the fifth year bringing our son. At the sight of him you will be glad when you behold him with your eyes, for he will be divinely fair, and you will lead him straightway to windy Ilios. But if any mortal asks of you what mother bore this your dear son, be mindful to answer him as I command: say that he is your son by one of the flower-faced Nymphs who dwell in this forest-clad mountain. But if in your folly you speak out and boast to have been the lover of fair-garlanded Cytherea, then Zeus in his wrath will smite you with the smoldering thunderbolt. Now all is told to you. Be wise, and keep your counsel; speak not my name, but revere the wrath of the gods.

So spoke she and soared up into the windy heaven.

Goddess, Queen of well-settled Cyprus, having begun with you, I shall pass on to another hymn.

6 To Aphrodite

I shall sing of the revered Aphrodite, the golden-crowned, the beautiful, who has for her portion the mountain crests of sea-girt Cyprus. There the strength of the West Wind moistly blowing carried her amid soft foam over the wave of the resounding sea. Her did the golden-hooded Horai gladly welcome and clad her about in immortal raiment and on her deathless head set a well-wrought crown, fair and golden, and in her pierced ears put earrings of orichalc and of precious gold. Her delicate neck and white bosom they adorned with necklaces of gold, which the golden-hooded Horai themselves wear when they come to the glad dance of the gods in their father's dwelling. As soon as they had thus adorned her in all finery, they led her to the immortals, who gave her greeting when they beheld her and welcomed her with their hands; and each god prayed that he might lead her home to be his wedded wife, so much they marveled at the beauty of fair-garlanded Cytherea. Hail, you of the glancing eyes, you sweet enchanting goddess, and grant that I bear off the victory in this contest, and lend grace to my song, while I shall both remember you and another song.

7 To Dionysos

Concerning Dionysos, the son of renowned Semele, shall I sing, how once he appeared upon the shore of the unharvested sea, on a jutting headland, in form like a man in the bloom of youth, with his beautiful dark hair waving around him, and on his strong shoulders a purple robe. Suddenly men from a well-wrought ship, pirates, came sailing swiftly over the dark seas: Tyrsenians were they, and an evil doom led them, for they, beholding him, nodded to one another and swiftly leapt forth, hastily seized him, and set him aboard their ship, rejoicing in heart, for they thought that he was the son of kings, the fosterlings Zeus, and they were minded to bind him with grievous bonds. But him the fetters did not hold, and the withes fell far from his hands and feet. There sat he smiling with his dark eyes, but the steersman saw it and spoke aloud to his companions: "Fools, what god have you taken and bound? He is a strong god; our well-built ship may not contain him. Surely this is Zeus or Apollo of the silver bow or Poseidon; for he is in no way like mortal man, but like the gods who have mansions in Olympos. Nay, come, let us instantly release him upon the dark mainland, and do not lay your hands upon him, lest, being wroth, he rouse against us mighty winds and rushing storm."

So spoke he, but their captain rebuked him with a hateful word: "Fool, look you to the wind and haul up the sail and grab all the hawsers; men will take care of this one. I think he will come to Egypt or to Cyprus or to the Hyperboreans or further still; and at the last he will tell us who his friends are and about his wealth and his brethren, for the god has delivered him into our hands."

So spoke he and went about raising the mast and hoisting the mainsail, and the winds filled the sail and made taut the ropes all around. But soon strange matters appeared to them. First, there flowed through all the swift black ship a sweet and fragrant wine, and the ambrosial fragrance arose, and fear fell upon all the mariners who beheld it. And straightway a vine stretched here and there along the sail, hanging with many a cluster, and dark ivy twined round the mast, blossoming with flowers and gracious fruit, and garlands grew on all the thole-pins, and they who saw it bade the steersman drive straight to land. Meanwhile within the ship the god changed into the shape of a lion at the bow; and loudly he roared, and amidships he made a shaggy bear, signs of his godhead. There it stood raging, and on the deck the lion glared terribly. Then the men fled in terror to the stern, and there stood in fear around the prudent pilot. But suddenly the lion sprang forth and seized the captain, and the men, when they saw, all at once leapt overboard into the strong sea, shunning dread doom, and there were changed into dolphins. But the god took pity upon the steersman and preserved him and gave him all good fortune and spoke, saying, "Be of good courage, kind sailor, you who are dear to me. I am Dionysos of the noisy rites, whom Cadmeian Semele bore after joining in love with Zeus." Hail, you child of beautiful Semele; none that is mindless of you can fashion sweet song.

8 To Ares

The Hymn to Ares *is unique in the collection. Several factors, most notably the astronomical lore within it, indicate that it is later than the other* Hymns. *One possible scenario even puts the work as late as the 5th century* AD *and attributes it to the philosopher Proclus. Since hymns written by Proclus were transmitted alongside the* Homeric Hymns *in the Middle Ages, perhaps this one was moved from one collection to another.*

Ares, you who excel in might, you lord of the chariot of war, god of the golden helm, you mighty of heart, you shield-bearer, you safety of cities, you who strikes in armor, strong of hand and a valiant spearman unwearied, bulwark of Olympos, father of Nike, champion of Themis! You who are tyrannous to them who oppose you with force; you leader of just men, you master of manliness, you who whirl your flaming sphere among the courses of the seven stars of the sky, where your fiery steeds ever bear you above the third orbit of heaven![20] Listen to me, helper of mortals, giver of the bright bloom of youth. Shed down a mild light from above upon this life of mine and my martial strength, so that I may be of avail to drive away bitter cowardice from my head and to curb the deceitful rush of my soul and to restrain the sharp stress of anger that spurs me on to take part in the dread din of battle. But give me heart, O blessed one, to abide in the painless measures of peace, avoiding the battle cry of foes and the violent fates of death.

9 To Artemis

Sing, Muse, of Artemis, the sister of the Far-darter, the archer maiden, fellow nursling with Apollo, who waters her steeds at the reedy wells of Meles, then swiftly drives her golden chariot through Smyrna to Claros of the many-clustered vines, where Apollo of the Silver Bow sits waiting for the far-darting archer maiden. And so hail to you, and hail to all goddesses in my song, but to you first, and beginning with you I will sing, and so pass on to another song.

10 To Aphrodite

I shall sing of Cytherea, the Cyprus-born, who gives sweet gifts to mortals. There is always a charming smile on her face, always a charming blush. Hail to you, Goddess, Queen of fair-settled Salamis and of all Cyprus, and give to me a desirable song. Now I will be mindful of you and of another song.

11 To Athena

Of Pallas Athena, the savior of cities, I begin to sing, dread goddess, who with Ares takes care of the works of war and of sacked cities and of the war cry and of battles.

[20] Ares is identified with the planet Mars, which, counting inward from the most distant planet known in antiquity, Saturn, is the third planet. This interest in astronomy is one of the marks of the *Hymn*'s late date.

It is she who protects the army as it goes and returns from the fight. Hail, Goddess, and give to us happiness and good fortune.

12 To Hera

Of Hera I sing, the golden-throned, whom Rhea bore, an immortal queen in beauty preeminent, the sister and the bride of loud-thundering Zeus, the lady renowned, whom all the blessed throughout high Olympos honor and revere no less than Zeus who delights in thunder.

13 To Demeter

Of fair-tressed Demeter the holy deity I begin to sing, of her and the Maiden, lovely Persephone. Hail, Goddess! Save this city and inspire my song.

14 To the Mother of the Gods

Sing for me, clear-voiced Muse, daughter of great Zeus, about the mother of all gods and all mortals, she who delights in the sound of rattles and drums and in the noise of flutes and in the cry of wolves and fierce-eyed lions and in the echoing hills and the woodland haunts. And so hail to you and to all the goddesses in my song.

15 To Heracles the Lion-Hearted

Of Heracles, the son of Zeus, I will sing, mightiest of mortals, whom Alcmene bore in Thebes of the fair-dancing places, for she had lain in the arms of the son of Cronos, the lord of the dark clouds. Of old did the hero wander endlessly over land and sea at the bidding of Prince Eurystheus and himself wrought many deeds of fateful might and many he endured. But now in the fair haunts of snowy Olympos he dwells in joy and has fair-ankled Hebe for his wife. Hail, Prince son of Zeus and grant me fame and fortune.

16 To Asclepios

Of the healer of diseases, Asclepios, I begin to sing, the son of Apollo, whom fair Coronis bore in the Dotian Plain, the daughter of King Phlegyas. A great joy to men is her son, and the soother of evil pains. And so hail to you, O Prince; I pray to you in my song.

17 To the Dioscouroi

Sing, clear-voiced Muse, of Castor and Polydeuces, the Tyndaridai sons of Olympian Zeus whom Lady Leda bore beneath the crests of Taygetos, having been secretly conquered by the desire of the son of Cronos of the dark clouds. Hail, Tyndaridai, you riders of swift steeds.

18 To Hermes

I sing of Cyllenian Hermes, slayer of Argos, prince of Cyllene and of Arcadia rich in sheep, the swift messenger of the immortals. Maia, the modest daughter of Atlas, bore him after joining in love with Zeus. The company of the blessed gods she shunned, and she dwelled in a shadowy cave where the son of Cronos used to lie with the fair-tressed Nymph in the dark of night, while sweet sleep held white-armed Hera, and neither immortals nor mortal men knew of it. Hail to you, son of Zeus and Maia, with you I will begin and pass on to another song. Hail, Hermes, giver of grace, guide, giver of good things.

19 To Pan

Tell me, Muse, about the dear son of Hermes, the goat-footed, the two-horned, the lover of the din of revel, who haunts the wooded dells with dancing Nymphs who tread the crests of the steep cliffs, calling upon Pan the pastoral god of the long wild hair. He is lord of every snowy crest and mountain peak and rocky path. Here and there he goes through the thick copses, sometimes being drawn to the gentle waters, sometimes faring through the lofty crags as he climbs the highest peak, from where he can see flocks below. Always he ranges over the high white mountains, and among the ridges he always chases and slays the wild beasts, the god, with keen eye, and at evening returns alone, piping from the chase, breathing sweet strains on the reeds. In song that bird cannot excel him that, among the leaves of the blossoming springtide, pours forth her lament and her honey-sweet song.

With him then the mountain Nymphs, the clear-voiced singers, go wandering with light feet and sing at the side of the dark water of the well, while the echo moans along the mountain crest, and the god leaps hither and thither and goes into the midst with many a step of the dance. On his back he wears the tawny hide of a lynx, and his heart rejoices with clear-voiced songs in the soft meadow where crocus and fragrant hyacinth bloom all mingled amidst the grass. They sing of the blessed gods and of high Olympos, and above all they sing of swift Hermes, how he is the fleet herald of all the gods, and how he came to many-fountained Arcadia, the mother of sheep, where is his Cyllenian sanctuary, and there he, though a god, shepherded the fleecy sheep, the servant of a mortal man. For soft desire had come upon him to unite in love with the fair-haired daughter of Dryops, and the glad nuptials he accomplished, and to Hermes in the hall she bore a dear son. From his birth he was a marvel to behold, goat-footed, two-horned, a loud speaker, a sweet laugher. Then the nurse leapt up and fled when she saw his wild face and bearded chin. But straightway did swift Hermes take him in his hands and carry him, and gladly did the god rejoice at heart. Swiftly to the dwellings of the gods he went, bearing the babe hidden in thick skins of mountain hare; there he sat down by Zeus and the other immortals and showed his child, and all the immortals were glad at heart and above all the Bacchic Dionysos. They called him Pan because he had made glad the hearts of them all.[21] Hail then to you, O Prince. I am your suppliant in song, and I will be mindful of you and of another song.

[21] The Greek word for "all" is *pan*.

20 To Hephaistos

Sing, clear-voiced Muses, of Hephaistos renowned in craft, who with gray-eyed Athena taught fine works to men on earth, who before were wont to dwell in mountain caves like beasts; but now, being instructed in craft by the renowned craftsman Hephaistos, lightly the whole year through they dwell happily in their own homes. Be gracious, Hephaistos, and grant me fame and fortune.

21 To Apollo

Phoibos, to you the swan also sings purely to the beating of his wings as he lights on the bank of the eddies of the river Peneios; and to you with his clear-voiced lyre the sweet-voiced singer always sings, both first and last. And so hail to you, Prince, I beseech you in my song.

22 To Poseidon

Concerning Poseidon, a great god, I begin to sing, the shaker of the land and of the unharvested sea, god of the deep who holds Helicon and wide Aigai. The gods have given you a double portion of honor, O shaker of the earth, to be tamer of horses and savior of ships. Hail, Poseidon, girdler of the earth, you dark-haired god, and with kindly heart, O blessed one, help those who sail.

23 To Highest Zeus

Of Zeus will I sing, the best and the greatest of the gods, the far-beholding lord who brings all to an end, who holds constant counsel with Themis as she reclines against him. Be gracious, far-beholding son of Cronos, most glorious and greatest.

24 To Hestia

Hestia, who tends to the sacred house of Prince Apollo the Far-darter in holy Pytho, ever does the oil drop moistly from your locks. Come to his house with a gracious heart; come with counseling Zeus and lend grace to my song.

25 To the Muses and Apollo

From the Muses I shall begin and from Apollo and Zeus. For it is from the Muses and far-darting Apollo that singers and lyre players are upon the earth, but from Zeus comes kings. Fortunate is he whomsoever the Muses love, and sweet flows his voice from his lips. Hail, you children of Zeus, honor my song, and now I will be mindful of you and another song.

26 To Dionysos

Of ivy-tressed uproarious Dionysos I begin to sing, the splendid son of Zeus and renowned Semele. Him did the fair-tressed Nymphs foster, receiving him from the king and father in their bosoms, and heedfully they nurtured him in the glens of Nysa. By his father's will he waxed strong in the fragrant cavern, being numbered among the immortals. When the goddesses had raised him up to be the god of many a hymn, then he went wandering in the woodland glades, draped with ivy and laurel, and the Nymphs followed with him where he led, and loudly rang the wild woodland. Hail to you, then, Dionysos of the clustered vine, and grant that we come gladly again to the season of the vintage, and afterward for many a year to come.

27 To Artemis

I sing of Artemis of the golden arrow, goddess of the loud chase, a modest maiden, the slayer of stags, the archer, very sister of Apollo of the golden blade. She through the shadowy hills and the windy headlands, rejoicing in the chase, draws her golden bow, sending forth shafts of sorrow. Then tremble the crests of the lofty mountains, and terribly the dark woodland rings with the howls of beasts, and the earth shudders, and the teeming sea. Meanwhile she of the stout heart turns about on every side slaying the race of wild beasts. When the archer huntress has taken her delight and has gladdened her heart, she slackens her bended bow and goes to the great hall of her dear brother Phoibos Apollo, to the rich Delphian land, and arrays the lovely dance of Muses and Charites. There she hangs up her bended bow and her arrows, and all graciously clad about she leads the dances, first in place, while the others utter their immortal voices in hymns to fair-ankled Leto, how she bore such children preeminent among the immortals in counsel and in deed. Hail, you children of Zeus and fair-tressed Leto, now I will be mindful of you and of another song.

28 To Athena

Of Pallas Athena, renowned goddess, I begin to sing, of the gray-eyed, the wise, her of the relentless heart, the maiden revered, the savior of cities, the mighty Tritogeneia. From his holy head Zeus the counselor himself begot her, all armed for war in shining golden armor, while in awe the other gods beheld it. Quickly did the goddess leap from his immortal head and stood before aegis-bearing Zeus, shaking her sharp spear, and high Olympos trembled in dread beneath the strength of the gray-eyed maiden, while the earth rang terribly around, and the sea roiled with dark waves. Then suddenly the sea grew still. The glorious son of Hyperion checked for a long time his swift steeds till the maiden, Pallas Athena, took from her immortal shoulders her divine armor, and Zeus the counselor rejoiced. Hail to you, child of aegis-bearing Zeus, now I will be mindful of you and of another song.

29 To Hestia

Hestia, you who have obtained an eternal place and the foremost honor in the lofty halls of all immortal gods and of all men who walk on earth, splendid is your glory and your gift, for there is no banquet of mortals without you, none where, Hestia, they are not accustomed first and last to make to you an offering of sweet wine. And you, slayer of Argos, son of Zeus and Maia, messenger of the blessed gods, god of the golden wand, giver of all things good; with kindly heart befriend us in company with dear and honored Hestia. For you both dwell in the fine homes of earthly men, dear to the other's heart, strong supports, and you accompany intelligence and youth. Hail, daughter of Cronos, you and Hermes of the golden wand, now I will be mindful of you and of another song.

30 To Gaia, the Mother of All

Of Gaia, the mother of all, shall I sing, firm foundation, eldest of gods, who nourishes all things in the world; all things that walk on the sacred land, all things in the sea, all flying things—all are fed from your bounty. Through you, revered goddess, are men happy in their children and fortunate in their harvest. Yours it is to give or to take livelihood from mortal men. Happy is he whom you honor with favoring heart; to him all good things are present in abundance: his fertile field is laden, his fields are rich in livestock, his house filled with goods. Such men rule righteously in cities of fair women, great wealth and riches are theirs, their children exult in youthful delights, and their maidens joyfully dance and sport through the soft meadow flowers in floral revelry. Such are those that you honor, holy goddess, generous spirit. Hail, mother of the gods, wife of starry Ouranos, and freely in return for my song give me sufficient livelihood. Now I will be mindful of you and of another song.

31 To Helios

Begin, O Muse Calliope, child of Zeus, to sing of Helios, the splendid Helios whom dark-eyed Euryphaessa bore to the son of Gaia and starry Ouranos. For Hyperion wedded famed Euryphaessa, his own sister, who bore him beautiful children, rosy-armed Eos and fair-tressed Selene and tireless Helios, like unto the immortals. Helios, mounted on his chariot, shines on mortals and on deathless gods, and dread is the glance of his eyes from his golden helm, and bright rays shine forth from him splendidly, and round his temples the shining locks flowing down from his fair head frame his far-shining face, and a beautiful garment, delicately wrought by the breath of the winds, shines about his body, and stallions speed beneath him when he, charioting his horses and golden-yoked car, drives down through heaven to ocean. Hail, Prince, and of your grace grant me livelihood enough; beginning from you I shall sing the race of heroes half divine, whose deeds the goddesses have revealed to mortals.

32 To Selene

You Muses, sing of the fair-faced, wide-winged Selene, you sweet-voiced daughters of Zeus son of Cronos, accomplished in song! The heavenly gleam from her immortal head circles the earth, and great beauty arises under her glowing light, and the sunless sky beams from her golden crown, and the rays dwell lingering when she has bathed her fair body in Oceanos' stream and clad herself in far-shining raiment, divine Selene, yoking her strong-necked glittering steeds. Then forward with speed she drives her deep-maned horses in the evening of the mid-month, when her mighty orb is full; then her beams are brightest in the sky as she waxes, a token and a signal to mortal men. With her once was the son of Cronos wedded in love, and she conceived and brought forth Pandia the maiden, preeminent in beauty among the immortal gods. Hail, Queen, white-armed goddess, divine Selene, gentle-hearted and fair-tressed. Beginning from you I will sing the renown of heroes half divine, whose deeds singers chant from their charmed lips, those ministers of the Muses.

33 To the Dioscouroi

Sing, fair-glancing Muses, of the sons of Zeus, the Tyndaridai, glorious children of fair-ankled Leda, Castor the tamer of steeds and faultless Polydeuces. These, after wedlock with the son of Cronos of the dark clouds, she bore beneath the crests of Taygetos, that mighty mountain, to be saviors of earthly men and of swift ships when the wintry storm winds rush along the pitiless sea. Then going up onto the stern deck, men call the sons of great Zeus, vowing white lambs in return. But the strong wind and the wave of the sea drive down their ship beneath the water, when suddenly appear the sons of Zeus rushing through the air with tawny wings,[22] and straightway they have stilled the tempests of terrible winds and have lulled the waves on the deep of the white sea; they are good portents to mariners, an ending of their labor, and men see them and are glad and cease from weary toil. Hail, Tyndaridai, you riders of swift steeds, now I will be mindful of you and of another song.

[22] The manifestation of the Dioscouroi is the electrical phenomenon known to us as "Saint Elmo's fire."

HORACE

(65–8 BC, wrote in Latin)

Horace, a contemporary and acquaintance of Vergil, is best known for his Odes, *poems that were modeled on those of the great Greek lyric poets such as Pindar, Bacchylides, and Alcaeus. Like those Greek lyricists, Horace often employed a mythical or religious topic as his main theme in a poem (as in 1.10 and 2.19 following) or as a secondary element (as in 3.11 in an erotic context).*

ODES

Ode 1.10

The present poem is based on a Greek hymn to Hermes by Alcaeus, but since that earlier hymn is only partially preserved, we do not know how closely Horace followed it. In any case, Horace's poem is successful at integrating the most important myths surrounding Hermes. The opening stanza emphasizes the god's role in human civilization; the second and third stanzas allude to the god's cleverness as it is reported in the Homeric Hymn to Hermes; *the fourth and fifth stanzas emphasize his role as guide: first, when he escorted Priam safely through the Greek camp (*Iliad *24), second, as* psychopompos, *the escort of souls to the world below.*

Mercury, eloquent grandson of Atlas!
You shrewdly refined the crude customs of early man
with gifts of voice and the institution of the glorious
    wrestling grounds.

I will sing of you, messenger of mighty Jove and the
other gods, you, the parent of the curved lyre,
clever at hiding whatever you want in
    playful thievery.

Once, while Apollo was threatening
you, still a child, to return his cattle, which
you had stolen through a trick, he laughed,
    because you filched his quiver.

It was also with you as guide that wealthy Priam
left Ilium and eluded the haughty sons of Atreus,
the Thessalian watch-fires, and the Greek encampment
hostile to Troy.

You restore dutiful souls to their blessed resting
places, and you conduct the weightless masses
with your golden wand, pleasing to the gods
above and below.

Ode 2.19

Starting with the perspective of a participant in Bacchic revelry, Horace here reflects upon the complex nature of Bacchus, a god capable both of great peacefulness and frenzied violence. Major themes from the myths surrounding Bacchus appear: the maenads, rejection of his worship by mortals (Pentheus and Lycurgus), his role in the Gigantomachy, and his retrieval of his mother, Semele, from the underworld in order to make her the immortal goddess Thyone.

While Bacchus taught his songs on secluded hills,
I watched on—future generations, believe me!
I saw the Nymphs and goat-footed Satyrs
with sharp ears learning from the god.

Euhoe! My mind shudders anew with fear!
My heart rumbles full of Bacchus, uneasily—
ecstasy! *Euhoe*, Liber, gentle now, gentle!
You are awesome with dread thyrsus.

It is right for me to sing of the tireless Thuiadae,[1]
to recount the fountain of wine and the thick
rivers of milk and the honey dripping
from the hollow tree trunks.

It is right to sing of your beatified wife's
crown, glory added to the stars,[2] and Pentheus'
house, torn apart with great destruction, and
Lycurgus' downfall.

You divert foreign rivers, you, the foreign sea.
Wine-soaked on desolate mountain heights you bind

[1] A name for the worshipers of Bacchus meaning "Possessed by god."

[2] His wife Ariadne's crown was placed among the stars (*corona borealis*).

back the hair of the Bistonidae[3] harmlessly
with bands of snakes.

You, when the lawless army of the Giants was
scaling your father's kingdom on high,
forced Rhoetus back with lion's claws and
frightening jaws.

Although men said that you were not up to the
fight (because they say you are more suited to
choruses, jokes, and laughter), you were the same
at the center of both war and peace.

While you were adorned with golden horn, Cerberus
watched on, harmless and gently wagging his tail, and
he licked with his three tongues your feet and
legs as you went away.

Ode 3.11

The structure of this poem, if the spurious fifth stanza is removed, falls into three parts of four stanzas each. The first part contains an invocation to Mercury and the lyre, ending with an allusion to the lyre in the hands of Orpheus in the underworld. This allows an easy transition to the second part, which transports the reader to the underworld, where the daughters of Danaus are punished for killing their husbands on their wedding night. The third section is the speech of Hypermestra (not named here), the only Danaid who spared her husband. But the myth, however, is not retold for its own sake, but for a rather different purpose: to provide Lyde (whoever this woman was) with examples of why she should give in to Horace's charms.

Mercury, I invoke you (for it was by your instruction
that skillful Amphion moved stones with his singing),
and I call on you, tortoise shell,[4] who are gifted in harmonizing
with seven strings.

Once you were neither garrulous nor pleasing, but now
you grace the tables of the wealthy and the temples—
so sing your rhythms, to which Lyde might lend
her obstinate ears.

[3] The Bistonidae were Thracian worshipers of Bacchus who often handled snakes.

[4] Mercury made the first lyre out of a tortoise shell. See *Homeric Hymn* 4.

She friskily sports about, just as a two-year-old
mare does on the wide plains, and balks at being touched,
since she has no experience in marriage and is not yet ripe
for a lusty husband.

You are able to charm tigers and forests into following you
and to halt swift rivers dead in their tracks.
The doorkeeper of the vast hall, Cerberus, gave way
to your enchanting,[5]

[Although he has a hundred serpents bracing
his Fury-like head and although there remains
foul breath and bloody slather
on his three-tongued face.][6]

Look! Ixion and Tityos are smiling broadly on
their unwilling faces; and the jar remains dry
for just a moment, while you soothe Danaus' daughters
with your pleasing song.

Let Lyde listen to the crime and the well-known
punishment of these damsels! Let her hear of the empty jar,
its water leaking from the very bottom, and those
postponed punishments

which await sins, even in the underworld.
Godless women (what greater crime could they commit?),
these godless women could kill their betrothed
with hardened steel.

Only one of these many maidens was worthy
of her marriage, the one who meritoriously
cheated her oath-breaking father, a maiden celebrated
for all eternity.

"Rise," she said to her young husband.
"Rise, lest your reward be that long sleep in which
there is no fear. No, elude your father-in-law
and wicked sisters,

[5] When he was charmed by the music of Orpheus, who traveled to the underworld to retrieve his wife, Eurydice.

[6] This stanza was later added by someone other than Horace.

who are, alas, slaughtering their husbands
like lionesses who have fallen upon calves. I am
gentler than they, and I will not strike at you
nor imprison you.

Let my father place cruel chains on me,
or banish me by ship to the most extreme fields of the
Numidians[7] because I showed mercy and spared
my wretched husband.

But go now, wherever your feet and the winds take you
while night and Venus are favorable. Go, while the omen is
auspicious, and upon some tomb in memory of us
chisel some expression of sorrow."

[7] The Numidians lived in northwest Africa, on the edges of the Roman world.

Hyginus

(perhaps 4th or 5th c. AD, wrote in Latin)

Hyginus' Stories (Fabulae) *are a series of more than two hundred more or less self-contained stories written in very simple Latin, derived from earlier Greek sources at some point and then abridged into the current form probably in the 4th or 5th century* AD. *It is a handbook of mythology void of any literary pretension. Although Hyginus does not always seem to have an overarching structure like other mythographers, we can identify groups centered around heroic myths: 1–11, early Thebes; 12–27, Jason and the Argonauts, Medea; 29–36, Hercules; 37–48, Athens and Crete, loosely organized; 66–76, Thebes from Laius to the Epigoni; 77–127, Trojan War. After 127, finding thematic connections is more difficult.*

*Although Hyginus is an important source for mythology, he must be used with caution. First, the text as we have it is full of problems, a legacy of the way it has come down to us from antiquity. Second, there are many mistakes, and some of the "alternate" versions may simply be errors caused by sloppiness, misunderstanding, or both. A good example comes from 25 (*Medea*), which diverges in three places from what may be called the standard version. First, Creon, the king of Corinth, is confused with the other famous Creon, the king of Thebes from the Oedipus cycle. Second, Hyginus only reports that Medea makes a poisoned crown, but all other sources include a dress as well. Finally, the* Story *claims that "Creusa . . . was consumed by fire along with Jason and Creon," although nowhere else is Jason a victim.*

FROM *STORIES*

2 Ino

Ino, the daughter of Cadmus and Harmonia, wanted to kill Phrixus and Helle, Athamas' children by Nebula. So she hatched a plan with the women of her family and made them all swear that they would parch the grain they were to hand over for sowing so that it would not sprout. Thus it happened that because of the crop failure and the resulting shortage of grain, the entire population was dying off, some because of starvation, some because of disease. Athamas sent one of his aides to Delphi to inquire about the matter, but Ino ordered him to deliver a false response: "If Athamas sacrifices Phrixus to Jupiter, there will be an end to the blight." When Athamas refused to do this, Phrixus willingly came forward of his own accord and declared that he would free the state from its plight. When he had been led to the altar dressed in the sacrificial headdress and his father was about to invoke Jupiter, Athamas' aide revealed Ino's scheme to Athamas out of pity for the boy.

When the king learned of the crime, he handed his wife, Ino, and her son, Melicertes, over to Phrixus for execution. As Phrixus led them to their punishment, Father Liber enveloped him in a mist and rescued Ino because she had raised him. Later, Athamas was driven mad by Juno and killed his son Learchus. As for Ino, she threw herself and her son Melicertes into the sea. Liber ordained that she be called Leucothea (we call her Mater Matuta) and that Melicertes be called the god Palaemon (we call him Portunus). In his honor every four years athletic games are held, which are called Isthmian.

3 Phrixus

Phrixus and Helle were driven mad by Liber. When they were wandering in the forest in this state, the story goes that their mother, Nebula, went there and brought them a golden ram, the offspring of Neptune and Theophane. She told her children to get on the ram and travel to the land of the Colchians and their king, Aeetes, the son of the Sun, and once there to sacrifice the ram to Mars. They followed orders, and when they had climbed on and the ram was carrying them over the sea, Helle fell off, and so the sea was named the Hellespont.

Phrixus, on the other hand, was carried all the way to Colchis by the ram. Once there he, following his mother's orders, sacrificed the ram and placed its golden fleece in the temple of Mars. (This is the one that Jason, the son of Aeson and Alcimede, went to retrieve though it was protected by a serpent.) Aeetes welcomed Phrixus kindly and gave his daughter Chalciope to him to be his wife, who later bore him children. But Aeetes feared that they would dethrone him; he had received ominous signs that he should beware of death at the hands of a foreigner, a son of Aeolus. So he killed Phrixus. The latter's sons (Argus, Phrontis, Melas, and Cylindrus), however, boarded a raft to cross the sea and rejoin their grandfather Athamas. They were shipwrecked on the island of Dia but were picked up by Jason while he was on his quest for the Fleece and transported back to their mother, Chalciope. In return for Jason's kind action, she put in a good word for him with her sister, Medea.

9 Niobe

At Apollo's command Amphion and Zethus, the sons of Jupiter and Antiope, enclosed Thebes in a wall that extended as far as Semele's grave, drove Laius son of King Labdacus into exile, and began their reign of power there. Amphion took Niobe, the daughter of Tantalus and Dione, in marriage, and they had seven sons and just as many daughters. Niobe threw the fact that she had so many children in Latona's face, arrogantly taunted Apollo and Diana (because she dressed like a man and because of Apollo's long dress and hair), and said that she was better than Latona because she had more children.

Because of this boast Apollo shot her sons dead with arrows while they were hunting in the forest, and Diana killed all her daughters, except Chloris, with arrows inside the palace. As for their mother, she, bereft of her children, turned into a stone from her weeping on Mount Sipylus, and her tears, they say, flow forth even to this day. Amphion was killed by Apollo's arrows since he intended to destroy Apollo's temple.

25 Medea

Medea (Aeetes and Idyia's daughter) and Jason had two sons, Mermerus and Pheres, and they lived in perfect harmony. But Jason was the object of constant ridicule; for although he was such a brave, handsome, and noble man, he had taken a foreign wife, and a witch at that. Creon, the son of Menoeceus and king of Corinth,[1] gave his younger daughter Glauce to him to be his wife. When Medea saw that she, though she had done Jason a good turn, had been slapped with such an insult, she made a poisoned golden crown and ordered her sons to give it to their stepmother as a gift. Creusa accepted the gift and was consumed by fire along with Jason and Creon.[2] When Medea saw the palace in flames, she killed Mermerus and Pheres, her sons by Jason, and escaped from Corinth.

28 Otos and Ephialtes

Otos and Ephialtes, the sons of Aloeus and Iphimede (Neptune's daughter), are said to have been extraordinarily huge. Each of them grew by nine inches every month. When they were nine years old, they tried to ascend into heaven. They made their approach like this: they placed Ossa on top of Pelion (this is the reason Mount Ossa is also called Pelion) and then heaped still other mountains on top of that. They ran into Apollo and were killed by him.

Other authors, however, say that they were invulnerable sons of Neptune and Iphimede. They wanted to ravish Diana, and when she was unable to resist their brute strength, Apollo sent a deer between them. They burned with a desire to kill it with their spears, and during their attempt they ended up killing each other instead. They are said to suffer the following punishment among the dead. They are bound, facing away from each other, to a pillar by snakes; there is an owl between them, sitting on the pillar to which they have been bound.

30 The Twelve Labors Imposed on Hercules by Eurystheus

When Hercules was an infant, he strangled the two snakes sent by Juno, one in each hand, and from this act it was realized that Hercules was the first-born.[3]

1. He killed the invulnerable Nemean Lion, which the Moon raised in a cave with two openings, and he used its skin as a protective covering.

2. He killed the nine-headed Lernaean Hydra, Typhon's daughter, at the Spring of Lerna. This beast had such powerful venom that she killed men just by breathing,

[1] The king of Corinth is Creon, but not Creon son of Menoeceus, who is a member of the royal family of Thebes.

[2] Jason is not usually killed in this manner.

[3] Heracles is usually said to have a younger twin, Iphicles, who was fathered by Amphitryon.

and if someone happened to pass by her while she was sleeping, she would breathe on his feet, and he would die an excruciating death. With Minerva's guidance, Hercules killed the Hydra, gutted her, and dipped his arrows in the venom. And so whatever he shot with his arrows thereafter did not escape death. This would also be the cause of his own death in Phrygia later on.[4]

3. He killed the Erymanthian Boar.

4. In Arcadia he captured alive the wild stag with golden horns and led it before King Eurystheus.

5. On the Island of Mars he shot and killed the Stymphalian Birds, which fired off their own feathers as arrows.

6. In a single day he cleaned out all of King Augeas' cow dung, the greater part with the help of Jupiter. He washed out all of the dung by diverting a river into the barn.

7. He brought back alive the bull Pasiphae slept with from the island of Crete to Mycenae.

8. Along with his servant Abderus he killed Diomedes, the king of Thrace, and his four horses that fed on human flesh. The names of the horses were Podargus, Lampon, Xanthus, and Dinus.

9. He also killed the Amazon Hippolyte, the daughter of Mars and Queen Otrera. He stripped the belt of the Amazon queen off of her; then he gave his prisoner, Antiope, to Theseus.

10. He killed three-bodied Geryon, the son of Chrysaor, with a single spear.

11. He killed the monstrous serpent (Typhon's offspring) whose task it was to guard the golden apples of the Hesperides at Mount Atlas, and he brought the apples to King Eurystheus.

12. He brought the dog Cerberus (also born of Typhon) back from the underworld and brought it to the king.

31 Hercules' Side-Labors

In Libya he killed Antaeus son of Earth, who compelled all visitors to wrestle with him, wore them down, and killed them. Hercules wrestled him and killed him. In Egypt he killed Busiris, who regularly sacrificed foreigners. When Hercules heard Busiris' decree, he allowed himself to be led to the altar dressed in the sacrificial headdress. But when Busiris was about to invoke the gods, Hercules killed both him and his sacrificial attendants with his club. He overcame Mars' son Cygnus in battle and killed him. When Mars arrived and was about to engage him in a battle over his son, Jupiter sent a thunderbolt between the two and so separated them. At Troy he killed the sea monster that was about to devour Hesione. He shot dead Hesione's father, Laomedon, with arrows because he refused to hand her over as agreed. He also shot dead the insatiable eagle that devoured Prometheus' heart. He killed Lycus son of Neptune because he was about to kill Hercules' wife, Megara (daughter of Creon), and his sons, Therimachus and Ophites.

[4] The scene of Heracles' death is usually Mount Oeta in Thessaly.

The river Achelous could change himself into any form he wanted, and when he and Hercules were fighting over the right to marry Deianira, he turned himself into a bull. Hercules broke off one of his horns and gave it to the Hesperides (or Nymphs); these goddesses filled the horn with fruit and called it the Cornucopia {"Horn of Plenty"}. He killed Neleus son of Hippocoon and his ten children because he was not willing to cleanse or purify him after he killed his wife, Megara (daughter of Creon), and his sons Therimachus and Ophites. Hercules killed Eurytus because he wanted to marry his daughter Iole and was rejected by him. He killed the Centaur Nessus because he tried to rape Deianira. He killed the Centaur Eurytion because he wanted to marry Deianira, Dexamenus' daughter, who was his fiancée.

47 Hippolytus

Phaedra, the daughter of Minos and wife of Theseus, fell in love with her stepson Hippolytus. When she was unable to win him over to her desire, she wrote and sent a message to her husband that said that she had been raped by Hippolytus. She then committed suicide by hanging. When Theseus heard about the affair, he ordered his son to leave the city and prayed to his father Neptune for his son's death. So when Hippolytus hitched up his horses and was driving his chariot out of town, a bull suddenly appeared out of the sea. Its bellowing spooked the horses, and they tore Hippolytus apart and took his life.

52 Aegina

Jupiter wanted to ravish Aegina, Asopus' daughter, but was afraid of Juno, so he brought her to the island of Delos and got her pregnant. From this, Aeacus was born. When Juno found this out, she sent a serpent into the water there, which poisoned it. All who drank from it paid their debt to nature. Soon Aeacus lost most of his men. When he could no longer hold out because of how few men he had left, he begged Jupiter to give him men for protection while watching some ants. Jupiter turned the ants into men, and these are called Myrmidons because the Greek word for ants is *myrmices*. The island took the name Aegina.

54 Thetis

It was fated that a son born from the Nereid Thetis would be greater than his father. No one but Prometheus knew this. When Jupiter was about to sleep with her, Prometheus promised to advise him on the matter if he would free him from his bonds. Jupiter gave his word, and Prometheus warned him not to sleep with Thetis, else someone greater than him would be born and overthrow him just as he had Saturn. So Thetis was given in wedlock to Peleus, Aeacus' son, and Hercules was sent to kill the eagle that kept devouring Prometheus' heart. With the death of the eagle, Prometheus was freed from Mount Caucasus after thirty thousand years.

57 Stheneboea

When the exiled Bellerophon came to stay at King Proetus' palace, the king's wife, Stheneboea, fell in love with him. He refused to sleep with her, so she lied to her husband and made up the story that Bellerophon had forced himself on her. When Proetus heard what was going on, he wrote a letter about it and sent Bellerophon to Stheneboea's father, King Iobates. When Iobates read the letter, he refused to be the one to kill such a great man, but rather sent him to his death against the Chimaera, who was said to breathe flames from her three mouths. Riding on the back of Pegasus, Bellerophon killed the Chimaera and, they say, fell onto the plain of Aleia and dislocated his hipbones. But the king praised his valor and gave him his other daughter in marriage. When Stheneboea heard this, she committed suicide.

66 Laius

Laius son of Labdacus received a prophecy from Apollo warning him to beware death at the hands of his own son. So, when his wife Jocasta, Menoeceus' daughter, gave birth, he ordered the child to be exposed. It just so happened that Periboea, King Polybus' wife, was at the shore washing clothes, found the exposed child, and took it in. When Polybus found out, because they had no children, they raised him as their own, naming him Oedipus because his feet had been pierced.[5]

67 Oedipus

When Oedipus, the son of Laius and Jocasta, reached manhood, he was the strongest of all his peers. As they were envious of him, they accused him of not really being Polybus' son because Polybus was so gentle yet he was so brash. Oedipus felt that their claim had some merit, and so he went to Delphi to inquire about his family. Laius was experiencing ominous signs that told him that death at his son's hands was near. So he too set out on his way to Delphi, and Oedipus ran into him on the way. The king's guards ordered him to make way for the king. Oedipus refused. The king drove the horses on anyway and ran over Oedipus' foot with the wheel. Oedipus grew angry and, not knowing who he was, threw his father from the chariot and killed him.

Upon Laius' death, Creon son of Menoeceus took power. Meanwhile, the Sphinx, the daughter of Typhon, was running loose in Boeotia and destroying the Thebans' crops. She issued a challenge to King Creon: if someone solved the riddle she posed, she would leave the area; if, however, the person did not solve the riddle, the Sphinx said she would devour him. Under no other circumstances would she leave the territory.

When the king heard these conditions, he made a proclamation throughout Greece. He promised to grant his kingdom and his sister Jocasta in marriage to the man who solved the riddle of the Sphinx. In their desire to be king many came and were devoured by the Sphinx. Oedipus son of Laius came and solved the riddle,

[5] Following a common Greek etymology of the name from *oideo,* "swell" + *pous,* "foot."

upon which the Sphinx threw herself to her death. Oedipus was given his father's kingdom and, not knowing who she was, his mother as wife. By her he fathered Eteocles, Polynices, Antigone, and Ismene.

Meanwhile, Thebes was stricken with a crop failure and a shortage of grain because of Oedipus' crimes. When he asked Tiresias why Thebes was plagued with this, he responded that if a descendant of the Sparti was still alive and died for his country, it would be freed from its problems. Then Menoeceus, Jocasta's father, threw himself from the city walls to his death.

While all of this was going on in Thebes, Polybus died in Corinth. When Oedipus heard this, at first he took it badly because he was under the assumption that it was his father who had died. But Periboea informed him that he was adopted, and at the same time the old man Menoetes (the one who exposed him) recognized from the scars on his feet and ankles that he was Laius' son. When Oedipus heard this and realized that he had committed so many horrible crimes, he removed the brooches from his mother's dress and blinded himself. He then handed his kingdom over to his sons to share in alternate years and went from Thebes into exile with his daughter Antigone as his guide.

68 Polynices

After a year had passed, Oedipus' son Polynices demanded back the throne from his brother Eteocles, but he refused to budge. So Polynices, with the help of King Adrastus, came with seven generals to attack Thebes. There Capaneus was struck down by a thunderbolt while scaling the wall because he said he would capture Thebes even in opposition to Jupiter's will. Amphiaraus was swallowed whole by the earth. Eteocles and Polynices fought and killed each other. The citizens of Thebes performed funeral sacrifices for them, and although there was a strong wind blowing, the smoke from the altars did not waft upward in a single direction but broke off into two separate streams. When the others assaulted Thebes and the Thebans were worried about their chances, the augur Tiresias son of Everes prophesied that the city would be saved from the slaughter if a descendant of the Sparti died. Menoeceus saw that he alone could secure his city's deliverance and so threw himself off the city walls to his death. The Thebans gained victory.

69 Adrastus

Adrastus, the son of Talaus and Eurynome, received an oracle from Apollo that foretold he would marry his daughters Argia and Deipyla to a boar and a lion. A short time later, Oedipus' son Polynices, who had been driven into exile by his brother Eteocles, arrived at Adrastus' court, as did Tydeus, the son of Oeneus by his captive slave Periboea, who had been banished by his father because he killed his brother Melanippus on a hunting expedition. When the king's guards announced that two young men had arrived in strange dress—one had on a boar's hide and the other that of a lion—Adrastus remembered the oracle and so ordered them to be brought before him. He asked them why they had come to his kingdom in such attire. Polynices explained to him that since he had come from Thebes, he put on a lion's skin because

Hercules' origins were in Thebes, and thus he was wearing a symbol of his heritage. Tydeus said that he was Oeneus' son and that his origins were in Calydon, and so he clothed himself in a boar's skin symbolic of the Calydonian boar. The king remembered the oracle and gave his older daughter, Argia, to Polynices (Thersander was their son) and the younger daughter, Deipyla, to Tydeus (Diomedes, who fought at Troy, was their son). Polynices asked Adrastus to furnish him with an army to take back his father's kingdom from his brother. Adrastus not only gave him an army, but himself went with six other generals because Thebes was enclosed by seven gates. When Amphion was putting the wall around Thebes, he constructed seven gates and named them after his daughters. These were Thera, Cleodoxe, Astynome, Astycratia, Chias, Ogygia, and Chloris.

72 Antigone

Creon son of Menoeceus issued a decree stating that no one was to bury Polynices or any other who had come along with him. His reason was that they had come to attack their own country. Polynices' sister Antigone and his wife, Argia, under the cover of night secretly lifted up and placed Polynices' body on the same pyre where Eteocles was cremated. When guards caught them in the act, Argia escaped, but Antigone was led before the king, who handed her over to his son Haemon, who had been her fiancé, to be killed. But Haemon, smitten by love, ignored his father's command and entrusted Antigone to some shepherds and deceitfully told his father that he had killed her. She gave birth to a son, and when he reached manhood, he went to Thebes for some athletic contests. Creon recognized him from the birthmark that all descendants of the Sparti have on their body. Hercules interceded on Haemon's behalf, asking Creon to forgive his son, but he was not successful. Haemon killed both himself and his wife, Antigone. As for Creon, he gave his daughter Megara to Hercules to marry, and she gave birth to Therimachus and Ophites.

75 Tiresias

They say that the shepherd Tiresias son of Everes took his staff and struck some snakes on Mount Cyllene while they were copulating; elsewhere it is said that he stepped on them. Because of this he was turned into a woman. Later, when on the advice of an oracle he stepped on some snakes in the same place, he returned to his earlier form. At the same time, a playful dispute arose between Jupiter and Juno as to which sex, male or female, got the most pleasure out of intercourse. They made Tiresias the judge of this dispute because he had expertise on both sides. When his verdict came down in Jupiter's favor, Juno grew angry, backhanded him across the face, and blinded him. But Jupiter in return brought it about that Tiresias lived for seven generations and was the best seer among mortals.

77 Leda

Jupiter changed his form into a swan and ravished Leda, Thestius' daughter, by the river Eurotas. By him she gave birth to Pollux and Helen; by Tyndareus, Castor and Clytaemnestra.

78 Tyndareus

Oebalus' son Tyndareus fathered Clytaemnestra and Helen by Leda daughter of Thestius. He betrothed Clytaemnestra to Agamemnon, Atreus' son. As for Helen, she was wooed by a great host of suitors from different cities because of her outstanding beauty. Tyndareus was afraid that Agamemnon would reject his daughter Clytaemnestra and feared that the whole thing would end in chaos, so he took Ulysses' advice and swore an oath, putting the decision in the hands of Helen herself, who was to place a crown on the head of the man she wanted to marry. She placed it on Menelaus' head, and Tyndareus gave her to him as his wife and on his deathbed bequeathed his kingdom to him.

79 Helen

Theseus, the son of Aegeus and Aethra (Pittheus' daughter), and Pirithous son of Ixion kidnapped from Diana's shrine the virgin Helen, the daughter of Tyndareus and Leda, while she was performing a sacrifice, and took her to Athens in the district of Attica. When Jupiter saw that these two men were so bold, willingly risking their lives, he came to them in their dreams and ordered them both to fetch Proserpina from Pluto and make her Pirithous' wife. When they descended into the underworld by way of Cape Taenarum and told Pluto why they had come, they were stretched out on the ground and tortured by the Furies for a long time. When Hercules came to fetch the three-headed dog, they begged him to save them. His negotiations with Pluto were successful, and he led the men out safe and sound. Castor and Pollux, Helen's brothers, went to war to get her back and captured Aethra, Theseus' mother, and Phisadie, Pirithous' sister, and gave them to their sister as slaves.

82 Tantalus

Tantalus, the son of Jupiter and Pluto, fathered Pelops by Dione. Jupiter used to confide his plans to Tantalus and let him come to the gods' feasts. Tantalus told all of this to mankind. Because of this, the story goes, he now stands in water up to his head and is constantly thirsty. When he wants to take a drink of water, the water recedes. Likewise, fruit hangs over his head, and when he wants to take some, the branches are blown out of reach by the wind. Also, a huge boulder hangs over his head, and he is constantly afraid that it will fall down on top of him.

83 Pelops

When Pelops, the son of Tantalus and Dione (Atlas' daughter), was chopped up by Tantalus and put out as a feast for the gods, Ceres ate his arm. He was brought back to life by the will of the gods; but when they were putting all the limbs back together as they had been, because part of his arm was missing, Ceres furnished an ivory one in its place.

84 Oenomaus

Oenomaus, the son of Mars and Asterope (Atlas' daughter), had as his wife Evarete, Acrisius' daughter. They had an exceptionally beautiful young daughter, Hippodamia. Oenomaus refused to allow her to marry anyone because he had received an oracle warning him to beware of death at the hands of his son-in-law. So when many suitors came seeking her hand in marriage, he issued a challenge, saying that he would give her to the man who contended with him in a chariot race and won—he chose this because he had horses faster than the North Wind. Whoever lost, however, would be put to death. Many came and were put to death. Finally, Tantalus' son Pelops came, and when he saw the human heads of Hippodamia's suitors affixed above the double-doors of the palace, he regretted having come, as the king's cruelty struck fear in his heart.

So he won over the king's charioteer, Myrtilus, and promised to give him half of the kingdom in return for his help. Myrtilus gave his word, and when he put together the chariot, he deliberately did not put the linchpins into the wheels. And so, when Oenomaus whipped the horses into a gallop, his chariot broke down, and his horses tore him apart. Now, when Pelops was returning home as victor with Hippodamia and Myrtilus at his side, he reckoned that Myrtilus would be a source of disgrace for him. So he refused to follow through on his promise and instead threw him into the sea named Myrtoan after him. Hippodamia he led back to his homeland, which is called the Peloponnese {"Island of Pelops"}. There he fathered Hippalcus, Atreus, and Thyestes by Hippodamia.

88 Atreus

Atreus, the son of Pelops and Hippodamia, desired to exact justice from his brother Thyestes for the outrages he committed against him. So he reconciled with Thyestes and brought him back into his kingdom. Then he killed Thyestes' infant sons, Tantalus and Plisthenes, and served them to his brother as a meal. After he had eaten them, Atreus ordered the hands and heads of the boys to be brought forth. Because of this crime even the Sun turned his chariot away.

When Thyestes realized the heinous crime that had transpired, he fled to King Thesprotus' land, where they say Lake Avernus is. From there he went to Sicyon, where his daughter Pelopia had been brought to ensure her safety. While he was there, he by chance came upon a nighttime sacrifice to Minerva and for fear of polluting the sacrifice hid in the woods. Pelopia, who was leading the choral procession, slipped on the sacrificial sheep's blood and soiled her dress. As she was going to the river to wash out the blood, she took off her stained dress. Thyestes covered his face and sprang from the woods. While she was being raped, Pelopia took his sword out of his sheath. Then, returning to the temple, she hid it beneath the pedestal of Minerva's statue. On the following day, Thyestes asked the king to send him to his homeland, Lydia.[6]

Meanwhile, the crops had failed in Mycenae because of Atreus' crime, and the citizens were experiencing a shortage of grain. He received an oracle telling him to bring Thyestes back into the kingdom. When he went to Thesprotus on the assumption that Thyestes was staying there, he caught sight of Pelopia and asked Thesprotus to give her to him in marriage (he thought she was Thesprotus' daughter). He did just that, so as not to raise suspicion, but Pelopia was already pregnant with her father Thyestes' son Aegisthus. When she came to Atreus, she gave birth and summarily exposed the baby. But shepherds found the child and placed him under a she-goat to suckle, and Atreus ordered him to be sought out and raised as his own.

Meanwhile, Atreus sent his sons Agamemnon and Menelaus to find Thyestes, and they went to Delphi to inquire into the matter. Thyestes by chance had also come there to consult the oracle about getting revenge on his brother. They arrested Thyestes and led him to Atreus, who ordered him to be thrown into prison. He then called Aegisthus, thinking he was his own son, and sent him to execute Thyestes.

When Thyestes saw Aegisthus and the sword he was carrying, he recognized it as the one he lost during the rape. So he asked Aegisthus where he had gotten it. He responded that his mother, Pelopia, had given it to him and ordered someone to go get her. She responded to their inquiry: she had taken it from someone—she did not know who—during a sexual encounter one night, and from that encounter she conceived Aegisthus. Then Pelopia took the sword (pretending to make sure it was the right one) and thrust it into her own chest. Aegisthus took the bloody sword from his mother's chest and took it to Atreus, who was delighted because he thought that meant Thyestes was dead. Aegisthus killed Atreus while he was performing a sacrifice on the shore and returned with his father, Thyestes, to their ancestral throne.

89 Laomedon

The story goes that Neptune and Apollo built the wall around Troy. King Laomedon promised to sacrifice to them all the livestock born in his kingdom that year. Laomedon reneged on his promise because of greed. (Others say it was gold that he promised.) Because of this violation Neptune sent a sea monster to ravage Troy. For this reason the king sent an envoy to consult Apollo, who angrily responded that the plague would end if they bound and offered up young Trojan women to the sea monster.

After a great many had been devoured, Hesione's name was drawn and she was bound to the rocks. Hercules and Telamon, who were on their way to Colchis with the Argonauts, arrived and killed the sea monster. They returned Hesione to her father on the condition that when they came back, they got to take back home both her and his horses that walked on water and stalks of wheat. Laomedon broke this promise too and refused to hand Hesione over as agreed. So Hercules prepared his ships and came to conquer Troy. He killed Laomedon and handed the throne over to

[6] His grandfather Tantalus' original home.

Laomedon's infant son Podarces, who later was named Priam from the fact that he was purchased {Greek *priasthai*}.[7] Hercules gave the now recovered Hesione to Telamon to marry, and she gave birth to Teucer.

91 Alexander Paris

Laomedon's son Priam had a great many children by sleeping with his wife, Hecuba, the daughter of Cisseus (or of Dymas). Once, while she was pregnant, she envisioned in her sleep that she was giving birth to a burning torch from which a great number of serpents emerged. She reported this vision to every soothsayer, and all of them told her to kill the newborn child to prevent it from bringing destruction to the country. When Hecuba bore Alexander, she handed him over to some of her men to be put to death, but out of pity they only exposed him. Shepherds found the exposed infant, raised him as one of their own, and named him Paris.

When Paris grew into a young man, he had a pet bull. Priam sent some men there to lead back a bull to be given as a prize at the funeral games being held in Paris' honor, and they started to lead Paris' bull away. He caught up to them and asked where they were taking it. They told him that they were taking the bull to Priam as a prize for the man who was victorious at the funeral games for Alexander. He, burning with a desire to get his bull back, went down to the contest and won every event, besting even his own brothers. Deiphobus grew resentful and drew his sword against him, but Paris leapt up to the altar of Jupiter Herceus. When Cassandra divined that he was Deiphobus' brother, Priam acknowledged him and welcomed him into his palace.

92 The Judgment of Paris

The story goes that when Thetis was getting married to Peleus, Jupiter summoned all the gods to the feast except for Eris (that is, Discord). When she arrived at the feast later and was not allowed in, she threw an apple from the doorway into the middle of them and said that the most beautiful woman was to take it. Juno, Venus, and Minerva asserted their claim to the title "beautiful," and great discord arose among the three of them. Jupiter ordered Mercury to lead them down to Alexander Paris on Mount Ida and make him be the judge.

Juno promised Alexander Paris, if he judged in her favor, that he would be king of all the lands and surpass everyone else in riches. Minerva promised, if she were to walk away victorious, to make him the bravest mortal of all and skilled at every craft. Venus, however, promised to give him Helen, Tyndareus' daughter, the most beautiful woman of all, to be his wife. Paris preferred the last gift to the previous two and judged Venus to be most beautiful. Because of this verdict, Juno and Minerva were hostile to the Trojans. Urged on by Venus, Alexander took Helen away from his host, Menelaus, and led her back from Lacedaemon to Troy, and made her his wife. He also took her handmaidens, Aethra and Thisadie, whom Castor and Pollux had captured and given to Helen as servants, though once they were queens.

[7] The details of Priam's "purchase" are to be found in Apollodorus' account of Heracles at K16.

93 Cassandra

Cassandra, the daughter of Priam and Hecuba, once fell asleep, they say, in the temple of Apollo after growing weary from play. Apollo wanted to ravish her, but she refused him access to her body. So he made it that no one believed her though she prophesied the truth.

94 Anchises

They say that Venus desired Anchises son of Assaracus, slept with him, and gave birth to Aeneas. She instructed Anchises never to reveal this to anyone. One day, however, he drank too much and blurted it out in front of his drinking buddies, and because of this Jupiter struck him down with a thunderbolt. Some say he died of natural causes.

95 Ulysses

When Agamemnon and Menelaus, the sons of Atreus, were leading the commanders who were bound by the oath to attack Troy, they came to Ulysses son of Laertes on the island of Ithaca. He had earlier received an oracle warning him that if he went to Troy, he would return home after twenty years, alone, destitute, and having lost his men. And so, when he found out that an embassy was on its way to him, he pretended to be crazy by putting on a felt hat and yoking a horse and a bull together to a plow. When Palamedes saw him, he sensed that he was faking it, so he took Ulysses' son Telemachus from the cradle, put him in front of the plow, and said, "Put aside your trickery and join the others bound by oath." Then Ulysses promised that he would go. From that time on he was hostile to Palamedes.

96 Achilles

The Nereid Thetis knew that Achilles, her son by Peleus, would die if he went to sack Troy, so she entrusted him to King Lycomedes on the island Scyros for safekeeping. The king had Achilles dress in women's clothing and kept him in the company of his young daughters under a different name—the young women called him Pyrrha because he had red hair (the Greek word for red is *pyrrhos*).

Well, when the Achaeans learned he was being hidden there, they sent an embassy to King Lycomedes with a request that he send Achilles to help the Danaans. The king said Achilles was not there and allowed them access to the palace to conduct a search. Since they could not tell which of the girls was in fact Achilles, Ulysses put in the courtyard gifts suitable for girls, in which he included a shield and spear. He then ordered his trumpeter to sound the call to arms abruptly and his men to produce the clanging and clashing of arms. Achilles thought that the enemy was at hand and so ripped off his woman's clothes and took up the shield and spear. In this way he was identified and promised the Argives his help and that of his soldiers, the Myrmidons.

98 Iphigenia

As Agamemnon was on his way to Troy with his brother Menelaus and Achaia's top commanders to fetch back Menelaus' wife, Helen, whom Alexander Paris had carried off, they were detained at Aulis by a storm caused by Diana. She was angry at Agamemnon because he had killed her sacred deer and insulted her. He called a meeting of the seers; Calchas said that Agamemnon could only appease the gods by sacrificing his own daughter, Iphigenia. When Agamemnon heard this, he at first refused, but then Ulysses advised him and convinced him to do what was best for everybody.

This same Ulysses was sent with Diomedes to bring Iphigenia back. When they came to her mother, Clytaemnestra, Ulysses lied to her and said that her daughter was to be married to Achilles. After he had brought her back to Aulis and her father was about to sacrifice her, Diana took pity on the girl, cast a mist around them, and replaced her with a deer. She took Iphigenia through the clouds to the land of the Taurians and there made her priestess of her temple.

102 Philoctetes

When Philoctetes, the son of Poeas and Demonassa, was on the island of Lemnos, a snake bit him on his foot. This snake had been sent by Juno, who was angry at him because he was the only one who had the nerve to build a pyre for Hercules when he discarded his human body and was made immortal. In return for his service, Hercules bequeathed to him his divine bow and arrows. But when the Achaeans could no longer put up with the foul odor that was coming from the wound, on King Agamemnon's orders he was abandoned on Lemnos along with his divine arrows. A shepherd of King Actor named Iphimachus, the son of Dolopion, found him abandoned and took care of him. Later it was revealed to the Greeks that Troy could not be taken without Hercules' arrows. Agamemnon then sent Ulysses and Diomedes to him as ambassadors. They convinced him to let bygones be bygones and help them sack Troy, and they took him back to Troy with them.

103 Protesilaus

The Achaeans received an oracle foretelling that the first one to touch the shores of Troy would die. When they brought their fleet to shore, everyone held back except for Iolaus, the son of Iphiclus and Diomedea, who was the first to leap from his ship and was summarily killed by Hector. All of them called him Protesilaus[8] because he had been the first man to die there. When his wife, Laodamia, Acastus' daughter, heard that her husband was dead, she wept and asked the gods for three hours' time in which to speak with him. They granted her request. Mercury led him back to the world of the living, and she talked with him for three hours. But when Protesilaus died a second time, Laodamia could not endure the pain.

[8] That is, "First of the army."

104 Laodamia

When Laodamia, Acastus' daughter, had used up the three hours she had received from the gods after the death of her husband, she could not endure the suffering and pain. So she made a golden statue in the likeness of her husband Protesilaus, put it in her chamber under the pretense it was a religious statue, and began to worship it.

Early one morning a servant of hers brought her some fruit for her sacrificial offering. He peered through the crack in the door and saw that she, far from Protesilaus' embrace, was holding and kissing the statue. Thinking that she was keeping a lover other than her husband, he reported it to her father, Acastus. When he arrived and burst into her chamber, he saw that it was a statue of Protesilaus; but in order to prevent her from prolonging her torture, he ordered that a pyre be built and that the statue and the sacred objects be burned. Laodamia, unable to endure the pain any longer, threw herself onto the pyre and was consumed by fire.

105 Palamedes

Ulysses plotted daily to find some way to kill Palamedes son of Nauplius because he had once foiled his scheme.[9] Finally, he put a plan into motion. He sent one of his men to Agamemnon to report that he had dreamed that the camp had to be moved in a single day. Agamemnon regarded this dream to be true and gave the orders to move the camp in a single day. That night, however, Ulysses secretly buried a great mass of gold at the site where Palamedes' tent had been the day before. In addition, he drew up a letter and gave it to a Phrygian captive to take to Priam; then he sent one of his soldiers ahead to kill the captive just a short distance from the camp.

The next day, when the army was returning to camp, a certain soldier brought Agamemnon the letter that had been written by Ulysses and planted on the Phrygian's dead body. It read, "From Priam to Palamedes," and promised Palamedes, if he betrayed Agamemnon's camp at an agreed upon time, the exact amount of gold that Ulysses had planted in his tent. So when Palamedes was led before the king and denied having anything to do with the conspiracy, they went to his tent and dug up the gold. When Agamemnon saw the gold, he believed that it really had happened. Thus Palamedes was tricked by Ulysses' scheme and was killed by the whole army though he was innocent.

106 The Ransoming of Hector

At the same time Agamemnon returned Chryseis to Chryses, the priest of Apollo Smintheus, he took away from Achilles Briseis, his captive from Moesia and the daughter of the priest Brisa because of her exceptional beauty. Enraged at this, Achilles refused to go forth into battle, choosing to spend time in his tent playing the cithara. But when Hector was driving the Argives back, Achilles, under harsh criticism from Patroclus, handed over his armor to him. With it Patroclus routed the Trojans, who thought he was Achilles, and killed Sarpedon, the son of Jupiter and Europa. Later, Patroclus himself was killed by Hector, and Achilles' armor was

[7] That is, his scheme to get out of the Trojan War (see *Story* 95).

stripped off his dead body.

Achilles reconciled with Agamemnon, who returned Briseis to him. Since he had gone forth to meet Hector without any armor, his mother, Thetis, got Vulcan to make him armor, which the Nereids carried across the sea. Clad in this armor, he killed Hector, tied him to his chariot, and dragged him around the walls of Troy. Achilles had no intention of handing over the body to his father for burial, so Priam, at Jupiter's behest and with Mercury as his guide, went into the Danaans' camp, where he ransomed his son's body with gold. Then he laid him to rest.

107 The Judgment over Achilles' Armor

After Hector was buried, Achilles ranged around the walls of Troy, boasting that he would sack Troy all by himself. Apollo grew angry at this, disguised himself as Alexander Paris, and struck him in the ankle—which they say was mortal—with an arrow, killing him. After Achilles' death and burial, Ajax son of Telamon demanded that the Danaans give him Achilles' armor on the grounds that he was his cousin. Because of Minerva's anger, however, Agamemnon and Menelaus rejected his claim and awarded the armor instead to Ulysses. Ajax was driven mad, and in a fit of insanity killed first his flock of sheep[10] and then himself, inflicting the wound with the same sword that he had received as a gift from Hector when they fought.

108 The Trojan Horse

When the Achaeans were unable to capture Troy after ten years, Epeus, following Minerva's guidance, built a wooden horse of awesome size. Inside it a force was assembled: Menelaus, Ulysses, Diomedes, Thersander, Sthenelus, Acamas, Thoas, Machaon, and Neoptolemus. On the outside of the horse they wrote, "THE DANAANS GIVE THIS OFFERING TO MINERVA," and then transferred their camp to the island of Tenedos. When the Trojans saw this, they concluded that the enemy had gone. Priam ordered the horse to be brought in and placed on the citadel of Minerva. He then proclaimed that there would be a great celebration. The seer Cassandra cried out that there were enemies inside the horse, but not one person believed her. After they had positioned the horse on the citadel and had themselves fallen asleep, exhausted by their drunken revelry, the Greeks were let out of the horse by Sinon. They slew the guards at the gates, and when the signal was given, they let in their fellow soldiers and took possession of Troy.

110 Polyxena

When the victorious Danaans were boarding their ships to leave Ilium and were getting ready to return, each to his own country with his share of the war-spoils, they say Achilles' voice emanated from his tomb and demanded his share of the spoils. So at his tomb the Danaans sacrificed Priam's daughter Polyxena. She was a most beautiful

[10] In his madness he believes the sheep are the Greek generals.

virgin, and it was on her account (that is, because he wanted to marry her) that Achilles had come to the parley at which he was killed by Alexander and Deiphobus.

111 Hecuba

When Ulysses was leading Hecuba, Priam's wife, Hector's mother and the daughter of Cisseus (other sources say of Dymas), home to a life of servitude, she hurled herself into the Hellespont and is said to have turned into a dog. Because of this, part of the sea is also called Cyneum.[11]

116 Nauplius

After Ilium had been taken and the spoils divvied up, the Greeks set out for home. Because the gods were angry at their desecration of the temples and Locrian Ajax's forceful removal of Cassandra from Pallas' icon, a hostile storm with adverse winds arose, and they were shipwrecked on the Capharean Rocks. In the storm Locrian Ajax was struck by lightning from Minerva's hand and dashed against the rocks by the surf; this is where the name Ajax's Rocks comes from.

The rest of them in the dark of night began to beg the gods for deliverance. Nauplius heard them and sensed that the time had come to get his revenge for the wrongs done to his son Palamedes. So, as if he were coming to their aid, he raised a burning torch where the rocks were sharp and the place was most perilous. The Greeks naturally thought that this was an act of human kindness and thus steered their ships in that direction. The result was that a great number of ships broke apart and a great many soldiers were killed in the storm beside their leaders, their limbs and guts smashed against the rocks. All who managed to make it to shore were killed by Nauplius. But the wind drove Ulysses to Maron and Menelaus to Egypt; Agamemnon made it home with Cassandra.

117 Clytaemnestra

Clytaemnestra, the daughter of Tyndareus and the wife of Agamemnon, heard from Oeax, Palamedes' brother, that Cassandra was being led home to be Agamemnon's mistress. This was a lie that Oeax made up to avenge the wrongs done to his brother. So Clytaemnestra plotted with Thyestes' son Aegisthus to kill Agamemnon and Cassandra; they killed them both with an ax while he was performing a sacrifice. Electra, Agamemnon's daughter, took her infant brother, Orestes, and placed him in the care of Strophius, who lived in Phocis and was married to Astyochea, Agamemnon's sister.

118 Proteus

It is said that in Egypt there lived Proteus, an old man, a mariner, and a seer, who could at will turn himself into all sorts of forms. Menelaus, acting on the advice of Proteus' daughter Idothea, tied him up in chains to force him to reveal when he would

[11] Because the Greek word for dog is *kyne*.

get back home. Proteus informed him that the gods were angry because Troy had been conquered and he should therefore perform the sacrifice that is in Greek called a *hecatomb*, in which a hundred head of cattle are killed. So Menelaus performed a *hecatomb*, and at last, eight years after he left Ilium, he returned home with Helen.

119 Orestes

When Orestes, the son of Agamemnon and Clytaemnestra, reached manhood, he made it his mission to avenge his father's death. So he formed a plan with Pylades: He returned to his mother, Clytaemnestra, in Mycenae, said that he was a visitor from Aetolia, and reported that Orestes, whom Aegisthus had handed over to the people to be killed, was dead. Not long afterward, Strophius' son Pylades came to Clytaemnestra carrying an urn he said held Orestes' remains. Aegisthus was overjoyed and welcomed them both into his house. Orestes seized upon the opportunity and with the help of Pylades killed his mother, Clytaemnestra, and Aegisthus during the night. When Tyndareus came to prosecute him, the Myceneans secured Orestes' escape because of their love for his father. Later, his mother's Furies tormented him.

120 Taurian Iphigenia

Since the Furies were tormenting Orestes, he set out for Delphi to inquire when he could expect an end to his affliction. The response was this: Orestes was to travel to the land of the Taurians and visit King Thoas (Hypsipyle's father), remove the cult statue of Diana from her temple, and bring it back to Argos; that would bring an end to his miseries. When he heard the response, he boarded a ship with his friend Pylades, Strophius' son, and quickly reached the land of the Taurians.

It was the custom of the Taurians to sacrifice in Diana's temple all foreigners who came to their land. Orestes and Pylades hid themselves in a cave and were waiting for an opportunity, but they were discovered by shepherds and brought before King Thoas. As was customary, he had them put in chains and taken to Diana's temple to be sacrificed. Orestes' sister happened to be the priestess there, and when she figured out who they were and why they had come based on clues and inferences, she cast aside her sacrificial instruments and began helping them pull up Diana's statue. But when the king arrived on the scene and asked her why she was doing that, she lied and said that these wicked men had defiled the statue. She went on: because sinful, wicked men had been led into the temple, the statue had to be carried down to the sea for purification. Then she ordered the king to forbid the citizens to go outside the city walls. The king obeyed the priestess' command. Iphigenia took advantage of the situation: she, Orestes, and Pylades picked up the statue and boarded the ship. They sailed under a favorable wind and were carried to the island Zminthe and came to Apollo's priest Chryses.

130 Icarius and Erigone

When Father Liber set out to show men the sweetness and pleasantness of his fruits, he found generous hospitality in the home of Icarius and Erigone. In return for their hospitality he gave them a gift, a wineskin full of wine, and told them to spread its cultivation over the rest of the lands. So Icarius loaded up his cart and came with his daughter Erigone and his dog Maera to some shepherds in Attica. He showed them the special nature of the grape's sweetness, but the shepherds drank too much, became drunk, and passed out. Thinking that Icarius had given them some evil drug, they pummeled him to death. His dog Maera howled over Icarius' dead body and thus showed Erigone where her father lay unburied. When she arrived, she hanged herself from a tree above her father's body.

Enraged at the Athenians' terrible actions, Father Liber afflicted their daughters with a similar punishment.[12] They went to Apollo to inquire about the problem, and they were told that it was because they had been indifferent to Icarius and Erigone's deaths. So after this reply, they punished the shepherds and established a holiday in honor of Erigone to commemorate the rash of hangings and to offer during the harvesting of the grapes the first-fruits to Icarius and Erigone. By the will of the gods they were given a place among the constellations: Erigone became the constellation Virgo, which we call Justice; Icarius, they say, became the constellation Arcturus; and the dog Maera became the star Canicula {"Little Dog"}.

135 Laocoon

Laocoon, the son of Capys, brother of Anchises and priest of Apollo, married and had children against Apollo's will. One day he was chosen by lot to perform a sacrifice to Neptune on the beach. Apollo seized this opportunity and sent two serpents across the sea from Tenedos to kill Laocoon's sons Antiphas and Thymbraeus. When Laocoon was on his way to help them, the serpents also wrapped him in their coils and killed him. The Phrygians thought this happened because Laocoon threw a spear into the Trojan horse.

136 Polyidus

Glaucus, the son of Minos and Pasiphae, fell into a big vat full of honey while playing ball. When his parents were looking for him, they asked Apollo about their son. Apollo responded to them, "A supernatural omen has been born unto you; whoever discovers its meaning will restore your son to you." After Minos heard the oracle, he asked his subjects if they knew of any supernatural occurrence. They told him that a calf had just been born that changed its color three times a day, every four hours: first white, then red, and finally black. Minos called together the augurs to figure out what it meant.

All of them were at a loss when Polyidus, Coeranus' son from Byzantium, demonstrated that the omen was similar to a blackberry bush: at first it is white, then it turns red, and finally completely black. Then Minos said to him, "According to Apollo's oracle, you are supposed to restore my son to me." While Polyidus was taking his augury, he saw an owl sitting above the wine cellar keeping the bees away. He interpreted this sign and pulled the dead boy from the vat.

Then Minos said to him, "Now that the body has been found, bring him back to life." When Polyidus said that this was not possible, Minos ordered him to be

[12] He caused them to hang themselves.

enclosed in the tomb along with the boy and a sword to be placed within. After they had been shut in, a serpent suddenly came toward the boy's body. Polyidus thought that the serpent was going to devour the boy, so he immediately struck it with the sword and killed it. When a second serpent seeking its mate saw that it had been killed, it came forth and applied an herb. At its touch, the serpent came back to life. Polyidus did the same thing. They called out from inside, and a passerby reported this to Minos. He ordered the tomb to be opened, and when he recovered his son alive and well, he sent Polyidus back home with many gifts.

153 Deucalion and Pyrrha

When the *cataclysmus* occurred, which we would call a deluge or a flood, the entire human race perished except for Deucalion and Pyrrha, who took refuge on Mount Aetna, which is said to be the highest mountain on Sicily. When they could no longer bear to live because of loneliness, they asked Jupiter either to give them some more people or to kill them off with a similar catastrophe. Then Jupiter ordered them to toss stones behind them. Jupiter ordered the stones Deucalion threw to become men and those Pyrrha threw to become women. From this comes the word *laos* {Greek "people"}, since the Greek word for stone is *laas*.

164 Athens

When an argument arose between Neptune and Minerva as to who would be the first to found a city on Attic soil, they made Jupiter judge of their dispute. The judgment fell in Minerva's favor because she planted the first olive tree in that land (which, they say, still stands there). Neptune grew angry over this and began flooding the land with the sea, but Jupiter ordered Mercury to prevent him from doing so. So Minerva founded a city and called it Athens after her own name;[13] this town is said to be the first one built in the land.

[13] Minerva is the Latin name for Athena.

LONGUS

(probably 2nd c. AD, wrote in Greek)

Longus was the author of the Greek novel, Daphnis and Chloe. *Nothing is known about the date of the author or the romance, but it is generally placed in the 2nd century AD. The story is set on the island of Lesbos, and much of the action takes place either on grazing pastures or in the woods. Pan, the god who haunts the countryside, naturally has a strong presence in the novel, including these two stories.*

FROM *DAPHNIS AND CHLOE*

2.34 Pan and Syrinx

[2.34] This syrinx was not originally an instrument, but a girl who was beautiful and had a lovely singing voice. She used to herd her goats, play with the Nymphs, and sing as she does now. Pan approached her while she was herding, playing, and singing, and tried to persuade her to do what he desired by promising that all her goats would bear twins. But she laughed at his love and said that she would not make someone who was neither wholly goat nor wholly human her lover. He set off to chase her and force her violently. Syrinx fled both him and his violence. Fleeing and tiring, she hid herself in some reeds, disappearing into a marsh. Pan cut down the reeds out of anger. When he did not find the girl, he learned what had happened, and with wax he joined together the reeds, which were uneven because their love had been unequal. So he invented the instrument. And the one who was then a beautiful girl is now a musical syrinx.

3.23 Pan and Echo

[3.23] The family of Nymphs is large, my girl. There are ash Nymphs, mountain Nymphs, marsh Nymphs. All are beautiful; all are musical. One of them gave birth to a daughter, Echo. She was mortal since she had a mortal father, and beautiful since she had a beautiful mother. She was raised by the Nymphs and taught by the Muses how to play the syrinx, how to play the flute, everything about the lyre, everything about the cithara, everything musical. So when she reached the peak of the bloom of her maidenhood, she danced with the Nymphs, sang with the Muses, and avoided every male, both mortal and immortal, loving her virginity. Pan was angry with the girl because he was jealous of her music and because he had failed to obtain her beauty. So he sent madness into the shepherds and goatherds. Like dogs or wolves they ripped her apart and scattered her still-singing limbs over all of Ge. As a favor to the Nymphs, Ge hid all of her limbs and preserved her music, and according to the wish of the Muses she sends forth sound and—just like the girl once did—she imitates everything: gods, humans, instruments, beasts. She even imitates Pan himself when he plays his pipe. And when he hears her, he leaps up and chases through the hills, not to seduce her, but just to find out who his hidden student is.

LUCIAN

(ca. AD 120–ca. 185, wrote in Greek)

Lucian was born in Syria but educated in the Greek manner. He produced a host of learned and witty works. Some of his best-known pieces are his Dialogues (of the Dead, of the Gods, *and* of the Sea Gods), *literary dramatizations in which he inventively traverses the territory of Greek myth, lightheartedly reinterpreting famous situations immortalized by earlier literary giants such as Hesiod and Homer. One of his favorite techniques is to take a moment just before or after a famous episode in a myth and allow the audience to peek behind the scenes, as it were. So we see Agamemnon and Ajax discuss Odysseus' visit to the underworld after he has left, and we do not just hear about Ixion's crime and punishment, but we get to listen in on Hera and Zeus as they discuss the situation. This is essentially the technique employed in the* Judgment of the Goddesses, *where we get to listen in on one of the most famous mythological moments, when Paris decides whether Hera, Athena, or Aphrodite is most beautiful. That impulse to view heroic and divine myth through the lens of everyday life also characterizes his other works, including his short essay* On Sacrifices, *which is a sarcastic and humorous piece with a more serious point—the criticism of popular attitudes toward gods and sacrifice.*

FROM *DIALOGUES OF THE DEAD*

23 Agamemnon and Ajax in the Underworld

After the death of Achilles, his arms were to pass to the next greatest hero among the Greeks at Troy. When Odysseus was chosen (some Trojans said that he had caused them more harm than Ajax), Athena made Ajax go insane. In his madness he killed a flock of sheep in the belief that they were the Greek leaders, and then killed himself. At Odyssey *11.543–11.560 the shade of Ajax refuses to talk to Odysseus when he visits the underworld to consult the prophet Teiresias. Lucian sets this short dialogue just after Odysseus has returned to the upper world.*

AGAMEMNON: Ajax, if you went crazy and killed yourself when you were planning to kill all of *us*, how can you blame Odysseus? You didn't even look at him just now when he came to question the prophet. You didn't deign to talk to a fellow soldier, a brother-in-arms. No respect. You just marched right by.

AJAX: That's right, Agamemnon. After all, he was the one responsible for my madness. He was the only one to challenge me for the arms.

AGAMEMNON: You didn't think anyone would oppose you? That you'd beat everyone without even working for it?

AJAX: Yes. Yes I did. The armor was mine by right of family. It belonged to my cousin. And the rest of you refused to compete. And you were far better than *him*. You all conceded the prizes to me. But Laertes' son—a guy I used to have to save all the time when he was in danger of being cut to pieces by the Phrygians—thought he was the better man and more fit to have the arms.

AGAMEMNON: Well then, noble hero, blame Thetis. She should've granted you the arms as an inheritance since you're a relative. Instead, she brought them and offered them as a prize for everyone.

AJAX: No, I blame Odysseus. He was the only one to challenge my claim.

AGAMEMNON: Ajax, he's only human. It's understandable if he grasped at glory, the sweetest thing. It's what we all risked our lives for. And he *did* get the better of you. And with Trojans doing the voting at that.

AJAX: I know exactly who condemned me, but it's not right to say anything about the gods. But as for Odysseus, I couldn't *not* hate him, Agamemnon, not even if Athena herself told me not to.

FROM *DIALOGUES OF THE GODS*

5 Prometheus and Zeus

Prometheus the Titan has been punished for stealing fire by being chained to the top of Mount Caucasus, where an eagle comes every day to eat out his liver, which regenerates during the night. In this dialogue, Lucian has Zeus pass by on his way to an amorous rendezvous with the Sea Nymph Thetis. The resolution of this dialogue, with Hephaistos ordered to release Prometheus, is not the usual ending of Prometheus' punishment. Rather, most versions have the hero Heracles performing that service.

PROMETHEUS: Let me go, Zeus. I've suffered terribly already.

ZEUS: I should free you, you say? When you should have been in even heavier shackles? When you should have had the whole of Caucasus put on top of your head? And sixteen vultures ripping up your liver? No, not just your liver, but they should have been gouging out your eyes too, for making humans such pesky animals, stealing fire, and creating women.[1] Not to mention the way you fooled me in the distribution of the meat by giving me bones covered with fat and keeping the better parts for yourself.[2]

[1] The creation of women is usually Zeus' deed undertaken to punish men for Prometheus' crime. It is perhaps possible that Lucian intends us to understand that Prometheus is responsible for the creation of women but did not himself create them.

[2] A reference to the trick at Mecone described by Hesiod, *Theogony* 537–559.

PROMETHEUS: Haven't I been punished enough by now? I've been nailed up for so long on the Caucasus, and all the while I've been feeding that eagle with my liver. Damned bird!

ZEUS: That's not even a fraction of what you deserve to suffer.

PROMETHEUS: All right then, you won't let me go without something in return. But I'll give you some information, Zeus. Something you really need to know.

ZEUS: You're trying to trick me, Prometheus.

PROMETHEUS: What good would that do me? It's not like you would forget where the Caucasus are, or run out of chains if I got caught playing a trick.

ZEUS: First, tell me what "something in return" you're going to give me that I "need to know."

PROMETHEUS: If I tell you why you're going where you're going right now, will you trust me when I give you a prophecy about the rest?

ZEUS: Why wouldn't I?

PROMETHEUS: You're going to visit Thetis. To sleep with her.

ZEUS: Got *that* right. So what about the rest? I believe you'll tell the truth.

PROMETHEUS: Don't mess with that Nereid at all, Zeus. If you get her pregnant, the child will do the same things to you that you did.

ZEUS: You mean to say that I'll be deposed from my kingship?

PROMETHEUS: Let's hope not, Zeus. But your union with her threatens *something* like that.

ZEUS: Well, so long to Thetis then. I'll have Hephaistos release you for this, Prometheus.

9 Zeus and Hera Discuss Ixion

The hunter Ixion was one of the few mortals honored by being invited to share in the feasts of the gods on Olympos. Famously, he took advantage of his closeness to the immortals to attempt to seduce Hera. For this offense he was punished in the underworld after sleeping with a cloud shaped like Hera, a union that produced the half-man and half-horse Centaurs. Much of the humor here derives from Zeus, himself a notorious philanderer (including Ixion's wife!), who is reluctant to punish someone for practicing his own favorite pastime. This cleverly plays up the absurdity of the myth—why would Zeus even bother with making a cloud figure once Ixion's intentions were clear?

HERA: This Ixion . . . What kind of person do you think he is, Zeus?

ZEUS: He's a good guy, Hera. Nice to have at a party. He wouldn't be here if he didn't deserve to be our guest.

HERA: But he doesn't deserve to be. He's behaved outrageously! So don't invite him anymore.

ZEUS: Really? What's he done that's outrageous? I think I should know.

HERA: Well, yes, you should. But I'm ashamed to talk about it. What he tried was awful!

ZEUS: And that's why if he tried to do something shameful, you'd better tell me about it. He hasn't been hitting on anyone, has he? Because I know that that's just the sort of disgraceful thing you'd be reluctant to discuss.

HERA: Not just anyone, Zeus, but *me*. And for a long time now. At first I didn't know what was the matter . . . why he would look over at me and stare. He would sigh and get misty-eyed, and if I happened to finish my drink and hand the cup to Ganymedes, he would ask for a drink in the same cup. And when he got it, in between drinks he would kiss the cup and bring it close to his eyes. Then he would look over at me again. That's when I understood that this was flirting. And for a long time I was ashamed to tell you, and I thought the man would stop this craziness. But after he dared to talk to me and propositioned me, I left him. He kept crying and begging on his knees, but I covered my ears so that I wouldn't have to listen to his outrageous pleas and came to tell you. You'll have to decide how to punish the man yourself.

ZEUS: Damn him, that's impressive! Messing with me and even going after an affair with Hera, eh? Was he that drunk on nectar? Well, it's our fault. We've been way too nice to humans. After all, we invited them as guests. After they drank like us and had a chance to see heavenly beauties who are unlike anything they saw on earth, they can't be blamed if they were overcome with desire and felt the urge to enjoy those beauties. Eros is a power to be reckoned with. And he doesn't just have power over humans, sometimes he even controls us.

HERA: Eros is definitely *your* master. He takes you and drags you along, leading you, as they say, by the nose. And you follow him wherever he guides you and happily transform yourself into whatever he commands. You're completely possessed by Eros. His toy. And now I know why you're forgiving Ixion—it's because you yourself once seduced his wife, and she bore you a son, Peirithous!

ZEUS: Wait. You still remember every single time I went down to earth and had some fun? Anyway, do you know what I think we should do about Ixion? I don't think we should punish him or keep him away from our parties. That has no finesse. Since he's in love and, as you say, weeps and suffers unbearably—

HERA: What, Zeus? I have a feeling that you're about to say something equally outrageous, and it scares me.

ZEUS: No, no. Let's make a figure out of clouds that looks just like you, then when dinner is over and he's lying awake, which of course he will be because he's in love, let's take it and put it in bed with him. That way he'll stop being troubled and think he's gotten what he's after.

HERA: For*get* it. Tough luck. He's after what's too good for him.

ZEUS: Let's do it anyway, Hera. What trouble can the model cause you if Ixion sleeps with a cloud?

HERA: Well, people will think the cloud is me. And I'll be ashamed because we look exactly alike.

ZEUS: You're making no sense. The cloud couldn't ever become Hera. And you couldn't become a cloud. Ixion will just be fooled.

HERA: But humans have no class. He'll go down and start bragging, maybe. And start telling everyone, saying that he slept with Hera and did it in Zeus' bed. And just maybe he'll say that I was in love with him. And they'll believe him, because they won't know that he was with a cloud!

ZEUS: All right, then. If he says anything like that, he'll get thrown into Hades. The wretch will be tied to a wheel and he'll spin around on it forever. He'll suffer endlessly, paying the price not for his love—there's nothing wrong with that—but for his big mouth.

16 Hermes and Apollo Discuss Hyacinthos

In Greek myths Apollo has a string of lovers, both male and female. Unfortunately, the majority of those love affairs end badly, often with the death of Apollo's beloved. Here Lucian describes the end of one of the most famous of these episodes, his short affair with a young Spartan man named Hyacinthos. Although earlier retellings of the myth speak of the great lamentation of Apollo and the creation of the hyacinth flower from the young man's blood, here we get to see Apollo just a bit later as he works his way through his grief with the help of the unsympathetic Hermes.

HERMES: Why are you depressed, Apollo?

APOLLO: Because I'm so unlucky in love, Hermes.

HERMES: That's worth hurting over. But how are you unlucky? Or do you just mean that you're still hurting about the whole Daphne thing?

APOLLO: No, I'm over that. But I'm grieving for a boyfriend—the Spartan, the son of Oibalos.

HERMES: Do tell. Is Hyacinthos dead?

APOLLO: *Very* dead.

HERMES: Who did it, Apollo? I mean, who could be so heartless that he would kill that beautiful guy?

APOLLO: *I* did it.

HERMES: Did you go crazy, Apollo?

APOLLO: No! It was a bit of an unfortunate accident.

HERMES: How? I want to hear how it happened.

APOLLO: He was learning to throw the discus and I was practicing with him. But that damned wind Zephyros—see, he had also been in love with the boy for a long time but the boy didn't pay attention to him, and he couldn't take being ignored. He did it. I threw my discus up, like I always do, but he blew down from Mount Taygetos, and moved it, and slammed it into the boy's skull so a lot of blood gushed from the wound and the boy died right then and there. Well, right away I shot an arrow at Zephyros and made him run off. I chased him all the way back to the mountain. As for the boy, I raised a tomb for him in Amyclai where the discus got him, and I made the earth send up a flower from his blood. The nicest and brightest flower of all, Hermes. It even has letters that spell out a lament for the deceased.[3] Do you think my grief is unreasonable?

[3] The Greeks thought that the pattern on this flower spelled out the lament "*Ai, ai!*"

HERMES: Yes I do, Apollo. You knew that you'd chosen a boyfriend who was mortal. So don't be upset because he died.

FROM *DIALOGUES OF THE SEA GODS*

2 Polyphemos and Poseidon

A fanciful account of the conversation between the Cyclops Polyphemos and his father, Poseidon. In typical fashion Lucian has chosen to give us insight into a moment just after Odysseus has blinded the former and escaped his clutches but before the latter punishes him. It thus complements and spoofs the famous recounting of Odysseus' adventures in the ninth book of Homer's Odyssey.

CYCLOPS: Dad, the things that damned foreigner did to me! He got me drunk, attacked me after I passed out, and completely blinded me.

POSEIDON: Who dared to do this, Polyphemos?

CYCLOPS: First he called himself Nowun,[4] but after he escaped and was too far away to throw rocks at, he said his name was Odysseus.

POSEIDON: Oh, I know the one you mean. The guy from Ithaca. He was sailing from Troy. But how did he manage this? He's not exactly brave.

CYCLOPS: I caught a bunch of them in my cave when I came back from grazing my animals. It was pretty obvious that they were after my flocks. You see, after I'd put the cover over my door—I've got a really big rock for that—and got the fire going again by lighting a tree that I'd brought from the mountain, I saw them trying to hide. I picked up a couple of them and ate them, naturally. I mean, they were robbers after all. Then that tricky son of a bitch, whatever his name is, Nowun or Odysseus, pours out some potion and gives it to me to drink. It tasted great and smelled fine, but it really snuck up on me. It got me totally messed up. As soon as I drank it, I thought everything was spinning. Even the *cave* flipped over. I was totally out of it. Finally, I fell asleep. He sharpened the stake and then, get this, he makes it red hot and then blinds me while I'm sleeping. He's the reason you've got a blind son, Poseidon.

POSEIDON: Kid, you must have been really passed out if you didn't wake up in the middle of him blinding you. Anyway, how did Odysseus get away? I'm positive that he couldn't have moved the rock from the door.

CYCLOPS: Well, I did that myself. I figured I could catch him easier when he was trying to get out. So I sat by the door, put my hands out, and tried to catch him. I only let out the sheep to graze and told the ram what I needed him to do for me.

POSEIDON: Ah, I see. They went out under your sheep and you didn't notice. You should've called out to the other Cyclopes to help with him.

[4] Homer's account hinges upon a pun that the clever Odysseus employs to escape: he tells Polyphemos that his name is Oûtis, which is, with a slight change of accent, "oútis," the word in Greek for "no one" (Nowun, here) or "nobody."

CYCLOPS: Oh, I called them, Dad. And they came. But when they asked what the name of the guy was who was hurting me and I said that his name was Nowun, they thought I was crazy and left me and went away. That's how the damned guy tricked me with his name. And what really gets me is that he even made fun of my injury. He said, "Not even your father Poseidon can heal you!"

POSEIDON: Buck up, son. I'll get him back. He'll learn that even if it's impossible for me to heal mutilated eyes, at least I have power over what happens to sailors. And he's still sailing. . . .

7 The Wedding of Peleus and Thetis

A description of the actions of Eris (Strife) at the wedding of the goddess Thetis and the mortal Peleus in Thessaly. The events described here led to the judgment of Paris on Ida and ultimately to the Trojan War. The conversation is between two daughters of Nereus, the Sea Nymphs Galene and Panope.

PANOPE: Galene, did you see what Eris did yesterday at the feast in Thessaly just because she hadn't been invited to the party?

GALENE: No. I wasn't there with you all. Poseidon ordered me to keep the sea calm during the ceremony, Panope. So what did Eris do if she wasn't even there?

PANOPE: Well, Thetis and Peleus had already retired to the bridal suite escorted by Amphitrite and Poseidon. Meanwhile, Eris—and nobody saw her, which wasn't hard because people were drinking and some were clapping, paying attention to Apollo while he played or to the Muses while they sang. Anyway, she threw a really beautiful apple into the party. It was solid gold, Galene. And it had written on it "The beautiful woman gets me." It rolled like it was all planned out and stopped where Hera, Aphrodite, and Athena were sitting. And when Hermes picked it up and read what was written on it, we Nereids just shut up. I mean, what could we do with those three there? Each of them said that she deserved the apple and claimed it. A fight would've broken out if Zeus hadn't gotten between them. But he said, "*I'm* not going to make this decision"—even though they demanded it. "No way. Go to Mount Ida to Priam's son. He's a great lover of beauty, so he knows how to judge it. He won't make a bad decision."

GALENE: So what did the goddesses do, Panope?

PANOPE: They're going to Ida today, I think. Someone will come in a little while and tell us who won.

GALENE: Oh, I can tell you that already. If Aphrodite's competing, no one else is going to win. Unless the ref is blind.

9 Delos

Here Lucian deflates the story of the birth of Apollo on the island of Delos by presenting us with a conversation between Iris and Poseidon. This version differs markedly from the one in Homeric Hymn *3 (to Apollo), the earliest and most famous account of how Delos came to be Apollo's birthplace.*

IRIS: Poseidon, that island that's moving around, the one that was ripped off from Sicily and has been swimming around under the sea? Zeus says you have to stop it now and bring it to the surface. Then you should fasten it really securely and make it stay put out in the open in the middle of the Aegean Sea. He needs it for something.

POSEIDON: Consider it done, Iris. But what's he going to do with it when it's out in the open and not sailing around?

IRIS: Leto needs it to give birth on. She's already in pretty bad shape from her labor pangs.

POSEIDON: How'd that happen? Isn't heaven big enough to give birth in? And couldn't the whole earth hold her children if heaven couldn't?

IRIS: No, Poseidon. Hera made Gaia swear a great oath not to offer Leto a place to give birth. But this island isn't covered by the oath since it was hidden.

POSEIDON: Gotcha. Hey, Island! Stand still! Rise up again from the deep and sink no more. Remain fixed in place and receive, very blessed island, my brother's two children, the most beautiful of the gods. And you, Tritons, ferry Leto over to it and let everything be calm. As soon as the newborns are delivered, they will chase after the serpent that is now driving their mother out of her mind with fear and avenge her. Iris, you tell Zeus that all is ready. Delos is stopped. Let Leto come now and give birth.

11 Io

Notos (the South Wind) and Zephyros (the West Wind) here watch as Hermes takes Io, an unfortunate woman seduced by Zeus and transformed into a cow, to Egypt, where she will give birth to Zeus' son Epaphos. The story's most important ancient occurrences are in Aeschylus' Prometheus Bound *and Ovid's* Metamorphoses. *In the current instance Lucian lingers on the general absurdity of her transformation into a cow and exploits the humor of the Greeks' equation of Io with the Egyptian goddess Isis and Hermes with the jackal-headed god Anubis.*

NOTOS: Hey, Zephyros. This heifer, the one that Hermes is leading across the sea to Egypt . . . Zeus was overcome by desire and ravished *her*?

ZEPHYROS: Yeah, Notos. Only she wasn't a heifer then. She was the daughter of the river Inachos. But now Hera made her like this out of jealousy because she saw that Zeus was really in love with her.

NOTOS: And he's still in love with the cow?

ZEPHYROS: Yes, indeed. That's why he sent her to Egypt and ordered us not to stir up the sea until she swims across. So when she gives birth there—she's already pregnant—she might become a god along with her child.

NOTOS: The heifer? A god?

ZEPHYROS: Yes, indeed. Hermes says she'll rule over people at sea. And she'll be our mistress, if she feels like sending one of us out or keeping us from blowing.

NOTOS: Well then, let's take care of her, Zephyros, since she's our mistress from now on. That way she'll be nicer to us.

ZEPHYROS: Well, she just got across and has swum to shore. Do you see how she no longer walks on four legs? Hermes has straightened her up and turned her back into a very beautiful woman.

NOTOS: How marvelous, Zephyros! No horns anymore. No tail. No legs with cloven hooves. Just a lovely girl! But wait—what's the matter with Hermes? He's changed himself. He's got a dog face when he used to look like a young man.

ZEPHYROS: Let's not get nosy. He knows what he needs to do better than we do.

12 Danae and Perseus in the Chest

Lucian presents us with a dramatized dialogue that occurs at the critical moment in the childhood of the hero Perseus, just before he and his mother are pulled in by Dictys' net on Seriphos thanks to the timely intervention of two Sea Nymphs. Lucian here dwells on the sentimental nature of the scene and seems most concerned with exploring the pity produced by the plight of mother and child. One can compare the touching poetic retelling of Simonides (fr. 543).

DORIS: Why are you crying, Thetis?

THETIS: Oh, Doris, I just saw the most beautiful girl being put into a chest by her father. Her and her newborn baby. The father ordered his sailors to take the chest and throw it into the sea when they were really far off shore so that the poor girl would die. Both her and the baby.

DORIS: But why, Sister? Tell me, if you know what really happened.

THETIS: I know the whole story. Because she was incredibly beautiful, her father Acrisios kept her a virgin by throwing her into a sort of bronze chamber. Then—I don't know if this is true, but they say that Zeus became gold and poured through the roof onto her and she caught him in her lap as he poured down and she became pregnant. When he learned of this, her father, a somewhat savage and jealous old man, grew angry. And, supposing that she'd been seduced by someone, he threw her into the chest just after she gave birth.

DORIS: And what did she do when she was being put in, Thetis?

THETIS: She didn't say anything about herself, Doris. She accepted her punishment. But she was begging for her baby not to be killed, weeping and showing it to its grandfather—it was a beautiful baby. And it was smiling at the sea because it didn't understand the terrible situation. My eyes fill with tears again when I remember them.

DORIS: You've made me start to cry, too. So . . . they're dead now?

THETIS: No, no! The chest is still floating around the island of Seriphos and it's keeping them alive.

DORIS: So why don't we save them by putting them into the nets of these fishermen from Seriphos? They'll certainly pull them in and save them.

THETIS: Good idea! Let's do it. She shouldn't die. Not her. And not her baby. It's so beautiful.

JUDGMENT OF THE GODDESSES

Although the Judgment of Paris is not told in either Homer's Iliad *or* Odyssey, *the event that ultimately led to the Trojan War was an enormously popular mythical subject in antiquity. Lucian has great fun with the situation by giving each of the participants in his dialogue a strong and distinct personality and by exploiting all the comic possibilities of a mortal being asked to judge three goddesses.*

ZEUS: Hermes, take this apple and go to Phrygia to Priam's son, the cowherd. He's got his herd on Gargaron, Mount Ida's highest peak. Tell him this: "Paris, Zeus orders you to judge which of the goddesses is the most beautiful because you yourself are handsome and wise in the ways of love. Let the winner take the apple as the prize." *[to the goddesses]* Now it's time for you to go to your judge because I refuse to make the decision. I love you all exactly the same. If it were only possible, I'd be happy to see you all win. And as it is, if I awarded one of you the prize, I would most definitely be completely hated by the other two. That's why I'm not a good judge for you. But the young man, this Phrygian you're going to, he's a prince and related to Ganymedes here. Besides, he's a simple man from the mountains, and you couldn't say he was unworthy of what he's about to see.

APHRODITE: Zeus, even if you made Momos[5] our judge, I'd be happy to go to the pageant. What fault could he find with me? But the mortal has to be acceptable to these ladies too.

HERA: We aren't afraid either, Aphrodite, not even if your Ares is trusted with the decision. Anyway, we also accept this Paris, whoever he might be.

ZEUS: *[to Athena]* Do you agree with that too, Daughter? What do you say? Are you turning away and blushing? Why, you're nodding! You virgins are normally so shy about such things! Off with you then. And the losers better not be mad at the judge. No causing trouble for him. It's just not possible for you all to be equally beautiful.

HERMES: Let's head straight for Phrygia. I'll lead and you follow me quickly. And cheer up. I know Paris. He's a handsome young man and passionate too. He's just the right kind of guy to make a decision like this. He won't judge badly.

APHRODITE: *[catching up to Hermes ahead of the other two]* When you say that our judge is just, that's really great. And it makes my chances look good. But is he single or does a woman live with him?

HERMES: He's not exactly single, Aphrodite.

APHRODITE: What do you mean?

HERMES: Well, apparently an Idaean woman is living with him.[6] She's okay, but she's rural and from the mountains. He doesn't seem to be all that committed to her. Why do you ask?

APHRODITE: Just asking.

[5] The personification of finding fault with or complaining about people.

[6] Oinone.

ATHENA: Hey! You're not doing your job very honestly. You're giving her all that private help.

HERMES: Athena, it wasn't anything bad about you two. She just asked me if Paris was single.

ATHENA: Now, why is she so curious about that?

HERMES: No idea. But she says she asked just because it occurred to her, not for any particular reason.

ATHENA: And? Is he single?

HERMES: He doesn't seem to be.

ATHENA: Who cares about that? Does he have any leanings toward matters of war? Is he at all fond of glory? Or is he just a cowherd through and through?

HERMES: I can't say for sure, but you have to suppose that since he's young he yearns to have these things and would want to be preeminent in battle.

APHRODITE: *[interrupting]* See? *I'm* not complaining at all or accusing you of talking to her in private. Only people who worry about what they've got behave like that. Aphrodite doesn't.

HERMES: She was asking me practically the same thing you did. So don't be angry or think you're getting the short end of the stick if I give her straight answers. Hey, while we've been talking, we've made good headway. We're out of the stars, practically over Phrygia. I see Ida and all of Gargaron clearly. If I'm not mistaken I also see your judge Paris.

HERA: Where is he? I can't see him.

HERMES: Look here to the left, Hera, not at the mountaintop, but to the side where the cave is. You can also see his herd there.

HERA: But I don't see his herd.

HERMES: What? Where I'm pointing, you don't see little cows coming out from the middle of the rocks? Or the man running down from his vantage point with a crook and trying to stop the herd from scattering too far?

HERA: I see him now. If that's him.

HERMES: That's him all right. Since we're close now, let's land on the ground and walk—if that's okay. That way we won't freak him out by dropping down from above out of the blue.

HERA: Good plan. Let's do it. And now that we've landed, it's time for you to take the lead, Aphrodite, and guide us. You're probably familiar with this place. You used to come down to Anchises all the time—or so they say.[7]

APHRODITE: These jokes of yours don't bother me, Hera.

HERMES: All right then, I'll lead. I personally spent some time on Ida back when Zeus was in love with the Phrygian boy. I used to come here all the time when he'd send me down to watch him. And after Zeus took the form of an eagle, I flew down with him and helped him lift the beautiful boy. And if I remember rightly, he

[7] Hera exaggerates. For Aphrodite's single visit to Anchises, see *Homeric Hymn* 5 (to Aphrodite).

snatched him up from this rock right here. He was playing his pipe to his flock just then, and Zeus dropped down behind him and put his claws around him. Holding the cap on the boy's head with his beak, he carried him up. The boy had his neck twisted around, looking at Zeus in terror. That was when I grabbed his panpipe—he'd let it drop from fear. Well, your referee is right here, so let's talk to him. *[to Paris]* Hello to you, cowherd!

PARIS: To you too, mister. But who are you, coming around to visit me? Who are these women you're bringing? They aren't the kind to be walking around the mountains. They're so beautiful.

HERMES: Well, they aren't mortal women. Paris, this is Hera and Athena and Aphrodite you're looking at. And I'm Hermes, sent by Zeus. Why are you shaking and all pale? Don't be afraid. It's no big deal. He just orders you to judge which of them is most beautiful. He says, "Since you are handsome and wise in the ways of love, I trust your judgment." If you read the apple, you'll know what the prize is.

PARIS: Here, let me see what it says. "Let the beautiful one take me." Now, how could I, Lord Hermes, be judge of such an incredible pageant? I'm mortal. I'm a bumpkin. This is too much for a cowherd to handle. You'd be better off having delicate city-folk judge such matters. Me? Now, I might knowledgeably be able to decide which of two she-goats was prettier. Or which heifer was prettier than another. But these goddesses are all just as beautiful as each other. I don't know how anyone could tear his eyes away from one to look at the next. Mine don't really want to move on. Wherever they land first they stick. And they like what's there. When they do look at something else, they see *that* beauty and stop, captivated by what's there. The goddesses' beauty is around me on all sides. It's surrounded me completely. It's terrible that I can't see with my whole body like Argos! I think it would be an excellent decision for me to give the apple to all of them. Oh, and now that I think about it, *she* happens to be Zeus' sister and wife and *they* are his daughters. That also makes the decision difficult, doesn't it?

HERMES: All I know is that it's impossible to refuse an order from Zeus.

PARIS: Hermes, get them to agree to this one condition: the two losers can't be mad at me. They should think of it as my eyesight's mistake, not mine.

HERMES: *[conferring with the goddesses]* They say that's what they'll do. Now it's time for you to make your decision.

PARIS: I'll do my best. What else can you do? But first I want to know whether it's enough for me to examine them as they are. Or do I have to have them take off their clothes for an accurate inspection?

HERMES: That's up to you. You're the judge. Tell them to do whatever you want.

PARIS: Whatever I want? Naked. I want to see them naked.

HERMES: *[to the goddesses]* You take off your clothes. *[to Paris]* You check them out. I've turned my back.

APHRODITE: Great, Paris! I'll strip first. That way you can find out that it's not just my arms that are white. And I'm not snooty about being "ox-eyed." *Every* part of me is beautiful to the exact same degree.

ATHENA: Paris, don't have her take off her clothes until she gets rid of her magical belt—she's a sorceress—that way she won't bewitch you. Also, she shouldn't take her turn all made up like that and painted with so much makeup. It really makes her look like a high-class hooker. She should show her beauty *au naturel.*

PARIS: They're right about the belt. Get rid of it.

APHRODITE: So, Athena, why don't *you* take off your helmet? Show your head bare instead of shaking your crest and scaring our judge. Or are you afraid that he'll criticize the grayness of your eyes when it's seen without the power to cause fear?

ATHENA: There you go. Helmet's off.

APHRODITE: My belt too!

HERA: Come *on*. Let's get these clothes off.

PARIS: O Zeus, god of marvels! The sight! The beauty! The pleasure! The virgin is so beautiful. And that one shines so royally and majestically. She's truly worthy of Zeus. And this other one looks sweet and smooth. She just gave me a come-hither smile. I don't think I could take any more bliss. But if it's okay, I want to view each of you individually. Right now I'm a bit overwhelmed. I don't know what to concentrate on. I can't keep my eyes in one place.

APHRODITE: Yes, let's do that!

PARIS: Then you two go away. Hera, you stay here.

HERA: I'm staying. And after you look me over carefully, you'll need to think about whether the other things you'll get as gifts for voting for me are also beautiful. If you decide that I am beautiful, Paris, you will be master of all Asia.

PARIS: I won't make a decision based on bribes. Just go. Whatever I decide is best will be done. Athena, your turn.

ATHENA: I'm right here by you. And if you decide that I'm beautiful you will never leave a battle defeated. You'll always be victorious. I will make you a conquering warrior!

PARIS: I don't need war or battle, Athena. As you can see we have peace here in Phrygia and Lydia. My father's kingdom has no enemies. But don't worry. You'll do fine even if I don't decide based on bribes. Well, get dressed now and put on your helmet. I've seen enough. It's time for Aphrodite's turn.

APHRODITE: Here I am, right beside you. Examine me carefully, one section at a time. Don't pass over any part of me too quickly. Take your time on every part of my body. And if it's all right with you, handsome, listen to what I have to say. Oh yes, I've been noticing this whole time that you are a handsome young man. I don't know if Phrygia is nurturing anyone else that compares to you. But while I congratulate you on your beauty, I think it's a problem that you haven't left the peaks and these cliffs to go live in the city. You're wasting your beauty out here in the boondocks. How can you enjoy the mountains? And what good does your beauty do the cows? You should have already been married by now. Not to some country girl like the ones they have here in Ida, but to someone from Greece. Maybe to an Argive girl or a Corinthian. Or to a Spartan girl like Helen. She's young and beautiful—as beautiful as I am. And most important, she's passionate. If she just laid eyes on you, I'm sure that she'd give up everything and be ready to marry you. She'd follow you and spend her life with you. No doubt you've heard about her.

PARIS: Not a word, Aphrodite. But I'd be happy to hear you tell me all about her right now.

APHRODITE: She's the daughter of Leda, the famous beauty that Zeus flew down to after turning himself into a swan.

PARIS: What does Helen look like?

APHRODITE: She's fair-skinned, as you'd expect from the daughter of a swan. And she's delicate since she hatched from an egg, but a highly trained wrestler. Men want her so badly that there was even a war over her after Theseus kidnapped her. That was when she was still a little girl. And there's more. When she finally did come of age, all of the noblest Achaians showed up to ask for her hand in marriage. Menelaos, one of Pelops' descendants, was selected. But if you want to marry her, I'll make it happen.

PARIS: What do you mean? Marry a married woman?

APHRODITE: You're young and from the country, but I know how to get such things done.

PARIS: How? I want to know too!

APHRODITE: You'll go to Greece as if on a sightseeing trip. When you get to Sparta, Helen will see you. From that point on it would be up to me to make sure she falls in love and goes with you.

PARIS: That's exactly what I find unbelievable—that she'll want to abandon her husband and sail off with a strange foreigner.

APHRODITE: Oh, don't worry about *that*. I've got two beautiful, lovely boys: Himeros {"Desire"} and Eros. I'll let you have the pair as guides. Eros will fill up her heart and force the woman to love you. Himeros will surround you with the very quality that he represents and make you desirable and lovely. And I'll be there, so I'll ask the Charites to come with me too. That way we'll all win her over.

PARIS: I don't know how this is going to turn out, Aphrodite, but I'm already in love with Helen. I don't know how, but I think I can actually see her . . . I'm sailing straight to Greece . . . I'm visiting Sparta . . . I'm coming back with the woman . . . and I'm upset because I'm *not* doing this stuff right now!

APHRODITE: Paris, don't fall in love until you trade me your vote. I'm your matchmaker, the one who'll be bringing you your bride. It would be right for me to be there with you, both of us winners. We could hold your wedding feast and my victory party at the same time. You can have it all. Her love. Her beauty. Her hand in marriage. You can buy it all for this apple.

PARIS: I'm afraid you'll forget about me after I make my decision.

APHRODITE: Well, do you want me to swear an oath?

PARIS: No, no! Just promise me again.

APHRODITE: I promise that I will give you Helen to be your wife and that she will follow you and come to your family in Troy. I myself will be there and will help accomplish everything.

PARIS: And you'll bring Eros and Himeros and the Charites?

APHRODITE: Don't worry about a thing. I'll bring Pothos {"Yearning"} and Hymenaios too.

PARIS: Then I grant you the apple on these conditions. You take it on the same ones.

ON SACRIFICES

The attitude expressed by Lucian in the Judgment of the Goddesses *and the* Dialogues *fundamentally opposes the traditional humanizing portrayal of the gods in Greek myth, which he thought absurd (compare Xenophanes, Plato, and others). In this short essay, Lucian makes a similar point about the religious nature of sacrifice, finding much to ridicule in popular attitudes toward the ritual. With consistent sarcasm Lucian exploits myths involving sacrifices to drive home the point that such stories mislead people into believing that the gods are greedy, petty, and influenced by human actions. There is a serious philosophical belief behind his ideas (compare his cynical reference to the sacrifice of Iphigenia with the horrified and more philosophically pointed description of it by Lucretius at* On the Workings of the Universe *1.82–101), but his tone is consistently derisive and humorous.*

[1] As for what fools do in their sacrifices, festivals, and processions for the gods, and what they ask them for and vow in return and what they think about them—well, I do not know if there is anyone who is so depressed or grief stricken that he is not going to laugh when he sees the stupidity of their actions. And I'm sure that *long* before he laughs, he will ask himself whether he should call them pious or, exactly the opposite, hostile to the gods and spiritually lacking since they assume that the divine is so base and disgraceful that it has need of mortals, takes pleasure when flattered, and grows angry when ignored.

Take, for example, the disasters that happened in Aitolia—the misfortunes of the Calydonians, the many murders, the destruction of Meleagros—all these things were, they say, the work of Artemis, who was complaining because she was not invited to the sacrifice held by Oineus. She was obviously deeply affected by the excellence of the animals he was offering! I can practically see her when it happened, alone in heaven because the rest of the gods had gone to Oineus' home, upset and whining about missing such a great festival.

[2] Conversely, you could say that the Ethiopians are both blessed and triply happy if, in fact, Zeus repays the favor they showed when they feasted him for twelve days despite the fact that he brought the rest of the gods too.

So the gods apparently don't do a single thing without getting something out of it. They sell their blessings to mortals; you can purchase from them the potential to be healthy in exchange for, say, the sacrifice of a calf. For four cows you can buy wealth. For one hundred you can be king. For nine bulls you will return safely from Troy to Pylos. And for a princess you can sail from Aulis to Troy. Once Hecuba paid twelve cows and a dress so Troy wouldn't be sacked. You have to figure that many things can be bought from the gods for a rooster or a garland or just some frankincense.

[3] I suppose that Chryses also knew this since he was a priest, an old man, and wise in divine matters. When he left Agamemnon without having ransomed his daughter, he asked for justice as if he had lent his favor to Apollo. He demanded payback and

all but insulted him when he said, "Noblest Apollo, I have often garlanded one of your temples that before had no garland. I have burned on the altars a great many thighs of bulls and goats for you. But you ignore me when I have suffered such awful things and do nothing for one who has done things for you."[8] As a result he made Apollo so uncomfortable with his words that the god picked up his bow and arrows, sat himself down by the anchored ships, and shot down with the plague the Achaians together with their mules and dogs.

[4] Since I have already brought up Apollo, I also want to talk about other things that wise men say about him. Not about how he was unlucky in love or about his killing of Hyacinthos or Daphne's disdain for him, but about how when he was condemned for the death of the Cyclopes and banished from heaven because of it, he was sent to earth to experience the life of a mortal. That was when he was a serf in Thessaly in Admetos' house and in Phrygia in Laomedon's. But he was not alone at Laomedon's. He had Poseidon with him, and because of their poverty both were making bricks and working on the city's wall. They didn't even get their whole price from the Phrygian, but they say that he still owed them more than thirty Trojan drachmas.

[5] Why, don't the poets solemnly declare these tales about the gods and far more holy stories than these about Hephaistos and Prometheus and Cronos and Rhea and practically the whole family of Zeus? What's more, they invite the Muses to sing along at the beginning of their poems and, supposedly inspired by them, they sing that Cronos, as soon as he castrated his father Ouranos, became king in his stead and then swallowed down his own children like Thyestes of Argos later did. Zeus was nursed by a goat after he was secreted away by Rhea when she substituted a stone for him and set him out in Crete, just as Telephos was nursed by a deer and the Persian Cyros the Elder by a dog. Then he drove his father out, threw him into prison, and seized power himself. He married many different women, and his sister last of all (a custom among the Persians and Assyrians). Since he was passionate and addicted to sex, he had no trouble filling heaven with children, producing some of them with females who were his peers and some illegitimately with mortal, earthly women, sometimes turning himself from a high-born god into gold, sometimes into a bull or swan or eagle—basically changing shapes more than Proteus. He produced Athena alone from his own head simply by conceiving her underneath his very brain. Dionysos, they say, he grabbed half-formed from his mother while she was still burning and took and buried him in his thigh. Then he cut him out when labor began.

[6] In the same way the poets also sing about Hera, telling how without intercourse with her husband she herself produced a child, Hephaistos, apparently fathered by the wind. They say he is not very well off, just a manual laborer, a smith and firestoker who lives his whole life in smoke, covered with embers, since he works in a furnace. And he is not even right in the legs since he was made lame from the fall he took when he was thrown out of heaven by Zeus. If the Lemnians had not done the good deed of catching him while he was still falling, Hephaistos would have been as dead for us as Astyanax after falling from the tower.

[8] Lucian quotes Chryses' prayer from book one of Homer's *Iliad.*

Still, Hephaistos' situation is not too bad. Prometheus, on the other hand—who does not know what he suffered because he loved mankind too much? Yes, taking him to Scythia, Zeus crucified him on Mount Caucasus and stationed the eagle near him to peck at his liver day after day.

[7] So Prometheus served out his sentence, but Rhea—to be fair I have to discuss this too—how can one say that she does not disgrace herself and behave badly? Although she's now an old woman past her years and the mother of so many gods, she still carries on with a boy, Attis, and acts jealously and takes him around on the backs of her lions even though he can no longer be of any use. So how can you criticize Aphrodite because she cheats on her husband, or Selene because she constantly leaves in the middle of her journey to go down to Endymion?

[8] Come, let us now leave these stories and go up to heaven itself, flying up poetically in the same way as Homer and Hesiod. Let us see how things are arranged above. We heard from Homer, who said it before us, that its outside is bronze. But to someone who crosses over it, emerges a bit into the upper side, and really gets onto its back, the light seems brighter, the sun purer and the stars more radiant. It is day all the time and the ground is made of bronze. As you go in, the Horai live closest, for they are the gatekeepers. Next live Iris and Hermes since they are the servants and messengers of Zeus. Then we have Hephaistos' forge, filled with every art, and after that the houses of the gods and the palace of Zeus, all of them incredibly beautiful since Hephaistos built them.

[9] "The gods, reclin'd round Zeus,"[9]—it is appropriate, I think, to use lofty words when one is high above—looked at the earth and look around everywhere, leaning over to see if they could spot a fire being lit anywhere or scent rising "wrapt around the smoke." And if anyone makes a sacrifice, they all feast by gulping the smoke and drinking the blood shed on the altars like flies. But if they eat at home, their meal consists of nectar and ambrosia. Now, long ago mortals too, Ixion and Tantalos, used to eat and drink with them. But because they overstepped their limits and could not control their tongues, those two are still being punished even now, and heaven is inaccessible and forbidden to the race of mortals.

[10] That is the way the gods live. Mortals, therefore, act in harmony and agreement with these things in regard to the way they worship. First, they set apart sacred groves, dedicated mountains, consecrated birds, and devoted plants to each god. Next, people divided the gods and worship them nationally and claim them as belonging to their cities. Someone from Delphi claims Apollo, as does someone from Delos. An Athenian claims Athena (she certainly shows her relationship through her name). An Argive claims Hera, a Mygdonian Rhea, and a Paphian Aphrodite. The Cretans not only say that Zeus was born and raised among them, but they even point out his tomb. So it turns out we have been deceived this whole time, supposing that Zeus has been thundering, raining, and getting everything else done when he had gone and died a long time ago and got buried in Crete without us knowing!

[11] Then people built temples so that the gods would not be without hearth and home, of course. They make likenesses of them, calling for Praxiteles, Polycleitos, or

[9] Here and at the end of the sentence Lucian quotes Homer, *Iliad* (4.1 and 1.317, respectively).

Pheidias,[10] men who must have seen them *somewhere*. They make Zeus bearded, Apollo always a boy, Hermes just getting his beard, Poseidon with blue hair, and Athena with gray eyes. In any case, those who enter the temple suppose they are looking not at ivory from India anymore, and not at gold mined in Thrace, but at the son of Cronos and Rhea, who has been moved to earth by Pheidias and commanded to watch over the deserted city of Pisa, happy if people sacrifice to him every four years just because they already happen to be visiting to watch the Olympics.

[12] When they have set up altars, posted temple regulations, and consecrated an area with holy water, they bring the sacrificial victims: the farmer a plowing ox; the shepherd a lamb; the goatherd a goat; someone else incense or cakes. The poor man wins the god's favor just by kissing his own right hand. But those who make sacrifices—to get back to them—put garlands on the animal's head, having examined it long before to see whether it is blemished so that they do not slaughter one that is unfit. They lead it to the altar and kill it before the god's eyes while it moos a little mournfully, apparently speaking praise of the god and accompanying the sacrifice with music, even though it is half-dead. Who would guess that the gods do *not* enjoy watching this?

[13] And the sign says that no one who has unclean hands is to enter the area sprinkled with holy water, but the priest himself stands covered in blood and like the famous Cyclops he cuts open the victim, pulls out the entrails, takes out the heart, and pours the blood around the altar. Why, what religious duty does he fail to perform? After all that he lights a fire. Then, carrying the goat in its own skin or the sheep in its own wool, he places it on the altar. The scent, being divine and holy, goes upward and gently wafts through heaven itself.

The Scythians, avoiding all animal offerings because they think them lowly, offer humans to Artemis. That is how they please the goddess.

[14] These things are also practiced more or less the same way by the Assyrians, Phrygians, and Lydians. But if you go to Egypt, *then* you will see many holy wonders that are truly worthy of heaven: Zeus with a ram's head. Most noble Hermes with a dog's head. Pan, who is completely a goat. Another god an ibis, still another a crocodile or a monkey. "And if you wish to ascertain these things to know them well,"[11] you will hear many wise men, scribes, and shaved-headed prophets explain—but first, as the saying goes, "Close your doors, you who are not initiated!"[12]—explaining that as the war and the revolt of the giants approached, the gods in their panic came to Egypt to hide from their enemies. Then one of them took on the form of a goat, and out of fear another became a ram and others beasts or birds. That is why even now to this day the gods keep the forms they had then. Of course, this information has been kept in the temples, recorded more than ten thousand years ago.

[15] In their culture sacrifices are the same except that they lament for the victim and beat their breasts while standing around the now-slain animal. They also just bury the animal after slaughtering it. As for Apis, the greatest god as far as they are

[10] Three of the most famous sculptors of classical antiquity.

[11] *Iliad* 6.150.

[12] A traditional cry at the start of many initiation rituals.

concerned, if he dies, there is no one who considers his own hair so valuable that he doesn't shave it off and show his grief plainly on his head, even if he happens to have the purple lock of Nisos. Apis is a god from a herd, chosen after his predecessor because he is far more handsome and holy than the regular cows.

When the rabble act this way and believe such things, I do not think we need someone to condemn them, but I think we do need a Heracleitos or a Democritos, someone to laugh at their lack of knowledge, someone to weep over their lack of understanding.[13]

[13] Democritos (5th c. BC) became known in antiquity as the "laughing philosopher," supposedly because he found human folly a source of amusement. Another early Greek philosopher, Heracleitos (late 6th c. to early 5th c. BC), who found such folly pitiable and sad, was paired with Democritos and became known as the "weeping philosopher" because of the contrasts between their philosophies.

LUCRETIUS

(ca. 94–ca. 55 BC, wrote in Latin)

Lucretius was an adherent of the Epicurean philosophical school, so-called because it was founded by Epicurus (341–270 BC). The Epicureans seem to have debated whether poetry was an appropriate vehicle for philosophy, but Lucretius seems to have had no such qualms himself, for he wrote On the Workings of the Universe (De Rerum Natura), *a poem in six books that sets forth the major beliefs of the school. The radical beliefs of the Epicureans had an impact on how they regarded myth. Two assumptions were crucial: 1) the world was made up of atoms (see 1.59–1.60), and 2) the gods were separated from and had no interest in mankind. For the Epicureans, then, mythology and religion arose from a fundamental misunderstanding of the nature of the world and gods, and what has been attributed to the gods can be explained rationally if one understands the way nature really works.*

FROM *ON THE WORKINGS OF THE UNIVERSE*

1.1–1.101 Lucretius Invokes Venus

The opening of the work sets the tone for the whole and is divided into three parts, each with its own purpose: an invocation to Venus, not the goddess as she is known from mythology, but the personification of desire, the force through which nature propagates itself (1–43); an exposition of the poet's goals, in which he explains atoms and Epicurus' great achievement in dispelling false ideas about the gods through his philosophy (50–79); and the cautionary tale of Aulis, a prime example of how traditional Greek religion can lead to horrible acts (80–101).

Mother of the Aeneadae,[1] pleasure of men and gods,
nourishing Venus, you who beneath the spinning stars of heaven
cause the ship-bearing sea and the fruitful lands
to throng with life! Through you all living creatures
are conceived and, once born, visit the sun's rays.
Before you the winds, before you and your advent the
clouds in heaven flee; for you the artful earth sends up
sweet flowers; for you the stretches of the sea laugh,

[1] "Descendants of Aeneas," i.e., the Romans.

and the peaceful sky shines in a bath of daylight.
For as soon as springtime's spectacle appears,
and the life-bringing West Wind begins to blow unfettered,
the birds on high announce you, goddess, and
your advent, their hearts smitten by your power.
The wild beasts prance through lush pastures
and ford raging streams, and, enchanted by your charm,
each beast through desire follows wherever you induce it to go.
Briefly put: from the seas, mountains, and racing rapids,
to the leaf-covered homes of birds and verdant meadows,
you, striking your luring love into the hearts of all, ensure that
every species through desire perpetually propagates itself.
Since you alone govern the workings of the universe
and without you nothing emerges into the shining realm of light
or becomes productive or pleasurable,
I am eager to have you as an ally in writing my poetry,
a work to establish the workings of the universe,
for our Memmius,[2] whom you, goddess, have ordained
to excel, endowed with every gift forevermore—
all the more may you, goddess, give eternal charm to my words!
May you meanwhile make sure that all wild works of war
grow silent in slumber over every sea and land.
For you alone have the power to grace mortals with peace
unbroken, because the wild works of war are guided by
Mavors,[3] mighty in war, and he often nestles himself in your arms,
smitten by an ever-fresh wound of love.[4]
He looks up, his head bent tenderly back, and feasts his ever-needy
eyes on your love, gazing at you, goddess, with parted mouth,
and his breath hangs forever on your lips.
Goddess, lean down and enfold him as he lies with your
holy body and whisper sweet nothings to him in your
quest, far-famed one, to bequeath tranquil peace to the Romans.
For in a time of stormy troubles for our country neither can we
execute our task undisturbed nor can renowned Memmius
amid such troubles turn his attention away from public safety.
<lines 44–49, repeated below at 2.646–2.651, probably do not belong here>

[2] An important politician to whom Lucretius dedicated his poem.

[3] Mars.

[4] Lucretius exploits the traditional Greek myth of the affair between Mars and Venus. Both divinities had great importance for the Romans: Venus was the mother of the Roman hero Aeneas and Mars was the father of Romulus and Remus, the legendary twin brothers who founded the city of Rome.

Now what is left for you is to dismiss your worries
and turn an open mind and ears to a true account,
lest you scorn and give up these gifts of mine, which I have
carefully set out for you, before you have understood them.
For I shall start my discussion of the supreme law of heaven and
the gods, and I shall reveal the basic elements of the universe
from which Nature creates, nourishes, and grows all things,
and into which the same, when they perish, are broken up by Nature.
These things I will in setting forth my account constantly call
"matter" or name "generative bodies" and
"seeds of things," or term "basic elements,"
because they exist first and the rest is made from them.

When human life on earth lay horribly crushed for all to see,
beaten down beneath oppressive Religion,
unveiling its face from the zones of heaven and
brooding over mortals with its terrifying gaze,
a Greek man[5] first dared to lift human eyes
against it, the first to take a stand against it,
a man unshaken by myths about the gods and by their thunderbolts
or by heaven and its threatening thunder. No, all this only
incited his mind to keen resolve, such that he desired
to be the first to break the tightly secured bolts of Nature's gates.
So the agile force of his mind prevailed, and he
traveled far beyond the flaming walls of the universe
and traversed the measureless expanse with his mind and soul.
Victorious, he brings back news to us about what can arise,
what cannot, and what law determines for each thing
its potential and its deeply rooted limitation.
This is why Religion instead lies trodden under foot,
and we by his victory stand equal to heaven.

My fear in all of this is that perhaps you might think
that you are learning the rudiments of a blasphemous system and
stepping onto a path of wickedness. On the contrary, all too often
Religion has given birth to wicked and blasphemous deeds,
as happened once on Aulis, when the altar of virgin Trivia[6]
was fouled, defiled by the blood of Iphianassa,[7]
an act perpetrated by the elite leaders of the Danaans, the best of men.
As soon as the sacred ribbons wreathed her virgin tresses,

[5] Epicurus.

[6] Diana.

[7] Iphigenia.

draping down over both her cheeks,
as soon as she saw her father grimly standing before the altar,
the priests beside him concealing the knife, and
her countrymen pouring forth a river of tears at the sight of her—
then she, mute with fear, dropped to the ground, sinking to her knees.
It availed the poor girl not at all at such an hour
that she was the first to bestow upon the king the name of father.
No, for she was hoisted up by those men's hands and led to the altars,
trembling, not so that she, the ritual sacraments of marriage complete,
might be surrounded with ringing shouts of "Hymenaeus,"
but so that she, pure in impure hands, in the very season to marry,
might fall a grim victim under her father's blow—
all so that his fleet might have a fortunate and felicitous launch!
This is how great a crime Religion could drive men to.

2.589–2.660 The False Myth of Mother Earth

This is one of the best examples in Lucretius of how humans invent false myths because of a fundamental misunderstanding of the workings of nature. The earth is, according to Epicureanism, an insensate body containing all sorts of atoms that make it fertile and fecund. But mankind, not understanding nature, has come to believe that Earth is a great and fertile goddess known as Cybele and worships her accordingly. The ritual celebration of her rites is full of pomp and circumstance, and Lucretius ridicules this exuberance of religious fervor to emphasize humankind's ignorance of nature. In the translation that follows, the pronouns "it" and "she" are used to distinguish between the insensate earth of the Epicureans and the personified goddess Earth of traditional myth.

To begin with, the earth has in itself elemental bodies.
From some of them fountains continually propel frigid waters
and renew the measureless sea, and from some fires arise.
For in many places the surface of the earth is kindled and burns,
and from its depths rage Aetna's fiery eruptions.
Further, it has the elements from which it is able to push up
shimmering grains and lush trees for mankind,
and also those from which it is able to offer
streams, foliage, and lush pastures for mountain-roaming animals.
This is why earth alone is called the Great Mother of gods,
Mother of beasts, and the Maker of our bodies.
The learned Greek poets of old have sung of this goddess,[8]
how she, seated upon her chariot, drives a pair of yoked lions.

[8] It is possible that two lines are missing after this one.

They teach us that the great earth is suspended in an expanse
of air, and that earth cannot rest upon earth.
The poets yoked wild beasts because offspring, however savage,
are sure to be subdued and tamed by the respect owed to their parents.
And they crowned her head with a wall[9]
because she, fortified in choice places, sustains cities.
Adorned with this symbol, the image of the Divine Mother
is even now carried through mighty lands producing awe.
Nations far and wide, following the ancient rituals,
call her the Idaean Mother and surround her with a great
retinue of Phrygians since they proclaim it was from Phrygia
that grain first grew and spread over all the earth.
They appoint *Galli*[10] to serve her since they wish to show
that all who have violated the Mother's divinity and have been
proven ungrateful toward their parents should be considered
unfit to bring living children into the realm of light.
Around her taut drums thump and cavernous cymbals crash
in their hands, and the harsh-sounding horns intone their warnings.
A hollow flute in Phrygian cadence goads on their minds,
and they carry weapons before her, signs of violent fury,
to terrorize the ungrateful minds and sinful hearts
of the masses with the fear of the goddess' powers.
So, as soon as she, carried through mighty cities,
silently graces mortals with an unspoken greeting,
they scatter bronze and silver on her whole route through town,
enriching her with bountiful offerings, and they release a flurry
of roses, casting shadows on the Mother and her retinue.
Then the armed band, given the title Phrygian Curetes
by the Greeks, sport amongst themselves
with weapons and leap to the rhythm, reveling in blood
and shaking their terrifying crests by nodding their heads.
They call to mind the Dictaean Curetes, who once in Crete,
the story goes, camouflaged the crying of Jupiter,
when around the boy the armed chorus of boys danced swiftly
<one nonsensical line omitted>
in rhythmic step and made bronze clash on bronze,
lest Saturn find and devour him with his jaws,
causing an everlasting wound deep in his mother's heart.
This is why armed men accompany the Great Mother,

[9] Artistic portrayals show the goddess with a crown crenellated like the walls of a city.

[10] The usual term for Cybele's eunuch priests.

or else it is to signify that the Goddess enjoins men to be ready
to defend their native land with arms and courage
and to be for their parents a source of protection and pride.
Now, although all of this has been nicely and neatly devised,
it is nevertheless far removed from a true account.
For the very nature of gods as gods must
enjoy everlasting life and unbroken peace,
separated from our lives in seclusion far away.
For they, subject to no pain, subject to no danger,
self-sufficient of themselves and needing nothing from us,
care not for our services nor do they feel anger.
And earth, to be sure, is perpetually insensate:
it is because it possesses the elemental bodies for many things
that it brings many things in many ways into the light of the sun.
If hereafter someone decides to call the sea Neptune and
grain Ceres and prefers to abuse the name Bacchus
instead of calling the liquid by its proper title,
let us grant him the right to say that the earth is
the Mother of the gods, so long as he in his heart
refrains from tarnishing his mind with sordid Religion.

5.1161–5.1240 The Origins of Religion

A fundamental tenet of Epicureanism is that gods are separated from humanity and take no interest, positive or negative, in mankind's affairs. Lucretius here details how primitive humans in the distant past came to invent religion (and myth alongside it) based upon consistently incorrect, even if understandable, assumptions about nature. Lucretius, following Epicurus, argues that the regularity of the heavenly bodies, the terrible crash of thunder, and the other phenomena that led to such beliefs have rational explanations without any connection to the divine, and therefore both myth and religion can be dispensed with.

Now, as for the reason why the worship of the gods spread through
the great nations of the world, and as for what filled our cities full of altars
and brought men to perform solemn rituals,
the same rituals that now flourish in mighty civilizations and states
and still to this day implant in mortal men awe,
awe that gives rise to new shrines to the gods over the whole world
and compels throngs to assemble there on holy days—
all of this is relatively easy to explain.
Very easy: For long ago generations of mortal men kept on seeing
extraordinary visions of the gods, bodies larger than life,
some while in a wakeful state, but even more in their sleep.

So they attributed sentience to them because
they appeared to move their limbs and emit lofty utterances
matching their splendid appearance and impressive strength.
They credited them with eternal life because their form
and beauty remained ever present and never changed,
but most important because they thought that beings endowed
with such strength could hardly be overcome by any force at all.
And men thought that the gods far excelled them in happiness
because the fear of death tormented not one of them,
and likewise because men saw in their dreams gods performing
many miracles without exerting themselves in the slightest.
Furthermore, men perceived that the heavenly systems and
the different seasons of the year revolved in a fixed order,
and they could not fathom the causes behind this.
So they escaped their dilemma by attributing everything to the gods
and having everything guided by the mere nods of their heads.
And they placed the homes and quarters of the gods in heaven
because night and moon were seen to glide through heaven,
the moon, the day, the night and the solemn signs of night,
the night-wandering torches of heaven and its flying flames,
clouds, sky, rain, snow, winds, thunder, hail,
the sudden crash and mighty menacing murmurs of thunder.
O misguided human race, to attribute such phenomena
to the gods and on top of this to assign them bitter anger!
What sorrows people produced for themselves! What
pains for us! What tears for our descendants!
Piety does not consist of being seen often veiling one's head,
turning toward a stone god, and approaching every altar,
or falling prostrate upon the ground before the gods' shrines
with palms held upward, or staining the altars with the blood
of many four-footed victims, or following one vow with another.
No, piety is the ability to contemplate the universe with a tranquil mind.
Of course, when we gaze up at the heavenly quadrants of the
mighty universe above, the aether studded with sparkling stars,
and when our thoughts turn to the paths of the sun and moon,
then in our hearts already burdened by other ills
this uneasiness too begins to stir and rear its head,
that there may be set over us some awesome divine power
that guides the bright celestial bodies on their various paths.
For it is our lack of understanding that disquiets our minds,
uncertain whether the universe had some moment of inception,
whether it will have some end when the walls of the universe

can no longer sustain the toil of this restless motion;
or if the world's walls, endowed with eternal sustainability
and gliding along over the never-ending passage of the ages,
can scorn the powerful force of boundless time.
Yet again, whose mind does not recoil in fear of the gods,
whose body does not shrink back in terror
when the earth, blasted by a terrifying lightning strike,
shudders deep, and thunder courses through the great heavens?
Do not whole peoples, whole nations tremble? Do not lofty kings
recoil and cower, struck with fear of the gods,
that the grave moment has finally come to pay the penalty
for some hideous crime or arrogant remark?
Likewise, when a tempest raging full fury over the sea
sweeps the fleet's admiral across its surface,
along with his stalwart legions and elephants,
does not he too try to win peace from the gods with promises,
and with prayers seek a treaty with the winds and favorable breezes?
All for naught, since often he, for all his prayers, is caught up
by a violent gale and carried toward the shallows of death.
To this extent a certain unseen force crushes human
affairs and seems to tread upon the noble *fasces*[11]
and menacing axes and make them its playthings.
Finally, when the whole earth totters beneath our feet,
and when shaken cities either fall or threaten to fall,
what wonder is it if humans think little of themselves
and give in to the belief that mighty and mysterious divine
forces are set over human affairs and govern everything?

[11] The *fasces* were rods bundled around an ax. They were carried before Roman magistrates as symbols of their power.

OVID

(43 BC–17 AD, wrote in Latin)

The poet Ovid wrote many mythological works, the most famous being the Metamorphoses, *one of the most influential mythological texts from antiquity. In addition to being remarkably productive, he was also extraordinarily creative, and no other work of his testifies to this better than the* Heroides, *a series of fictitious letters from famous mythological heroines to their absent lovers. Ovid more or less invented a new genre. He takes the great literary tradition of the Greeks (e.g., Homer and the tragedians) and transforms it by adding the female voice where earlier writers were largely silent. Thus the achievement of the* Heroides *is the sustained exploration of the mythical tradition from a perspective that had not been consistently exploited previously.*

FROM *HEROIDES*

1 Penelope to Ulysses

Serving as a backdrop to this poem is Homer's Odyssey, *which portrays Penelope as the paragon of wifely virtue, suffering and waiting for twenty years for her husband to return home from the Trojan War. Ovid carefully chooses the moment he wishes to dramatize. The war is over. The other Greek kings have returned from the war to their wives and families. Suitors have taken control of the palace. Where is Ulysses? What is taking him so long? As she wavers between despair (what if something happened?) and anger (what if he chooses to stay away?), Ovid shows us Penelope in a new light.*

Your Penelope sends this letter to you, her dallying Ulysses.
  A return-letter will not do; you must come yourself.
Troy has surely fallen, city hateful to Greek girls—
  Priam and all of Troy could hardly have taken so long.
How I wish that that adulterer had drowned in raging seas
  while on his voyage to Sparta with his fleet!
Then I would not have had to lie in a cold, empty bed, or have
  complained of passing monotonous days deserted,
or of having exhausted these widowed hands working on my
  dangling loom, a vain attempt to while away long nights.
Tell me, when did I not fear dangers worse than real?
  Love's an emotion that's full of anxious fears.

I envisioned Trojans about to make a rush at you;
at every mention of Hector's name I grew pale.
If someone recounted how Antilochus was subdued by Hector,
Antilochus was the reason for my fears.
Or if he told how Menoetius' son[1] fell in deceptive armor,
I wept that the ploy couldn't have met with success.
When Tlepolemus made the Lycian's[2] spear warm with his blood,
Tlepolemus' death revived my worry for you.
In short, whenever one of the Greeks fell to the slaughter,
this lover's heart felt the chill of fear colder than ice.
But as it turns out, a kindly god looked out for my faithful love:
Troy was reduced to ashes, and my husband survived safe and sound.
The Greek chieftains have come home. Smoke is rising from the altars.
The spoils of a foreign war lie before the ancestral gods.
Every wife gives thank-offerings for her husband's deliverance,
while the men sing how their comrades put an end to Troy's days.
Real old-timers and timorous girls listen in awe, while
wives hang on every word of their storytelling husbands.
Now someone reconstructs fierce battles upon the table before him
and sketches out all of Troy with a touch of wine:
"Here the river Simois flowed. This is the area called Sigea.
Here elderly Priam's towering palace once stood.
Here were the camps of Aeacus' grandson,[3] there Ulysses',
and here Hector's mangled body spooked the horses to a gallop."
All of this venerable Nestor told to your son
when I sent him to find you, and he passed it on to me.
[He also told how Rhesus and Dolon were cut down by the sword,
the former in his sleep, the latter by deceit.][4]
Did you dare—ever too forgetful of your family!—
to undertake a night raid on the Thracian camp,
slaying so many heroes, aided by just a single man?
Yet once you were quite cautious, thoughtful, mindful of me.
My heart didn't stop racing with fear until I'd heard
you rode through friendly ranks on those Ismarian steeds.
But what good does it do me that Troy was razed by your stout arms
and flat ground now sits where the walls once stood,
when my plight remains the same as it was when Troy endured?

[1] Patroclus.

[2] Sarpedon.

[3] Achilles.

[4] This couplet was likely added later by someone other than Ovid.

I must endlessly feel the loss of an absent husband.
The towers of Troy have been razed; for me alone, they still remain,
though a victorious settler plows the land with a captured ox.
Where Troy once stood there's only a field of grain. The earth flourishes,
fertilized by Phrygian blood, awaiting the harvesting sickle.
Curved plowshares strike the half-buried bones of men,
and the ruins of fallen houses lie hidden among the weeds.
Though victorious, you are still gone, and I have no way of knowing
why the delay, or where your unfeeling heart is hiding.
Every sailor who turns a foreign ship to these shores leaves
only after answering numerous questions about you,
and I give them a letter written by these fingers
for them to deliver if they should happen to see you.
For news we sent to Pylos, the Neleian lands of venerable Nestor,
but we received no clear word from them.
We also sent to Sparta, but Sparta too had no knowledge of the truth.
Where are you staying? Where do you dally away from home?
I'd be better off if the walls Phoebus built still stood.
I'm mad at myself for my earlier prayers—ah, fickle woman!
At least then I'd know where you were fighting, war my only worry,
my lament joined by those of many other women.
What I should fear, I don't know. Yet I, out of my mind, fear everything,
and my worries have many places in which to roam.
Whatever perils the lands and the sea pose for you,
these I presume are the reasons for your long delay.
Yet, while I stupidly dream up these fears, knowing the lust of you men,
you could be ensnared in a foreign woman's embrace!
Perhaps you're telling her how backward a wife you have,
how the only thing not coarse in her world is her wool.
Oh, I hope I'm mistaken, that my accusation vanishes in the wind,
that you, if you are free to return, do not *choose* to stay away.
As for me, my father, Icarius, has been pressing me hard to give up
my widow's bed, ceaselessly chiding me for my perpetual delays.
Let him chide all he wants! I am yours and should be spoken of as such—
I shall always be Ulysses' wife, Penelope!
All the same, he is being won over by my loyalty and my virtuous
pleas; his forceful demands have softened.
But suitors from Dulichium, Samos, and lofty Zacynthus—
that whole wanton mob—have descended upon me.
They are playing king in *your* palace, and there's no one here to stop them.
Your wealth, our sustenance, is being gutted.
Why speak of those dreadful suitors, Pisander, Polybus, and Medon?

Or of Eurymachus and Antinous' ever grabbing hands?
Or all the rest whom you in your absence are allowing to grow fat
on the treasures won at the cost of your blood?
Your final humiliation? Add to your losses the beggar Irus and
Melanthius, who drives your flocks to feed the suitors' bellies.
We are only three in number, all unsuited for war—a powerless wife,
your old father, Laertes, and Telemachus, just a boy, and him
I almost lost recently to a treacherous plot as he was preparing
to sail to Pylos against the will of all the others.
I pray that the gods preserve the natural order of the Fates, that
he will close both my eyes and yours on our final days.
On our side are the guardian of your cattle, your elderly nurse,
and a third ally, the faithful caretaker of your filthy sties.[5]
But even so, Laertes—seeing that he is unfit to fight—is not
strong enough to hold power surrounded by enemies.
In time Telemachus will grow into a brave man (provided he lives),
but his tender years should be protected by a father's care.
I certainly don't have strength to drive the enemy from the palace.
You must come quickly. You are your family's shelter and sanctuary.
You have a son (and I pray you may still), who in his tender years
ought to have been reared in his father's ways.
Have regard for Laertes. He's holding off his dying day,
hoping that you will close his eyes for the last time.
And as for me, I was but a girl when you left.
Even if you came home right away, I would seem old and gray.

3 Briseis to Achilles

The most famous (one could almost say the only) story of Briseis, Achilles' slave and lover, is from Homer's Iliad. *Though she is central to the action—Agamemnon's seizure of her from Achilles leads to the latter's great anger and withdrawal from the war—she is largely silent, almost more a piece of property than a human being. What better opportunity could have presented itself to Ovid, who has* carte blanche *to dramatize Briseis' feelings? The setting is carefully chosen. It is not immediately after she is seized (*Iliad *1), but days later, just after the Greek kings have sent an embassy of Achilles' peers, who, in order to reconcile with him, offer among other things the return of Briseis (*Iliad *9). Achilles refuses. Ovid's poem is a vivid investigation of what Briseis might have felt at that moment.*

The letter you now read has been sent by your stolen Briseis,
written in Greek, but poorly by her barbarian hand.
All the smears you see have been made by my tears,

[5] The three are, respectively, Philoetius, Eurycleia, and Eumaeus.

yet tears too have the weight of words.
If I am allowed to complain a bit about you, my lord and lover,
I shall raise a few complaints about my lord and lover.
It is not your fault that I was quickly handed over to the king
on demand, but this is your fault:
When Eurybates and Talthybius came to demand me, *immediately*
I was handed over to go back with Eurybates and Talthybius.
Each turned to the other and cast a puzzled glance,
silently wondering where our love had gone.
I did not have to go so soon; a moment's delay would have been nice.
Alas for me, I could give you not a single kiss as I departed.
No, I shed an endless flood of tears and rent my hair.
An unfortunate lot, it seemed, to be taken a second time!
[Often have I wished to elude my guard and return to you,
but the enemy was always present to grab me in my fear—
I was afraid that, if I did set out at night, I would be captured and
sent as a prize to one of Priam's daughters.][6]
But suppose I *had* to be handed over—still I've been gone so many nights
and have gone unclaimed! You do nothing. Your anger is slow.
Menoetius' son[7] himself, as I was being handed over, whispered in my ear,
"Why weep? You'll be back in no time!"
Unclaimed is one thing, Achilles, but you actively oppose my return!
So go ahead, claim the title of an eager lover now!
The sons of Telamon and Amyntor[8] came to you
(the former related by blood, the latter your friend),
as did Laertes' son[9]—all to secure my return!
Magnificent gifts added weight to their coaxing entreaties:
twenty burnished cauldrons made of finely-wrought bronze,
seven tripods identical in weight and craftsmanship.
Added to these were twice-five talents of gold,
twice-six stallions that have never known defeat,
girls of outstanding beauty (completely unnecessary!) from Lesbos,
bodies enslaved when their house was taken,
and, along with all this, a wife (no need for *this*),
one of Agamemnon's three daughters.
All of this—the price you should have *paid* to Atreus' son to
buy me back—you refuse to accept!

[6] Some scholars think these lines were added later.

[7] Patroclus.

[8] Ajax and Phoinix, respectively.

[9] Ulysses.

What sin did I commit that I now seem so cheap in your eyes, Achilles?
Where has that fickle love fled so swiftly away from me?
Or is it that the downtrodden are doggedly haunted by grim fortune
and enjoy no moment of respite once their evils have begun?
I witnessed the razing of Lyrnessus' walls in your onslaught—
I, who was an important person in my country.
I witnessed three men fall, three who were joined in kinship and
death, three whose mother was also my own.
I witnessed the death of my husband fully stretched out on the
gory earth, chest heaving and soaked in blood's crimson.
For so many lost I have but one to compensate, you.
You were my master, my husband, my brother.
You yourself swore on your sea-mother's power and kept telling me
that my capture was to my advantage.
Advantage? So you can spurn me now, though I come with a dowry,
and avoid me and the riches I bring?
There's even a rumor floating about that tomorrow at dawn's first rays
you intend to hoist your sails to the cloud-bearing South Wind.
When my anxious, wretched ears caught wind of that villainous plan,
all blood, all life drained out of my heart.
You'll leave and—Oh, woe!—to whom are you leaving me, you destructive man?
Who will be my source of soothing solace in my desolation?
Would that a wide chasm suddenly gape open and swallow me whole
or a heaven-sent thunderbolt obliterate me with its ruby fire
before Phthia's ships churn the waters white without me on board,
and I, deserted, am forced to look upon the ships as they sail away.
If you are now bent on returning home to your ancestral gods,
well, I am not a lot of cargo for your ships to carry!
I will follow you as a captive does her captor, not as a bride her husband;
my hands are deft at spinning wool that is soft.
No, it will be the most beautiful Achaean woman who will come
into your chamber as your bride—and may she come!—
a worthy daughter for her new father-in-law, Jupiter and Aegina's grandson,
and one that old Nereus would want to be his grandson's wife.[10]
I'll be content to spin my daily share of wool as your humble slave.
My ball of wool will diminish as my hands draw off the thread.
All I ask you is that you not let your wife abuse me—
somehow I know that she will not be fair to me—
nor let her tear at my hair in your presence. And do *not*
offhandedly say, "She too was once mine."

[10] The father-in-law is Peleus, Achilles' father; Nereus is the father of Achilles' mother, Thetis.

Then again, let her do it—just do not shun and leave me;
this (oh, the pain!) is the fear that shivers my bones.
Anyway, what are you waiting for? Agamemnon regrets his anger,
and all of Greece mourns, lies prostrate at your feet.
Conquer that pride, that anger of yours. You conquer everything else!
Why do you let Hector tirelessly maul the Danaan army?
Take up your arms, grandson of Aeacus[11]—but take me back first!—
and with Mars' support drive the enemy back in panic.
Let the anger that was roused on my account subside on my account;
let me be both the beginning and the end of your sullen mood.
Do not think it dishonorable to give in to my pleas—
Oeneus' son[12] was roused to fight by his wife's pleading.
I've heard the story; you know it well. His mother cursed the head
and hopes of her son because he deprived her of her brothers.
War was afoot. He defiantly withdrew from battle and put down his arms.
Stubbornly he refused to help his country.
Only his wife could bend her husband's resolve. She met with more success;
my words fall for naught because you give them no weight.
And yet, I'm not angry or behaving as if I were your wife just because
I, a slave, have been called many times to my master's bed.
A certain captive girl, I recall, used to call me "Lady."
I said to her, "To my servitude you now add the burden of a title."
Still, by my husband's bones, scarcely covered by a tomb hastily made,
always to be held hallow in my heart;
by my three brothers' stout souls, now my guardian spirits,
who fell in honor for their country and with their country;
by your head and mine, which we joined together as one,
and by your sword, that weapon known to my family,
I *swear* that the Mycenean never shared a bed with me.
If I am lying, you have every right to desert me.
And yet, if I should say to you, "Bravest of men, now swear to me
that you have not enjoyed another woman," you couldn't!
The Danaans think you're miserable. Ha! You're playing the lyre,
held in the warm arms of some supple girlfriend!
And if someone asks why you refuse to fight? It's because fighting brings
pain, while the cithara, night, and Venus bring pleasure.
It's safer to lie in bed with a girl in your arms and
to strum the Thracian lyre with your fingers

[11] Achilles' paternal grandfather.

[12] In *Iliad* 9, Phoinix uses the famous story of Meleager son of Oeneus (in this volume see Antoninus Liberalis 2 and Apollodorus F) to try to persuade Achilles to return to battle.

than it is to have a shield on your arm, a spear in your hand,
  or a helmet on your matted-down hair.
Yet there was a time you prized deeds that brought glory, not safety.
  It was the fame won on the battlefield that was sweet.
Or did you like fierce battles only until you took me captive?
  Does your passion for glory now lie dead with my country?
God forbid! I pray that you cast Pelion's spear from your stout arm
  and drive it through Hector's side!
Danaans, send me as ambassador! I shall appeal to my master and
  bring your message, but mixed with many kisses.
Trust me, I will accomplish more than Phoenix, eloquent Ulysses,
  and Teucer's brother could have combined.
Something will come from having familiar arms around his neck,
  having his memories stirred at the sight of my breast.
Achilles, though you are cruel, fiercer than your mother's waves,
  even if I should say nothing, you would still crumble under my tears.
Even now (so may your father, Peleus, fulfill all his allotted years and
  may Pyrrhus[13] take up arms following in your example),
show some courtesy to your anxious Briseis, brave Achilles.
  Don't heartlessly torture a broken woman with drawn-out delays.
Or, if your love for me has turned tiresome, force the woman
  you now force to live without you to meet her death.
And you will if you keep this up. My body and complexion have withered,
  yet my hope in you has sustained what little is left of my soul.
And if I lose that, I shall reunite with my brothers and my husband.
  No great boast for you, ordering a woman to die!
But why give the order? Draw the sword yourself and strike me.
  There's blood in my body to shed from a pierced chest.
When you attack, use the sword you would have plunged into the chest
  of Atreus' son had the goddess sanctioned his death.[14]
No! Preserve my life, the gift I owe to your generosity. As your lover I ask
  for that kindness you, my captor, gave to me when I was your enemy.
Pergamum, the citadel Neptune built, offers you men more suitable to kill.
  If you need an object for your slaughter, look to the enemy to find it.
Whether you are planning to launch your ships under oar or to stay,
  I beg you, as is your right as my master, beckon me to come!

[13] Achilles' son.

[14] In *Iliad* 1, Athena prevents Achilles from killing Agamemnon.

4 Phaedra to Hippolytus

In Euripides' Hippolytos *Phaidra falls in love with her stepson Hippolytos but refuses to reveal her love to him. Her nurse, however, does so, and to preserve her honor Phaidra kills herself, leaving a letter accusing Hippolytos of trying to rape her. Ovid, however, has a different version of the story, in which Phaedra actually decides to confess her love to Hippolytus, here through a letter presumably to be delivered by the nurse. It is not clear whether the existence of this letter was Ovid's invention or derives from an earlier tradition.*

The Cretan maiden sends greetings to you, the Amazonian hero.[15]
  Her welfare, unless you provide it, will be wholly lost.
Read this letter through—what harm can reading a letter do?
  You too may find something pleasing within.
These characters convey secrets over land and sea.
  Even enemies look at letters from each other.
Three times I tried to speak to you. Three times my tongue stopped cold,
  useless. Three times my voice failed to pass beyond my lips.
Modesty, when possible and natural,[16] must be united with Love;
  what Modesty kept me from saying, Love ordered me to write.
Love's commands cannot be safely ignored, since he is king
  and has absolute mastery over the gods almighty.
When at first I was uncertain if I should write, he said to me,
  "Write! That iron-hearted man will surrender to you."
May he aid me and, just as he kindles the flame of desire in my marrow,
  may he prompt your thoughts to respond to my prayers!
It won't be out of wantonness that I break my marriage vows.
  My reputation—ask around—has never been compromised.
Desire is upon me, more oppressive for having come late. I burn inside,
  I burn, and an invisible wound rests within my heart.
Of course, just as soft necks of bulls chafe beneath their first yoke,
  and as a colt captured from a wild herd bucks at the reins,
so too does my inexperienced heart ill endure its first feelings of desire,
  and the weight does not sit well on my mind.
It becomes routine when intrigue is learned well from one's tender years,
  yet when a woman loves past her prime, her love's all the worse.
You will receive the first-fruits of my long-guarded reputation.
  Both of us will become guilty side by side.
There is something to plucking fruit from branches that are full
  and cutting the first rose of spring with a delicate nail.
Yet if that spotless and unsullied purity with which I once lived

[15] Hippolytus' mother was the Amazon Antiope (or Hippolyte).

[16] The text and exact meaning of the Latin here is uncertain.

had to be marred by some unaccustomed stain,
at least it turned out well in this: worthy is the flame with which I burn.
Worse than adultery is to commit it with an adulterer who is base.
If Juno were to offer up to me her brother and husband,
I believe I would choose Hippolytus over Jupiter!
Now (you'd hardly believe it) I'm even taking a plunge into new pursuits!
I have the urge to go into the wild among the animals.
The chief goddess for me is the one preeminent with her curved bow,
the Delian—I am merely following your lead.
I enjoy outings to the woods, harrying deer into nets
and spurring on swift hunting dogs along mountain ridges,
or flinging from whirling arm a missile that quivers in flight,
or laying my body down upon the grassy earth.
Often I take delight in turning the nimble chariot in the dust,
twisting the mouth of the racing steed with the reins.
And then I rush wildly, like the Eleleidae[17] driven on by their god's madness,
or like the drum-beating women at the foot of Mount Ida's slopes,[18]
or like those who the half-divine Dryads and the double-horned Fauns
have stricken with their powers and driven out of their minds.
I know. My attendants, after that madness of mine has passed, tell me
everything. I do not reply, burned by desire, my accomplice.
Perhaps this desire is the debt I pay in accordance with my family's fate,
and Venus is exacting payment from my entire family.
Europa—who is the first of our line—was Jupiter's
beloved, and a bull was the god's disguise.
Pasiphae, my mother, was mounted by a bull fooled by her ploy
and gave birth from her womb to her disgraceful burden.[19]
Aegeus' son[20] was a traitor, who by following the guiding thread
escaped out of the winding walls with my sister's help.
And look, now I (lest people by chance think I am not Minos' daughter)
am the last of my family to meet the fate we all share.
This too was destined: one house would capture two girls' hearts.
I am taken by your good looks, my sister was taken by your father.
Theseus and Theseus' son took two sisters captive—
set up your twin trophies in honor of sacking our house!
The moment I entered Eleusis, city sacred to Ceres
(how I wish Cnossus' soil had held me back!),

[17] Bacchae.

[18] A reference to the ecstatic worship of Cybele.

[19] The Minotaur.

[20] Theseus.

I was smitten by you—not that I wasn't attracted before—
    and within my bones a love that cuts deep took hold.
You were dressed in shining white, your hair bound in a wreath of flowers,
    and a modest blush graced your suntanned cheeks.
The features other women call "stiff" and "severe"
    are not stiff at all (if Phaedra's to judge), but *strong*.
Keep those men gussied up like women away from me!
    A man's natural looks are suited best by few accessories.
That ruggedness serves you well, as does your simply arranged hair
    and that light layer of dust upon your gorgeous face.
If you turn the straining neck of your high-spirited stallion,
    I marvel at its feet turning in so tight a circle.
Or if you hurl a pliant shaft with your mighty arm or brandish
    cornel-wood spears tipped with wide iron blades,
that strong arm of yours draws my eyes that way.
    Put simply, my eyes take pleasure in everything you do.
But you—just leave that toughness in the hillside forests!
    I am not fit prey for your hunting prowess.
Why do you delight in that zealous devotion to agile Diana
    and steal from Venus one of her rightful subjects?
Whatever does not enjoy periods of repose cannot last forever.
    Rest renews strength and refreshes wearied limbs.
Your bow—and you ought to imitate your goddess' weapons—
    if you never cease drawing it back, it will grow flaccid.
Cephalus was a man renowned in the forests, and he felled many beasts
    in the field by the stroke of his spear.
And yet, he did not offer himself reluctantly to the love of Aurora;
    The wise goddess left her old husband and came to him.
Often Venus and Cinyras' son[21] lay on the earth beneath some holm-oak,
    their bodies propped up on some patch of grass.
Oeneus' son[22] too burned, he for Maenalian Atalanta, and
    she has as a token of his love the hide of the wild beast.
It's high time we too were counted in that company of lovers!
    Take Venus away and that forest of yours has no romance.
I'll be your squire—no rocky, lurking lair will daunt me,
    no boar with its fearful side-slashing tusks.
I'll dwell with you in Troezen, Pittheus' realm, where the
    two seas batter with salty waves the Isthmus,
where that thin slip of land listens to the sea-roar of both,

[21] Adonis.

[22] Meleager.

land that now means more to me than my own.
For the time being his heroship, Neptune's son, is gone, and long will be—
he's being detained in his good friend Pirithous' land.
Theseus—unless we deny what is completely obvious—prefers
Pirithous to Phaedra, Pirithous to you.
And this is not the only injury we have suffered at his hands.
Oh no, both of us have been mightily abused.
My brother's bones he shattered with a triple-knotted club,
littering the ground with them. He left my sister for wild beasts.
Your mother was foremost in valor among the ax-wielding
women,[23] a parent with the vigor to match her son's.
Want to know where she is? Well, Theseus drove a sword into her side.
So great a bond as a son's birth did not protect her!
She was never married, never brought home under the marriage torch.
Why? Lest you, a bastard son, inherit the family throne.
What's more, he gave you brothers from my womb; yet all these he
raised as heirs not for my sake, but for his.
How I wish the womb destined to harm you, handsomest of men,
had ruptured in the midst of its delivery!
So go on, respect the bed of a father who *so* deserves it,
the bed *he* is avoiding and rejecting by his actions!
And about the appearance of incest between stepmother and stepson,
well, don't let those meaningless names scare you away!
That old-fashioned, prudish respect for family you adhere to prevailed
when Saturn ruled and was doomed to die out in a generation.
Jupiter gave new meaning to "familial respect"—whatever was pleasing!
Everything was fair game once sister married brother.
Family bonds are held fast by a solid chain only
if Venus herself binds them with her knots.
It will not be hard to hide our love either, though we sin.
Our guilt will be hidden under the name of family.
Should someone see us in an embrace, we will both be praised.
I will be called a stepmother devoted to her stepson.
No need to slink through shadows, waiting for the door of your mistress'
heartless husband to be unbarred. There will be no guard to elude!
We've lived under one roof, and we'll continue to live under one roof.
You used to kiss me openly, and you'll continue to kiss me openly.
You will be safe with me, and through sin you will earn praise,
though people see you in my bed.
Just stop with the delays; hurry up and affirm this bond of love!

[23] The Amazons.

So may the desire that now rages in my heart be gentle to you.
It is not beneath me to entreat you as a suppliant on bent knees.
Alas, where is that former pride, those lofty words? Humbled.
And there I was, resolved—if lust carries with it any "resolve"—
to put up a long fight and not to give in to sin.
I am beaten. So I beg you, I stretch out my royal arms to your knees.
Proper behavior? A lover doesn't give a damn.
Gone is all modesty—it's deserted the field, abandoned the standards.
Pity a woman baring her soul. Soften your hard, hard heart.
My father is Minos, who controls the high seas, and his father's hand
hurls the mighty stroke of the lightning bolt.
My mother's father is wreathed in a palisade of pointed rays and
guides the warming daylight on his shining chariot.
So what? My nobility has been crushed by Desire. Pity my ancestors.
If you will not spare me, then spare my family!
With my dowry comes a land, Crete, Jupiter's island—let them all,
palace and country, bow to my Hippolytus' wishes!
Let go of your obstinacy. Stop being defiant. My mother could seduce a
bull. Are you going to be crueler than a savage bull?
I beg you by Venus, who is strongest in me now, spare me!
In return may you never feel love for one who could reject it,
and may the swift goddess aid you in remote woodlands.
May the deep forest present wild game for you,
may Satyrs and Pans, mountain deities, favor you, and may the boar fall
pierced by your spearpoint as he rushes at you.
May the Nymphs (though they say you hate women) give to you
waters to quench your thirst when you are parched.
I also add tears to these prayers, so when you read the words
of my prayer, imagine that you see my tears as well!

10 Ariadne to Theseus

The standard version of Ariadne's myth runs in general terms like this. She falls in love with Theseus and saves him from the labyrinth, is summarily abandoned by him on the island of Naxos, and is then saved by Dionysus, who makes her his immortal wife. The setting of Ovid's poem is Naxos, some days after she is abandoned, but before her rescue by Dionysus. Ariadne's plight is worse than those of the other women in the Heroides; *in addition to losing her lover, she is left on a desert island with no means of survival. While we know she is to be saved, she does not, and Ovid exploits her feelings of isolation and terror.*

I've found that every species of wild beast is less cruel than you;
I'd have been better off trusting them.
These words that you are reading, Theseus, I send from that very shore

from which your ship set sail without me.
It was here that I was betrayed by sleep, and by you too, who
waited for me to fall asleep with villainy in your heart.
It was the time of year when the glassy frost first covers the lands,
when birds on their leaf-covered perch begin their lament.
I, on my side, only half-awake and groggy from sleep,
reached over to embrace my Theseus—
he wasn't there! I drew my hands back and tried again
and ran my hands all over the bed—he wasn't there!
Panic shook me from sleep. Terrified, I rose up and
threw my body out of that deserted bed.
At once my breast resounded with blows from my hands,
and I tore at the hair on my head, unkempt as it was from sleep.
By the full moon I looked out, perhaps to see something besides the shore,
yet the shore was all that my eyes could see.
I ran this way and that, and back again, without direction or purpose,
the deep sand slowing my girlish feet.
All the while I filled the whole shore with shouts of "Theseus,"
but the rocky hollows only echoed your name.
As many times as I called out to you, so too did the place itself,
as if it wanted to offer aid to me in my misery.
There was a mountain. Shrubs occasionally broke the line of the slope,
and a rocky crag, eroded by the hoarse waves, hung over the sea.
I climbed up (my love gave me strength), and from this vantage point
I surveyed the deep seas far and wide.
It was then I found out that the winds too were cruel,
when I saw your canvas sails taut with the rushing South Wind.
Either I saw, or else it had been what I thought I had seen,
and I became colder than ice, all but dead.
But my pain did not allow me to languish too long, but spurred me on
and made me call out "Theseus" at the top of my voice,
shouting, "Where are you fleeing? Theseus, you scoundrel, come back!
Turn that ship around—it's missing a passenger!"
That was my cry. What I could not put into words, I beat out on my chest.
Coupled together were my beatings and my pleadings.
And so that you might be able to see me, in case I was not heard,
as a signal I waved my hands in a wide swath and
attached my white veil to a long branch to draw
your attention. After all, you had simply forgotten me.
Soon you were wrenched from my sight. Only then did I weep.
Until then my eyes had been weak and numb with grief.
What else could my eyes do except shed tears for my lot

when they no longer looked upon your sails?
I spent my days all alone, now wandering with loose hair
like a Bacchant in the Ogygian god's[24] frenzy,
now sitting on a rock, cold, staring out to sea;
I was as much a rock as that upon which I sat.
Many times I returned to the bed that once embraced us both,
a bed destined never to show us together again.
Instead of you I touch what I can, the imprint you left
and the coverings made warm by your body.
I lie down upon the bed now drenched with my many tears:
"Two of us lay upon you," I shout at it. "Make us two again!
We both came here, so why didn't we leave together?
Traitorous bed! Where is my better half?"
What will I do? Where will I go all alone? The island isn't civilized;
I see neither feat of mankind nor achievement of oxen.
The land on every side is girt by the sea, nowhere a sailor,
no ship likely to make a journey through these winding paths.
Suppose I am given some comrades, a good wind, and a ship.
What am I to make for? My homeland denies me entry.
Suppose I do glide along over peaceful waters on a happy voyage,
with Aeolus calming his winds for me. I will be an exile.
I will not ever look upon you, Crete, your hundred cities,
the land known to Jupiter when he was but a boy.
My father and the land that was justly ruled by him,
names dear to me, were betrayed by my actions.
Remember when I gave you thread to guide your steps lest you
die, though victorious, in the winding labyrinth?
You kept promising me, "I swear by the perils I am about to face
that you will be mine so long as we both shall live."
Well, we are still alive, Theseus, and I am not yours—if you can call
a woman buried by her treacherous husband's fraud alive.
Wretch, you should have slain me with a club like my brother,
then your promise would have been voided with my death.
[Now I recall not only what I am about to endure,
but what any deserted woman could endure.][25]
A thousand forms of death occur to my mind, yet
death would be less punishment than putting it off.
I envision wolves about to appear at any moment

[24] The first king of Thebes was Ogyges; the epithet applies to Dionysus because his mother, Semele, was Theban.

[25] This couplet was likely added later by someone other than Ovid.

to eviscerate my bowels with ravenous jaws.
This land might support tawny lions too, and
who knows if Dia harbors savage tigresses?
And (they say) from the sea leap mighty seals!
What is to keep someone from planting a sword in my side?
I just hope I'm not captured, shackled with hard chains,
forced to spin out many yards of wool with my hands enslaved!
My father is Minos, my mother Phoebus' daughter, and—
this is ever more on my mind—I was once betrothed to you!
Whenever I look to the sea, the land, or the sprawling beaches,
I feel the many threats posed by both land and sea.
That leaves only the heavens, yet I fear visions of the gods—
I am deserted, left to be prey for savage beasts to feed on!
If men inhabit and cultivate this land, they will not have my trust.
Burned once is enough—I've learned to fear foreign men.
If only Androgeos were alive![26] Then, Land of Cecrops,[27] you wouldn't have
atoned for these impious deeds with the lives of your citizens;
nor would you, Theseus, have raised the knotty club in your hand
and smitten that beast, part man, part bull;
nor would I have given you thread to show your escape,
thread often retraced as your hands pulled it in.
But I'm not surprised that Victory stood by your side, that the beast
toppled and crashed down dead upon the Cretan soil.
Why? Your iron heart could not have been pierced by mere horn.
You had no armor, but your chest was safe from harm,
for there you wore the hardest stone, the hardest steel—
there you had *Theseus*, which is harder than any stone.
Aegeus is not your father; your mother is not Pittheus' daughter,
Aethra. No, your parents are the rocks and sea.
O cruel sleep, why did you hold me powerless? Better yet, night
should have buried me in its embrace once and for all.
Winds, you too were cruel, far too prepared to blow,
and you, breezes, were all too eager for my tears.
Cruel you were, right hand, who put an end both to me and my brother.
Cruel too, that promise you gave when I asked—just an empty word!
Sleep, wind, promise—all conspired against me,
all three responsible for the betrayal of a single girl.
And so I shall not see my mother's tears upon my deathbed,
nor will I have a son whose hand will close my eyes in death.

[26] Son of Minos and brother of Ariadne; see Apollodorus N2 for his death.

[27] Cecrops was the first king of Athens.

Is my luckless spirit to pass into the breezes of a foreign land?
Will no kindly hand anoint my settled limbs?
Will my bones lie unburied for seagulls to perch upon?
Is this the burial I deserve in return for my services?
You, of course, will reach Cecrops' harbor. You'll be welcomed home.
And when you assume your lofty position before your flock
and tell the glorious story about the destruction of the bull-man,
about his stone house cut into perplexing passageways,
remember to tell them about *me* too, about how you abandoned me on a
desolate island. Do not silently leave me off your list of conquests!
If only the gods had you notice me from your lofty stern!
My lonesome figure would surely have made you turn back.
Look even now—not with your eyes, but as you can, with your mind's eye:
I cling to this rocky crag beaten by the roving sea.
Look at my hair let down as if in mourning, at this dress
drenched in tears shed as if in a rainstorm.
My body shivers like fields of grain rippling in the winds,
my writing unsteady from my trembling hand.
I do not entreat you by the help I gave to you (*that* has turned out badly),
for I do not deserve any credit for what I have done.
But I do not deserve punishment either. If I was not the one who saved you,
this is yet no grounds for you to be the cause of my death.
These hands exhausted from beating my breast in mourning
I extend to you across these vast seas in my misery.
In my sadness I show you what little hair remains.
I beg you by these tears brought on by *your* actions:
turn your ship around, Theseus. Turn the sails around and glide back.
If I die first, at least it will be you who lay my bones to rest.

12 Medea to Jason

Medea betrayed her father, murdered her brother, contrived Pelias' death, poisoned King Creon and his daughter, and killed her own children. She would, therefore, seem to be an unsympathetic figure, and one unlikely to fit in with the other heroines of the Heroides. *Her story is told most famously in Euripides'* Medea *and Apollonius of Rhodes'* Argonautica *(Ovid's own play,* Medea, *is lost), both of which Ovid clearly exploits in his characterization of Medea. This letter is set, we are to imagine, right after Jason has abandoned Medea and married another woman, the Corinthian king's daughter. Ovid traces Medea's thought in this letter from sad disbelief at her abandonment to indignation that culminates in her plan to kill the new bride and her father. The last line, however, hints horrifically at a worse intention that is not yet fully formed in her mind: to kill her two sons by Jason.*

And yet I, a Colchian princess, had time for you, I recall,
when you came begging me to use my magic to help you.
Then the sisters who portion out the thread of mortality
should have unwound my spool.
Then I, Medea, would have died well. All the life I have drawn out
since that moment has been punishment.
Alas! Why was that ship ever built from Mount Pelion's wood
and driven by young men's arms in search of Phrixus' ram?
Why did we Colchians ever set our eyes on the Magnesian Argo?
Why did you and your Greek crew drink from Phasis' waters?
Why was I all too smitten with your golden locks, your good looks,
and that sweet-talking charm of your tongue?
Otherwise, as soon as that strange ship of yours landed on our
shores, bringing with it men brave and bold,
Aeson's forgetful son would've faced fiery blasts from the scorched
snouts of those bulls without the protection of my salve.
He would have sown the seeds—and as many enemies as seeds—
and fallen victim, the farmer to his own crops.
How much treachery, scoundrel, would have died along with you!
How many woes this head would not have suffered!
It feels good to reproach an ingrate for what you've done for him.
This is my pleasure, this, the only joy I take from you.
Under orders to guide your untested ship to Colchis' shores,
you entered into the blessed kingdom of my country.
There I, Medea, played the part that your new bride is playing here.
My father was as rich as hers is now.
Her father rules Ephyre of the two seas, but mine controls the whole span
on the left side of Pontus as far as snowy Scythia.
O Aeetes, you received these Pelasgian youths into your house,
and you, Greek bodies, lay down upon his embroidered couches.
That was when I saw you and began to know what you were;
that was the beginning of my mind's downfall.
I saw. I was done for. I burned with a fire I had not known before,
like a pine-torch blazes before the mighty gods.
You were handsome, and my fate was already working against me.
Your eyes stole away my ability to see.
And you knew it too, traitor—after all, who can really conceal love?
Its treacherous flame shines forth and gives itself away.
Meanwhile, the conditions were dictated to you: Submit the
wild bulls' unyielding necks to a yoke they had never felt,
the wild bulls of Mars, and it was not just horns that made them fierce;

their breath was terrifying fire.
Their hooves were made of solid bronze, bronze covered their snouts,
which had also been scorched black by their breath.
Then sow over the wide fields, with a hand doomed to death,
the seeds that would give birth to men,
men destined to assail your body with weapons sprouting beside them,
an unequal match, that harvest, for its harvester.
Your final task was by some skill to elude the guardian's eyes
that knew not how to succumb to sleep.
Aeetes had spoken. All of you rose shrouded in gloom, and the high table
was taken away from the purple couches.
How useless then was Creusa's dowry, that kingdom,
your new father-in-law, mighty Creon, and his daughter!
You left despondent, and as you left I followed you with misty eyes,
and my tongue said in a soft whisper, "Farewell."
When I reached the bed made up in my chamber, deeply wounded in my
heart, I spent the whole night long in tears.
Before my eyes flashed bulls and baleful harvests,
before my eyes the never-sleeping serpent.
I was torn between love and fear, and fear made love all the stronger.
Night became morning. Let into my chamber, my sister found
me lying face down upon the bed, my hair all disheveled,
everything drenched with my tears.
She begged me to help the Minyans. She asked, but another received:
what she asked for I granted to the Aesonian youth.
There is a grove plunged in the somber shadows of pines and dark oaks,
where the sun's rays rarely make their way.
In it there is—or, at least, *was*—a shrine sacred to Diana, where stands
a golden statue of the goddess molded by barbarian hands.
Remember? Or have memories of the place fallen from your mind as I have?
That's where we met. You spoke first from your deceitful mouth:
"Fortune has handed over to you the power to decide our fate.
In your hands lies the decision whether we live or die.
If it is power that gives you pleasure, then to be *able* to destroy is enough,
but your glory will be all the greater should you save me.
By our hardships—which you have the power to lighten—
by your lineage, by the power of your all-seeing grandfather,
by the countenance of three-formed Diana and her sacred mysteries,
by whatever gods you people worship, I beg you,
O maiden: take pity upon me, take pity upon my men.
Help me, make me indebted to you forevermore!
And if by chance you think a Pelasgian is good enough to be your husband—

ah, why hope that the gods will listen and respond to my prayers?—
may my spirit fade away into the light breezes before
anyone but you is bride in my bedchamber!
Let our witnesses be Juno, the protectress of holy matrimony,
and the goddess in whose marble shrine we stand."
These, and many more, were the words that stirred the soul of this
simple girl, and you clasped your right hand to mine.
I saw tears, too—they had their own part to play in your deception.
Just like that I, but a girl, was quickly taken in by your words.
You yoked the bronze-footed bulls, your body untouched by flames.
You split the solid earth with the plow as was ordered.
You filled the furrows with venomous teeth in place of seed,
and up grew an army holding sword and shield.
I, the very one who gave you the protective salve, sat white with dread
when I saw the sudden-born men with weapons in their hands,
until those earth-born brethren—a remarkable event!—
drew weapons against each other and began to skirmish.
Suddenly that never-sleeping guardian bristling with rippling scales
hissed as it swept along the ground on its coiling chest.
Where was your dowry's help then? Or that royal spouse of yours?
Or the Isthmus that cleaves the waters of two seas?
No, I, who now in the end have come to be barbaric in your eyes,
who seem poor to you, and guilty too—
I was the one who with drugged sleep made the flaming eyes unable to see
and gave you the Fleece to take away unscathed.
I betrayed my father, gave up my kingdom and country.
My reward? I am allowed to live in exile.
My virginity has become the spoil of a bandit from abroad.
I left my good sister and dear mother behind.
But I did not leave you behind as I fled, Brother—
my writing falters only at this one place.[28]
My right hand does not dare to write what it dared to do.
I should have been torn apart, but alongside you!
And still I was not afraid (after all, what fear had I after what I had done?)
to trust myself to the deep sea, a woman, and now a criminal!
Where is the power of heaven? The gods? We deserve to be punished
on the sea, you for your treachery, I for my credulity.
If only the Symplegades had clashed, smashing us both together,
and my bones now clung fast to yours!
If only voracious Scylla had drowned us for her dogs to feed on

[28] A reference to her murder of her brother Absyrtus (Apsyrtos).

(Scylla has the right to harm ungrateful men)![29]
If only the creature that gulps down and disgorges the sea over and over[30]
had plunged us too beneath the Trinacrian waves!
But *you* returned to Haemonia's cities safe and triumphant;
the Golden Fleece was laid out before your country's gods.
Why mention Pelias' daughters, who brought harm through their devotion,
or their father's limbs cut by their maidenly hands?
Though others may fault me, you must give me praise.
I have often been forced to do harm on your behalf.
But you had the gall—no words to express my righteous indignation—
you had the gall to say, "Take your leave of Aeson's house."
So ordered, I vacated the house, accompanied by our two sons and
that ever-faithful companion, my love for you.
Then suddenly I heard the sound of Hymen's wedding song.
Flames danced from the flickering lamps,
and a flute poured forth its songs—for you, of nuptial bliss,
but for me, more mournful than a trumpet's dirge of death.
I was stricken with fear, but did not think such an outrage was possible.
Yet my heart was all encased in ice.
The crowd swarmed onward, oft raising their cry, "Hymen, O Hymenaeus."
The closer the voices came, the worse it got for me.
My slaves wept, withdrawing from me, trying to conceal their tears;
no one wanted to be the bearer of such bad news.
I too knew it was just as well that I did not know, whatever it was;
yet my mind, as though it did, was weighed down with gloom.
Right then our younger boy (who by chance or out of a desire to see
was standing right outside the double-doors of the house)
said, "Come here, Mom! There's a parade, and dad—Jason—is out front
leading it. He's dressed in gold, driving a team of horses!"
Right then and there I ripped my dress and beat my breast,
and my cheeks were not safe from my fingernails.
I felt the urge to plunge into the middle of the crowd,
to fling that crown off her nicely coiffed hair.
It was all I could do, my hair all a mess, to stop myself from
shouting, "He's mine," and laying my hands on you as my own.
Father whom I injured, rejoice! Colchians whom I abandoned, rejoice!
Shade of my brother, accept this funeral offering:
I have lost my kingdom, country, and home, and now I have been

[29] Because of her treatment at Minos' hands (see Apollodorus N2).

[30] The creature is Charybdis.

abandoned by my husband, who was everything to me.
So I was able to subdue serpents and raging bulls;
my husband alone lay outside my powers.
So I repelled raging fires with skillful salve;
I cannot escape the flames of my own love.
My very spells, herbs, skills in magic have left me in the lurch;
neither powerful Hecate nor her sacred rites help at all.
Day brings me no pleasure. Nights I spend in bitter wakefulness.
My ailing heart knows no gentle sleep.
Once I buried a serpent in slumber, but I cannot bring myself to sleep;
my anxious concerns help everyone else more than me.
A mistress now embraces the limbs I once saved,
and she enjoys the fruits of my labor.
Perhaps, while you flaunt yourself in front of your stupid wife
and speak the words her biased ears want to hear,
you will invent new slurs against my looks and my behavior.
Let her laugh and take pleasure in my faults.
Let her laugh while lying high up on her Tyrian purple.
She *will* weep, in flames that will exceed the heat of my passion.
So long as iron, flames, and magical poisons are at my disposal,
no enemy of Medea will go unpunished.
But if by chance iron hearts are stirred by prayers,
hear now these words that are beneath my proud spirit.
I submit myself, a suppliant, to you now as you often did to me,
and I do not hesitate to lay myself down at your feet.
If I mean nothing to you, consider our children:
their awful new stepmother will be cruel to my offspring.
They look too much like you. I am moved by the sight of them.
Each time I look upon them, my eyes well up with tears.
I beg you by the gods in heaven, by the light of my grandfather's flame,
by my service to you and our two sons, the bonds that join us,
restore my marriage, for which I madly left behind so much,
and make good on your word and aid me as I did you.
I do not implore you to face off against bulls and men,
to use your powers to overcome a serpent with sleep.
No, *you* are my request. I earned you, and you gave yourself over to me.
With you I became a parent as you became one.
Where is my dowry, you ask? We tallied it up on that field that
you had to till if you were to take away the Fleece.
That golden ram, illustrious with its deep, shaggy coat is my dowry,
and if I were to say, "Give it back," you'd say no!
My dowry? That you're alive and well. My dowry? Your Greek crew.

Go on now, you ingrate, compare Sisyphus' wealth[31] with that!
The fact that you are alive, that you have a royal bride and father-in-law,
the very fact that you *can* be an ingrate—this is all owed to me.
And them I shall now—but what good does it do to foretell their
punishment? Great are the threats with which my anger is pregnant.
Where my anger leads, I shall follow. Perhaps I'll regret my actions.
But right now I regret having protected a traitorous husband.
Let this be the concern of the god that now stokes my heart.
Be sure, though, something truly momentous is stirring in my soul.

[31] Sisyphus was the founder and first king of Corinth, so his wealth is that of the royal family of the city.

PALAEPHATUS

(perhaps 4th or 3rd c. BC, wrote in Greek)

Palaephatus—the name might be a pseudonym—is a shadowy figure about whom everything is uncertain. One possible scenario is this: He lived sometime in the 3rd century BC *and wrote* On Unbelievable Things (Peri Apiston) *in five books. These were later summarized in the epitome (abridged version) we currently have. Palaephatus' work is an excellent example of mythological rationalization, an ancient method of interpretation that attempts to see in myths mere erroneous accounts of situations that were originally ordinary events with rational explanations. Most often for Palaephatus the transformation of something ordinary into the extraordinary is due to misunderstanding of one sort or another. Language, in particular, is liable in his mind to give rise to later interpretations made out of context. For instance, the hero Bellerophontes did not ride a winged horse Pegasos, but captained a ship called* Pegasos. *Although this approach sometimes produces absurd results—more absurd, in fact, than the myths themselves—it is one that was clearly at work in the thinking of many other Greek writers. It should be also noted that dim reflections of rationalization are at the heart of many more modern approaches to myth.*

FROM *ON UNBELIEVABLE THINGS*

Prologue

I have written this work about unbelievable things because gullible people, unacquainted with wisdom and scientific knowledge, believe everything they are told, while those who are naturally more intelligent and analytical disbelieve that any of these things happened at all. I think that all the stories happened since names do not appear in isolation without any story behind them. No, first there was the reality, then accordingly the story about it. Whatever physical shapes and forms are said to have actually existed in the past but that do not exist now—such things never existed, for anything that has ever come into existence at any time both exists now and will exist in the future. I, at any rate, am constantly commending the writers Melissos and Lamiscos of Samos for saying, "What came into existence in the beginning exists and so will exist." The poets and chroniclers distorted certain events into something more incredible and astonishing so that people would be thrilled. I recognize that such things cannot happen as they are described, but I have also grasped this separate fact: if they had not happened at all, they would not have been turned into stories. I went to numerous lands and asked the old people what they had been told about each of the stories. I am writing what I learned from them. I personally saw what each of the locations is like today, and I have written these accounts not as they had been told to me, but after I visited and investigated them in person.

1 The Centaurs

They say that the Centaurs were beasts that had the overall form of a horse except for the head, which was that of a man's. Now, in case anyone believes such a beast existed, it is an impossibility. The natures of horse and man are not at all harmonious, their food is not the same, and it is not possible for a horse's food to pass through a human mouth and throat. Besides, if there had been such a form then, it would also exist now.

The truth of the matter is this. When Ixion ruled Thessaly, a herd of bulls had gone wild on Mount Pelion, rendering the rest of the mountain range impassable as well. The bulls came down into the inhabited regions and devastated the orchards and crops along with the beasts of burden. So Ixion proclaimed that if anyone destroyed the bulls, he would give him a lot of money. Some young men from a village in the foothills called Nephele {"Cloud"} came up with the idea of training horses for riding (previously people had not understood how to ride on horseback; they just used wagons). So they mounted their riding horses and set off for where the bulls were. They attacked the herd using javelins. When they were chased by the bulls, the young men would pull back a little, for their horses were more fleet-footed than the bulls. And when the bulls stopped chasing, the men would turn around and throw their javelins. In this way they destroyed them. From that the Centaurs {*Kentauroi*} got their name since they had shot {*kentannumi*} down the bulls {*tauroi*}. It has nothing to do with the form of the bulls, for there is nothing bull-like about the Centaurs. They are shaped like horses and humans. So they took their name from their deed.

Now, the Centaurs got their money from Ixion and prided themselves on what they had done and on their wealth. They grew arrogant and committed many base acts, even against Ixion himself, who lived in the city that is now called Larissa (at the time those who lived there were called Lapiths). When the Lapiths invited them to a feast, the Centaurs got drunk and kidnapped their womenfolk. Loading them up onto their horses, they rode off to their own village. After that they attacked the Lapiths and made war upon them. They would descend during the night to the plains and set ambushes. When day came, they would burn and pillage and then run off to the mountains. While they were heading off like this, those looking at them from behind and from far away could only see the backs of the horses, not their heads, and the upper part of the men, not their legs. Seeing this strange sight, they said, "The Centaurs from Nephele are overrunning us!" From this image and saying there was fashioned the unbelievable myth, that a horse-man was born from the cloud {*nephele*} on the mountain.

2 Pasiphae

A myth is told about Pasiphae that she fell in love with a grazing bull, that Daidalos made a wooden cow and enclosed Pasiphae in it, and in this way the bull mounted and mated with the woman. It is said that she became pregnant and gave birth to a son with a man's body and a bull's head. I deny that this happened. First, it is impossible for one animal to make love to another if the female does not have a vagina that matches the male's genitals. It is not possible for a dog and a monkey or a wolf and a hyena to mate with each other. Even an antelope cannot mate with a deer, for they are of different species. Even if they did mate with each other, it is not possible for them to produce young. I do not think a bull had intercourse with a wooden cow in the first place, for all four-legged animals smell the genitals of the animal before mating with it and only then mount it. And the woman could not have endured a bull mounting her. A woman could also not carry a fetus with horns.

The truth of the matter is this. They say that Minos had pain in his genitals and was being treated by Procris daughter of Pandion for the price of the puppy and the javelin < . . . > Cephalos.[1] During this time a young man of exceptional beauty was working for Minos. His name was Tauros {"Bull"}. Pasiphae conceived a passion for him, persuaded him to sleep with her, and had a son fathered by him. Minos counted from the time he had had the pain in his genitals and realized that the child could not be his because he had not slept with her. Through careful comparison he discovered that the child was Tauros'. He decided not to kill the boy because he considered him a brother to his own children. He did, however, send him away into the mountains so that he could be a servant for the shepherds after he grew up.

When the boy became a man, though, he would not listen to the herders. When Minos learned of this, he gave orders to arrest and bring him back to the city. If he came willingly, he was to come without being tied up, but otherwise he was to be bound. The young man learned what was happening and withdrew to the mountains. He stole livestock and in that way sustained himself. Minos sent a larger company to capture him, but the young man dug a deep pit and shut himself in it. He lived in it the rest of his life. They used to throw sheep and goats to him, and he lived by feeding on them. Whenever Minos wished to have a person punished, he would send him to this one shut up in his cell, and in that way the person would be killed. When Minos captured his enemy Theseus, he brought him to the place to be killed. Ariadne, however, sent a sword into the prison ahead of time, and Theseus killed the "Minotaur" with it. < . . . > Such was the event as it occurred, but the poets transformed it into the myth.

4 The Cadmeian Sphinx

It is told of the Cadmeian Sphinx that she was a beast with a dog's body, a girl's head and face, a bird's wings, and a human's voice. She sat on Mount Phicion and sang a riddle to each of the citizens, killing whoever could not solve it. When Oidipous solved the riddle, she killed herself by throwing herself off the mountain. This is an unbelievable and impossible story. Such a bodily structure could not exist. Besides, it is infantile that they were eaten up by her because they could not solve riddles, and it

[1] Though we cannot be certain, it is likely that relatively little is missing from our text, for instance, " . . . the puppy and the javelin <that she later gave to> Cephalos." For the story, see Antoninus Liberalis 41.

is idiotic that they did not shoot the beast dead with arrows instead of standing around and watching while people got eaten up as though they were enemies and not fellow citizens.

The truth is this. Cadmos came to Thebes with an Amazon wife, whose name was Sphinx. He killed Dracon and took his property and kingdom,[2] including Dracon's sister, whose name was Harmonia. When Sphinx discovered that he had married another woman, she persuaded many of the citizens to move away with her. She absconded with most of Cadmos' money and also took the fast-running dog he had brought when he came to Thebes. She moved away with these to the mountain called Phicion, and from there she waged war on Cadmos. Setting up ambushes during the day, she would kill whomever she seized and then get away. Since the Cadmeian word for ambush is "riddle," the citizens commonly used to say, "The wild Sphinx sets up a riddle, plunders us, and sits on her mountain. No one is able to figure out her riddle, and it is impossible to fight her in the open, for she does not just run, she flies, both dog and woman."[3] Cadmos proclaimed that he would give a lot of money to the man who killed Sphinx. Then Oidipous, a Corinthian who was good at waging war, came and brought a swift-running horse. By organizing the Cadmeians into units, going out during the night, and setting an ambush for her, he solved the Sphinx's "riddle" and killed her. This is what happened; the rest has been mythologized.

6 Actaion

They say that Actaion was eaten up by his own dogs. That is a falsehood, for a dog loves its master and provider above all. This is especially true in the case of dogs trained for hunting, for they fawn upon all people. Some say that Artemis changed him into a deer and the dogs destroyed him as a deer. I think that Artemis is capable of doing what she wishes; nevertheless, it is not true that a man can be turned into a deer or a deer into a man. The poets composed these myths so that their listeners would not act with hubris toward the divine.

The truth of the matter is this. Actaion was a descendant of Arcas and a real lover of hunting. He always kept a lot of dogs and hunted in the mountains, completely ignoring his own affairs. The people at that time all did their own work because they did not have slaves. The richest man was the hardest working one. Now since Actaion paid no attention to his own property and preferred to go hunt, his life was ruined. When he no longer had anything left at all, the people said, "Poor Actaion. He's been eaten up by his own dogs." It is the same way now if someone falls on hard times because he spends all his money on prostitutes. In that case we usually say,

[2] This rationalizes another incident of Cadmos' myth, his killing of the serpent (*drakon*) guarding the Castalian Spring and subsequent foundation of Thebes. Here, the city already exists and is ruled by a King Dracon.

[3] Palaephatus as usual is depending on a word play in Greek that is hard to capture in English. Greeks could say "he's flying" and mean "he's running *really* fast." The real ambiguity lies in the phrase "both dog and woman." The Thebans mean, "She flies. She does and her dog too." But the Greek and English can both (just barely) be understood to mean, "She flies, a dog-woman."

"He's been eaten up by the prostitutes." That is just the sort of thing that happened to Actaion too.

15 Europa

They say that Europa daughter of Phoinix came across the sea from Tyre to Crete by riding on a bull. I do not think that a bull (or even a horse) would cross so much open sea. I also do not think that a girl would climb onto the back of a wild bull. And Zeus, if he wanted Europa to go to Crete, would have found a better way for her to cross.

The truth of the matter is this. A man from Cnossos named Tauros {"Bull"} was waging war against the land of Tyre. He ended up kidnapping many girls from Tyre, most notably the king's daughter Europa. So people said, "Tauros left and took Europa, the king's daughter." These are the events that happened; the myth was based on them.

21 Daidalos

It is said of Daidalos that he made statues that moved on their own. But I think that it is impossible for a statue of a person to walk on its own.

The truth is as follows. The sculptors of the time, both those who worked on statues of people and those who worked on statues of gods, sculpted the feet attached to one another and the hands held by the sides. Daidalos was the first to make a statue with one foot taking a step forward. Because of that people said, "Daidalos made this statue that walks and does not stand still." In the same way we now say of a work of art that it shows "men who fight" or "horses that run" or "a ship that is storm-tossed." So they said that he made statues "that walk."

24 Geryones

They say that Geryones was three-headed, but it is impossible for a body to have three heads. It was like this. There is a city on the Euxine Sea called Three Peaks.[4] Geryones was famous among the people of those times for surpassing everyone else in wealth and in other ways too. He also had a marvelous herd of cows. Heracles came to get this herd, fought Geryones, and killed him. People who saw the cows being driven along were astounded, for they were small as far as height goes, but from head to haunch they were long and sleek. They had no horns, but their bones were big and thick. People said to anyone who asked about them, "Heracles is driving these cows. They belong to the Three Peaker Geryones." Some assumed from this statement that he had three heads.

[4] Once again Palaephatus relies on a wordplay that is impossible to render in English. The word he uses above for Geryones is *trikarenos*, which means "having three heads." He calls the city *Trikarenia*, which is a plausible name that would mean something like "built on three hills" or "having three citadels."

28 Bellerophontes

They say that Pegasos, a winged horse, used to carry Bellerophontes. I do not think that a horse could ever do this, not even if it got all birds' wings in the world, for if such an animal ever existed, it would also exist now. They also say that Bellerophontes destroyed Amisodaros' Chimaira. The Chimaira was "in front a lion, in back a serpent, in between a goat."[5] Some think that such a beast existed, only with three heads and one body. But it is impossible for a serpent, a lion, and a goat to digest the same food, and the idea of a mortal creature breathing fire is silly. And which of the heads did the body obey?

The truth of the matter is this. Bellerophontes was a Corinthian gentleman who lived in exile. He built a long ship and sailed around making raids and plundering the coastal regions. The name of this ship was *Pegasos*. In the same way even now every ship has a name, and I think Pegasos is a name more likely to be given to a ship than to a horse.[6] King Amisodaros lived by the river Xanthos on a high mountain covered by the Telmissis Forest. There are two approaches to this mountain, one from in front that comes from the city of the Xanthians and one from behind that comes from Caria. Otherwise, the cliffs are high, and in the middle of them there is a huge chasm in the earth from which fire pours forth. The name of this mountain is Chimaira. At that time, according to those who live in the area, there was a lion living along the front approach and a serpent living along the rear, and these terrorized the woodcutters and herdsmen. It was then that Bellerophontes arrived. He set fire to the mountain, burned down the Telmissis, and destroyed the beasts. So the people of the area said, "Bellerophontes came with *Pegasos* and destroyed Amisodaros' Chimaira." This happened and the myth was based on it.

30 Phrixos and Helle

The account they give of Phrixos is that the ram foretold to him that his father was going to sacrifice him and his sister. Phrixos grabbed his sister and climbed onto the ram with her. They went across the deep to the Euxine Sea after traveling for three or four days in all. It is hard to believe that a ram swam faster than a ship can sail. And it was carrying two people and, I suppose, food and water for itself and for them to boot (they certainly could not have lasted for so long a time without nourishment)! Then Phrixos slaughtered the ram—the ram that had told him how to save himself and had then carried him to safety—then removed its fleece and gave it as bride-price to Aietes for his daughter (Aietes was then king in those parts). You can see that animal skins were so rare at the time that a king took the fleece as bride-price for his own daughter! Did he think that his own daughter was worth nothing? To avoid this ridiculous conclusion, some people now say, "This fleece was golden." Even if the skin were golden, the king would not have had any reason to accept it from some foreigner.

[5] Palaephatus quotes Homer, *Iliad* 6.181–6.182.

[6] Because *pegai* in Greek means "streams" or "waters." Pegasos the horse was supposed to have been so named because he was born near the *pegai* of Ocean.

It has also been said that Jason readied the *Argo* and recruited the heroes of Greece for an expedition to get this fleece. But Phrixos would not have been so ungrateful as to kill his benefactor, nor would the *Argo*, even if the fleece were made of emeralds, have sailed after it.

The truth of the matter is this. Athamas son of Aiolos (who was the son of Hellen) ruled Phthia. He had a man whom he entrusted with his finances and his authority, a man whom he considered extraordinarily trustworthy and valuable. His name was Crios {"Ram"}. After Phrixos' mother died, Athamas made Phrixos heir to the kingdom because he was the eldest. < . . . >[7] Learning of this, Crios said nothing to Athamas, but did speak to Phrixos, urging him to leave the land. Crios personally equipped a ship and loaded onto it whatever Athamas had that was of value. He filled the ship full with all possible treasures and money. Among these was a statue. Merops' mother (her name was Cos {"Fleece"}), a daughter of Helios, had commissioned a statue of herself—life-sized and made of gold that she herself owned. There was a lot of gold in the statue and it was a big topic of conversation. Crios put these things on board the ship, along with Phrixos and Helle, then departed and got away. Now Helle fell sick during the voyage and died (and the sea is called the Hellespont after her), but they made it to Phasis and settled there. Phrixos married the daughter of Aietes, the king of the Colchians, and gave him the golden statue of Cos as bride-price. Later, after Athamas was dead, Jason sailed on the *Argo* to get the gold of Cos {"Fleece"}—not a ram's skin. That is the truth.

32 The Amazons

I have this to say about the Amazons: these women warriors were not women, but barbarian men who used to wear full-length tunics (like Thracian women), put their hair up in headbands, and shave their beards (like the <*name of a foreign people missing*> do even today). Because of this they were called women by their enemies, but the Amazons were, as a nation, good at fighting battles. There probably never was an army of women, for there are none anywhere now.

33 Orpheus

The myth about Orpheus is also false, that four-legged animals, crawling things, birds, and trees followed him when he played his cithara. I think this is what it was. Some raving Bacchai tore up some sheep on Mount Pieria. They would do many other things in their violent state and then go to the mountain and spend their days there. While they were staying there, the townsmen, afraid for their wives and daughters, sent for Orpheus and asked him to think of some way he could bring them down from the mountain. He offered sacrifices to Dionysos and led the frenzied women down by playing the cithara. The women came down the mountain

[7] Something is obviously missing from the text here and the sentence preceding this gap may well also be damaged. If we fill in the gap with the usual account, Athamas remarries, and his new wife, Ino, plots the death of Phrixos and Helle so that her own children will inherit the kingdom.

holding for the first time fennel stalks and branches from all sorts of trees. The pieces of wood seemed a miracle to the men who saw them on that occasion, and they said, "Orpheus even brings the forest down from the mountain with his cithara playing!" From this the myth was formed.

34 Pandora

The story about Pandora, that she was fashioned from earth and then passed along her physical form to others, is intolerable. I do not think this happened. Rather, Pandora was a Greek woman of very great wealth. Whenever she would go out, she would make herself up and rub herself with a lot of white earth.[8] She was the first woman to discover how to color one's skin by using a large quantity of white earth as many women do nowadays. In fact, none of them is singled out today because most do it. That is what really happened, but the story took a turn toward the impossible.

38 The Hydra

It is also said of the Lernaian Hydra that it was a snake with fifty heads but one body. And when Heracles removed one of its heads, two would grow back. A crab supposedly also came to the aid of the Hydra. Then Iolaos helped Heracles because the crab was helping the Hydra. If anyone believes any of this happened, he is a fool. It is ridiculous at first glance. How is it, when he cut off one head, that did he not suffer from the rest of them and get eaten?

It was like this. Lernos was king of a certain place, and the place had in fact gotten its name from him. Today the spot is in Argive territory, but everyone back then lived in separate villages. So Argos, Mycenae, Tiryns, and Lerna were independent cities at the time, and a king was in charge of each of them. Now, the other kings were subordinate to Eurystheus, the son of Sthenelos and the grandson of Perseus, because he controlled the greatest and most populous of these places, Mycenae. But Lernos did not wish to remain his subordinate, so he therefore went to war against him.

At one of the approaches to his territory Lernos had a sturdy little fort that was garrisoned by fifty elite archers who manned the tower night and day without break. The name of the fort was Hydra {"Water-Snake"}. Now, Eurystheus sent Heracles to sack the fort. Heracles' troops tried to set fire to the archers on the tower, and whenever one of them would get hit with the fire and fall, two regular archers would rise up in place of the one (because the man who had just been killed was one of the elite ones). When Lernos was hard-pressed by Heracles in the war, he hired some mercenaries from Caria. A great warrior, Carcinos {"Crab"} by name, came and brought his troops to him, and with Carcinos' help, Lernos held off Heracles. Then Iolaos son of Iphicles (Iolaos was Heracles' nephew) helped Heracles by bringing some troops from Thebes. He came to Hydra and set fire to the tower. With the help of this force Heracles

[8] The Greek simply says "earth" here, but it very likely refers to ceruse, or white lead, which was (and still is) employed as a paint pigment and was used before modern times to whiten the skin.

sacked the fort, destroyed Hydra, and wiped out the opposing army. This is what happened, but they write that the Hydra was a snake, and build the myth on that.

39 Cerberos

It has been said of Cerberos that he was a dog with three heads. It is clear that he too was called this from the city called Three Peaks, just like Geryones.[9] People used to say, "The Three-Peaker dog is large and fine-looking." It has also been said—mythically—that Heracles brought him up out of Hades.

It happened as follows. Geryones had large, fearless dogs who looked after his cattle. One was named Cerberos, the other Orthos. Heracles killed Orthos in Three Peaks before he drove off the cattle, but Cerberos followed along with the cattle. A Mycenaean named Molossos decided he wanted the dog. First, he asked Eurystheus to sell it to him, but when Eurystheus refused, he bribed the cattle herders and confined the dog in a cave in Tainaron in Laconia[10] with the intention of using him as a stud dog. He put many females down in the cave for Cerberos to mount. Eurystheus sent Heracles to look for the dog. Heracles went around the whole Peloponnese, came to where he had been told the dog was, went down into the cave, and brought out the dog. People said, "Heracles brought up the dog after descending to Hades through the cave."

40 Alcestis

A myth fit for a tragedy has been told about Alcestis, that once when Admetos was about to die, she chose to die in his place, and that Heracles took her away from Thanatos {"Death"} because of her piety and returned her to Admetos. I do not think that anyone is capable of bringing a dead person back to life.

No, it happened like this. When the daughters of Pelias killed their father, his son, Acastos, chased them with the intention of killing them for killing their father. He caught the others, but Alcestis fled to Pherai to her cousin Admetos. Acastos asked for her to be handed over, but Admetos could not do so because she had taken a seat on his hearth as a suppliant. Acastos positioned a large army around the city and began to devastate the inhabitants with fire. Admetos went out on a night attack, but ran into the enemy commanders and was captured alive. Acastos threatened to kill him if he did not hand over Alcestis, even if she was a suppliant. When Alcestis found out that Admetos was going to be killed on her account, she went out and surrendered herself. Acastos released Admetos and took Alcestis into custody. So people said, "Alcestis is courageous. She willingly died for Admetos."

But it did not happen as the myth says. At just this moment Heracles came from somewhere bringing the horses of Diomedes, and Admetos entertained him when he arrived there. Admetos kept lamenting the misfortune of Alcestis. Heracles now considered himself Admetos' friend and so attacked Acastos and destroyed his army. He

[9] See Palaephatus' discussion of Geryones (24).

[10] A cave there was said to be an entrance to the underworld.

distributed the spoils to his own army, but handed Alcestis over to Admetos. So people said that Heracles happened to deliver Alcestis from death. This happened, then the myth was based on it.

41 Zethos and Amphion

Hesiod and others give an account about Zethos and Amphion, that they built the city walls of Thebes with a cithara. Some take this to mean that they played the cithara and the stones rose up of their own accord and put themselves on the walls.

The truth of the matter is this. These men were excellent citharists and put on shows for a price. The people back then did not have money, so Amphion and his brother told anyone who wanted to hear them to come and work on the walls. (But the stones did not listen to the music and follow along!) So people said—accurately—that the walls were built with a lyre.

42 Io

They say that Io was turned from a woman into a cow and then crossed the sea from Argos to Egypt because she was stung by a gadfly. It is unbelievable that she < . . . > and remained for so many days without food.

The truth of the matter is this. Io was the daughter of the king of the Argives. They gave her the honor of being the priestess of Argive Hera at her temple outside the city. She became pregnant and fled the city in fear of her father and the citizens. The Argives set out in search of her, and wherever they found her, they would try to catch her and put her in chains. So they said, "She keeps getting away, like a cow stung by a gadfly!" < . . . > Eventually, she handed herself over to some foreign merchants and begged them to take her away to Egypt. When she got there, she gave birth. The myth was based on that.

43 Medeia

Medeia, they say, made old people young by boiling them, but it has not been proved that she made anyone young. She certainly killed anyone she boiled.

It happened like this. Medeia was the first to discover red and black dye, so she would make the elderly seem to be young by dying their gray hairs black or red. Dipping their white hairs into black and red dyes, she transformed them. < . . . > Medeia was the first to discover the benefits of a steam bath for people. She would give steam baths to anyone who wanted, but not openly so no doctor would find out about it. And while she gave them the bath, she made them swear to tell no one. She called her steam treatments "boiling." Now, people were emerging from the steam baths happier and healthier. Because of this, when people saw that there were cauldrons and fire at her house, they became convinced that she was boiling the people. Pelias, an old and sickly man, died while undergoing the steam treatment. Hence the myth.

45 The Horn of Amaltheia

They say that Heracles carried around the so-called Horn of Amaltheia everywhere, and he got from it everything he wanted just by praying.

This is the truth. Heracles was traveling in Boiotia with his nephew Iolaos and rented a room in a certain inn in Thespiai. A very beautiful young woman named Amaltheia happened to be the innkeeper here. She delighted Heracles, so he took advantage of her hospitality for a little longer than planned. Iolaos did not take it very well, so he decided to steal the profits Amaltheia stashed in a horn. From these profits Iolaos procured whatever he wanted for himself and for Heracles. So the other travelers said, "Heracles got Amaltheia's horn and procured whatever he wanted from it." The myth was based on this, and painters who paint Heracles paint the Horn of Amaltheia next to him.

Parthenius

(1st c. BC, wrote in Greek)

One of the most celebrated Greek poets of his time, Parthenius of Nicaia was captured and taken to Rome. After gaining his freedom he became a friend and acquaintance of many Roman poets, including Cornelius Gallus. It was to him that Parthenius sent his Sentimental Love Stories (Erotika Pathemata), *a collection of abridged tales taken from earlier Greek poetry. Although this collection was designed to provide Gallus with material for composing new poems, none of Gallus' compositions survive.*

FROM *SENTIMENTAL LOVE STORIES*

Introductory Letter

Greetings from Parthenius to Cornelius Gallus.

I thought that the collection of sentimental love stories was particularly fitting for you, Cornelius Gallus, and I have sent them to you after abridging them as much as possible. For even if they are not told in their entirety, you will for the most part be able to tell from what follows what is in the various poets, and it will be up to you to recast the ones you find particularly appealing into hexameters and elegiacs. Do not think worse of them because they do not have the splendor that you seek. For I have collected them after the manner of notes, and they will, I think, prove their usefulness to you as such.

2 Polymele

As Odysseus was wandering around Sicily and the Tyrrhenian and Sicilian seas, he arrived at the island of Meligounis, where there lived Aiolos, who took great care of Odysseus because of his fame for wisdom. He questioned him about the capture of Troy and about how the Greeks' ships were scattered as they sailed away from Ilion. Aiolos entertained Odysseus as his guest for a long time, and it turns out that the delay was enjoyable for Odysseus too, for Polymele, one of Aiolos' daughters, fell in love with him and was secretly sleeping with him. When Odysseus sailed off, taking with him the winds shut up in a bag, the girl was caught with some of the spoils from Troy, rolling around tearfully among them. Aiolos then heaped abuse on Odysseus, even though he was not there, and intended to punish Polymele, but her brother, Diores, happened to be in love with her. He pleaded on her behalf and persuaded their father to marry her to him.

3 Euippe

Odysseus did not commit a transgression only against Aiolos,[1] but after he was done with his wandering and after he killed the suitors, he also went to Epeiros on account of some oracles and seduced Euippe, the daughter of Tyrimmas. This man had dutifully received Odysseus into his home and hosted him with every kindness. Odysseus had a son named Euryalos by this girl. When the boy grew up, his mother sent him off to Ithaca after giving him a sealed letter that proved his identity. It chanced that Odysseus at that time was not home, but after Penelope learned of these things (in any case, she already knew of his tryst with Euippe), she urged Odysseus on his return—before he realized what the situation was—to kill Euryalos, saying that he was plotting against him. Odysseus, because he could not control his temper and was not a reasonable man even at the best of times, killed his son with his own hands. Not long after carrying out this deed he was wounded by his own offspring with a stingray's spine and died.[2]

4 Oinone

When Alexander son of Priam was a cowherd on Mount Ida, he fell in love with Oinone, the daughter of Cebren. It is said that, in addition to being widely famed for her intelligence, she used to become possessed by one of the gods and give prophecies about the future. Alexander brought her from her father's house to Ida, where he had his corrals, and kept her as his wife. Meaning every word of it, <he used to promise> never to abandon her and to treat her with the greatest possible honor. She would say that she understood for the time being that he really loved her very much, but there would come a time when he would leave her and cross over to Europe. Falling passionately for a foreign woman there, he would bring war on his friends and family. She explained that he was doomed to be wounded in the war and that no one would be able to make him healthy except her. Each time she tried to say more, he would not allow her to go on.

Time passed. When Alexander married Helen, Oinone blamed Alexander for what he had done and went back to Cebren and her family. When the war was almost over, Paris engaged in an archery duel with Philoctetes and was wounded. Recalling what Oinone had said when she used to claim that he could only be healed by her, he sent a messenger to beg her to hurry and mend him and forget about the past since it had happened in accordance with the will of the gods. Rather stubbornly, she answered that he should go to Helen and beg her. When the messenger swiftly returned with report of what Oinone had said, Alexander grew discouraged and breathed his last. When Oinone arrived and saw that he was already lying dead on the ground, she gave out a wail and, agonizing greatly, killed herself.

[1] See previous selection.

[2] A reference to his death at the hands of Telegonos, his son by the sorceress Circe.

12 Calchos

They say that a man named Calchos from Daunia fell in love with Circe (the one that Odysseus visited), offered to give her the kingdom of the Daunians, and presented her many other gifts to win her over. But since she was burning for Odysseus (he happened to be there at that time), she detested him and forbade him from setting foot on her island. But when he would not give up visiting and calling out "Circe!" she grew very annoyed and set out to trap him. Right then and there, she invited him in and set a table before him after filling it with all sorts of tidbits. The food was tainted with magical drugs, and when Calchos ate it, he went immediately out of his mind, and she drove him to the pigsties. After a time, however, when a Daunian army attacked the island to conduct a search for Calchos, she released him after making him swear oaths that he would never return to her island, neither to ask for her hand nor for any other reason.

13 Harpalyce

In Argos, Clymenos son of Teleus married Epicaste and fathered children, sons Idas and Theragros, and a daughter, Harpalyce, who was far more beautiful than the other girls of her age. Clymenos came to love her erotically, but held out for some time and resisted his passion. When his illness finally undermined his resolve, he got hold of the girl through her nurse and secretly slept with her. But when it was time for her marriage and her fiancé, Alastor, one of the sons of Neleus, came to lead her away, Clymenos handed her over without delay, throwing a very magnificent wedding feast. But soon he changed his mind because he was crazy and set off in pursuit of Alastor. When they were already halfway home, he took the girl back, brought her to Argos, and slept with her without trying to conceal the fact. She believed that she had suffered terrible and monstrous things at the hands of her father, so she dismembered her younger brother. There was a certain festival and sacrifice being held among the Argives at which everyone feasted at public expense. On that occasion, she cooked the flesh of the boy and set it before her father. Having done these things, she prayed to the gods to be removed from humanity and was changed in appearance into a *chalkis* bird.[3] As for Clymenos, when he realized his plight, he killed himself.

15 Daphne

The following story is told about Daphne, the daughter of Amyclas. She absolutely refused to go down to the city and would not mingle with the other girls. She acquired a lot of dogs and used to hunt in Laconia, and sometimes she would go hunting in the other mountains of the Peloponnese. For this reason she was very close to Artemis' heart and the goddess made her shoot straight. While Daphne was wandering near Elis, Oinomaos' son, Leucippos, came to desire her. Despairing of getting her in any normal way, he dressed himself in women's clothing, made himself look

[3] Unknown bird.

like a girl, and went hunting with her. He managed to get close to her heart, and she always kept him around, embracing and hanging on him all the time.

But Apollo himself was inflamed with desire for the girl and was full of anger and envy that Leucippos was with her. The god put into the girl's mind the idea of bathing with the rest of the girls, who had gone to a spring. After they had arrived, they disrobed and saw that Leucippos was not willing to do so. So they tore his clothes off. Learning of his deception and how he had plotted against them, they all hurled their spears at him. While he disappeared in accordance with the will of the gods, Daphne caught sight of Apollo coming after her and fled with great vigor. When she was going to be overtaken in the chase, she asked Zeus if she could be removed from humanity. They say that she became the tree that is called *daphne* {"laurel"} after her.

20 Leiro

It is said that Leiro was the daughter of Oinopion and the Nymph Helice. Orion son of Hyrieus fell in love with her and asked her father for the girl. For her sake Orion cleared the island, which at that time was filled with beasts, and he gathered a great deal of plunder from those who lived around and offered it as bride-price. But on each occasion Oinopion put off the marriage because of his disgust at the thought of having such a son-in-law. When Orion was out of his wits with wine, he broke into the bedroom where the girl was sleeping and, as he tried to rape her, had his eyes burned out by Oinopion.

29 Daphnis

In Sicily a son, Daphnis, was born to Hermes. Daphnis was skilled at playing the syrinx and was remarkably good-looking. He did not go among the great throng of men, but herded cows on Mount Aitna and lived outdoors both winter and summer. They say that the Nymph Echenais fell in love with him and warned him not to have sex with a woman; for if he did not heed her, it would come about that he would lose his eyesight. He held out steadfastly for a time, even though more than a few women were crazy about him, but later one of the princesses in Sicily plied him with a lot of wine and made him desire to sleep with her. He, because of this, was blinded because of his thoughtlessness, like Thamyras the Thracian.[4]

[4] Who was blinded because he challenged the Muses to a musical contest.

PAUSANIAS

(2nd c. AD, wrote in Greek)

Pausanias is known for his Description of Greece, *the only complete travel guide that we have from antiquity. Although he lived in the 2nd century* AD, *his primary interest was in the monuments and history of early Greece, particularly major temples, famous statues, and religious sites such as Epidauros, Olympia, and Delphi. Pausanias had access to guides at the various sites and gives us interesting local variants of well-known myths as well as those that are elsewhere unknown to us. He also had at his disposal many relatively obscure written resources (such as epic works on Oidipous, for example) that are now lost. He is one of our most trustworthy sources from antiquity. Whenever we have been able to compare archaeological finds with his account, we have discovered that Pausanias' description of these monuments is for the most part accurate and reliable.*

FROM *DESCRIPTION OF GREECE*

A The Sanctuary of Theseus in Athens (1.17.2–1.17.3)

[1.17.2] Beside the gymnasium is a sanctuary of Theseus, with paintings of the Athenians fighting the Amazons. This war is represented also on the shield of Athena and on the pedestal of Olympian Zeus. In the sanctuary of Theseus there is also painted the battle of the Centaurs and Lapiths. Theseus has already slain a Centaur, but the others are fighting on equal terms. To those who may be unacquainted with the legend, the painting on the third wall is not clear, partly, no doubt, because of the effects of time, but partly also because Micon has not painted the whole story. When Minos brought Theseus and the rest of the youthful band to Crete, he fell in love with Periboia; and when Theseus stoutly withstood him, Minos broke into angry abuse of him, and said he was no son of Poseidon, "For," said he, "if I fling into the sea the signet ring I wear on my finger, you could not bring it back to me." With these words, so runs the tale, he flung the ring into the sea, from which Theseus emerged with it, as well as a golden crown, a gift of Amphitrite.[1]

B Sanctuary of Dionysos in Athens (1.20.3)

[1.20.3] But the oldest sanctuary of Dionysos is beside the theater. Within the enclosure there are two temples and two images of Dionysos, one surnamed

[1] A poetic recounting of this scene is found in Bacchylides, *Dithyramb* 17.

Eleuthereus {"Deliverer"}, the other made by Alcamenes of ivory and gold. Here, too, are pictures representing Dionysos bringing Hephaistos up to heaven. For the Greeks say that Hera flung Hephaistos down as soon as he was born, and that he, bearing her a grudge, sent her as a gift a golden chair with invisible bonds. When Hera sat down on it, she was held fast, and Hephaistos would not listen to the intercession of any of the gods until Dionysos, his trustiest friend, made him drunk, and so brought him to heaven. There are also depicted Pentheus and Lycourgos suffering retribution for the insults they offered to Dionysos, Ariadne asleep with Theseus putting to sea, and Dionysos having come to carry Ariadne off.

C The Tomb of Medeia's Children in Corinth (2.3.6–2.3.9)

[2.3.6] We now leave the marketplace by another road, the one that leads to Sicyon. On the right of the road we see a temple with a bronze image of Apollo, and a little farther on a water-basin named after Glauce; for they say she threw herself into it, thinking the water would be an antidote to Medeia's drugs.[2] Above this water-basin stands the Odeon {"Music Hall"}, as it is called. Beside it is the tomb of the children of Medeia. Their names were Mermeros and Pheres. They are said to have been stoned to death by the Corinthians on account of the gifts they brought to Glauce.[3] And because their death had been violent and unjust, they caused the infant children of the Corinthians to pine away, till, at the bidding of the oracle, yearly sacrifices were instituted in their honor, and an image of Deima {"Terror"} was set up. That image remains to this day. It is a likeness of a woman of terrifying aspect. But since the destruction of Corinth by the Romans and the extinction of its old inhabitants,[4] the sacrifices in question have been discontinued by the new inhabitants; and the children no longer cut their hair and wear black garments in honor of the children of Medeia. Medeia thereupon went to Athens and married Aigeus; but afterward being detected plotting against Theseus, she fled from Athens also, and coming to the land that was then called Aria, she caused the people to be called Medes after herself. The child whom she took with her in her flight to the Arians is said to have been her son by Aigeus, and to have been named Medos. But Hellanicus calls him Polyxenos, and says that his father was Jason. There is an epic poem current in Greece called the *Naupactia*. In this poem it is said that Jason migrated from Iolcos to Corcyra after the death of Pelias, and that his elder son, Mermeros, was killed by a lioness while he was hunting on the opposite mainland; but of Pheres nothing is recorded. Cinaithon the Lacedaimonian, who also composed genealogies in verse, said that Jason had a son, Medeios, and a daughter, Eriopis, by Medeia; but he has said nothing more about the children.

[2] This Glauce (other versions call her Creousa) is Jason's bride, who was killed by Medeia.

[3] Some accounts offer a version different than that in Euripides' *Medea*, in which Medeia herself kills her sons (Aelian 5.21, Apollodorus G5).

[4] In 146 BC.

D The Temple of Hera near Mycenae (2.17.1–2.17.4)

[2.17.1] To the left of Mycenae, at a distance of fifteen furlongs, is the Heraion {"Temple of Hera"}. Beside the road flows a stream that is called the Water of Freedom.[5] The women who minister at the sanctuary employ it for purifications and for the secret sacrifices. The sanctuary itself is on the lower slope of Euboia. For they name this mountain Euboia, saying that the river Asterion had three daughters, Euboia, Prosymna, and Acraia, and that they were nurses of Hera. The mountain opposite the Heraion is named after Acraia. The ground about the sanctuary is called after Euboia; and the district below the Heraion is called Prosymna. The Asterion flowing above the Heraion falls into a gully and disappears. On its banks grows a plant that they also name Asterion. They offer the plant to Hera, and twine its leaves into wreaths for her. They say that the architect of the temple was Eupolemos, an Argive. Some of the sculptures over the columns represent the birth of Zeus and the battle of the gods and giants, others the Trojan War and the taking of Ilion. Before the entrance stand statues of women who have been priestesses of Hera, and statues of heroes, including Orestes; for they say that the statue, which the inscription declares to be the Emperor Augustus, is really Orestes. In the forepart of the temple are ancient images of the Charites on the left; and on the right is a couch of Hera[6] and a votive offering consisting of the shield that Menelaos once took from Euphorbos at Ilion. The image of Hera is seated on a throne, and is of colossal size. It is made of gold and ivory, and is a work of Polycleitos.[7] On her head is a crown with the Charites and the Horai wrought on it in relief; in one hand she carries a pomegranate, in the other a scepter. The story about the pomegranate I shall omit as it is of a somewhat mystic nature;[8] but the cuckoo perched on the scepter is explained by a story, that when Zeus was in love with the maiden Hera, he changed himself into this bird and that Hera caught the bird to play with it. This and similar stories of the gods I record, though I do not accept them.

E The Grave of Thyestes Between Mycenae and Argos (2.18.1–2.18.2)

[2.18.1] In the Argolid, going on a little way from this shrine, we come to the grave of Thyestes on the right. Over the grave is the stone figure of a ram because Thyestes obtained the golden lamb after he had committed adultery with his brother's wife.[9] Prudence did not restrain Atreus from retaliating. He murdered the children of Thyestes and served up the notorious banquet. Afterward, I cannot say for certain

[5] So-called because slaves would drink from it when being freed.

[6] A couch was used in the dramatic recreation of the ritual of the *hieros gamos*, the sacred marriage of Zeus and Hera.

[7] Polycleitos was one of the most famous sculptors from antiquity. Strabo, another late geographer, claimed that the works of Polycleitos in the Heraion were the most beautiful in the world.

[8] The pomegranate that Hera is often shown holding has been variously interpreted by scholars as a representation of, among other things, either fertility, blood, or death.

[9] The lamb was important because whichever of the two brothers possessed it would be king. The dispute between the two brothers continues in the next generation with Atreus' son Agamemnon and Thyestes' son Aigisthos.

whether Aigisthos was the aggressor, or whether Agamemnon began the feud by murdering Tantalos son of Thyestes. They say that Tantalos was Clytaimnestra's first husband, Tyndareos having given her to him in marriage. I do not wish to charge them with having been by nature wicked; but if the guilt of Pelops and the avenging ghost of Myrtilos dogged their steps so long, it at least jibes with what the Pythian Priestess told to the Spartan Glaucos son of Epicydes, when he was considering committing perjury, that vengeance would pursue his descendants.[10]

F Three-eyed Zeus in Larisa near Argos (2.24.3–2.24.4)

[2.24.3] On the summit of Larisa is a temple of Larisian Zeus. The roof is gone, and the image, which is made of wood, no longer stands on its pedestal. There is also a temple of Athena that is worth seeing. Amongst the votive offerings it contains is a wooden image of Zeus with two eyes in the usual place, and a third eye on the forehead. They say that this Zeus was the ancestral god of Priam son of Laomedon and stood in the courtyard under the open sky; and when Ilion was taken by the Greeks, Priam fled for refuge to this god's altar. In the division of the spoils Sthenelos son of Capaneus got this image, and that is why it stands here. The reason why it has three eyes may be conjectured to be the following. All men agree that Zeus reigns in heaven, and there is a verse of Homer that gives the name of Zeus also to the god who is said to rule under the earth:

> Both underground Zeus and august Persephone.

Further, Aeschylus son of Euphorion applies the name of Zeus also to the god who dwells in the sea. So the artist, whoever he was, represented Zeus with three eyes because it is one and the same Zeus who reigns in all three realms of nature, as they are called.

G Epidauros and Asclepios (2.26.3–2.27.4)

[2.26.3] The country is sacred in a very high degree to Asclepios, and this is how it is said to have come about. The Epidaurians say that Phlegyas came to the Peloponnese nominally to view the land, but really to spy out the number of the people and see whether they were a fighting race. For Phlegyas was the greatest warrior of the age and made forays in all directions, carrying off the crops and driving away the cattle. When he came to the Peloponnese, his daughter {Coronis} came with him. She, all unknown to her father, was with child by Apollo. In the land of Epidauros she gave birth to a male child, whom she exposed upon the mountain that is named Titthion {"Nipple"} in our day, but then it was called Myrtion. But one of the goats that browsed on the mountain gave suck to the forsaken baby, and a dog, the guardian of

[10] Glaucos inquired of the Delphic oracle whether he should cheat a man's sons out of the money that had been entrusted to him. The god responded that considering such a crime was tantamount to committing it, and within a few generations the whole of Glaucos' family died off.

the flock, watched over it. Now, when Aresthanas—for that was the name of the goatherd—perceived that the tally of the goats was not full, and that the dog too kept away from the flock, he went up and down, they say, looking everywhere. At last he found the baby and desired to take it up in his arms. But as he drew near, he saw a bright light shining from the child. So he turned away, "For surely," thought he, "this was something divine," as indeed it was. And soon the fame of the child went abroad over every land and sea, how he had all power to heal the sick and that he raised the dead.

Another story told of him is this: While he was still in the womb of his mother, Coronis, she had sex with Ischys son of Elatos. Artemis avenged the insult offered to Apollo by slaying her. The pyre was already lit when Hermes, they say, snatched the infant from the flames.

The third story, which represents Asclepios as the son of Arsinoe daughter of Leucippos, is to my mind the most unlikely of them all. For when Apollophanes the Arcadian, came to Delphi and inquired of the god whether Asclepios was the son of Arsinoe and therefore a Messenian, the Pythian Priestess gave answer:

> O born to be the world's great joy, Asclepios,
> Offspring of love, whom Phlegyas' daughter,
> Fair Coronis, bore to me in rugged Epidauros.

This oracle is the best proof that Asclepios was not the son of Arsinoe, but that Hesiod or some other interpolator of Hesiod composed the verses to please the Messenians.

Another proof that the god was born in Epidauros is this. I find that his most famous sanctuaries are offshoots from the one at Epidauros. For instance, the Athenians professedly assign to Asclepios a share in the mysteries, and name the day on which they do so Epidauria; and they date their worship of Asclepios as a god from the time when this practice was instituted. Again, the worship of Asclepios was introduced into Pergamos by Archias son of Aristaichmos because, hunting on Pindasos, he had strained a limb and had been healed in Epidauros. And in our time the sanctuary of Asclepios beside the sea at Smyrna was founded from the one at Pergamos. Again, at Balagrai in the land of Cyrene, Asclepios is worshiped under the title of Iatros {"Healer"}, and this worship also came from Epidauros. And from this Cyrenean sanctuary, again, is derived the one at Lebene in Crete. The Cyreneans differ from the Epidaurians in this, that whereas the Cyreneans sacrifice goats, it is against the Epidaurian custom to do so. That Asclepios was held to be a god from the first, and did not merely acquire this reputation in the course of time, I find from various evidence, in particular from the words that Homer puts in the mouth of Agamemnon about Machaon:

> Talthybios, hither call with speed Machaon,
> The mortal who is son to Asclepios,[11]

[11] *Iliad* 4.193–4.194.

Which is as if he said, "a man the son of a god."

[2.27.1] The sacred grove of Asclepios is surrounded by mountains on every side. Within the enclosure no death or birth takes place. The same rule is observed in the island of Delos. The sacrifices, whether offered by a native or foreigner, are consumed within the bounds. I know that the same thing is done at Titane. The image of Asclepios is half the size of the image of Olympian Zeus at Athens. It is of ivory and gold. An inscription sets forth that the sculptor was Thrasymedes, a Parian, the son of Arignotos. The god is seated on a throne, grasping a staff in one hand and holding the other over the head of the serpent; a dog crouches at his side. On the throne are carved in relief the deeds of the Argive heroes: Bellerophontes killing the Chimaira, and Perseus after he has cut off Medousa's head. Over against the temple is the place where the suppliants of the god sleep. Near it is a round building of white marble called the Tholos, and it is worth seeing. It contains a picture of Eros by Pausias. The god has thrown away his bow and arrows, and has picked up a lyre instead. Here, too, is another painting by Pausias. It represents Drunkenness drinking out of a crystal goblet. In the picture you can see the crystal goblet and a woman's face through it.

Tablets stood within the enclosure. There used to be more of them. In my time six were left. On these tablets are engraved the names of men and women who have been healed by Asclepios, together with the disease from which each suffered, and the manner of the cure.[12] The inscriptions are in the Doric dialect. Apart from the others stands an ancient tablet with an inscription stating that Hippolytos dedicated twenty horses to the god. The people of Aricia tell a tale that agrees with the inscription on this tablet. They say that Hippolytos, done to death by the curses of Theseus, was raised from the dead by Asclepios. After he had come to life again, he refused to forgive his father and, disregarding his entreaties, went away to Aricia in Italy. There he reigned, and there he consecrated to Artemis a precinct, where down to my time the priesthood of the goddess is the prize of victory in a single combat. The competition is not open to free men, but only to slaves who have run away from their masters.

H Poseidon and Horses (7.21.7–7.21.8)

[7.21.7] Beside the harbor {in Patrai} is a temple of Poseidon with a standing image of stone. Besides the names that poets have bestowed on Poseidon to trick out their verses, and the special local names that are given to him in various places, the following surnames are universally applied to him: Pelagaios {"Marine"}, Asphalios {"Securer"}, and Hippios {"of Horses"}. Various reasons might be given why Poseidon is called Hippios; for my part, I conjecture that he got the name as the inventor of horsemanship. Certainly Homer, in the description of the chariot race, puts into the mouth of Menelaos a challenge to swear by this god:

> Lay your hand on the horses, and by the Earth-holding, Earth-shaking god
> Swear that you did not guilefully obstruct my car.[13]

[12] One such inscription is given in Appendix Two, O.

[13] Pausanias quotes *Iliad* 23.583–23.584.

And Pamphos, who composed for the Athenians their most ancient hymns, says that Poseidon is the

> Giver of horses and of ships with spread sails.

Thus he got the name of Hippios from horsemanship, and for no other reason.

I The Oracle of Hermes (7.22.2–7.22.4)

[7.22.2] The marketplace at Pharai is spacious and in the old style. In the middle of it is a stone image of Hermes with a beard. It stands on the ground and is of the square shape, but of no great size. An inscription on it states that it was dedicated by Simylos, a Messenian. It is called Agoraios {"of the Market"}, and beside it an oracle is established. In front of the image is a hearth made of stone, with bronze lamps clamped to it with lead. He who would inquire of the god comes at evening and burns incense on the hearth, fills the lamps with oil, lights them, lays a coin of the country called a copper on the altar to the right of the image, and whispers his question, whatever it may be, into the ear of the god. Then he stops his ears and leaves the marketplace; and when he is gone a little way outside, he takes his hands from his ears, and whatever words he hears he regards as an oracle. The Egyptians have a similar mode of divination at the sanctuary of Apis. At Pharai there is also a sacred water. The spring is named the Stream of Hermes, and they do not catch the fish in it because they esteem them sacred to the god. Close to the image stand about thirty square stones; these the people of Pharai revere, giving each stone the name of a god. In the olden time all the Greeks worshiped unwrought stones instead of images.

J Lycanthropy in Arcadia (8.2.3–8.2.7)

[8.2.3] Lycaon brought a human baby to the altar of Zeus Lycaios {"Wolfish"}, and sacrificed it, and poured out the blood on the altar; and they say that immediately after the sacrifice he was turned into a wolf {*lycos*}. For my own part I believe the tale. It has been handed down among the Arcadians from antiquity, and probability is in its favor. For the men of that time, by reason of their righteousness and piety, were guests of the gods and sat with them at table; the gods openly bestowed honor upon the good and their displeasure upon the bad. Indeed, men were raised to the rank of gods in those days, and are worshiped down to the present time. Such were Aristaios; the Cretan maiden Britomartis; Hercules son of Alcmene; Amphiaraos son of Oicles; and finally, Polydeuces and Castor. So we may well believe that Lycaon was turned into a wild beast, and Niobe daughter of Tantalos into a stone. But in the present age, when wickedness is growing to such a height, and spreading over every land and every city, men are changed into gods no more, save in the hollow rhetoric that flattery addresses to power. And the wrath of the gods at the wicked is reserved for a distant future when they shall have gone hence. In the long course of the ages, many events in the past and not a few in the present have been brought into general discredit by persons who build a superstructure of falsehood on a foundation of truth.

For example, they say that from the time of Lycaon downward a man has always been turned into a wolf at the sacrifice of Zeus Lycaios, but that the transformation is not for life; for if, while he is a wolf, he abstains from human flesh, in the ninth year afterward he changes back into a man, but if he has tasted human flesh, he remains a beast forever. In like manner they say that Niobe on Mount Sipylos sheds tears in summer. I have also been told that griffins are spotted like leopards and that Tritons speak with a human voice, though others say they blow through a pierced shell. Lovers of the marvelous are too prone to heighten the marvels they hear by adding touches of their own, and thus they debase truth by alloying it with fiction.

K Black Demeter near Phigalia in Arcadia (8.42.1–8.42.4)

[8.42.1] The other mountain, Mount Elaios, is about thirty furlongs from Phigalia. There is a cave there sacred to Demeter surnamed the Black. All that the people of Thelpousa say concerning the loves of Poseidon and Demeter is believed by the Phigalians; but the Phigalians say that Demeter gave birth, not to a horse, but to her whom the Arcadians name the Mistress.[14] They say that afterward Demeter, angry with Poseidon and mourning the rape of Persephone, put on black raiment, and, entering this grotto, tarried there in seclusion a long while. But when all the fruits of the earth were wasting away, and the race of man was perishing still more of hunger, none of the other gods, it would seem, knew where Demeter was hidden; but Pan, roving over Arcadia, and hunting now on one mountain, now on another, came at last to Mount Elaios, and spied Demeter and saw the plight she was in and the garb she wore. So Zeus learnt of this from Pan, and sent the Moirai to Demeter, and she hearkened to the Moirai, and swallowed her wrath, and abated even from her grief.

For that reason the Phigalians say that they accounted the grotto sacred to Demeter and set up in it an image of wood. The image, they say, was made in this manner: it was seated on a rock, and was in the likeness of a woman, all but the head; the head and the hair were those of a horse, and attached to the head were figures of serpents and other wild beasts; she was clad in a tunic that reached even to her feet; on one of her hands was a dolphin, and on the other a dove. Why they made the image thus is plain to any man of ordinary sagacity who is versed in legendary lore. They say they surnamed her Black because the garb the goddess wore was black. They do not remember who made this image, nor how it caught fire.

L Actaion's Bed near Plataia in Boiotia (9.2.3–9.2.4)

[9.2.3] On the road from Megara there is a spring on the right, and a little farther along a rock. They call the rock Actaion's bed, for they say that he slept on this rock when he was weary with the chase. They also say that he looked into the spring while Artemis was bathing in it. Stesichoros of Himera says that the goddess threw a deerskin around Actaion to ensure his death by the dogs, so that he would not marry Semele. I am persuaded that without the intervention of the goddess the dogs went

[14] In some versions, Demeter gives birth to the horse Areion; see Apollodorus M9.

mad, and in this condition they would be sure to rend in pieces without distinction whomsoever they fell in with.

M The Reconciliation of Zeus and Hera in Plataia (9.2.7–9.3.1)

[9.2.7] There is another statue of Hera here. It is seated and is by Callimachos. The Plataians name the goddess "the Bride" for the following reason. [9.3.1] They say that Hera, enraged at Zeus for some reason, retired to Euboia and that Zeus, when he could not persuade her to return to him, came to Cithairon, who then ruled in Plataia. For Cithairon was second to none in craft. He accordingly advised Zeus to have an image made of wood, to convey it, wrapped up, in an ox cart,[15] and to say that he was marrying Plataia daughter of Asopos. Zeus did as Cithairon advised him, and no sooner had Hera heard of it than she flew to the spot, and going up to the wagon tore the dress off the image. And finding a wooden image instead of a bride, she was pleased with the trick and made up with Zeus.

In memory of this reconciliation they celebrate a festival called Daidala, because people long ago called the wooden statues *daidala*. I believe that they called these statues this even before Daidalos[16] son of Palamaon was born at Athens, and I think that Daidalos was a surname subsequently given to him from the *daidala*, and not a name bestowed on him at birth.

N Did Oidipous Have Children By His Mother? (9.5.10–9.5.11)

[9.5.10] While Laios sat on the throne and was married to Jocaste, there came to him an oracle from Delphi, that if Jocaste should bear a son, that son would be his father's death. Therefore, he exposed Oidipous. But as fate would have it, when Oidipous was grown to manhood, he slew his father and married his mother. But I think he had no children by her, and Homer is my witness, who says in the *Odyssey*:[17]

> And the mother of Oidipous I saw, fair Epicaste,
> who all unwitting wrought a fearful deed,
> wedding her son. But he his father slew
> and wedded her, and straightway the gods revealed it to mankind.

Now, how could they have revealed it straightway if Jocaste was the mother of four children by Oidipous? In point of fact, the mother of his children was Euryganeia daughter of Hyperphas. This is proved by the author of the poem they call the *Oidipodia*; and Onasias has painted a picture at Plataia of Euryganeia bowed with grief at the battle between her children.

[15] Greek brides were heavily veiled, and part of the marriage ceremony involved a procession, here on ox cart, from the bride's house to the groom's home.

[16] Daidalos was said to have invented a new kind of statue (see Palaephatus 21).

[17] Homer, *Odyssey* 11.271.

O The Sphinx (9.26.2–9.26.4)

[9.26.2] Farther on we come to the mountain from which they say the Sphinx used to sally, reciting a riddle that proved fatal to those whom she caught. Others say that she was a pirate who, roving with a naval force, touched at Anthedon, and seizing this mountain, engaged in pillage till Oidipous conquered her by the superior numbers of an army that he brought from Corinth.[18] Another story is that she was a bastard daughter of Laios, who because he loved her, revealed to her the oracle that had been given to Cadmos at Delphi.[19] No one knew the oracle except the royal family. Now, Laios had sons by concubines, but knowledge of the Delphic oracle went only so far as Epicaste and her children. So when any of Sphinx's half-brothers came to claim the throne from her, she dealt subtly with them, pretending that, as sons of Laios, they must surely know the oracle given to Cadmos. And when they could not answer, she put them to death on the ground that their claim to the blood royal and the kingdom was baseless. But when Oidipous came, it appears that he had learned the oracle in a dream.

[18] A similarly rationalizing version can be seen in Palaephatus 4.

[19] That is, he was supposed to settle where a cow led him.

Pherecydes

(5th c. BC, wrote in Greek)

Pherecydes of Athens, one of the most important early mythographers to judge by how often he was cited by later writers such as Apollodorus, wrote extensively on mythological matters in his Histories, *a work that was organized by genealogies. Unfortunately, this work has only survived in fragmentary form, mostly in quotations and in summaries of his accounts in* scholia *(ancient footnotes), such as the fragments provided here.*

FROM *THE HISTORIES*

10 The Story of Danae (fr. 10 Fowler)

Pherecydes in his second book gives the account that Acrisios married Eurydice daughter of Lacedaimon. They had a daughter, Danae. When Acrisios consulted the oracle about having male children, the god in Pytho responded that he would have no male child, but his daughter would have a son by whom he would be killed. Upon his return to Argos, he had constructed in the courtyard of his home an underground bronze chamber and placed Danae in it with a nurse. He had her guarded in this chamber so that no son might be born of her. But Zeus fell in love with the girl and flowed through the thatched roof in a form like gold; she caught him in her lap. Zeus revealed himself and had sex with the girl; they had a son, Perseus. Danae raised him, and she and her nurse kept him out of Acrisios' sight. But when Perseus was three or four years old, Acrisios heard his voice while he played and had his attendants summon Danae and her nurse. He killed the nurse, but took Danae down to the altar of Zeus Herceios with her son. When alone, he asked her who could possibly have fathered her son; she replied that Zeus was the father. He did not believe her and loaded her into a chest with her child, locked it, and cast it into the sea.

They floated all the way to the island of Seriphos, where Dictys son of Peristhenes dragged them out of the water as he fished with a net. Then Danae begged him to open the chest, and when he had done so and found out who they were, he brought them home and took them in because of their family connection; for Dictys and Polydectes were the sons of Androthoe daughter of Castor and Peristhenes son of Damastor (son of Nauplios, the son of Poseidon and Amymone). This genealogy is given by Pherecydes in his first book.

11 The Story of Perseus (fr. 11 Fowler)

When Perseus, who was by now grown up, was living on Seriphos with his mother in the house of Dictys, Polydectes (he and Dictys had the same mother) happened to be king of Seriphos. He fell in love with Danae at first sight but had no idea how he could sleep with her. He arranged a feast and invited many men, including Perseus himself. Perseus asked him what each man was supposed to contribute in return. When Polydectes answered that each should bring a horse, Perseus said he would bring the Gorgon's head. The day after the feast all the contributors brought back their horses, and Perseus did too, but Polydectes would not accept his. He demanded the Gorgon's head, as Perseus had promised, and said that he would take his mother if he did not bring it. Sorely troubled, Perseus bemoaned his plight and went off to the end of the island.

Hermes appeared to him and, asking, learned the reason for his lamentation. Telling him to cheer up, Hermes led him first to the Graiai, the daughters of Phorcys, that is, Pemphredo, Enyo, and Deino. Athena went before them. Perseus took the eye and tooth as they were passing them around to each other. When they realized it, they cried out and begged him to give back their eye and tooth, for the three used one of each, taking turns. Perseus said that he had them and would give them back if the Graiai showed him the way to the Nymphs who had Hades' cap, the winged sandals, and the *kibisis*. They told him and he returned their eye and tooth. He went with Hermes to the Nymphs, asked for the objects, and got them. He strapped on the winged sandals, slung the *kibisis* over his shoulders, and put Hades' cap on his head. Accompanied by Hermes and Athena, he then flew to Oceanos and the Gorgons, whom he found sleeping. The two gods advised him that he had to face away while he cut off the head and pointed out Medousa, who was the only one of the Gorgons who was mortal. He drew near, cut off her head, put it in the *kibisis,* and fled. Realizing what was happening, they chased after him but could not see him.

When Perseus reached Seriphos, he went to Polydectes' house and told him to call his men to an assembly so that he could show them the Gorgon's head. Perseus was fully aware that if they looked upon it, they were going to turn to stone. When he had gathered the crowd, Polydectes told Perseus to show the head. Perseus turned away, pulled it out of the *kibisis,* and showed it. Those who looked upon it and were turned to stone.

Athena took the head from Perseus and placed it onto her aegis. Hermes returned the *kibisis*, sandals, and cap to the Nymphs. Pherecydes gives the account in his second book.

12 The Death of Acrisios (fr. 12 Fowler)

Next Pherecydes tells of the death of Acrisios. After Polydectes and those with him were turned to stone by the Gorgon's head, Perseus left Dictys as king of the remaining people on the island of Seriphos, while he himself sailed to Argos with the Cyclopes, Danae, and Andromeda. When he arrived, he did not find Acrisios in Argos since he had withdrawn to the Pelasgians in Larissa out of fear of Perseus. Failing to find him, he left Danae with her mother, Eurydice, along with Andromeda and the Cyclopes. He himself went to Larissa, and when he got there, he recognized Acrisios and persuaded him to accompany him back to Argos. Just when they were about to depart, they stumbled upon some young men holding an athletic competition in Larissa. Perseus stripped down for the competition, took the discus, and threw it (for the pentathlon did not yet exist, and they held each one of the events individually instead). The discus spun against Acrisios' foot and wounded him. Falling ill as a result of this, Acrisios died there in Larissa. Perseus and the Larissans buried him outside the city, and the locals built a hero's shrine for him. Perseus withdrew from Argos.

PINDAR

(ca. 518–ca. 438 BC, wrote in Greek)

Pindar was the leading lyric poet of his time, having been commissioned to compose his first epinicion *(victory ode) at the age of twenty and continuing his career for some sixty years. In the Hellenistic age, his poems were collected into seventeen books, but only his four books of* epinicia *survive. These are arranged according to the major festival for which these odes were performed (Olympian, Pythian, Nemean, and Isthmian). Below is one of the earliest and most famous of the* Olympians. *Like Bacchylides'* Ode *5, this poem celebrates Hieron of Syracuse's victory in the horse race at the Olympic Games in 476* BC. *It begins (1–27) and ends (97–118) with praise for the victor and more generally for the Olympic Games. In the central mythological piece, which is characteristic of* epinicia, *Pindar turns to the myth of Pelops, but he rejects the story that he was fed to the gods by his father Tantalos (28–53). More important for the* epinicion *itself, Pindar connects Pelops to the site of Olympia, and by extension to the Olympic Games, by recounting the myth of his winning Hippodameia's hand in marriage. This tale, involving a chariot race, links the mythical world of Tantalos and Pelops to the real celebration held in Olympia. Furthermore, Pindar's account is interesting for two other reasons. First, he attributes Pelops' victory not to trickery, as is the case in other ancient versions (see Hyginus 84), but to Poseidon's help; second, he mentions Pelops' tomb at Olympia, which visitors could see near the Temple of Zeus.*

OLYMPIAN 1

For Hieron son of Deinomenes, from Syracuse,
victor in the horse race

Best is water, and gold, like blazing fire by night, [Str. 1]
shines forth preeminent amid the lordliness of wealth.
But if it is contests that you wish
to sing of, O my heart,
do not look further than the sun
for warmth and brilliance in a star amid the empty air of day,
nor let us herald any games as superior to Olympia's,
from which comes glorious song to cast itself about
the intellects of skillful men, to celebrate
the son of Cronos when they have arrived, amid abundance,
at the blessed hearth of Hieron,

who wields his scepter lawfully amid the fruitful fields [Ant. 1]
of Sicily. He culls the foremost of all excellences,
and he is made resplendent too
by music's choicest strains,
such songs as we men often sing
in playful fashion around his friendly table. But from its peg take down
the Dorian lyre, if both Pisa's grace and Pherenicos'
have placed your mind beneath the spell of sweetest thoughts,
recalling how beside the Alpheos he rushed,
giving his body's strength ungoaded to the race,
and so infused his lord with mastery,

the Syracusan king whose joy is horses. Bright for him shines fame [Ep. 1]
in the brave-hearted settlement of Lydian Pelops,
with whom the mighty Earthholder fell in love,
Poseidon, when from the pure cauldron Clotho took him out,
his shoulder marked with gleaming ivory.[1]

Truly, wonders are many, yet doubtless too men's talk,
tales embellished beyond the true account
with lies of cunning pattern, cheat and lead astray.

And Charis, which fashions all that pleases mortals, [Str. 2]
by adding her authority makes even what outstrips belief
be frequently believed.
But future days remain
the wisest witnesses.
It is fitting for a man to say good things about the gods, for so
the blame is less.
Son of Tantalos, contrary to earlier accounts I shall proclaim
how when your father called the gods to that
most orderly of feasts at his dear Sipylos,
offering them a banquet in return,
then it was that he of the splendid trident snatched you up,

his mind subdued by longing, and on golden horses [Ant. 2]
brought you aloft to the house of august Zeus,
where at a later time

[1] In the traditional myth, which Pindar rejects, Tantalos cut up his own son and fed him to the gods. Only Demeter took a bite, and when he was reconstituted, she furnished him a shoulder of ivory (see Hyginus 83).

Ganymedes came as well,
to render Zeus the selfsame service.
But when you disappeared, and those who sought you long failed to return you to your mother,
at once some envious neighbor told a tale in secret,
how into water brought to the fullest boil by fire
they cut you with a knife, limb by limb,
and then among the tables, as the final course,
they portioned out your flesh and ate.

For me, however, it is impossible to call any of the blessed gods a glutton: I stand apart. [Ep. 2]
Often a lack of profit falls to slanderers.
But truly, if the watchers of Olympos ever held a mortal man
in honor, Tantalos was he—but all in vain, for he could not digest
his great good fortune. In his greed he gained
excess of ruin, for the Father
hung over him a mighty rock,
and being always eager to cast it from his head, he strays exiled from merriment.

He has this helpless life of lasting toil, [Str. 3]
a fourth trial with three others, since he cheated the immortals
by sharing with his drinking friends and age-mates
the nectar and ambrosia
with which they had made him
free from decay. But if in any action any man hopes to elude divinity, he is in error.
Therefore, the immortals sent his son back once again
to dwell among the short-lived race of men.
And when, toward the time of his youth's flowering,
his chin and jaw were darkening with soft hair,
he sent his thoughts upon the ready marriage

that might be his by wrestling fair-famed Hippodameia from her father, [Ant. 3]
the king of Pisa.[2] Drawing near the white-flecked sea, alone in dark of night,
he hailed the loud-resounding

[2] In most versions Pelops has to resort to guile to win the chariot race (Hyginus 84), but here his victory is owed to Poseidon.

god of the trident, who close by
the young man's feet revealed himself.
To him he said: "Come, if in any way the Cyprian's affectionate gifts lay claim, Poseidon,
to gratitude, then shackle Oinomaos' brazen spear;
dispatch me on the swiftest of all chariots
to Elis; draw me near to mastery.
For thirteen men, all suitors, he has killed,
and so puts off the marriage

of his daughter. Great risk does not place its hold on cowards. [Ep. 3]
Since we must die, why sit in darkness
and to no purpose coddle an inglorious old age,
without a share of all that's noble? But for me, this contest is a task that I
must undertake; may *you* bring to fulfillment that which I hold dear."
Thus he spoke, and the words that he laid hold of
were not without effect. Exalting him, the god
gave him a golden chariot and a team of tireless winged horses.

He took strong Oinomaos down and took the maiden as his bride, [Str. 4]
begetting six sons, leaders eager to excel.
But now he has a share
in splendid acts of sacrifice,
reclining by the course of Alpheios,
in his well-tended tomb beside the altar that many strangers visit.[3] Fame
gleams far and wide from the Olympic races
of Pelops, where the speed of feet contends,
and utmost strength courageous to bear toil.
Throughout the rest of life the one who wins
enjoys a honeyed calm,

at least as regards games. That good, however, which comes day by day [Ant. 4]
is always uppermost for every mortal. As for me, to crown
that man with music in the Aiolian mode,
a tune fit for a horseman, is
my duty. I am confident that no host
exists who can lay claim to deeper knowledge of noble ends or yet to greater power,

[3] Pausanias records that "the Eleans honor Pelops as much above all the heroes of Olympia as they honor Zeus above the rest of the gods."

at least among those living now, to be embellished with loud folds of song.
Having this as his special care,
a guardian god takes thought
for your ambitions, Hieron. Unless he should leave suddenly,
I hope to honor a still sweeter victory

with a swift chariot, discovering a path of words to lend assistance [Ep. 4]
as I approach the sunny hill of Cronos. Now for me
the Muse fosters in her reserves of force the mightiest arrow:
in different matters different men show greatness, but the utmost peak belongs
to kings. Extend your gaze no further.
May your lot be to walk on high throughout the time you have;
may mine be to keep company with those who win
on each occasion, foremost in poetic skill among Greeks everywhere.

Plato

(ca. 429–347 BC, wrote in Greek)

Plato, the student of Socrates and the teacher of Aristotle, may be labeled with some confidence as the most important philosophical thinker in the western world. He contributed to many areas of philosophic thought, including ethics, law, and theology. Early philosophers, notably the 6th-century thinker Xenophanes (see fragments), were the first in Greek society to challenge the authority and validity of myths. Plato, however, grew up in a period when philosophers were even more inclined to subject myth to rigorous analysis and criticism, and he was no exception, as is shown by his rejection of the stories told by earlier poets in the selection below from the second book of the Republic. *Nevertheless, Plato himself employed myth in a variety of ways, including having characters in his dialogues provide mythic accounts as contributions to a philosophic discussion (see the excerpts from the* Protagoras *and* Symposium*). Plato also invented or adapted myths to lend authority to his own arguments, as can be seen in the selection from book 10 of the* Republic.

FROM *PROTAGORAS*

320c–322d The Origin of Justice Among Mankind

*Protagoras (ca. 480–ca. 410 BC) was a successful sophist, a name given to teachers who traveled and lectured around the Greek world for a fee. Although some of these professional teachers were among the first to reject traditional notions of the divine—Protagoras himself claimed that he did not know whether gods exist or not—they nevertheless created and narrated their own myths as instruments to instruct their students. A prime example is found in the excerpt below (as is Prodicus' lecture on the Choice of Heracles in Xenophon), where Protagoras tells a story (*mythos*) in order to prove that all humans share a sense of justice. The story he relates is an elaboration of the creation myth of humankind hinted at in earlier poems such as Hesiod's* Theogony, *but his main point is the importance of justice and shame in human civilization. Since Zeus here is the benefactor of humankind—justice and shame are his gifts to mortals—Protagoras seems to have found a neat way to mend the traditional rift between man and Zeus caused by Prometheus' theft of fire.*

320C "Well, Socrates," he said, "I won't refuse your request. Should I prove my point by telling a story {*mythos*}, as elders do to the young, or by giving a rational argument {*logos*}?"

Many in the audience responded that he should give his account in whatever way he wished.

"Then it seems to me," he said, "that it would be more pleasant if I told you a story. There was once a time when there were gods but no mortal creatures. When the appointed time came to create them, the gods formed them within the earth using a combination of earth, fire, and matter created by a mixture of fire and earth. When they were about to lead them into the light, they ordered Prometheus and Epimetheus to furnish and distribute capabilities to each species as was fitting. Epimetheus begged Prometheus to let him conduct the distribution by himself and said, 'Once I have distributed them, you can check my work.' He persuaded him and began distributing them.

"During the distribution he provided some with strength but not speed; on the weaker ones he bestowed speed. Some he armed; for others, since he gave them a defenseless nature, he furnished some other capability for survival. To the ones he endowed with a diminutive stature he allotted escape on wing or an underground lair; to those he enlarged with great stature he provided protection by that very quality.

"Likewise, he distributed the other capabilities in a balanced way and furnished 321A
them taking care that no species would become extinct. Once he had assured them the means to escape mutual slaughter, he furnished protection from the heaven-sent seasons, covering them with thick fur and tough hides sufficient for warding off the winter cold and capable of resisting the summer heat. He also did this so that when they retired to their lairs, these same things would function as personal, built-in bedding for each. He equipped some with hooves and others with tough and callous pads of skin.

"Then he furnished different means of nourishment for the different species—for some it was grass from the earth, for others fruit on trees, and for still others roots from the ground. And then there were those to whom he granted the flesh of other animals as food. To these carnivores he furnished the capacity to produce few offspring, while he gave the animals eaten by them the capability to produce many, thereby ensuring the survival of the species. Since he was not particularly intelligent, however, Epimetheus used up all the capabilities without realizing it. The human race, however, was still without endowments, and Epimetheus had no idea what to do about it.

"While he was puzzling over the matter, Prometheus came to check out the distribution of capabilities and saw that while the rest of the living animals had their proper share of everything, humankind remained naked and unshod, without bedding or protection. And yet the appointed day had already arrived when mankind too was to proceed from the earth into the light. So Prometheus, at a loss to find mankind some means of preservation, stole Hephaistos and Athena's technical wisdom along with fire (without fire no one could possess or use that wisdom) and without delay bestowed it upon humankind. In this way men obtained wisdom in providing for their lives, but they did not yet possess political wisdom, for that resided at the side of Zeus. Prometheus was no longer permitted to enter the citadel of Zeus' dwelling; moreover, Zeus' guards were formidable. So he sneaked into Hephaistos and Athena's shared residence, where they practiced their art, stole Hephaistos' skill with fire and Athena's as well, and gave them to humankind. With this gift humankind provides for itself with ease, but Prometheus, as the story goes, thanks to Epimetheus later paid the penalty for this theft.

322A “Since man received a portion of the divine, they were, first of all, the only living beings who worshiped the gods and undertook to set up altars and statues of the gods. Then, with their skill they quickly invented articulate speech and names for things, and they devised houses, clothes, shoes, beds, and nourishment from the earth. Having provided for themselves in this way, men at first lived scattered about; there were no cities. So they were constantly killed off by wild animals since they were weaker in every way than the beasts. Their technical skill was a suitable aid for sustaining themselves but was insufficient for warring against wild beasts. For they did not yet have political skill, and skill in war is a part of that. They tried to band together and protect themselves by building cities, but then, when they did band together, they injured each other since they did not possess any political skill. The result was that they dispersed again and were killed off.

“So Zeus, afraid that our race would be exterminated, sent Hermes to bring Shame and Justice to men so that there might be order in our cities and binding ties of friendship. Hermes asked Zeus how he was to bestow Justice and Shame onto mankind: ‘Am I to distribute these as the other skills have been distributed? They have been distributed like this: A single man possessing skill in healing is sufficient for many regular people. The same goes for the other experts in the technical arts. Am I to ration Shame and Justice to men along these lines? Or should I distribute them to all men?’

“ ‘To all men,’ Zeus said, ‘and give all men the chance to accept their share. For no cities would arise if few men have a share in these as they do in the case of other skills. And you will establish a law under my authority, that anyone incapable of accepting his share of Shame and Justice is to be killed as a plague upon the city.’ ”

FROM *REPUBLIC*

2.376d–2.380c The Role of Poets and Myth in an Ideal State

In the following excerpt from Republic *2 Socrates discusses with Glaucon and Adeimantos the creation of the ideal state, and they have come to the important topic of how its leaders are to be educated. Since myth and the poets who told myths were an important part of early Greek education, the subject of myth had to be dealt with in a systematic manner. Socrates argues that the myths of Homer and Hesiod are unsuitable for early education because they lead the young to improper behavior. It is also worth noting that in the discussion prior to the beginning of this excerpt Adeimantos himself had used the myths of self-serving gods as told by Homer and Hesiod to justify a self-serving lifestyle. This leads to Plato's contention that the storytellers must be censored for content, and he gives an account of individual passages from authors that prove his case. So powerful was Plato's condemnation of Homer that later thinkers such as Heraclitus sought to defend the epic poet against his denunciations.*

SOCRATES: Come, then, and just as if we had the leisure to make up stories, let's describe in theory how to educate our men.

376E ADEIMANTOS: All right.

What will their education be? Or is it hard to find anything better than that that has developed over a long period—physical training for bodies and music and poetry for the soul?

Yes, it would be hard.

Now, we start education in music and poetry before physical training, don't we?

Of course.

Do you include stories under music and poetry?

I do.

Aren't there two kinds of story, one true and the other false?

Yes.

And mustn't our men be educated in both, but first in false ones? 377A

I don't understand what you mean.

Don't you understand that we first tell stories to children? These are false, on the whole, though they have some truth in them. And we tell them to small children before physical training begins.

That's true.

And that's what I meant by saying that we must deal with music and poetry before physical training.

All right.

You know, don't you, that the beginning of any process is most important, especially for anything young and tender? It's at that time that it is most malleable and takes on any pattern one wishes to impress on it.

Exactly.

Then shall we carelessly allow the children to hear any old stories, told by just anyone, and to take beliefs into their souls that are for the most part opposite to the ones we think they should hold when they are grown up?

We certainly won't.

Then we must first of all, it seems, supervise the storytellers. We'll select their stories whenever they are fine or beautiful and reject them when they aren't. And we'll persuade nurses and mothers to tell their children the ones we have selected, since they will shape their children's souls with stories much more than they shape their bodies by handling them. Many of the stories they tell now, however, must be thrown out.

Which ones do you mean?

We'll first look at the major stories, and by seeing how to deal with them, we'll see how to deal with the minor ones as well, for they exhibit the same pattern and have the same effects whether they're famous or not. Don't you think so?

I do, but I don't know which ones you're calling major.

Those that Homer, Hesiod, and other poets tell us, for surely they composed false stories, told them to people, and are still telling them.

Which stories do you mean, and what fault do you find in them?

The fault one ought to find first and foremost, especially if the falsehood isn't well told.

For example?

When a story gives a bad image of what the gods and heroes are like, the way a painter does whose picture is not at all like the things he's trying to paint.

You're right to object to that. But what sort of thing in particular do you have in mind?

First, telling the greatest falsehood about the most important things doesn't make a fine story—I mean Hesiod telling us about how Ouranos behaved, how Cronos
378A punished him for it, and how he was in turn punished by his own son.[1] But even if it were true, it should be passed over in silence, not told to foolish young people. And if, for some reason, it has to be told, only a very few people—pledged to secrecy and after sacrificing not just a pig but something great and scarce—should hear it, so that their number is kept as small as possible.

Yes, such stories are hard to deal with.

And they shouldn't be told in our city, Adeimantos. Nor should a young person hear it said that in committing the worst crimes he's doing nothing out of the ordinary, or that if he inflicts every kind of punishment on an unjust father, he's only doing the same as the first and greatest of the gods.

No, by god, I don't think myself that these stories are fit to be told.

Indeed, if we want the guardians of our city to think that it's shameful to be easily provoked into hating one another, we mustn't allow *any* stories about gods warring, fighting, or plotting against one another, for they aren't true. The battles of gods and giants, and all the various stories of the gods hating their families or friends, should neither be told nor even woven in embroideries. If we're to persuade our people that no citizen has ever hated another and that it's impious to do so, then *that's* what should be told to children from the beginning by old men and women; and as these children grow older, poets should be compelled to tell them the same sort of thing. We won't admit stories into our city—whether allegorical or not—about Hera being chained by her son, nor about Hephaistos being hurled from heaven by his father when he tried to help his mother, who was being beaten, nor about the battle of the gods in Homer. The young can't distinguish what is allegorical from what isn't, and the opinions they absorb at that age are hard to erase and apt to become unalterable. For these reasons, then, we should probably take the utmost care to insure that the first stories they hear about virtue are the best ones for them to hear.

That's reasonable. But if someone asked us what stories these are, what should we say?

You and I, Adeimantos, aren't poets, but we *are* founding a city. And it's appropri-
379A ate for the founders to know the patterns on which poets must base their stories and from which they mustn't deviate. But we aren't actually going to compose their poems for them.

All right. But what precisely are the patterns for theology or stories about the gods?

Something like this: Whether in epic, lyric, or tragedy, a god must always be represented as he is.

Indeed, he must.

Now, a god is really good, isn't he, and must be described as such?

What else?

[1] See Hesiod, *Theogony* 137–187, 458–508.

And surely nothing good is harmful, is it?

I suppose not.

And can what isn't harmful do harm?

Never.

Or can what does no harm do anything bad?

No.

And can what does nothing bad be the cause of anything bad?

How could it?

Moreover, the good is beneficial?

Yes.

It is the cause of doing well?

Yes.

The good isn't the cause of all things, then, but only of good ones; it isn't the cause of bad ones.

I agree entirely.

Therefore, since a god is good, he is not—as most people claim—the cause of everything that happens to human beings but of only a few things, for good things are fewer than bad ones in our lives. He alone is responsible for the good things, but we must find some other cause for the bad ones, not a god.

That's very true, and I believe it.

Then we won't accept from anyone the foolish mistake Homer makes about the gods when he says:

> There are two urns at the threshold of Zeus,
> One filled with good fates, the other with bad ones. . . .[2]

and the person to whom he gives a mixture of these

> Sometimes meets with a bad fate, sometimes with good,[3]

but the one who receives his fate entirely from the second urn,

> Evil famine drives him over the divine earth.[4]

We won't grant either that Zeus is for us

> The distributor of both good and bad.[5]

And as to the breaking of the promised truce by Pandarus,[6] if anyone tells us that it was brought about by Athena and Zeus or that Themis and Zeus were responsible

[2] *Iliad* 24.527–24.528.

[3] *Iliad* 24.530.

[4] *Iliad* 24.532.

[5] This quotation comes from an unknown source.

[6] *Iliad* 4.

for strife and contention among the gods, we will not praise him. Nor will we allow
380A the young to hear the words of Aeschylus:

> A god makes mortals guilty
> Men he wants utterly to destroy a house.[7]

And if anyone composes a poem about the sufferings of Niobe, such as the one in which these lines occur, or about the house of Pelops, or the tale of Troy, or anything else of that kind, we must require him to say that these things are not the work of a god. Or, if they are, then poets must look for the kind of account of them that we are now seeking, and say that the actions of the gods are good and just, and that those they punish are benefited thereby. We won't allow poets to say that the punished are made wretched and that it was a god who made them so. But we will allow them to say that bad people are wretched because they are in need of punishment and that, in paying the penalty, they are benefited by the gods. And, as for saying that a god, who is himself good, is the cause of bad things, we'll fight that in every way, and we won't allow anyone to say it in his own city, if it's to be well governed, or anyone to hear it either—whether young or old, whether in verse or prose. These stories are not pious, not advantageous to us, and not consistent with one another.

10.614a–10.621d The Myth of Er

At the end of the Republic, *Plato rounds off his discussion of justice by having Socrates narrate the famous myth (as Socrates calls it) of Er. Er was a man who, after having been wounded in war and thought dead, traveled into the beyond only to return to tell what he had seen of the afterlife. It is uncertain whether Plato invented this myth entirely or adapted it to fit his own purpose. What is certain is that the myth is forcefully employed to drive home the importance of justice on earth since punishments and rewards in the afterlife are meted out based upon the extent to which one has lived a life of wickedness or justice. The philosophical conception of the afterlife was influential for later authors, not least of whom was Vergil (*Aeneid *6).*

SOCRATES: Then these {good reputation, chance to rule in their cities, etc.} are the prizes, wages, and gifts that a just person receives from gods and humans while he
614A is alive and that are added to the good things that justice itself provides.

GLAUCON: Yes, and they're very fine and secure ones too.

Yet they're nothing in either number or size compared to those that await just and unjust people after death. And these things must also be heard, if both are to receive in full what they are owed by the argument.

Then tell us about them, for there aren't many things that would be more pleasant to hear.

It isn't, however, a tale of Alcinoos that I'll tell you but that of a brave Pamphylian man called Er, the son of Armenios, who once died in a war. When the rest of the

[7] It is uncertain from which play of Aeschylus this quotation comes.

dead were picked up ten days later, they were already putrefying, but when he was picked up, his corpse was still quite fresh. He was taken home, and preparations were made for his funeral. But on the twelfth day, when he was already laid on the funeral pyre, he revived and, having done so, told what he had seen in the world beyond. He said that, after his soul had left him, it traveled together with many others until they came to a marvelous place, where there were two adjacent openings in the earth, and opposite and above them two others in the heavens, and between them judges sat. These, having rendered their judgment, ordered the just to go upward into the heavens through the door on the right, with signs of the judgment attached to their chests, and the unjust to travel downward through the opening on the left, with signs of all their deeds on their backs. When Er himself came forward, they told him that he was to be a messenger to human beings about the things that were there, and that he was to listen to and look at everything in the place. He said that he saw souls departing after judgment through one of the openings in the heavens and one in the earth, while through the other two souls were arriving. From the door in the earth souls came up covered with dust and dirt and from the door in the heavens souls came down pure. And the souls who were arriving all the time seemed to have been on long journeys, so that they went gladly to the meadow, like a crowd going to a festival, and camped there. Those who knew each other exchanged greetings, and those who came up from the earth asked those who came down from the heavens about the things there and were in turn questioned by them about the things below. And so they told their stories to one another, the former weeping as they recalled all they had suffered and seen on their journey below the earth, which lasted a thousand years, 615A
while the latter, who had come from heaven, told about how well they had fared and about the inconceivably fine and beautiful sights they had seen. There was much to tell, Glaucon, and it took a long time, but the main point was this: For each in turn of the unjust things they had done and for each in turn of the people they had wronged, they paid the penalty ten times over, once in every century of their journey. Since a century is roughly the length of a human life, this means that they paid a tenfold penalty for each injustice. If, for example, some of them had caused many deaths by betraying cities or armies and reducing them to slavery or by participating in other wrongdoing, they had to suffer ten times the pain they had caused to each individual. But if they had done good deeds and had become just and pious, they were rewarded according to the same scale. He said some other things about the stillborn and those who had lived for only a short time, but they're not worth recounting. And he also spoke of even greater rewards or penalties for piety or impiety toward gods or parents and for murder with one's own hands.

For example, he said he was there when someone asked another where the great Ardiaios was. (This Ardiaios was said to have been tyrant in some city in Pamphylia a thousand years before and to have killed his aged father and older brother and committed many other impious deeds as well.) And he said that the one who was asked responded: "He hasn't arrived here yet and never will, for this too was one of the terrible sights we saw. When we came near the opening on our way out, after all our sufferings were over, we suddenly saw him together with some others, pretty well all of whom were tyrants (although there were also some private individuals among them who had committed great crimes). They thought that they were ready to go up, but

the opening wouldn't let them through, for it roared whenever one of these incurably wicked people or anyone else who hadn't paid a sufficient penalty tried to go up. And there were savage men, all fiery to look at, who were standing by, and when they heard the roar, they grabbed some of these criminals and led them away, but they
616A bound the feet, hands, and head of Ardiaios and the others, threw them down, and flayed them. Then they dragged them out of the way, lacerating them on thorn bushes, and telling every passerby that they were to be thrown into Tartaros, and explaining why they were being treated in this way." And he said that of their many fears the greatest each one of them had was that the roar would be heard as he came up and that everyone was immensely relieved when silence greeted him. Such, then, were the penalties and punishments and the rewards corresponding to them.

Each group spent seven days in the meadow, and on the eighth they had to get up and go on a journey. On the fourth day of that journey, they came to a place where they could look down from above on a straight column of light that stretched over the whole of heaven and earth, more like a rainbow than anything else, but brighter and more pure. After another day, they came to the light itself, and there, in the middle of the light, they saw the extremities of its bonds stretching from the heavens, for the light binds the heavens like the cables girding a trireme and holds its entire revolution together. From the extremities hangs the spindle of Necessity, by means of which all the revolutions are turned. Its stem and hook are of adamant, whereas in its whorl[8] adamant is mixed with other kinds of material. The nature of the whorl was this: Its shape was like that of an ordinary whorl, but, from what Er said, we must understand its structure as follows. It was as if one big whorl had been made hollow by being thoroughly scooped out, with another smaller whorl closely fitted into it, like nested boxes, and there was a third whorl inside the second, and so on, making eight whorls altogether, lying inside one another, with their rims appearing as circles from above, while from the back they formed one continuous whorl around the spindle, which was driven through the center of the eighth. The first or outside whorl had the widest circular rim; that of the sixth was second in width; the fourth was third; the eighth was fourth; the seventh was fifth; the fifth was sixth; the third was seventh; and the second was eighth. The rim of the largest was spangled; that of
617A the seventh was brightest; that of the eighth took its color from the seventh's shining on it; the second and fifth were about equal in brightness, more yellow than the others; the third was the whitest in color; the fourth was rather red; and the sixth was second in whiteness. The whole spindle turned at the same speed, but, as it turned, the inner spheres gently revolved in a direction opposite to that of the whole. Of these inner spheres, the eighth was the fastest; second came the seventh, sixth, and fifth, all at the same speed; it seemed to them that the fourth was third in its speed of revolution; the fourth, third; and the second, fifth. The spindle itself turned on the lap of Necessity. And up above on each of the rims of the circles stood a Siren, who accompanied its revolution, uttering a single sound, one single note. And the concord of the eight notes produced a single harmony. And there were three other beings sitting at equal distances from one another, each on a throne. These were the Moirai,

[8] A whorl is the weight that twirls a spindle.

the daughters of Necessity: Lachesis, Clotho, and Atropos. They were dressed in white, with garlands on their heads, and they sang to the music of the Sirens. Lachesis sang of the past, Clotho of the present, and Atropos of the future. With her right hand, Clotho touched the outer circumference of the spindle and helped it turn, but left off doing so from time to time; Atropos did the same to the inner ones; and Lachesis helped both motions in turn, one with one hand and one with the other.

When the souls arrived at the light, they had to go to Lachesis right away. There a Speaker arranged them in order, took from the lap of Lachesis a number of lots and a number of models of lives, mounted a high pulpit, and spoke to them: "Here is the message of Lachesis, the maiden daughter of Necessity: 'Ephemeral souls, this is the beginning of another cycle that will end in death. Your *daimon* or guardian spirit will not be assigned to you by lot; you will choose him. The one who has the first lot will be the first to choose a life to which he will then be bound by necessity. Virtue knows no master; each will possess it to a greater or less degree, depending on whether he values or disdains it. The responsibility lies with the one who makes the choice; the god has none.'" When he had said this, the Speaker threw the lots among all of them, and each—with the exception of Er, who wasn't allowed to choose—picked up the one that fell next to him. And the lot made it clear to the one who picked it up where in the order he would get to make his choice. After that, the models of lives were placed on the ground before them. There were far more of them than 618A
there were souls present, and they were of all kinds, for the lives of animals were there, as well as all kinds of human lives. There were tyrannies among them, some of which lasted throughout life, while others ended halfway through in poverty, exile, and beggary. There were lives of famous men, some of whom were famous for the beauty of their appearance, others for their strength or athletic prowess, others still for their high birth and the virtue or excellence of their ancestors. And there were also lives of men who weren't famous for any of these things. And the same for lives of women. But the arrangement of the soul was not included in the model because the soul is inevitably altered by the different lives it chooses. But all the other things were there, mixed with each other and with wealth, poverty, sickness, health, and the states intermediate to them.

Now, it seems that it is here, Glaucon, that a human being faces the greatest danger of all. And because of this, each of us must neglect all other subjects and be most concerned to seek out and learn those that will enable him to distinguish the good life from the bad and always to make the best choice possible in every situation. He should think over all the things we have mentioned and how they jointly and severally determine what the virtuous life is like. That way he will know what the good and bad effects of beauty are when it is mixed with wealth, poverty, and a particular state of the soul. He will know the effects of high or low birth, private life or ruling office, physical strength or weakness, ease or difficulty in learning, and all the things that are either naturally part of the soul or are acquired, and he will know what they achieve when mixed with one another. And from all this he will be able, by considering the nature of the soul, to reason out which life is better and which worse and to choose accordingly, calling a life worse if it leads the soul to become more unjust, better if it leads the soul to become more just, and ignoring everything else: We have seen that this is the best way to choose, whether in life or death. Hence, we

must go down to Hades holding with adamantine determination to the belief that
619A this is so, lest we be dazzled there by wealth and other such evils, rush into a tyranny or some other similar course of action, do irreparable evils, and suffer even worse ones. And we must always know how to choose the mean in such lives and how to avoid either of the extremes, as far as possible, both in this life and in all those beyond it. This is the way that a human being becomes happiest.

Then our messenger from the other world reported that the Speaker spoke as follows: "There is a satisfactory life rather than a bad one available even for the one who comes last, provided that he chooses it rationally and lives it seriously. Therefore, let not the first be careless in his choice nor the last discouraged."

He said that when the Speaker had told them this, the one who came up first chose the greatest tyranny. In his folly and greed he chose it without adequate examination and didn't notice that, among other evils, he was fated to eat his own children as a part of it. When he examined at leisure the life he had chosen, however, he beat his breast and bemoaned his choice. And, ignoring the warning of the Speaker, he blamed chance, *daimons,* or guardian spirits, and everything else for these evils but himself. He was one of those who had come down from heaven, having lived his previous life under an orderly constitution, where he had participated in virtue through habit and without philosophy. Broadly speaking, indeed, most of those who were caught out in this way were souls who had come down from heaven and who were untrained in suffering as a result. The majority of those who had come up from the earth, on the other hand, having suffered themselves and seen others suffer, were in no rush to make their choices. Because of this and because of the chance of the lottery, there was an interchange of goods and evils for most of the souls. However, if someone pursues philosophy in a sound manner when he comes to live here on earth and if the lottery doesn't make him one of the last to choose, then, given what Er has reported about the next world, it looks as though not only will he be happy here, but his journey from here to there and back again won't be along the rough underground path, but along the smooth heavenly one.

Er said that the way in which the souls chose their lives was a sight worth seeing,
620A since it was pitiful, funny, and surprising to watch. For the most part, their choice depended upon the character of their former life. For example, he said that he saw the soul that had once belonged to Orpheus choosing a swan's life, because he hated the female sex because of his death at their hands, and so was unwilling to have a woman conceive and give birth to him. Er saw the soul of Thamyris[9] choosing the life of a nightingale, a swan choosing to change over to a human life, and other musical animals doing the same thing. The twentieth soul chose the life of a lion. This was the soul of Ajax son of Telamon. He avoided human life because he remembered the judgment about the armor. The next soul was that of Agamemnon, whose sufferings also had made him hate the human race, so he changed to the life of an eagle. Atalante had been assigned a place near the middle, and when she saw great honors being given to a male athlete, she chose his life, unable to pass them by. After her, he saw the soul of Epeios,[10] the son of Panopeus, taking on the nature of a

[9] See Apollodorus B3.

[10] Epeios is mentioned at *Odyssey* 8.493 as the man who helped Athena make the Trojan Horse.

craftswoman. And very close to last, he saw the soul of the ridiculous Thersites clothing itself as a monkey.[11] Now, it chanced that the soul of Odysseus got to make its choice last of all, and since memory of its former sufferings had relieved its love of honor, it went around for a long time, looking for the life of a private individual who did his own work, and with difficulty it found one lying off somewhere neglected by the others. He chose it gladly and said that he'd have made the same choice even if he'd been first. Still other souls changed from animals into human beings, or from one kind of animal into another, with unjust people changing into wild animals, and just people into tame ones, and all sorts of mixtures occurred.

After all the souls had chosen their lives, they went forward to Lachesis in the same order in which they had made their choices, and she assigned to each the *daimon* it had chosen as guardian of its life and fulfiller of its choice. This *daimon* first led the soul under the hand of Clotho as it turned the revolving spindle to confirm the fate that the lottery and its own choice had given it. After receiving her touch, he led the soul to the spinning of Atropos, to make what had been spun irreversible. Then, without turning around, they went from there under the throne of Necessity and, when all of them had passed through, they traveled to the Plain of Forgetfulness in burning, choking, terrible heat, for it was empty of trees and earthly vegetation. And 621A
there, beside the River of Unheeding, whose water no vessel can hold, they camped, for night was coming on. All of them had to drink a certain measure of this water, but those who weren't saved by reason drank more than that, and as each of them drank, he forgot everything and went to sleep. But around midnight there was a clap of thunder and an earthquake, and they were suddenly carried away from there, this way and that, up to their births, like shooting stars. Er himself was forbidden to drink from the water. All the same, he didn't know how he had come back to his body, except that waking up suddenly he saw himself lying on the pyre at dawn.

And so, Glaucon, his story wasn't lost but preserved, and it would save us, if we were persuaded by it, for we would then make a good crossing of the River of Forgetfulness, and our souls wouldn't be defiled. But if we are persuaded by me, we'll believe that the soul is immortal and able to endure every evil and every good, and we'll always hold to the upward path, practicing justice with reason in every way. That way we'll be friends both to ourselves and to the gods while we remain here on earth and afterward—like victors in the games who go around collecting their prizes—we'll receive our rewards. Hence, both in this life and on the thousand-year journey we've described, we'll do well and be happy.

[11] Thersites is a soldier who criticizes Agamemnon at *Iliad* 2.211–2.277. Odysseus beats him for his presumption and is widely approved for doing so.

FROM *SYMPOSIUM*

189d–193b A Myth About the Origin of the Sexes

In this dialogue Plato describes the probably fictitious symposium ("drinking party") attended by some of the leading intellectuals in Athens, including Socrates, the tragedian Agathon, and the writer of comedies Aristophanes. The topic of discussion is the nature of Eros, and each of the participants takes turns stating their views on love. The excerpt below is from the speech Plato puts in the mouth of Aristophanes. As befits his profession, he narrates a rather humorous story in mythic form that relates the original creation of the sexes and the development of both hetero- and homosexual love.

First, you must learn what Human Nature was in the beginning and what has happened to it since, because long ago our nature was not what it is now, but very different. There were three kinds of human beings, that's my first point—not two as there are now, male and female. In addition to these, there was a third, a combination of those two; its name survives, though the kind itself has vanished. At that time, you see, the word "androgynous" really meant something: a form made up of male and female elements, though now there's nothing but the word, and that's used as an insult. My second point is that the shape of each human being was completely round,
190A with back and sides in a circle; they had four hands each, as many legs as hands, and two faces, exactly alike, on a rounded neck. Between the two faces, which were on opposite sides, was one head with four ears. There were two sets of sexual organs, and everything else was the way you'd imagine it from what I've told you. They walked upright, as we do now, whatever direction they wanted. And whenever they set out to run fast they thrust out all their eight limbs, the ones they had then, and spun rapidly, the way gymnasts do cartwheels, by bringing their legs around straight.

Now, here is why there were three kinds, and why they were as I described them: The male kind was originally an offspring of the sun, the female of the earth, and the one that combined both genders was an offspring of the moon, because the moon shares in both. They were spherical, and so was their motion, because they were like their parents in the sky.

In strength and power, therefore, they were terrible, and they had great ambitions. They made an attempt on the gods, and Homer's story about Ephialtes and Otos was originally about them: how they tried to make an ascent to heaven so as to attack the gods.[12] Then Zeus and the other gods met in council to discuss what to do, and they were sore perplexed. They couldn't wipe out the human race with thunderbolts and kill them all off, as they had the giants, because that would wipe out the worship they receive, along with the sacrifices we humans give them. On the other hand, they couldn't let them run riot. At last after great effort, Zeus had an idea.

"I think I have a plan," he said, "that would allow human beings to exist and stop their misbehaving: they will give up being wicked when they lose their strength. So I shall now cut each of them in two. At one stroke they will lose their strength and also

[12] *Iliad* 5.385 ff.; *Odyssey* 112.308 ff.

become more profitable to us, owing to the increase in their number. They shall walk upright on two legs. But if I find they still run riot and do not keep the peace," he said, "I will cut them in two again, and they'll have to make their way on one leg, hopping."

So saying, he cut those human beings in two, the way people cut sorb-apples before they dry them or the way they cut eggs with hairs. As he cut each one, he commanded Apollo to turn its face and half its neck toward the wound, so that each person would see that he'd been cut and keep better order. Then Zeus commanded Apollo to heal the rest of the wound, and Apollo did turn the face around, and he drew skin from all sides over what is now called the stomach, and there he made one mouth, as in a pouch with a drawstring, and fastened it at the center of the stomach.
This is now called the navel. Then he smoothed out the other wrinkles, of which 191A
there were many, and he shaped the breasts, using some such tool as shoemakers have for smoothing wrinkles out of leather on the form. But he left a few wrinkles around the stomach and the navel, to be a reminder of what happened long ago.

Now, since their natural form had been cut in two, each one longed for its own other half, and so they would throw their arms about each other, weaving themselves together, wanting to grow together. In that condition they would die from hunger and general idleness, because they would not do anything apart from each other. Whenever one of the halves died and one was left, the one that was left still sought another and wove itself together with that. Sometimes the half he met came from a woman, as we'd call her now, sometimes it came from a man; either way, they kept on dying.

Then, however, Zeus took pity on them, and came up with another plan: he moved their genitals around to the front! Before then, you see, they used to have their genitals outside, like their faces, and they cast seed and made children, not in one another, but in the ground, like cicadas. So Zeus brought about this relocation of genitals, and in doing so he invented interior reproduction, by the man in the woman. The purpose of this was so that, when a man embraced a woman, he would cast his seed and they would have children; but when male embraced male, they would at least have the satisfaction of intercourse, after which they could stop embracing, return to their jobs, and look after their other needs in life. This, then, is the source of our desire to love each other. Love is born into every human being; it calls back the halves of our original nature together; it tries to make one out of two and heal the wound of human nature.

Each of us, then, is a "matching half" of a human whole, because each was sliced like a flatfish, two out of one, and each of us is always seeking the half that matches him. That's why a man who is split from the double sort (which used to be called "androgynous") runs after women. Many lecherous men have come from this class, and so do the lecherous women who run after men. Women who are split from a woman, however, pay no attention at all to men; they are oriented more toward women, and lesbians come from this class. People who are split from a male are male-oriented. While they are boys, because they are chips off the male block, they love
men and enjoy lying with men and being embraced by men; those are the best of 192A
boys and lads, because they are the most manly in their nature. Of course, some say such boys are shameless, but they're lying. It's not because they have no shame that such boys do this, you see, but because they are bold and brave and masculine, and

they tend to cherish what is like themselves. Do you want me to prove it? Look, these are the only kind of boys who grow up to be politicians. When they're grown men, they are lovers of young men, and they naturally pay no attention to marriage or to making babies, except insofar as they are required by local custom. They, however, are quite satisfied to live their lives with one another unmarried. In every way, then, this sort of man grows up as a lover of young men and a lover of Love, always rejoicing in his own kind.

And so, when a person meets the half that is his very own, whatever his orientation, whether it's to young men or not, then something wonderful happens: the two are struck from their senses by love, by a sense of belonging to one another, and by desire, and they don't want to be separated from one another, not even for a moment.

These are the people who finish out their lives together and still cannot say what it is they want from one another. No one would think it is the intimacy of sex—that mere sex is the reason each lover takes so great and deep a joy in being with the other. It's obvious that the soul of every lover longs for something else; his soul cannot say what it is, but like an oracle it has a sense of what it wants, and like an oracle it hides behind a riddle. Suppose two lovers are lying together and Hephaistos stands over them with his mending tools, asking, "What is it you human beings really want from each other?" And suppose they're perplexed, and he asks them again: "Is this your heart's desire, then—for the two of you to become parts of the same whole, as near as can be, and never to separate, day or night? Because if that's your desire, I'd like to weld you together and join you into something that is naturally whole, so that the two of you are made into one. Then the two of you would share one life, as long as you lived, because you would be one being, and by the same token, when you died, you would be one and not two in Hades, having died a single death. Look at your love, and see if this is what you desire: Wouldn't this be all the good fortune you could want?"

Surely you can see that no one who received such an offer would turn it down; no one would find anything else that he wanted. Instead, everyone would think he'd found out at last what he had always wanted: to come together and melt together with the one he loves, so that one person emerged from two. Why should this be so? It's because, as I said, we used to be complete wholes in our original nature, and now
193A "Love" is the name for our pursuit of wholeness, for our desire to be complete.

Long ago we were united, as I said; but now the god has divided us as punishment for the wrong we did him, just as the Spartans divided the Arcadians. So there's a danger that if we don't keep order before the gods, we'll be split in two again, and then we'll be walking around in the condition of people carved on gravestones in bas-relief, sawn apart between the nostrils, like half dice. We should encourage all men, therefore, to treat the gods with all due reverence, so that we may escape this fate and find wholeness instead. And we will, if Love is our guide and our commander. Let no one work against him. Whoever opposes Love is hateful to the gods, but if we become friends of the god and cease to quarrel with him, then we shall find the young men that are meant for us and win their love, as very few men do nowadays.

Plutarch

(ca. 50–ca. 120 AD, wrote in Greek)

Plutarch was a remarkably prolific author, writing in many prose genres, from popular philosophy to historical and literary criticism. His most famous works are the Parallel Lives, *pairs of biographies matching a famous Greek with a Roman counterpart. The* Life of Theseus *is particularly interesting because of the way the figure of Theseus is treated as both a subject of myth and a definite historical figure; in the* Lives *Theseus is the Greek counterpart to Romulus, the legendary founder of Rome, who is likewise for Plutarch a real figure whose historicity has been somewhat obscured by myths. Plutarch at the beginning of his* Life of Theseus *recognizes the difficulty in dealing with such figures, but expresses the hope "that I can purify the mythical and make it submit to reason and take on the appearance of history." In the following excerpt Theseus is credited with an historical event, the* synoikismos, *or "unification" of the independent cities in Attica into a single city-state, Athens.*

FROM *LIFE OF THESEUS*

24.1–25.2 The Synoikismos {"Unification"} of Attica

[24] After Aigeus' death Theseus came up with a grand and marvelous project. He brought the inhabitants of Attica into one city, making them a single people {*demos*} of a single city-state, whereas they had up until then been scattered and difficult to assemble for the common benefit of all; there were even times when they disputed and fought wars with each other. So Theseus went around and tried to convince them one village and clan at a time. The average people and the poor quickly accepted his appeal, but to the powerful he offered a form of government without a king, a democracy in which his only role was to be a leader in war and guardian of the laws, and a government that in all other matters would afford everyone an equal share. Some he persuaded of these matters; the rest, afraid of his power (which was already considerable) and his boldness, preferred to be persuaded rather than to be forced to concede to them. He got rid of the local town halls, council-chambers, and political offices and built for everyone a single shared town hall and council-chamber where the modern city is located. He called the city-state Athens and instituted the communal festival of the Panathenaia. On the sixteenth day of the month of Hecatombaion he also celebrated the Metoicia {"Festival of Living Together"}, which they celebrate even today. He gave up royal power, as he had promised, and organized the government by following the lead of the gods. For when he consulted the oracle about the city, a reply came from Delphi:

Theseus son of Aigeus, offspring of Pittheus' daughter,
For many cities my father has placed
the limits and fates in your city.
Do not pain overmuch your heart within—
just advise. For the wineskin will traverse the sea amidst the swells.[1]

They give the account that later the Sibyl also recited this to the city, with the cry:

Let the wineskin be dunked; it is not ordained that it sink!

[25] Since he wanted to enlarge the city even more, he invited everyone to come and enjoy equal rights. They say that the proclamation "All you people, come hither!" was what Theseus said because he had established a sort of all-inclusive body politic. However, he did not allow the democracy to become unruly or mixed with a confused mass of people flooding in. He was the first to divide the populace into separate categories of nobles, landowners, and craftsmen. He gave to the nobles the right to be the experts in religion, to provide the office-holders, to be teachers of the law, and to interpret sacred and holy matters. For the other citizens he set up a sort of balance: the nobles were thought to excel in honor, the landowners in usefulness, and the craftsmen in number. Homer also seems to be a witness that Theseus was the first to favor the masses (as Aristotle says) and give up the right to rule as a monarch; in his "Catalogue of Ships" he calls the Athenians alone a "people" {*demos*}.

[1] The oracles compare the fortunes of the city of Athens with an inflated wineskin, which, like a balloon, will always rise to the surface.

Proclus

(410–485 AD, wrote in Greek)

The epic cycle was a series of independent poems written by various authors of the 7th and 6th centuries BC. The poems of the cycle covered many of the major myths of the Greeks, including such events as the birth of the gods and the Titanomachy, as well as the stories of the heroes. While neither as early nor as authoritative as the Iliad *or* Odyssey, *themselves part of the epic cycle, some of these poems were nevertheless well known in antiquity and provided a great deal of material for later writers. Unfortunately, save for the* Iliad *and* Odyssey, *all of these early epics have now been lost, but we do have summaries of the contents of several of them made by Proclus, a philosopher from late antiquity, who wrote the* Chrestomathy, *a literary handbook. These summaries involve those epics that describe the events before, during, and after the Trojan War.*

FROM *CHRESTOMATHY*

A The *Cypria*

Next[1] is the poem called the *Cypria,* which is circulated in eleven books. It encompasses the following events:

Zeus makes plans with Themis for the Trojan War. Eris arrives while the gods are feasting at the wedding of Peleus and instigates a quarrel between Athena, Hera, and Aphrodite over beauty. At Zeus' command they are taken by Hermes to Alexander on Mount Ida to be judged by him. Alexander chooses Aphrodite, his vote secured by marriage to Helen. Then at Aphrodite's suggestion he has ships built. Helenos foretells the future to him. Aphrodite commands Aineias to sail with him. Cassandra makes clear what the future will bring. Alexander goes to Lacedaimonia and is received as a guest by the sons of Tyndareos. After that he goes to Sparta and is a guest in the palace of Menelaos. Alexander gives Helen gifts while they feast. After this Menelaos sails away to Crete, bidding Helen to provide their guests with whatever they might require until their departure. During this time Aphrodite leads Helen to Alexander, and after they have intercourse, they load up as much wealth as they can and sail off during the night. Hera sends a storm against them. Sailing to Sidon, Alexander captures the city. Sailing off to Ilion, he celebrates his marriage to Helen.

[1] After an earlier poem in the cycle that has been lost.

In the meantime, Castor and Polydeuces are caught while trying to steal the cattle of Idas and Lynceus. Castor is killed by Idas, and Lynceus and Idas are killed by Polydeuces. Zeus grants them immortality on alternate days.

After this Iris tells Menelaos what has happened in his house. He goes back and makes plans for an expedition to Ilion with his brother. Menelaos goes to Nestor. In a digression Nestor tells the story of how Epopeus seduced the daughter of Lycos and was undone. He also tells him the tale of Oidipous and of the madness of Heracles, and the story of Theseus and Ariadne. Then they travel throughout Greece and gather the leaders. They catch Odysseus when he pretends to be crazy because he does not want to campaign with them. At Palamedes' suggestion they snatch his son Telemachos to punish him.

After this they come together at Aulis and make a sacrifice. They see what happens with the serpent and the sparrows,[2] and Calchas foretells to them what the results will be. Then they set sail, land at Teuthrania, and sack it in the belief that it is Ilion. Telephos marches out in defense of the city, kills Thersandros son of Polyneices, and is himself wounded by Achilles. As they sail away from Mysia, a storm falls upon them and scatters them. Achilles lands on Scyros and marries Deidameia, the daughter of Lycomedes. Then, following a prophecy, Achilles heals Telephos when he comes to Argos so that he will be their guide on the voyage to Ilion.

When the fleet had assembled for the second time at Aulis, Agamemnon said that he was greater even than Artemis after he shot a deer while hunting. The goddess grew wrathful and prevented them from sailing by sending storms against them. When Calchas told them of the goddess' wrath and ordered them to sacrifice Iphigeneia to Artemis, they sent for her on the pretext that she was to marry Achilles and tried to sacrifice her. But Artemis snatched her away, transported her to the land of the Taurians, and made her immortal. She substituted a deer for the girl on the altar.

Then they sail to Tenedos. While they were feasting, Philoctetes was bitten by a water snake. He got left behind on Lemnos because of the foul odor.[3] Achilles quarrels with Agamemnon because he is summoned late. Then when they try to go ashore, the Trojans stop them, and Protesilaos is killed by Hector. Then Achilles kills Cycnos son of Poseidon and routs the Trojans. They recover their dead and send an embassy to the Trojans to demand Helen and the wealth back. The Trojans refuse to comply, and at that point the Greeks besiege them. Then they go out and plunder the land and the neighboring cities. After this Achilles wants to see Helen, and Aphrodite and Thetis bring the two face to face. Then Achilles restrains the Achaians when they are eager to return home. Then he drives off the cattle of Aineias, sacks Lyrnessos, Pedasos, and many neighboring cities, and kills Troilos. Patroclos takes Lycaon to Lemnos and sells him. From the spoils Achilles gets Briseis as his prize and Agamemnon gets Chryseis. Next are Palamedes' death, Zeus' plan to relieve the Trojans by removing Achilles from the Greek alliance, and the catalog of those who will become allies of the Trojans.

[2] A mother sparrow and her eight fledglings were eaten by the serpent, an omen that the Greeks would fight at Troy for nine years before capturing it in the tenth (*Iliad* 2.301–2.329).

[3] His wound putrefied and gave off a foul stench.

B The *Aithiopis*

The *Iliad* of Homer follows the *Cypria*, which I described in the last book. After the *Iliad* come the five books of the *Aithiopis* of Arctinos of Miletos. They encompass the following events:

The Amazon Penthesileia arrives to help the Trojans. She is the Thracian daughter of Ares. While she is displaying her prowess, Achilles kills her. The Trojans bury her. Achilles kills Thersites because he insulted him and attributed to him a supposed love for Penthesileia. Consequently, conflict arises among the Greeks over the murder of Thersites. Afterward, Achilles sails to Lesbos and, after sacrificing to Apollo, Artemis, and Leto, is purified of the murder by Odysseus.

Memnon, the son of Eos, arrives with armor made by Hephaistos to aid the Trojans. Thetis foretells to her son what will happen to Memnon. When there is an engagement, Antilochos is killed by Memnon, then Achilles kills Memnon. Eos asks Zeus for permission, then gives her son immortality. Achilles routs the Trojans and is killed by Paris and Apollo when he is rushing into the city. A fierce battle ensues over his corpse. Ajax recovers it and brings it to the ships while Odysseus fights off the Trojans. Then they bury Antilochos and lay out Achilles' body. Thetis, who comes with the Muses and her sisters, laments for her son. After this Thetis snatches her son out of the funeral pyre and carries him across to the White Island.[4] The Achaians heap up a tomb and hold games. A conflict breaks out between Odysseus and Ajax over the arms of Achilles.

C The *Little Iliad (Ilias Mikra)*

Next are the four books of the *Little Iliad* of Lesches of Mytilene. They encompass the following events:

The judgment over the arms happens, and Odysseus gets them in accordance with the will of Athena. Ajax becomes crazed and commits outrages against the Achaians' herd of captured livestock. He kills himself. After this Odysseus sets an ambush and captures Helenos. After Helenos gives a prophecy about the capture of Troy,[5] Diomedes brings Philoctetes over from Lemnos. Philoctetes is healed by Machaon and kills Alexander in single combat. After the corpse is disfigured by Menelaos, the Trojans recover and bury it. After this Deiphobos marries Helen, and Odysseus brings Neoptolemos from Scyros and gives him the arms of his father. Achilles' spirit appears to him.

Eurypylos son of Telephos comes as an ally of the Trojans. While he is displaying his prowess, Neoptolemos kills him, and the Trojans are besieged. Epeios follows Athena's plan and builds the wooden horse. Odysseus disfigures himself and goes into Ilion as a spy. He is recognized by Helen, and they plan the capture of the city. He kills some Trojans and returns to the ships. After this, he along with Diomedes

[4] A legendary place (though sometimes thought of as being in the Black Sea) where some heroes lived in eternal bliss.

[5] The prophecy was that Troy would fall if the Greeks fetched Heracles' bow (and perhaps its current owner Philoctetes), brought Achilles' son Neoptolemos to Troy, and could remove the Palladion from Troy.

brings the Palladion out of Ilion. Then the Greeks load their best men into the wooden horse. The rest burn their tents down and sail to Tenedos. The Trojans, assuming that they are rid of their troubles, bring the wooden horse into the city by taking down part of the wall. They feast in the belief that they are victorious over the Greeks.

D The *Sack of Ilion (Iliou Persis)*

Following the *Little Iliad* are the two books of the *Sack of Ilion* by Arctinos of Miletos. They encompass the following events:

Since the Trojans are suspicious concerning the matter of the horse, they stand around it and discuss what they should do. Some think it best to throw it off a cliff; some think it best to destroy it by fire. Others say that it should be dedicated to Athena as an offering. Finally, the opinion of this last group wins out. Turning to celebration, they hold a feast, thinking that they have been delivered from the war. At that very moment two snakes appear and destroy Laocoon and one of his sons. Aineias and his followers are distressed at the portent and escape to Mount Ida. Sinon, having earlier gotten in under false pretenses, raises the signal-torches to the Achaians. Having sailed in from Tenedos, they and the men from the wooden horse fall upon the enemy and, killing many, take the city by force. Neoptolemos kills Priam, who had fled to the altar of Zeus Herceios. Menelaos discovers Helen and takes her off to his ships after killing Deiphobos. Ajax son of Ileus, while violently dragging off Cassandra, also pulls along the wooden statue of Athena. The Greeks grow angry at this and plan to stone Ajax, but he escapes to the altar of Athena and is saved from the impending danger. Then, after burning the city, they sacrifice Polyxena at the grave of Achilles. Neoptolemos takes Andromache as a prize after Odysseus kills Astyanax, and the rest of the spoils are divided up. Demophon and Acamas discover Aithra and take her with them, then the Greeks sail off, and Athena devises their destruction at sea.

E The *Returns (Nostoi)*

Following closely upon the *Sack of Ilion* are the five books of the *Returns* by Agias of Troizen. They encompass the following events:

Athena makes Agamemnon and Menelaos quarrel about the ships' departure. So Agamemnon remains to appease the anger of Athena, but Diomedes and Nestor set sail and make it home safely. Menelaos sails out after them and arrives in Egypt with five ships (the rest of his ships are destroyed at sea). The parties of Calchas, Leontes, and Polypoites proceed on foot to Colophon and bury Teiresias, who dies there. When Agamemnon's party is setting sail, the ghost of Achilles appears and tries to prevent them from doing so by foretelling what is going to happen. Then the storm around the Capherian rocks is described, as is the death of Locrian Ajax. Neoptolemos makes the journey on foot (because he is warned by Thetis), gets to Thrace, where he catches up to Odysseus at Maroneia, finishes the rest of the trip, and buries Phoinix, who dies. He himself comes to the land of the Molossians and is recognized by Peleus. Then we have the revenge that Orestes and Pylades take for Agamemnon after he is murdered by Aigisthos and Clytaimnestra, as well as Menelaos' return to his home.

F The *Telegony*

After the *Returns* is Homer's *Odyssey*. Then come the two books of the *Telegony* of Eugammon of Cyrene. They encompass the following events:

The suitors are buried by their relatives. Odysseus makes sacrifice to the Nymphs and sails off to Elis to inspect his herds. He is received as a guest in the house of Polyxenos and receives a wine bowl as a gift. After this comes the story of Trophonios, Agamedes, and Augeas. Then Odysseus sails back to Ithaca and performs the sacrifices prescribed by Teiresias. After this he goes to Thesprotis and marries Callidice, the queen of the Thesprotians. Then a war takes place between the Thesprotians (led by Odysseus) and the Brygians. Then Ares routs Odysseus and his men. Athena comes to fight Ares. Apollo reconciles them. After Callidice's death Polypoites, the son of Odysseus, succeeds to the kingdom, while Odysseus himself goes to Ithaca. In the meantime, Telegonos,[6] while sailing in search of his father, comes to Ithaca and lays waste to the island. Odysseus comes out to stop him and is killed by his son out of ignorance. Telegonos realizes his error and transports his father's body, Telemachos, and Penelope to his mother. She makes them immortal. Telegonos marries Penelope, and Telemachos marries Circe.

[6] The son of Odysseus and Circe.

SALLUSTIUS

(4th c. AD, wrote in Greek)

In 361 AD the emperor Julian attempted to reverse the Christianization of the Roman Empire by restoring paganism. One obstacle was the criticism of mythological stories and their contents. These had been attacked by many pagan philosophers through the centuries, and the Christians eagerly adopted those criticisms and added their own. The following excerpt is from a treatise believed to be by one of Julian's supporters, who sets about to defend mythology in an unusual manner.

Sallustius starts his treatise, On the Gods and the Cosmos (Peri theon kai kosmou), *by stating certain philosophical principles held by many pagan intellectuals of the time that are incompatible with the portrait painted by traditional mythology. For instance, he asserts that gods are good and unchangeable (so how could a god change his mind?); that they never come into existence, but always exist (so how could a god be born?); that they do not have bodies (so how could they visit earth?); that they are not limited by space (so how could they be in one place and not another?). Sallustius, like many other pagans in antiquity (see Cornutus, for instance), finds allegorical truth in the myths. But in the following passage, which comes immediately after he outlines these principles, he goes on to argue a deeper question: Why would such truths be encoded in myth when they can be stated so simply and discussed rationally? He argues that myths are in fact an appropriate and excellent way to convey such truths, for they force mortals to seek actively, philosophically, and intellectually for the true meanings. He then goes on to classify different sorts of myths, each of which must be investigated in different ways.*

FROM *ON THE GODS AND THE COSMOS*

3–4 The Purpose and Types of Myth

[3] So then why ever did the ancients neglect these principles and begin to make use of myths? This is worth investigating so as to gain the first benefit that can be derived from myths: the very act of investigation itself and of not leaving the intellect idle. We can say that myths are divine because of who has made use of them: the poets who were divinely inspired, the best of the philosophers, and also those who introduced the mysteries. Even the gods themselves have made use of myths in oracles. It is philosophy's role to investigate why the myths are divine. Now, since everything that exists enjoys similarity and avoids dissimilarity, the stories about the gods must also be similar to the gods so that the stories will be worthy of their true nature and make them favorably disposed to those telling the stories, which can only happen by

means of myths. And myths represent the gods themselves in terms of the speakable and unspeakable, the obscure and the obvious, and the clear and the hidden. The myths also represent the gods' goodness: just as the gods produce the benefits that come from the senses for all men alike but the benefits that come from the mind only for the wise, so myths tell everyone of the gods' existence but tell who they are and what they are like only to those capable of understanding.

Myths also represent the activities of the gods. For one can call the cosmos a myth because bodies and things can be seen in it, but souls and minds are hidden. What is more, the desire to teach everyone the truth about the gods brings about scorn in foolish people (because they cannot learn) and laziness in good people. But concealing the truth through myths prevents the former from feeling scorn and forces the latter to practice philosophy. But why in their myths have they spoken of infidelities, thefts, imprisoning of fathers, and every other absurdity? Is this not, in fact, a marvelously fitting way to make the soul, because of the apparent absurdity, believe that the stories are veils and think that the truth is secret knowledge?

[4] Some of the myths are theological, some are physical, some psychic, some material, and some mixed from these.

Theological myths are those that involve no body but contemplate the very nature of the gods. Take, for instance, Cronos' swallowing of his children. Since god is intellectual and all mind turns to itself, the myth allegorizes the nature of god.

One can look at myths physically when one of them speaks of the gods' activities in regard to the cosmos, just as some have before now thought that Cronos was time {*chronos*} and, calling the divisions of time the children of the whole, said that the children are swallowed by their father.

The psychic way is to look at the activity of the soul itself since the thoughts of our souls, even if they go forth to others, nevertheless remain in the ones who produced them.

The material is the worst way. The Egyptians make most use of it out of ignorance, believing material objects themselves are gods and calling the earth Isis, moisture Osiris, and heat Typhon—or water Cronos, crops Adonis, and wine Dionysos. To say that these things are sacred to gods, like plants, stones, and animals are, is something sensible men can do. But to call them gods is the mark of madmen, unless, that is, it is part of everyday speech, like calling the sun's {*helios*} sphere and the light from the sphere "Helios."

One can see the mixed form of myths in many different cases. For example, in the symposium of the gods, they say, Eris tossed a golden apple, and the goddesses who quarreled over it were sent by Zeus to be judged by Paris. Aphrodite seemed beautiful to him, so he awarded her the apple. Here the symposium shows the hypercosmic powers of the gods, and this is why they associate with each other. The golden apple is the cosmos, which, being made up of opposites, is reasonably said to be "tossed by strife {*eris*}." Since the different gods grant different things to the cosmos, they are thought to quarrel over the apple. The soul that lives by physical perception (this is Paris) cannot see any other power in the cosmos but beauty, so it says that the apple belongs to Aphrodite.

Theological myths are suitable for philosophers; the physical and psychic are suitable for poets; and the mixed are suitable for priests of the mysteries (since the goal of every initiation into the mysteries is really to unite us with the cosmos and the gods).

Sappho

(late 7th–early 6th c. BC, wrote in Greek)

Sappho was born into an aristocratic family on the island of Lesbos sometime in the late 7th century. Much of her poetry centers on erotic themes and the private relationships (including homoerotic relationships) of a group of women with which Sappho was associated. Called the "tenth muse" by Plato, her numerous poems were collected into nine books in the Hellenistic period. Although some fragments, a few extensive, are preserved in quotations of later authors or on papyrus scraps, this is the only one of Sappho's poems to have survived in its entirety. In formal terms it is a prayer and most of the standard elements of the prayer are present: (a) an invocation (1–2), including such conventional elements as genealogy and honorific epithets; (b) an initial statement of the request (3–5); (c) a lengthy "reminder" of previous assistance rendered by the goddess (5–24); and (d) a second and fuller statement of the request (25–28).

1 Prayer to Aphrodite (1 L-P)

Immortal Aphrodite on your richly crafted throne,
daughter of Zeus, weaver of snares, I beg you,
do not with sorrows and with pains subdue
my heart, O Lady,

but come to me, if ever at another time as well,
hearing my voice from far away,
you heeded it, and leaving your father's house
of gold, you came,

yoking your chariot. Graceful sparrows
brought you swiftly over the black earth,
with a thick whirring of wings, from heaven down
through the middle air.

Suddenly they were here, and you, O Blessed,
with a smile on your immortal face
asked me what was wrong *this* time, and why
I called you *this* time,

and what in my maddened heart I wanted most
to happen. "Whom shall I persuade *this* time
to welcome you in friendship? Who is it,
    Sappho, that wrongs you?

For if she flees now, soon she shall pursue;
if she refuses presents, she shall give them;
if she does not love, soon she shall love
    even against her will."

Come to me now as well; release me from
this agony; all that my heart yearns
to be achieved, achieve, and be yourself
    my ally in arms.

Semonides

(late 7th c. BC, wrote in Greek)

*Semonides—not to be confused with the other similarly named lyric poet, Simonides—is one of the earliest extant poets from Greece. The most famous of his works is an elaboration of the motif found in Hesiod that womankind is evil (*Theogony *570–589 and* Works and Days *60–82). The fragment, which breaks off in the middle of an interesting allusion to the Trojan War and Helen's role in it, is found in a collection of quotations made in late antiquity.*

7 The Different Kinds of Women (fr. 7 West)

The god made women's minds separately
in the beginning. One he made from the bristly sow:
everything in her house lies in disorder,
smeared with dirt, and rolls about the floor,
while she herself, unbathed, in unwashed clothes,
sits upon the dung heap and grows fat.
Another the god made from the wicked vixen,
a woman who knows all things. Whether bad
or good, nothing escapes her notice;
for often she calls a good thing bad
and a bad thing good; her mood keeps changing.
Another is from the bitch, a mischief-maker just like her mother,
who wants to hear all things and see all things.
Peering and roaming everywhere, she yelps
even when she sees no person there;
and no man can stop her, either by uttering threats
or, in a fit of rage, by knocking out her teeth
with a stone, or yet by speaking to her gently,
even if she happens to be sitting with guests—
no, she keeps up her constant useless howling.
Another the Olympians fashioned out of earth
and gave to man with wits impaired; for such a woman
understands nothing, bad or good.
The only thing she knows how to do is eat:
not even when the god brings on a bad winter
does she feel the cold and draw her stool nearer to the fire.

Another is from the sea: she has two minds.
One day she smiles and beams with joy;
a stranger, seeing her in the house, will praise her:
"There is no woman more estimable than this
among all humankind, nor one more beautiful."
The next day, though, she is unbearable to lay eyes on
or to come near to; at that time she rages
unapproachably, like a bitch with puppies,
proving implacable and repulsive
to everyone, enemies and friends alike.
So too the sea often stands in unmoved
calm, harmless, a great joy to sailors,
in the summer season; but often too it rages,
borne along by loud-thundering waves.
This is what such a woman most resembles
in mood; the sea too has its different natures.
Another is from the ash-gray obstinate ass.
Under compulsion and rebuke, reluctantly,
she puts up with everything after all and does
acceptable work; meanwhile, she eats in the innermost room
all night and all day, and she eats beside the hearth;
just so, as her companion in the act of love,
she also welcomes any man who comes.
Another is from the weasel, a wretched, miserable sort.
She has nothing beautiful or charming
about her, nothing delightful or lovely.
She is mad for bed and lovemaking,
but any man who lies with her she sickens with disgust.
Her thieving does great harm to her neighbors,
and she often eats up offerings left unburned.
Another the delicate, long-maned mare brought forth.
She turns away from menial tasks and trouble;
she won't lay a finger on a mill, nor pick up
a sieve, nor throw the dung outside the house,
nor, being anxious to avoid the soot, sit near
the oven. Yet she compels a man to be her own:
every day she washes herself clean
twice, sometimes three times, and rubs herself with perfumes;
she wears her mane of thick long hair
well-combed and shadowy with flowers.
A beautiful sight indeed is such a woman
to others; to her husband, though, she proves disastrous,

unless he is a tyrant or a sceptered king,
whose heart takes pride in such ornaments.
    Another is from the ape. This is, above all others,
the greatest evil that Zeus has given to men.
Her face is ugly in the extreme: when such a woman
walks through the city, everyone laughs at her.
She's short in the neck; she moves with difficulty;
she's rumpless, nothing but legs. Pity the wretched man
who holds in his arms a calamity like that!
She knows all arts and wily ways,
just like an ape, and doesn't mind being laughed at.
She won't do anyone a kindness; all her attention,
all her planning throughout the day is fixed on this:
how she can do a person the greatest possible harm.
    Another is from the bee. Happy is he who gets her,
for on her alone no censure settles.
In her care his property flourishes and prospers;
she grows old loving a husband who loves her,
a mother of noble and illustrious offspring.
She is conspicuous among all women,
and a godlike grace suffuses her.
She takes no pleasure sitting among women
in places where they tell tales of lovemaking.
Such women are the best and wisest wives
that Zeus in his graciousness bestows on men.
    All these other kinds, however, Zeus
has contrived to be with men and there remain.
No greater plague than this has Zeus created—
women. Even if they may seem to be of some service
to him who has them, to him above all they prove a plague.
He who lives with a woman never passes through
an entire day in a state of cheerfulness;
nor will he quickly push away Hunger from his house,
that hated housemate, that malevolent god.
Whenever a man means to enjoy himself
at home, by divine dispensation or human favor,
she finds a reason to criticize him and arms herself for battle.
Wherever a woman is, men cannot give a hearty welcome
even to a stranger who has come to the house.
She who seems to be most self-controlled
turns out to commit the greatest outrages:
as her husband stands there open-mouthed, the neighbors

take delight in seeing how yet another has gone astray.
Every man will do all he can to praise
his own wife and find fault with another's,
but we fail to recognize that our lots are equal.
No greater plague than this has Zeus created,
and he has bound us to them with unbreakable shackles,
ever since Hades welcomed those
who fought a war for a woman's sake. . . .

SIMONIDES

(mid-6th–early 5th c. BC, wrote in Greek)

Simonides, a lyric poet from Cios, was a remarkably prolific writer and seems to have been a sort of mercenary poet, spending time as the court poet in the service of many Greek kings and rulers. No complete poem of his survives intact, and we rely heavily on papyrus fragments and quotations for knowledge of his work. The fragment below, preserved in a later Greek author, is an expressive piece narrating the moment when Danae and her baby, Perseus, have been put in a chest and are floating on the sea. Simonides effectively contrasts the motherly anxiety of Danae with the peacefulness of the sleeping infant Perseus, who is unaware of his predicament.

543 Perseus in the Chest (fr. 543 PMG)

. . . when in the chest,
intricately fashioned,
the blowing wind
and the sea stirred into motion
cast her down in fear, with cheeks not free from tears
she put her loving arm around Perseus
and said: "My child, what pain and trouble I have!
But you are asleep, and in your milk-fed
baby's way you slumber
in this cheerless brass-bound box
gleaming amid the night,
stretched out under the blue-black gloom.
The thick spray that looms over
your curly head as the wave
passes by means nothing to you, nor the wind's
clamorous voice, as you lie wrapped
in a crimson cloak, with only your lovely face showing.
If to you what is fearsome were truly fearsome,
then you would turn that delicate ear
to hear my words.
But I tell you: sleep, my baby!
Let the sea sleep, let this unmeasured evil sleep!
May some shift in purpose appear,
Father Zeus, from you;
and if I pray too boldly here,
or ask for other than what is right,
forgive me. . . ."

Sophocles

(ca. 495–406/5 BC, wrote in Greek)

Sophocles, most famous for his plays about the family of Oidipous, was an extremely prolific and successful Athenian tragedian. He wrote more than 120 plays, of which only seven survive. In addition to the extant plays, we also have over one thousand fragments, most of them short, from various sources.

FROM *NAUPLIOS*

432 Nauplios on the Achievements of His Son, Palamedes (fr. 432 Radt)

Nauplios' son Palamedes was an important hero credited with numerous accomplishments, as is evident from this fragment. Palamedes came into conflict with Odysseus (Hyginus 95), who later brings about Palamedes' downfall (Hyginus 105). Nauplios eventually gets revenge on the Greeks for killing his son (Hyginus 116).

NAUPLIOS: He hit upon the idea of a wall for the Argive army.
Weighing, counting, measuring—these were his discoveries,
as were these military formations and the heavenly constellations.
He was also the first to count from one to ten,
and then further from ten to fifty
and one thousand. He demonstrated the use of army
beacon-signals and revealed what had not been revealed.
He discovered the positions and courses of the stars,
reliable marks for those who guard others' sleep,
and found for those at sea who shepherd ships
the Bear's revolutions and the Dog Star's frigid setting.

FROM *TEREUS*

583 Procne Laments the Life of Women (fr. 583 Radt)

The story of Procne and Philomela is best known from Ovid's Metamorphoses, *but Sophocles was one of the earliest if not the earliest playwright to dramatize the Thracian Tereus' barbaric rape of his wife's sister. Here Procne, Tereus' wife, laments her lot as his wife. One can see similar statements by Euripides' characters Medea and Melanippe (for the latter, see Euripides fr. 660).*

PROCNE: On my own now, I am nothing. But I have
often seen the nature of woman in this way,
I mean, that we are nothing. While young in our father's
house, I think we live the most pleasant life a person can lead,
for naiveté always makes children grow up in constant bliss.
But when we reach adolescence, we understand.
We are kicked out and sold to different buyers,
away from our ancestral gods and parents,
some to strange men, some to barbarians,
some to joyless houses, some to abusive ones.
And after a single night binds us,
we have to praise it and believe that it is fine.

FROM AN UNKNOWN TRAGEDY

941 The Power of Aphrodite (fr. 941 Radt)

A description of Aphrodite's power over all living things. One can compare both the opening to Homeric Hymn *5 (to Aphrodite) and Lucretius' invocation to Venus.*

[UNKNOWN]: Children, Cypris is not just Cypris,
but she is known by many names.
She is Hades; she is immortal life.
She is the frenzy of madness; she is desire
unmixed; she is lamentation. In her is everything
active, everything serene, everything that leads to violence.
She sinks deep into the hearts of everything that
lives. What does not crave this goddess?
She enters into the swimming race of fish,
she is among the four-footed family on land,
and she plies her wing among the birds.
< . . . *a line, perhaps two, missing* . . . >
among beasts, among mortals, and among the gods above.
Which of the gods does she not throw three times while wrestling?
If it is right for me—and it is—to speak the truth,
she lords it over Zeus' heart without spear,
without sword. Cypris cuts all of the plans
of mortals and of gods to her own pattern.

FROM AN UNKNOWN SATYR PLAY

1130 Satyrs as Suitors (fr. 1130 Radt)

In the major dramatic festival in Athens, the City Dionysia, each playwright presented three tragedies followed by a Satyr play, a type of drama that was named after the Satyrs who comprised the chorus. Although Satyr drama has many of the formal features of tragedy (choruses, a mythological setting, poetic meter, the three-actor rule, and so forth), the content and tone of a Satyr play are comic and crude. This led one ancient critic to define Satyr drama as "tragedy at play." In this selection the playwright, probably but not definitely Sophocles, has taken a common mythological situation—suitors presenting themselves and competing for the hand of a king's daughter—and turned it on its head by having the Satyrs of the chorus put themselves forward as candidates. The king is Oineus and the maiden in question is his daughter, Deianeira,[1] and so the suitor who enters the stage at the end of this fragment could well be Heracles. The ribald and absurd nature of much of the dialogue of Satyr plays is apparent even in an excerpt this short—one need only look at a few of the "qualifications" the Satyrs present: "testicle twisting" and the ability to "speak with our nether regions," the latter a euphemism for farting.

< . . . *a few damaged lines omitted* . . . >
OINEUS: Well, I will tell you. But first I want
to know who you are who have come and from what family
you sprout. For I do not yet know this even now.

CHORUS OF SATYRS: You will learn everything. We come as suitors,
children of Nymphs, servants of Bacchos,
neighbors of gods. Every noble pursuit is in our
repertoire: the art of spear-fighting, contests of wrestling,
of horse-racing, of foot-racing,
of boxing, of biting, of testicle-twisting.
We have musical songs; we have
oracles that have never been heard—and they are not fakes.
We have ways of testing medications and of
measuring the heavens. We can dance. We can talk
with our nether regions. Is our mission fruitless?
You can take for yourself whichever of these things
you want if you give me your daughter.
[Another actor enters the stage]

OINEUS: Well, your lineage is beyond reproach, but I first
want to give consideration also to this man who is coming.

[1] It is possible that the king is Schoineus, which would make the daughter Atalante.

Statius

(48–96 AD, wrote in Latin)

Statius wrote two epic works on mythological subjects that survive: the Thebaid, *which recounts the story of the Seven against Thebes, and the* Achilleid, *an unfinished poem about the hero Achilles (only one book and part of another survive), which details the attempts of his mother, Thetis, to save him from fighting in the Trojan War, in which he was fated to die. The two passages below describe her plan to dress him in women's clothing and to hide him among the girls in Lycomedes' palace on Scyros (1.242–1.282), as well as his subsequent discovery by a trick of Ulysses and Diomedes (1.819–1.882). The central feature of these two selections is the conflict between Thetis' motherly love and Achilles' manly nature.*

FROM *ACHILLEID*

1.242–1.282 Thetis Takes Achilles to Scyros

Already daylight was dispelling the stars, and out of the low-lying sea
Titan rolled his dripping team, and from the wide expanse above
fell the seawater borne aloft by the chariot. But Achilles' mother
long before had traversed the waves, reached the shallows of Scyros,
and released the weary dolphins from their yoke.
Then the boy was stirred awake, and his opening eyes
felt the daylight pouring in. He was bewildered at his first sight:
"Where am I? What waters are these? Where is Pelion?" Everything was
strange, unfamiliar, and it took a moment to recognize his mother.
She embraced her frightened son and with coaxing words addressed him:
"Dear child, if my destiny had given me the marriage it originally
ordained,[1] then in the celestial regions I would embrace you,
a brilliant star, and as a mother in the mighty heavens
I would fear neither the earthly Parcae nor the deathly Fates.
But, son, your line is unbalanced, and only on your mother's side
is the way of death barred. Moreover, perilous times are drawing near,
and dangers have reached their final turning point.
Let us rest. For a little while relax that manly spirit of yours.

[1] Instead of marrying a god, Thetis was forced by Zeus to marry a mortal because it was prophesied that she would produce a son greater than his father.

Take these clothes. Do not scorn them. If the Tirynthian held
Lydian wool and women's spears in his calloused hand,
if it befits Bacchus to sweep away his footprints with a golden
dress, if Jupiter assumed the form of a maiden,
and if changing genders did not enervate great Caeneus,[2]
I beg you, do this and let this threat, this menacing cloud, pass.
Soon I will return you to the fields, to the haunts of the Centaurs.
I beg you, by this beauty of yours and the joys of youth soon to be,
if I endured the earth and a lowly mortal husband for your sake,
if I armed you as a newborn babe in the grim waters of the river Styx[3]
(if only completely!) then take for just a little while these clothes
that will in no way weaken your courage. Why are you drawing back?
What does that look mean? Are you ashamed to look soft in this garb?
Dear, I swear by you and these kindred seas, Chiron will not know of this."
    In such a way she worked on his stubborn spirit, trying in vain
to coax him. But thoughts of his father and his great mentor
opposed his mother's request, as did the first inklings of his bold nature.
It was like someone for the first time trying to subject to the reins
an unbroken horse, inflamed with the blaze of uncontrolled youth.
This horse, long relishing the pastures, streams, and his proud dignity,
offers neither neck to the yoke nor untamed mouth to the bridle;
a captive, he snorts, refusing to surrender to the dominance
of a master, and is surprised to learn another's gait.

1.819–1.885 Achilles' True Identity Is Uncovered by Ulysses and Diomedes

Dawn had barely broken and already the son of Tydeus, accompanied
by Agyrtes, had arrived, bringing with him the agreed-upon gifts.
The Scyrian maidens too emerged from their bedrooms
and set out to display their dances and the sacred rites promised
to the revered guests. Escorted by Peleus' son, Queen Deidamia
outshone the rest, just as Diana and fierce Pallas
and the wife of the Elysian king surpass the Nymphs of Enna
in their radiance beneath the cliffs of Sicily's Mount Aetna.
At once they began to move, and the Ismenian pipe called for
Bacchic dance. Four times Rhea's cymbals and the frenzied drums
they struck, and four times they traced their winding steps.

[2] The preceding examples emphasize males in feminine roles: Hercules (the Tirynthian) as servant of Queen Omphale, Dionysus who is often portrayed as feminine, Jupiter who turned into a female to seduce Callisto, and the sex-shifting Caeneus/Caenis.

[3] This is the earliest literary reference to Thetis' dipping Achilles in the Styx to make him invulnerable.

Then in unison they lifted their thyrsi up and in unison lowered them,
and they quickened their steps, now in the manner of the Curetes,
now the pious Samothracians, and now facing each other
for the Amazonian Comb Dance, now in a ring as when Delia stirs up
Laconian girls and whirls them around in dance in her own Amyclae.
Then especially Achilles, for all to see, cared not at all
to keep step or link arms with his fellow-dancers.
More than ever he scorned womanly steps and womanly garb:
he disrupted the dance and caused great chaos.
Just so did sorrowing Thebes witness Pentheus scorning
the thyrsus and cymbals that his mother had willingly received.
The troop dispersed amid applause and returned to their father's
threshold, where in the central courtyard of the palace
the son of Tydeus had earlier set up gifts designed to tempt the eyes
of young maidens, a token of hospitality and a reward for their toil.
He urged them to choose, and the appeasing king did not stand in the way.
Alas! Simple-minded, so very naive is the man who is unaware
of the clever gifts and cunning deceit of the Greeks and crafty Ulysses.
Then the others, led by their inactive nature and sex,
tested out the smooth thyrsi and the resounding drums,
and wreathed their temples with jewel-lined bands.
The weapons they saw, but thought them gifts for their mighty father.
But as soon as the wild grandson of Aeacus caught sight of the gleaming
shield engraved with battle scenes—it happened to be tinged
red with the savage stains of war—and the spear it was leaning upon,
he growled and widened his eyes, and the hair on his brow
bristled on end. Gone were his mother's instructions,
gone the love he had kept secret. Troy consumed his whole heart.
He was like a lion who, when taken young from its mother's teat, submits
to being tamed: he learns to have his mane combed, to respect man,
and to lose control of his rage only when ordered.
Yet once the flash of a sword meets his eye, loyalty is forsworn
and his tamer becomes his foe as for the first time he hungers
to eat his master, ashamed of having submitted to a timid ruler.
As Achilles came closer, the mimicking light cast his reflection,
and he saw his image reproduced in the gold. He bristled
with excitement and blushed all at once. On cue, sharp Ulysses
sidled up to him and whispered, "Why do you hesitate?
We know. You are the protégé of the half-beast Chiron.
You are the descendant of sky and sea. It is you whom the Doric fleet
and your homeland Greece await with anxious standards,
and already Pergamum shudders with trembling walls awaiting.

Come on! No more delays! Let treacherous Ida grow pale in fright,
let it delight your father to hear these words and let deceitful
Thetis be ashamed to have feared for your safety." Already he was
loosening the dress, when on command Agyrtes blew a great blast
from his trumpet. The maidens fled, gifts scattered everywhere,
imploring their father, believing that the battle had already begun.
Achilles' dress fell away from his chest on its own,
the shield and too-short spear were dwarfed by his massive hand—
unbelievable!—he seemed to tower head and shoulders over
the Ithacan and Aetolian leaders. A sudden flash of arms and the fire
of Mars filled the whole hall with an awesome glow.
He strode mightily, as if demanding Hector on the spot,
and stood in the middle of the trembling palace, and the Pelian
maiden was nowhere to be seen.

THEOCRITUS

(early 3rd c. BC, wrote in Greek)

One of the most celebrated poets of the Hellenistic Age, Theocritus is best known for writing pastoral poetry centering on the theme of rustic life. One of these pastoral poems is this famous appeal by the Cyclops Polyphemos to his would-be lover Galateia, a Sea Nymph. Polyphemos, so grimly portrayed in the Odyssey, *has here been humanized by Theocritus, who delights in the Cyclops' clumsy attempts to seduce Galateia with his promises of the advantages of his life as a shepherd over her life in the sea. Particular fun is had with ironic references, such as those to burning his eye and a stranger arriving by ship, which recall Polyphemos' fate at the hands of Odysseus. The setting is on Sicily, Theocritus' own home island and the place where Homer's Cyclopes were said to have lived. This is the one of two poems (the other is* Idyll *6) that Theocritus wrote about the bizarre love of Polyphemos and Galateia, a theme he took from Philoxenos, an earlier poet who seems to have invented the affair between the two.*

FROM *IDYLLS*

11 Polyphemos' Love for Galateia

There is no other remedy for love,
Nicias, no ointment, I think, nor any powder—
nothing but the Pierides.[1] This is a painless and pleasant
remedy for people, but it is not easy to find.
I expect that you know this well, being a doctor
who is greatly beloved by the nine Muses.
That's how the Cyclops had it quite easy, the one who lived here,
Polyphemos of old, when he loved Galateia,
his whiskers just coming in round his mouth and temples.
He did not show his love with apples, roses, or locks of hair,
but with real madness. All else he thought trifles.
Often his sheep came home to their fold by themselves
from the green pasture. But he, singing of Galateia,
wasted away on the seaweed strewn beach by himself,
starting at dawn, a most bitter wound beneath his heart,

[1] The Muses.

which mighty Cypris' arrow fixed fast in his liver.
But he found the remedy, and sitting on the lofty
cliff, looking out to sea, he sang this song:
"O white Galateia, why do you reject the one who loves you,
who are whiter than cottage cheese to behold, softer than a lamb,
more skittish than a calf, more glistening than an unripe grape?
Why do you come at once when sweet sleep holds me,
but go off immediately when sweet sleep frees me
and flee like a ewe that's spotted a gray wolf?
I fell in love with you, girl, when for the first time
you came with my mother, wanting to pluck
hyacinths from the mountain, and I was your guide.
I laid eye on you, and ever since then—even now I can't
stop loving one bit. But you don't care. Oh, Zeus, not at all!
I know, lovely girl, why you avoid me—
because of the shaggy brow across my whole forehead,
which stretches from this ear to that, one long line,
and the single eyeball below, and the wide nose above my lip.
But even though I am like I am, I herd one thousand animals
and draw the finest milk from them to drink.
And I don't lack for cheese, not in the summer, not in the fall,
and not in the dead of winter. My cheese racks are overloaded.
I know how to play the syrinx like no other Cyclops here,
and about you, my dear sweetie-apple, and also about me, I sing
often, at all hours of the night. For you I am raising eleven fawns,
all wearing collars, and four bear cubs.
Just come to me and you will lack for nothing,
and let the gray sea stretch up onto the dry land!
You'll spend the night more pleasantly with me in my cave.
There are laurels here; there are slender cypresses;
there is dark ivy; there is the sweet-fruited vine;
there is chill water that tree-rich Aitna pours
for me, a divine drink from white snow.
Who would choose the sea and waves over these things?
And if I seem to you overly hairy,
I've got oak firewood and beneath the ashes a fire that never goes out.[2]
I'd even put up with you setting my soul on fire
and my one eye too, and nothing is sweeter to me than that.
Alas that my mother bore me with no gills,

[2] Polyphemos may be inviting Galateia to singe off his excess hair, a common procedure in antiquity. In the next line he turns to the figurative fires of love.

else I could have dived down to you, kissed your hand
(if your mouth is forbidden), and brought you white lilies
or soft poppies with their broad red petals—
well, except one is a summer flower, and the other comes in winter,
so I couldn't have brought you both together.
But now, my darling, oh, right now I will learn to swim,
if some stranger comes sailing here on a ship.
That way I can see why it is you like inhabiting the deep.
Oh, come out, Galateia, and once you've come out, forget—
as I, sitting here now, have forgotten—to go back home.
Desire to herd sheep along with me and milk them
and make cheese by adding pungent rennet.
My mother is the only one wronging me, and I blame her.
She has never said anything nice to you at all on my behalf,
even though she sees me growing thinner day after day.
I will tell her that my head and both my feet
are throbbing so that she will feel bad, since I too feel bad.
O Cyclops, Cyclops, where have your wits flown off to?
Go. You'd show more sense if you were to weave your baskets,
and cut branches and bring them to your lambs.
Milk the ewe you've got! Why chase the one who flees you?
Perhaps you will find another Galateia, one even more beautiful.
Many girls call me to play with them through the night,
and they all giggle whenever I answer them.
It's obvious I too, on land, seem to be someone important."
In that way did Polyphemos shepherd his love
by singing, and had an easier time of it than if he'd paid gold.

THEOPHRASTUS

(ca. 371–ca. 287 BC, wrote in Greek)

Theophrastus studied with the philosopher Aristotle and succeeded him as head of the Lyceum, his philosophical school. In his Characters *he gives sketches of thirty different personality types, one of which is "the superstitious man." It is a remarkable document that exaggerates and parodies Athenian popular piety of the day, particularly with regard to the concept of pollution. In it he attributes to a single fictional man all of the irrational behaviors that superstitious people could exhibit in everyday life as they attempted to avoid running afoul of the divine. In fact, the Greek word for superstition,* deisidaimonia, *literally means "fear of the divine."*

FROM *CHARACTERS*

16 The Superstitious Man

Superstition will manifest itself as excessive fear in regard to divine matters. The superstitious person is the sort who <*unintelligible word*> washes his hands, purifies himself with water from a shrine, pops a laurel leaf into his mouth, and walks around like that throughout the day. And if a weasel runs across his path, he cannot continue until someone else goes first or he throws three rocks across the path. And if he sees a snake in his house, he calls on Sabazios if it is a red snake,[1] and right then and there he dedicates a shrine for a hero if it is a sacred snake. As he goes by the anointed stones at the crossroads, he pours oil on them from his oil-flask and leaves only after falling to his knees and performing obeisance. If a mouse chews through a sack holding barley,[2] he goes to the temple interpreter and asks what he should do. Even if the interpreter tells him to send it to the leather-worker to be patched up, he ignores this advice, goes off, and makes a sacrifice to atone for his sin.

He is prone to purify his house all the time, claiming that Hecate has put it under a spell. And if owls hoot as he walks by, he is shaken and only goes on after saying, "Great Athena!" He is unwilling to set foot on a grave monument or to go to the viewing of a corpse or to visit a woman in her childbed. He says that the best policy

[1] Red snakes were used in the rituals of Sabazios, a Phrygian deity the Athenians began to worship in the 5th c. BC.

[2] Presumably an issue because barley was part of the sacrificial ritual.

is for him to not incur pollution in the first place. On both the fourth and the seventh day of the month he orders his family to boil wine. He then goes to the market for myrtle, frankincense, and sacrificial cakes. After his return he spends the whole day putting garlands on the Hermaphrodites.[3]

Whenever he has a dream, he goes to the dream-interpreters, the diviners, and the observers of birds to find out what god or goddess he needs to pray to. He goes every month with his wife to the Initiators of Orpheus to be initiated. If his wife does not have time, he takes the wet-nurse and the children. He will make sure to be there when people are purifying themselves at the seashore. If he ever observes someone at the crossroads with a string of garlic around his neck, he leaves, washes from head to toe, and then calls priestesses and orders a complete purification with a squill or puppy.[4] Catching sight of a lunatic or an epileptic, he gives a shudder and then spits on his chest.[5]

[3] Probably statues of some sort, but this is the first recorded use of the word and the exact reference is uncertain.

[4] Sacrificed puppies were part of some purificatory rituals, as was the squill, the bulb of the sea-onion plant.

[5] The action is supposed to avert the "evil eye."

THUCYDIDES

(ca. 460–ca. 400 BC, wrote in Greek)

Thucydides was the author of the History of the Peloponnesian War, *an account of the war between Athens and Sparta (431–404 BC). He emphatically and completely distanced himself from mythical accounts of the past, something that his predecessor Herodotus had begun to do in a limited fashion some years earlier. In an important passage about his method he is clear about how earlier historians (Herodotus among them) were insufficiently critical of myth. He claims that a reader would not be misled by his own account of early events "as he would if he believed what the poets have sung about them, which they have much embellished, or what the prose-writers have strung together, which aims more to delight the ear than to be true. Their accounts cannot be tested, you see, and many are not credible, as they have achieved the status of myth over time" (1.21, trans. Woodruff). The passage given below is taken from the first part of Thucydides'* History, *which is traditionally called the Archaeology ("An Account of Ancient Times"). It is his reassessment of Greek prehistory, which for the Greeks naturally involved myths, and in it we can see Thucydides' method at work. He takes a purely critical and rational approach to the past and rejects all unlikely stories, although he accepts that some historical truth underlies most myths. This tendency to rationalize myth can also be seen in later authors such as Diodorus of Sicily and Palaephatus.*

FROM *HISTORY OF THE PELOPONNESIAN WAR*

1.1–1.12 Thucydides Reassesses Greek Prehistory

Thucydides, an Athenian, wrote up the war of the Peloponnesians and the Athenians as they fought against each other. He began to write as soon as the war was afoot, with the expectation that it would turn out to be a great one and that, more than all earlier wars, this one would deserve to be recorded. He made this prediction because both sides were at their peak in every sort of preparation for war, and also because he saw the rest of the Greek world taking one side or the other, some right away, others planning to do so.

This was certainly the greatest upheaval there had ever been among the Greeks. It also reached many foreigners—indeed, one might say that it affected most people everywhere. Because of the great passage of time it is impossible to discover clearly what happened long ago or even just before these events; still, I have looked into the evidence as far as can be done, and I am confident that nothing great happened in or out of war before this.

[2] It is evident that what is now called "Hellas"[1] was not permanently settled in former times, but that there were many migrations, and people were ready to leave their land whenever they met the force of superior numbers. There was no trade, and they could not communicate with each other either by land or over the sea without danger. Each group used its ground merely to produce a bare living; they had no surplus of riches, and they planted nothing, because they could not *know* when someone would invade and carry everything away, especially since they had no walls. They counted themselves masters of just enough to sustain them each day, wherever they were, and so made little difficulty about moving on. Because of this they had no strength, either in the size of their cities or in any other resources. The best land was always the most subject to these changes of inhabitants: what is now called Thessaly, also Boiotia, most of the Peloponnese except for Arcadia, and whatever was most fertile in the rest of Greece. For the excellence of the land increased the power of certain men, and this led to civil wars, by which they were ruined; and all this made them more vulnerable to the designs of outsiders. Accordingly, Attica has been free from civil war for most of its history, owing to the lightness of its soil; and that is why it has always been inhabited by the same people.[2]

Here is strong support for this account: because of the migrations, the rest of Greece did not develop at the same rate as Athens, since the most able refugees from wars and civil strife all over Greece retired to the safety of Athens. There they became citizens, and they added so much to the citizen population that Attica could no longer support them, and colonies were sent out to Ionia.

[3] I am further convinced of the weakness of Hellas in ancient times by this fact: before the Trojan War, Hellas evidently took no action in common. I do not believe, either, that the name "Hellas" was yet applied to the whole country. Before the time of Hellen, the son of Deucalion, there was no such name at all, but the various regions took the names of their own inhabitants, with "Pelasgian" naming the largest. When Hellen and his sons came to power in Phthiotis, however, they were called in to the aid of other cities, which one by one came to be called Hellenes because of their association with them. That name cannot have prevailed over all of Greece until much later, however. The principal evidence for this is from Homer, who does not ever give them that name in general, though he was born long after the Trojan War. He does not use the name for anyone but those who came from Phthiotis with Achilles (who were the very first Hellenes); but he calls the others "Danaans," "Argives," or "Achaians" in his poems. He does not use the term "foreigner" {*barbaros*} either, because, it seems to me, the Hellenes were not yet marked off by one name in opposition to them. City by city, then, they came to be called Hellenes if they understood each others' language, and later they all had this name; but before the Trojan War they did not enter into any action with their forces joined, owing to their lack of strength and communication; and they joined in that expedition only because they had learned to make more use of the sea.

1 "Hellas" is the Greek name for Greece.

2 Athenians believed they had always lived in Attica.

[4] Minos, by all reports, was the first to build a navy; he made himself master of most of what is now the Hellenic Sea, ruled the islands called the Cyclades, and sent colonies to most of them, expelling the Carians and setting up his own sons there as governors. Also, as one would expect, he freed the seas from piracy as much as he could, so that his revenue could reach him more easily.

[5] In ancient times, you see, the Greeks had turned to piracy as soon as they began to travel more in ships from one place to another, and so had the foreigners who lived on the mainland shore or on the islands. Their most powerful leaders aimed at their own profit, but also hoped to support the weak; and so they fell upon cities that had no walls or were made up of settlements. They raided these places and made most of their living from that. Such actions were nothing to be ashamed of then, but carried with them a certain glory, as we may learn from some of the mainlanders for whom this is still an honor, even today, if done nobly. The same point is proved by the ancient poets, who show that anyone who sails by, anywhere, is asked the same question—"Are you a pirate?"—and that those who are asked are not insulted, while those who want to know are not reproachful.

They also robbed each other on the mainland, and even now much of Greece follows this old custom—the Ozolean Locrians, for example, and the Aetolians and Acarnanians and mainlanders near them. The fashion of carrying iron weapons survives among those mainlanders as well, from their old trade of thieving. [6] All of Greece used to carry arms, you see, because houses were unfenced and travel was unsafe; and so they became accustomed to living every day with weapons, as foreigners do. The fact that some parts of Greece still do so testifies that the practice was once universal.

The Athenians were the first Greeks to put their weapons away and change to a more relaxed and luxurious lifestyle. It was due to this refinement that the older men among the rich there only recently gave up the fashion of wearing long linen robes and tying up the hair on their heads in knots fastened with golden cicadas.[3] (From them, because of their kinship with Athens, the same fashion spread to the older men of Ionia and lasted a long time.) The moderate sort of clothing that is now in style was first used by the Lacedaimonians, who had made the lifestyle of the rich equal to that of ordinary people, especially in regard to dress. They were also the first to strip themselves naked for exercise and to oil themselves afterward. In the old days athletes used to wear loincloths around their private parts when they competed, even at the Olympic Games, and it has not been many years since this custom ended. Even now there are foreigners, especially in Asia, whose athletes wear loincloths in boxing matches. And in many other ways one could show that the lifestyle of the ancient Greeks was similar to that of foreigners today.

[7] As for the cities, those that were settled more recently—since the advance of navigation—had a surplus of money and so were built with walls right on the coasts. They took over the isthmuses both for commercial reasons and to strengthen themselves individually against their neighbors. The older cities, however, were built further from the sea, owing to the greater danger of piracy on the islands as well as on

[3] As cicadas seem to be born from the ground, they represented the Athenian belief that they had themselves sprung from the ground on which they lived.

the mainland. They robbed each other and any nonseamen who lived by the coast, with the result that even today those people are still settled inland.

[8] Most of the pirates were islanders, the Carians or Phoenicians who had settled most of the islands. The evidence for this is as follows: when the Athenians purified Delos during this war,[4] they dug up the graves of those who had died on the island and found that more than half were Carian. They knew this by the style of the weapons that were buried with them and by the burial customs, which are still in use.

Once Minos' navy was afloat, navigation became easier, since he expelled the evil-doers from the islands and planted colonies of his own in many of them. And as those who lived along the coasts became more addicted to acquiring wealth, their settlements became more stable. Some, who had become richer than before, threw up walls around their towns. In their desire for gain, the weaker cities let themselves be subject to the stronger ones, while the more powerful cities used their surplus wealth to bring weaker ones under their rule. And that was the situation later, when they sent the expedition against Troy.

[9] In my view Agamemnon was able to get the fleet together because he had more power than anyone else at that time, and not so much because he was the leader of the suitors of Helen who were bound by oaths to Tyndareos.

Those who received the clearest account of the Peloponnesians from their predecessors say that Pelops used the great wealth he brought from Asia and was the first to win power among the Peloponnesian people (who were very poor at the time). Because of this he gave his own name to the land, though he was an outsider. Afterward, his descendants became still more powerful. After Eurystheus was killed in Attica by the Heracleidai, Atreus made himself king of Mycenae and the other lands Eurystheus had ruled. (Eurystheus had entrusted the rule of Mycenae to him when he set off on campaign, because of their family relationship. Atreus was his mother's brother and happened to be living at the time with Eurystheus, in exile from his father for the death of Chrysippos.)[5] When Eurystheus did not come back, the Mycenaeans wanted Atreus to be king, partly out of fear of the Heracleidai and partly because they thought Atreus was an able man and, at the same time, because he had served the interests of the majority. That is how the descendants of Pelops became greater than those of Perseus.

Now, Agamemnon was the son of Atreus and inherited this power; and besides this he had a stronger navy than anyone else. That is why I think he assembled his forces more on the basis of fear than good will. It is evident that most of the ships were his and that he had others to lend to the Arcadians, as Homer declares (whose evidence should be good enough for anyone).[6] Besides, in the "Giving of the Scepter" Homer says that Agamemnon was lord "of many islands and all Argos.[7] Now, since he lived on the mainland, he could not have controlled islands (except for the neighboring ones, of which there were only a few) unless he had a navy. And we should infer the character of earlier enterprises on the basis of that expedition.

[4] The Peloponnesian War.

[5] See Hyginus 85.

[6] *Iliad* 2.612.

[7] *Iliad* 2.108.

[10] Of course Mycenae was small, and the cities of that time may not seem to be worth very much; but such weak evidence should not count against believing that the expedition was as great as the poets have said it was, and as tradition holds. For if the Lacedaimonians' city were wiped out, and if only their temples and building foundations remained, I think people in much later times would seriously doubt that their power had matched their fame; and yet they own two-fifths of the Peloponnese and are leaders of the rest, along with many allies outside. Still, it would seem to have been rather weak, since it was not settled as one city around the use of costly temples or other buildings, but was made up of villages in the old Greek style.[8] If the same thing were to happen to Athens, however, one would infer from what was plain to see that its power had been double what it is.

We have no good reason, then, to doubt those reports about the size of the army in the Trojan War, or to measure a city more by its appearance than its power. We should think of that army as indeed greater than those that went before it, but weaker than those we have now. This depends on our trusting Homer again on this point, where he would be expected as a poet to exaggerate; but on his account that army was still much weaker than modern ones: he makes the fleet consist of 1200 ships and reports that the Boiotian ships carried 120 men each, while those of Philoctetes carried 50. I think he did this to show the maximum and minimum, but he makes no mention at all in his catalogue of the size of the other ships.[9] He does, however, show that all the rowers in Philoctetes' ships were also fighters, for he writes that all the oarsmen were archers. As for passengers on the ships, it is not likely that there were many, aside from the kings and other top people, especially since they had to cross the sea with military equipment on board, and in ships without the protection of upper decks, built in the old pirate fashion. So if we take the mean between the largest and smallest ships, we find that not many went to Troy, considered as a joint expedition from all of Greece.

[11] This is to be explained more by lack of wealth than by a shortage of men. Because of their lack of rations, they brought a smaller army—just the size they expected would be able to support itself while fighting. When they landed, they got the upper hand in fighting. (That is obvious; otherwise they could not have fortified their camp.) After that, apparently, they did not use all their power, because they had to turn partly to farming in the Chersonese, and partly to piracy. Because they were dispersed in this way, the Trojans were better able to hold them off for those ten years and were an equal match for those Greeks who were left near Troy at any one time.

If they had gone out with plenty of rations, however, and concentrated their forces on continuous warfare without farming or piracy, they would easily have taken the city once they'd gotten the upper hand in fighting, since they were a match for the Trojans with the portion of the army that was present at any time. If they had settled down in a siege, they would have taken Troy in less time with less trouble.

[8] Sparta was not enclosed by a wall until Roman times. The Athenians, by contrast, believed that Theseus had gathered their villages into one city at a very early date. See Plutarch.

[9] *Iliad* 2.484 ff.

All enterprises were weak before the Trojan War for want of money, and this one was too, for all that it was the most famous expedition of ancient times. The facts show clearly that it was weaker than its fame would have it, and weaker than the verbal tradition that has come down to us from the poets.

[12] After the Trojan War the Greeks were still in motion, still resettling, and so could not make progress in one place. The Greeks came back from Troy after a long absence, and this brought about many changes: civil war broke out in most cities, and the people who were driven out founded new cities. The people now known as Boiotians were thrown out of Arne by the Thessalians in the sixtieth year after Troy was taken; they settled in what is now Boiotia, but was then called Cadmeis. (Only a portion of them were in that country before then, some of whom fought against Troy.) And in the eightieth year the Dorians seized the Peloponnese along with the Heracleidai.[10]

With much ado, then, and after a long time, peace came with security to Greece; and now that they were no longer being uprooted they began to send colonies abroad. The Athenians settled Ionia and most of the islands, while the Peloponnesians planted colonies in most of southern Italy and Sicily, as well as in some other parts of Greece. And all these were founded after the Trojan War.

[10] The Dorian invasion is probably historical, though not as early as Thucydides puts it. According to legend, the Heracleidai, who claimed descent from Heracles, were driven out of the Peloponnese by the sons of Pelops and found asylum among the Dorians. Later, they reclaimed their thrones with the aid of the Dorians, who took over the Peloponnese and reduced the local population to a status like that of sharecroppers.

VERGIL

(70–19 BC, wrote in Latin)

Vergil, generally regarded as the greatest Latin poet, is best known for his Aeneid, *the national epic of Rome. The* Aeneid *is a reinterpretation of the myth of Aeneas, the great Trojan hero, one of a few who escaped the sack of Troy. In this poem, the hero travels to Italy after Troy's fall to establish a new kingdom. Both Julius Caesar and his adopted son, Augustus, traced their family name Julius back to Aeneas' son, Iulus. It has been argued that Augustus, at the beginning of his reign as the first emperor of Rome, urged the poet to compose the* Aeneid *to legitimize his reign and, more generally, to create a heroic past for the Roman people. In promoting the Romans' Trojan past, Vergil relies heavily on Greek myth, but he is also influenced by his own poetic purpose and philosophical ideas. Vergil also produced two other major poetic works, the* Eclogues *on pastoral life and the* Georgics *on agriculture. In a passage from the latter, which is given below, he relates the story of Orpheus and Eurydice.*

FROM *AENEID*

2.1–2.558 Aeneas Escapes from Troy

The second book of the Aeneid *is the earliest surviving full account of the Trojan Horse and the sack of Troy. It was a story familiar to the Greeks and often told, but the ravages of time have left us with very little besides summaries (see Proclus' summary of the* Iliou Persis*) and tempting allusions. Aeneas was destined to survive the destruction of Troy (this is mentioned as early as Homer's* Iliad*), but subsequent tradition varies widely concerning the details of his actions before his escape. Vergil, however, chooses to emphasize his heroic nature by showing him fighting desperately to save the city. But the gods have decreed that Troy must fall, and Aeneas must follow his destiny, so he ultimately flees the doomed city with his father, his son, and the* Penates, *the sacred icons of Troy. This devotion to family, country, and gods is central to Aeneas' character (one can compare the portrait in Aelian 3.22).*

Aeneas recounts the fall of Troy at the court of the Carthaginian queen, Dido, who has fallen in love with him. She is summarily abandoned by him and then kills herself out of grief. Aeneas will meet her again in the underworld (see 6f). The following excerpt ends with the dramatic death of King Priam, before Aeneas leaves the city.

2a Aeneas Begins to Describe the Fall of Troy (1–39)

Your Majesty, you ask me to revisit an unspeakable pain, to recall how the Danaans demolished the Trojans' power and their unhappy kingdom. I was myself witness to these horrible events and involved in a great many of them. What soldier from the Myrmidons or Dolopians could hold back his tears when speaking of such horrors?

Could even brutal Ulysses? And now the damp night hurries down the sky, and the sinking constellations urge us to go to sleep. But if you have such a strong desire to know about our misfortunes and to hear a brief account of Troy's final struggle, I shall begin, although my mind shudders at the thought and cringes in sorrow.

War-torn and broken by the Fates, the Danaan leaders after many years constructed a horse as great as a mountain with the help of Pallas' divine skill and interlaced its ribs with wood cut from fir trees. They pretended that it was a votive offering for a safe return home. At least that was the rumor being spread about. Their leaders chose select men and secretly hid them in the dark interior; they filled the huge hollows of the belly deep within with an armed body of men.

There is a well-known island within sight of Troy, and it was wealthy so long as the kingdom of Priam stood. Now it is just seacoast, a treacherous anchorage for ships. The Greeks set out to this island and hid themselves on the deserted coast. We thought that they had gone away and were sailing for Mycenae. And so, all of Teucria was freed from its long sorrow; the gates were thrown wide open, and everyone felt the urge to go out and see the Dorian camps, the deserted places, and the abandoned shore. Here the troops of the Dolopians were encamped, over there was the tent of savage Achilles. Here their ships were docked, and over there they used to fight. Some of us stood dumb in awe of the fatal gift for Maiden Minerva and marveled at the massive size of the horse.

Thymoetes was the first to advocate bringing the horse within the walls of the city and placing it on the citadel; either it was a trick on his part or the Fates of Troy had willed it so. But Capys—and others who had a better opinion in mind—directed us to toss the contrivance of the Danaans, a suspicious gift, headlong into the sea or set fire to it or bore through and examine the hollow recesses of the belly. The crowd that had assembled was split into opposing factions, undecided.

2b Laocoon Advises the Trojans to Destroy the Horse (40–56)

There in front of all the others, accompanied by a great entourage, Laocoon, incensed, ran down from the citadel and from a distance cried out:

"O you miserable citizens, what awful madness has seized you? Do you really think that the enemy has sailed away? Do you really think that any gift from the Danaans is free of treachery? Is Ulysses known for his innocence? Either Achaeans have been enclosed and are hidden within these planks, or this is a device created to breach our walls, to look down on our homes, and to come into the city from above. Or some such ruse lurks within. Do not trust the horse, Trojans. Whatever it is, I fear the Danaans, especially when they bring gifts."

Thus he spoke, and he hurled with mighty force a huge spear into the side of the beast, where the belly curved at the joints. The spear stood there, shaking, and the cavernous hollows let out a crash and a groan as the belly was struck. And, if our destiny and the gods' intentions had not been hostile toward us, he would have driven us to lay waste to the hiding places of the Argives with our swords, and Troy would now stand, and you, lofty citadel of Priam, would still remain.

2c The Greek Sinon Is Captured and Led to the King (57–198)

Suddenly some Dardan shepherds amid a great uproar hauled in to the king a young man with his hands bound behind him. As it turns out, when these men approached, this stranger surrendered himself for just this purpose, to be brought to the king and to open Troy to the Achaeans. He was resolved and prepared for either eventuality, to carry out his deception or to meet certain death. The Trojan youths, in their desire to see the captive, rushed in from all sides and surrounded him, and they made their mockery of the captive a contest.

Now listen to the Danaans' ambush and, from a single crime, come to know them all. As he stood there, distressed, unarmed, in full view of us all, and as he surveyed the Phrygian ranks, he spoke:

"Alas, in what land, on what seas am I welcome now? What is in store for me in my misery? I have no place anywhere among the Danaans. Worse still, the Dardanians themselves are hostile and demand punishment from me, with blood."

His anguished sobbing abolished all of our tense hostility toward him. We urged him to tell us who his parents were and what news he could provide, and to remember just how little credibility a captive commands. He remained silent for a long time. Finally, he put aside his fear and said the following:

"I will indeed tell you the whole story, King, whatever may come, and it will be the truth. First things first: I am a Greek, from Argos. And even if Fortune has made me, Sinon, a pathetic creature, she will not be greedy and make me false and deceptive as well.

"Perhaps in conversation the name of Palamedes, descendant of Belus, has reached your ears, as well as his far-renowned glory. With falsified evidence, the Pelasgians sent him down to death on a false charge of treason (because he opposed the war), although he was innocent. Now that he is dead, they mourn his loss. When I was very young, my destitute father sent me here to be this man's squire, as he was a close relative of ours. As long as he possessed a kingdom undiminished and was influential in the assemblies of kings, I too shared in his good reputation and glory. But after he left this land of the living because of resourceful Ulysses' grudge[1]—you know what I am referring to—I, broken, dragged my life out in mournful shadows, and I privately resented the tragedy of my guiltless friend. But foolishly I did not remain quiet, and I swore that if by some chance I ever reached our homeland of Argos in victory, I would avenge him. With these words I inflamed Ulysses' bitter animosity.

"This was my first step into misfortune. From then on, Ulysses was constantly threatening me with fresh recriminations and spreading suggestive words through the rank and file; he was looking for accomplices for his plan. In fact, he did not stop searching until he had Calchas in his pocket and—why am I revisiting this unhappy story? Why do I put off the inevitable? If you think all the Achaeans are the same, and all you need is to hear that I am a Greek, then go on, take your revenge. Ithacan Ulysses and the Atridae indeed would pay a great price to do just that."

Then, oblivious to the clever, horrible Pelasgian deception, we eagerly sought to know more and asked him what he meant. Sinon continued to tell his story with false words and feigned fear:

"Often the Danaans felt a great desire to abandon Troy, retreat, and give up the long war out of exhaustion. If only they had! But often a severe storm on the sea

[1] Because Palamedes had seen through Ulysses' attempt to get out of going to Troy. See Hyginus 95 and 105.

blocked their retreat, or a stiff south wind discouraged them from going. And it was when this horse was complete, its maple beams well-fitted, that the thunderclouds crashed most violently throughout the whole sky. We did not know what to do, and so we sent Eurypylus to consult the oracle of Phoebus Apollo, and that god sent forth these grim words from the inner sanctum:

> With blood you, Danaans, placated the winds with a maiden sacrificed
> when you first came to these regions of Ilium.
> With blood now must you seek your returns home by sacrificing
> the soul of an Argive.

"When the god's response reached the ears of the rank and file, their minds were struck with horror, and an icy chill ran deep down into their bones. Whose end was being readied? Whom was Apollo demanding?

"Then there was a great commotion, and the Ithacan dragged the seer Calchas before us all. He pressed him to reveal the will of the gods. Already many were predicting the cruel deed that the schemer had in store for me; they saw what was coming but said nothing in opposition. For ten days the seer remained silent. Shut in his tent, he refused to name anyone or subject him to death with his own utterance. At last the plan was afoot: at the agreed time Calchas, provoked by the Ithacan's great cries of outrage, broke his silence and designated me for the altar. Everyone approved, and since they had feared this evil for themselves, they did not protest when it fell onto the head of a single, miserable man.

"Already that awful day was at hand. They had prepared the sacred rites for me, the salted grains, the ribbons to fit around my head. I saved myself from this death—I admit it—and I broke my bonds. I hid myself in the reeds of a muddy pond, veiled by the night, waiting for them to set sail, if only they would! No longer could I hope to see my ancient homeland, my sweet children, or beloved father. The Greek leaders will probably demand punishment from them on account of my escape, and they will avenge this transgression with the death of my poor, innocent family. Therefore, I beg you, by the gods above and the powers that protect the truth, and by good faith, if any remains undefiled among mortals: please take pity on hardships so great, take pity on a soul that has suffered what it has not deserved."

Because of these tears we spared his life. Worse, we began to feel pity for him. Priam was the first to come forward, and he ordered the handcuffs and the tight chains to be removed, and he addressed him with the following kindly words:

"Whoever you are, from this point on, forget the Greeks. They are lost to you. You will be one of us. Please tell me the truth about these matters. Why did they erect this massive, hulking horse? Who built it? What do they want with it? Is there some religious purpose? Or is it a machine of war?"

He had spoken. And the captive, trained in Pelasgian trickery and deception, raised up his hands, now removed from the chains, to the sky and said:

"I call upon you, eternal fires of heaven, and your inviolable power to be my witness, and you, altar and ghastly swords that I fled, and the ribbons of the gods that I wore as a sacrificial victim: I have every right to break my hallowed allegiance to the Greeks, I have every right to hate those men and to bring everything to light, whatever they are concealing. I am no longer bound to my country's laws. You, Troy, make sure you keep your promises and your word in return for your salvation, if I report the truth, if I greatly repay you now.

"All the Danaans' hopes and confidence in undertaking the war resided in the aid of Pallas Athena. Now, ever since the time when Tydeus' son, a godless man, and Ulysses, the inventor of wickedness, undertook the mission to wrest the fateful Palladium from its sacred shrine, when they slaughtered the guards of the lofty citadel, stole the sacred statue, and dared to touch the virginal ribbons of the goddess with bloodied hands—from this time on the hopes of the Danaans slipped and faded away. Their forces were broken, the goddess' goodwill turned to hate. Tritonia made it known to us by omens by no means ambiguous. No sooner had the icon been put in the camp when fire flashed from her steely eyes and a salty sweat beaded on her body. Three times (an awesome sight) the goddess herself blazed up from the ground, bearing shield and shaking spear.

"Calchas divined that the Greeks should immediately take to flight over the seas and that the Pergamene towers could not be taken with Argive weapons, unless they were to consult oracles back in Argos and return the icon they had carried off over the sea on curved ships. Now the fact is that they have set sail for Mycenae and are preparing for a renewed war with the gods as their allies. They will soon cross the seas again and come upon you unexpectedly. Thus Calchas interpreted the omens. So advised, they erected this horse, as reparation for the Palladium and for the slighted goddess, to atone for their grim crime.

"Calchas, however, gave orders to raise this massive structure on frames of oak beams and to make it reach the sky so that it could not be admitted through the gates and led into the city and thus protect the people in place of the old religious icon. For if your hand were to violate the gift to Minerva, he said, then great destruction would rain down on Priam's kingdom and the Phrygians. But if your hand were to place it in your city, Asia would instead reach Pelops' walls in a great war, and this would be the destiny that awaits our grandchildren."

Through Sinon's exceptional skill at trickery and lies the story was believed. We were taken in by guile and forced tears—we who had never been conquered by Tydeus' son or Larisaean Achilles, by ten years or a thousand ships!

2d The Death of Laocoon (199–267)

Then our luckless men encountered something far more terrible, and it troubled our unsuspecting souls. Laocoon, chosen to be priest by lot, was sacrificing a huge bull to Neptune at the altars. Suddenly, two serpents with huge coils were coming across the calm seas from Tenedos. I shudder at the thought. They streaked across the sea, both going for the shoreline, side by side. Their chests and blood-red crests rose above the waves; the rest of them glided on top of the sea, their tails winding in sinuous curves. The choppy surf thundered.

Already they were on dry land. Their eyes were burning with blood and fire, and they were licking their lips with flickering tongues. We scattered, terrified. But the snakes never changed their course; they were heading straight for Laocoon. First, the snakes wound their way around the bodies of his two small children, squeezed, and fed on their limbs. Then they caught and bound with their huge coils Laocoon himself, who was rushing to their aid with spear in hand. They wrapped their scaly coils around his torso twice, his neck twice, and still their heads and necks towered high above him.

Laocoon raised awful cries to the heavens while he tried to pull the snakes from around his neck with his hands, his headdress covered with gore and black venom. His cries were like the bellowing of a wounded bull that has fled the altar after shaking from his neck the ax that missed its mark. The two serpents slithered up to the lofty shrine and citadel of savage Tritonia and hid themselves beneath the goddess' feet and the orb of her shield.

A new dread ran through our shaking hearts, and the explanation being bandied about was that Laocoon had paid the penalty for his wickedness because he had injured the sacred oak with a spear point. Shouts went up that the horse should be taken to its rightful place in the city and that the goddess' divinity should be supplicated.

So we opened up the walls and fortifications of the city. We all helped out with the work, some putting wheels under the horse, others tying thick ropes around its neck. The fateful machine, packed with soldiers, came through the walls. Boys and girls sang sacred songs and joyfully touched the ropes with their hands. It slipped in, towering over and threatening the middle of the city. O homeland! O Ilium, home of the gods! O Dardanian walls, renowned in war! Four times it halted on the very threshold of the gate, and four times the weapons rang out from inside the belly! Still, we pressed on, mindless, blinded by madness, and we placed the unhappy beast on the citadel. Then too did Cassandra, compelled by the god, begin to utter prophecies of what was to come, never believed by the Teucrians. No, we went around the city wreathing the sanctuaries of the gods with garlands of thanksgiving—pitiful fools, for this would be our final day.

Meanwhile the sky was turning and night was rushing down toward Ocean, covering the lands and sky—and the tricks of the Myrmidons—with a great shadow. The Teucrians throughout the city fell silent. A deep, sound sleep embraced their weary limbs. But already the Argive battalion was proceeding by ship from Tenedos through the friendly stillness of a silent moon. They were making for familiar shores. The flagship lit a signal fire, and Sinon, protected by the unfair practices of the gods, removed the bolts made of pine and let out the Danaans hidden inside the belly. The opened horse gave birth to those men, and happily they came out of the hollowed oak. The generals Thessandrus, Sthenelus, and dreadful Ulysses let down a rope and slithered down, as did Acamas, Thoas, Peleus' grandson Neoptolemus, foremost Machaon, Menelaus, and the fabricator of the plot himself, Epeos. They invaded the city, which was buried in sleep and wine. These men slaughtered the guards and threw open the gates to let in all of their comrades. The two conspiring parties were united.

2e Hector Appears in a Dream to Aeneas (268–301)

It was the time of night when the first, most welcome moments of rest begin to creep upon wearied mortals, a gift sent by the gods. Suddenly, in my dreams before my eyes stood Hector, gravely downcast, heaving great sobs of distress. He looked just like he had when he was brutally dragged behind the chariot, blackened by dark, bloody grime, the leather strap driven through his swollen feet. Alas, what a sight! How different he was from the Hector who returned to us in Achilles' armor or that had hurled Phrygian torches onto the ships of the Danaans! His beard was rough and unkempt, his hair matted with blood, his body bearing the numerous wounds he received fighting around his city's walls.

In my dreams I appeared to weep and address the man with these gloomy words:

"O light of Dardania, you most steadfast hope for the Teucrians, what has held you up for so long? From what place do you now come, Hector, long-awaited? How good it is for us in our utter exhaustion to look upon you now after the many deaths of your men, after the many hardships suffered by both men and city! What has caused your beaming face to become disfigured? What do these wounds I see mean?"

He did not respond to this, nor did he allow me to keep on asking meaningless questions. He let out a groan from deep within his chest and spoke:

"Flee, goddess-born! Save yourself from these flames. The enemy holds the city. Troy is utterly and completely fallen. This is it for Priam and his country. If the Pergamene towers could be saved by someone's right hand, it would have already been saved by this one, mine. To you Troy entrusts her sacred possessions and her Penates. Take these as comrades of your destiny. Go find for them a great city that you will build after you have covered the whole sea in your wanderings."

Thus he spoke, and with his own hands he brought forth from the inner chambers of the temple potent Vesta, festooned in ribbons, and the eternal flame.

Meanwhile, the city's walls were resounding with shouts of lamentation coming from all sides, and although my father Anchises' house was set away from the city and hidden from view by a screen of trees, the chill clanging and clashing of weapons grew ever clearer as it advanced toward us.

2f Aeneas Awakens and Enters the Fray (302–346)

I was driven from my slumber. I climbed to the highest point on the roof and stood there listening with ears alert. It sounded like it does when raging winds drive fire onto the crops or when mountain floods in a raging torrent lay waste to the lush fruits in the fields, the efforts of oxen, uprooting trees. The shepherd perched on a rocky point, when he hears this sound, is dumbstruck and helpless.

Then the Danaans' guile was exposed, their ambush revealed. Deiphobus' grand house was already overwhelmed by Vulcan's fire and had collapsed. Ucalegon's was already ablaze next door. The wide Sigean waters were aglow with fire.

Then arose the shouts of men and the blasts of trumpets. Blindly I took up my arms—there is no reasoning in war. No, my thoughts burned to amass a band of men for war and to rally our allies on the citadel. My good judgment was thrust out by madness and rage. Death on the battlefield was glorious.

Suddenly, Panthus son of Othryas, priest of Phoebus' temple on the citadel, slipped out of the Greeks' onslaught, running madly toward my father's door. He was lugging the sacred objects, the conquered gods, and his small grandson.

"Where is the worst fighting, Panthus? What stronghold do we possess?"

I had barely gotten this out when he groaned and responded:

"The final day, the last, unavoidable day of Dardania is upon us! We Trojans are done for! Ilium and the Teucrians' glory are lost! Savage Jupiter has transferred all of our power to Argos. The Danaans are masters over a city in flames. Armed men are pouring out of the horse that towers over the city center. Sinon triumphantly hurls torches and mocks us. All the rest stand at the double gates of the city, however many thousands came from great Mycenae. Still others have set up a blockade along the narrow streets, their weapons set out in front. A line of steel stands there, sharp edges gleaming, ready for slaughter. The sentries at the gates are trying to make a battle out of it, but show little resistance because they are fighting blindly."

Panthus' words of desperation and the will of the gods drove me into the fires and fray, wherever grim Fury called, wherever the roar and shouts of war reached the heavens. Joining me were Rhipeus and Epytus, an awesome fighter, who surfaced in the moonlight. Hypanis and Dymas also assembled at our side, along with Mygdon's young son, Coroebus, who had by chance just recently arrived at Troy, burning with a mad lust for Cassandra. In hopes of marriage he was offering his assistance to Priam and the Phrygians—unlucky soul, if only he had listened to his raving fiancée's predictions!

2g Aeneas Addresses His Men, and the Battle Begins (347–434)

When I saw that all of them were assembled in tight quarters and were yearning for battle, I began:

"Men! Hearts hopelessly brave! If you have resolved to risk everything and follow me, consider what the situation is. Gone are all the gods on which our power depended. They have abandoned our temples and altars. You are bringing help to a city already in flames. Let us die and rush into the fray. The only salvation for the conquered is to expect none."

This added rage to my men's bravery. Just like voracious wolves in a dark mist who are driven blindly by a gnawing hunger and whose cubs wait for them with thirsty throats, we charged through the enemy's weapons into death that was assured, and we held a steadfast course to the city's center. The dark night embraced us with its enveloping shadow.

Who could with mere words describe the carnage? Who could possibly find enough tears for our troubles that night? Our venerable city came crashing down after many years of supremacy. Our streets, homes, and temples sacred to the gods were littered with lifeless bodies. And it was not only the Teucrians who paid the price with their blood; sometimes courage even returns to the hearts of the vanquished, and even though victorious, Danaans fell too. Everywhere you looked there was grim lamentation, everywhere dread and the pervasive image of death.

The first Danaan to present himself to us was Androgeos with his large contingent. He thought that the two units were allies, and he spurred us on with encouraging words:

"Hasten, men! Has some laziness kept you from the action for so long? The others are already sacking and looting the blazing Pergamene towers. Have you just now come from the tall ships?"

He spoke, and immediately (our reaction was suspicious) it struck him that he had stumbled upon the enemy. In shock he checked his step and choked back his voice, just like a man who steps on a snake lurking beneath the brush on the ground and jumps back in terror when it raises its swollen, bluish head in anger. Just so Androgeos was trying to fall back, shaking from the sight.

We charged upon them and surrounded them with a dense field of weapons. They were in disorder, unsure of where they were, stricken with terror, and we struck them down. Fortune blessed our first encounter.

Then Coroebus, triumphant and confident after our victory, spoke:

"Comrades! Let us follow the path to safety that favorable fortune is providing us and put on the Danaans' shields and their uniforms. Guile or valor? No one asks in war. The Greeks themselves will provide us weapons."

He spoke and then put on Androgeos' crested helmet and his beautiful, distinctive shield. He clipped an Argive sword to his side. Rhipeus followed suit, as did Dymas and the whole battalion of men. Each armed himself with the spoils from his recent kill.

We charged in, intermingled with the Greek ranks, under the protection of a power not our own. Many were the encounters, many were the battles we fought during the shadowy night, and many were the Danaans we sent to Orcus. Others scattered and ran away to their secure beachhead and their ships; still others disgracefully fell back to the huge horse, climbed in, and hid in the familiar womb.

Alas! No one should have confidence in unwilling gods. No! Priam's young daughter, Cassandra, her hair disheveled, was dragged away from the inner chamber of Minerva's temple. She hopelessly held her burning eyes heavenward, yes, her eyes, since bonds were preventing her from using her tender hands. Coroebus could not endure this sight and, his mind blinded with fury, threw himself into the middle of the swarm, death in sight. We all followed after him, and then two things happened. First, we were assailed by friendly fire from the high rooftop of the temple; a most pitiful slaughter erupted because of the shape of our weapons and the confusion caused by the Greeks' helmets. Then the angry uproar over our rescuing Cassandra brought the Danaans together from all sides—the extremely fierce Ajax, the twin Atridae, the whole army of the Dolopians. They attacked us, just as when opposing winds, Zephyrus, Notus, and Eurus, joyful on Eos' horses, collide in a great stormburst; trees ripple and crack; and foamy Nereus whips up the seas top to bottom with his trident.

Also appearing on the scene were all those men we had earlier routed and driven over the whole city in the dark night's shadow. They were the first to recognize the deceptive shields and weapons and to note that our speech seemed strange. Immediately, we were overwhelmed by their sheer number. Coroebus was the first to fall under Peneleus' blow at the altar of the all-powerful goddess. Rhipeus too fell, although he was the fairest and most just there ever was among the Teucrians. The gods thought otherwise. Both Hypanis and Dymas perished, impaled by the spears of our own men. Neither your great piety, Panthus, nor the wreath of Apollo could save you from passing on from this world.

Ashes of Troy, the final fire that consumed my people! You are my witnesses that during your collapse I never avoided any weapon, any exchange with the Danaans, and that if I had been fated to die, I would have earned it by my actions.

2h The Battle Around Priam's Palace (434–505)

We were torn away from that spot, drawn by the uproar that erupted around Priam's palace. Iphitus and Pelias were with me, but the former was hobbled by old age, the latter by a wound from Ulysses. There we saw a truly awesome battle, as if no other battles were being fought in the city, as if no one anywhere else was dying. We saw a mighty battle: The Danaans were charging the walls, besieging the city in the tortoise-formation. Ladders clung to the walls. Men stood on the rungs just in front of the doorways, holding out with their left hands shields against the enemy's weapons and grasping the rooftop with their right.

The Dardanians on the other side were pulling apart the towers and the whole roof. These were the weapons that they readied in their last-ditch defense, in the very jaws of death, when they saw what was coming. They sent down gilded beams, the proud ornaments of their ancient forefathers. Others drew their swords and blockaded the entranceway in tight formation. My resolve was renewed to relieve the king's palace, to bring aid and assistance to our men, to add vigor to the vanquished.

Priam's palace had a hidden entrance, unseen doors with service passageways that linked the different buildings together. In the rear there was an abandoned side door, which Andromache used when she went alone to visit her in-laws or take her boy Astyanax to see his grandfather. I used this to go up to the rooftop, where the miserable Teucrians were vigorously hurling missiles down, in vain. A tall tower, built on top of the highest part of the palace, reaching for the stars, stood precariously on the edge. From this vantage they used to survey all of Troy, the Danaan ships, and their camps. We set upon the tower on all sides with crowbars, where the upper stories offered loose joints. We wrenched it off its lofty perch and pushed it over. It suddenly slipped off its foundation and collapsed with a crash, coming down in a wide swath on the ranks of the Danaans. But others came up and replaced them, and in the meantime neither rocks nor other missiles ceased to fall.

Right at the front entrance to the palace Pyrrhus ran amok, shaking his weapon, bronze light glinting from his armor. He was just like a poisonous snake returning to the light from its hibernating hole where it has spent frigid winter nights. Now renewed, its old skin shed and shining anew, it unrolls its slippery body and thrusts its underside high toward the sun, licking its mouth with the flicker of its forked tongue.

With Pyrrhus were giant Periphas and Automedon, once the charioteer and arms-bearer of Achilles, and all the Scyrian men. They advanced as one on the palace and hurled torches onto the rooftops. In the front ranks Pyrrhus himself with ax in hand hacked through the hard doors, wrenching the bronze pins from their hinges. Soon he had cut out a wooden beam, boring through the hard timber, making a wide, gaping breach.

The house inside came into view and the long hallways were revealed. The sanctum of Troy's venerable kings was visible, and the Greeks saw armed men standing just inside the door. The interior of the palace was filled with commotion and pitiful groans, and deep within the hollow halls echoed the howls of women's lamentation. Their cries struck against the fiery stars above. Terror-stricken mothers wandered throughout the huge palace or held onto the doorways and kissed them.

Pyrrhus pressed on with violence matching his father's. Neither the bars on the doors nor the guards could hold him off. The doorway shook with frequent blows from the battering ram. The doors lay flat, knocked off their hinges. Force made a way. The Danaans burst through the entry, slaughtered the forward guard, and flooded the palace with soldiers. It was worse than when a foaming river has broken through the levies and the flood waters have poured over the barriers in a massive rush, when they rage and rush down into the tilled fields in a mass and tow the livestock along with their stables over the plains.

I myself saw Neoptolemus seething for slaughter and the Atridae too. I saw Hecuba, one hundred young women, and Priam, defiling with his blood the fires he had himself consecrated. The hundred bedchambers, the great hopes for grandchildren, and the magnificent doorways adorned with the golden spoils of the barbarians—all were destroyed. The Danaans occupied what the fire had not burned.

2i Aeneas Describes the Death of Priam (506–558)

Perhaps you would like to know what happened to Priam. When he saw the doom of the captured city and that the enemy had crashed through the entrance and now occupied the inner parts of his palace, he armed himself with the weapons of his youth, shoulders trembling, now too old. He attached to his side a useless sword. He headed out into the great host of the enemy and into certain death.

In the middle of the palace there was a huge altar beneath the open sky. Nearby an ancient laurel tree hung over it and embraced the household gods with its shadow. Here Hecuba and her daughters sat close together, embracing the statues of the gods. When she saw Priam wearing the armor fit for a young man, she said:

"What grim intention, miserable soul, has compelled you to arm yourself with these weapons? Where are you going? This is not the time for this kind of help or defense. No, not even if my Hector were here now. Come, retreat to this spot. Either this altar will protect us all, or we will all die together."

Thus she spoke and sat the old man down by the altar.

Suddenly, Polites, one of Priam's sons, slipped away from Pyrrhus' onslaught and was fleeing through the missiles, through the enemy, along the broad colonnades and the empty rooms, wounded. Pyrrhus was ablaze and pursuing him with a weapon poised to kill. Now and again he almost had him, pressing hard on his heels with his spear. When Polites eventually reached the eyes of his parents, he fell, pouring out his life in a great deal of blood. Then Priam, although in the grip of death, did not hold off or refrain from expressing his anger:

"May the gods above repay your crime with just punishments, since you forced me to view the death of my son and defiled a father's countenance with his death. And yet, that famous man, whom you falsely swear is your father, Achilles, was not so heartless toward me, Priam, though I was his enemy. No, he respected the rights and good faith of a suppliant, and so he returned Hector's lifeless body to me for burial and sent me back to my kingdom."

Thus the elder man spoke and weakly threw a spear that did not penetrate the clanging shield but was beaten back, and it stuck on the surface of its boss.

Pyrrhus responded:

"You, then, will go to my father, the son of Peleus, and take him this message yourself. Remember to tell him about my awful deeds and how Neoptolemus is worse than his father. Now die!"

As he spoke, he dragged Priam to the altar, trembling and slipping in the great pool of his son's blood. Neoptolemus gripped Priam's hair with his left hand; with his right he unsheathed his flashing sword and buried it to the hilt in his side.

This was the last moment of Priam's appointed destiny, this was the fated end that stole him away as he gazed upon Troy in flames and the Pergamene towers in ruins. The man who once ruled so proudly over so many lands and peoples of Asia, his huge torso now lies on the shore, head wrenched from shoulders, a body without name.

6.237–6.755 Aeneas Goes to the Underworld

Odysseus' visit to the underworld in Homer's Odyssey *is Vergil's model, but with many important differences. Homer in no uncertain terms treats the underworld as a grim place; we are all subject to death, and death brings no joy. Vergil, on the other hand, incorporated philosophical ideas about death and the underworld, not least of which is the Pythagorean notion of metempsychosis, whereby souls of certain men are reborn in new bodies on earth (compare the Myth of Er in Plato,* Republic *10). Further, Vergil gives a coherent picture of the underworld, dividing it into three sections: Limbo, where the souls of the unfortunate are located; Tartarus, where the wicked are punished; and the Blessed Groves, where heroes enjoy a blissful afterlife (**see Map of the Underworld, p. xli**). Aeneas is guided through the underworld by the Sibyl, Apollo's priestess at Cumae in southern Italy, who has already helped Aeneas get the Golden Bough, a magical branch required for the living to visit the underworld.*

6a The Way to the Underworld (237–268)

The cave of Avernus was deep, gaping monstrously like jaws, jagged and sheltered by a dark pool and the shadows of the forest. No winged creature could direct its flight safely above it, so noxious were the fumes pouring forth from its dark fissures into the dome of heaven.[2] Here the priestess first set out four steers with hides of black and tipped out wine upon their brows. Then she clipped the ends of the bristles between their horns and placed them, the first offerings, onto the sacred fires, voicing an invocation to Hecate, powerful in heaven as in Erebus. Her attendants put the sacrificial knives beneath their necks and caught the warm blood in bowls. Aeneas himself struck with his sword a black-fleeced lamb for the mother of the Eumenides and her great sister,[3] and for you, Proserpina, a sterile cow. Then he fashioned nocturnal altars for the Stygian king and placed the carcasses of the bulls upon the flames whole, pouring luxurious oil over their burning entrails. Then suddenly, just before the first rays of the rising sun, the ground beneath their feet began to moan, the treetops swayed, and the sound of howling dogs was heard through the shadows as the goddess drew nearer.

"Away! O stand away, all who are impure," cried the priestess. "Step not into the grove. But you, Aeneas, enter upon this path and unsheathe your sword. Now, Aeneas, is the time for courage, now, for a stout heart."

So much she spoke, seized by madness, and she hurled herself through the open cave. Aeneas kept pace with his guide as she went, with strides that showed no fear.

Gods who lord over spirits! Souls of the silent dead! Chaos and Phlegethon, wide expanses plunged in the silence of night! Sanction me to tell what I have heard. Sanction me by your will to reveal the secrets hidden deep within the murky darkness of the earth.

6b The Descent into the Underworld (269–294)

They, but dim silhouettes, made their way beneath the lonely night through the shadows, through the empty lands of Dis, his lifeless kingdom, as if on a journey

[2] The line, "This is why the Greeks called the place 'Aornos,' " was added here, most likely by a later scribe, to make explicit Vergil's allusion to the origin of the name Avernus, for *aornos* means "birdless."

[3] Night and Earth, respectively.

through a forest beneath the stingy light of a shrouded moon when Jupiter has buried the heavens in shadows and black night has robbed the world of its colors. Before the very courtyard, in the outer jaws of Orcus, Mourning and avenging Guilts have their quarters. Beside them dwell pale Diseases, grim Old Age, Fear, evil-urging Hunger, disgraceful Poverty—terrible apparitions all—Death and Toil, then Death's own brother Sleep, and the evils of men's minds, Joys. In the entranceway before them sit War the death-bearer, the Eumenides in their iron chambers, and demonic Discord, who ties back her hair of snakes with gore-soaked bands of wool. In the middle, a dark massive elm spreads out its branches, its ancient arms, and it is here—so common legend says—that false Dreams have their perch, clinging upside down beneath every leaf. There are many other monstrous beasts too: along the doorway the Centaurs have their stalls, as do the double-formed Scyllas, hundred-bodied Briareus, the dreadfully hissing beast of Lerna, the flame-breathing Chimaera, Gorgons, Harpies, and the shadowy, three-bodied shade.[4]

Here, trembling in sudden terror, Aeneas ripped his sword from its sheath and held the blade before him to meet the advancing shades, and if his wise companion had not told him that they were tenuous life forces without body, fluttering beneath the empty appearance of form, he would have rushed upon them, hacking vainly through the shadows with his sword.

6c The Ferryman Charon and the Crowd of Souls (295–336)

From here leads the way to the waters of Tartarean Acheron. This deep-swirling, murky abyss boils and bubbles and belches all of its silt into Cocytus. The waters of this stream are watched by the ferryman Charon, a ghastly, squalid figure: upon his chin sits an unkempt mass of white hair, his eyes are fixed and fiery, and a filthy cloak drapes down from a knot on his shoulder. Alone, he pushes the boat away from shore with a pole. Alone, he attends to the sails. And, alone, he conveys the bodies across in his dusky boat, an old man now, but his is a god's old age, robust and vigorous.

Here a great throng was swarming down to the shores to meet him: mothers and husbands, bodies of great-hearted heroes robbed of life, young boys and unmarried girls, men in the prime of their lives placed on pyres before their parents' eyes—as many souls as leaves that fall in the forests under autumn's first freeze, or birds that flock together on land coming off the deep sea when the wintry season forces them across the main in search of sunny climes. They stood there, pleading to be the first to cross, and they stretched out their hands, yearning for the bank on the other side. But the grim captain took on some passengers here, some there, and all the rest he warded off, keeping them far away from the sandy bank.

Aeneas looked on in wonder, moved by the commotion, and said, "Tell me, O virgin priestess, what does this rush to the river mean? What do these souls want? Why do some souls walk away from the shore, while others sweep across the deep-hued river under oar?"

To him did the aged priestess return this brief reply, "Son of Anchises, true scion of the gods, what you see are the pools of Cocytus and the marshes of Styx, on whose divine waters the gods fear making and breaking their oaths. The whole crowd you see

[4] Geryon.

here on the shore are the destitute and unburied souls. The ferryman is Charon. Those who you see ferried upon the water are the buried—he is forbidden to ferry souls across these raucous waters to the distant dread banks until their bones have found rest in their graves. For one hundred years these souls flit about upon these shores. Only then are they at last allowed to come back to the pools that they long to cross."

Anchises' son stopped and checked his step, deep in thought and feeling pity for their hard lot. There he made out two gloomy figures, men unburied, without death's honor, Leucaspis and the Lycian fleet's commander, Orontes, who sailed from Troy together over the blustery seas until the South Wind overwhelmed them, swamping both ships and men with water.

6d Aeneas Meets with Palinurus, His Former Helmsman (337–383)

Suddenly, Aeneas saw his helmsman Palinurus drawing near. Just days before, he had fallen from the stern while observing the stars on their journey from Libya, sent sprawling amidst the swells of the sea. When Aeneas made out the dim figure of his gloomy comrade in the thick shadows, he addressed him, "What god was it, Palinurus, who stole you from us and drowned you in the middle of the sea? Come, tell us. Never before has Apollo been found deceitful, yet in this one oracle have I been misled: he prophesied that you would not be harmed on the sea and would make it to the land of Ausonia[5]—and this is how he keeps his word!"

Palinurus answered, "Phoebus' tripod did not mislead you, my leader, son of Anchises, nor was I drowned in the sea by a god. No, it was the rudder, my assigned post. I was holding on to it, guiding the ship's course, when it was wrenched off by some great force, and I fell with it headfirst overboard. I swear on the harsh seas that I did not fear for myself as much as for your ship, that, stripped of its controls and bereft of its pilot, it might falter amidst such mighty swells. For three stormy nights the South Wind tossed me violently across the vast open seas. On the fourth day, when the crest of a wave lifted me skyward, I could barely make out Italy in the distance. Gradually I paddled toward shore. Finally, I was on dry land and safe, I thought, when the savage inhabitants, mistaking me for some worthy prey, swept down upon me with swords as I, weighed down in water-logged clothes, clutched at the jagged top of the headland crag with grasping hands. Now the surf holds me, and the winds buffet me on the shore. Therefore, I beg you, invincible spirit, by the sweet light and air of heaven, by your father, and by your son Iulus' bright future, save me from my evils! Either seek out Velia's port and toss some earth upon me—for you can—or if there is some way, if your divine mother shows you some way (and it is not, I think, without the gods' will that you intend to sail on these dreadful streams and the marshes of Styx), offer me, a pitiful soul, your right hand and take me along with you over the waters, so that at least in death I might find some peaceful resting place."

This much he had spoken when the prophetess broke in, "Whence did such a dreadful desire come upon you? Do you, though unburied, intend to behold the waters of Styx and the merciless stream of the Eumenides? Or to approach the bank unbidden? Give up your hopes that prayer can alter the gods' decrees. But take you these words to heart as solace for your hard trial: Neighboring peoples in cities far

[5] Italy.

and wide will be driven by heaven-sent omens to appease your bones. They will build you a tomb, and at that tomb they will perform yearly rituals, and the place will forever bear Palinurus' name."[6]

Palinurus' cares were soothed by her words, and for a moment in time his sullen heart felt no pain, only joy at the land that bears his name.

6e Aeneas and the Sibyl Present the Golden Bough and Cross the River (384–425)

They continued on their journey and approached the river. When the boatman caught sight of them from the Stygian marsh as they made their way through the silent grove and turned their steps to the riverside, he spoke first, upbraiding Aeneas with menacing words, "Whoever you are who approach our streams with sword drawn, stay where you are. Tell me why have you come. Come no further! This is the realm of shades, sleep, and drowsy night. It is forbidden to ferry living bodies upon my Stygian vessel. When Alcides came, I did not delight in taking him on board, or Theseus and Pirithous, although they were born of gods and were of indomitable strength. Hercules sought to put the guard of Tartarus in chains and dragged the trembling beast away from the throne of the king himself. The other two attempted to lead our queen out of Dis' bedchamber."

The Amphrysian priestess gave this brief reply, "We bring no such tricks here—do not be alarmed—nor does his weapon bring violence. Let the massive warden of this realm forever terrify the bloodless shades by barking in his cave. Let Proserpina remain chaste and watch over her uncle's home. This is Trojan Aeneas, renowned for his devotion and valor, who has journeyed down into the deepest darkness of Erebus to find his father. And if the image of such devotion does not move you at all, then perhaps"—she took out the bough hidden in her dress—"you might recognize this bough."

And at that, the anger that swelled in Charon's heart subsided. No more was said. He gazed in wonder at the venerable gift, the fateful bough, now seen again after so long a time, and he turned and brought his dark-blue vessel to the shore. Then he shoved aside the other souls seated on the long benches and cleared the gangways to let great Aeneas onto the vessel. The boat, its planks roped together, groaned under the weight, and the craft let in a flood of marsh water through its cracks. At length Charon safely ferried both hero and seer across the river's expanse and unloaded them upon the formless mud and the drab reeds on the other side.

Massive Cerberus makes this realm resound with his three-throated barking. His monstrous frame lay in the cave before them. When the seer saw that the snakes upon his necks were already hissing and bristling, she threw him a cake drugged with honey and magical flour. Ravenous with hunger, Cerberus opened wide his three jaws and wolfed down the treat. His monstrous backside went limp, and he collapsed upon the ground, his hugeness extending across the whole cave. Aeneas raced through the entrance now that the guard was buried in sleep, escaping the bank of the river that allows no return.

[6] The place is still known in Italy as Capo Palinuro.

6f Aeneas Enters Limbo (426–493)

Cries were heard immediately in the first area, great wailing, the souls of infants weeping, souls never tasting sweet life, snatched from their mothers' breasts, stolen by the black day of doom, buried in bitter death. Next were those condemned to death under false accusations, but their resting places were not allotted without a trial, without a judge. For the inquisitor Minos presides over the court. He controls the selection of judges, convenes the jury of silent dead, and learns of their lives and the charges against them. The next region was occupied by those guiltless but unhappy souls who brought death unto themselves by their own hand and in their loathing of the light threw away their lives on earth. How they would now choose to endure poverty and hard toil under the skies above! But immutable law stands in their way. The grim marsh, that hateful water, hems them in, and the nine winding circles of the Styx confine them.

Not far from here, spreading as far as the eye can see, the Fields of Mourning—the name given to them in stories—came into view. Here, concealed in secret groves and hidden by a forest of myrtle, reside those consumed by the savage wasting caused by pitiless love. Their pangs of love do not leave them even in death. In these places Aeneas saw Phaedra, Procris, and gloomy Eriphyle, revealing the wounds inflicted by her hard-hearted son, as well as Evadne and Pasiphae. Beside them walked Laodamia, and the once male Caeneus, now a woman, returned by fate to her original form.

Among them was Phoenician Dido, wandering through the great forest, her wound still fresh. As soon as the Trojan hero stopped and made out her barely visible figure through the dim shadows—just like when a man either sees, or thinks he has seen, the moon rise through the clouds at the month's beginning—he released a flood of tears and spoke to her out of sweet love, "Ill-starred Dido, so the message that came to me was true after all, that you brought an end to your life with a sword. Alas, was I the cause of your death? I swear by the stars and the gods above, and by whatever faith resides in earth's depths, it was against my will, Queen, that I left your shores. It was the gods' orders—the same that now compel me to go through these shadows, these moldering, rough places, and the deep night—that drove me to do their bidding. I could not have fathomed that my departure would bring such great pain to you. Stop! Don't take yourself from my sight! Why are you running away? This is the final time the fates will allow me to address you."

With such words Aeneas tried to comfort the soul of the seething, glaring woman, and he began to weep. She turned away and kept her eyes fixed firmly on the ground, and as Aeneas spoke, her expression changed no more than if she were hard flint or the ragged cliffs of Marpessus. At last she tore herself away, full of hate, and retreated to the shade-giving grove, where her former husband, Sychaeus, soothed her cares and requited her love. Shaken by her hard lot, Aeneas followed after her at a distance as she went, with tears in his eyes and pity in his heart.

From there he pressed on his appointed journey. Soon they reached the last of the fields, the secluded haunts of celebrated warriors. He first encountered Tydeus, then Parthenopaeus, renowned in war, and the pale ghost of Adrastus. He then met men much wept for among the living, the war-fallen, his fellow Dardanians. When he saw them all filing out in one long train, he gave out a deep groan, Glaucus, Medon, Thersilochus, Antenor's three sons, Ceres' priest Polyboetes, and Idaeus, who even in death still held fast to his chariot and his war gear. The souls crowded around him on his left and right, and it was not enough just to see him once; they delighted in detaining him, walking alongside him, and learning the reasons why he had come. But when the leaders of the Danaans and Agamemnon's battalions saw the man and the flash of his weapons through the shadows, they quaked in great fear. Some ran away as they once had run for their ships; others tried to raise their war cry, a pitiful whimper, their shout cut short, mocking their gaping mouths.

6g Aeneas Meets His Fellow Trojan Deiphobus (494–547)

Then he saw Priam's son Deiphobus, his whole body mutilated. His face was savagely cut up, his face and both hands, his ears torn from his ravaged head, and his nose lopped off to the nostrils, a dishonorable wound. Thus Aeneas barely recognized him as he cowered and tried to cover up his grisly punishments. He went out of his way to address him in a familiar voice, "Valiant Deiphobus, descendant of great Teucer's bloodline! Who chose to exact their revenge in so cruel a fashion? Who could have treated you like this? Word came to me that on Troy's final night you, with nothing left to give after your great slaughter of Pelasgians, fell dead atop the great tangled mountain of carnage. Then with my own hands I built an empty tomb on the Rhoetean shore, and I hailed your spirit three times in a great voice. There your name on stone and a tribute of arms mark the spot. I was unable, friend, to find you as I left and lay your bones to rest in our native land."

To these words Priam's son responded, "You, friend, have left nothing undone. You have performed every rite owed to Deiphobus, to the ghost of his corpse. No, it was my fate and the deadly crime of the Spartan woman that drowned me in these evils. It was she who left me these mementos. You know that we spent our last night amidst misguided happiness—it is all too deeply etched in our minds. When that fateful horse bounded up the lofty towers of Pergamum and produced armed infantry from its pregnant belly, that woman in a mock choral procession led Phrygian women around the city chanting "*Euhoe*" in Bacchic frenzy. She herself stood in the middle and from the highest point in the city hoisted a huge torch above her, a beacon for the Danaans. Then, exhausted from toil and overpowered by sleep, I was held fast in an ill-omened bridal chamber, where I lay, subdued by a sweet deep stillness, very much like peaceful death.

"Meanwhile, that outstanding wife of mine took every weapon from my halls—she even slipped my trusty sword out from under my pillow! She then called Menelaus into my house, opening up the doors for him in the hope, of course, that her actions would be a great peace-offering to her lover and that the infamy of her past ills would be erased. But why drag the story out? They burst into my bedchamber, together with that inciter of crimes, Aeolus' descendant, Ulysses. Gods, pay back the Greeks in kind if I demand these punishments with a pure mouth! But you, Aeneas, come, tell us in turn what has brought you here while you are still alive. Have you been driven here off-course in your wanderings over the sea? Were you directed by the gods? Or have you been dogged by such misfortune that you have come to these homes without sun, these dismal places?"

At this point of their conversation, Aurora upon her rosy chariot had already crossed the midpoint of her heavenly circuit, and they would have spent all the allotted time talking like this, if Aeneas' companion, the Sibyl, had not admonished him tersely, "Night is falling, Aeneas, and we are drawing out the hours in tears. Here is the spot where the road forks. The right path leads down to the walls of mighty Dis. This is the one that will take us to Elysium. But the left path—that one leads the wicked to their punishments and sends them along to unholy Tartarus."

Deiphobus replied, "No need for wrath, great priestess. I will depart, take my proper place, retire to the shadows. Onward, glory of our race, onward! And may you enjoy a better fate." He spoke, and as he did, he turned and walked away.

6h The Sibyl Describes Tartarus (548–627)

Aeneas turned and suddenly saw, down beneath the cliff on the left, an extensive fortress encircled by three walls. Around it flowed a violent river, licking the walls with its scorching flames, Tartarean Phlegethon, tossing crashing boulders as it went. The massive gate faced them, a gate with pillars of solid adamantine, which neither mortal force nor the dwellers of heaven themselves could tear down in war. An iron turret towered above the rest, and Tisiphone, wrapped in her bloody robe, sat perched upon it, watching over the entryway sleeplessly, both night and day. From here you could hear groans, the lashes of brutal beatings, the screech of grating iron too, and chains being dragged. Aeneas stopped and took in the noises, terrified: "What kind of crimes are here? Please tell me, virgin priestess. What punishments cause their suffering? What is the reason for this terrible lamentation?"

The seer spoke, "Renowned leader of the Teucrians, no pure person is allowed to step through the Gateway of Wickedness. But when Hecate put me in charge of Avernus' sacred grove, she herself taught me the punishments that the gods dole out and took me through it all. This hard, brutal realm is under the dominion of Cnossian Rhadamanthus. He reprimands them, listens to their web of lies, and forces each to confess what sins they committed in the world above, thinking they had gained happiness with their hollow deceit, only to atone for it later in death. Upon the guilty the Avenger Tisiphone, armed with a whip, immediately leaps down and lashes them, thrusting menacing snakes in their faces with her left hand and summoning her grim band of sisters. Finally, with a frightening grating sound, the Gates of the Damned swing open. You see what sort of guard looms over the courtyard, what grim shape watches over the doors—well, something even more savage resides inside, the monstrous Hydra, her fifty black jaws gaping wide. Behind her, Tartarus itself falls off sharply, plunging deep beneath the shadows of the underworld twice as far as the distance of a man's gaze heavenward into aethereal Olympus. Here dwells the ancient brood of Earth, the band of Titans, cast down by the thunderbolt's blast, wallowing in the deep abyss.

"Here too I saw the twin sons of Aloeus, monstrous bodies, who tried to tear down mighty heaven with their bare hands and topple Jupiter from his lofty throne. I also saw Salmoneus suffering cruel punishments, retribution for his sins, as he mimicked Jupiter's flames and Olympus' rumblings. Through the peoples of Greece, through the city in the heart of Elis, he rode upon a four-horse chariot, brandishing a torch, exulting and demanding to be honored like a god—lunatic, mimicking the storms and inimitable thunder with bronze and the galloping of hooved horses! The almighty Father from the dense cloud cover hurled his missile—no firebrand or smoky pine-torch this—and threw him head over heels in a mighty whirlwind. There too Tityos, the nursling of all-creating Earth, could be seen, his body lying outstretched over six entire acres. A monstrous vulture, its hooked beak plucking out his immortal liver and intestines, fertile for punishment, probes for its feast and lives deep inside his chest, and there is no rest for his organs ever renewed. Why should I tell of the Lapiths, Ixion and Pirithous, over whom hangs a dark boulder, always on the verge of falling, appearing as if it were? The golden frames of the festal couch gleam, and a sumptuous banquet prepared in royal style is set out before them. But the eldest of the Furies crouches nearby and prevents the meal from being touched. She rears up, holding her torch up high, and booms in a thunderous voice.

"Here too reside those who in life hated their brothers, beat a parent, or cheated a dependent; those who stingily guarded the riches they acquired and refused to set aside a share for their families (this group of sinners is enormous). Then there are adulterers cut down for their crimes, generals who prosecuted wars against their country, and men who felt no shame in breaking the promises they made to their masters. Jailed, they await their punishment. Do not ask what punishment they face or what sort of fashion or fortune has buried these men in ruin. Some roll huge rocks. Others hang suspended, bound spread-eagle on the spokes of wheels. Ill-starred Theseus sits eternally anchored to his seat. Phlegyas in the depths of woe issues his warning to all. He spreads his message through the shadows with his loud voice, 'Learn righteousness—be you warned—and do not scorn the gods!' Another sold out his country for gold and installed a powerful master; for a price he enacted laws, and for a price he annulled them. Then there is the one who violated his daughter's bedchamber, engaging in forbidden nuptials. All dared monstrous crimes, all accomplished what they dared. I could not, even if I had one hundred tongues, one hundred mouths, and a voice of iron, recount every form of crime or name every punishment."

6i Aeneas Enters the Blessed Groves (628–678)

When the venerable priestess of Phoebus finished her account, she said, "But come now, push on and complete the mission you have undertaken. We must move faster. I can see the walls forged in the Cyclopes' forges and the gates in the archway before us. This is where we have been directed to place this gift as an offering."

She had spoken. Going side by side through the dark ways, they hurried across the intervening space and approached the doors. Aeneas quickly took up position at the entrance and sprinkled his body with fresh water. Then he planted the bough in the doorway before him. With this done at last, his duty to the goddess fulfilled, they came to the lush lands, the charming greenery of the Blessed Groves, blissful resting places. Here a loftier expanse of air embraced the fields and clothed them in a brilliant light. They enjoy their own sun, their own stars. Some were exercising in the grassy yards, competing in sport or wrestling on golden sand. Others were pounding the earth with their feet in dance as they sang. There too the Thracian priest,[7] dressed in a long robe, accompanied their rhythms with seven notes, playing the same notes now with his fingers, now with his ivory pick. Here lay the ancient race of Teucer, a most beautiful brood, great-hearted heroes born in a better age, Ilus,

[7] Orpheus.

Assaracus, and Dardanus, the founder of Troy. Aeneas admired the men's weapons and their empty chariots. Spears stood fixed in the ground, and their teams, unharnessed, grazed here and there over the fields. The same joy they took from their arms and chariots while they were alive, the same care they took in pasturing their sleek steeds, followed them to their resting places beneath the earth.

Suddenly he saw others picnicking in the grass on his right and left, and still others singing in unison a festive paean to Apollo in a grove fragrant with laurel. From here the flow of the Eridanus, at its most powerful, streams through the forest on its way to the world above. Assembled here were those who suffered wounds while fighting for their country, priests who remained pure in life, pious poets with eloquence worthy of Phoebus, those who improved life by discovering new knowledge, and those who by their service to others made themselves unforgettable. The brows of all were wreathed in a crown of snow-white wool. When they had gathered around, the Sibyl addressed them all, directing her words to Musaeus most of all since he was surrounded by a great throng and stood head and shoulders above the rest, "Tell me, blessed souls, and you, noble prophet, in what place, in what region is Anchises? It is for him that we have come and sailed across the mighty streams of Erebus."

The hero gave his brief response to her, "No one here has a fixed home. We live in shady groves and rest upon soft riverbanks and meadows watered by rivulets. But if your heart is bent on finding him, climb over this ridge, and before long I shall set you upon a path that is easy." After he spoke, he went before them as guide and from the ridge showed them the shimmering fields down below them. Then they descended, leaving the mountaintops behind them.

6j Aeneas Meets His Father (679–755)

Father Anchises was in a deep, lush valley of green, surveying with careful consideration the souls kept there awaiting their journey to the light above. By chance he was reviewing the full roster of his own family, his beloved descendants, their fates and fortunes, their dispositions and deeds. When he saw Aeneas drawing across the fields toward him, he eagerly stretched out both hands, tears drenching his cheeks, and let out a cry, "Have you come at last? Has your devotion to your father, long awaited, overcome this hard journey? Can it be that I am allowed to gaze upon your face, Son, to hear your familiar voice and respond to it in kind? This is how I kept thinking it would turn out, how I reckoned it would be as I counted off the days, and my anxious concern was not deceived. What lands you must have crossed, what seas you must have sailed to greet me! How great must the dangers have been that tormented you, Son! How I feared that Libya's kingdom might bring you harm!"

Aeneas answered, "It was your image, Father, your sad image, so often seen, that drove me to follow this course. My fleet stands anchored on the Tyrrhenian Sea. Let me clasp your right hand, Father, please, and do not draw back from my embrace." As he spoke, a wide flow of tears streamed down his cheeks. Three times he tried to put his arms around his father's neck; three times the ghost, embraced in vain, slipped through his hands like weightless breezes and winged sleep.

Now Aeneas saw a secluded grove in a withdrawn hollow where the forest's branches were rustling and the river Lethe lazily drifted past peaceful abodes. Along this river countless races, countless peoples fluttered, as when bees in the meadows on a clear summer's day alight upon the myriad of colorful flowers and swarm about the white lilies, and the whole field is abuzz with humming. Startled by this sudden sight, Aeneas asked his father the reasons for it, for he did not know the stream in the distance or the men who had swarmed to the banks in such a multitude.

Then father Anchises answered, "The souls that by fate's decree are owed another body, here, at the bank of the river Lethe, drink its care-releasing waters, the deep erasures of the mind. These souls I have long wanted to tell you about, to show them to you face to face, to relate to you the descendants of my family, so that you might better rejoice with me now that you have found Italy."

"Father," said Aeneas, "am I really to think that some exalted souls leave here to go into the world above and return to sluggish bodies? What dread desire of the light do these poor souls feel?"

"I will tell you, Son. I will not keep you in suspense," Anchises responded and revealed each detail in order. "First, heaven and earth, the fluid fields of the sea, the shining orb of the moon, and the Titan sun are nourished by a spirit within them, and an intelligence permeating the parts drives the whole mass and mingles with the great body of the universe. From this mingling are born the races of men and beasts, the lives of flying creatures, and all the monsters the sea holds beneath its marble surface. Their seeds have a fiery force, and their origin is divine, but harmful bodies blunt their powers—their earthly frame, their dying limbs dull them. From this come fear and desire, pain and pleasure, and they do not perceive the pure air of heaven because they are imprisoned in the blinding darkness of their dungeons. Yes, and even when life has left them on their final day, they are not liberated from every defect, every bodily scourge—the many defects are so long attached that they by necessity become deeply and mysteriously infused into their very being. So they are purged by punishment, paying the penalty for their old evils: some are suspended and exposed to the weightless winds; for others the guilty stain is leeched out beneath a mighty deluge or burned away by fire. Each of us endures our own afterlife. Then we are sent through the wide expanse of Elysium. A few of us live here in the Blessed Groves until the circuit of the ages is complete and the long passage of time has cleansed that ingrained pollution from our souls and left behind only the pure ethereal consciousness and fiery spirit unsullied. But all of these souls, when they have turned the wheel over a thousand years, are summoned by the god to the stream of Lethe in mighty throngs, so that, you see, without memory they will visit the dome of the upper world again and want to return to flesh."

FROM *GEORGICS*

4.453–4.527 Orpheus in the Underworld

The Georgics, *a four-book poem on agricultural life, ends with the beautiful but heartbreaking story of Orpheus and Eurydice. Vergil's account describes the complete story of these two unfortunate lovers, but the dramatic highpoint is the description of Orpheus' loss of his beloved wife for the second and final time as he tries to lead her back from the underworld. The story is told by Proteus, a prophetic sea god, to Aristaeus, a rustic beekeeper who has lost all of his bees and is at a loss as to why. The reason is, of course, that it was his pursuit of Eurydice that caused her death, and now Orpheus is gaining revenge for his transgression.*

Indeed, it is the wrath of a great spirit that torments you; grievous are the sins you are atoning for. Orpheus, that pitiable soul, who suffers unjustly, sets these punishments on you, should the Fates not oppose, and rages passionately for his wife. Yes, while running headlong along the river to escape from you, that girl destined for death did not see the monstrous serpent before her feet, lurking by the riverbank in the deep grass. A band of Dryads, her companions, filled the mountaintops with their cries: the peaks of Rhodope wailed, as did lofty Pangaea, Rhesus' land sacred to Mars, the Getae, the river Hebrus, and Athenian Orithyia.[8] But Orpheus, soothing his aching love with his hollow tortoiseshell, sang of you, his sweet wife, you as he sat alone on the desolate shore, you as the day arrived, you as the day departed.

He even entered the jaws of Taenarum, the deep doorway of Dis, and the grove shrouded in black terror. He dared to approach the spirits of the dead, the terrifying king, hearts that know not how to be softened by human prayers. Yet, moved by his song, the insubstantial shades and the ghosts of those deprived of light came from the deepest region of Erebus, like many thousands of birds taking cover in the woods when evening or the winter rains drive them down from the mountains: mothers and husbands, bodies of great-hearted heroes robbed of life, young boys and unmarried girls, men in the prime of their lives placed on pyres before their parents' eyes—those whom the black mire and murky reeds of Cocytus and the hateful marsh with its sluggish waters hem in and the nine winding circles of the Styx confine. Even the very halls, the innermost depths of Death, and the Eumenides with bluish snakes entwined in their hair were entranced. Cerberus held his three jaws agape, and the wheel that spun Ixion ceased to turn with the wind.

At last he had overcome all obstacles and was making his way back. Eurydice, now returned to him, was nearing the air above, following behind her husband (for this was the condition Proserpina had set), when her unsuspecting lover was seized by a sudden madness, a forgivable one to be sure, if only the spirits of the dead knew how to forgive. Orpheus stopped just short of the light itself and, (alas!) forgetful, his will overcome, looked back at Eurydice, who was his own again. Right then all his hard toil was wasted, his compact with the pitiless tyrant broken. Three times thunder reverberated throughout the pools of Avernus. She spoke, "What madness, Orpheus, what awful madness has destroyed my miserable life and yours? Behold, a second time the cruel Fates call me back, and sleep falls over my swimming eyes. And now, farewell. I am swept away, shrouded by deep night, stretching out to you—though, alas!, I am no longer yours—these helpless hands."

She spoke, and suddenly she slipped away from his sight like smoke dissipating into thin air, and she did not see him thereafter as he grasped at the shadows in vain,

[8] All of these names are geographical markers related to Thrace, the land sacred to Mars from which Orpheus hailed: Rhesus was the famous Thracian ally of the Trojans; Rhodope is a mountain range; the Getae dwelled along the lower Danube; the Hebrus River runs through Thrace; and Orithyia, the daughter of the Athenian king, Erechtheus, was married to Boreas, the North Wind who dwelled in Thrace.

wanting to say much more. The ferryman of Orcus would not allow him to cross the barrier of the marsh again. What was he to do? Where turn now that his wife had been wrested from him a second time? What tears could win over the spirits of the dead? What prayer the gods? No matter. She, now cold, was floating across on the Stygian vessel.

They say that for seven whole months unceasing, beneath a tall crag beside the lonely waters of the Strymon River, Orpheus wept for himself and beneath the frigid stars spun out this tale of woe, soothing tigers and moving oak trees with his song. He was like the mournful nightingale, who beneath the poplar's shade grieves over her lost young, those that a hard-hearted ploughman spotted in their nest and pulled down before feathers even graced their bodies. She weeps the whole night through and, perched upon a branch, repeats her sad song, filling the places far and wide with her forlorn laments. But Orpheus cared not for Venus or for marriage. Alone, he wandered over the Hyperborean ice, the snowy Tanais, and the fields ever under the Riphaean frost, in mourning over his stolen Eurydice and the gifts of Dis that might have been.

Feeling scorned by his tribute to her, the Ciconian mothers, during the sacred rites of the gods and the rituals of nocturnal Bacchus, ripped apart the young man and scattered him over the wide fields. Even then, as the Oeagrian Hebrus flowed along, carrying the head torn from his marble-white neck amidst its waters, the selfsame voice, his death-cold tongue called out "Eurydice! Poor Eurydice!" as his spirit departed, and the riverbanks echoed "Eurydice" all along the stream.

Xenophanes

(6th c. BC, wrote in Greek)

Xenophanes, an early poet and thinker, hailed from Colophon, a city in Ionia on the west coast of Asia Minor, one of the centers of philosophical enlightenment in the 6th and 5th centuries BC. *Although he left Ionia in his mid-twenties, it is likely that the time he spent in this intellectual climate led to some of his criticism of conventionally held beliefs, most notably of the depictions of gods handed down by the poets Homer and Hesiod (see fr. 11). The following nine poetic fragments not only deconstruct the idea that the gods are anthropomorphic, but also give a picture of Xenophanes' conception of the divine, which shows monotheistic tendencies similar to some other Greek authors (for example, Aeschylus fr. 70 and Cleanthes'* Hymn to Zeus*).*

11 Homer and Hesiod on the Gods (11 D-K)

Both Homer and Hesiod ascribed to the gods all things
that evoke reproach and blame among human beings,
theft and adultery and mutual deception.

14 What Humans Believe About the Gods (14 D-K)

But mortals believe that gods are begotten
and have clothing, voice, and body like their own.

15 If Animals Worshiped Gods (15 D-K)

But if oxen and horses and lions had hands
and so could draw and make works of art like men,
horses would draw pictures of gods like horses,
and oxen like oxen, and they would make their bodies
in accordance with the form that they themselves severally possess.

16 Foreign Gods (16 D-K)

Ethiopians say that their gods are snub-nosed and black;
Thracians say that theirs have blue eyes and red hair.

18 The Gods Withhold Things from Men (18 D-K)

The gods have not, of course, revealed all things to mortals
from the beginning;
but rather, seeking in the course of time, they discover
what is better.

23 God Is Unlike Man (23 D-K)

There is one god, greatest among gods and human beings,
not at all like mortals in form nor yet in mind.

24 God Perceives Everything (24 D-K)

All of him sees, all of him thinks, all of him hears.

25 God Sets Everything in Motion (25 D-K)

But, far from toil, with the thought of his mind he puts all
things in motion.

26 God Is Motionless (26 D-K)

Always he remains in the same place, moving not at all,
nor does it befit him to go at different times in different
directions.

XENOPHON

(ca. 430–ca. 355 BC, wrote in Greek)

In the Memorabilia, *Xenophon gave his recollections of his great teacher, Socrates. The famous philosopher had been put to death in 399 BC by his fellow citizens in Athens while Xenophon was away on a military expedition in Persia (described in his most famous work, the* Anabasis*). In the following passage Socrates urges an acquaintance to live a virtuous life by recounting the famous allegory of "The Choice of Heracles," as told by the philosopher and teacher Prodicus. Plato, another student of Socrates, also represents philosophers as rendering philosophical ideas in the form of myths. See his* Protagoras, *where the title character is shown telling a myth, and the Myth of Er from the tenth book of the* Republic, *where Plato has Socrates himself tell a philosophical myth.*

FROM *MEMORABILIA*

2.1.21–2.1.34 The Choice of Heracles

[21] Prodicus the wise gives the same sort of account of virtue as we have been discussing in his piece about Heracles, the one that he also delivers as a speech to large audiences. As far as I can remember, he says something along the following lines:

He says that when Heracles was moving from boyhood to adolescence—the time of life when the young, as they are beginning to become independent, show whether they will approach life by the path through virtue or by the path through vice—he went out to a quiet spot and sat, at a loss over which of the two paths to follow.

[22] He saw two tall women approaching him. One was lovely to behold and noble in stature, her body adorned with purity, her eyes with modesty, her figure with chastity, her clothes with whiteness. The other had grown to plumpness and softness, her skin and figure decked out, her skin so that she would seem to be both paler and pinker than she really was, her figure so that she would seem to be taller than she naturally was. She kept her eyes open wide—and her clothes too so that her beauty could be readily seen underneath them. Often she looked herself over, and looked around to see if anyone else was looking at her, and many times she looked at her own shadow. [23] When they drew closer to Heracles, the woman who was mentioned first continued to approach just as she had been doing, but the other one, wishing to get there first, ran to Heracles and began to speak:

"Heracles, I see that you are at a loss as to which path to follow in life. If you make me your friend, I will lead you along the most pleasant and easiest path. You will taste every pleasure; you will spend your life without experiencing difficulty.

[24] First of all, you will not think of wars or troubles. You will spend your time considering what food or drink you might want to get. Or what sight or sound you would enjoy. Or what smell or touch would please you. Or what lover you would spend the most enjoyable time with. Or how you would sleep most comfortably. Or how you would achieve all these pleasures without lifting a finger. [25] If you ever suspect that you might run into a lack of what makes this lifestyle possible, do not be afraid that I will lead you to procure them by toiling or laboring with your body or mind. No, you will have at your disposal what the rest of the world produces. You will have access to everything that might profit you. I give my associates *carte blanche* to help themselves however they want to."

[26] Heracles heard this and said, "Ma'am, what is your name?"

She replied, "People who like me call me Happiness, but people who hate me call me by the nickname Vice."

[27] Meanwhile, the other woman approached him and said, "Heracles, I have also come to you. I know those who gave you life and I observed your character while you were growing up. From what I know I have hopes, if you take my path, that you might become a great doer of noble and righteous deeds and that I might be thought even more honored and distinguished for goodness. But I will not try to fool you by talking first about pleasure.

[28] No, I will truly tell you about reality exactly as the gods have arranged it. The gods do not give anything that is really good and noble to mortals without labor and effort. If you wish the gods to be favorable to you, you must serve the gods. If you want to be loved by friends, you must do nice things for your friends. If you desire to be honored by some city, you must be of service to the city. If you want to be respected by the whole of Greece for your virtue, you must try to be a benefactor to Greece. If you wish the earth to produce abundant crops for you, you must cultivate the earth. If you think you need to grow wealthy from livestock, you must take care of your livestock. If you are eager to grow strong in war and want to be able to set your friends free and subjugate your enemies, you must learn the arts of war from those who have real knowledge of them and train yourself in how they are to be employed. And if you want to be physically powerful, you must accustom your body to serve your intelligence and exercise it with hard work and sweat."

[29] According to Prodicos, Vice interrupted and said, "Heracles, do you realize what a difficult and long path to happiness this woman is describing to you? I will lead you along one that is easy and short."

[30] Virtue said, "Wretch! What do you have that is good? What do you know about pleasant things when you are unwilling to do anything to get them? You do not even wait for the urge for something pleasant! No, even before you want something, you gorge yourself on everything. Before you are hungry, you eat. Before you are thirsty, you drink. So that you can enjoy eating, you get yourself chefs. Then, so you can enjoy drinking, you acquire expensive wines and run around looking for snow during summertime. So that you can enjoy sleeping, you do not just get comforters that are soft, but you obtain special bed supports. After all, you do not want to sleep because you are tired from hard work, but because you have nothing to do. You force yourself to have sex before you need it, employing any means necessary and

using men as women. That is how you teach your friends, by acting wantonly during the night and sleeping away the most useful part of the day.

[31] "Though you are immortal, you have become an outcast from the gods and are disdained by good men. The most pleasant of all sounds is someone praising you, but you have not heard it. Nor have you seen the most pleasant of all sights, for you have never seen a noble deed that you yourself have performed. Who would believe anything you say? Who would give you anything you ask for? Who in his right mind would dare to be part of your entourage? Your followers, when they are young, are physically weak, and when they grow older, they are deficient in character. In their youth they grow up in comfort without any hard work, but they pass their old age laboriously in misery, ashamed of what they have done and worn out by what they are doing. Their life might pass pleasantly in their youth, but they are just saving up their difficulties for old age.

[32] "I associate with gods and with good men. No noble deed, divine or mortal, happens without me. I am honored above all, both among the gods and among the mortals who belong to me. To artisans I am a beloved coworker. To masters I am a trusted guardian of houses. To slaves I am a kindly protector. I am a good assistant in the hard work of peace. I am a steadfast ally in war. I am the finest partner in friendship.

[33] My friends have the pleasant reward of simple food and drink, for they wait until they desire these things. A more pleasant sleep comes to them than to the lazy. They neither get annoyed when they leave it behind, nor for its sake do they put off what needs to be done. Those who are young rejoice in the praise of their elders. The older ones exult in the honors paid to them by the young, and while they recall their old actions with pleasure, they also take pleasure in performing their current ones well, because on my account they are dear to the gods, beloved by their friends, and honored by their countries. When their fated end comes, they do not lie forgotten in dishonor, but they flourish, remembered for all time, and have songs sung about them. Heracles, you child of good parents, the most blessed happiness lies within your grasp if you work hard as I have described."

[34] That is essentially how Prodicus describes Virtue's education of Heracles. Of course, he adorned the ideas with even more splendid words than I have just now.

Appendix One: Linear B Sources

Thomas G. Palaima

The earliest written evidence we have for Greek language and culture, and for Greek mythology and religion, is found in economic texts on clay tablets written in a writing system known as Linear B. The first tablets were found in 1900 AD by Sir Arthur Evans excavating at Cnossos,[1] the chief center of Minoan and later Mycenaean culture on Crete.[2] Other tablets, too, come exclusively from the environs of Mycenaean palatial sites that flourished for approximately two centuries (1400–1200 BC) near the end of the Aegean Bronze Age.[3]

It took more than fifty years for the Linear B script to be deciphered. The decipherment was achieved without the aid of any bilingual text.[4] The most productive work on decipherment was done beginning in the late 1940s by two American scholars, Alice E. Kober and Emmett L. Bennett, Jr., and British architect Michael Ventris. In June 1952, Ventris offered solid evidence that the language of the texts written in Linear B was Greek. His proposal has since been proved by more than fifty years of careful work interpreting both the texts he had available to him and many more texts discovered in the course of continuing excavations.[5]

The tablets themselves (see photos of Tn 316 front side and Fr 1226) are fragile and are only preserved for us by being accidentally baked, just as moist clay is intentionally fired into hardened pottery, when the rooms or buildings in which they were left were destroyed by fire. Most tablets suffered serious damage in such destructions, so that it is not unusual for tablets to be partially preserved or pieced together from fragments through the process that Mycenaean inscription experts call making "joins."

[1] In tablet translations here Cnossos is abbreviated with the prefix KN (= Knossos) in conformity with the conventions of Mycenaean textual editing.

[2] W. A. McDonald and C. G. Thomas, *Progress into the Past: The Rediscovery of Mycenaean Civilization,* 2nd ed. (Bloomington, Ind. 1990), 113–169.

[3] Cf. J. Chadwick, *The Mycenaean World* (Cambridge 1976).

[4] A. Robinson, *The Man Who Deciphered Linear B: The Story of Michael Ventris* (London and New York 2002).

[5] T. G. Palaima, "Archaeology and Text: Decipherment, Translation and Interpretation," in *Theory and Practice in Mediterranean Archaeology: Old World and New World Perspectives,* eds. J. K. Papadopoulos and R. M. Leventhal (Los Angeles 2003), 45–73.

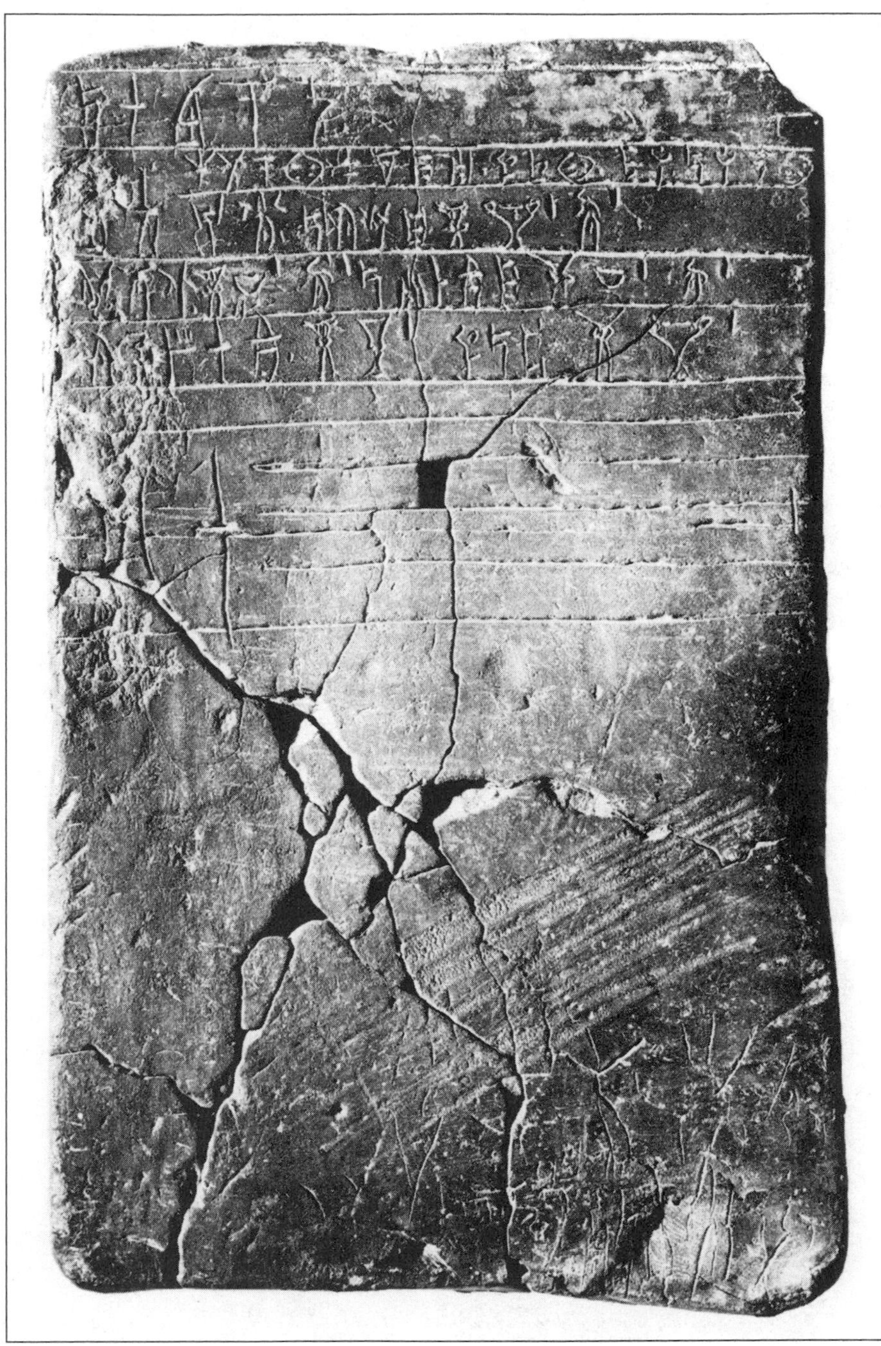

Front side of Pylos tablet Tn 316, recording offerings to gods like Zeus, Hermes, Hera, and Potnia of gold vessels carried by cult officials of the Palace of Nestor to the Mycenaean sanctuary area known as Sphagianes. (Photograph courtesy of the Department of Classics, University of Cincinnati, from the photographic archives of the Program in Aegean Scripts and Prehistory, University of Texas at Austin.)

Tablet Fr 1226 recording the offering of sage-scented oil "to the gods." (Photograph courtesy of the Department of Classics, University of Cincinnati, from the photographic archives of the Program in Aegean Scripts and Prehistory, University of Texas at Austin.)

One spectacular join in recent years has yielded a clear reference to a "fire altar" of the god Dionysos, whose historical myths were once thought to identify a deity whose worship entered Greece well after the Bronze Age, perhaps from Anatolia.

The Linear B writing system[6] has a repertory of approximately eighty-seven phonetic signs (phonograms) that stand for open syllables (single consonants or consonant clusters followed by vowels) e.g., *pa, do, ta, nwa, dwo.*[7] It also uses about two hundred signs, known as ideograms or logograms, to represent materials and commodities, animate or inanimate, that were important within the regional economic and political systems of the Mycenaean palatial period. The ideograms are represented in our translations here by smaller-sized capital letters, e.g., OIL, HONEY, GOLD CUP, MAN, SHEEP, WHEAT. Some phonograms are used as ideograms. Such phonetic ideograms generally represent the first syllables of the words for the objects they designate, whether the words are derived from Minoan (*NI* = "figs" from the Cretan word *nikuleon*) or Mycenaean Greek (*WI* = *wi-ri-no* "oxhide," historical Greek *rhinos*). The phonetically written words are here either translated into English or, where appropriate and necessary, transcribed in Latin according to the conventional values for individual signs. Signs within word-units are connected by hyphens. So, for example, *po-ti-ni-ja* = *Potnia* (literally, "The Female God Who Has Power," conventionally translated here as "Lady").

We now have roughly five thousand Linear B tablets from the major centers of the Greek Bronze Age. These are the same centers that gave rise to the great mythical story cycles, a fact first observed by the Swedish scholar of ancient Greek religion M. P. Nilsson.[8] Mycenae, Tiryns, Cnossos, Pylos, and Thebes have yielded appreciable to extensive archives. Other key "mythological" sites like Eleusis and Orchomenos have produced inscribed oil-transport vessels known as stirrup jars. The hazards of excavation

[6] M. G. F. Ventris and J. Chadwick, *Documents in Mycenaean Greek*, 2nd ed. (Cambridge 1973), 28–66, 387–395.

[7] A few rarer signs have not had their values determined. These are identified numerically, e.g., **22*.

[8] See his groundbreaking *The Mycenaean Origin of Greek Mythology* (Berkeley, Calif. 1932).

and site settlement patterns explain the absence of Linear B tablets at other centers of early Greek myths like Sparta (Menelaos), Athens (Aigeus and Theseus), and Iolcos (Jason and the Argonauts).

The Linear B texts were written as internal administrative records that would have been consulted by officials and agents within the intensively exploitative economic systems of the period.[9] As such, they have the quality of very condensed accounting, auditing, or inventory notes. Therefore, we do not always grasp the precise nuances or specialized meanings of the vocabulary, effectively a bureaucratic or economic jargon, used by the tablet writers. In interpreting the texts, we are working with a prealphabetic script that is not so precise at representing *for us* the words the scribes are writing. Finally, we are trying to make sense out of Greek at a stage four hundred to five hundred years earlier than the stage represented by our earliest texts of the historical period.

Despite difficulties of interpretation, the Linear B texts offer us a good deal of solid information relevant to Greek myth and religion, and they give us a partial view of elements of myth about half a millennium earlier than historical Greek myths. The earliest alphabetic Greek inscriptions cannot be pushed back further than the second quarter of the 8th century BC; and the poems of Homer and Hesiod, as we have them, were written down in the 8th century BC or later. Ruijgh has established, by applying our knowledge of Mycenaean Greek to the Homeric texts, that oral hexameter verse was already being generated as early as the 15th century BC.[10] As we shall see below in the "Personnel List," Linear B texts and the iconography of Mycenaean palatial culture confirm that the palatial centers held periodic communal feasts, complete with "Homeric-style" animal sacrifices and bardic performances.[11]

The tablets keep track of raw materials, finished products, agricultural commodities, animals, and human beings, who was responsible for them, where they were or were supposed to be, and what was happening or had happened or would happen to them. Consequently, more than seventy percent of the words on the tablets are personal names (anthroponyms) or place names (toponyms) or gods' names (theonyms). Important are anthroponyms formed from divine names (theophorics, literally names "bearing the god"), since they reflect the pious feelings that parents, clan groups, and the general culture had for individual deities in this period.

The tablets do not give us the narrative stories, histories, or legends that the Greeks of the early historical period called *muthoi*, the word that gives us our word *myths*. Nor do they explicitly describe religious rituals. In this they differ greatly from our standard written sources for "myth" in historical Greek culture. But studied carefully, the data of the tablets can shed light on the earliest phases of Greek mythology, as the following selection of tablets will show.

[9] Cf. T. G. Palaima, "'Archives' and 'Scribes' and Information Hierarchy in Mycenaean Greek Linear B Records," in *Ancient Archives and Archival Traditions*, ed. Maria Brosius (Oxford 2003), 153–194, figs. 8.1–8.9.

[10] C. J. Ruijgh, "D'Homère aux origines proto-mycéniennes de la tradition épique," in *Homeric Questions*, ed. J. P. Crielaard (Amsterdam 1995), 1–96.

[11] See most recently I. Mylonas Shear, *Tales of Heroes: The Origins of the Homeric Texts* (New York and Athens 2000); with the sober review by J. Burgess, *Bryn Mawr Classical Review* 2002.10.18. http://ccat.sas.upenn.edu/bmcr/2002/2002-10-18.html; I. Morris and B. Powell, *A New Companion to Homer* (1997); A. J. B. Wace and F. H. Stubbings, *A Companion to Homer* (London 1962).

THE GODS IN LINEAR B TABLETS

The tablet data reveal which deities from later Greek mythology were worshiped by the Mycenaeans, where they were worshiped, and some forms that their worship took. We begin with a full, up-to-date list of gods' names (theonyms) attested in Linear B (parentheses contain explanations of epithets or of Mycenaean transcriptions). An asterisk means that a proposed form or attestation is based on the interpretation, often conjectural, of incomplete evidence. A question mark or question marks mean that identification of a Mycenaean word as a deity is moderately to seriously doubtful.

Deities Common to Cnossos and Mainland Greece

Cnossos	**Pylos**	**Mycenae**	**Thebes**	**Khania**
Poseidon	Poseidon			
Zeus (Diktaios)				
Zeus (F 51)	Zeus		Zeus	
Ares	Ares[a]			
di-wi-ja	*di-wi-ja*			
Dionysos[b]	Dionysos[b]			Dionysos[b]
ma-ri-ne-u?		**ma-ri-ne-u?*	*ma-ri-ne-u?*	
Hermes (D 411?)	Hermes		Hermes	
te-o / *te-o-i* (god, gods)	*te-o* / *te-o-i*			
ma-ka (F 51)???[c]			*ma-ka???*[c]	

[a] Attested in an epithet derived from the theonym ("god's name").

[b] Attested mostly in theophoric anthroponyms (human names derived from gods' names) and now at Khania and Pylos as a clear theonym.

[c] Interpreted by some as *Mā Gā* (= "Mother Earth"), but the textual contexts do not support identification of the term as a deity. It is better interpreted as an action noun = **magā* = "the action of kneading barley into barley cakes." There are other possibilities.[12]

Conspicuously absent from the gods attested in Linear B texts are the later canonical deities Demeter, Aphrodite, Hephaistos (perhaps attested indirectly in a theophoric anthroponym), and Hestia.

The special word the Greeks use for god, *theos*, is attested,[13] mainly in the pious catch-all plural phrase "to all the gods." (It is typical of hymns and prayers in almost all cultures to make sure that no appropriate divine power is "left out" on ritual occasions.) Other elements of interest are the "free-standing" deities (e.g., *Enualios, Paiawon*) from the Bronze Age who are later reduced to epithets, e.g., Paieon Apollo or Ares Enyalios; the number of female counterparts to male gods who are still objects

[12] Cf. T. G. Palaima, review of eds. V. L. Aravantinos, L. Godart and A. Sacconi, *Les tablettes en linéaire B de la Odos Pelopidou, Édition et Commentaire.* Thèbes Fouilles de la Cadmée 1. Istituti Editoriali Poligrafici Internazionali (Pisa and Rome 2001), in *American Journal of Archaeology* 107.1 (2003), 113–115; and in *Minos* 35–36 (2000–2001), 475–486.

[13] W. Burkert, "From Epiphany to Cult Statue: Early Greek *Theos*," in *What Is a God?*, ed. A. B. Lloyd (London 1997), 15–34, links *theos* to the notion of sudden manifestation or apparition of divine power, a key concept in Minoan religious iconography.

Deities Occurring Either Only at Cnossos or Only on the Mainland

Cnossos	Pylos	Mycenae	Thebes	Khania
	po-ti-ni-ja		*po-ti-ni-ja*	
a-ta-na-po-ti-ni-ja (the Lady of Athens)				
da-pu$_2$-ri-to-jo po-ti-ni-ja (the Lady of the Labyrinth)				
	e-re-wi-jo-po-ti-ni-ja			
	ne-wo-pe-o po-ti-ni-ja			
	u-po-jo po-ti-ni-ja			
		si-to-po-ti-ni-ja (the Lady of Grains)		
	po-ti-ni-ja i-qe-ja (the Lady of Horses)			
	po-ti-ni-ja a-si-wi-ja (the Lady of Asia)			
	ma-te-re te-i-ja (the divine Mother)			
pa-de				
qe-ra-si-ja (the hunter goddess)				
pi-pi-tu-na				
Eleuthia				
Erinus				
Enualios				
Paiawon				

Deities Occurring Either Only at Cnossos or Only on the Mainland (continued)

Cnossos	Pylos	Mycenae	Thebes	Khania
	Hera		Hera	
	Artemis			
	Posidaeia			
	Trisheros			
	Iphimedeia			
	ma-na-sa			
	*pe-re-*82*			
	do-po-ta (the "House-Master")			
	di-ri-mi-jo			
	qo-wi-ja (the bovid female deity) ?			
	ko-ma-we-te-ja (the fair-tressed female deity) ?		*ko-ma-we-te-ja* ?	
	a-ma-tu-na ? (Fn 187.11)[a]			

[a] *a-ma-tu-na* has a form similar to *pi-pi-tu-na*. Both are thought to be Minoan deities. Compare the structure of the historical Greek *Diktynna*.

of cult (female Zeus = *Diwia*, female Poseidon = *Posidaeia*); and the associations between deities and specific locales that are preserved in the historical mythological tradition, e.g., Eileithyia and the site of Amnisos on Crete.

The above information has been extracted from texts such as the following. By convention, the signs [and] mark the place in lines of text where the tablet is broken away to the right and to the left, respectively. Texts are preceded by abbreviation of site and are identified by contents as belonging to series, designated by capital letter followed by small letter, e.g., Fp is a series of texts dealing with the agricultural commodity olive oil. Another such set at Pylos is designated as Fr. The sets are distinguished conventionally as coming from KN (Cnossos), PY (Pylos), KH (Khania), and TH (Thebes).

1 Allocations of Olive Oil to Deities and Sanctuaries

The following text from Cnossos (KN) is part of a fuller set of similar records. It is a good example of the kind of economic record that gives us information about the gods whom the inhabitants of Crete during the Mycenaean palatial period (ca. 1400–1200 BC) worshiped. The record was drawn up to record the disbursement of oil and fulfillment of a ritual obligation to deities, here identified as located in specific sanctuaries. OIL is olive oil, one of the main agricultural products (along with barley, wheat, figs, and wine) produced in large quantities for consumption and trade. We do not know how this oil would have been used within the sacred place where the individual recipient deities are located. But the large quantities and the inclusion of a human priestess among the recipients would seem to argue for some use besides token ritual offering.

Note the references to a sanctuary of Daidalos, to Diktaean Zeus, to a divine being known as Erinys, and to a priestess of the winds in the vicinity of the Cnossian port town of Amnisos.

KN Fp(1) 1 + 31

.1	in the month of Deukios[a]	
.2	to Diktaean Zeus	OIL 9.6 liters
.3	to the sanctuary of Daidalos	OIL 19.2 liters
.4	to "pa-de"[b]	OIL 9.6 liters
.5	to all the gods	OIL 28.8 liters
.6	to Therasia[c]	OIL 9.6 liters[[d]
.7	at Amnisos, to all the gods	OIL 9.6 liters[[d]
.8	to Erinus[e]	OIL 4.8 liters
.9	to the site of "*47-da"[f]	OIL 1.6 liters
.10	to the priestess of the winds	6.4 liters
.11	**blank line**	
.12	so much	OIL 108.8 liters

[a] One of six or seven month names at Cnossos. Month names only occur on "ritual" texts, where the completion of an action within a particular time period is important. Consequently month names are most often in the grammatical case that specifies "occurring *within*" a given time period.

[b] "pa-de" seems to be a Minoan divinity.

[c] *Therasia* is a goddess of the hunters. Cf. Greek *theratās*, "hunter."

[d] On one of these lines, another 9.6 liters is to be restored after the tablet break.

[e] The word *Erinus* is the singular of the Greek word for the Furies who in historical Greek myth and religion pursue those who are guilty of kindred murder. They are most notably treated in the *Eumenides* of Aeschylus. The Erinyes in Hesiod's *Theogony* 176–187 are primordial divinities born from the earth and the blood from the castrated sexual organs of Ouranos. They are the powers who avenge kindred murder, and they assist at the birth of "Oath," who springs from "Strife" (Hesiod's *Works and Days*, 803–804).

[f] "*47-da" seems to be a Minoan place name.

---

2 Oil Allocations at Cnossos and Pylos

Besides the larger-sized shipments of olive oil to sanctuaries examined above, the palatial centers also record disbursements of smaller quantities of precious perfumed oils.

KN Fh <390>[a] to Erinu[s

[a] Fh <390> is known only from a drawing, hence the angle brackets. It is also part of a group of texts recording larger disbursements of oil.

PY Fr 1226	.1 The Lousian fields to the gods sage-scented	OIL+sage	4.8 liters
	.2 blank line		
	(see the photo of Fr 1226, p. 399)		
PY Fr 1224	.a sage-scented and treated with henna		
	in the Sphagianian[a] month to Poseidon	OIL+sage	0.8 liters
PY Fr 1231	.1 for the Lady[b] to the Thirsty Ones[c] [		
	.2 for guests [ ] OIL 9.6 liters[		
	.3 blank line		
PY Fr 1230	to the sanctuary of Zeus	OIL+ "anointing"	1.6 liters

[a] The month name derives from the sacred area in the kingdom of Pylos known as *Sphagianes*, or "the place of ritual slaughter."

[b] *po-ti-ni-ja*, translated here as "Lady," appears elsewhere with many epithets. See the above tables of attested deities.

[c] The "Thirsty Ones" are some kind of *daimones*, supernatural forces that interact with human lives and affairs.

3 Honey Offering Texts from Khania and Cnossos

A relatively recent surprise is the firm evidence that the cult of Dionysos was active in the 13th century BC.[14] From the site of Khania (KH) in western Crete, we have a tablet that records offerings of amphorae (two-handled transport-storage jars) of honey to Zeus and to Dionysos in a sanctuary of Zeus.

This tablet from Khania conforms to the pattern of a fuller series of honey offering texts from Cnossos, of which we provide one example. Given how honey has to be extracted and prepared, it would have been a special treat and a fitting offering to the deity (perhaps to be consumed by his sacred officials or worshipers during rituals). The Linear B texts refer to officials known as "honey masters" and "honey men," and honey is listed among the ingredients for large-scale ritual banquets.

KH Gq 5

.1 to the precinct of Zeus	to Zeus	AMPHORA of honey 1
.2 to Dionysos		AMPHORA of honey 2

The following two Cnossos "honey-offering" texts are remarkable for the reference to *Eileuthia* (compare historical Eileithyia, the goddess of childbirth associated with Artemis) and the *potnia* of the Labyrinth. In Homer, *Odyssey* 19.188, Odysseus is said to have been driven by storms to Amnisos where there is a cave sanctuary of Eileithyia. One Linear B tablet, Cn 1287 from Pylos, has a scribal drawing or "doodle" of a maze or labyrinth on the back.

KN Gg(3) 705

.1] at Amnisos	/ to Eileuthia	HONEY AMPHORA 1
.2] to all the gods	HONEY AMPHORA 1	
.3 to Posei?]don	HONEY AMPHORA 1	

KN Gg(1) 702

.1 to all the gods /	HONEY AMPHORA 1
.2 to the Lady of the Labyrinth	HONEY AMPHORA 1

4 Landholding Records from Pylos

Dionysos is also found now at Pylos. Mycenaean palatial culture, like the contemporary Hittite civilization in Anatolia, operated on an elaborate system of various grades of obligations and corresponding rewards or entitlements. Chief among the benefits for work service or production or for noble or sacred status was the privilege of "holding" land, part of the produce of which could be used for the personal benefit of the landholder. The palatial centers monitored landholdings, both to ascertain that their own obligations to specialist workers and palatial officials were discharged,

[14] T. G. Palaima, "Linear B and the Origins of Greek Religion: '*di-wo-nu-so*,'" in *The History of the Hellenic Language and Writing: From the Second to the First Millennium BC: Break or Continuity?*, eds. N. Dimoudis and A. Kyriatsoulis (Altenburg 1998), 205–222.

and as a way of calculating contributions that would be made from the produce of the land held.

This tablet is part of a set monitoring landholdings, measured in terms of amounts of seed grain. Among these landholders are specialist crafts personnel associated with the presumed "military leader" or *lawagetas* at Pylos (PY). Here a parcel of land containing a fire altar of Dionysos out in the Messenian countryside is recorded.

PY Ea 102

.1 of Dionysos the fire altar BARLEY 249.6 liters of seed grain

5 The Room of the Chariot Tablets at Cnossos: Our Earliest References to the Gods

The two tablets here come from our earliest collection of tablets in Linear B, the Room of the Chariot tablets at Cnossos (ca. 1400 BC). The location gets its name because of the concern for military equipment, including chariots and sets of armor, on over 20 percent of the tablets. Records from this location also have a high incidence of Greek names of an aristocratic type.[15] (The context may explain why, remarkably, on this text all preserved theonyms are attested in the historical Greek tradition.)

KN V 52 + 52 bis + 8285

.1 to the Lady of Athens 1 [ ] *traces* [

.2 to Enualios 1 to Paiawon 1 to Poseid[on

bottom edge {to Erinus^{erased} , pe-ro?^{erased}}

Note that, as with the reference to the Lady or *potnia* of the Labyrinth, here we get Mycenaean corroboration that the Homeric phrase "Athenian potnia" reflects the origin of this major Greek deity as the "powerful female goddess" of a settlement with the name *Athene*.[16] Most of the Mycenaean remains on the acropolis of Athens have been obliterated by long and continuous habitation of the locale and successive major building programs, but the mythical tradition alone (compare Theseus and the Minotaur) suggests that, like its neighbor Eleusis, the site must have been significant in the late Bronze Age.

KN F 51 reverse side

.1 to? the king WHEAT 14.4 liters for the preliminary meal ? 4 liters

.2 to Zeus WHEAT 9.6 liters WHEAT 38.8 liters for kneading ? WHEAT 9.6 liters

[15] J. Gulizio, K. Pluta, and T. G. Palaima, "Religion in the Room of the Chariot Tablets," in *Potnia, Deities and Religion in the Aegean Bronze Age*, eds. R. Hägg and R. Laffineur (Liège and Austin 2001), 453–461; and T. G. Palaima, "Mycenaean Militarism from a Textual Perspective. Onomastics in Context: *lawos, damos, klewos*," in *Polemos: Warfare in the Aegean Bronze Age*, ed. R. Laffineur (Liège and Austin 1999), 367–378.

[16] W. Burkert, *Greek Religion*, trans. J. Raffan (Cambridge, Mass. 1985), 139.

WHEAT (or perhaps BARLEY) is here allotted to the king or *wanaks* and, in a pair of allotments, to Zeus. At the same time smaller allotments are designated for a preliminary banquet and for kneading into cakes, perhaps for ceremonial use.

6 Tn 316: The Famous *Sphagianes* "Human Sacrifice" Tablet[17]

Given the Greek mythical traditions for human sacrifice (most notably the sacrifice of Iphigeneia at Aulis and the sacrifice of Trojan youths at the funeral pyre of Patroclos) and the controversial Bronze Age evidence from Crete for the same practice,[18] it is understandable that scholars looked to this tablet for textual corroboration.

Some scholars have argued[19] that the term on tablet Tn 316 from Pylos transliterated as *po-re-na* (*phorenas* meaning either "those brought" or "those bringing") identifies human sacrificial victims. According to this line of interpretation, the text of Tn 316 was written as one of many extreme emergency measures just before the destruction of the palace. Tn 316 would then reflect a desperate, and abnormal, attempt to placate divine powers through the sacrifice of male victims to male gods and female victims to female gods.

But the term *po-re-na* more likely refers to "human sacristans" who are identified as "bearers."[20] Thus it is more plausible[21] that tablet Tn 316 records a ritual procession with sacristans carrying gold heirloom vessels from the stores of the palatial center out to sanctuaries located in the district known as *Sphagianes* ("the place of ritual slaughter"). *Sphagianes* is where the Pylian "Lady" (*potnia*) was the primary deity. This goddess and this religious district are closely linked with palatial cult and power.

The divine recipients on this text are recorded in a hierarchy that privileges female deities, beginning with *potnia*. Poseidon himself is absent from his own sanctuary. Notice, too, the female counterparts to Zeus (line v.6) and Poseidon (line .4), and the reference to the concept of hero in the recipient *Thrice-Hero*.[22]

Of further mythological interest here is the pairing of Zeus and Hera in Zeus' sanctuary, and the isolation of the feminine counterpart of Zeus, *Diwia*, in her own sanctuary. Hermes here is either worshiped in *Diwia*'s shrine (with suggestions that he is her son, in contrast with the later tradition in Hesiod and the *Homeric Hymns*, which makes him the son of Zeus and Maia) or he is, as god of boundaries, placed outside any defined sanctuary.

[17] Cf. T. G. Palaima, "Kn02–Tn 316," in *Floreant Studia Mycenaea*, vol. 2, eds. S. Deger-Jalkotzy, S. Hiller and O. Panagl (Vienna 1999), 437–461; and J. C. Wright, "Empty Cups and Empty Jugs: The Social Role of Wine in Minoan and Mycenaean Societies," in *The Origins and Ancient History of Wine*, eds. P. E. McGovern, S. J. Fleming, and S. H. Katz (Philadelphia 1995), 287–309.

[18] Reviewed in D. D. Hughes, *Human Sacrifice in Ancient Greece* (London 1991).

[19] E.g., Chadwick, *The Mycenaean World*, 91–92.

[20] Compare later Greek *kanephoroi*, "basket-bearers."

[21] Palaima, "Kn02–Tn 316."

[22] Wright, "Empty Cups and Empty Jugs: The Social Role of Wine in Minoan and Mycenaean Societies," links the notion of "hero" in this period to ancestor worship that is so important in legitimizing power and status.

PY Tn 316 (see the photo of Tn 316 frontside, p. 398)

front side

.1	Within [the month] of Plowistos? (or Phlowistos? or Prowistos?)[a]	
.2		performs a holy ritual[b] at *Sphagianes*, and brings gifts and leads *po-re-na*
.3	PYLOS[c]	to *potnia* GOLD CUP 1 WOMAN 1
.4	to *Manassa* GOLD BOWL 1 WOMAN 1 to *Posidaeia* GOLD BOWL 1 WOMAN 1	
.5	to *Thrice-Hero* GOLD CHALICE 1 to *House-Master* GOLD CUP 1	
.6		narrow/ **blank line**
.7		**blank line**
.8		**blank line**
.9		**blank line**
.10	PYLOS	**blank line**

remaining portion of this side of tablet without rule lines

reverse side

v.1		**phr** at the *sanctuary of Poseidon* and the town leads
v.2		and brings gifts and leads *po-re-na*
v.3a	PYLOS	*a*
v.3		GOLD CUP 1 WOMAN 2 to *Bowia* and X of *Komawentei-*
v.4		**phr** at *sanctuary of pe-re-*82* and at *sanc. of Iphemedeia* and at *sanc. of Diwia*
v.5		and brings gifts and leads *po-re-na* to *pe-re-*82* GOLD BOWL 1 WOMAN 1
v.6	PYLOS	to *Iphimedeia* GOLD BOWL 1 to *Diwia* GOLD BOWL 1 WOMAN 1
v.7		to *Hermes Areias* GOLD CHALICE 1 MAN 1
v.8		**phr** at the *sanctuary of Zeus* and brings gifts and leads *po-re-na*
v.9		to *Zeus* GOLD BOWL 1 MAN 1 to *Hera* GOLD BOWL 1 WOMAN 1
v.10	PYLOS	to *Drimios*[d] *the son of Zeus* GOLD BOWL 1
v.11		**blank line**
v.12		narrow/ **blank line**
v.13		**blank line**
v.14		**blank line**
v.15	PYLOS	**blank line**
v.16		**blank line**

[a] Given other occurrences of this word in the "recipient" slot of oil-offering texts, it is most reasonable to interpret it as the name of a deity, linked alternatively with "sailing" or "flowering" or "knowing."

[b] Hereafter abbreviated **phr**. The word thus translated may also simply refer to ritual "sending." It is typical in ritual texts in many cultures to have an unspecified subject of a verb that designates

(*continues*)

ritual actions. For a complete interpretation of Tn 316 with a full review of scholarly theories, see Palaima, "Kn02–Tn 316."

[c] PYLOS is everywhere written in extra-large letters. Its syntactical function is ambiguous. It may represent the collective subject of the ritual action expressed in each section, or it may somehow designate location.

[d] Attempts have been made to link this deity with later epithets of Dionysos.

MYTHICAL NAMES AND OTHER TEXTUAL EVIDENCE RELATED TO MYTHOLOGY

It is significant that approximately seventy human names in the tablets are also found in the Homeric texts,[23] famous names like Hector and Achilles among them. Given that these names were not given by parents to their children in the historical period,[24] the Linear B evidence alone demonstrates that the Homeric tradition was not "coining" these mainly compound names, but was freely drawing from the repertory of names borne by real human beings in the Bronze Age, but not the historical period. Moreover, the tablets and material record give sufficient evidence to prove that a mythological performance tradition, complete with lyre players (now attested on a Thebes tablet) at aristocratic banquets (attested on tablets and sealings and frescoes from many sites[25]), was already under way in the Bronze Age.

7 Landholding Tablets from the *Sphagianes* District

These two tablets, from a series dealing with landholdings in the sacred district of Sphagianes (see the discussion in section 6), contain two famous mythological names from Homer, here borne by relatively low-ranking individuals who have some form of religious affiliation as "servants of the deity" known as *Potnia*, or "Lady."

PYLOS En 609

.1 at *Sphagianes* so many households HOUSEHOLD 40

.2 so many *telestai*[a] are in (*Sphagianes*) MAN 14

.3 of *Warnataios* the settled land so much seed grain BARLEY 193.6 liters

.4 thus the benefited landholders have land from *Warnataios*

Here follows a list of five individuals who hold plots of land from *Warnataios*. I give one example:

.6 *Inia* the servant of the god(dess) has a beneficial plot of land so much seed grain BARLEY 25.8 liters of seed grain

[23] Ventris and Chadwick, *Documents in Mycenaean Greek*, 104–105.

[24] A. Morpurgo Davies, "Greek Personal Names and Linguistic Continuity," in *Greek Personal Names*, eds. S. Hornblower and E. Mathews (Oxford 2000), 15–39.

[25] T. G. Palaima, "Sacrificial Feasting in the Linear B Tablets," *Hesperia* 73.2 (2004), 217–246.

[a] The term *telestās* is found in historical Greek inscriptions. Here it seems to mean "agent of the *telos*, man of service," i.e., a functionary who performs services on behalf of local communities. In the En series, the *telestai*, like *Warnataios*, control land that they in turn sublease.

PYLOS En 74 has the same structure. Here are three entries of benefited landholders.

.3 *Pekitas*, the dry-cleaner of the *king*, has a beneficial plot of land so much seed grain BARLEY 9.6 liters

.5 *Theseus*, the servant of the god(dess), has a beneficial plot of land so much seed grain BARLEY 38.4 liters

.7 *Hektor*, the servant of the god(dess), has a beneficial plot of land so much seed grain BARLEY 4.8? liters

Theseus and *Hektor*, then, are names of ordinary Mycenaeans in the Linear B texts. These references prove that Homer and the singers of early Greek traditional legend were drawing upon a stock of common names for the heroes they treated.

8 Personnel List

Here is a personnel list from the site of Thebes (TH) with significant names and occupational titles, including fullers (otherwise known as "dry cleaners," see En 74.3 in section 7) and a pair of lyre players. The significant names include *Smintheus*, found as an epithet of Apollo in Homer and also attested twice at Cnossos in the Linear B corpus, and *Nestianor* ("he who causes men to return safely").[26] *Nestianor* is found twice at Pylos. The **nes* root occurs as an element in "speaking" names like Neleus (*ne-e-ra-wo* in a text from Pylos below) and Nestor in the Neleid dynasty at Pylos. Nestor is the archetype among all the Greek heroes of the pious and wise elder statesman who brings himself and his troops back home and rules over them and his children in a harmonious kingdom.

TH Av 106

.1]		Nestianor		MAN 1
.2]	MAN 1	Omphialos		MAN 1
.3]*ke-re-u-so*	MAN 1	Smintheus		MAN 1
.4]*na-e-si-jo*	MAN 1	*te-u-ke-i-jo*		MAN 1
.5]*ta-me-je-u*	MAN 1	fullers	MAN 6	
.6]*sa-nwa-ta*	MAN 1	*a-re-pe-se-u*		MAN 1
.7]	MAN 1	lyre players		MAN 2
.8		]*-ra* MAN 1		

There are also some other tantalizing mythological names, like the personal name *Tantalos* itself on tablets from Pylos and Cnossos. The word "hero" (in section 6) appears in the name of a minor deity, where it is emphasized by the intensifying prefix *tris-*.

[26] Cf. the category of mythic songs, like the *Odyssey*, known as *nostoi* or "songs of return." It is a normal pattern in Greek for verbal elements to have an *e* vowel and noun elements to have an *o* vowel.

9 Mythical Names on Other Tablets

Achilles appears on two tablets, one at Pylos and one at Cnossos. At Cnossos, his name is entered on a tablet in the series of tablets from the Room of the Chariot Tablets (see section 5) that record individuals who are already in possession of a chariot, two horses, and two sets of body armor. These individuals are warriors of high status who command military equipment of top palatial quality.

KN Vc 106

] Achilles

At Pylos, Achilles occurs, along with other personal names, including Neleus, and occupational terms, such as "yoke-men" (probably individuals who control teams of worker oxen) and "horse-feeders," as recipients of WHEAT and OLIVES. Here are excerpts:

PY Fn 79

.2 to Achilles	WHEAT 48 liters
.5 to Neleus	WHEAT 64 liters OLIVES 96 liters
.10 to the "yoke-men" and "horse-feeders"	WHEAT 163.2 liters

Finally, we should note the presence of names, scattered throughout the Mycenaean corpus, connected with the legend of Jason and the Argonauts, which is centered on the site of Iolcos in northern Greece and Colchis at the extreme eastern limit of the Black Sea. Notable among these names[27] are Jason (PY Cn 655), Mopsos (seer of the Argonauts, KN Dc 1381) and perhaps even *Kolkhidas* ("the man from Colchis"?, PY Ea 59 and elsewhere).[28]

[27] S. Hiller, "The Mycenaeans and the Black Sea," in *Thalassa: L'Egée prehistorique et la mer*, eds. R. Laffineur and L. Basch (Liège 1991), 214.

[28] For a full list of Homeric names in Linear B, see Ventris and Chadwick, *Documents in Mycenaean Greek*, 103–105.

Appendix Two: Inscriptions

The way most people today encounter inscriptions—texts inscribed on stone or other imperishable materials—is on tombstones. The Greeks likewise used inscriptions to record the names of the dead, their accomplishments, and their hopes in this lifetime and the next. But from the time the Greek alphabet came into use in the 8th century BC, inscriptions were often employed to record many other types of documents, including laws, religious regulations, dedications of buildings (another common use of inscriptions today), and records of the offerings set up by an individual or a city in a particular shrine. Because the gods were so much a part of Greek life, they figure as prominently in inscriptions as they do in literary texts.

The evidence provided by inscriptions is of a different sort than we gain from literary texts. Literary texts for the most part were preserved specifically because they were found to have artistic merit or were informative or provocative. Their survival is usually due to their unique character and the stamp that a particular author put on them. While what we learn about mythology from these texts may reflect actual practices and beliefs, one must always take into account that the views may be very much a product of the author's imagination. In contrast, inscriptions are chance finds and represent a random and somewhat more representative sample of what the average Greek, at least those wealthy enough to set up inscriptions, believed about the gods. Another difference is that when an inscription mentions the gods (and it is nearly always the gods; references to heroes are unusual), rarely does it explain why a religious rite was carried out as it was, as a philosophical text might. Nor do they provide any extended narrative, like the stories told by the poets, which can be subjected to detailed analysis. To a large degree, then, inscriptions provide insight as to what the Greeks believed but not why. In the end, though, it is precisely because inscriptions differ from literary texts that they are useful for the study of Greek mythology. At times they confirm the portrait of the gods presented by Greek poets, philosophers, and historians. More often they extend or challenge what we are told about the gods by those sources.

One of the major issues in dealing with inscriptions as evidence is that they tend to have suffered damage, especially at the top edge, where important information is often recorded, such as who set up the inscription, when they set it up, or why they set it up. Sometimes these gaps can be reconstructed using the various techniques that make up the discipline of epigraphy (the study of inscriptions). For example, the number of letters lost can often be determined, or other documents of the same type will indicate what the missing text is likely to have said. Epigraphers have a complex system of marking exactly what can be seen on the stone and what parts of a text represent restorations. For the reader's convenience we have not followed that system but have marked in brackets < > only those parts of the text requiring substantial restoration. It must be remembered that these restorations are only skilled guesses as to what originally was on the stone and that our understanding of an inscription often depends on the study of hundreds of other inscriptions and other types of evidence.

DEDICATIONS

It was common practice throughout Greek history for cities, groups (such as the young men who trained together in the gymnasium), and individuals to make gifts to a god or gods. These gifts might be intended to thank the god for a particular service or more generally to establish and maintain the god's goodwill. The gifts most often took the form of statues or fine objects, such as bowls and woven goods that might play a role in the worship of the gods. So common was the practice of making these dedications to the gods that a sanctuary such as the Athenian Acropolis or Delphi would have been packed with statues—for instance, despite the ravages of time we have nearly four hundred inscriptions recording dedications made on the Acropolis. Likewise, the inventories of the Parthenon and other temples belonging to Athena, again in the form of inscribed documents, indicate that the storerooms of the goddess' temples were packed with gold and other precious offerings.

Dedications were often accompanied by inscriptions, either on the object itself or, especially in the case of statues, on the base on which the statue stood. In their simplest form, these inscriptions record who made the dedication, the god to whom the dedication was made, and a detail or two about the reason for the dedication. The following three inscriptions are samples of the many such dedications found on the Acropolis, most of which were made to Athena.

A Dedication of a Marble Basin to Athena, Before 480 BC (Raubitschek, *DAA* 353)

> Onesimos, the son of <S>micythos de<dicated> this as a first<-fruits offering> to Athena.

The term "first-fruits offering" is common in dedications. In a literal sense it means that the god (or goddess) should receive the first share of the harvest because of his help, and in a more general sense, it is an acknowledgment that the god was responsible for an individual's success.

B Dedication of a Statue to Athena Parthenos, ca. 470–460 BC (*CEG* 272)

> Ecphantos' father, along with his son,[1] dedicated me to Athena Parthenos
> here as a remembrance of the labors of Ares.

[1] The relationship of the names on this inscription has been debated. Our interpretation is this: the son of Ecphantos' father is, of course, Ecphantos. So this is a riddling way of saying "Hegelochos, along with his son, Ecphantos, dedicated . . . "

Hegelochos, possessing a share of great love for his new country
and every virtue, is a resident in this city.
Critios and Nesiotes made this work.

The statue (here speaking to the reader, hence "me") probably represented either a striding warrior or Athena dressed in armor. The "labors of Ares" might refer to the Persian Wars, in which Hegelochos (who seems to have been a foreigner residing permanently in Athens) perhaps fought on the Athenian side. This is one of the earliest references to Athena as Athena Parthenos. In other early dedications she is referred to as Pallas and the daughter of Zeus.

C Dedication of a *Kore* (Statue of a Girl) to Poseidon, ca. 480–475 BC (*CEG* 266)

<Nau>lochos dedicated this *kore* as a first-fruits offering of his catch,
which the lo<rd> of the sea with the <gol>den trident provided.

The relations between the humans and gods expressed in these dedications seem perfunctory at best. Yet the two following inscriptions are not unusual in mentioning that the dedication would be a source of *charis*. In the strict sense, *charis* is the beauty exhibited by an object or person. It was personified in mythology as the Charites. In a more general sense, though, *charis* can mean the gratitude and goodwill created when gifts and favors are exchanged. These dedicators, then, conceived of the gods in somewhat human terms and were attempting to establish the same sort of long-term beneficial relationship as they would with a human benefactor.

D Dedication of a *Herm* (a Pillar Topped with Hermes' Head) on the Acropolis, ca. 500–480 BC (*CEG* 234)

To Hermes he dedicated this <fine> gift here, <providing> *charis*,
Oin<obio>s, the herald, for the sake of remembrance.

E Dedication of a Statuette to Apollo in Thebes, ca. 700–675 BC (*CEG* 326)

Manticlos dedicated me to the far-shooter, silver-bowed god,
as a tithe. Phoibos, provide *charis* in return!

Although not common, a dedication will sometimes indicate the features or power of a god that the dedicator found especially attractive. A case in point is the following dedication from Side in southern Turkey, which presents several other interesting features. It is relatively late, being six or seven centuries after Homer and Hesiod, but it reflects the continuing relevance of the gods. Some of this relevance derived from the fact that, as here, considerable honor accrued to those who served the gods.

F Dedication of a Statue of Eros to Aphrodite, late 1st c. BC or early 1st c. AD (*SEG* 34 1308 = Nollé, *EA* 4 [1984] 17–25)

Dionysios dedicated me, Eros <the child of Chaos>,
having obtained <the same office> as his father, Pa<ion>.
I carry in my hand the fire-flaming thunderbolt,
which once the Cyclopes forged for the lord of the gods,
Zeus the deep-thundering, demonstrating that, even though small,
I, the well-winged one, have awesome power.
Dionysios Maleis, the son of Paion
son of Polychares,
when he was temple steward
for Aphrodite.

The reference to the Cyclopes as the makers of Zeus' thunderbolt recalls Hesiod, *Theogony* 140–142, suggesting that the gap in the first line might be restored to coincide with Hesiod's view in the first lines of the *Theogony* that Eros was the child of Chaos.

FUNERARY MONUMENTS

Early Greek *epitaphs* (inscriptions on tombstones or the vessels designed to hold the ashes of the dead) tended to record little more than the name of the deceased. As time went on, epitaphs became much fuller and sometimes reflected the deceased's or his family's view about the nature of the gods and the roles they might play in an individual's life on earth and in the hereafter. As the following three epitaphs indicate (see also Inscription S), the views expressed could vary greatly, partially because the diverse nature of the Greek pantheon allowed for considerable divergence in religious beliefs.

G Epitaph for a Teacher from Rhodes, 2nd c. BC (Peek, *GV* 1916)

This man taught school for fifty years
plus two, and he <has reached> the land of the pious.
Plouton and Kore have given him a home.
Hermes and torch-bearing Hecate have rendered him
beloved to all and made him steward of the mysteries
due to his complete belief.

Stranger, approach this monument and learn clearly <how many>
have crowned these gray temples of mine.

H Epitaph for a Skeptic from Rome, 3rd or 4th c. AD (Peek, *GV* 1906.1–1906.8)

Do not pass my epitaph by, traveler,
but stop and listen, and only when you understand, move on.

There is no boat in Hades, no ferryman Charon,
no Aiacos, keeper of the key, no hound Cerbelos.[2]
All of us who have died and gone below are
bones, ashes, not one thing else.
I have spoken to you truly. Leave, traveler,
lest even dead I appear to you to be a chatterbox.

I Epitaph for a Wife from Pergamon, 1st or 2nd c. AD (Peek, *GV* 2040.23–2040.36)

Farewell, Pantheia, my wife, from me, your husband, who
suffers inconsolable sorrow since you met your woeful fate.
Never has Hera, the marriage goddess, seen such a wife,
noted for her beauty, her prudence, her faithfulness.
You bore me children all like myself.
You took care of your spouse and children,
holding straight the rudder of our lives at home
and increasing the public reputation of our art.
Although a woman, you never fell short of me in skill.
So your husband, Glycon, built for you this tomb,
which also hides the body of immortal Philadelphos.
Here too will I lie when I die.
As I duly shared my bed with you alone,
so too I <will cover myself> with the same earth.

This inscription was set up by a physician to honor his dead wife, who was also a physician ("our art"). Buried in the same tomb was Glycon's father, Philadelphos. Glycon calls upon Hera because she was considered the guardian and promoter of wifely virtue ("children all like myself" means that his children were truly his).

RELIGIOUS REGULATIONS

While not all Greeks were as strict as the superstitious man described by Theophrastus (see the main part of the volume), they did acknowledge that great care and exactness were needed in dealing with the gods. This concern was reflected in the many regulations set up in cities and sanctuaries governing how gods were to be worshiped and how worshipers should act. Because sacrifices were such an integral part of the worship of the gods and were the major source of meat in Greek cities, inscriptions often give detailed instructions about how, once the god received his portion, the sacrifice was to be divided, e.g., what parts the priest or priestess received (also see Inscription R below). As well, instructions were often given to ensure that

[2] As recorded on the stone for Cerberos.

the worshipers were not polluted and did not damage the purity of the sanctuary. As laws passed by the states where the cults were located, these regulations demonstrate the importance of the gods not just to individuals but to the whole political community. They also reflect the relative importance of ritual (as opposed to doctrine) in Greek religion.

J Sacrifices for Heracles on Thasos, ca. 440 BC (*LSCG* suppl. 63)

> For <Hera>cles of Thasos it is not right to sacrifice a <goa>t or a pig. Nor is it right for a woman to take part. A ninth part is not to be set aside; nor are honorary portions to be cut; nor is the meat to be used for prizes in athletic contests.

The prohibition against using the sacrifice for athletic prizes is interesting because Heracles was a favorite god of athletes. We have other documents prohibiting the participation of women in the worship of Heracles, but most documents are entirely silent on the matter.

K Sacrifices for Athena Patroia ("Ancestral") on Thasos, 5th c. BC (*LSCG* 113)

> For Athena Patroia sacrifices are to be performed every other year. And women get a share.

L Regulations for the Sanctuary of Athena Nicephoros ("Victory Bringer") in Pergamon, after 133 BC (Dittenberger, *SIG*^{3} 982.I–982.II)

> (I) Dionysios son of Menophilos was commissioner of sacred affairs for the People.
>
> (II) Let the citizens and all others perform religious rites and enter the temple of the goddess only after purifying themselves by washing from any sexual contact with their wives or husbands on that day, or from any contact with any other woman or man in the last two days. Likewise, they must purify themselves from any participation with preparing a corpse or contact with a woman giving birth in the last two days. After being at a funeral or funeral procession, they must be pure that day by sprinkling themselves with water and entering through the gate where the vessels for purification stand.

M Women at the Festival of Demeter at Patrai, 3rd c. BC (*LSCG* suppl. 33A)

> At the festival of Demeter women are not allowed to wear gold jewelry weighing more than five carats, wear embroidered cloaks or those dyed with purple, wear makeup, or play the flute. If someone breaks these regulations, the sanctuary must be purified because she has been impious.

N Maintaining Purity of Religious Areas on Delos, 3rd c. BC (*LSCG* suppl. 53)

Resolved by the Council and the People. Telemnestos son of Aristeides made the motion: That in the future the place <near> <Dio>nysos will remain pure and that nobody will toss anything into the purified place, nor into the sanctuary of Leto, neither <dung>, nor ashes, nor any<thing else>. This was decided by the Council and the People: If someone is caught doing any of these things, the one catching him is allowed to bring him before the Council and report him. The Council can have a slave beaten with fifty lashes in the stocks or fine a free man ten drachmas and summarily exact payment. Half of the silver is to be given to the temple wardens, half to the informer. The councilors are to have this decree engraved on a stele and set up next to the altar of Dionysos. The treasurers Tlepolemos and Nicarchos are to pay the expense of setting it up. Anphithales <son of> Praxon put the motion to the vote.

INSCRIPTIONS INVOLVING INDIVIDUAL GODS

As the selections from Pausanias included in this volume indicate, there was great variation in the way in which particular gods were worshiped by different Greek cities and in the stories told to explain those different rituals. Sometimes these variations reflect older, or at least different, views of a god than we would derive from literary accounts alone. In a similar fashion, inscriptions detailing how gods were to be worshiped in particular cites can provide us with information that we would not otherwise have. The following is a sample of what we can learn from inscriptions about Asclepios, Dionysos, and Zeus.

Asclepios

Epidauros, a city in the Argolid, was the most important site in the Greek world for the worship of the healing god Asclepios. During the 4th century BC (about the time the inscription below was set up) the sanctuary at Epidauros underwent a massive expansion marked by a building program that included an extensive temple for Asclepios and facilities for the worshipers who came there to be cured. At the same time Asclepios' cult was spreading throughout the Greek world. The importance Asclepios had in religion contrasts sharply with his relatively minor role in Greek myth (see Pausanias G), while the expansion in his worship testifies to the fact that Greek religion did undergo change over time.

O Cures Performed By Apollo and Asclepios at Epidauros, late 4th c. BC (Dittenberger, *SIG*^{3} 1168–1169)

This inscription is an official document set up in the sanctuary of Asclepios at Epidauros. When Pausanias toured the site in the 2nd century AD (the passage is included in the main part of the volume), six documents like this one could still be seen. Ostensibly, this document represented an official acknowledgment of the god's help, but it also served to advertise the power of Asclepios, especially as it was demonstrated at Epidauros. Of the more than forty cures described in this document we have here provided translations of eight. The description of each cure begins with a title listing the name of the person cured (men, women, and children all appear), the city from which the person came (from all over the Greek world), and the patient's medical problem. Then comes a description of how the god cured them. Sometimes thank-offerings in return for the god's services were recorded. What is not mentioned is that the priests are likely to have provided some medical treatment.

The patient's cure normally took place during "incubation" ("sleeping in"), the technical term for the period when a patient slept in the *abaton* ("place not to be entered") of the god's sanctuary in order to be cured. The *abaton* was a separate building from the temple. Patients could not enter it until they had ritually bathed to remove pollution and had made sacrifice. During incubation the god appeared to the patients in dreams and cured them in various ways. Sometimes the god would perform surgery or apply a medicine himself. At other times, a sacred animal, most often a snake, would be used to effect the cure. Asclepios was closely associated with snakes in myth, art, and cult.

(I) The God. Good Fortune. The Cures of Apollo and Asclepios.

<Cl>eo, pregnant for five years.

She had already been pregnant for five years when she came as a suppliant to the god and went to sleep in the *abaton*. As soon as she left the *abaton* and had gotten outside the sanctuary, she bore a boy. Right after his birth he washed in the spring and walked around with his mother. Having obtained these results, she had inscribed on her dedication: "Marvel not at the size of the tablet but at the god's power, how Cleo carried this weight in her stomach for five years until she went to sleep and he made her healthy."

(IV) Ambrosia from Athens, having the use of only one eye.

She came as a suppliant to the god. Walking around the sanctuary, she laughed at some of the cures as being unbelievable and impossible—that the lame and blind became healthy just from seeing a dream. Falling asleep, she had a dream. The god seemed to stand next to her and <say> that he would make her healthy, but as recompense she would have to dedicate a silver pig as a reminder of her ignorance. After he said <this,> he cut open her diseased eye and poured in medicine. When day came, she came out cured.

(VI) <Pandar>os of Thessaly, having marks from a tattoo[3] on his forehead.

<Falling asleep,> he had a dream. <The god> seemed to bind his marks with a bandage and ordered him, when he went <outside> the *abaton*, <to remove> the bandage and dedicate it in the temple. When day came,

[3] Criminals and slaves were sometimes marked on their foreheads.

> he <rose> and removed the bandage. His forehead <had been cleared> of the marks, and in the temple he dedicated the bandage <with> the letters from his forehead on it.

After Pandaros left, he sent his friend Echedoros, who was interested in having his own tattoos removed, to Epidauros with money for a thank-offering to the god. As the next passage shows, Echedoros tried to cheat both his friend and Asclepios but got his just rewards.

> (VII) Echedoros, received the <marks> of Pandaros in addition to his existing ones.
>
> Although he had gotten <money from Pandaros> to make a dedication to the god in Epidauros on his behalf, he did <not> deliver it. Falling asleep, he had a dream. It seemed that the god stood next to him and asked if he had some money from Pandaros from the town of Euthenai for a dedication in the sanctuary. He said that he had not gotten anything of the sort from Pandaros, but that if the god made him healthy, he would set up an image with an inscription. After this the god bound Pandaros' bandage over Echedoros' marks and ordered him, when he had left the *abaton*, to remove the bandage, wash his face with water from the spring, and then to look at himself in the water. When day came, he left the *abaton* and removed the bandage, which no longer had the letters on it. Gazing into the water, he saw his face had acquired the letters of Pandaros in addition to his own.
>
> (XV) Hermodicos of Lampsacos, lacking control of his body.
>
> The god cured him as he slept and ordered him, when he had left, to carry into the temple as large a stone as he could. He carried it and left the stone lying in front of the *abaton*.

A huge stone with a poem inscribed on it describing Hermodicos' accomplishment and attributing it to Asclepios' skill has been found at Epidauros, but the poem seems to date considerably later than this inscription.

> (XIX) Heraieus from Mytilene.
>
> He had no hair on his head but a whole lot on his face. Ashamed <because> people made fun of him, he went to sleep. The god smeared his head with medicine and caused it to have hair.
>
> (XXIII) Arista<gora of Troiz>en.
>
> She, having worms in her abdomen, went to sleep in the sanctuary of Asclepios in Troizen and saw a dream. It seemed that the sons of the god (he himself was not there but was in Epidauros) cut off her head but were not able to put it back on. So they sent someone to Asclepios so that he would come. Meanwhile, day caught up with them and the priest <clearly> saw the head separated from the body. The next night Aristagora had a dream. It seemed that the god arrived from Epidauros and put her head back on her neck. After this, he cut open her abdomen, removed the worms, and stitched her up. And after that she became healthy.

Troizen, a city not far from Epidauros, also had a sanctuary of Asclepios. At many sanctuaries of Asclepios, his sons Machaon and Podaleirios, already known for their skill in medicine in Homer's *Iliad*, were worshiped alongside him. Stories of the god cutting off a part of a patient's body were not unusual, and a much less contorted version of this story, without any mention of Troizen, is preserved by an author who wrote considerably before the previous inscription was set up.

> (XLII) Nicasiboula of Messenia, concerning having children.
> <Falling asleep> she had a dream. The god appeared <to come> to her bearing a snake; she had intercourse with it. <And after this> she had two male children within the year.

Dionysos

The impression gained from many stories told about Dionysos is that his worship was viewed as threatening, in part because it might lead women to be out of control. The inscriptions mentioning the cult of Dionysos, which are admittedly much later than many of the stories, paint a different picture. Three of the inscriptions given here show that cities were welcoming to his cult, even seeking it out, and that participation in his worship was quite acceptable for women, many of whom served as cult officials. The fourth reveals (and at least one other implies) Dionysos' connection with mysteries that were thought to provide the initiates some solace in the afterlife.

P Epitaph for a Priestess of Dionysos from Miletos, 3rd or 2nd c. BC (Henrichs, *HSCP* 82 [1978] 148)

> Bacchai of the City, say, "Farewell, pious
> priestess!" This is fitting for a good woman.
> She led you to the mountain, and she carried all the apparatus
> and sacred objects in procession before the whole city.
> If a stranger asks her name—Alcmeionis
> daughter of Rhodios, assured of her share of blessings.

When alive this woman had two separate duties: leading Bacchai into the mountains for rites there and taking part in a festival the city held for Dionysos. The last line implies (as does Inscription S below) that Dionysos has provided this woman some solace after death due to her worship. The "Bacchai of the City" may not mean the worshipers of Dionysos who happened to be living in Miletos but officially sanctioned priestesses like those mentioned below in Inscription R.

Q Establishment of Bacchic Rites in Magnesia on the Maeander (Henrichs, *HSCP* 82 [1978] 123–125 = *I.Magn.* 215A.24–215A.41, B)

> [*On the stele*]
> "Go to the sacred plain of Thebes to get
> Mainads of the race of Cadmean Ino.

They will give you the rites and noble customs
And establish *thiasoi* of Bacchos in the city."

In accordance with the oracle, through the agency of the messengers sent to Delphi, three Mainads from Thebes were granted: Cosco, Baubo, and Thettale. Cosco assembled the "Plane Tree" *thiasos*, Baubo the one outside the city, and Thettale the "Cataibatai" *thiasos*. When these women died, they were buried by the people of Magnesia. Cosco is buried in Cosco Hill, Baubo in the place called Tabarnis, and Thettale near the theater.
[On the base on which the stele stood]
For the god Dionysos, Apollonios Mocolles, head mystic, had the ancient oracle inscribed on the stele and dedicated it along with the base.

The first part of the oracle (not translated here) describes how the people of Magnesia were prompted to send to Delphi for advice because an image of Dionysos was found in a plane tree after a storm, hence the reference to the "'Plane Tree' *thiasos*." A *thiasos* (plural: *thiasoi*) was a group of people who joined together to worship a god; most often the term was applied to worshipers of Dionysos. The first two *thiasoi* were likely made up of women only, but the third included men ("Cataibatai" is masculine in form). "Cataibatai" may be a reference to Zeus Cataibates, "Zeus who descends as lightning," and hence this *thiasos* may have met where lightning had struck. The oracle from Delphi dates to the third century BC, while the inscription itself dates to the 2nd century AD. Apollonios seems to have done some historical research to locate the oracle and determine where the priestesses were buried. During the Roman Empire many Greeks looked to their past, religious and otherwise, to affirm their sense of identity.

R Regulations for the Cult of Dionysos at Miletos, 3rd c. BC (*LSAM* 48)

Whenever the priestess <performs> the sacrifices on behalf of the city < . . . > it is not permitted for anyone to put the raw meat sacrifice in <before the prie>stess has done so for the city. Nor is it permitted for anyone to assemble his or her *thiasos* before the public one is assembled. If a man or woman wants to sacrifice to Dionysos, let him or her designate whichever of the two he or she prefers to perform the sacrifice,[4] and let the one designated take the honorary portion. The payment for the priesthood is to be paid in installments over ten years, with a tenth part each year. *<what follows is a schedule for paying the installments, after which the inscription is heavily damaged>*

< . . . > the priestess to appoint women < . . . > to prov<ide the women> with the instruments required for initiation for all *orgia*. If a woman wants to sacrifice to Dionysos, let her give honorary portions to the

[4] The person is choosing whether the priest or the priestess will perform the sacrifice.

> priestess: the spleen, the kidneys, the intestines, the sacred portion, the tongue, and the part of the leg cut off at the hip-joint. And if a woman wants to perform initiations for Dionysos Bacchios in the city, in the country, or in the islands, she must give the priestess a stater {a gold coin} at each triennial festival.[5] And at the Catagogia the priests and priestesses of Dionysos Bacchios are to lead back {*katagein*} Dionysos with the <priest> and priestess[6] in a procession that lasts from before dawn until sunset. *<the inscription is heavily damaged at this point>*

Some priesthoods were inherited in antiquity; others were sold, as here, with the buyer obtaining the honor of the position and a share of the sacrifices. This inscription details the regulations governing the chief priestess of Dionysos, particularly her relationship to the chief priest and to her subordinates. While damaged, the text makes it quite clear, contrary to what is sometimes claimed, that the worshipers did not eat the raw meat sacrifice (*omophagion*), although we do not know where the meat was to be put.

The Catagogia ("Festival of the Return") was celebrated in Miletos and several nearby cities. As to the nature of this festival, one can only guess. One possible scenario is that during this festival a statue of Dionysos was brought into the city on a chariot or wheeled ship, possibly marking the renewal of the seasons.

S Dedication of a Statue to Dionysos from Nicomedeia, Unknown Date (*SEG* 34 1266 = Cole, *EA* 4 [1984] 37–49)

> Dionysos—I, Dion, was dear to you when alive, dancing with my young
> fellow carousers holding Bromios' nectar.
> And now I have set you beside my grave, beside me, for all to see,
> so that I, dead but not gone, may look upon you.

Zeus

The following inscription comes from a shrine on Mount Dicte, located in eastern Crete and identified by some ancients as the birthplace of Zeus (see Apollodorus A1). The inscription was inscribed in the 3rd century AD, but the poem is much older, dating to at least the 3rd century BC and perhaps even earlier. The inscription gives a hymn to Dictaean Zeus, although the name Zeus never actually appears; the poet only uses the title Greatest Kouros {"Youth"}. The Zeus worshiped on Crete was very different from the older, bearded Zeus of mainland Greece. In this hymn Zeus is presented as a vegetation god who dies (hence "you have gone to earth" in the refrain) and is reborn each year. His rebirth, the central feature of the poem, brings with it regeneration of nature, fertility, and prosperity for humankind.

The hymn likely reflects a ritual that was performed yearly by a chorus at the altar of Dictaean Zeus. The first six lines are repeated as a refrain following each of the six

[5] Every two years, counting inclusively.

[6] That is, the minor priests and priestesses alongside the chief priest and priestess.

stanzas. In order, the stanzas provide: (7–10) the setting; (17–20; perhaps the missing 27–30) a narrative of the god's birth on Crete, with perhaps mention of the Couretes (hence "shield" in line 19); (37–40) mention of peace and prosperity, perhaps owed to the god's presence on earth; (47–50, 57–60) the actual prayer to the god, an appeal for him to make his epiphany in many forms on earth.

T Hymn to the Dictaean Kouros (West, *JHS* 85 [1965] 149–150 = *I.Cret.* III.ii.2)

Io, Greatest Kouros!
Hail, Son of Cronos,
all powerful, who have gone to earth,
leading spirits divine!
Come to Dicte again this year
and rejoice in our song!
We are weaving it for you,
a knit of strings and flutes,
singing as we stand
around your well-walled altar.

[*Repeat lines 1–6 as refrain*]

For there they took you, a child divine,
shield < . . . >
from Rhea < . . . >
< . . . >

[*Repeat lines 1–6 as refrain*]

< . . . *three verses missing* . . . >

< . . . > of fair Eos.

[*Repeat lines 1–6 as refrain*]

< . . . > teeming yearly,
and man possessed Justice
< . . . > outside
prosperity-loving Peace.

[*Repeat lines 1–6 as refrain*]

Now, <Lord, spring up in the wine> jugs,

spring up in the deep-fleeced <flocks>,
spring up <in the field>s of grain,
and in the family th<at flourishes!>

[*Repeat lines 1–6 as refrain*]

<Spring up in> our cities,
spring up in our sea-going ships,
spring up in y<oung cit>izens,
spring up in re<nowned> law and order!

[*Repeat lines 1–6 as refrain*]

Appendix Three: Papyri

The most common material for writing in antiquity was papyrus, a material produced by pressing fibers from the papyrus plant together into sheets that were then assembled into a scroll. Because papyrus was no more resistant to damage than modern paper, most of the written works of antiquity we possess are not preserved on the material on which they were originally written. Rather, they survive because they were copied by hand over the centuries, eventually being transferred to books made of parchment and preserved in the libraries of medieval Europe and the Arab world. The major exceptions to this rule are inscriptions, the records written on stone that are discussed in Appendix Two, and papyri that were buried in Egypt, where dry conditions increased the odds of survival. Occasionally, nearly complete works have been found. More often all that we have to work with are scraps, especially since papyrus was recycled for various purposes, for instance, to make *cartonnage*, the papier-mâché casing of mummies. To make matters worse, when scholars and museums acquired papyri, they were sometimes purchased in random lots, which means that pieces that belonged together were often separated.

By their nature these scraps of papyrus often have large gaps that challenge our understanding of the meaning. In many cases papyrologists, the scholars who study papyri, have been able to fill in gaps using many techniques, such as by estimating how many letters have been lost or by comparing similar documents. Papyrologists also take great care to indicate what is actually found on a papyrus, what might have been on it, and what is not. We have not used their scholarly system of notation, but we have put major restorations of the text in brackets < > to alert the reader that this material is not certain or cannot be restored.

LITERARY PAPYRI

The majority of papyri are business or governmental documents, such as contracts and tax records. A significant number, however, contain literary material, some of which is useful for studying mythology. In some cases papyrologists have been able to assign fragments to well-known authors using an understanding of what their lost works covered and what was typical about their language and expression. Examples in this volume of papyri assigned to famous authors include Bacchylides' poem describing the adventures of Theseus and some portions of lost Greek tragedies. Yet not all papyri can be attributed to a particular author, and some are so fragmentary that the most that can be said is that they treated a mythological topic. If nothing else, they testify to myth's widespread appeal.

A Helen's Lament to Menelaos, ca. 100 BC (Powell, *CA* 185 = *P.Tebt. I.*1)

This papyrus, found in the wrappings of a mummified crocodile, preserves what may be a complete poem in two stanzas. In it, Helen addresses Menelaos after the fall of Troy. Menelaos has decided not to take Helen back, although it is not clear whether they are still at Troy or somewhere else. In the first part Helen reflects on Menelaos' love for her in the past; in the second she relates her shock when she discovers he intends to abandon her. We cannot say whether the poet was following an earlier tradition where Menelaos abandoned or thought about abandoning her or whether this was his own invention. However, the fact that Helen is allowed to give voice to her feelings is striking and calls to mind Ovid's *Heroides*, where famous female mythological figures are given a chance to express their complaints to their absent lovers, especially those who have abandoned them.

I once thought you my beloved source of
joy, back when you loved me,
when with the spear of war
you sacked the city of
the Phrygians, only
wanting to bring me,
your wedded wife, back home.

But now, heartless man, you're going away,
deserting me, your wife,
the one the army of the Danaans
came <to get,>
and because of whom Artemis took
the unmarried child,
Agamemnon's sacrificial victim.

B Boys Loved By Gods, Hellenistic (after 323 BC) or Roman Empire (*P.Oxy.* 3723)

This papyrus, recovered from a trash dump in the Egyptian town Oxyrhynchos, illustrates the difficulties scholars have in understanding papyri because of the damage they have suffered. What is clear about this poem is that it listed the boys with whom various gods fell in love. Since much of the papyrus has been lost, however, we are uncertain whether the poet listed these divine love affairs as a way of excusing his own infatuation with a particular boy or as examples illustrating the power of Eros. The poem is sometimes dated to the Roman Empire, but it might as easily belong to the Hellenistic period when, as may be happening here, poets looked for innovative ways to rework mythological themes.

Because we have at best only parts of lines left and often only single words, the following translation attempts to give the sense of the passage without adding more than we can safely say. Lines 1–2 might refer to Hephaistos' love of Peleus. Lines 3–10 may possibly have read something like (following J. L. Butrica's reconstruction)

"Apollo no longer wreaths the tripod with laurel or utters oracles from his sanctuary at Delphi but has placed as sign of his power his lyre/bow at the feet of Hyacinthos as a suppliant." Lines 11–16 concern a boy loved by Dionysos (from other sources likely to have been named Ampelos). In lines 17–22 the poet fancifully suggests that Heracles' love for Hylas was so overwhelming that it could be ranked among his labors. In line 23 the author may be addressing himself and his situation.

< . . . > quenched his fire
< . . . > foam-born
< . . . > he, having wreathed around
< . . . > tripod
< . . . > from the sanctuary
< . . . >ing with his mouth
<text is uncertain>
< . . . > suffering
< . . . > he placed at the feet of Hyacinthos
< . . . > as a suppliant
< . . . > and the foothills of Mount Tmolos
and of Cithairon where the woods dance < . . . >
with the initiated Bacchai < . . . >
clear crashing sound at his heels < . . . >
for the Indian boy as the spoils of love he placed < . . . >
the thyrsos that accompanies the dance < . . . >
O, yes, Alcmene's powerful <offspring . . .>
and who slew the lion's m<ight . . .>
pined away for the fair-haired Thracian Hylas' < . . . >
taking on love as his <thirtee>nth labor < . . . >
having known all lands < . . . >
to save his heart from harsh < . . . >
"Soul, to what story can I < . . . >"

C Eutychides Practices Penmanship, 3rd c. AD (Daniel, *ZPE* 49 [1982] 43–44 = *P.Mich.* inv. 4953)

This papyrus was an exercise designed to let a student, Eutychides, practice his cursive handwriting by copying out his schoolmaster's example. The text used is four lines of poetry, each of which treats a famous hero. Most of the fourth line is lost, but this is no matter because Eutychides gave up on his assignment even before reaching the end of the first line! Each line of the schoolmaster's text starts with a different letter of the alphabet, like a modern children's book "A is for . . ." (we have duplicated this feature below but with the English, not Greek, alphabet). What is interesting about this and similar exercises is that myth was so much a part of ancient culture that it was used in schools somewhat akin to the way material drawn from the Bible formed the basis of reading and writing exercises in the 17th and 18th centuries AD.

[*model written by the teacher*]
Althaia destroyed Meleagros with the ruthless firebrand.
Best of Bebryces, Amycos, did <Polydeuces> beat.
Cut off the dire Gorgon's head did Pers<eus>.
Detained with chains < . . . >

[*student's copy*]
Althaia destroyed Meleagros with the ruthless
[*signed*]
Eutychides son of Kalopos

MAGICAL PAPYRI

A considerable number of papyri record spells that an individual could use to make someone fall in love with him or her, prevent someone from doing something e.g., winning a chariot race, or injure an enemy. The power to accomplish these aims was expected to come from the gods, and a considerable portion of a spell was devoted to laying out the rites and sacrifices that would convince or compel the appropriate god. Spells might also explain what power a god possessed that made him or her suitable for the task at hand. A single spell might call on gods drawn from the Greek pantheon, as well as those from Egyptian and other Near Eastern mythologies.

Spells often include magical names or words that probably did not make sense to the person who used the spell, somewhat like a modern magician's abracadabra. These phrases, some nonsense and some drawn from languages like Persian and Hebrew, are printed here in capital letters. These were generic spells, and the user was expected to fill in the name of the person at whom the spell was directed or similar details. "NN" marks the places where the user needs to add the required information. Many of these spells were probably collected over a long period of time and may even have undergone changes. As a result, it is nearly impossible to date them.

D All-Purpose Magical Prayer to Selene[1] (*PGM* IV 2785–2890)

Selene does not have a prominent place in literary works but was important in the world of magic in part because she was equated with Hecate, a goddess much associated with the underworld and nighttime activities such as magic. (Hecate was also associated with things that come in three, hence the references to "triple ways," "three-faced," etc.). As a further sign of her power Selene is also equated here with Artemis, several other goddesses, and even forces of nature. Some spells call upon a god for a specific purpose, usually connected with matters appropriate to that god. Here, however, Selene-Hecate's power is so extensive that this spell can accompany any sort of request, with a minor variation in the offering depending on whether the user wanted to help or hurt someone.

[1] Translated by Richard L. Philips.

Prayer to Selene for any ritual:
"Come, dear Mistress, Selene triple-faced,
And heed my incantations with goodwill,
Glory of night, new one, bringing mortals light,
Child of morn, queen who sit upon fierce bulls,
Driving your chariot in a course equal to Helios,
Who dance with triple Graces triple-formed,
Rev'ling with stars. Justice and the Moirai's threads
You are, Clotho, Lachesis, Atropos,
Triple-headed, you are Persephone,[2]
Megaira, Allecto, with many forms,
Who arm your hands with dark, terrible lamps,
Who on your brow shake locks of fright'ning snakes,
Who from your mouths unleash the bellowings of bulls,
Whose womb is girded with scales of creeping things,
And rows of vipers from your shoulders hang,
Bound down your backs by bonds detestable,
Night-crier, bull-faced, lover of solitude,[3]
Bull-headed, bull-eyed, with a puppy's cry,
Hiding your forms 'midst the legs of lions,
Having ankles wolf-shaped, attended by wild dogs,
Wherefore, they call you Hecate, having
Many names, O Mene,[4] cleaving the air,
Like arrow shooting Artemis, goddess
Four-faced, four-named, inhabiting the crossing of four ways,
Artemis,[5] Persephone, deer-shooter,
Night-shining, triple-sounding, triple-voiced,
Triple-headed, triple-named Selene,
Triple-pointed, triple-faced, triple-necked,
Frequenting the triple ways, holding in
Triple baskets untiring flaming fire,
You who guard the crossing of triple ways,
You who are the ruler of three decades,
Favor me as I invoke you and kindly give heed,
O you who guard the vast cosmos by night,
Before whom daimons quake, immortals shake,
O goddess bringing glory unto men,
Called by many names, bearing fair offspring,

[2] Tisiphone, not Persephone, is traditionally one of the three Furies.

[3] Lit. the text reads, "lover of silence."

[4] Another Greek word meaning "moon."

[5] Some editors excise the wording, "Four-faced, four-named, inhabiting the crossing of four ways,/Artemis," since it does not appear in a parallel passage found earlier in the same manuscript (*PGM* IV 2523–28).

Bull-faced, horned, begetting gods and men, All-
Mother Nature; frequenting Olympos,
You traverse the wide and boundless abyss.
You are both the beginning and the end
And you alone are mistress of all things.
For all is from you and in you all ends,
Eternal One. On your temples you wear,
As everlasting diadem, chains of
Great Cronos, not to be broken or loosed,
And a golden scepter you hold in hand,
'Round which Cronos himself incised letters,
That he presented for you to bear in
Order that all things might remain steadfast:
"DAMNŌ DAMNOMENEIA DAMASANDRA DAMNODAMIA."[6]
And chaos you rule, ARARACHARARA ĒPHTHISIKĒRE,
Welcome, goddess, and hearken to your names,
This spice I burn for you, O child of Zeus,
Arrow shooting and goddess heavenly,
Presiding over harbors everywhere,
Mountain-roaming and dwelling at crossroads,
Nether and nocturnal, Hades-dwelling,
Goddess of darkness, quiet and frightful,
O you who hold your feasts amid the tombs,
Night, Erebos, and Chaos stretching-wide;
You are Necessity, hard to escape,
And you are Moira, Erinys, Inquisitor,
Destroyer, Justice. You hold Cerberos
In chains, you are dark with scales of serpents,
With snaky hair, by serpents encircled,
Imbiber of blood and bringer of death,
Breeding ruin and feasting on men's hearts,
Flesh-eating, devouring the untimely dead,
causing cries of mourning and the wanderings of madness,
come in return for my offerings, do this deed for me."

Offering for the ritual: For those who are doing good, offer storax, myrrh, sage, frankincense, and a fruit pit, but for those doing evil, offer magical material of a dog and a dappled goat, likewise that of a virgin who has died an untimely death.

[6] Perhaps with the meaning, "O you who are subduer are subdued, Subduer of men, O you who subdue."

Amulet for the ritual: Take a lodestone, on which let three-faced Hecate be engraved. And let the middle face be that of a horned virgin, and the left that of a dog, and the right that of a goat. After engraving the stone, clean it with natron and water and dip it into the blood of someone who has died a violent death. Then make an offering of food to it and utter the same invocation during the rite.

E Spell to Make Aphrodite Attract One's Lover[7] (*PGM* IV 2891–2942)

Aphrodite was a logical goddess to call upon for a love spell. This spell, like others, assumes that a god could be compelled to come to the aid of the user. In this respect it differs from the previous spell, which took the form of a prayer and hoped to obtain Selene's help by praising her power rather than by coercion.

Ritual for attracting someone:

Offering to the star of Aphrodite:[8] [Take] blood and fat of a white dove, unprocessed myrrh and dry wormwood. Form small pellets and offer them to the star on vine wood or coals. And also have a vulture's brain ready to offer for the ritual utterance of compulsion. In addition take as an amulet a tooth from the upper right jawbone of a female ass or a tawny heifer that has been sacrificed. Bind it on your left arm with thread of Anubis.[9]

Ritual utterance of compulsion for the rite:
"If as goddess you act at all slowly,
You'll not see Adonis rise from Hades.
For running straightway, I'll bind him with adamantine chains,
Having done so I will tie him to a second Ixion's wheel,
Ne'er more to come to light, chastized, subdued.
Wherefore, act, lady, I beg, lead NN,
Whom NN bore, to come very quickly
To my door, me, NN, whom NN bore,
Driven by madness to my love and bed
With violent goads, by compulsion led.
Today, now, quick, you, Cythere, I summon.
NOUMILLON BIOMBILLON AKTIŌPHI ERESCHIGAL NEBOUTOSOULALĒTH PHROURĒXIA THERMIDOCHĒ BAREŌ NĒ

Ritual utterance of compulsion:
"Foam-born Cythereia, both gods and men

[7] Translated by Richard L. Phillips.

[8] The planet Venus.

[9] Jackal-headed Egyptian god who is patron of emblamers, protector of the necropolis, and guide of the deceased.

Begetting, ethereal and chthonic,
All-Mother Nature, goddess unsubdued,
Binding all things, making great fire orbit,
You keep BARZA[10] in round, constant motion,
Unbroken. You complete all, head to toe,
And by your will holy water is mixed,
When you stir the one 'mid the stars with your hands, ROUZŌ,[11]
Center of the cosmos, whom you hold fast.
Into men's souls you move holy desire,
Likewise, attract women to men, making
Woman desirous to man ever more.
Our queen, goddess, mistress, by these incantations come,
ARRŌRIPHRASI, GŌTHĒTINI Cyprus-born, SOUÏ ĒS THNOBOCHOU THORITHE
STHENEPIŌ, mistress, SERTHENEBĒÏ, and smite with flaming desire NN, whom NN bore,
So that for me NN, whom NN bore,
Through the force of love she melt ever more.
You, blessed one, ROUZŌ, grant me, NN, these things,
Just as into your chorus 'mid the stars,
You lured an unwilling man to your bed.
And he, once led, made the great BARZA turn,
Who, once turned, ceased not, but whirling, is never at rest.
So lead NN, whom NN bore, to me,
My love and bed. You, Cyprus-born goddess,
Bring to fruition this incantation through and through."

If you see the star shining steadily, it is a sign that she has been smitten, but if it is sparkling, she is on the road, and if it is lengthened as a lamp, the ritual has already attracted her.

F Spell to Compel Cronos to Reveal the Truth[12] (*PGM* IV 3086–3124)

While the user of this spell grinds salt in a mill, Cronos is supposed to appear behind him ghost-like and dressed in the chains with which Zeus bound him. Cronos will then reveal to the person what he wants to know. It is not clear if Cronos will tell him about the future or give him the facts about some past event. To guard himself against Cronos and force him to help, the user must carve a picture of Zeus on the rib of a pig.

Sought after Oracle of Cronos, called "little mill": Take two liters of salt and grind them with a hand mill, repeating the ritual utterance until

[10] A magical word presumably tied to the Persian phrase, "shining light."

[11] Another magical word—perhaps of Persian origin—with unknown meaning.

[12] Translated by Richard L. Phillips.

you see the god. Do it at night in a place where grass grows. If, while saying this, you hear the sound of a heavy step and clanging iron, the god is coming, bound with chains and holding a sickle. But do not be alarmed, since you are protected by the amulet that is about to be revealed to you. Clothe yourself in clean linen with the attire of a priest of Isis. Offer the god sage with a cat's heart and horse manure.

This is the ritual utterance to be spoken while you are grinding: Ritual utterance: "I summon you, the great holy one, you who created the entire inhabited world, you who suffered the unlawful act at the hands of your own son, you whom Helios bound with adamantine bonds in order that the whole world might not collapse in disorder, hermaphrodite, father of the thunderbolt, the one who is master of all who lie beneath the earth, AÏE OI PAIDALIS PHRENOTEICHEIDŌ STUGARDĒS SANKLEON GENECHRONA KOIRAPSAÏ KĒRIDEU THALAMNIA OCHTOTA ANEDEÏ; come, master, god, and under compulsion tell me about the NN matter at hand. For I am the one who revolted against you, PAIDOLIS MAINOLIS MAINOLIEUS." These are to be spoken, while the salt is being ground.

The ritual utterance that compels him is: "KUDOBRIS KODĒRÏEUS ANKURIEUS XANTOMOULIS." When he enters in a threatening manner, you are to say these things so that he will be pacified and will address the matters about which you are inquiring.

The sought after amulet against him: Onto a piglet's broad rib, carve Zeus holding a sickle and this name "CHTHOUMILON." Or let it be the broad rib of a black, scaly, castrated boar.

Ritual utterance for dismissal: "ANAEA OCHETA THALAMNIA KĒRIDEU KOIRAPSIA GENECHRONA CANĒLON STUGARDĒS CHLEIDŌ PHRAINOLE PAIDOLIS IAEI, go away, master of the cosmos, forefather; and withdraw to your own places in order that the universe might be protected. Be favorable to us, lord."

G Spell to Catch a Thief[13] (*PGM* V 172–212)

This spell seeks Hermes' help in locating a thief. The spell also enlists the aid of all-seeing Helios, Themis (the personification of justice and right action), Erinys (Avenging Fury), Ammon (an Egyptian god equated with Zeus), and Parammon (an Egyptian god sometimes equated with Hermes). The suspects are required to drink a special mixture, and Hermes is supposed to keep the thief from drinking his serving.

Another way:[14] "To catch a thief, I summon you, Hermes, immortal god, who cut a furrow down Olympos, and a sacred barge, light-burning Iao,[15] the great immortal one, awesome to behold and awesome to hear. Hand

[13] Translated by Richard L. Phillips.

[14] In ritual handbooks such a title generally implies that a spell has the same intent as the one preceding it.

[15] Iao, derivec from the name of the Hebrew god Yahweh, appears frequently in magical texts.

over the thief whom I am seeking ABERAMENTHŌOULERTHE XENAX SONELUSŌTHNEMAREBA."[16] This ritual utterance is to be spoken twice during the act of purification.

Ritual utterance of the bread and cheese: "Come to me, LISSOIN MATERNA MAUERTĒ PREPTEKTIOUN INTIKIOUS OLOKOTOUS PERIKLUSAI. May you bring me what has been lost and make the thief known on this very day. I call upon Hermes, finder of thieves, and Helios and Helios' pupils, two illuminators of unlawful deeds, and Themis and Erinys and Ammon and Parammon, to take control of the thief's ability to swallow and make him known on this very day, in this very hour.

Procedure for the ritual: The same ritual utterance during the act of purification. Take a blue-green, glazed vessel[17] and add water, myrrh, and kynokephalion plant.[18] Wet a laurel branch and [sprinkle], cleansing each individual. Take a tripod and place it on an earthen altar. Offer myrrh, frankincense, and a frog's tongue. Take unsalted winter wheat and 8 drams of cheese, while saying the following ritual utterance (inscribe this name and glue it underneath the tripod): "Master Iao, bringer of light, hand over the thief, whom I am seeking." If one of them does not swallow what has been given to him, *he* is the thief.

[16] It appears as if these magical words once formed a palindrome that has since been corrupted. The appearance of such palindromes in the magical texts is quite common.

[17] Most likely Egyptian faïence.

[18] Ancient sources identify this plant as calf's snout and fleawort.

Appendix Four: Near Eastern Myth

General Introduction

Our understanding of ancient history, literature, language, and culture was transformed dramatically in the 19th century by the discovery of cities, monuments, and texts from the ancient Near East, that is, from Egypt, Mesopotamia (Iraq), Anatolia (Turkey), Persia (Iran), and the Levant (Syria, Lebanon, Israel, and Jordan). In a few short decades the range of evidence and the area of the world we could study on the basis of its own sources expanded drastically. Since this first period of discovery, scholars working on these archaeological sites and texts have continued to increase our knowledge of Near Eastern cultures and their languages. These new discoveries have had an enormous effect on the study of antiquity and in particular have changed our view of how Greek culture developed. Rather than envisioning Greece as closed off from its neighbors, we now view ancient Near Eastern cultures as having vigorous communication and interchange both amongst themselves and with other areas of the Mediterranean, including Greece. It was inevitable that Greece, whose culture developed later than the other Near Eastern cultures, would adopt technologies and ideas from its neighbors. Mythical stories were naturally part of this process of borrowing and adaptation.

With regard to myth, the most important new evidence came in the form of previously unknown images and especially texts from the Near East.[1] As Mesopotamian documents were deciphered in the mid-19th century, an enormous corpus of new sources, including many that were clearly mythological in nature, came to light and began to be translated. Many of these showed that motifs in Greek myth were already found in Near Eastern texts from several centuries earlier, perhaps most obviously the myth of the catastrophic flood already known from the Greek story of Deucalion and the biblical tale of Noah in the book of *Genesis*. But scholars have established many other points of contact between Greek and Near Eastern myth, and as we find and decipher more texts we likely will discover further ways in which the Greeks adapted mythical material from their eastern neighbors.

For students of classical myth the similarities between Greek and Near Eastern myth will become obvious almost immediately. Three examples can be seen in the selections

[1] While this appendix treats only literary texts that provide parallels with Greek myth, there are images and inscriptions that provide further points of contact. Perhaps the most compelling are the images found on Mesopotamian seals that show a god, probably Ninurta, who wears an animal's skin and carries a club and a bow, reminiscent of Heracles. In an inscription found on the Gudea cylinders (ca. 2100 BC) we find a list of Ninurta's conquered foes, the eleven Slain Warriors (Heracles' twelve labors?), among whom are found a seven-headed serpent (Hydra?), a bison (Cretan Bull?), and a "terrible" lion (Nemean Lion?).

given below: (1) the flood stories in the *Epic of Gilgamesh*, *Atrahasis*, and *Genesis* will call to mind the great flood that Deucalion and Pyrrha survive in Greece; (2) the accounts of generational conflict among the gods in the Babylonian *Epic of Creation* and especially the Hittite *Song of Emergence* resemble similar narrative structures in Hesiod's *Theogony*; (3) the antagonism between gods and mortals (and between Zeus and Prometheus), featured in so many Greek myths, is found explicitly in the *Atrahasis* and implicitly in other texts. Of course, these narratives differ from Greek myths in many important ways, but the parallels between Greek and Near Eastern myth certainly raise the question of how Greek myth came to be influenced by these cultures.

Despite the clear similarities in Greek and Near Eastern myths, and despite the certainty that in the early period the Greeks borrowed motifs from the Near East and not the other way around, we unfortunately cannot determine how or when these motifs from the Near East made their way into Greek myth. The most likely period of transmission was from the 10th to 7th centuries BC, when there was renewed vigorous communication between Greece and the Near East, but it is also possible that some of the motifs had already made their way to Greece in the Mycenaean period (15th–13th c. BC) and perhaps even before. Indeed, by the 17th century BC we already find valuable objects imported from the East in the shaft graves in the Greek city of Mycenae. If goods were traded, it makes sense that ideas could be traded alongside them.

We also do not know the precise process by which mythological elements "migrated" from the Near East to the Greek world. Was it through iconography, that is, the pictures found on Mesopotamian seals or other ceramics that found their way to Greece? Was it from traveling storytellers visiting Greece from the East, even though they probably did not speak Greek? Or did Greek travelers to the East bring back stories that were transformed into Greek tales? Again, differences in language may have made this a challenge. Or did migrants from the Near East who settled in Greece bring the rich tradition of stories with them? We do know of one example of an eastern Greek moving to the Greek mainland: Hesiod (*Works and Days* 633–40), who lived perhaps between the end of the 8th century and the beginning of the 7th century BC, tells us that his father migrated from the Greek city Cyme in Asia Minor to Ascra in mainland Greece. Is it coincidence that Hesiod's *Theogony* shares motifs with the Hittite *Song of Emergence*, which also originated in Asia Minor, though centuries before Hesiod's time?

It is telling, however, that as far as the evidence allows us to judge, there is no single Greek myth that was adopted in its entirety from the Near East. To take one example, the succession of divine kings in the Hittite *Song of Emergence* is not the result of sons deposing their fathers, as in Hesiod's *Theogony*, but of two families overthrowing each other until the emergence of the supreme god, Teshub. Thus, it is clear that the Greeks did not simply copy any particular Near Eastern myth, but likely borrowed parts of stories, or motifs, that suited their own purposes. In other words, even when Near Eastern influence is evident, Greek storytellers clearly adapted the narrative elements to fit a specifically Greek context.

Our understanding of Greek myth is thus enhanced by understanding its place within the broader context of the Mediterranean and the Near East. And yet, we must resist the impulse to regard any mythical tradition as less original because it drew from a web of ideas that circulated from place to place as people moved about. To some extent all mythical traditions are fluid. The story of Noah and the flood in *Genesis* is clearly derived from Mesopotamian predecessors (see *Atrahasis* and *The Epic of Gilgamesh*), but it has been adapted to fit its Hebraic context. In the same way, Greek myth reflects, and frequently self-consciously explains, specifically Greek practices, attitudes, rituals, and place names—even if the Greeks borrowed many of the underlying motifs from other cultures.

In this appendix we provide a selection of the most important Near Eastern texts for the study of Greek and Roman myth. First is the account of the flood myth told by Utanapishtim in the *Epic of Gilgamesh* (Tablet XI), followed by excerpts from the *Atrahasis* (Atrahasis is another name for Utanapishtim), which recounts the creation of humans to relieve the gods of their labor, the attempts of Enlil to destroy humans after they multiply and become too loud, and finally Atrahasis' survival of the flood. Next, we offer excerpts from the creation story in the Babylonian *Epic of Creation* (*Enuma Elish*), which narrates a series of divine conflicts until the installment of the Babylonian god Marduk as the supreme deity. The notion of divine conflict is also at the center of the next text, the Hittite *Song of Emergence*, which recounts the violent succession of kings of heaven until the emergence of the storm god Teshub. Finally, we offer the opening chapters of *Genesis* from the Hebrew Bible, which narrates the creation of the world and of humans, God's attempt to destroy humanity because of its wicked nature, and Noah's survival of the flood.

Readers encountering these works for the first time will perhaps be intimidated by their language and extremely fragmentary state. With the exception of *Genesis*, which has been continuously transmitted from antiquity onward as the first book of the Bible, these texts were written in cuneiform ("wedge-writing") on clay tablets, whose survival was accidental. As one might imagine, these clay tablets were prone to damage when walls fell in on top of them, and many of those translated here are quite fragmentary. Because of the limited number of texts from these cultures, we also do not know everything about the languages found on the tablets (Sumerian, Akkadian, Hittite). Thus, sometimes we do not know what a word or phrase means even when we can read the tablet clearly. As elsewhere in this book, material in brackets "< . . . >" must be treated as uncertain.

Major Cultures of Mesopotamia, Syria, and Anatolia

Before introducing the texts, it may be helpful to have an overview of some major Near Eastern cultures and some of their gods.

Sumerians: The oldest identifiable ethnic group of Mesopotamia, the Sumerians lived in the far south of the land between the Euphrates and Tigris rivers. In the first half of the third millennium BC they lived in independent city-states like Gilgamesh's city of Uruk until the creation of the Old Akkadian empire in the 24th century BC. They established the major patterns of civilization for the western world, including a sedentary agricultural economy, urbanization, specialization of labor, organized politics, organized military, writing, and the oldest literary tradition in the world.

The Sumerians were the first culture to invent writing, possibly as early as 3400 BC. Their language is a language isolate, which means that it is not related to any other known language. The Sumerian writing system itself is called cuneiform ("wedge-shaped") and consists of hundreds of symbols, all formed by pressing wedges onto soft clay tablets. The earliest Sumerian texts are primarily accounting and administrative records, but by about 2600 BC the Sumerians had begun to record literary texts (hymns, wisdom literature, and narratives like the *Epic of Gilgamesh*). After a period of subjugation under the Old Akkadian empire (see below), the Sumerians and their literary tradition flourished again in the 21st to 20th centuries BC under the Third Dynasty of Ur. Under this dynasty's most prosperous king, Šulgi, Sumerian literature revived, not only in copying down older stories but also in the composition of new works. Extant copies of Sumerian texts are found even long after the end of the Third Dynasty of Ur, down into the 17th century BC, when Sumerian as a spoken language was dead.

Old Akkadian: The Akkadians, named after their capital city Agade (which has never been found) and the land they called Akkad, were Semitic immigrants who moved into Mesopotamia in the middle of the third millennium BC. Eventually, under their first king, Sargon (24th to 23rd century BC), they achieved political autonomy. Sargon's conquests resulted in the first empire in human history, and he promoted his native Semitic language, Akkadian, over the language of the Sumerians. In the process he initiated the first instance in human history of the adaptation of an existing writing system (cuneiform) to a new language. This began an Akkadian scribal and literary tradition that lasted for two thousand years, through many dynasties and over a huge area. After the breakup of the Old Akkadian empire due to pressure from outside invaders, Sumerian experienced a revival under the Third Dynasty of Ur, as mentioned above. When that empire also fell to outside pressure, Akkadian speakers again asserted their cultural dominance, controlling both northern Mesopotamia (Assyria) and southern (Babylonia). These eventually became separate languages and cultures, although Assyrian and Babylonian are recognizable as dialects of Akkadian.

Old Babylonian: Partly responsible for the fall of the Third Dynasty of Ur were the Amorites, a second wave of Semitic invaders from the Semitic homeland in Syria. After the fall of the last Sumerian dynasty, the Amorites established themselves at Babylon, building it into the greatest city of southern Mesopotamia and promoting its god Marduk as the chief god of the pantheon, as can be seen below in the *Epic of Creation (Enuma Elish)*. The old Babylonian dynasty is also famous for the Code of Hammurabi, created by the sixth king of the dynasty. This dynasty was destroyed by a Hittite raid led by King Muršili I (ca. 1595 BC).

Middle Babylonian: After the fall of the Old Babylonian dynasty, Babylon was controlled for about four hundred years (to the mid-12th century BC) by Kassites, newcomers from the Zagros mountains to the north. Their language is another language isolate, although Babylonian Akkadian also continued to be used in Babylon. The Middle Babylonian period corresponds with the period of Kassite rule.

Neo-Assyrian: The greatest period in Assyrian history is its last, the Neo-Assyrian empire, which lasted from 911 to 609 BC. Assyria was centered around the traditional capital of Ashur, although wealthy Neo-Assyrian kings built other capitals, at Nineveh, Kalhu (Nimrud), and Dur-Sharrukin. In this period the Assyrians created the largest empire the world had ever known, including the conquest of Palestine mentioned in the Hebrew Bible. Although the Assyrians themselves did not produce major literary works, the later kings consciously collected many Mesopotamian literary texts in the great library of Nineveh, started by Sennacherib (704–681 BC) and built up by his grandson Ashurbanipal (668–627 BC). The Neo-Assyrian empire, which ruled by terror and constant warfare, was destroyed by a coalition that included the Medes, relatively recent Indo-European immigrants in Iran, and the Kaldu (Biblical Chaldeans) from southern Mesopotamia. So loathsome was the Assyrians' reign that the memory of them was all but lost to history after their fall, with only references in the Hebrew Bible attesting to their existence until the excavation of ancient Assyrian cities in the late 19th century.

Neo-Babylonian: After their success in toppling the Neo-Assyrians, the Kaldu established the last native Mesopotamian dynasty ever, the Neo-Babylonian dynasty. This dynasty is famous primarily for its conquest of the southern Hebrew kingdom of Judah and the sacking of Jerusalem and the Hebrew temple. The Neo-Babylonian king Nebuchadnezzar II (reigned ca. 605–562 BC) deported many of the conquered Hebrews to Babylon, in the Babylonian Exile. In 539 BC Babylon was conquered by the Persian king Cyrus the Great, ending forever native Mesopotamian rule over Mesopotamia and allowing the Jews to return to their home city to rebuild Jerusalem and the second Temple.

Hittites/Hurrians: The Hittite language is the oldest known Indo-European language (the language family that includes Greek, Latin, and English) preserved in texts. The Hittites migrated into Anatolia in the Middle Bronze Age, around 2000 BC. Originally settling an area south of their later capital, at a place called Kanesh (modern Kültepe), their probable first king Anitta created the first empire in Anatolia sometime in the 17th century BC. The Hittites later moved their capital to Hattuša (modern Boğazkale), where a large number of tablets have been found. The Hittite empire varied in size and strength over its history from 1600 to ca. 1180 BC, but generally controlled its homeland in central Anatolia plus much of the southern Anatolian coast and also south into Syria. Their treaty with a northwestern Anatolian state called Wiluša (Greek *Ilion*) is probably our earliest written evidence for Troy.

The Hittites as immigrants borrowed heavily from their neighbors. Early in their history they borrowed the Babylonian cuneiform writing system, which they used alongside a hieroglyphic system developed later. They also depended culturally on existing Anatolian cultures in their early history, eventually falling under the cultural sway of the Hurrians. The Hurrians, who spoke a language unrelated to any other Near Eastern language except for its descendant language Urartian, lived in northern Syria and Mesopotamia and southern Anatolia from the early second millennium BC. Sometime in the 13th century BC the Hittites captured the Hurrian capital, and soon afterwards the Assyrians annexed their territory, ending Hurrian political independence and their cultural identity.

The Hurrian influence on the Hittite state was extensive, as can be seen from the number of Hurrian or bilingual Hittite-Hurrian texts discovered at the Hittite capital of Hattuša. Some later Hittite kings may even have been ethnic Hurrians. This influence can be seen in the mythological narratives of the Hittite Empire period, all of which depend on Hurrian prototypes, as is evident in the Hurrian names and themes in the narratives. This is apparent in the *Song of Emergence* myth translated below, which favors the Hurrian name for the storm god, Teshub, over the native Hittite name Tarhun.

Primary Deities of the Ancient Near East

Note: In the following list, the names of Sumerian deities are by convention printed in all capital letters, whereas the names of Akkadian/Babylonian and Hittite gods are printed in lower case. In the translations which follow, however, nearly all names are printed in lower case script, with the exception of a few gods only known by their Sumerian names.

Adad: See (H)adad.

AN/Anu: Literally, "Sky." In the division of the cosmos he takes the heavens, and is a central character in the *Epic of Gilgamesh*, partly as the father of INANNA/Ishtar (see below). His sacred city was Uruk, also Gilgamesh's home city. The oldest Sumerian deity worshiped by Mesopotamians, he is one of the four primary deities in their pantheon.

Ba'al: A title, "lord," in Northwest Semitic languages (Hebrew, Aramaic). In Syria this title became associated with the storm god Hadad, and eventually became a divine name of a god associated with fertility. The Akkadian cognate Belu, also meaning "lord," came to be associated with Marduk, the victorious god of the *Epic of Creation (Enuma Elish)* and the chief deity of Babylon.

Belet-ili: See NINTU.

DAMKINA: See NINTU.

Ea: See ENKI.

ENKI/Ea: He is the god of the Apsu, the freshwater deep. His Sumerian name, ENKI, may mean "Lord Earth." He is adopted by the Akkadians/Babylonians as Ea, a name that may ultimately be Hurrian. His cult center was in the ancient Sumerian city of Eridu. He is the god of wisdom and cunning, and he helps humans survive the flood. As Anu is god of the sky and ENLIL of the earth, ENKI/Ea is the god of (fresh) waters. He is one of the four primary deities in the Mesopotamian pantheon.

ENLIL: Arguably the most powerful god in the Sumerian pantheon, his name "Lord Wind" denotes his sphere of influence as a storm god. His sacred city was Nippur, an ancient Sumerian city. His domain is the earth. Borrowed by Akkadians without a name change, he is one of the four primary deities of the Mesopotamian pantheon. He is the father of the moon god NANNA/Sin, the grain goddess NISABA, and the god of disease NAMTAR, among others.

(H)adad: The Akkadian storm god Adad reflects the Northwest Semitic (Amorites, Hebrews, Aramaeans) storm god Hadad. The Amorites brought this deity with them in their migration from Syria to Mesopotamia. The Sumerian storm god IŠKUR is less important than this imported storm god Adad, probably reflecting the fact that Sumerian agriculture in southern Mesopotamian is based not on rainfall but on bringing water from the great rivers to the crops, whereas Semites living in areas where weather was more unpredictable developed a very important storm god in their pantheon. In some traditions IŠKUR is the son of AN/Anu.

INANNA/Ishtar: The Mesopotamian goddess of erotic love and fertility on the one hand, and war on the other. She plays a major role in the *Epic of Gilgamesh* as the goddess who propositions and is rejected by Gilgamesh. She is the daughter of Anu, with whom she shared the cult sanctuary of Uruk. Associated with the planet we now call Venus (the Roman goddess of erotic love), she is one of the lesser of the seven major gods of Mesopotamia.

Kumarbi: The primary deity in the pantheon of the Hurrians (see above, "Hittites"). In the *Song of Emergence* he is the next-to-last king of heaven and the unwilling father of the storm god, whose Hurrian name is Teshub, who evidently then overthrows him.

MAMI: See NINTU.

Marduk: This Babylonian name probably derives from the original Sumerian AMAR. UTU, "calf of the sun." He is a later-generation deity who became the head of the Babylonian pantheon probably in the Old Babylonian period (see above). The *Epic of Creation* describes his rise to supreme power in the cosmos. He is the son of Ea and DAMKINA (see "NINTU" below).

NAMTAR: Son of ENLIL, he is the Sumerian bringer of pestilence in the form of sixty demons that attack the body (the Sumerian conception of disease), also adopted by the Babylonians. These demons also carried out his decisions on human fate. He could attack deities as well as mortals.

NINTU/MAMI/Belet-ili: All of these are secondary names for NINHURSAG (NIN, "lady" + HUR.SAG, "mountain"). NINTU means "lady of birth," MAMI (also written MAMMA) is the "Mother," and Belet-ili is an Akkadian name meaning "mistress of the gods." She is the only female deity of the four primary deities of Mesopotamia, and her sphere of influence is primarily birth and motherhood. Also called DAMKINA, she is the wife of ENKI and the mother of some of his children. She is also the mother of, among others, Ninurta, the god of hunting and war.

Tarhun: Also occurring in the form Tarhunza, this is the Hittite name for the storm god. From archaeological evidence the storm god is clearly the most important male god in the Hittite pantheon. In the Hittite Empire period, the Hittites increasingly referred to this god by his Hurrian name Teshub (see next).

Teshub: The Hurrian name of the storm god. In the *Song of Emergence*, Teshub is apparently the final successor to the kingship of heaven, the last victor in a struggle over succession that lasted at least four generations. The Hittite name of the storm god is Tarhun/Tarhunza (see previous).

UTU/Shamash: The sun god, considered the god of justice because he sees and illuminates everything; as such he is portrayed at the top of the Code of Hammurabi stele. He is one of the lesser of the seven primary gods of Mesopotamia, and in some traditions he is the offspring of the moon god NANNA/Sin.

The Epic of Gilgamesh: Tablet XI
Introduction

The *Epic of Gilgamesh* is the most famous work of Mesopotamian literature, and rightly so. It is the longest poem written in cuneiform Akkadian, as well as the most emotional and human of the mythical works from the Near East. It tells of the adventures of Gilgamesh, who was a real or at least legendary king of Uruk in the 2600s BC, but it is not a historical document. Instead, it is a mythological celebration of a determined man who, in his search for fame and immortality, overcomes challenges set by the gods, forges a friendship, suffers loss, and eventually realizes and confronts his own mortality. While there were individual stories about Gilgamesh written in Sumerian, it was not until the first Babylonian Dynasty (19th–16th c. BC) that an extended narrative evolved. This "epic" of Gilgamesh was extremely popular and became what might be called an international sensation; copies, or at least fragments of copies, have been found in many different locations in several of the main Near Eastern literary languages. The most important sources for the epic are the extensive fragments discovered in the Library of Ashurbanipal (668–627 BC) in Nineveh, from which the tablet translated below comes.

In Tablet XI, the discovery of which caused a great stir in London in 1872, Gilgamesh asks Utanapishtim ("He who found life," also called Atrahasis, "Exceedingly Wise") his great question: How were he and his wife the only ones to escape the universal fate of the human race? In answer, Utanapishtim relates the story of the flood, which is found in its original context in *Atrahasis* (see next selection). In the *Atrahasis*, humans have multiplied so much and become so rowdy that Enlil, the chief god on earth, tries to obliterate the human race in a number of ways, culminating in a destructive flood. His plans are frustrated by Ea (Enki), god of wisdom, who warns the mortal Utanapishtim of the impending flood, as is also the case in *Gilgamesh*. Because he has taken an oath not to reveal Enlil's plan to mortals, Ea directs his warning to the wall of a reed enclosure that Utanapishtim had built near the water. He advises Utanapishtim to build a boat, and he loads onto it his family, possessions, every type of animal, and skilled individuals. In the ark they survive the deluge sent by the rain god Adad, and after disembarking from the boat, which had come to rest on Mount Nimush, he prepares sacrifices for the gods, who "crowded round the sacrificer like flies" (line 166). The gods decide to keep the human population in check by other, less catastrophic means, and they make Utanapishtim and his wife immortal.

After Utanapishtim tells his story, he tells Gilgamesh that he must remain awake for six days and seven nights to obtain the eternal life he seeks. Gilgamesh instead sleeps for the entire period, and Utanapishtim orders his boatman, Ur-Shanabi, to take Gilgamesh away, both never to return. Thus, Gilgamesh is denied eternal life and humans no longer have access to Utanapishtim. As the two prepare to embark, Utanapishtim's wife asks him to give Gilgamesh something to show for his quest. He tells Gilgamesh where he could find the "plant of rejuvenation," which Gilgamesh obtains by diving into the depths of the sea, but as he bathes on his homeward journey, a snake devours the plant and rejuvenates itself by shedding its skin. Having lost eternal life and eternal youth, Gilgamesh returns to Uruk.

Text

Gilgamesh Asks Utanapishtim How He Gained Eternal Life

Gilgamesh said to him, to Utanapishtim the Distant One:
As I look upon you, Utanapishtim,
Your limbs are not different, you are just as I am.
Indeed, you are not different at all, you are just as I am!
Yet your heart is drained of battle spirit,
You lie flat on your back, your arm <idle>.
You then, how did you join the ranks of the gods and find eternal life?"
Utanapishtim said to him, to Gilgamesh:
I will reveal to you, O Gilgamesh, a secret matter,
And a mystery of the gods I will tell you.
The city Shuruppak, a city you yourself have knowledge of,
Which once was set on the <bank> of the Euphrates,
That aforesaid city was ancient and gods once were within it.
The great gods resolved to send the deluge,
Their father Anu was sworn,
The counselor the valiant Enlil,
Their throne-bearer Ninurta,
Their canal-officer Ennugi,
Their leader Ea was sworn with them.
He repeated their plans to the reed fence:
'Reed fence, reed fence, wall, wall!
Listen, O reed fence! Pay attention, O wall!
O Man of Shuruppak, son of Ubar-Tutu,
Wreck house, build boat,
Forsake possessions and seek life,
Belongings reject and life save!
Take aboard the boat seed of all living things.
The boat you shall build,
Let her dimensions be measured out:
Let her width and length be equal,
Roof her over like the watery depths.'
I understood full well, I said to Ea, my lord:
'Your command, my lord, exactly as you said it,
I shall faithfully execute.
What shall I answer the city, the populace, and the elders?'
Ea made ready to speak,
Saying to me, his servant:
'So, you shall speak to them thus:
"No doubt Enlil dislikes me,
I shall not dwell in your city.
I shall not set my foot on the dry land of Enlil,

I shall descend to the watery depths and dwell with my lord Ea.
Upon you he shall shower down in abundance,
A windfall of birds, a surprise of fishes,
He shall pour upon you a harvest of riches,
In the morning cakes in spates,
In the evening grains in rains."

Gilgamesh Builds a Boat

At the first glimmer of dawn,
The land was assembling at the gate of Atrahasis:[2]
The carpenter carried his axe,
The reed cutter carried his stone,
The old men brought cordage(?),
The young men ran around < . . . >,
The wealthy carried the pitch,
The poor brought what was needed of < . . . >.
In five days I had planked her hull:
One full acre was her deck space,
Ten dozen cubits, the height of each of her sides,
Ten dozen cubits square, her outer dimensions.
I laid out her structure, I planned her design:
I decked her in six,
I divided her in seven,
Her interior I divided in nine.
I drove the water plugs into her,[3]
I saw to the spars and laid in what was needful.
Thrice thirty-six hundred measures of pitch I poured in the oven,
Thrice thirty-six hundred measures of tar <I poured out> inside her.
Thrice thirty-six hundred measures basket-bearers brought aboard for oil,
Not counting the thirty-six hundred measures of oil that the offering consumed,
And the twice thirty-six hundred measures of oil that the boatbuilders made off with.
For the <builders> I slaughtered bullocks,
I killed sheep upon sheep every day,
Beer, ale, oil, and wine

[2] Another name ("Exceedingly Wise") for Utanapishtim.

[3] The reference to "water plugs" is obscure but may refer to caulking, stabilizers, depth markers, water taps, or bilge drains.

<I gave out> to the workers like river water,
They made a feast as on New Year's Day,
< . . . > I dispensed ointment with my own hand.
By the setting of Shamash,[4] the ship was completed.
<Since boarding was(?)> very difficult,
They brought up gangplanks(?), fore and aft,
They came up her sides(?) two-thirds (of her height).
<Whatever I had> I loaded upon her:
What silver I had I loaded upon her,
What gold I had I loaded upon her,
What living creatures I had I loaded upon her,
I sent up on board all my family and kin,
Beasts of the steppe, wild animals of the steppe, all types
of skilled craftsmen I sent up on board.
Shamash set for me the appointed time:
 'In the morning, cakes in spates,
 In the evening, grains in rains,
 Go into your boat and caulk the door!'
That appointed time arrived,
In the morning cakes in spates,
In the evening grains in rains,
I gazed upon the face of the storm,
The weather was dreadful to behold!
I went into the boat and caulked the door.
To the caulker of the boat, to Puzur-Amurri the boatman,
I gave over the edifice, with all it contained.

The Storm God Adad and Other Gods Cause the Flood

At the first glimmer of dawn,
A black cloud rose above the horizon.
Inside it Adad was thundering,
While the destroying gods Shullat and Hanish went in front,
Moving as an advance force over hill and plain.
Errakal tore out the mooring posts (of the world),
Ninurta came and made the dikes overflow.
The supreme gods held torches aloft,
Setting the land ablaze with their glow.
Adad's awesome power passed over the heavens,
Whatever was light was turned into darkness,
<He flooded> the land, he smashed it like a <clay pot>!

[4] The references to Shamash (see UTU in list in the introduction to this appendix) here and in line 87 suggest that in some version of this story, now lost, Shamash, rather than Enki, warned Utanapishtim of the flood and told him how much time he had to build his ship. In the oldest account of the Babylonian story of the flood, Enki sets a timing device, apparently a water clock, to tell Utanapishtim how much time he has before the coming of the deluge.

For one day the storm wind <blew>,
Swiftly it blew, <the flood came forth>,
It passed over the people like a battle,
No one could see the one next to him,
The people could not recognize one another in the downpour.
The gods became frightened of the deluge,
They shrank back, went up to Anu's highest heaven.
The gods cowered like dogs, crouching outside.
Ishtar screamed like a woman in childbirth,
And sweet-voiced Belet-ili wailed aloud:
'Would that day had come to naught,
When I spoke up for evil in the assembly of the gods!
How could I have spoken up for evil in the assembly of the gods,
And spoken up for battle to destroy my people?
It was I myself who brought my people into the world,
Now, like a school of fish, they choke up the sea!'
The supreme gods were weeping with her,
The gods sat where they were, weeping,
Their lips were parched, taking on a crust.
Six days and seven nights
The wind continued, the deluge and windstorm leveled the land.
When the seventh day arrived,
The windstorm and deluge left off their battle,
Which had struggled, like a woman in labor.
The sea grew calm, the tempest stilled, the deluge ceased.
I looked at the weather, stillness reigned,
And the whole human race had turned into clay.
The landscape was flat as a rooftop.
I opened the hatch, sunlight fell upon my face.
Falling to my knees, I sat down weeping,
Tears running down my face.
I looked at the edges of the world, the borders of the sea,
At twelve times sixty double leagues the periphery emerged.
The boat had come to rest on Mount Nimush,
Mount Nimush held the boat fast, not letting it move.
One day, a second day Mount Nimush held the boat fast, not letting it move.
A third day, a fourth day Mount Nimush held the boat fast, not letting it move.
A fifth day, a sixth day Mount Nimush held the boat fast, not letting it move.
When the seventh day arrived,
I brought out a dove and set it free.
The dove went off and returned,
No landing place came to its view, so it turned back.
I brought out a swallow and set it free,
The swallow went off and returned,

No landing place came to its view, so it turned back.
I brought out a raven and set it free,
The raven went off and saw the ebbing of the waters.
It ate, preened, left droppings, did not turn back.
I released all to the four directions,
I brought out an offering and offered it to the four directions.
I set up an incense offering on the summit of the mountain,
I arranged seven and seven cult vessels,
I heaped reeds, cedar, and myrtle in their bowls.[5]
The gods smelled the savor,
The gods smelled the sweet savor,
The gods crowded round the sacrificer like flies.

Ea Soothes Enlil's Anger; Utanapishtim Is Given Eternal Life

As soon as Belet-ili arrived,
She held up the great fly-ornaments that Anu had made in his ardor:
'O gods, these shall be my lapis necklace, lest I forget,
I shall be mindful of these days and not forget, not ever!
The gods should come to the incense offering,
But Enlil should not come to the incense offering,
For he, irrationally, brought on the flood,
And marked my people for destruction!'
As soon as Enlil arrived,
He saw the boat, Enlil flew into a rage,
He was filled with fury at the gods:
'Who came through alive? No man was to survive destruction!'
Ninurta made ready to speak,
Said to the valiant Enlil:
'Who but Ea could contrive such a thing?
For Ea alone knows every artifice.'
Ea made ready to speak,
Said to the valiant Enlil:
'You, O valiant one, are the wisest of the gods,
How could you, irrationally, have brought on the flood?
Punish the wrongdoer for his wrongdoing,
Punish the transgressor for his transgression,
But be lenient, lest he be cut off,
Bear with him, lest he < . . . >.
Instead of your bringing on a flood,
Let the lion rise up to diminish the human race!
Instead of your bringing on a flood,
Let the wolf rise up to diminish the human race!

[5] The Mesopotamians sometimes burned various plants in order to produce an attractive odor when making offerings to the gods.

Instead of your bringing on a flood,
Let famine rise up to wreak havoc in the land!
Instead of your bringing on a flood,
Let pestilence rise up to wreak havoc in the land!
It was not I who disclosed the secret of the great gods,
I made Atrahasis have a dream and so he heard the secret of the gods.
Now then, make some plan for him.'
Then Enlil came up into the boat,
Leading me by the hand, he brought me up too.
He brought my wife up and had her kneel beside me.
He touched our brows, stood between us to bless us:
'Hitherto Utanapishtim has been a human being,
Now Utanapishtim and his wife shall become like us gods.
Utanapishtim shall dwell far distant at the source of the rivers.'
Thus it was that they took me far distant and had me dwell at the source of the rivers.
Now then, who will convene the gods for your sake,
That you may find the eternal life you seek?
Come, come, try not to sleep for six days and seven nights.

Gilgamesh Fails to Gain Eternal Life and Eternal Youth

As he sat there on his haunches,
Sleep was swirling over him like a mist.
Utanapishtim said to her, to his wife:
'Behold this fellow who seeks eternal life!
Sleep swirls over him like a mist.
His wife said to him, to Utanapishtim the Distant One:
'Do touch him that the man may wake up,
That he may return safe on the way whence he came,
That through the gate he came forth he may return to his land.'
Utanapishtim said to her, to his wife:
'Since the human race is duplicitous, he'll endeavor to dupe you.
Come, come, bake his daily loaves, put them one after another by his head,
Then mark the wall for each day he has slept.'
She baked his daily loaves for him, put them one after another by his head,
Then dated the wall for each day he slept.
The first loaf was dried hard,
The second was leathery, the third soggy,
The crust of the fourth turned white,
The fifth was gray with mold, the sixth was fresh,
The seventh was still on the coals when he touched him, the man woke up.
Gilgamesh said to him, to Utanapishtim the Distant One:
'Scarcely had sleep stolen over me,
When straightaway you touched me and roused me.'

Utanapishtim said to him, to Gilgamesh:
'<Up with you>, Gilgamesh, count your daily loaves,
<That the days you have slept> may be known to you.
The first loaf is dried hard,
The second is leathery, the third soggy,
The crust of the fourth has turned white,
The fifth is gray with mold,
The sixth is fresh,
The seventh was still in the coals when I touched you and you woke up.'
Gilgamesh said to him, to Utanapishtim the Distant One:
'What then should I do, Utanapishtim, whither should I go,
Now that the Bereaver[6] has seized my <flesh>?
Death lurks in my bedchamber,
And wherever I turn, there is death.'
Utanapishtim said to him, to Ur-Shanabi the boatman:
'Ur-Shanabi, may the harbor <offer> you no <haven>,
May the crossing point reject you,
Be banished from the shore you shuttled to.
The man you brought here,
His body is matted with filthy hair,
Hides have marred the beauty of his flesh.
Take him away, Ur-Shanabi, bring him to the washing place.
Have him wash out his filthy hair with water, clean as snow,
Have him throw away his hides, let the sea carry them off,
Let his body be rinsed clean.
Let his headband be new,
Have him put on raiment worthy of him.
Until he reaches his city,
Until he completes his journey,
Let his garments stay spotless, fresh and new.'
Ur-Shanabi took him away and brought him to the washing place.
He washed out his filthy hair with water, clean as snow,
He threw away his hides, the sea carried them off,
His body was rinsed clean.
He renewed his headband,
He put on raiment worthy of him.
Until he reaches his city,
Until he completes his journey,
His garments would stay spotless, fresh and new.
Gilgamesh and Ur-Shanabi embarked on the boat,
They launched the boat, they embarked upon it.
His wife said to him, to Utanapishtim the Distant One:
'Gilgamesh has come here, spent with exertion,

[6] An epithet for death.

What will you give him for his homeward journey?'
At that he, Gilgamesh, lifted the pole,
Bringing the boat back by the shore.
Utanapishtim said to him, to Gilgamesh:
'Gilgamesh, you have come here, spent with exertion,
What shall I give you for your homeward journey?
I will reveal to you, O Gilgamesh, a secret matter,
And a mystery of the gods I will tell you.
There is a certain plant, its stem is like a thornbush,
Its thorns, like the wild rose, will prick <your hand>.
If you can secure this plant, < . . . >
< . . . >'
No sooner had Gilgamesh heard this,
He opened a shaft, <flung away his tools>.
He tied heavy stones <to his feet>,
They pulled him down into the watery depths < . . . >.
He took the plant though it pricked <his hand>.
He cut the heavy stones <from his feet>,
The sea cast him up on his home shore.
Gilgamesh said to him, to Ur-Shanabi the boatman:
'Ur-Shanabi, this plant is cure for heartache,
Whereby a man will regain his stamina.
I will take it to ramparted Uruk,
I will have an old man eat some and so test the plant.
His name shall be "Old Man Has Become Young-Again-Man."
I myself will eat it and so return to my carefree youth.'
At twenty double leagues they took a bite to eat,
At thirty double leagues they made their camp.
Gilgamesh saw a pond whose water was cool,
He went down into it to bathe in the water.
A snake caught the scent of the plant,
<Stealthily> it came up and carried the plant away,
On its way back it shed its skin.
Thereupon Gilgamesh sat down weeping,
His tears flowed down his face,
He said to Ur-Shanabi the boatman:
'For whom, Ur-Shanabi, have my hands been toiling?
For whom has my heart's blood been poured out?
For myself I have obtained no benefit,
I have done a good deed for a reptile!
Now, floodwaters rise against me for twenty double leagues,
When I opened the shaft, I flung away the tools.
How shall I find my bearings?
I have come much too far to go back, and I abandoned the

boat on the shore.'
At twenty double leagues they took a bite to eat,
At thirty double leagues they made their camp.
When they arrived in ramparted Uruk,
Gilgamesh said to him, to Ur-Shanabi the boatman:
'Go up, Ur-Shanabi, pace out the walls of Uruk.
Study the foundation terrace and examine the brickwork.
Is not its masonry of kiln-fired brick?
And did not seven masters lay its foundations?
One square mile of city, one square mile of gardens,
One square mile of clay pits, a half square mile of Ishtar's dwelling,
Three and a half square miles is the measure of Uruk!'

Atrahasis
Introduction

Atrahasis, named after the central character Atrahasis ("Exceedingly Wise") who saves humanity from destruction, is the longest surviving narrative poem on humanity from Mesopotamia. It narrates, in a tightly knit plot, the creation of humans, their dynamic increase in numbers, the gods' hostile reaction to their rise in numbers and loudness and their attempts to destroy humanity in a variety of ways, culminating in a catastrophic flood, and finally the origins of human birth, marriage, procreation, and death. Like Gilgamesh, Atrahasis was a legendary figure, found on a list of Sumerian kings (under his Sumerian name Ziusudra) and said to have ruled the city of Shuruppak in southern Mesopotamia around the same time as a great flood is recorded to have taken place. He is known as Utanapishtim in the Gilgamesh epic, and the story of the flood myth found in that epic is derived from a fuller flood-myth narrative, such as the one here in *Atrahasis*, which offers the reasons and motivations for attempting to destroy the human race.

The story begins in the middle of the action. Exhausted from hard labor, the lesser gods rebel: Why should any god have to toil? The greater gods are threatened by the rebellion, and in an attempt to solve the problem, they create humanity to act as servants for the lesser gods and to relieve them of work. Birth is instituted to allow humans to reproduce. But without natural death, reproduction gets out of hand, and the human race grows too numerous and noisy, which brings great annoyance to Enlil, the chief god on earth. He tries in a number of ways to destroy the human race, unsuccessfully, leading to the decision to flood the earth—a severe attempt at population control. When the flood proves too drastic a measure, population control is achieved by forbidding marriage and procreation to certain groups of people and ordaining mortality for all.

There are several versions of the epic. Below we offer selections from the earliest text, the Old Babylonian version. The primary text for this version comprises three tablets, originally containing 1245 lines of poetry, which can be dated to the 17th century BC. Each tablet is divided into eight columns, four on the front, and four on the back. At times they are quite fragmentary (only about 60 percent survives), and where possible these lost parts are supplemented with other copies of the same version, or from the late Assyrian version, which uses the Old Babylonian version as its base. Because the colophon (brief concluding paragraph, or "author's note") survives intact for the third and last tablet, we know the name of the scribe who copied out the Old Babylonian version and the date of composition: Nur-Aya, junior scribe, in the reign of Ammi-ṣaduqa, king of Babylon from 1702 to 1682 BC.

Text

The Anunna-Gods Force the Lesser Igigi-Gods to Work

(I.i) When gods were man,[7]
They did forced labor, they bore drudgery.
Great indeed was the drudgery of the gods,
The forced labor was heavy, the misery too much:
The seven(?) great Anunna-gods were burdening
The Igigi-gods with forced labor.
Anu their father was king,
Their counselor was the warrior Enlil,
Their prefect was Ninurta,
<And> their bailiff(?) <En>nugi.
They had taken the < . . . > by the < . . . >
They cast lots, the gods took their shares:
Anu went up to heaven,
<Enlil too>k the earth for his subjects(?),
<The bolt>, the closure of the sea,
<They had gi>ven to Enki the leader.
<The Anunna-gods?> went up to heaven,
<The gods of the de>pths had descended.
<The Anunna-gods> in the he<ights> of heaven
<Burdened> the Igigi-gods <with forced labor>.
<The gods> were digging watercourses,
<Canals they opened, the> life of the land.

<Those gods> were digging watercourses,
<Canals they opened, the> life of the land.
<The Igigi-gods dug the Ti>gris river,
<And the Euphrates there>after.
<Springs they opened up from> the depths,
<Wells . . . > they established.
< . . . > the depth

[7] The line is a metaphor, meaning "when gods were (like) men," in that they had to work.

< . . . > of the land
< . . . > within it
< . . . > they lifted up,
<They heaped up> all the mountains.
< . . . years> of drudgery,
< . . . > the vast marsh.
They <cou>nted years of drudgery,
< . . . and> forty years, too much!
< . . . > forced labor they bore night and day.
<They were com>plaining, denouncing,
<Mut>tering down in the ditch,
"Let us face up to our <foreman> the prefect,
He must take off (this) our <he>avy burden upon us!
< . . . >, counselor of the gods, the warrior,
Come, let us remove (him) from his dwelling;
Enlil, counselor of the gods, the warrior,
Come, let us remove (him) from his dwelling!"
< . . . > made ready to speak,
<And said to the> gods his brethren,
"< . . . > the prefect of olden days(?)

<gap>

The Igigi-Gods Revolt

(I.ii) "The counselor of the go<ds>, the warrior,
Come, let us remove (him) from his dwelling.
Enlil, counselor of the gods, the warrior,
Come, let us remove (him) from his dwelling!
Now then, call for battle!
Battle let us join, warfare!"
The gods heard his words,
They set fire to their tools,
They put fire to their spades,
And flame to their workbaskets.
Off they went, one and all,
To the gate of the warrior Enlil's abode.
It was night, half-way through the watch,
The house was surrounded, but the god did not know.
It was night, half-way through the watch,
Ekur was surrounded, but Enlil did not know!
Kalkal noticed it and < . . . >,
He touched the bolt and examined the < . . . >.
Kalkal woke <Nusku>,
And they listened to the clamor of <the Igigi-gods>.

Nusku woke <his> lord,
He got <him> out of bed,
"My lord, <your> house is surrounded,
Battle has run right up <to your gate>.
Enlil, your house is surrounded,
Battle has <ru>n right up to your gate!"
Enlil had < . . . > to his dwelling.
Enlil made ready to speak,
And said to the vizier Nusku,
"Nusku, bar your gate,
Get your weapons and stand before me."
Nusku barred his gate,
Got his weapons and stood before Enlil.
Nusku made ready to speak,
And said to the warrior Enlil,
"My lord, your face is (gone pale as) tamarisk,
Your own offspring! Why did you fear?
My lord, your face is (gone pale as) tamarisk,
Your own offspring! Why did you fear?
Send that they bring Anu down <here>,
And that they bring Enki be<fore yo>u."
He sent and they brought Anu down to him,
They brought Enki before him.
Anu, king of <hea>ven, was seated,
The king of the depths, Enki, was < . . . >.
With the great Anunna-gods present,
Enlil arose, the debate <was underway>.
Enlil made ready to speak,
And said to the great <gods>,
"Against me would they be <rebelling>?
Shall I make battle <against my own offspring>?
What did I see with my very own eyes?
Battle ran up to my gate!"
Anu made ready to speak,
And said to the warrior Enlil,
(I.iii) "The reason why the Igigi-gods
Surrounded(?) your gate,
Let Nusku go out <to discover it>,
<Let him take> to <your> so<ns>
<Your great> command."
Enlil made ready to speak,
And said to the <vizier Nusku>,
"Nusku, open <your gate>,
Take your weapons, <stand before them>.

In the assembly of <all the gods>
Bow down, stand up, <and expound to them> our <words>:
‘Anu, <your father>,
Your counselor, <the warrior> Enlil,
Your prefect, Ninurta,
And your bailiff Ennugi have sent me (to say),
“Who <is instigator of> battle?
Who <is instigator of> hostilities?
Who <declared> war,
<(That) battle has run up to the gate of Enlil>?”
<Nusku opened> his gate,
<Took his weapons> and w<ent . . . > Enlil.
<In the assembly of a>ll the gods,
<He knelt, s>tood up, expounded the c<omm>and,
“Anu, your father,
<Your counselor, the> warrior Enlil,
<Your prefect>, Ninurta,
And <your bailiff> Ennugi <have sent me (to say)>:
‘Who is <instigator of> battle?
Who is <instigator of> hostilities?
Who <declared> war,
<(That) battle has run up to the gate of Enlil>?
In < . . . >
He trans<gressed the command of> Enlil.’[8]
“Every <one of us gods has declared> war;
We have set < . . . > in the e<xcavation>.
<Excessive> drudgery <has killed us>,
<Our> forced labor was heavy, <the misery too much>!
Now, every <one of us gods>
Has resolved on <a reckoning?> with Enlil.”
Nusku took <his weapons . . . >,
He went, he < . . . to his lord>,
“My lord, <you sent> me to the < . . . >,
I went < . . . >
I expounded <you>r great <command>,
< . . . trans>gressed it.
‘<Every one of us> gods has declared war,
We <have set . . . > in the excavation.
Excessive <drudgery> has killed us,
Our forced labor <was heavy>, the misery too much!
<Now, every> one of us gods
Has resolved on a reckoning(?) with Enlil.’”

[8] See above, Tablet I line 116. Perhaps this was given in Tablet I lines 144ff.

When Enlil heard that speech,
His tears flowed.
Enlil < . . . > his speech(?),
And addressed the warrior Anu,
"I will go up with you, to heaven.
(I.iv) Bear your authority, take your power,[9]
With the great gods in session before you,
Summon one god, let them put a burial mound over him."
Anu made ready to speak,
And addressed the gods his brethren,
"Why do we blame them?
Their forced labor was heavy, their misery too much!
<Every day . . . >,
<The outcry was> loud, <we could> hear the clamor.
< . . . > to do,
< . . . assigned> tasks . . . "

[*There is a gap in the main text, which is filled partly by the following fragment from another copy.*]

The God Ea Proposes the Creation of Humans

Ea made ready to speak,
And said to the gods <his brethren>,
"What calumny do we lay to their charge?
Their forced labor was heavy, <their misery too much>!
Every day < . . . >
The outcry <was loud, we could hear the clamor>.
There is < . . . >
<Belet-ili, the midwife>, is present.
Let her create, then, a hum<an, a man>,
Let him bear the yoke < . . . >,
Let him bear the yoke < . . . >!
<Let man assume the drud>gery of god . . . "

[*As the main text resumes, Enki is speaking.*]
"<Belet-ili, the midwife>, is present,
Let the midwife create < . . . >,
Let man assume the drudgery of god."
They summoned and asked the goddess,
The midwife of the gods, wise Mami,
"Will you be the birth goddess, creatress of mankind?
Create a human being that he bear the yoke,

[9] Lines 181a–l are restored from the Late Assyrian Version.

Let him bear the yoke, the task of Enlil,
Let man assume the drudgery of god."
Nintu made ready to speak,
And said to the great gods,
"It is not for me to do it,
The task is Enki's.
He it is that cleanses all,
Let him provide me the clay so I can do the making."
Enki made ready to speak,
And said to the great gods,
"On the first, seventh, and fifteenth days of the month,
Let me establish a purification, a bath.
Let the one god be slaughtered,
Then let the gods be cleansed by immersion.
Let Nintu mix clay with his flesh and blood.
Let that same god and man be thoroughly mixed in the clay.
Let us hear the drum for the rest of time,
From the flesh of the god let a spirit remain,
Let it make the living know its sign,
Lest he be allowed to be forgotten, let the spirit remain."
The great Anunna-gods, who administer destinies,
Answered, "Yes!" in the assembly.
On the first, seventh, and fifteenth days of the month,
He established a purification, a bath.

The Gods Create Humans from We-Ilu; They Grow and Multiply

They slaughtered We-ilu,[10] who had the inspiration, in their assembly.
Nintu mixed clay with his flesh and blood.
<That same god and man were thoroughly mixed in the clay.>
For the rest <of time they would hear the drum>.[11]
From the flesh of the god <the> spi<rit remained>.
It would make the living know its sign,
Lest he be allowed to be forgotten, <the> spirit remained.
After she had mixed that clay,
She summoned the Anunna, the great gods.
The Igigi, the great gods, spat upon the clay.
Mami made ready to speak,
And said to the great gods,
"You ordered me the task and I have completed (it)!
You have slaughtered the god, along with his inspiration.

[10] We-ilu may be a play on the Akkadian word for "man" (*awēlu*).

[11] Or "heartbeat."

I have done away with your heavy forced labor,
I have imposed your drudgery on man.
You have bestowed(?) clamor upon mankind.
I have released the yoke, I have <made> restoration."[12]
They heard this speech of hers,
They ran, restored, and kissed her feet, (saying),
"Formerly <we used to call> you 'Mami,'
Now let your n<am>e be 'Mistress-of-All-the-Gods' (Belet-kala-ili)."

[*The tablet breaks off; the missing section, supplied by another version, describes the production of seven male and seven female fetuses.*]

<And the young girl . . . > her breasts,[13]
<The youth . . . > a beard,
<And hair . . . > the cheek of the young man.
<In the . . . > and street
Wife and husband were <bliss>ful.
The birth goddesses were assembled,
And Nintu <sat rec>koning the months.
<At the> destined <time> they summoned the tenth month.
The tenth month[14] arrived;
< . . . > opened the womb.
Her face beaming and joyful,
She covered her head
And performed the midwifery.
She girded (the mother's) middle
As she pronounced a blessing.
She drew (a circle?) with meal and placed the brick,[15]
"I am the one who created, my hands have made it!
Let the midwife rejoice in the sacrosanct woman's house.[16]
Where the pregnant woman gives birth,
And the mother of the baby is delivered,
Let the brick be in place for nine days,

[12] That is, returned matters to their original state before the great gods had imposed labor on the lesser gods.

[13] The first pair of human beings has grown from babyhood to adolescence and matured enough to reproduce. At line 277 the first mother-to-be is about to give birth.

[14] Forty weeks = ten lunar months = nine calendrical months.

[15] The text implies that the placing of a brick in the room where a woman was about to give birth was to be a common practice, but it is unknown outside of this composition.

[16] It is possible that this refers to a woman who has just given birth, so she could not have intercourse for a taboo period. The next line refers to resumption of intercourse after delivery.

Let Nintu, the birth goddess,[17] be honored.
Always call Mami their < . . . >,
<Always pra>ise the birth goddess, praise Kesh.[18]
On <the tenth day?>, when the bed is laid,
(Then) let wife and her husband reach bliss together,
At the time for being man and wife,
They should heed Ishtar in the < . . . > chamber.
For the nine days let there be rejoicing,
Let them <cal>l Ishtar Ishara.[19]
< . . . > at the destined time"

[*After a long gap, humankind has reproduced and is put to work to feed the gods.*]

A man < . . . >
Cleanse the dwelling (?) < . . . >
The son to <his> father < . . . >
< . . . >
They sat and < . . . >
He it was who was carrying < . . . >
He saw and < . . . >
Enlil < . . . >
They took up < . . . >
They made n<e>w hoes and shovels,
They built the big canal banks.
For food for the peoples, for the sustenance of <the gods>.

<large gap>

Enlil Attempts to Destroy Humankind by Disease

(I.vii) <Twel>ve hundred years <had not gone by>.
<The land had grown wide>, the peoples had increased,
The <land> was bellowing <like a bull>.
The god was disturbed with <their uproar>.
<Enlil heard> their clamor.
<He said to> the great gods,
"The clamor of mankind <has become burdensome to me>,
I am losing sleep <to their uproar>.
< . . . > let there be ague . . . "
<three lines lost>

17 Variant: Belet-ili.

18 Sanctuary of the birth goddess.

19 Lines 301ff. refer to consummation of marriage. Ishara was another name for Ishtar.

But he, <Atrahasis>, his god was Enki,
<He was exceedingly wise>.
He would speak <with his god>,
And his god <would speak> with him!
Atrahasis <made> ready to speak,
And said to <his> lord,
"How long < . . . >
Will they impose the disease on us <forever>?"
Enki made ready to speak
And said to his servant,
"The elders < . . . >
< . . . > in < . . . >
<Command>:
'Let heralds proclaim,
raise a loud clamor in the land.'
"Do not reverence your (own) gods,
Do not pray to your (own) goddesses,
Seek the door of Namtar,
Bring a baked (loaf) before it."
"May the flour offering please him,
May he be shamed by the gift and suspend his hand."
Atrahasis received the command,
And assembled the elders to his gate.
Atrahasis made ready to speak,
And said to the elders,
"Elders < . . . >
(I.viii) < . . . >
<Command>:
'Let heralds proclaim,
Let them raise a loud <clamor> in the land.
"<Do not reverence> your (own) gods,
<Do not> pray to your (own) <goddesses>,
<Seek> the door of <Namtar>,
<Bring a baked (loaf) before it.'"
"May the flour offering please him,
May he be shamed by the gift and suspend his hand,"
The elders heeded <his> words,
They built a temple for Namtar in the city.
They commanded and the <heralds> proclaimed,
They made a loud clamor <in the land>.
They did <not> reverence their (own) gods,
They did <not> pray to <their (own) goddesses>,
They sought <the door> of Namtar,
They <brought> a baked (loaf) before <it>.

The flour offering pleased him,
<He was shamed> by the gift and suspended his hand.
<The ague> left them,
They resumed <their clamor?>,

<two fragmentary lines>

Tablet II

Enlil Tries to Destroy Humankind Again with Drought and Famine

(II.i) Twelve hundred years had not gone by,
The land had grown wide, the peoples had increased,
The land was bellowing like a bull.
The god was disturbed by their uproar,
Enlil heard their clamor.
He said to the great gods,
"The clamor of mankind has become burdensome to me,
I am losing sleep to their uproar.
Cut off provisions for the peoples,
Let plant life be too scanty <fo>r their hunger.
Let Adad withhold his rain,
Below, let the flood not come up from the depths.
Let the wind come to parch the ground,
Let the clouds billow but discharge not a drop.
Let the field reduce its yields,
Let the grain goddess close her bosom.
Let there be no rejoicing for them,
Let <their faces?> be gloomy,
Let there not < . . . >"
[*A large gap follows; in the intervening period Enki likely told Atrahasis how to save humanity by supplicating Adad, the Rain God.*]

(II.ii) "<Command:
'Let heralds proclaim>,
<Let them make a loud> cl<amor> in the land.
"Do not reverence your (own) gods,
Do not pray to your (own) <goddesses>,
Seek <the door of> Adad.
Bring a baked (loaf) <before it>.'"
"<May the flour offering> please him,
May he be shamed <by the> gift and suspend his hand.
May he rain down mist in the morning,

May he stealthily rain down dew in the night,
May the fields just as stealthily bear ninefold."
They built a temple for Adad in the city.
They commanded and the heralds proclaimed,
They made a loud clamor in the land.
They did not reverence their (own) gods,
They did <not> pray to their (own) goddesses,
They <sought> the door <of Adad>,
<They brought> a baked (loaf) before it.
The flour offering pleased him,
He was shamed by the gift and suspended his hand.
He rained down mist in the morning,
He stealthily rained down dew in the night,
<The fields just as> stealthily bore ninefold.
<The famine?> left them,
They resumed their <clamor?>

[*We skip forward in the narrative, omitting the repeated attempts of Enlil to destroy humankind with disease and drought—seemingly coming close to succeeding since people are said to be "shriveled" and "hunched over as they walk." He decides to send a flood to do the job. Enlil is speaking when we pick up the narrative.*]

Enlil Proposes to Destroy Humankind with a Flood

(II.vii) "<She? imposed> your drudgery <on man>,
<You> have bestowed(?) clamo<r upon mankind>.
You slaughtered <the god>, together with <his inspiration>,
<You> sat down and bath<ed yourselves>.
< . . . > it will bring < . . . >
You resolved on <a rule . . . >,
Let (mankind) return to <its> la<ir?>.
Let us be sure to bind the leader Enki < . . . > by an oath so that(?) he < . . . >"
Enki made ready to speak,
And said to the gods <his brethren>,
"Why would you bind me by oath < . . . >?
Am I to bring my hands against <my own peoples>?
The flood that you are speaking of <to me>,
Who is that? I <do not know>.
Am I to produce <a flood>?
The task of that is <Enlil's>.
Let him < . . . > choose,
Let Shullat and <Hanish> go <in front>,
Let Errakal <tear out> the mooring poles,
Let <Ninurta> go make <the dikes> overflow.

<large gap>

(II.viii) "Assemble < . . . >
Do not obey . . . < . . . >."
The gods commanded annihilation,
E<nlil> committed an evil deed against the peoples.

Tablet III

Atrahasis Receives a Dream and Asks Enki for Its Meaning

(III.i) Atrahasis made ready to speak,
And said to his lord,

<gap of about eight lines>

Atrahasis made ready to speak,
And said to his lord,
"Make me know the meaning <of the dream>,
< . . . > let me know, that I may look out for its consequence."
<Enki> made ready to speak,
And said to his servant,
"You might say, 'Am I to be looking out while in the bedroom?'
Do you pay attention to the message that I speak for you:
'Wall, listen to me!
Reed wall, pay attention to all my words!
Flee house, build boat,
Forsake possessions, and save life.
The boat which you build,
< . . . > be equal < . . . >
<small gap>
'Roof her over like the depths,
So that the sun shall not see inside her,
Let her be roofed over fore and aft.
The gear should be very firm,
The pitch should be firm, make (her) strong.
I will shower down upon you later
A windfall of birds, a spate(?) of fishes.'"
He opened the water clock and filled it,
He told it (the wall?) of the coming of the seven-day deluge.
Atrahasis received the command,
He assembled the elders at his gate.
Atrahasis made ready to speak,

And said to the elders,
"My god <does not agree> with your god,
Enki and <Enlil> are constantly angry with each other.
They have expelled me from <the land?>.
Since I have always reverenced <Enki>,
<He told me> this.
I can<not> live in < . . . >
Nor can I <set my feet on> the earth of Enlil.
<I will dwell?> with <my> god in(?) the depths.
<This> he told me < . . . >"

<gap of about 14 lines>

Atrahasis Builds a Boat

(III.ii) The elders < . . . >
The carpenter <carried his axe>,
The reed-worker <carried his stone>.
<The rich man? carried> the pitch,
The poor man <brought the materials needed>.
<gap>
Atrahasis < . . . >
<gap>
Bringing < . . . >
Whatever he <had . . . >
Whatever he had < . . . >
Pure (animals) he sl<aughtered, cattle . . . >
Fat (animals) <he killed, sheep(?) . . . >
He chose <and brought on> board.
The <birds> flying in the heavens,
The cattle(?) <and . . . of the cat>tle god,
The <creatures(?) . . . > of the steppe,
< . . . > he brought on board
< . . . >
< . . . > he invited his people
< . . . > to a feast.
< . . . > his family he brought on board.
While one was eating and another was drinking,
He went in and out; he could not sit, could not kneel,
For his heart was broken, he was retching gall.
The outlook of the weather changed,
Adad began to roar in the clouds.
The god they heard, his clamor.
He brought pitch to seal his door.
By the time he had bolted his door,

Adad was roaring in the clouds.
As the furious wind rose,
He cut the mooring rope and released the boat.

<*gap of four lines*>

The Earth Is Flooded

(III.iii) < . . . > the storm
< . . . > were yoked
<Anzu rent> the sky with his talons,
<He . . . > the land
And broke its clamor <like a pot>.
< . . . > the flood <came forth>,
Its power came upon the peoples <like a battle>.
One person did <not> see another,
They could <not> recognize each other in the catastrophe.
<The deluge> bellowed like a bull,
The wind <resound>ed like a screaming eagle.
The darkness <was dense>, the sun was gone,
< . . . > like flies
< . . . the clamor(?)> of the deluge

<*two fragmentary lines*>

< . . . > the clamor of the de<luge>
It was trying < . . . > of the gods.
<Enki> was beside himself,
<That> his sons were carried off before him.
Nintu, the great lady,
Gnawed her lips in agony.
The Anunna, the great gods,
Were sitting in thirst and hunger.
The goddess saw it, weeping,
The midwife of the gods, the wise Mami,
"Let the day grow dark,
Let it turn back to gloom!
In the assembly of the gods,
How did I agree with them on annihilation?
Was Enlil so strong that he forced <me> to speak?
Like that Tiruru, did he make <my> speech confused?[20]
Of my own accord, from myself alone,
To my own charge have I heard (my people's) clamor!

[20] Tiruru is otherwise unknown.

My offspring—with no help from me—have become like flies.
And as for me, how to dwell in (this) abode of grief, my clamor fallen silent?
Shall I go up to heaven,
As if to live in a house of <plentiful store>s?
Where has Anu gone to, the chief decision-maker,
Whose sons, the gods, heeded his command?
He who irrationally brought about the flood,
And relegated the peoples to ca<tastrophe>?"

<gap of four lines>

(III.iv) Nintu was wailing < . . . >
"< . . . > gave birth to(?) < . . . >
As dragonflies a watercourse, they have filled the sea.
Like rafts they lie against the e<dg>e,
Like rafts capsized they lie against the bank.
I saw and wept over them,
I have exhausted my lamentation for them."
She wept, giving vent to her feelings,
While Nintu wailed, her emotion was spent.
The gods wept with her for the land.
She had her fill of woe and thirsted for beer.
Where she sat, they too sat weeping,
Like sheep, they filled a streambed.[21]
Their lips were agonized with thirst,
They were suffering pangs of hunger.
Seven days and seven ni<ghts>
There came the deluge, the storm, <the flood>.
Where it < . . . >
< . . . > was thrown down

<large gap>

Atrahasis Offers Sacrifice to the Gods, Who Decide on Less Destructive Means for Population Control

(III.v) To the <four> winds < . . . >
He cast < . . . >
Providing food < . . . >
< . . . >
<The gods sniffed> the savor,
They were gathered <like flies> around the offering.
<After> they had eaten the offering,

[21] The gods are hoping to find something to drink.

<Nin>tu arose to rail against all of them,
"Where has Anu come to, the chief decision-maker?
Has Enlil drawn nigh the incense?
They who irrationally brought about the flood,
And relegated the peoples to catastrophe?
You resolved upon annihilation,
So now (the people's) clear countenances are turned grim."
Then she drew nigh the big < . . . s>
Which Anu had and < . . . >
"Mine is <their> woe! Proclaim my destiny!
Let him get me out of my misery, let him show me the way(?).
Let me go out < . . . >"
< . . . >
(III.vi) "In < . . . >
Let <these> flies[22] be jewelry around my neck,
That I may remember it <every?> day <and forever?>."
<The warrior Enlil> saw the vessel,
And was filled with anger at the Igigi-gods.
"All we great Anunna-gods
Resolved together on an oath.
Where did life(?) escape?
How did a man survive the catastrophe?"
Anu made ready to speak,
And said to the warrior Enlil,
"Who could do this but Enki?
< . . . > he revealed the command."
<Enki> made ready to speak,
<And said to> the great gods,
"I did it <indeed> for your sakes!
<I am responsible> for safeguarding li<fe>.
< . . . > gods < . . . >
< . . . > the flood
< . . . > brought about
<O Enlil, . . . > your heart
< . . . > and relax.
Impose your penalty <on a wrong-doer>,
<For> who is it that disregards your command?[23]
< . . . > the assembly < . . . >"

<gap of thirteen lines>

[22] The episode is obscure and seems to contain a play on words.

[23] The thrust of the argument may be that he had sworn not to tell mankind of the flood, but did not swear to annihilate life.

<Enlil> made ready to speak,
And said to Ea the leader,
"<Come>, summon Nintu the birth goddess,
<Do you> and she take counsel together in the assembly."
<Enki> made ready to speak,
And <said to> Nintu the birth goddess,
"<You>, birth goddess, creatress of destinies,
<Establish death> for all peoples!
< . . . >
< . . . > let there be."
<one line missing?>

(III.vii) "Now then, let there be a third (woman) among the people,
Among the people are the woman who has borne and the woman who has not borne.
Let there be (also) among the people the (she)-demon,
Let her snatch the baby from the lap of her who bore it,
Establish high priestesses and priestesses,
Let them be taboo, and so cut down childbirth."

<large gap>

(III.viii) "How we brought about <the flood>,
But man survived the <catastrophe>,
You, counselor of the <great> gods,
At <your> command have I brought a < . . . > to be,
This <my> song (is) for your praise.
May the Igigi-gods hear, let them extol your great deed to each other.
I have sung of the flood to all peoples:
Listen!"

[*A colophon ends the text, naming the scribe who copied it (Nur-Aya), the total length of the poem (1245 lines) and the king's name, which allows us to date the copy to the reign of Ammi-ṣaduqa, king of Babylon 1702–1682 BC.*]

The Babylonian *Epic of Creation (Enuma Elish)*
Introduction

This mythological poem, also called *Enuma Elish* ("When on High") after the first two words of the work, celebrates the exaltation of the Babylonian god Marduk to supreme deity of the Mesopotamian pantheon after he had saved the gods from an attack by Tiamat, the female goddess "Ocean." The entire poem, in fact, can be viewed as a panegyric of Marduk. Even as the song recounts the intergenerational struggle between the primeval gods, Tiamat and Apsu, and their progeny, there is never really any doubt that Marduk will emerge victorious. Instead, Apsu's and Tiamat's hostility toward the younger generation of the gods is a symptom of the unavoidable disorder that is endemic in the universe until a god capable of creating order emerges. This is Marduk, and once he defeats Tiamat and her army of fearsome monsters, he then turns his attention to bringing order to the universe by creating Esharra, the abode of the gods, by organizing the seasons and the stars, and by building Babylon, the most important city and the gods' abode on earth. Marduk is also behind the creation of mankind in order to sustain the gods. Because of Marduk's capable leadership, the other gods willingly put supreme power in his hands (Tablet VI, lines 95–100):

> Then the great gods convened,
> They made Marduk's destiny highest, they prostrated themselves.
> They laid upon themselves a curse (if they broke the oath),
> With water and oil they swore, they touched their throats.
> They granted him exercise of kingship over the gods,
> They established him forever for lordship of heaven and netherworld

Readers of Hesiod's *Theogony* will find familiar the emergence of order and permanence at the same time that a supreme being arises. After all, Zeus emerges victorious after a period of intergenerational strife, and even though he does not actively organize the universe, his offspring (such as the Horai, "Seasons," or Moirai, "Fates") often serve as avatars for the orderliness of the world.

Despite the confident tone celebrating Marduk, the Babylonian *Epic of Creation* should not be considered "the" Mesopotamian creation story. Rather, it is the individual work of a poet who viewed Babylon as the center of the universe, and Marduk, god of Babylon, as head of the pantheon. The poem may be a product of Babylonian nationalistic revival at the time of Nebuchadnezzar I (ca. 1125–1104 BC), though there is no firm evidence for its date of composition. To judge from its language and content, the poem indeed dates to the latter part of the second millennium BC, though it is possible that the story may have first been created in the Old Babylonian period.

Text
Tablet I

Tiamat (Mother Ocean) and Apsu (Fresh Water?) Produce the First Gods

> When on high no name was given to heaven,
> Nor below was the netherworld called by name,
> Primeval Apsu, their progenitor,

And matrix-Tiamat,[24] who bore them all,
Were mingling their waters together,
No cane brake was intertwined nor thicket matted close.[25]
When no gods at all had been brought forth,
None called by names, none destinies ordained,
Then were the gods formed within the(se two).
Lahmu and Lahamu[26] were brought forth, were called by name.
When they had waxed great, had grown up tall,
Anshar and Kishar were formed, greater than they,
They grew lengthy of days, added years to years.
Anu their firstborn was like his forebears,
Anshar made Anu, his offspring, his equal.
Then Anu begot in his image Nudimmud,[27]
Nudimmud was he who dominated(?) his forebears:
Profound in wisdom, acute of sense, he was massively strong,
Much mightier than his grandfather Anshar,
No rival had he among the gods his brethren.

Apsu, Annoyed with His Offspring, Plots to Destroy Them

The divine brethren banded together,
Confusing Tiamat as they moved about in their stir,
Roiling the vitals of Tiamat,
By their uproar distressing the interior of the Divine Abode.[28]
Apsu could not reduce their clamor,
But Tiamat was silent before them.
Their actions were noisome to her,
Their behavior was offensive, (but) she was indulgent.
Thereupon Apsu, begetter of the great gods,
Summoned Mummu[29] his vizier, saying to him,
  "Mummu, vizier who contents me,
  Come, let us go to Tiamat."
They went, took their places facing Tiamat,
They took counsel concerning the gods their offspring.
Apsu made ready to speak,

[24] Tiamat is the name of the ocean; Apsu is generally taken to refer to fresh water. The word rendered here "matrix" is *mummu*, meaning "wisdom" or "skill," hence "creator" or "craftsman." *Mummu* can also mean "noise."

[25] That is, nothing divided or covered the waters.

[26] Lahmu and Lahamu are likely primeval figures that represent pillars (or possibly primeval mud). Anshar and Kishar are the circle and horizon of heaven and earth.

[27] Another name for Ea, god of wisdom.

[28] Andurna, a cosmic locality, perhaps an abode of the gods.

[29] The same word, *mummu*, translated above as "matrix," is here the personal name of Apsu's advisor.

Saying to her, Tiamat, in a loud voice,
"Their behavior is noisome to me!
By day I have no rest, at night I do not sleep!
I wish to put an end to their behavior, to do away with it!
Let silence reign that we may sleep."
When Tiamat had heard this,
She grew angry and cried out to her spouse,
She cried out bitterly, outraged that she stood alone,
(For) he had urged evil upon her,
"What? Shall we put an end to what we formed?
Their behavior may be most noisome, but we should bear it in good part."
It was Mummu who answered, counseling Apsu,
The vizier was not receptive to the counsel of his creatrix,[30]
"Put an end here and now, father, to their troublesome ways!
By day you should have rest, at night you should sleep."
Apsu was delighted with him, he beamed.
On account of the evils he plotted against the gods his children,
He embraced Mummu, around his neck,
He sat on his knees so he could kiss him.[31]
Whatever they plotted between them,
Was repeated to the gods their offspring.
The gods heard it as they stirred about,
They were stunned, they sat down in silence.

Ea Thwarts Apsu's Plans

Surpassing in wisdom, ingenious, resourceful,
Ea was aware of all, recognized their stratagem.
He fashioned it, he established it, a master plan,
He made it artful, his superb magic spell.
He recited it and brought (him) to rest in[32] the waters,
He put him in deep slumber, he was fast asleep,
He made Apsu sleep, he was drenched with slumber,
Mummu the advisor was drowsy with languor.
He untied his sash, he stripped off his tiara,
He took away his aura, he himself put it on.
He tied up Apsu, he killed him,
Mummu he bound, he locked him securely.
He founded his dwelling upon Apsu,
He secured Mummu, held (him) firm by a leadrope.

[30] Play on words between Mummu-Tiamat and Mummu the vizier.

[31] As interpreted here, Apsu bends down to kiss Mummu, so is presumably taller; another possibility is that Mummu is sitting on Apsu's knees.

[32] Variant: "on the waters."

After Ea had captured and vanquished his foes,
Had won the victory over his opponents,
In his chamber, in profound quiet, he rested.
He called it "Apsu," which he assigned sanctuaries.
He established therein his chamber,
Ea and Damkina his wife dwelt there in splendor.

The Great God Marduk Is Born

In the cella of destinies, the abode of designs,
The most capable, the sage of the gods, the Lord was begotten,
In the midst of Apsu Marduk was formed,
In the midst of holy Apsu was Marduk formed!
Ea his father begot him,
Damkina his mother was confined with him.
He suckled at the breasts of goddesses,
The attendant who raised him endowed him well with glories.
His body was magnificent, fiery his glance,
He was a hero at birth, he was a mighty one from the beginning!
When Anu his grandfather saw him,
He was happy, he beamed, his heart was filled with joy.
He perfected him, so that his divinity was strange,
He was much greater, he surpassed them in every way.
His members were fashioned with cunning beyond comprehension,
Impossible to conceive, too difficult to visualize:
Fourfold his vision, fourfold his hearing,
When he moved his lips a fire broke out.
Formidable[33] his fourfold perception,
And his eyes, in like number, saw in every direction.
He was tallest of the gods, surpassing in form,
His limbs enormous, he was surpassing at birth.
"The son Utu, the son Utu,[34]
The son, the sun, the sunlight of the gods!"
He wore (on his body) the auras of ten gods, had (them) wrapped around his head too,
Fifty glories[35] were heaped upon him.
Anu formed and produced the four winds,
He put them in his hand, "Let my son play!"[36]

[33] "Formidable" is an attempt to render a pun in the original between *rabû*, "great," and *erbu*, "four."

[34] A series of interlingual puns on son and sun, only one level of which can be rendered in English. The cuneiform signs used to write the name Marduk, AMAR.UD, are here construed as *māru*, "son," and Utu, "sun."

[35] These refer to the fifty epithets or other names of Marduk, listed at the end of Tablet V (not translated here).

[36] Or: "My son, let them whirl."

He fashioned dust, he made a storm bear it up,
He caused a wave and it roiled Tiamat,
Tiamat was roiled, churning day and night,
The gods, finding no rest, bore the brunt of each wind.

The Gods Convince Tiamat to Confront Marduk

They plotted evil in their hearts,
They said to Tiamat their mother,
"When he killed Apsu your husband,
You did nothing to save him but sat by, silent.
Now he has made four terrible winds,
They are roiling your vitals so we cannot sleep.
You had no care for Apsu your husband,
As for Mummu, who was captured, you remained aloof.
You are <no mo>ther, you churn back and forth, confused.
As for us, who cannot lie down to rest, you do not love us!
Our < . . . >, our eyes are pinched,
Lift this unremitting yoke, let us sleep!
<Rai>se a <storm>, give them what they deserve,
<Ma>ke a <tempest>, turn them into nothingness."
When Tiamat <heard> these words, they pleased her,
"<As y>ou have counseled, we will make a tempest,[37]
<We will . . . > the gods within it,
<For> they have been adopting <wicked ways> against the gods <thei>r parents.
<They clo>sed ranks and drew up at Tiamat's side,
Angry, scheming, never lying down night and day,
<Ma>king warfare, rumbling, raging,
Convening in assembly, that they might start hostilities.
Mother Hubur,[38] who can form everything,
Added countless invincible weapons, gave birth to monster snakes,
Pointed of fang, with merciless incisors(?),
She filled their bodies with venom for blood.
Fierce dragons she clad with glories,
Causing them to bear auras like gods, (saying,)
"Whoever sees them shall collapse from weakness!
Wherever their bodies make onslaught, they shall not turn back!"
She deployed serpents, dragons, and hairy hero-men,
Lion monsters, lion men, scorpion men,
Mighty demons, fish men, bull men,

[37] Or: "monsters," but this would leave the reference in line 127 unclear.

[38] Another epithet of Mummu-Tiamat, as a proper name suggesting a creative force, more commonly a name of the netherworld river, construed here by one scholar as "Mother Noise."

Bearing unsparing arms, fearing no battle.
Her commands were absolute, no one opposed them,
Eleven indeed on this wise she crea<ted>.[39]
From among the gods her offspring, who composed her assembly,
She raised up Qingu[40] from among them, it was he she made greatest!
Leadership of the army, command of the assembly,
Arming, contact, advance of the melee,
Wardenship of the (spoils?) of battle,
(All) she entrusted to him, made him sit on the dais.
"I cast your spell. I make you the greatest in the assembly of the gods,
Kingship of all the gods I put in your power.
You are the greatest, my husband, you are illustrious,
Your command shall always be greatest, over all the Anunna-gods."
She gave him the tablet of destinies,[41] had him hold it to his chest, (saying)
"As for you, your command will not be changed, your utterance will be eternal.
Now that Qingu is the highest and has taken <supremacy>,
And has <ordained> destinies for his divine children,
Whatever you (gods) say shall cause fire to <subside>,[42]
Your concentrated venom shall make the mighty one yield."

Tablet II

Ea Seeks Help from Anshar against Tiamat

Tiamat assembled her creatures,
Drew up for battle against the gods her brood.
Thereafter Tiamat, more than(?) Apsu, was become an evildoer.[43]
She informed Ea that she was ready for battle.
When Ea heard this,
He was struck dumb with horror and sat stock still.
After he had thought and his distress had grown calm,
He made straight his way to Anshar his grandfather.
He came in before his grandfather, Anshar,

[39] This number was reached by adding the "monster snakes" of 134, the "Fierce dragons" of 137, and the nine creatures of 141–43.

[40] A male deity about whom little otherwise is known. His name is possibly derived from the Sumerian word for "work," and hence Qingu's blood, used to create humans, gave them their working capacities.

[41] The tablet of destinies, though not a clearly defined concept in Mesopotamian tradition, was sometimes considered to be in the netherworld and was presumably inscribed with a person's destiny and day of death. In the Anzu story, on which this episode is based, the tablet gave the power to control divine spheres of responsibility and thus universal authority.

[42] Contrast Tablet I line 96.

[43] One could also understand "on account of Apsu" or "against Apsu" (in that case the domain of Ea).

All that Tiamat plotted he recounted to him,
"My father, Tiamat our mother has grown angry with us,
She has convened an assembly, furious with rage.
All the gods rallied around her,
Even those you created are going over to her side,
They are massing around her, ready at Tiamat's side.
Angry, scheming, never lying down night and day,
Making warfare, rumbling, raging,
Convening in assembly, that they might start hostilities.
Mother Hubur, who can form everything,
Added countless invincible weapons, gave birth to monster serpents,
Pointed of fang, with merciless incisors(?),
She filled their bodies with venom for blood.
Fierce dragons she clad with glories,
Causing them to bear auras like gods, (saying)
'Whoever sees them shall collapse from weakness!
Wherever their bodies make onslaught, they shall not turn back!'
"She deployed serpents, dragons, and hairy hero-men,
Lion monsters, lion men, scorpion men,
Mighty demons, fish men, bull men,
Bearing unsparing arms, fearing no battle.
Her commands were absolute, no one opposed them,
Eleven indeed on this wise she created.
From among the gods her offspring, who composed her assembly,
She raised up Qingu from among them, it was he she made greatest!
Leadership of the army, command of the assembly,
Arming, contact, advance of the melee,
Wardenship of the (spoils?) of battle,
(All) she entrusted to him, made him sit on the dais.
'I cast your spell. I make you the greatest in the assembly of the gods,
Kingship of all the gods I put in your power.
You are the greatest, my husband, you are illustrious.
Your command shall always be greatest, over all the Anunna-gods.'
"She gave him the tablet of destinies, had him hold it to his chest, (saying)
'As for you, your command will not be changed, your utterance will be eternal.
Now that Qingu is the highest and has taken <supremacy>,
And has <ordained> destinies for his divine children,
Whatever you (gods) say shall cause fire to <subside>,
Your concentrated venom shall make the mighty one yield.'"

Anshar Reacts Desperately; Ea Reassures Him He Is Up to the Task

<When Anshar heard> the speech, he was deeply distressed,
He cried out "Woe!"; he bit his lips,

His spirits were angry, his mind was uneasy,
His cries to Ea his offspring grew choked,
"My son, you yourself were instigator of battle!
Do you bear the consequences of your own handiwork!
You went forth and killed Apsu,
So Tiamat, whom you have enraged, where is one who can face her?"
The sage counselor, wise prince,
Producer of wisdom, divine Nudimmud.
Answered his father Anshar gently,
With soothing words, calming speech,
"My father, inscrutable, ordainer of destinies,
Who has power to create and destroy,
O Anshar, inscrutable, ordainer of destinies,
Who has power to create and destroy,
I will declare my thoughts to you, relent for a moment,
Recall in your heart that I made a good plan.
Before I undertook to kill Apsu,
Who had foreseen what is happening now?
Ere I was the one who moved quickly to snuff out his life,
I indeed, for it was I who destroyed him, <wh>at was there?"
When Anshar heard this, it pleased him,
He calmed down, saying to Ea,
"Your deeds are worthy of a god,
You can(?) < . . . > a fierce, irresistible stroke,
Ea, your deeds are worthy of a god,
You can(?) < . . . > a fierce, irresistible stroke,
Go then to Tiamat, sub<due> her onslaught,
May her anger <be pacified> by <your> magic spell."

Ea Finds That He Is No Match for Tiamat; Neither Is Anu

When he heard the command <of his father> A<nshar>,
He set off, making straight his way,
Ea went to seek out Tiamat's stratagem.
He stopped, horror-stricken, then turned back.
He came before Anshar the sovereign,
He beseeched him with entreaties, saying,
"<My father>, Tiamat has carried her actions beyond me,
I sought out her course, but my spell cannot counter it.
Her strength is enormous, she is utterly terrifying,
She is reinforced with a host, none can come out against her.
Her challenge was in no way reduced but overwhelmed me,
I became afraid at her clamor, I turned back.
My father, do not despair, send another to her,
A woman's force may be very great, but it cannot match a man's.

Do you scatter her ranks, thwart her intentions,
Before she lays her hands on all of us."
Anshar was shouting, in a passion,
To Anu his son he said these words,
"Stalwart son, valiant warrior,
Whose strength is enormous, whose onslaught is irresistible,
Hurry, take a stand before Tiamat,
Soothe her feelings, let her heart be eased.
If she will not listen to what you say,
Say something by way of entreaty to her, so that she be pacified."
When he heard what his father Anshar said,
He set off, <made str>aight his way,
Anu went to seek out Tiamat's stratagem.
He stopped, horror-stricken, then turned back.
He came before <Ansha>r, <his father who begot him>,
He beseeched him with entreaties, s<aying>,
"My father, Tiamat has carried her actions beyond me,
I sought out her course, but my s<pell cannot counter it>.
Her strength is enormous, she is utterly terrifying,
She is reinforced with a host, none can <come out against> her.
Her challenge was in no way reduced, but overwhelmed me.
I became afraid at her clamor, I turned back.
My father, do not despair, send another to her,
A woman's strength may be very great, but it cannot match a man's.
Do you scatter her ranks, thwart her intentions,
Before she lays her hands on all of us."
Anshar fell silent, gazing at the ground,
Nodding towards Ea, he shook his head.
The Igigi-gods and Anunna-gods were all assembled,
With lips closed tight, they sat in silence.
Would no god go out <at his> command?
Against Tiamat would none go as <he> ordered?
Then Anshar, father of the great gods,
His heart was angry, he <would not summon> anyone!

Ea Summons Marduk to Face Tiamat; He Agrees on Condition that He Gain Supremacy among the Gods

The mighty firstborn, champion of his father,
Hastener to battle, the warrior Marduk
Did Ea summon to his secret place,
Told him his secret words,[44]
"O Marduk, think, heed your father,

[44] Uncertain. It could be a reference to magic words, or to Marduk's demand.

You are my son who can relieve his heart!
Draw nigh, approach Anshar,
Make ready to speak. He was angry, seeing you he will be calm."
The Lord was delighted at his father's words,
He drew near and waited upon Anshar.
When Anshar saw him, his heart was filled with joyful feelings,
He kissed his lips, he banished his gloom.
"My father, let not your lips be silent but speak,
Let me go, let me accomplish your heart's desire.
<O Anshar>, let not your lips be silent but speak,
Let me go, let me accomplish your heart's desire!
What man is it who has sent forth his battle against you?"
"< My son>, Tiamat, a woman, comes out against you to arms."
"<My father>, creator, rejoice and be glad,
Soon you will trample the neck of Tiamat.
<Anshar>, creator, rejoice and be glad,
Soon you will trample <the neck> of Tiamat!"
"<Go>, son, knower of all wisdom,
Bring Tiamat to rest with your sacral spell.
Make straight, quickly, with the storm chariot,
Let it not veer from its <course>, turn (it) back!"
The Lord was delighted at his grandfather's words,
His heart was overjoyed as he said to his grandfather,
"Lord of the gods, of the destiny of the great gods,
If indeed I am to champion you,
Subdue Tiamat and save your lives,
Convene the assembly, nominate me for supreme destiny!
Take your places in the Assembly Place of the Gods, all of you, in joyful mood.
When I speak, let me ordain destinies instead of you.
Let nothing that I shall bring about be altered,
Nor what I say be revoked or changed."

Tablet III

[We skip ahead to the end of Tablet III. In the omitted portion, Anshar sends out his messenger to all the gods, reporting Tiamat's threat and the inability of Anu and Ea to stop her, as well as Marduk's offer to confront Tiamat—provided that the gods make him supreme deity. We resume with the reaction of the gods to Anshar's report, their assembly, and their feasting—the last a sign of their confidence in Marduk.]

When Lahmu and Lahamu heard, they cried aloud,
All of the Igigi-gods wailed bitterly,

"What (is our) hostility, that she has taken a<ct>ion (against) us?[45]
We scarcely know what Tiamat might do!"
They swarmed together and came.
All the great gods, ordainers of <destinies>,
Came before Anshar and were filled with <joy>.
One kissed the other in the assembly < . . . >,
They conversed, sat down at a feast,
On produce of the field they fed, imbibed of the vine,
With sweet liquor they made their gullets run,
They felt good from drinking the beer.
Most carefree, their spirits rose,
To Marduk their champion they ordained destiny.

Tablet IV

Marduk Is Made King and Sets Off against Tiamat

They set out for him a princely dais,
He took his place before his fathers for sovereignty.
"You are the most important among the great gods,
Your destiny is unrivalled, your command is supreme.
O Marduk, you are the most important among the great gods,
Your destiny is unrivalled, your command is supreme!
Henceforth your command cannot be changed,
To raise high, to bring low, this shall be your power.
Your command shall be truth, your word shall not be wrong.
Not one of the gods shall go beyond the limits you set.
Support is wanted for the gods' sanctuaries,
Wherever their shrines shall be, your own shall be established.
O Marduk, you are our champion,
We bestow upon you kingship of all and everything.
Take your place in the assembly, your word shall be supreme.
May your weapon never strike wide but dispatch your foes.
O Lord, spare his life who trusts in you,
But the god who has taken up evil, snuff out his life!"
They set up among them a certain constellation,
To Marduk their first born said they (these words),
"Your destiny, O Lord, shall be foremost of the gods',
Command destruction or creation, they shall take place.
At your word the constellation shall be destroyed,
Command again, the constellation shall be intact."
He commanded and at his word the constellation was destroyed,

[45] Or, "Why be opposed?" The second half of the line is problematic.

He commanded again and the constellation was created anew.
When the gods his fathers saw what he had commanded,
Joyfully they hailed, "Marduk is king!"
They bestowed in full measure scepter, throne, and staff,
They gave him unopposable weaponry that vanquishes enemies.
"Go, cut off the life of Tiamat,
Let the winds bear her blood away as glad tidings!"
The gods, his fathers, ordained the Lord's destiny,
On the path to success and authority did they set him marching.
He made the bow, appointed it his weapon,
He mounted the arrow, set it on the string.
He took up the mace, held it in his right hand,
Bow and quiver he slung on his arm.
Thunderbolts he set before his face,
With raging fire he covered his body.
Then he made a net to enclose Tiamat within,
He deployed the four winds that none of her might escape:
South Wind, North Wind, East Wind, West Wind,
Gift of his grandfather Anu;[46] he fastened the net at his side.
He made ill wind, whirlwind, cyclone,
Four-ways wind, seven-ways wind, destructive wind, irresistible wind:
He released the winds which he had made, the seven of them,
Mounting in readiness behind him to roil inside Tiamat.
Then the Lord raised the Deluge, his great weapon.
He mounted the terrible chariot,[47] the unopposable Storm Demon,
He hitched to it the four-steed team, he tied them at his side:[48]
"Slaughterer," "Merciless," "Overwhelmer," "Soaring."
Their lips are curled back, their teeth bear venom,
They know not fatigue, they are trained to trample down.
He stationed at his right gruesome battle and strife,
At his left the fray that overthrows all formations.
He was garbed in a ghastly armored garment,[49]
On his head he was covered with terrifying auras.
The Lord made straight and pursued his way,
Toward raging Tiamat he set his face.
He was holding a spell ready upon his lips.
A plant, antidote to venom, he was grasping in his hand.

[46] The gift refers to the four winds (see Tablet I lines 105–6), not the net. The original has an elaborate poetic structure that cannot be reproduced clearly in translation. "At his side" could also mean "on his arm."

[47] Literally: "the storm chariot . . . the terrible one."

[48] Apparently the ends of the reins, normally held by an attendant, are here strapped to him, to keep both hands free for fighting. Balancing in a chariot with weapons in both hands and guiding a four-steed team by the belt is, of course, a heroic feat of the first order.

[49] This line is a remarkable example of alliteration, a device esteemed by this poet: *naḫlapti apluḫti pulḫāti ḫalipma.*

At that moment the gods were stirring, stirring about him,
The gods his fathers were stirring about him, the gods stirring about him.

Marduk Engages in Battle with Tiamat, Kills Her, and Takes the Tablet of Destinies

The Lord drew near, to find out the intent(?) of Tiamat,
He was looking for the stratagem of Qingu her spouse.
As he looked, his tactic turned to confusion,[50]
His reason was overthrown, his actions panicky,
And as for the gods his allies, who went at his side,
When they saw the valiant vanguard, their sight failed them.
Tiamat cast her spell pointblank,
Falsehood, lies she held ready on her lips.
"< . . . > lord, the gods rise against you,
They assembled <where> they are, (but) are they on your side?"[51]
The Lord <raised> the Deluge, his great weapon,
To Tiamat, who acted conciliatory,[52] sent he (this word),
"Why outwardly do you assume a friendly attitude,
While your heart is plotting to open attack?
Children cried out as their parents were deceitful,
And you, their own mother, spurned all natural feeling.[53]
You named Qingu to be spouse for you,
Though he had no right to be, you set him up for chief god.
You attempted wicked deeds against Anshar, sovereign of the gods,
And you have perpetrated your evil against the gods my fathers.
Though main force is drawn up, though these your weapons are in array,
Come within range, let us duel, you and I!"
When Tiamat heard this,
She was beside herself, she turned into a maniac.
Tiamat shrieked loud, in a passion,
Her frame shook all over, down to the ground.
He was reciting the incantation, casting his spell,
While the gods of battle were whetting their blades.
Tiamat and Marduk, sage of the gods, drew close for battle,
They locked in single combat, joining for the fray.
The Lord spread out his net, encircled her,
The ill wind he had held behind him he released in her face.
Tiamat opened her mouth to swallow,

[50] Marduk is temporarily discomfited by the sight of his enemy.

[51] Uncertain: Tiamat evidently tells Marduk that the gods he is championing are actually disloyal to him.

[52] Or: "who was furious."

[53] The precise significance of Marduk's remarks is not clear. While he may refer to Tiamat's natural goodwill towards her children (Tablet I lines 28, 46), it seems more likely that he refers to her insinuation that he had best beware the loyalty of those he championed.

He thrust in the ill wind so she could not close her lips.
The raging winds bloated her belly,
Her insides were stopped up, she gaped her mouth wide.
He shot off the arrow, it broke open her belly,
It cut to her innards, it pierced the heart.
He subdued her and snuffed out her life,
He flung down her carcass, he took his stand upon it.
After the vanguard had slain Tiamat,
He scattered her forces, he dispersed her host.
As for the gods her allies, who had come to her aid,
They trembled, terrified, they ran in all directions,
They tried to make a way out(?) to save their[54] lives,
There was no escaping the grasp that held (them)!
He drew them in and smashed their weapons.
They were cast in the net and sat in a heap,
They were heaped up in the corners, full of woe,
They were bearing his punishment, to prison confined.
As for the eleven creatures, the ones adorned with glories,
And the demonic horde(?), which all went at her side,
He put on leadropes, he bound their arms.
He trampled them under, together with their belligerence.
As for Qingu, who was trying to be great among them,
He captured him and reckoned him among the doomed.
He took away from him the tablet of destinies that he had no right to,
He sealed it with a seal and affixed it to his chest.

Marduk Creates the Heavens from Tiamat's Corpse and Builds Esharra

Having captured his enemies and triumphed,
Having shown the mighty(?) foe subservient(?),[55]
Having fully achieved Anshar's victory over his enemies,
Valiant Marduk having attained what Nudimmud desired,
He made firm his hold over the captured gods,
Then turned back to Tiamat whom he had captured.
The Lord trampled upon the frame of Tiamat,
With his merciless mace he crushed her skull.
He cut open the arteries of her blood ,
He let the North Wind bear (it) away as glad tidings.
When his fathers saw, they rejoiced and were glad,
They brought him gifts and presents.
He calmed down. Then the Lord was inspecting her carcass,
That he might divide(?) the monstrous lump

[54] Text has "his life."

[55] This may refer to a triumphal parade.

and fashion artful things.
He split her in two, like a fish for drying,
Half of her he set up and made as a cover, (like) heaven.[56]
He stretched out the hide and assigned watchmen,
And ordered them not to let her waters escape.
He crossed heaven and inspected (its) sacred places,[57]
He made a counterpart of Apsu, the dwelling of Nudimmud.
The Lord measured the construction of Apsu,
The Great Sanctuary, its likeness, he founded, Esharra.[58]
The Great Sanctuary, Esharra, which he built, (is) heaven,[59]
He made Ea, Enlil, and Anu dwell in their holy places.

Tablet V

Marduk Organizes the Stars and Seasons

He made the position(s) for the great gods,
He established (in) constellations the stars, their counterparts.
He marked the year, described its boundaries,
He set up twelve months of three stars each.[60]
After he had patterned the days of the year,
He fixed the position of Nebiru to mark the (stars') relationships.[61]
Lest any make an error or go astray,
He established the position(s) of Enlil and Ea in relation to it.
He opened up gates on both (sides of her) ribs,
He made strong bolts to left and right.
In her liver he established the zenith.
He made the moon appear, entrusted (to him) the night.
He assigned to him the crown jewel of nighttime to mark the day (of the month):
"Every month, without ceasing, start off with the (crescent) disk.
At the beginning of the month, waxing over the land,
You shine with horns to mark six days,
At the seventh day, the disk as <ha>lf.

[56] That is, he made a cover to the watery deep that serves as the "sky" for it.

[57] Marduk models his new home after the domain of Ea, the Apsu.

[58] Esharra means "The House of Totality," the domain of Enlil.

[59] Or, perhaps, "(as in) heaven."

[60] Babylonian astrolabes assign three stars to each month; here Marduk is portrayed as creating this pattern.

[61] Refers to the daily rotation of the stars. The planet Mercury best fits the astronomical data for Nebiru, though in another translation the planet could also have referred to Jupiter or the central area in the sky where Jupiter was to be found.

At the fifteenth day, you shall be in opposition, at the midpoint of each <month>.
When the sun f<ac>es you from the horizon of heaven,
Wane at the same pace and form in reverse.
At the day of di<sappeara>nce, approach the sun's course,
On the < . . . > of the thirtieth day, you shall be in conjunction with the sun a second time.
I d<efined?> the celestial signs, proceed on their path,
< . . . > approach each other and render (oracular) judgment.
The sun shall < . . . > killing, oppression."

<The tablet becomes very fragmentary for about twenty lines.>

He compacted (the foam) into c<louds> and made (them) billow.
To raise the wind, to cause rainfall,
To make mists steam, to pile up her spittle (as snow?),
He assigned to himself, put under his control.
He set down her head and piled < . . . >[62] upon it,
He opened underground springs, a flood was let flow(?).
From her eyes he undammed the Euphr<ates> and Tigris,
He stopped up her nostrils, he left < . . . >
He heaped up high-peaked mo<unt>ains from(?) her dugs.
He drilled through her waterholes to carry off the catchwater.
He coiled up her tail and tied it as(?) "The Great Bond."[63]
< . . . > Apsu beneath, at his feet.
He set her crotch as the brace of heaven,
He set <half of> her as a roof, he established the netherworld.
< . . . t>ask, he caused the oceans to surge within her.
<He spre>ad his net, let all (within) escape,
He formed the < . . . > of heaven and netherworld,
Tightening their bond < . . . >

Marduk Distributes Trophies, Parades His Defeated Enemies, and Is Proclaimed King

After he had designed his prerogatives and devised his responsibilities,
He founded (their) <sanc>tuaries, entrusted (those) to Ea.
<The tablet> of destinies, which he took from Qingu and brought away,
As the foremost gift he took away, he presented (it) to Anu.
The < . . . > of battle, which dangled and fluttered about (in the net),
< . . . > he led before his fathers.
<And as for> the eleven creatures which Tiamat created < . . . >

[62] On the basis of Tablet VII line 71 one may restore "mountain" here, but this is not assured.

[63] That is, the link that holds heaven and the world below together.

He smashed their <wea>pons, he tied them to his feet.
He made images <of them> and set them up at the <Gate of> Apsu:
"Lest ever after they be forgotten, let this be the sign."
When <the gods> saw, they rejoiced and were glad,
Lahmu, Lahamu, and all his fathers.
Anshar <embra>ced him, proclaimed (his) salutation (to be) "king."
<A>nu, Enlil, and Ea gave him gifts,
< . . . > Damkina his mother made cries of joy over him,
She(?) made his face glow with (cries of) "Good . . . !"[64]
To Usmu,[65] who brought (Damkina's) gift at the glad tidings,
<He en>trusted the ministry of Apsu and care of the sanctuaries.
All the Igigi-gods together prostrated before him,
<And> the Anunna-gods, all there are, were doing him homage,
The whole of them joined together to pay him reverence,
<Before him> they stood, they prostrated, "This is the king!"

Marduk Dons His Insignia; the Gods Swear Allegiance to Him

<After> his fathers had celebrated him in due measure,
< . . . > covered with the dust of battle.
< . . . >
With cedar <oil> and < . . . > he anoi<nted> his body,
He clothed himself in <his> princely <gar>ment,
The kingly aura, the awe-inspiring tiara.
He picked up the mace, he held it in his right hand,
< . . . > he held in his left hand.
< . . . >
< . . . > he made firm at his feet.
He set over < . . . >
The staff of success and authority <he hung> at his side.
After he <had put on> the aura of <his kingship>,
His netted sack, the Apsu < . . . > awesomeness.
He was seated like < . . . >
In <his> throne room < . . . >
In his cella < . . . >
The gods, all there are, < . . . >
Lahmu and Lahamu < . . . >
Made ready to speak and <said to> the Igigi-gods,
"Formerly <Mar>duk was 'our beloved son,'
Now he is your king, pay heed to his command."
Next all of them spoke and said,
"'Lugaldimmerankia' is his name, trust in him!"

[64] This is evidently a congratulatory exclamation, with a play on Damkina and *dumqu* ("good").

[65] Advisor or messenger god to Ea, a Janus-like figure with a double head.

When they had given kingship over to Marduk,
They said to him expressions of good will and obedience,
"Henceforth you shall be provider for our sanctuaries,
Whatever you shall command, we will do."

Marduk Creates Babylon

Marduk made ready to speak and said
(These) words to the gods his fathers,
"Above Apsu, the azure dwelling,
Opposite Esharra, which I built above you,
Below the sacred places, whose grounding I made firm,
A house I shall build, my favorite abode.
Within it I shall establish its holy place,
I shall appoint my (holy) chambers, I shall establish my kingship.
When you go up from Apsu to assembly,
Let your stopping places be there to receive you.[66]
When you come down from heaven to <assembly>,
Let your stopping places be there to receive all of you.
I shall call <its> name <Babylon>, Abode of the Great Gods,
We shall all hold fe<stival>s with<in> it."

[*We omit a fragmentary portion at the end of the tablet in which the gods prostrate themselves before Marduk. The tablet breaks off after that.*]

Tablet VI

Human Beings Are Created from the Blood of Qingu

When <Mar>duk heard the speech of the gods,
He was resolving to make artful things:
He would tell his idea[67] to Ea,
What he thought of in his heart he proposes,
"I shall compact blood, I shall cause bones to be,
I shall make stand a human being, let 'Man' be its name.
I shall create humankind,
They shall bear the gods' burden that those may rest.[68]
I shall artfully double the ways of the gods:
Let them be honored as one but divided in twain."[69]

[66] That is, when the gods or their cult images travel in Babylonia, they can find accommodation in specific chambers of the Babylonian temples.

[67] Literally: "his utterance," but to judge from the context, the utterance is so far purely internal.

[68] From the necessity of providing for themselves; see *Atrahasis* Tablet I, lines 39ff.

[69] A reference to two main divisions of the Mesopotamian pantheon, Anunna-gods and Igigi-gods, or to the supernal and infernal deities.

Ea answered him, saying these words,
He told him a plan to let the gods rest,[70]
  "Let one, their brother, be given to me,
  Let him be destroyed so that people can be fashioned.
  Let the great gods convene in assembly,
  Let the guilty one be given up that they may abide."
Marduk convened the great gods in assembly,
He spoke to them magnanimously as he gave the command,
The gods heeded his utterance,
As the king spoke to the Anunna-gods (these) words,
  "Let your first reply be the truth!
  Do you speak with me truthful words!
  Who was it that made war,
  Suborned Tiamat and drew up for battle?
  Let him be given over to me, the one who made war,
  I shall make him bear his punishment, you shall be released."
The Igigi, the great gods, answered him,
To Lugaldimmerankia, sovereign of all the gods, their lord,
  "It was Qingu who made war,
  Suborned Tiamat and drew up for battle."
They bound and held him before Ea,
They imposed the punishment on him and shed his blood.
From his blood he made mankind,
He imposed the burden of the gods and exempted the gods.
After Ea the wise had made mankind,
They imposed the burden of the gods on them!
That deed is beyond comprehension,
By the artifices of Marduk did Nudimmud create!

Marduk Assigns the Gods Their Lot; the Gods Build Esagila, Marduk's Temple in Babylon

Marduk the king divided the gods,
The Anunna-gods, all of them, above and below,
He assigned to Anu for duty at his command.
He set three hundred in heaven for (their) duty,
A like number he designated for the ways of the netherworld:
He made six hundred dwell in heaven and netherworld.
After he had given all the commands,
And had divided the shares of the Anunna-gods of heaven and netherworld,

[70] The text assigns Marduk primacy in the creation of man by giving him the "idea," since Mesopotamian tradition, established centuries before this text was written, agreed that Ea/Enki had been the actual creator, along with the Mother Goddess.

The Anunna-gods made ready to speak,
To Marduk their lord they said,
"Now, Lord, you who have liberated us,
What courtesy may we do you?
We will make a shrine, which is to be called by name
'Chamber that shall be Our Stopping Place,' we shall find rest therein.
We shall lay out the shrine, let us set up its emplacement,
When we come thither (to visit you), we shall find rest therein."
When Marduk heard this,
His features glowed brightly, like the day,
"Then make Babylon the task that you requested,
Let its brickwork be formed, build high the shrine."
The Anunna-gods set to with hoes,
One (full) year they made its bricks.
When the second year came,
They raised up Esagila, the counterpart of Apsu,
They built the high ziggurat of (counterpart-)Apsu,
For Anu-Enlil-Ea[71] they founded his house and dwelling.
Majestically he took his seat before them,
Its pinnacles were facing toward the base of Esharra.
After they had done the work of Esagila,
All the Anunna-gods devised their own shrines.
The three hundred Igigi-gods of heaven and the six hundred of Apsu all convened.
The Lord, in the Highest Shrine, which they built as his dwelling,
Seated the gods his fathers for a banquet,
"This is Babylon, your place of dwelling.
Take your pleasure there, seat yourselves in its delights!"
The great gods sat down,
They set out cups, they sat down at the feast.
After they had taken their enjoyment inside it,
And in awe-inspiring Esagila had conducted the offering,
All the orders and designs had been made permanent,
All the gods had divided the stations of heaven and netherworld,
The fifty great gods took their thrones,
The seven gods of destinies were confirmed forever for rendering judgment.

Marduk's Bow Becomes a Constellation

The Lord took the bow, his weapon, and set it before them,
The gods his fathers looked upon the net he had made.
They saw how artfully the bow was fashioned,
His fathers were praising what he had brought to pass.

[71] The three divine names together may here be taken as a syncretism for Marduk.

Anu raised (it), speaking to the assembly of the gods,
He kissed the bow, "This be my daughter!"
He named the bow, these are its names:
"'Longwood' shall be the first, 'Conqueror' shall be the second."
The third name, 'Bow Star,' he made visible in heaven,
He established its position with respect to the gods his brethren.

Marduk Is Made Supreme God

After Anu had ordained the destinies of the bow,
He set out the royal throne which stood highest among the gods,
Anu had him sit there, in the assembly of the gods.
Then the great gods convened,
They made Marduk's destiny highest, they prostrated themselves.
They laid upon themselves a curse (if they broke the oath),
With water and oil they swore, they touched their throats.[72]
They granted him exercise of kingship over the gods,
They established him forever for lordship of heaven and netherworld.
Anshar gave him an additional name, Asalluhi,
"When he speaks, we shall all do obeisance,
At his command the gods shall pay heed.
His word shall be supreme above and below,
The son, our champion, shall be the highest.
His lordship shall be supreme, he shall have no rival,
He shall be the shepherd of the black-headed folk,[73] his creatures.
They shall tell of his ways, without forgetting, in the future.
He shall establish for his fathers great food offerings,
He shall provide for them, he shall take care of their sanctuaries.
He shall cause incense burners to be savored, he shall make their chambers rejoice.
He shall make on earth the counterpart of what he brought to pass in heaven,
He shall appoint the black-headed folk to serve him.
Let the subject peoples be mindful that their gods should be invoked,
At his command let them heed their goddess(es).
Let their gods, their goddesses be brought food offerings,
Let (these) not be forgotten, let them sustain their gods.
Let their holy places be apparent(?), let them build their sanctuaries.[74]
Let the black-headed folk be divided as to gods,
(But) by whatever name we call him, let him be our god."[75]

[72] A symbolic slashing gesture meaning that they may die if they break the oath.

[73] The Mesopotamians.

[74] The holy places show forth their own qualities of holiness so that mankind builds shrines there.

[75] That is, Marduk is to be the one god of all the gods, no matter how many gods mankind may serve.

The Hittite *Song of Emergence*
Introduction

The Hittite *Song of Emergence*,[76] formerly called *Kingship in Heaven* or the *Song of Kumarbi*, narrates a generational conflict among the gods that has many parallels in Hesiod's *Theogony*. In it, the first god of heaven, Alalu, is deposed by his cupbearer Anu ("Sky"), who is in turn overthrown, in spectacular fashion, by his cupbearer Kumarbi, Alalu's son. Kumarbi, who had bitten off and swallowed Anu's genitals as the latter tried to flee, was impregnated with three gods: Teshub, the storm god; the "irresistible" Tigris River; and the god Tashmishu. After the birth of Teshub, perhaps but not certainly from the head of Kumarbi, Kumarbi apparently demands that the newborn be given to him to devour, but is instead given a diorite stone that breaks his teeth. After the birth of the Tigris and Tashmishu, the tablet, very fragmentary at this point, seems to tell of an impending battle between Teshub and Kumarbi and of concerns about keeping Teshub's power in check. The tablet ends with an intriguing reference to the birth of two sons of Earth, followed by a colophon (an author's or copyist's note) that dates the tablet to about 1220 BC.

The story has to do with the conflict over kingship of heaven: How is the king of the gods chosen, and how secure is his control over the world? Here, the king of heaven is overthrown three times in violent fashion. This motif of generational conflict and challenges to established power among the gods is a common one both in the Ancient Near East and in Greek mythology. The best example of this conflict among generations of gods from Babylon may be seen in the *Epic of Creation* (see selection above), where previous generations of gods are replaced until the emergence of the chief Babylonian god, Marduk. When one reads Hesiod's *Theogony*, parallels to both the *Epic of Creation* and especially the Hittite *Song of Emergence* can be found. In the *Theogony* it is clear that the older gods are perfectly aware of the threat their progeny pose as they seek the power of the older generation. This is why Ouranos and Cronos attempt to neutralize (but not kill) their children, and Zeus' special status is emphasized by his ability to avoid the threats posed by his children. The *Song of Emergence* likewise shows parallels to this narrative of generational conflict over control of the cosmos, without any of the interest in describing the creation of the universe as found in both the *Epic of Creation* and the *Theogony*. It should be noted, however, that this text is not complete, as the colophon makes clear; it is only the first tablet of a series, which presumably told the rest of the story and may also have included information about how this conflict affected the cosmos and its creation.

This is a particularly difficult text to translate for several reasons. It exists almost exclusively in one damaged tablet that has been supplemented by a few other small fragments that have been identified as belonging to the same tablet and a duplicate text containing a few lines that are missing from the main tablet. Most of the narrative must, therefore, be reconstructed from the one main tablet. This would be fine except that the main tablet is in terrible condition. Large portions of the clay have simply

[76] The new title is found in the recently discovered fragment that contains the colophon (see section 29 of the translation at the end of this selection).

broken off, leaving parts of many lines lost forever. In addition, much of the tablet that is preserved is badly abraded, making it difficult to read the signs on the surface. We have been careful to note where we have reconstructed the lost text in brackets < . . . >. The new translation provided here attempts to avoid reconstruction based on circular reasoning—that is, we do not assume that the Hittite myth must look like Hesiod's *Theogony* if the text is not clear. We also incorporate a recently discovered join piece that helps complete the colophon and reveals the ancient Hittite title. In addition, recent research in Hittite lexicography, the study of the meaning of words, has allowed us to propose new restorations of missing or difficult passages. While we have added a few words (where the meaning is obvious) to make the translation more idiomatic, we try to retain the flavor of the original, which abounds in short declarative sentences.

Text

1 (i 1–11) <I sing of Kumarbi, father of the gods.> May the older generations of gods, who are <in the dark earth>, may <those> mighty <primev>al gods listen attentively! May Na<ra, Napshara, Mink>i, and Amunki listen! May Ammezzadu and <*name lost*>, the father and mother of <*name lost*>, listen! **2** <May Enlil and Apan>du, the father and mother of Ishara, listen! May Enlil and <Ninlil, below and on h>igh, who are mighty and unchanging gods, < . . . > and quiet,[77] listen! Formerly, in the ear<lie>st years, Alalu was king in heaven. Alalu sat on the throne, and Anu, foremost among the gods, stood before him. He always bowed down at (his) feet, and he placed the drinking cups in his hand.

3 (i 12–17) For a mere nine years Alalu was king in heaven. In the ninth year, however, Anu declared war against Alalu and defeated him. Alalu fled before him. He went down into[78] the dark earth, down he went into the dark earth. Anu sat on the throne. While Anu was on his throne, powerful Kumarbi served him his drink. He would bow down at his feet and put the drinking cups in his hand.

4 (i 18–29) For a mere nine years Anu was king in heaven. In the ninth year, however, Anu declared war against Kumarbi, and Kumarbi, the offspring of Alalu, returned battle against Anu. When Anu could no longer withstand the gaze of Kumarbi, he escaped from Kumarbi's grasp. He fled, did Anu, and went to heaven, and Kumarbi rushed on after him. He seized Anu by the feet and pulled him down from heaven, **5** and bit his genitals.[79] Anu's manhood united with Kumarbi, in his insides, like bronze.[80] When Kumarbi swallowed down Anu's manhood, he rejoiced and laughed.

Anu turned back towards Kumarbi and began to speak to him: "You are rejoicing at your insides, because you swallowed my manhood." **6** (i 30–46) "Do not rejoice at your insides, for I have placed a heavy burden in your insides. First I have impregnated you with the mighty Storm God. Second, however, I impregnated you with the irresistible

[77] Or "bright, shining?"

[78] Or "to."

[79] Compare Cronos' castration of Ouranos in Hesiod's *Theogony*.

[80] That is, analogous to the alloying process of combining copper and tin to make bronze, the primary metal of that period.

Tigris River. And third I impregnated you with the mighty god Tashmishu. I have put three fearsome deities (in)to you, burdens to your insides, and you will end up striking the stones of Mount Dassha with your head (in pain)." **7** When Anu finished speaking, he went up to heaven and concealed himself. Kumarbi the wise king spat out his mouth, he spat his mouth out, spittle and manhood mixed together. But what Kumarbi spat up, Mount Kanzura received, a fearsome god.[81] **8** Kumarbi, recovering, went to the city of Nippur, and he sat down in a lordly <place>. Kumarbi did not < . . . Kumarbi> continued to count <the months>. The seventh month arrived. < . . . > Inside him, . . . <*column i breaks off*>

[When column ii begins, someone is apparently addressing the gods growing inside the pregnant Kumarbi.]

9 (ii 1–3) "Come forth from Kumarbi, from his strong < . . . >. Or come forth from him through the flesh,[82] or come forth from him through the good place."[83]

10 (ii 4–15) The god A.GILIM[84] spoke the(se) words before Kumarbi, to his insides. "May you live, you lord of wisdom and the watery depths.[85] If for coming out, < . . . > Kumarbi" <*too damaged to translate*> "Earth will give her strength to me. Sky will give me his courage. Anu will give me his manliness, Kumarbi will give me his wisdom. Nara will give me his strength, Napshara will give me < . . . > . . . <*Another name and gift is lost*>. Enlil will give me his strength, his < . . . >, his majesty, and his wisdom." <*Two more lines of text are too broken to translate; "all of his insides" and "spirit/soul" are discernible.*>[86]

*[**Paragraph 11** (ii 16–22) is too damaged to translate. The bull Šeri, one of the bulls that pull the Storm God's chariot, and who will appear later as an advisor to the Storm God, appears. There is also a reference to a wagon, or possibly the Storm God's chariot, depicted throughout Hittite art pulled by the bulls Šeri and Ḫurri. A wagon, possibly this wagon, will also appear later in the narrative.]*

12 (ii 23–28) Anu began to speak: "< . . . > come! I feared your gaze. < . . . > All that < . . . > which I gave. < . . . > come! As a woman <for giving birth brings> forth, just so come forth! Come <like(?)> the Storm God of the city < . . . >. < . . . > come

[81] Perhaps, following one scholar's interpretation, "Mount Kanzura <was impregnat>ed with the fearsome god Ta<shmi>." Either way, Mount Kanzura was impregnated by the semen that was spat out.

[82] Or possibly "hump," that is, "pregnant belly."

[83] This phrase is understood as "skull" by earlier translators, but this is based solely on an analogy with the birth of Athena from the head of Zeus as depicted in Hesiod's *Theogony*. Their proposed interpretation is in no way certain.

[84] A god attested only in this text.

[85] This may be addressed to Ea, the Sumerian god of wisdom. An alternative translation would be "lord of the source of wisdom."

[86] In this paragraph the god A.GILIM is apparently speaking not to Kumarbi, but to the god(s) growing inside him. It is presumably the Storm God who is citing the various attributes he will receive when he comes out of Kumarbi.

forth through the mouth(?). < . . . > all the < . . . >, come! If it is good,[87] come (forth) through the good place."

13 (ii 29–38) He began to speak from within Kumarbi: "< . . . > place is standing." "If I come out <from . . . >, he will break <*me*(?)>[88] off like a reed. If I come out through the good place, it will defile me within that (place) as well. < . . . >, it will defile me through the ear.[89] If, however, I come forth through the good place, (Kumarbi) will pant like a woman in labor (?). When I < . . . > the Storm God of Heaven, < . . . >." He readied it inside. He split his head like a stone. He released him, Kumarbi. He released him upward and the god KA.ZAL (= Teshub), the hero king, came out.

14 (ii 39–54) When KA.ZAL went forth, he stood before Ea. Kumarbi tottered,[90] he fell down. Kumarbi was transformed through <*anger*>. He sought the trail of NAM.ḪE,[91] and he spoke to Ea. "Give me the child, and I will utterly devour him.[92] Whoever < . . . > me like a woman, < . . . >. I will eat up Teshub < . . . >. I will chew <him> like a <broken> reed. < . . . > I will damage <him> before <you>. < . . . > order <it>." He finished <speaking>. Ea, ask < . . . >! He gathered him with his mind. < . . . > Kumarbi. The Sun-god of Heaven observed him, and Kumarbi began to eat. However the <dior>ite stone <cracked> the teeth in Kumarbi's mouth.[93] When it <crack>ed his teeth in his mouth, he began to cry out.

15 (ii 55–75) Kumarbi < . . . >. He said, "<Of wh>om was I afraid?" < . . . > As in old age, Kumarbi < . . . >. He began to speak to Kumarbi. "Let them call it the < . . . st>one. Let it be placed < . . . >." The diorite stone, however, he pushed into the hole and said, "Let them in the future call you <the . . . stone>. May the wealthy men, the heroic lords, continue to slaughter cattle <and rams> to you. May the poor men, however, make offerings to you with meal." When it <is> not < . . . >, that which <*verb lost*> Kumarbi from the mouth, no one will < . . . > behind him. Kumarbi spoke with <his mouth>. <What> happened in his body, the lands above and below will <revere>. **16** <The wealthy men> began to make blood sacrifices with cattle and rams. The poor men began to make offerings with meal. They began to < . . . >. They stitched together Kumarbi's skull like a garment. And the heroic Storm God came forth from the <good> place.

17 (ii 76–87) The Birth Goddesses <arrived>. His good place like a garment <they stitched up>. His < . . . > place like a < . . . >, as a second place <they opened>. But the Tigris River, lo and behold, however, came forth <from that second place>. They helped him to give birth, <Kumarbi>. <The Birth Goddesses helped> Kumarbi <to give birth> like a woman of the bed. <They took Kumarbi>, however, to Mount Kanzura, and <they helped> Mount Kanzura <to give birth>, and the heroic <Tashmishu> came

[87] That is, "if you prefer."

[88] Or: "He will snap <my knee>s like a reed."

[89] Perhaps meaning that it will deform him?

[90] The verb *hink-* normally means to bow or prostrate oneself, but in this case it seems unlikely.

[91] Apparently another epithet for the storm god Teshub.

[92] Compare Cronos swallowing his offspring in *Theogony*, except that Cronos swallows his offspring, which allows them to be brought up alive, but here they are to be utterly devoured and presumably destroyed.

[93] Compare the stone that Rhea gives Cronos in place of Zeus, allowing Zeus to survive.

(forth). <Tashmishu> came forth from the good place (of Mount Kanzura). And <he rejoic>ed, did Anu. <When Anu> saw <his three heroic progeny>, he said:

[Column ii breaks off. There must be another line or two in column ii detailing what Anu said, probably to his three offspring. As for column iii, there are two paragraphs missing at the beginning. From what follows it is probable that this missing section describes how the newly born Teshub overcame Kumarbi and effected a change in the kingship of heaven. The last word of ***paragraph 18*** *is "strike/kill."*>

19 (iii 2'–19') "We shall des<troy . . . >." Anu <said> "We shall destroy him. < . . . > in our midst, < . . . > we will destroy the god NAM.ḪE (= Teshub) Like an <enemy> we will k<ill him>." The <wo>rds which <Anu?> spoke <to his offspring>: "You shall destroy Kumarbi. < . . . > He w<ho sits> on my throne <shall . . . > him, Kumarbi. Who <will> dest<roy> him, the Storm God, for us? If he grows up, however, they will make someone el<se king>. He will permit < . . . >. Leave him be! < . . . > Lord of wisdom and the watery depths:[94] Make < . . . > king! < . . . > of the words. He will < . . . > him on the footstool."

(iii 20'–29') When Teshub <heard this>, he grew sad in his heart. He spoke to the bull Šeri:[95] **20** <Who> will come against <me> in battle? <Who will con>quer <me?> Even Kumarbi will <not> rise up <against me>. Ea as well <will not oppose me>. The son < . . . >. The Sun-god also <will . . . >. "I pursued <him> in the time of < . . . >. <Him> I conquered < . . . >. I h<ave cut> even Zababa, god of war, and brought him to Banapi, to the city. Who now will come <again>st me in battle?"

21 (iii 30'–39') Šeri r<esponded> to the Storm God. "My lord: Why do <you> curse them? <The . . . > gods. My lord: Why <do you curse> them? And the god Ea as well, why do you curse (him)? < . . . > You will be heard! Ea will not in that way < . . . >. <E>a's great mind is as big as the lands; <once> agreeable to you, <angry> he will come." It will come to pass that you will not be able to lift <your> neck." <Šeri> continued to speak. < . . . > "He is perceptive, is Ea." < . . . >

[At this point the tablet is completely broken away, and an unknown number of paragraphs have been lost. The next two paragraphs, ***23*** *and* ***24****, are too broken to make sense of.]*

25 (iii 67"–72") When Ea heard (these) words, he became wroth in his heart. And Ea in turn began to speak words in response to the protective deity of the field: "Do not speak curses to me! He who has cursed me, curses me <at his own risk.> Even you who repeat <these curses> to me are in fact cursing me.[96] A pot of beer <which is put> down <on the fire>, that pot will boil over."

End of column iii

[94] Or: "lord of the source of wisdom."

[95] One of the two bulls who pull the storm god's chariot.

[96] Ea seems to be telling the tutelary deity not even to repeat the curses of someone else to him, because even that can be understood as cursing him.

[The beginning of column iv is lost. The text picks up with a very fragmentary paragraph, followed by two somewhat well-preserved paragraphs and then the colophon, the ending section which provides the name of the scribe who wrote it and other information about the text. ***Paragraph 26*** *(iv 1'–5') provides two references to a wagon, important because of its role in the next paragraph. The second reference to the wagon may be "by means of the wagon"; from what follows it is possible to surmise that some deity sent his manhood (semen) in the wagon to impregnate Earth.]*

27 (iv 6'–16') <When> the sixth month was over, the wagon <arrived>.[97] <Earth received the> man<hood> of the wagon. The wagon retu<rned> to the Ap<su>.[98] She (Earth) acquired understanding in her soul.[99] < . . . > Ea <lord of> wis<dom, heard of this.> Earth went to the Apsu. "<Ea> will know (about) <it (the pregnancy).>" And Ea, <lord of> wisd<om,> counted <the months.> The first, <second, and third month passed.> The fourth, fifth, and sixth month passed. <The seventh>, eighth, and ninth month passed. The tenth month <arrived. In> the tenth month, Earth <began to c>ry out (with labor pains).

28 (iv 17'–27') When the Earth cried out in labor, she gave birth to <two> sons. A messenger went forth. A messenger went forth, and *<name lost>* on his throne approved and sent forth the good news: "Earth has given birth to two sons." <Wh>en <Ea>, king of wisdom, heard these words, he sent a gift to the messenger who had gone down to him. <He placed> a garment on <his bo>dy, as well as a shirt for his chest. An *ipantu*-garment of silver he wrapped around the messenger's waist and made it tight.

29 (iv 28'–35') (Colophon) First tablet of the Song of Emergence, unfinished.[100] (Copied by) the hand of Ašḫapala, son of Tarḫuntaššu, grandson of Kuruntipiya, descendant of Waršiya. (He was) the apprentice scribe of Ziti. This tablet was damaged. I, Ašḫapala, wrote it in the presence of Ziti.[101]

Genesis
Introduction

The stories in *Genesis* concerning the creation of the world, Adam and Eve, and Noah's survival of the great flood are some of the most familiar narratives from the ancient world. The Israelites told other stories about creation, but because of the placement of *Genesis* at the beginning of the Bible, this version has become the most prominent and important account, overshadowing the rest. In this monotheistic

[97] The wagon apparently traveled for six months, possibly carrying some god's "manhood" with which to impregnate Earth.

[98] The watery home of the god Ea.

[99] An understanding that she was pregnant.

[100] That is, "to be continued."

[101] Scholarly work on the history of scribes in the Hittite world dates Ašḫapala, and therefore this tablet, to the last half of the reign of Tudḫaliya IV, ca. 1220 BC. This dating would put this copy of the tablet near the very end of the Hittite Empire.

account, the world is created by a single god over the course of seven days. The physical features we associate with gods in other Near Eastern texts—the sky, the earth, and so on—are not endowed with divinity but are the inanimate result of the sole creator's power. The creation of Adam and Eve, the first man and woman, follows, as does Eve's fateful eating of the fruit from the tree of knowledge, which brings suffering and toil to humankind. After several generations, God then resolves to use a worldwide flood to obliterate the human race, which has grown wicked, but he saves the last righteous man on earth, Noah, along with his family, by instructing him to build an ark and to put his family and animals on board. After the flood Noah and his family emerge and repopulate the earth after making a covenant with God.

The text of *Genesis* that we have, perhaps dating to as late as the 4th century BC, is the result of a compositional process that took a long period of time, probably from the era of David and Solomon (11th–10th c. BC) to the exile in Babylon (6th c. BC) and perhaps even later. Meticulous study of the text indicates that *Genesis* as we have it is a compilation of numerous earlier sources that have been stitched together somewhat awkwardly. This explains the different names used for God (Yahweh and Elohim), as well as the repetition of stories with different details. For example, in chapter 1 God creates both man and woman (unnamed) on the sixth day, but in chapter 2 a fuller story is told where Adam is created first, followed by Eve. Despite being firmly locked into a monotheistic tradition, *Genesis* shows obvious connections to the other Near Eastern texts found in this appendix and surely derives, at least in part, from that earlier Mesopotamian tradition.

Text

The Creation

(1) In the beginning God created the heavens and the earth. The earth was formless and void, and darkness was over the surface of the deep, and the Spirit of God was moving over the surface of the waters. Then God said, "Let there be light"; and there was light. God saw that the light was good; and God separated the light from the darkness. God called the light day, and the darkness He called night. And there was evening and there was morning, one day.

Then God said, "Let there be an expanse in the midst of the waters, and let it separate the waters from the waters." God made the expanse, and separated the waters which were below the expanse from the waters which were above the expanse; and it was so. God called the expanse heaven. And there was evening and there was morning, a second day.

Then God said, "Let the waters below the heavens be gathered into one place, and let the dry land appear"; and it was so. God called the dry land earth, and the gathering of the waters He called seas; and God saw that it was good. Then God said, "Let the earth sprout vegetation, plants yielding seed, and fruit trees on the earth bearing fruit after their kind with seed in them"; and it was so. The earth brought forth vegetation, plants yielding seed after their kind, and trees bearing fruit with seed in them, after their kind; and God saw that it was good. There was evening and there was morning, a third day.

Then God said, "Let there be lights in the expanse of the heavens to separate the day from the night, and let them be for signs and for seasons and for days and years; and let them be for lights in the expanse of the heavens to give light on the earth"; and it was so. God made the two great lights, the greater light to govern the day, and the lesser light to govern the night; He made the stars also. God placed them in the expanse of the heavens to give light on the earth, and to govern the day and the night, and to separate the light from the darkness; and God saw that it was good. There was evening and there was morning, a fourth day.

Then God said, "Let the waters teem with swarms of living creatures, and let birds fly above the earth in the open expanse of the heavens." God created the great sea monsters and every living creature that moves, with which the waters swarmed after their kind, and every winged bird after its kind; and God saw that it was good. God blessed them, saying, "Be fruitful and multiply, and fill the waters in the seas, and let birds multiply on the earth." There was evening and there was morning, a fifth day.

Then God said, "Let the earth bring forth living creatures after their kind: cattle and creeping things and beasts of the earth after their kind"; and it was so. God made the beasts of the earth after their kind, and the cattle after their kind, and everything that creeps on the ground after its kind; and God saw that it was good.

Then God said, "Let Us make man in Our image, according to Our likeness; and let them rule over the fish of the sea and over the birds of the sky and over the cattle and over all the earth, and over every creeping thing that creeps on the earth." God created man in His own image, in the image of God He created him; male and female He created them. God blessed them; and God said to them, "Be fruitful and multiply, and fill the earth, and subdue it; and rule over the fish of the sea and over the birds of the sky and over every living thing that moves on the earth." Then God said, "Behold, I have given you every plant yielding seed that is on the surface of all the earth, and every tree which has fruit yielding seed; it shall be food for you; and to every beast of the earth and to every bird of the sky and to every thing that moves on the earth which has life, I have given every green plant for food"; and it was so. God saw all that He had made, and behold, it was very good. And there was evening and there was morning, the sixth day.

The Creation of Man and Woman

(2) Thus the heavens and the earth were completed, and all their hosts. By the seventh day God completed His work which He had done, and He rested on the seventh day from all His work which He had done. Then God blessed the seventh day and sanctified it, because in it He rested from all His work which God had created and made.

This is the account of the heavens and the earth when they were created, in the day that the Lord God made earth and heaven. Now no shrub of the field was yet in the earth, and no plant of the field had yet sprouted, for the Lord God had not sent rain upon the earth, and there was no man to cultivate the ground. But a mist used to rise from the earth and water the whole surface of the ground. Then the Lord God formed man of dust from the ground, and breathed into his nostrils the breath of life; and man became a living being. The Lord God planted a garden toward the east, in Eden; and there He placed the man whom He had formed. Out of the ground the Lord God caused to grow every tree that is pleasing to the sight and good for food; the tree of life also in the midst of the garden, and the tree of the knowledge of good and evil.

Now a river flowed out of Eden to water the garden; and from there it divided and became four rivers. The name of the first is Pishon; it flows around the whole land of Havilah, where there is gold. The gold of that land is good; the bdellium and the onyx stone are there. The name of the second river is Gihon; it flows around the whole land of Cush. The name of the third river is Tigris; it flows east of Assyria. And the fourth river is the Euphrates.

Then the Lord God took the man and put him into the garden of Eden to cultivate it and keep it. The Lord God commanded the man, saying, "From any tree of the garden you may eat freely; but from the tree of the knowledge of good and evil you shall not eat, for in the day that you eat from it you will surely die."

Then the Lord God said, "It is not good for the man to be alone; I will make him a helper suitable for him." Out of the ground the Lord God formed every beast of the field and every bird of the sky, and brought them to the man to see what he would call them; and whatever the man called a living creature, that was its name. The man gave names to all the cattle, and to the birds of the sky, and to every beast of the field, but for Adam there was not found a helper suitable for him. So the Lord God caused a deep sleep to fall upon the man, and he slept; then He took one of his ribs and closed up the flesh at that place. The Lord God fashioned into a woman the rib which He had taken from the man, and brought her to the man. The man said,

> "This is now bone of my bones,
> And flesh of my flesh;
> She shall be called Woman,
> Because she was taken out of Man."

For this reason a man shall leave his father and his mother, and be joined to his wife; and they shall become one flesh. And the man and his wife were both naked and were not ashamed.

The Fall of Man

(3) Now the serpent was more crafty than any beast of the field which the Lord God had made. And he said to the woman, "Indeed, has God said, 'You shall not eat from any tree of the garden'?" The woman said to the serpent, "From the fruit of the trees of the garden we may eat; but from the fruit of the tree which is in the middle of the garden, God has said, 'You shall not eat from it or touch it, or you will die.'" The serpent said to the woman, "You surely will not die! For God knows that in the day you eat from it your eyes will be opened, and you will be like God, knowing good and evil." When the woman saw that the tree was good for food, and that it was a delight to the eyes, and that the tree was desirable to make one wise, she took from its fruit and ate; and she gave also to her husband with her, and he ate. Then the eyes of both of them were opened, and they knew that they were naked; and they sewed fig leaves together and made themselves loin coverings.

They heard the sound of the Lord God walking in the garden in the cool of the day, and the man and his wife hid themselves from the presence of the Lord God among the trees of the garden. Then the Lord God called to the man, and said to him, "Where are you?" He said, "I heard the sound of You in the garden, and I was afraid because I was naked; so I hid myself." And He said, "Who told you that you were naked? Have you eaten from the tree of which I commanded you not to eat?" The man said, "The woman whom You gave to be with me, she gave me from the tree, and I ate." Then the Lord God said to the woman, "What is this you have done?" And the woman said, "The serpent deceived me, and I ate." The Lord God said to the serpent,

"Because you have done this,
Cursed are you more than all cattle,
And more than every beast of the field;
On your belly you will go,
And dust you will eat
All the days of your life;
And I will put enmity
Between you and the woman,
And between your seed and her seed;
He shall bruise you on the head,
And you shall bruise him on the heel."

To the woman He said,

"I will greatly multiply
Your pain in childbirth,
In pain you will bring forth children;
Yet your desire will be for your husband,
And he will rule over you."

Then to Adam He said, "Because you have listened to the voice of your wife, and have eaten from the tree about which I commanded you, saying, 'You shall not eat from it';

Cursed is the ground because of you;
In toil you will eat of it
All the days of your life.
Both thorns and thistles it shall grow for you;
And you will eat the plants of the field;
By the sweat of your face
You will eat bread,

Till you return to the ground,
Because from it you were taken;
For you are dust,
And to dust you shall return."

Now the man called his wife's name Eve, because she was the mother of all the living. The Lord God made garments of skin for Adam and his wife, and clothed them.

Then the Lord God said, "Behold, the man has become like one of Us, knowing good and evil; and now, he might stretch out his hand, and take also from the tree of life, and eat, and live forever"—therefore the Lord God sent him out from the garden of Eden, to cultivate the ground from which he was taken. So He drove the man out; and at the east of the garden of Eden He stationed the cherubim and the flaming sword which turned every direction to guard the way to the tree of life.

Cain and Abel

(4) Now the man had relations with his wife Eve, and she conceived and gave birth to Cain, and she said, "I have gotten a manchild with the help of the Lord." Again, she gave birth to his brother Abel. And Abel was a keeper of flocks, but Cain was a tiller of the ground. So it came about in the course of time that Cain brought an offering to the Lord of the fruit of the ground. Abel, on his part also brought of the firstlings of his flock and of their fat portions. And the Lord had regard for Abel and for his offering; but for Cain and for his offering He had no regard. So Cain became very angry and his countenance fell. Then the Lord said to Cain, "Why are you angry? And why has your countenance fallen? If you do well, will not your countenance be lifted up? And if you do not do well, sin is crouching at the door; and its desire is for you, but you must master it." Cain told Abel his brother. And it came about when they were in the field, that Cain rose up against Abel his brother and killed him.

Then the Lord said to Cain, "Where is Abel your brother?" And he said, "I do not know. Am I my brother's keeper?" He said, "What have you done? The voice of your brother's blood is crying to Me from the ground. Now you are cursed from the ground, which has opened its mouth to receive your brother's blood from your hand. When you cultivate the ground, it will no longer yield its strength to you; you will be a vagrant and a wanderer on the earth." Cain said to the Lord, "My punishment is too great to bear! Behold, You have driven me this day from the face of the ground; and from Your face I will be hidden, and I will be a vagrant and a wanderer on the earth, and whoever finds me will kill me." So the Lord said to him, "Therefore whoever kills Cain, vengeance will be taken on him sevenfold." And the Lord appointed a sign for Cain, so that no one finding him would slay him.

Then Cain went out from the presence of the Lord, and settled in the land of Nod, east of Eden.

Cain had relations with his wife and she conceived, and gave birth to Enoch; and he built a city, and called the name of the city Enoch, after the name of his son. Now to Enoch was born Irad, and Irad became the father of Mehujael, and Mehujael became the father of Methushael, and Methushael became the father of Lamech. Lamech took to himself two wives: the name of the one was Adah, and the name of the other, Zillah. Adah gave birth to Jabal; he was the father of those who dwell in tents and have livestock. His brother's name was Jubal; he was the father of all those who play the lyre and pipe. As for Zillah, she also gave birth to Tubal-cain, the forger of all implements of bronze and iron; and the sister of Tubal-cain was Naamah.

Lamech said to his wives,

"Adah and Zillah,
Listen to my voice,
You wives of Lamech,
Give heed to my speech,
For I have killed a man for wounding me;
And a boy for striking me;
If Cain is avenged sevenfold,
Then Lamech seventy-sevenfold."

Adam had relations with his wife again; and she gave birth to a son, and named him Seth, for, she said, "God has appointed me another offspring in place of Abel, for Cain killed him." To Seth, to him also a son was born; and he called his name Enosh. Then men began to call upon the name of the Lord.

Descendants of Adam

(5) This is the book of the generations of Adam. In the day when God created man, He made him in the likeness of God. He created them male and female, and He blessed them and named them Man in the day when they were created.

When Adam had lived one hundred and thirty years, he became the father of a son in his own likeness, according to his image, and named him Seth. Then the days of Adam after he became the father of Seth were eight hundred years, and he had other sons and daughters. So all the days that Adam lived were nine hundred and thirty years, and he died.

Seth lived one hundred and five years, and became the father of Enosh. Then Seth lived eight hundred and seven years after he became the father of Enosh, and he had other sons and daughters. So all the days of Seth were nine hundred and twelve years, and he died.

Enosh lived ninety years, and became the father of Kenan. Then Enosh lived eight hundred and fifteen years after he became the father of Kenan, and he had other sons and daughters. So all the days of Enosh were nine hundred and five years, and he died.

Kenan lived seventy years, and became the father of Mahalalel. Then Kenan lived eight hundred and forty years after he became the father of Mahalalel, and he had other sons and daughters. So all the days of Kenan were nine hundred and ten years, and he died.

Mahalalel lived sixty-five years, and became the father of Jared. Then Mahalalel lived eight hundred and thirty years after he became the father of Jared, and he had other sons and daughters. So all the days of Mahalalel were eight hundred and ninety-five years, and he died.

Jared lived one hundred and sixty-two years, and became the father of Enoch. Then Jared lived eight hundred years after he became the father of Enoch, and he had other sons and daughters. So all the days of Jared were nine hundred and sixty-two years, and he died.

Enoch lived sixty-five years, and became the father of Methuselah. Then Enoch walked with God three hundred years after he became the father of Methuselah, and he had other sons and daughters. So all the days of Enoch were three hundred and sixty-five years. Enoch walked with God; and he was not, for God took him.

Methuselah lived one hundred and eighty-seven years, and became the father of Lamech. Then Methuselah lived seven hundred and eighty-two years after he became the father of Lamech, and he had other sons and daughters. So all the days of Methuselah were nine hundred and sixty-nine years, and he died.

Lamech lived one hundred and eighty-two years, and became the father of a son. Now he called his name Noah, saying, "This one will give us rest from our work and from the toil of our hands arising from the ground which the Lord has cursed." Then Lamech lived five hundred and ninety-five years after he became the father of Noah, and he had other sons and daughters. So all the days of Lamech were seven hundred and seventy-seven years, and he died.

Noah was five hundred years old, and Noah became the father of Shem, Ham, and Japheth.

The Corruption of Mankind

(6) Now it came about, when men began to multiply on the face of the land, and daughters were born to them, that the sons of God saw that the daughters of men were beautiful; and they took wives for themselves, whomever they chose. Then the Lord said, "My Spirit shall not strive with man forever, because he also is flesh; nevertheless his days shall be one hundred and twenty years." The Nephilim were on the earth in those days, and also afterward, when the sons of God came in to the daughters of men, and they bore children to them. Those were the mighty men who were of old, men of renown.

Then the Lord saw that the wickedness of man was great on the earth, and that every intent of the thoughts of his heart was only evil continually. The Lord was sorry that He had made man on the earth, and He was grieved in His heart. The Lord said, "I will blot out man whom I have created from the face of the land, from man to animals to creeping things and to birds of the sky; for I am sorry that I have made them." But Noah found favor in the eyes of the Lord.

These are the records of the generations of Noah. Noah was a righteous man, blameless in his time; Noah walked with God. Noah became the father of three sons: Shem, Ham, and Japheth.

Now the earth was corrupt in the sight of God, and the earth was filled with violence. God looked on the earth, and behold, it was corrupt; for all flesh had corrupted their way upon the earth.

Then God said to Noah, "The end of all flesh has come before Me; for the earth is filled with violence because of them; and behold, I am about to destroy them with the earth. Make for yourself an ark of gopher wood; you shall make the ark with rooms, and shall cover it inside and out with pitch. This is how you shall make it: the length of the ark three hundred cubits, its breadth fifty cubits, and its height thirty cubits. You shall make a window for the ark, and finish it to a cubit from the top; and set the door of the ark in the side of it; you shall make it with lower, second, and third decks. Behold, I, even I am bringing the flood of water upon the earth, to destroy all flesh in which is the breath of life, from under heaven; everything that is on the earth shall perish. But I will establish My covenant with you; and you shall enter the ark—you and your sons and your wife, and your sons' wives with you. And of every living thing of all flesh, you shall bring two of every kind into the ark, to keep them alive with you; they shall be male and female. Of the birds after their kind, and of the animals after their kind, of every creeping thing of the ground after its kind, two of every kind will come to you to keep them alive. As for you, take for yourself some of all food which is edible, and gather it to yourself; and it shall be for food for you and for them." Thus Noah did; according to all that God had commanded him, so he did.

The Flood

(7) Then the Lord said to Noah, "Enter the ark, you and all your household, for you alone I have seen to be righteous before Me in this time. "You shall take with you of every clean animal by sevens, a male and his female; and of the animals that are not clean two, a male and his female; also of the birds of the sky, by sevens, male and female, to keep offspring alive on the face of all the earth. "For after seven more days, I will send rain on the earth forty days and forty nights; and I will blot out from the face of the land every living thing that I have made." Noah did according to all that the Lord had commanded him.

Now Noah was six hundred years old when the flood of water came upon the earth. Then Noah and his sons and his wife and his sons' wives with him entered the ark because of the water of the flood. Of clean animals and animals that are not clean and birds and everything that creeps on the ground, there went into the ark to Noah by twos, male and female, as God had commanded Noah. It came about after the seven days, that the water of the flood came upon the earth. In the six hundredth year of Noah's life, in the second month, on the seventeenth day of the month, on the same day all the fountains of the great deep burst open, and the floodgates of the sky were opened. The rain fell upon the earth for forty days and forty nights.

On the very same day Noah and Shem and Ham and Japheth, the sons of Noah, and Noah's wife and the three wives of his sons with them, entered the ark, they and every beast after its kind, and all the cattle after their kind, and every creeping thing that creeps on the earth after its kind, and every bird after its kind, all sorts of birds. So they went into the ark to Noah, by twos of all flesh in which was the breath of life. Those that entered, male and female of all flesh, entered as God had commanded him; and the Lord closed it behind him.

Then the flood came upon the earth for forty days, and the water increased and lifted up the ark, so that it rose above the earth. The water prevailed and increased greatly upon the earth, and the ark floated on the surface of the water. The water prevailed more and more upon the earth, so that all the high mountains everywhere under the heavens were covered. The water prevailed fifteen cubits higher, and the mountains were covered. All flesh that moved on the earth perished, birds and cattle and beasts and every swarming thing that swarms upon the earth, and all mankind; of all that was on the dry land, all in whose nostrils was the breath of the spirit of life, died. Thus He blotted out every living thing that was upon the face of the land, from man to animals to creeping things and to birds of the sky, and they were blotted out from the earth; and only Noah was left, together with those that were with him in the ark. The water prevailed upon the earth one hundred and fifty days.

The Flood Subsides

(8) But God remembered Noah and all the beasts and all the cattle that were with him in the ark; and God caused a wind to pass over the earth, and the water subsided. Also the fountains of the deep and the floodgates of the sky were closed, and the rain from the sky was restrained; and the water receded steadily from the earth, and at the end of one hundred and fifty days the water decreased. In the seventh month, on the seventeenth day of the month, the ark rested upon the mountains of Ararat. The water decreased steadily until the tenth month; in the tenth month, on the first day of the month, the tops of the mountains became visible.

Then it came about at the end of forty days, that Noah opened the window of the ark which he had made; and he sent out a raven, and it flew here and there until the water was dried up from the earth. Then he sent out a dove from him, to see if the water was abated from the face of the land; but the dove found no resting place for the sole of her foot, so she returned to him into the ark, for the water was on the surface of all the earth. Then he put out his hand and took her, and brought her into the ark to himself. So he waited yet another seven days; and again he sent out the dove from the ark. The dove came to him toward evening, and behold, in her beak was a freshly picked olive leaf. So Noah knew that the water was abated from the earth. Then he waited yet another seven days, and sent out the dove; but she did not return to him again.

Now it came about in the six hundred and first year, in the first month, on the first of the month, the water was dried up from the earth. Then Noah removed the covering of the ark, and looked, and behold, the surface of the ground was dried up. In the second month, on the twenty-seventh day of the month, the earth was dry. Then God spoke to Noah, saying, "Go out of the ark, you and your wife and your sons and your sons' wives with you. Bring out with you every living thing of all flesh that is with you, birds and animals and every creeping thing that creeps on the earth, that they may breed abundantly on the earth, and be fruitful and multiply on the earth." So Noah went out, and his sons and his wife and his sons' wives with him. Every beast, every creeping thing, and every bird, everything that moves on the earth, went out by their families from the ark.

Then Noah built an altar to the Lord, and took of every clean animal and of every clean bird and offered burnt offerings on the altar. The Lord smelled the soothing aroma; and the Lord said to Himself, "I will never again curse the ground on account of man, for the intent of man's heart is evil from his youth; and I will never again destroy every living thing, as I have done.

"While the earth remains,
Seedtime and harvest,
And cold and heat,
And summer and winter,
And day and night
Shall not cease."

Covenant of the Rainbow

(9) And God blessed Noah and his sons and said to them, "Be fruitful and multiply, and fill the earth. The fear of you and the terror of you will be on every beast of the earth and on every bird of the sky; with everything that creeps on the ground, and all the fish of the sea, into your hand they are given. Every moving thing that is alive shall be food for you; I give all to you, as I gave the green plant. Only you shall not eat flesh with its life, that is, its blood. Surely I will require your lifeblood; from every beast I will require it. And from every man, from every man's brother I will require the life of man.

"Whoever sheds man's blood,
By man his blood shall be shed,
For in the image of God
He made man.
As for you, be fruitful and multiply;
Populate the earth abundantly and multiply in it."

Then God spoke to Noah and to his sons with him, saying, "Now behold, I Myself do establish My covenant with you, and with your descendants after you; and with every living creature that is with you, the birds, the cattle, and every beast of the earth with you; of all that comes out of the ark, even every beast of the earth. I establish My covenant with you; and all flesh shall never again be cut off by the water of the flood, neither shall there again be a flood to destroy the earth." God said, "This is the sign of the covenant which I am making between Me and you and every living creature that is with you, for all successive generations; I set My bow in the cloud, and it shall be for a sign of a covenant between Me and the earth. It shall come about, when I bring a cloud over the earth, that the bow will be seen in the cloud, and I will remember My covenant, which is between Me and you and every living creature of all flesh; and never again shall the water become a flood to destroy all flesh. When the bow is in the cloud, then I will look upon it, to remember the everlasting covenant between God and every living creature of all flesh that is on the earth." And God said to Noah, "This is the sign of the covenant which I have established between Me and all flesh that is on the earth."

Note on the Texts and Translation

The following list contains the texts used as the basis of the translations in this volume. Whenever possible we attempted to key our translations to texts that would be widely available in university libraries in the United States. Where those texts were accompanied by introductions, commentaries, and translations, it can be assumed that we consulted them. The translator of each text, if one of the editors, is identified by initials in parentheses. Where we have with permission reprinted the translation of other scholars, no initials appear and the citation indicates the source.

Acusilaus (SMT)	*Early Greek Mythography Volume I: Text and Introduction,* ed. R. L. Fowler (Oxford 2000).
Aelian (SMT)	*Aelian Historical Miscellany,* ed. N. G. Wilson. Loeb Classical Library (Cambridge, Mass. 1997).
Aeschylus (RSS)	A. Nauck, *Tragicorum Graecorum Fragmenta Supplementum adiecit Bruno Snell* (Hildesheim 1983). Also consulted: *Aeschylus II Agamemnon, Libation-Bearers, Eumenides, Fragments,* ed. H. W. Smyth and H. Lloyd-Jones. Loeb Classical Library (Cambridge, Mass. 1983).
Andron (SMT)	*Early Greek Mythography Volume I: Text and Introduction,* ed. R. L. Fowler (Oxford 2000).
Antoninus Liberalis (SMT)	*Antoninus Liberalis Les Métamorphoses,* ed. M. Papathomopoulos (Paris 1968). Also consulted: F. Celoria, *The Metamorphoses of Antoninus Liberalis* (London 1992).
Apollodorus (SMT)	*Apollodorus The Library,* 2 vols., ed. J. G. Frazer. Loeb Classical Library (London/New York 1921). Also consulted: *Mythographi Graeci,* vol. 1, ed. R. Wagner (Stuttgart/Leipzig 1996).
Archilochus	From: *Greek Lyric: An Anthology in Translation,* trans. A. M. Miller (Indianapolis/Cambridge, Mass. 1996). Reprinted by permission of Hackett Publishing Company, Inc. All rights reserved.
Arrian (SMT)	*Arrian History of Alexander and Indica,* vol. 1, ed. P. A. Brunt. Loeb Classical Library (Cambridge, Mass. 1976).
Babrius (SMT)	*Babrius and Phaedrus,* ed. B. E. Perry. Loeb Classical Library (Cambridge, Mass. 1984).
Bacchylides	From: *Greek Lyric: An Anthology in Translation,* trans. A. M. Miller (Indianapolis/Cambridge, Mass. 1996). Reprinted by permission of Hackett Publishing Company, Inc. All rights reserved.

Bion (SMT)	*Bion of Smyrna: The fragments and the Adonis,* ed. with introduction and commentary by J. D. Reed (Cambridge 1997).
Callimachus (RSS)	*Callimachus: The Fifth Hymn,* ed. with introduction and commentary by A. W. Bulloch (Cambridge 1985). *Hymn to Demeter: Callimachus,* ed. with an introduction and commentary by N. Hopkinson (Cambridge 1984).
Cleanthes (RSS)	*Stoicorum Veterum Fragmenta, vol. 1: Zeno et Zenonis discipuli,* ed. J. von Arnim (Leipzig 1905).
Conon (SMT)	M. K. Brown, *The Narratives of Konon* (Munich 2002).
Cornutus (SMT)	*Cornuti Theologiae Graecae Compendium,* ed. Carolus Lang (Leipzig 1881). Also consulted: Robert Stephen Hays, *Lucius Annaeus Cornutus'* Epidrome (Introduction to the Traditions of Greek Theology): *Introduction, Translation, and Notes* (Diss., University of Texas 1983).
Critias (SMT)	A. Nauck, *Tragicorum Graecorum Fragmenta Supplementum adiecit Bruno Snell* (Hildesheim 1983).
Diodorus of Sicily (SMT)	*Diodorus Siculus Library of History,* ed. C. H. Oldfather, 3 vols. Loeb Classical Library (Cambridge, Mass. 1998–2000).
Eratosthenes (RSS)	*Mythographi Graeci* vol. III, fasc. I: *Pseudo-Eratosthenis Catasterismi,* ed. A. Olivieri (Leipzig 1897).
Euripides (SMT)	*Euripides Selected Fragmentary Plays,* with introductions, translations, and commentaries by C. Collard, M. J. Cropp and K. H. Lee. Also consulted: A. Nauck, *Tragicorum Graecorum Fragmenta Supplementum adiecit Bruno Snell* (Hildesheim 1983).
Fulgentius (RSS)	*Fabii Planciadis Fulgentii V.C. Opera,* ed. R. Helm (Stuttgart 1970).
Hellanicus (SMT)	*Early Greek Mythography Volume I: Text and Introduction,* ed. R. L. Fowler (Oxford 2000).
Heraclitus (SMT)	*Héraclite Allégories D'Homère,* ed. F. Buffière (Paris 1962).
Herodorus (SMT)	*Early Greek Mythography Volume I: Text and Introduction,* ed. R. L. Fowler (Oxford 2000).
Herodotus, 2.113–120 (SAB)	*Herodoti Historiae,* ed. C. Hude, vol. 1 (Oxford 1960). Other selections from: *Herodotus on the War for Greek Freedom Selections from the* Histories, trans. S. Shirley, ed. with introduction and notes by J. Romm (Indianapolis/Cambridge, Mass. 2003). Reprinted by permission of Hackett Publishing Company, Inc. All rights reserved.
Hesiod	From: *Hesiod Works & Days Theogony,* trans. S. Lombardo (Indianapolis/Cambridge, Mass. 1993). Reprinted by permission of Hackett Publishing Company, Inc. All rights reserved.
Homeric Hymns	Modernized and adapted from: *Homer, The Homeric Hymns,* trans. A. Lang (London 1899). Translation updated in places to match the text in *Homeric Hymns Homeric Apocrypha Lives*

	of Homer, ed. M. L. West. Loeb Classical Library (Cambridge, Mass. 2003).
Horace (RSS)	*Q. Horati Flacci Opera,* ed. D. R. Shackleton Bailey (Stuttgart 1995).
Hyginus (RSS)	*Hyginus Fabulae.* editio altera, ed. P. K. Marshall (Munich/Leipzig 2002).
Longus (SMT)	*Longus Daphnis et Chloe,* ed. M. D. Reeve (Stuttgart/Leipzig 1994).
Lucian (SMT)	For the *Dialogues*: Lucian, vol. 7, ed. M. D. MacLeod. Loeb Classical Library (Cambridge, Mass. 1998). For *Judgment* and *Sacrifices*: Lucian, vol. 3, ed. A. M. Harmon. Loeb Classical Library (Cambridge, Mass. 1995).
Lucretius (RSS)	*Lucreti De Rerum Natura Libri Sex,* ed. Cyril Bailey (Oxford 1922).
Ovid (RSS)	*P. Ovidi Nasonis Heroides,* ed. A. Palmer (Hildesheim 1967). Also consulted: *Ovid Heroides Select Epistles,* ed. P. E. Knox (Cambridge 1995).
Palaephatus (SMT)	*Mythographi Graeci,* vol. III, fasc. II: *Palaephati* ΠΕΡΙ ΑΠΙΣΤΩΝ, ed. N. Festa (Leipzig 1902). Also consulted: J. Stern, *Palaephatus: On Unbelievable Tales* (Wauconda 1996).
Parthenius (SMT)	*Parthenius of Nicaea: The poetical fragments and the* Ἐρωτικὰ Παθήματα, ed. with introduction and commentaries by J. L. Lightfoot (Oxford 1999).
Pausanias	Adapted from: *Pausanias' Description of Greece*, trans. with a commentary by J. G. Frazer, 6 vols. (London/New York 1898).
Pherecydes (SMT)	*Early Greek Mythography Volume I: Text and Introduction*, ed. R. L. Fowler (Oxford 2000).
Pindar	From: *Greek Lyric: An Anthology in Translation*, trans. A. M. Miller (Indianapolis/Cambridge, Mass. 1996). Reprinted by permission of Hackett Publishing Company, Inc. All rights reserved.
Plato, *Protagoras* (RSS)	*Plato Protagoras,* with introduction, notes, and appendices by J. Adam and A. M. Adam (Cambridge 1984). *Republic*, from: *Readings in Ancient Greek Philosophy from Thales to Aristotle*, ed. S. M. Cohen, P. Curd, and C. D. C. Reeve (Indianapolis/Cambridge, Mass. 2000). Reprinted by permission of Hackett Publishing Company, Inc. All rights reserved. *Symposium*, from: *Plato Symposium,* trans. with introduction and notes by A. Nehamas and P. Woodruff (Indianapolis/Cambridge, Mass. 1989). Reprinted by permission of Hackett Publishing Company, Inc. All rights reserved.
Plutarch (SMT)	*Plutarch Parallel Lives,* vol. 1, ed. B. Perrin. Loeb Classical Library (Cambridge, Mass. 1969).

Proclus (SMT)	*Homeri Opera,* vol. 5, ed. T. W. Allen (Oxford 1959). Also consulted: *Hesiod, The Homeric Hymns, and Homerica,* trans. H. G. Evelyn-White. Loeb Classical Library (Cambridge, Mass. 1982).
Sallustius (SMT)	*Sallustius Concerning the Gods and the Universe,* ed. with prolegomena and translation by A. D. Nock (Hildesheim 1966).
Sappho	From: *Greek Lyric: An Anthology in Translation*, trans. A. M. Miller (Indianapolis/Cambridge, Mass. 1996). Reprinted by permission of Hackett Publishing Company, Inc. All rights reserved.
Semonides	From: *Greek Lyric: An Anthology in Translation*, trans. A. M. Miller (Indianapolis/Cambridge, Mass. 1996). Reprinted by permission of Hackett Publishing Company, Inc. All rights reserved.
Simonides	From: *Greek Lyric: An Anthology in Translation*, trans. A. M. Miller (Indianapolis/Cambridge, Mass. 1996). Reprinted by permission of Hackett Publishing Company, Inc. All rights reserved.
Sophocles (SMT)	*Sophocles Fragments*, ed. H. Lloyd-Jones. Loeb Classical Library (Cambridge, Mass. 1996). Also consulted: A. Nauck, *Tragicorum Graecorum Fragmenta Supplementum adiecit Bruno Snell* (Hildesheim 1983).
Statius	Translated by N. K. Zeiner based on the Latin text of *Statius: Thebaid 5–12 Achilleid,* ed. J. H. Mozley, vol. 2, Loeb Classical Library (Cambridge, Mass. 1969).
Theocritus (SMT)	*Theocritus Select Poems*, ed. with introduction and commentary by K. J. Dover (Wauconda 1994). Also consulted: A. S. F. Gow, *Theocritus*, 2 vols., second edition (Cambridge 1952).
Theophrastus (SMT)	*Theophrastus Characters Herodas Mimes Cercidas and the Choliambic Poets,* ed. J. Rusten, I. C. Cunningham, and A. D. Knox. Loeb Classical Library (Cambridge, Mass. 1993).
Thucydides	From: *Thucydides On Justice Power and Human Nature Selections from* The History of the Peloponnesian War, trans., with introduction and notes, by P. Woodruff (Indianapolis/Cambridge, Mass. 1993). Reprinted by permission of Hackett Publishing Company, Inc. All rights reserved.
Vergil (RSS)	*P. Vergili Maronis Opera,* ed. R. A. B. Mynors (Cambridge 1969). Also consulted: *The Aeneid of Virgil Books 1–6,* ed. with introduction and notes by R. D. Williams (New York 1992); *Virgil Georgics*, vol. 2, ed. R. F. Thomas (Cambridge 1988).
Xenophanes	From: *Greek Lyric: An Anthology in Translation,* trans. A. M. Miller (Indianapolis/Cambridge, Mass. 1996). Reprinted by permission of Hackett Publishing Company, Inc. All rights reserved.

Xenophon (SMT)	*Xenophon IV Memorabilia Oeconomicus Symposium Apology,* trans. E. C. Marchant and O. J. Todd. Loeb Classical Library (Cambridge, Mass. 1979).

Additional Notes to Appendix Four

Gilgamesh: From *The Epic of Gilgamesh,* translated by Benjamin R. Foster. Copyright © 2001 by W. W. Norton & Company. Used by permission of W. W. Norton & Company, Inc.

"Hittite *Song of Emergence*": Translated by Gregory McMahon.

For all other translations in Appendix Four: Selections from *Before the Muses: An Anthology of Akkadian Literature, vol. 1*, by Benjamin R. Foster (Bethesda, MD: CDL Press, 1993). Used by permission.

Names and Transliteration

The readings in this book present different forms of names depending on whether the text was originally written in Greek or Latin. What this means is that a character like Medeia will appear as Medea in Latin texts, Oidipous as Oedipus, Iocaste as Jocasta, and so on. English has traditionally favored Latinized spellings of Greek names, but recently direct transliteration (see below) has become common. In most cases the names are recognizably the same, but students of myth will profit from studying what follows. A little familiarity dispels a great deal of confusion down the road.

In Greek texts we use direct transliteration (conversion from one writing system to another) to convert names from the Greek to the English alphabet. There are some exceptions, based mainly on English pronunciation (among the heroes, for instance, we use Achilles instead of Achilleus, Jason instead of Iason, Ajax instead of Aias). We have also chosen the letter C to represent Greek kappa (κ), since many Greek names containing this letter are traditionally pronounced with the C soft in English (Eurydice is pronounced Yu-ri-di-see not Yu-ri-di-kee). In other cases, where we thought the C looked odd or misleading, or where the pronunciation requires it, we render kappa with a K (Dike not Dice; Nike not Nice).

Another warning: sometimes the Latin names of Greek figures differ substantially (Greek Heracles = Latin Hercules; Odysseus = Ulysses) or entirely, as in cases where the Romans equated a native Italic divinity with a Greek god (Greek Zeus = Latin Jupiter; Greek Artemis = Latin Diana). For ease we have cross-listed these names in the index, which also supplies both the Greek and (where appropriate) Latinate spellings.

Below is a chart detailing our transliteration scheme and showing how Greek names are usually Latinized. If you know the names of the letters of the Greek alphabet, you actually already know how to do this because the first letter (plus an H if that is the second letter, so theta = TH) of each letter's name shows its value in transliteration.

Letter Forms	**Name**	**Latin Equivalent**
Α α	<u>a</u>lpha (ἄλφα)	a
Β β	<u>b</u>eta (βῆτα)	b
Γ γ	<u>g</u>amma (γάμμα)[1]	g
Δ δ	<u>d</u>elta (δέλτα)	d

[1] But γγ = <u>ng</u>, γκ = <u>nk</u> and γχ = <u>nch</u>.

Letter Forms	Name	Latin Equivalent
Ε ε	epsilon (ἒ ψιλόν)	e
Ζ ζ	zeta (ζῆτα)	z
Η η	eta (ἦτα)	e[2]
Θ θ	theta (θῆτα)	th
Ι ι	iota (ἰῶτα)	i (*or* j[3])
Κ κ	kappa (κάππα)	c[4]
Λ λ	lambda (λάμβδα)	l
Μ μ	mu (μῦ)	m
Ν ν	nu (νῦ)	n
Ξ ξ	xi (ξεῖ)	x
Ο ο	omicron (ὂ μικρόν)	o
Π π	pi (πεῖ)	p
Ρ ρ	rho (ῥῶ)	r *or* rh[5]
Σ σ ς[6]	sigma (σῖγμα)	s
Τ τ	tau (ταῦ)	t
Υ υ	upsilon (ὖ ψιλόν)	u *or* y
Φ φ	phi (φεῖ)	ph
Χ χ	chi (χεῖ)	ch
Ψ ψ	psi (ψεῖ)	ps
Ω ω	omega (ὦ μέγα)	o[7]

The standard Greek alphabet has no letter representing H. Instead, breathing marks show the presence or lack of an H sound at the start of a Greek word (over/before initial vowel and over initial rho).

’ [no H] (smooth breathing)

‘ H (rough breathing)

so ’Αφροδίτη = Aphrodite and ‘Ερμῆς = Hermes.

[2] Eta is a longer sound than epsilon, so it is sometimes transliterated with a mark to show the difference (ê or ē).

[3] In English, I before another vowel in a Greek or Latin word sometimes becomes J.

[4] It is common in English now to represent kappa with a k, but generally we have used the traditional Latin c.

[5] Rho is represented by r in most positions, but rh at the beginning of words (this survives compounding, so *Calli* + *rhoe* remains Callirhoe, not Calliroe) and after another rho (so ‘rrh’ is a common sight in Greek names).

[6] Sigma has an alternate lower case form (ς), which is only used at the end of words.

[7] Omega is a longer sound than omicron, so it is sometimes transliterated with a mark to show the difference (ô or ō).

VOWEL COMBINATIONS

This system is pretty straightforward. Much of the time, the Latin name looks different from transliterated Greek because of the changes to two-vowel combinations (diphthongs).

Greek		Latin	
ai	=	ae	(Aithra/Aethra)
oi	=	oe	(Oineus/Oeneus)
eu	=	ev	(Euadne/Evadne)
au	=	av	(Agaue/Agave)
ei	=	i *or* e	(Teiresias/Tiresias) or (Medeia/Medea)
ou	=	u	(Ouranos/Uranus)

WORD ENDINGS

The endings of Greek words and names are often changed when Latinized:

Greek		Latin	
-os	=	-us	(Oceanos/Oceanus)
-ous	=	-us	(Oidipous/Oedipus)
-on	=	-o	(Plouton/Pluto)
-ros	=	-er	(Meleagros/Meleager)
-e	=	-a	(Atalante/Atalanta)

Index/Glossary

This index/glossary contains, in addition to a few important terms frequently used, entries for most mythological figures that occur in two or more authors in this volume. All references to an individual have been grouped together, e.g., Aphrodite, Venus, Cypris, Cyprogenes, and Cythereia are all listed under Aphrodite. Ancient authors and places have not been indexed. This index/glossary is also designed to be used as a short mythological dictionary, though space has limited the amount of information given for each entry. Names are listed by their Greek spelling, though where alternate names exist or Latin or English spellings are notably different, we have included cross-references, as well as the alternatives within the entry. References are alphabetically arranged, just as the authors are in the volume. The abbreviations are as follows:

Acus.	Acusilaus	Hes.	Hesiod	*Symp.*	*Symposium*
Ael.	Aelian	(no letter)	*Theogony*	Plut.	Plutarch
Aes.	Aeschylus	W	*Works & Days*	Proc.	Proclus
And.	Andron	*HH*	*Homeric Hymns*	Sall.	Sallustius
A.L.	Antoninus Liberalis	Hor.	Horace	Sapph.	Sappho
Apd.	Apollodorus	Hyg.	Hyginus	Sem.	Semonides
Arch.	Archilochus	Long.	Longus	Sim.	Simonides
Arr.	Arrian	Luc.	Lucian	Soph.	Sophocles
Bab.	Babrius	*DD*	*Dial. of the Dead*	Stat.	Statius
Bac.	Bacchylides	*DG*	*Dial. of the Gods*	Theoc.	Theocritus
Bion	Bion	*DSG*	*Dial. of the Sea Gods*	Thph.	Theophrastus
Call.	Callimachus	*Jud.*	*Judgment of the Goddesses*	Thu.	Thucydides
Cle.	Cleanthes			Ver.	Vergil
Con.	Conon	*Sac.*	*On Sacrifices*	*G*	*Georgics*
Corn.	Cornutus	Lucr.	Lucretius	Xen.	Xenophon
Crit.	Critias	Ov.	Ovid	Ap1	Appendix 1
Diod.	Diodorus of Sicily	Pal.	Palaephatus	Ap2	Appendix 2
Erat.	Eratosthenes	Par.	Parthenius	Ap3	Appendix 3
Eur.	Euripides	Paus.	Pausanias	AP4	Appendix 4
Fulg.	Fulgentius	Pher.	Pherecydes	Ap4 *Gilg.*	*Epic of Gilgamesh*
Hell.	Hellanicus	Pi.	Pindar	AP4 *Atr.*	*Atrahasis*
Herac.	Heraclitus	Pl.	Plato	Ap4 *EoC*	*Epic of Creation*
Hdr.	Herodorus	*Prt.*	*Protagoras*	Ap4 *SoE*	*Song og Emergence*
Hdt.	Herodotus	*Rep.*	*Republic*	Ap4 *Gen.*	*Genesis*

Abderos (Ἄβδηρος): son of Hermes, Heracles' companion when he went after the Mares of Diomedes: Apd. K10| Hyg. 30.

Abel: Ap4 *Gen.* 4.

Absyrtus: see Apsyrtos.

Acamas (Ἀκάμας): son of Theseus, took part in the Trojan War: Apd. N7| Hyg. 108| Proc. D| Verg. 2d.

Acastos (Ἄκαστος): son of Pelias, king of Iolcos, an Argonaut: Apd. G1, G5| Hyg. 103, 104| Pal. 40.

Achaios (Ἀχαιός): son of Xouthos, eponymous ancestor of the Achaians: Apd. E3| Con. 27.

Acheloos (Ἀχελῷος): son of Oceanos & Tethys, a river god who wrestled Heracles for the hand of Deianeira & was father of the Sirens: Apd. B3, E3, F, K19| Hes. 342| Hyg. 31.

Acheron ('Αχέρων): river in the underworld: Apd. C, K14| Bion| Ver. 6c.

Achilles ('Αχιλλεύς, strictly Achilleus): son of Peleus & Thetis, the best Greek warrior in the Trojan War. He killed Hector & was killed by Paris: A.L. 27| Diod. 2.46| Hell. 145| Hes. 1015| Hyg. 96, 98, 106, 107, 110| Ov. 1.35, 3 *passim*| Proc. A–E| Stat. *passim*| Thu. 1.3| Ver. 2a, 2c, 2e, 2h–i. See also Ap1.9.

Acrisios ('Ακρίσιος): king of Argos, fated to be killed by his grandson, Perseus: Apd. J1–2| Hyg. 84| Luc. *DSG* 12| Pher. 10, 12.

Actaion ('Ακταίων): son of Aristaios & Autonoe, consumed by his own dogs: Apd. M3| Call. 5| Pal. 6| Paus. L.

Actor ("Ακτωρ): ***I*** son of Peisidice & Myrmidon, father of Eurytion: Apd. E3, F, K17| ***II*** son of Hippasos, father of Menoitios: Apd. G1| ***III*** a king of Lemnos: Hyg. 102.

Adad: Mesopotamian storm-god: Ap4 *Atr.* II.i.11, II.ii.11–25, III.ii.49–55; Ap4 *Gilg.* 99–166.

Adam: ***I*** first man, created by God: Ap4 *Gen.* 2–5| ***II*** unnamed, as generic "man:" Ap4 *Gen.* 1.

Admetos ("Αδμητος): king of Pherai under whom Apollo served. His wife Alcestis died for him: Apd. F, G1, K15| Hell. 125| Luc. *Sac.* 4| Pal. 40.

Adonis ("Αδωνις): son of the incestuous union between Cinyras & his daughter Smyrna, loved by Aphrodite, died while hunting: A.L. 34| Apd. B3| Bion| Ov. 4.97| Sall.| Ap3 E.

Adrastos ("Αδραστος): king of Argos who led the Seven against Thebes, the only one to survive: Apd. M7, M9–10| Hyg. 68–69| Ver. 6f.

Ae-: see Ai-

Aello ('Αελλώ) or Aellopous: one of the Harpies, also called Nicothoe: Apd. A2, G2| Hes. 268.

Aesculapius: see Asclepios.

Aethlios ('Αέθλιος): son of Zeus by Protogeneia: Apd. E3.

Agamedes ('Αγαμήδης): son of Erginos, a famous architect: *HH* 3g| Proc. F.

Agamemnon ('Αγαμέμνων): son of Atreus, brother of Menelaos, leader of Greek forces at Troy, killed by his wife, Clytaimnestra, or her lover, Aigisthos, upon returning home from Troy: Aes. 99| A.L. 27| Hyg. 78, 88, 95, 98, 102, 105–107, 116, 117, 119–120| Luc. *DD* 23, *Sac.* 3| Ov. 3.38, 3.83| Paus. E, G| Pl. *Rep.*10| Proc. A, E| Thu. 1.9| Ver. 2c, 2g–h, 6f| Ap3 A.

Agaue ('Αγαύη), Agave: ***I*** daughter of Cadmos & Harmonia, by Echion mother of Pentheus, whom she killed: Apd. M2, M4| Fulg. 2.12| Hes. 984| ***II*** a Nereid: Apd. A2| Hes. 248.

Ageleos ('Αγέλεως) or Agelaos: brother of Meleagros: A.L. 2| Bac. 5.117.

Agenor ('Αγήνωρ): ***I*** son of Poseidon & Libya, ruler of Tyre, father of Cadmos, Europa, Phoinix, & Cilix: Apd. L1| ***II*** father of Phineus: Apd. G2| ***III*** son or grandson of Niobe & Amphion: Apd. M5.

Aglaia ('Αγλαΐα): one of the Charites: Apd. B1| Hes. 914, 953.

Aglauros ("Αγλαυρος): daughter of King Cecrops of Athens: Fulg. 2.11.

Agrios ("Αγριος): ***I*** a Giant: Apd. D1| ***II*** a Centaur: Apd. K6| ***III*** son of Circe & Odysseus: Hes. 1021.

Aiacos (Αἰακός): son of Zeus & Aigina, father of Telamon & Peleus: Apd. F, G1| Arr.| Hes. 1012| Hyg. 52, 54| Ov. 1.35, 3.87| Stat. 1.852| Ap2 H.

Aidoneus: see Hades.

Aietes (Αἰήτης): son of Helios, king of Colchis, father of Medeia, received the Golden Fleece from Phrixos: Apd. G3–5| Erat. 19| Hes. 964, 965, 1000, 1001| Hyg. 3| Ov. 12.29, 12.51| Pal. 30.

Aigeus (Αἰγεύς): father of Theseus & king of Athens. He killed himself when Theseus forgot to change the color of the sails after defeating the Minotaur: Apd. F, G1, G5,

N1–2, N4–5| Hyg. 79| Ov. 4.59, 10.111| Paus. C| Plut.

Aigialeus (Αἰγιαλεύς): *I* early king of Sicyon: Acus. 23| *II* one of the Epigonoi, son of Adrastos: Apd. M10.

Aigina (Αἴγινα): mother of Aiacos by Zeus, who gave her name to the island: Apd. G4| *HH* 3b| Hyg. 52| Ov. 3.73.

Aigipan (Αἰγίπαν): son of Zeus & a she-goat (or otherwise explained): Apd. D2| Erat. 27.

Aigisthos (Αἴγισθος): son of Thyestes & his daughter, Pelopeia, killed Agamemnon: Hyg. 88, 117, 119| Paus. E| Proc. E.

Aigle (Αἴγλη): one of the Hesperides: Apd. K13.

Aigoceros (Αἰγόκερως): the constellation Capricorn: Erat. 27.

Aineias (Αἰνείας), Aeneas: son of Aphrodite & the mortal Anchises, warrior in the Trojan War, destined to survive Troy's fall and establish a new kingdom: Acus. 39| Ael. 3.22| Hes. 1016| *HH* 5d| Hyg. 94| Proc. A, D| Ver. 2 *passim*, 6 *passim*.

Aiolos (Αἴολος): son of Hellen, the eponymous ancestor of the Aiolians, sometimes identified as the god of the winds: Apd. E3| Call. 6| Con. 27| Hell. 125| *HH* 3b| Hyg. 3| Ov. 10.66| Pal. 30| Par. 2, 3| Ver. 6g.

Aison (Αἴσων): king of Iolcos & father of Jason: Apd. F, G1, G5| Hes. 1000, 1005| Hyg. 3| Ov. 12.15, 12.134.

Aithra (Αἴθρα): daughter of Pittheus & mother of Theseus: Apd. N1, N4| Bac. 17.58| Hyg. 79, 92| Ov. 10.112| Plut.| Proc. D.

Ajax (Αἴας, strictly Aias): *I* son of Telamon: Hyg. 107| Luc. *DD* 23| Ov. 3.27, 3.130| Pl. *Rep*.10| Proc. B–D| Ver. 2g| *II* son of Oileus, also called Locrian: Hyg. 116| Proc. D, E| Ver. 2g.

Alalu: first god in Hittite/Hurrian myth: Ap4 *SoE* 2–4.

Al(l)ecto (Ἀληκτώ): one of the Erinyes: Apd. A1| Ap3 D.

Alceides (Ἀλκείδης), Alcides: "Descendant of Alcaios," original name of Heracles: Apd. K2| Ver. 6e.

Alcestis (Ἄλκηστις): daughter of Pelias, the only daughter who did not slay her father under Medeia's trick. She died for her husband, Admetos: Apd. K15| Pal. 40.

Alcides: see Alceides.

Alcinoos (Ἀλκίνοος): king of the Phaiacians who entertained Odysseus on his way home: Apd. G4| Pl. *Rep*.10.

Alcmaion (Ἀλκμαίων), Alcmaeon: son of Amphiaraos & Eriphyle, led the Epigonoi to victory against Thebes & killed his mother: Apd. M10.

Alcmene (Ἀλκμήνη): mortal mother of Heracles: Apd. K1–2, L1| Bac. 5.72| Diod. 2.46| Hdr. 14| Hes. 529, 950, 957| *HH* 15| Paus. J| Ap3 B.

Alcyone (Ἀλκυόνη): daughter of Aiolos, turned into the halcyon bird: Apd. E3.

Aleos (Ἀλεός): father of Auge: Apd. G1, K18.

Alexander (Ἀλέξανδρος): see Paris.

Althaia (Ἀλθαία), Althaea: mother of Meleagros: A.L. 2| Bac. 5.120| Ap3 C.

Amaltheia (Ἀμάλθεια): goat that suckled Zeus on Crete. The Horn of Amaltheia, or "cornucopia" ("horn of plenty"), is one of her horns & provided the owner with whatever was wanted: Apd. A1, K19| Diod. 5.70| Hyg. 31| Pal. 45.

Amazons (Ἀμαζόνες): tribe of women warriors who were located in various places often visited by Greek heroes: Apd. I, K11, N7| Diod. 2.45–46| Hyg. 30| Ov. 4.1, 4.118| Pal. 4, 32| Paus. A| Proc. B| Stat. 1.833.

Amisodaros (Ἀμισώδαρος): raised the Chimaira: Apd. I| Pal. 28.

Amphiaraos (Ἀμϊάραος): son of Oicles & Hypermestra, a seer who took part in the Seven against Thebes. His wife, Eriphyle, tricked him into going although he knew he was fated to die there: Apd. F, G1, M7, M9–10| Hyg. 68| Paus. J.

Amphidamas (Ἀμιδάμας): ***I*** son of Bousiris: Apd. K13| ***II*** father of Cleisonymos: Hell. 145.

Amphion (Ἀμφίων): son of Zeus & Antiope, twin brother of Zethos. Exposed at birth, the two eventually became corulers of Thebes, and built the city's walls. He later married Niobe: Apd. M5–6| Hor. 3.11.2| Hyg. 9, 69| Pal. 41.

Amphitrite (Ἀμιτρίτη): the Nereid (or Oceanid) wife of Poseidon: Apd. A2, B5| Bac. 17.111| Hes. 244, 254, 935| *HH* 3b| Luc. *DSG* 7| Paus. A.

Amphitryon (Ἀμιτρύων): the husband of Alcmene & the mortal father of Heracles: A.L. 41| Apd. F, K1–2| Bac. 5.85, 5.155| Hes. 317.

Amyclas (Ἀμύκλας): ***I*** son of Niobe & Amphion: Apd. M5| ***II*** father of Daphne: Par. 15.

Amycos (Ἄμυκος): enormous son of Poseidon & king of the Bebryces who forced all strangers to box with him. Polydeuces defeated him: Apd. G2, K11| Ap3 C.

Amymone (Ἀμυμώνη): daughter of Danaos who slept with Poseidon & bore Nauplios *I*: Apd. K4| Call. 5| Pher. 10.

Amyntor (Ἀμύντωρ): king of Ormenion, father of Phoinix *II*: Apd. K20| Ov. 3.27.

Ancaios (Ἀγκαῖος): ***I*** son of Lycourgos, participant in the hunt for the Calydonian Boar & the voyage of the Argo: Apd. F, G1–2| ***II*** brother of Meleagros: Bac. 5.117.

Anchises (Ἀγχίσης): father of Aineias by Aphrodite: Acus. 39| Hes. 1017| *HH* 5b–d| Hyg. 94, 135| Luc. *Jud.*| Ver. 2e, 6i–j.

Androgeos (Ἀνδρόγεως): ***I*** son of Minos & Pasiphae: Apd. K11, L1–2, N2| Ov. 10.99| ***II*** Greek general at Troy: Ver. 2g.

Andromache (Ἀνδρομάχη): daughter of Eetion, wife of Hector, mother of Astyanax: Proc. D| Ver. 2h.

Andromeda (Ἀνδρομέδη, strictly -mede): daughter of Cepheus & Cassiepeia, rescued by & married Perseus: Apd. J2| Con. 40| Pher. 12.

Anshar: circle or horizon of heaven in Babylonian myth: Ap4 *EoC* I.12, 15, 19, II *passim*, III.131, IV.83, 125, V.79, VI.101.

Antaios (Ἀνταῖος): giant son of Poseidon & Gaia killed by Heracles: Apd. K13| Hyg. 31.

Anticleia (Ἀντίκλεια): mother of Periphetes: Apd. N4.

Antigone (Ἀντιγόνη): daughter of Oidipous & Iocaste who buried her brother's corpse against King Creon's orders: Apd. M6, M9| Hyg. 67, 72.

Antilochos (Ἀντίλοχος): Nestor's son, Greek warrior at Troy, killed by Memnon: Proc. B| Ov. 1.15–16.

Antiope (Ἀντιόπη): mother of Amphion & Zethos: Apd. M5, N7| Hyg. 9, 30.

Anu: "Sky," Sumerian/Mesopotamian god of sky: Ap4 *Atr.* I *passim*, III.iii.51, III.v.40, 48| Ap4 *EoC* I.14, 89, II.96–126, IV.44, 146| V.8, 70, 80, VI.41, 86–94| Ap4 *Gilg.* 15, 117, 168| Ap4 *SoE* 2–5, 7, 10, 12, 17, 19.

Anunna-gods: greater gods of Mesopotamian pantheon: Ap4 *Atr.* I.5–22, 103, 219–223, 233, III.iii.30, III.vi.7| Ap4 *EoC* I.155, II.42, 121, V.82, VI.20, 40–69.

Anzu: divine storm-bird: Ap4 *Atr.* III.iii.7.

Aphareus (Ἀφαρεύς): father of Idas & Lynceus: Apd. F, G1.

Aphrodite (Ἀφροδίτη), Venus: goddess of love, sexual desire, & human fertility, born either from Ouranos' genitals or from Zeus & Dione. She was married to Hephaistos, but had a love affair with Ares (among other gods) & had children with him, including Eros. Among mortals she had affairs with Adonis & Anchises, by whom she had the Trojan hero Aineias, the ancestor of the Romans. One of her major religious centers was on the island of Cyprus, hence her names Cypris & Cyprogenes: Acus. 39| A.L. 1, 34| Apd. B1, B3, B5, G2, G4, M1| Bac. 5.175, 17.10, 17.116| Bion| Call. 5| Con. 37, 40| Corn. 30| Diod. 5.72–73| Herac. 54, 69| Hes. 17, 195, 197, 828, 939, 969, 982, 988,

997, 1013, 1016, 1022, W84| *HH* 2b, 3d, 5a–d, 6, 10| Hor. 3.11.50| Hyg. 92, 94| Luc. *DSG* 7, *Jud.*, *Sac.* 7, 10| Lucr. 1.2| Ov. 3.116, 4.54, 4.88, 4.97, 4.102, 4.136, 4.167| Pi. 75| Proc. A| Sall.| Sapph.| Soph. 941| Theoc.| Ver. *G*| Ap2 F| Ap3 E.

Apis (Ἆπις): Egyptian god: Luc. *Sac.* 15| Paus. I.

Apollo (Ἀπόλλων): god of, among other things, music, prophecy, & medicine. The son of Zeus & Leto, his & his twin sister's (Artemis') birth was delayed by Hera but eventually took place on Delos, where the god established an oracle. At Delphi he killed the Python & established his most important oracle. He gave Cassandra, the Sibyl & other mortal prophets the ability to foretell the future. As the god of music he was associated with the lyre, which he received from Hermes & with which he bested Marysas in a contest. His love affairs (e.g., Daphne, Hyacinthos) usually turned out badly, but by Coronis he was the father of Asclepios. He was armed with bow & arrows, which were sometimes said to cause disease: A.L. 1, 4, 6, 28| Apd. B2–3, B5, D1, G4, K2, K5, K11, K15, K20, L1, M5, M10| Bab. 68| Call. 6| Diod. 5.67, 5.72| Eur. 660| Herac. 56| Hdr. 34| Hes. 15, 96, 349, 923| *HH* 3 *passim*, 4a–b, 4d–h, 5a, 5c, 7, 9, 16, 21, 24, 25, 27| Hor. 1.10.9| Hyg. 9, 28, 66, 89, 93, 106, 107, 120, 130, 135, 136| Luc. *DG* 16, *DSG* 7, *Sac.* 3, 4, 10, 11| Ov. 1.67| Par. 15| Paus. C, G| Pl. *Symp.*| Proc. B, F| Ver. 2c, 2f–g, 6d, 6i| Ap2 E, O.I| Ap3 B. See also Ap1.8.

Apples of the Hesperides: Heracles' Eleventh Labor: Apd. K13| Hyg. 30.

Apsu: ***I*** Babylonian god of the freshwater deep: Ap4 *EoC* I.1–78 *passim*, I.113–117, II.3, 55, 67| ***II*** the freshwater deep itself: Ap4 *EoC* I.76–81, IV.142, V.60, 75, 84, 102, 119, VI.62–63.

Apsyrtos (Ἄψυρτος), Absyrtus: son of Aietes & brother of Medeia, killed by his sister or Jason: Apd. G3–4| Ov. 10.114.

Aquilo: see Boreas.

Arcas (Ἀρκάς): son of Zeus & Callisto: Pal. 6.

Arceisios (Ἀρκείσιος), Arcesius: father of Laertes & grandfather of Odysseus: Apd. G1.

Archemoros: see Opheltes.

Ares (Ἄρης), Mars, or Mavors: son of Zeus & Hera. He was the god of war, particularly its destructive frenzy. He produced children with Aphrodite & several mortal women, but does not figure in myth much outside of war. When he was put on trial in Athens for murder, he was acquitted & the site of the trial became known as the Areopagos ("Hill of Ares"): Aes. 99| A.L. 2, 28| Apd. B1, B5, F, G1, K10–11, K13, K20, M1, M5, M8| Bac. 5.130, 5.166| Con. 37| Diod. 2.45–46, 5.72| Herac. 54, 69| Hes. 927, 939, 941, W168 [War]| *HH* 3d, 5a, 8, 11| Hyg. 3, 30, 31, 84| Luc. *Jud.*| Lucr. 1.33| Ov. 3.88, 12.41| Proc. B, F| Stat. 1.882| Ver. *G*| Ap2 B. See also Ap1.5.

Arestor (Ἀρέστωρ): ***I*** father of Argos *IV*: Apd. H| ***II*** important early figure in Argos: Call. 5.

Arete (Ἀρήτη): Alcinoos' wife: Apd. G4.

Argeia (Ἀργεία): daughter of Adrastos, wife of Polyneices: Apd. M7| Hyg. 69, 72.

Argeios (Ἀργεῖος): son of Licymnios who fought with Heracles: And.| Apd. K21.

Argeiphontes: see Hermes.

Arges (Ἄργης): see Cyclopes *I*.

Argiope (Ἀργιόπη): ***I*** mother of Thamyris: Apd. B3| ***II*** mother of Cercyon: Apd. N4.

Argo (Ἀργώ): ship built by Argos *II* (with the help of Athena) on which the Argonauts sailed: Apd. G1–4| Erat. 28| Ov. 12.9| Pal. 30.

Argonauts (Ἀργοναῦται): "Sailors on the *Argo*," a band of heroes assembled by Jason to retrieve the Golden Fleece: A.L. 26| Apd. G2, G4–5| Diod. 4.25| Hyg. 89.

Argos (Ἄργος): ***I*** grandfather of Io: Apd. H| ***II*** son of Phrixos: Apd. G1| Hyg. 3| ***III*** all-seeing warden of Io, slain by Hermes: Apd.

Thph.| Ver. 2a, 2c, 2g| Ap2 A, B, K, L. See also Ap1.5.

Atlas ("Ατλας): son of Iapetos & Clymene, forced to hold up the heavens on his shoulders. He is identified with the Atlas Mts. in N. Africa: Apd. A2, K13| Hdr. 13| Hes. 511, 519, 751| *HH* 18| Hor. 1.10.1| Hyg. 30, 83, 84.

Atrahasis (see also Utanapishtim): man who survives great flood: Ap4 *Atr.* I.365–387, III *passim*| Ap4 *Gilg.* 49.

Atreidai ('Ατρεῖδαι), Atridae: "sons of Atreus" (see Agamemnon & Menelaos).

Atreus ('Ατρεύς): son of Pelops & Hippodameia, king of Argos (or Mycenae). After his brother Thyestes seduced his wife & stole his throne, he killed his brother's sons & fed them to him: Hell. 157| Hor. 1.10.14| Hyg. 78, 84, 88, 95| Ov. 3.39| Paus. E| Thu. 1.9.

Atropos ("Ατροπος): one of the Moirai.

Auge (Αὔγη): raped by Heracles & bore Telephos: Apd. K18| Proc. F.

Augeias (Αὐγείας), Augeas: son of Helios (or Poseidon or Phorbas), king of Elis who participated in the voyage of the *Argo*. Heracles was ordered to clean his stables as his Fifth Labor: Apd. G1, K7, K17| Hyg. 30.

Aurora: see Eos.

Autolycos (Αὐτόλυκος): son of Hermes & Chione, grandfather of Odysseus. He received from his father the ability to steal without being caught: Apd. G1, K2, K15.

Autonoe (Αὐτονόη): ***I*** daughter of Cadmos, wife of Aristaios: Apd. M2–M3| Call. 5| Fulg. 2.12| Hes. 984| ***II*** a Nereid: Apd. A2| Hes. 259.

Avengers: see Erinyes.

Bacchai (Βάκχαι): female worshipers of Dionysos (see also Mainads): A.L. 10| Apd. M4| Corn. 30| Fulg. 2.12| Ov. 4.47, 10.48| Pal. 33| Ap2 P| Ap3 B|.

Bacchos/Bacchios: see Dionysos.

Belet-ili (see also Nintu): mistress of the gods, midwife: Ap4 *Atr.* I.181h, 189| Ap4 *Gilg.* 120, 167.

Bellerophontes (Βελλεροφόντης), Bellerophon: son of Glaucos *II* or of Poseidon, this hero rode Pegasos. He killed the Chimaira & performed other dangerous tasks, including fighting the Amazons. He rejected the advances of Stheneboia, who then accused him of trying to seduce her. He later rode Pegasos up to the heavens, but was thrown down to earth & lived out the rest of his life a hated outcast: Apd. I, L1| Eur. 286| Hes. 326| Hyg. 57| Pal. 28| Paus. G.

Belos (Βῆλος): ***I*** son of Poseidon & Libya, king of Egypt, father of Danaos & Aigyptos: Apd. L1| Ver. 2c| ***II*** father of Theias: A.L. 34.

Bia (Βία): the personification of Force: Apd. A2| Hes. 386.

Boreas (Βορέας), Aquilo: the North Wind, son of Eos & Astraios: Apd. G1–2| Hes. 380, 876| Hyg. 84.

Bousiris (Βούσιρις), Busiris: son of Poseidon & Lysianassa. King of Egypt, sacrificed all strangers who entered his realm, killed by Heracles: Apd. K13| Hyg. 31.

Briareos (Βριάρεως): see Hundred-Handers.

Briseis (Βρισηίς): female slave of Achilles captured in war, later taken from him by Agamemnon: Hyg. 106| Ov. 3 *passim*| Proc. A.

Bromios: see Dionysos.

Brontes (Βροντής): see Cyclopes *I*.

Busiris: see Bousiris.

Cadmos (Κάδμος): son of Agenor, founder & first king of Thebes. By Harmonia he fathered Semele, Ino, Autonoe, & Agaue. Later, he & his wife were changed into serpents: Apd. G3, L1, M1–2, M4| Call. 5| Con. 37| Hes. 328, 943, 946, 983, W184| Hyg. 2| Pal. 4| Paus. O| Ap2 Q.

Cain: Ap4 *Gen.* 4–5.

Caineus (Καινεύς), Caeneus: Cainis, a woman, became the man Caineus after be-

ing raped by Poseidon: A.L. 17| Apd. G1| Stat. 1.264| Ver. 6f.

Cainis (Καινίς): see Caineus.

Calais (Κάλαϊς): son of Boreas & Oreithyia: Apd. G1–2.

Calchas (Κάλχας): Greek seer at Troy: Con. 34| Hyg. 98| Proc. A, E| Ver. 2c.

Callidice (Καλλιδίκη): ***I*** daughter of Celeos & Metaneira: *HH* 2b| ***II*** queen of the Thesprotians, marries Odysseus: Proc. F.

Calliope (Καλλιόπη): a Muse, according to some the mother of Orpheus: Apd. B1–3| Bac. 5.176| Hes. 80| *HH* 31.

Callir(r)hoe (Καλλιρ(ρ)όη): ***I*** Oceanid, mother of Geryones: Apd. K12| Hes. 289, 987| *HH* 2f| ***II*** Nereid, Hes. 353.

Calydonian Boar: sent by Artemis to ravage Calydon after Oineus forgot to sacrifice to her. Many great Greek heroes assembled to kill this beast: Apd. K15| Hyg. 69.

Calypso (Καλυψώ): ***I*** an Oceanid: Apd. A2| Hes. 361| *HH* 2f| ***II*** daughter of Atlas, goddess who entertained Odysseus on the island of Ogygia: Ael. 13.1| Hes. 1025.

Canace (Κανάκη): daughter of Aiolos: Apd. E3| Call. 6.

Capaneus (Καπανεύς): one of the Seven against Thebes: Apd. M7–10| Hyg. 68| Paus. F.

Capys (Κάπυς): a Trojan, father of Laocoon Hyg. 135| Ver. 2a.

Cassandra (Κασσάνδρα): daughter of Priam & Hecuba, had prophetic powers but was never believed: Hyg. 91, 93, 108, 116, 117| Proc. A, D| Ver. 2d, 2f–g.

Cassiepeia (Κασσιέπεια), Cassiopia: mother of Andromeda: Apd. J2, L1.

Castor (Κάστωρ): one of the Dioscouroi.

Cattle of Augeias: Heracles' Fifth Labor: Apd. K7, K13| Hyg. 30.

Cattle of Geryones: Heracles' Tenth Labor: Apd. K12| Hyg. 30.

Cecrops (Κέκροψ): early Athenian king: A.L. 6| Ov. 10.99, 10.127.

Celeos (Κελεός): king or leading figure of Eleusis, husband of Metaneira: Apd. C| *HH* 2b–c, 2g.

Centaurs (Κένταυροι): mythical creatures, half man & half horse, mostly known for their violence (although see Cheiron): Ael. 13.1| Apd. A2, K6, K14, K19| Erat. 28| *HH* 4e| Pal. 1| Paus. A| Stat. 1.266| Ver. 6b.

Cephalos (Κέφαλος): husband of Procris, seduced by Eos: A.L. 41| Hes. 994| Ov. 4.93| Pal. 2.

Cepheus (Κηφεύς): ***I*** son of Aleos, participant in the hunt for Calydonian Boar: Apd. G1| ***II*** son of Lycourgos, an Argonaut: Apd. F, K17| ***III*** king of Ethiopia, son of Belos & father of Andromeda: Apd. J2| Con. 40.

Cerberos (Κέρβερος): three-headed guard dog of the underworld: Apd. K14–15| Bac. 5.60| Hes. 312| Hor. 2.19.29, 3.11.15| Hyg. 30| Pal. 39| Ver. 6e, *G*| Ap2 H| Ap3 D.

Cercyon (Κερκύων): bandit killed by Theseus: Apd. N4.

Ceres: see Demeter.

Cerynitian Deer: Heracles' Third Labor: Apd. K5| Hyg. 30.

Ceto (Κητώ): "Sea-monster," daughter of Pontos & Gaia, mother of many horrible creatures: Apd. A2, J1| Hes. 238, 271, 334, 338.

Ceyx (Κῆυξ): king of Trachis, father of Hylas: A.L. 26| Apd. K19–21.

Chalciope (Χαλκιόπη): ***I*** wife of Aigeus: Apd. N1| ***II*** daughter of Aietes, wife of Phrixos: Hyg. 3.

Chaos (Χάος): "Abyss" or "Gaping Void," from which the rest of the gods come: Hes. 116, 123, 704, 820| Ver. 6a| Ap2 F| Ap3 D.

Chariclo (Χαρικλώ): Nymph companion of Athena, the mother of Teiresias: Apd. M8| Call. 5.

Charites (Χάριτες), Graces: daughters of Zeus & Eurynome, goddesses of grace & beauty (Euphrosyne, Thaleia, Aglaia): Apd. B1, N2| Bac. 5.10| Bion| Diod. 5.72–73| Hdr. 34| Hes. 65, 913, 953, W92| *HH* 3d,

5b–c, 27| Luc. *Jud.*| Paus. D| Pi. 30| Ap2 D–E| Ap3 D.

Charon (Χάρων): boatman of the underworld who ferried the souls of the dead across the Acheron river: Ver. 6c, 6e, *G*| Ap2 H.

Charybdis (Χάρυβδις): monstrous daughter of Gaia & Poseidon who three times daily swallowed & disgorged masses of water, usually located across from Scylla at the Straits of Messina: Apd. G4| Herac. 70| Ov. 12.126.

Cheiron (Χείρων): Centaur known for kindness & wisdom, especially in music & medicine: Apd. A2, K6, K13, M3| Hes. 1009| Stat. 1.273, 1.868.

Chimaira (Χίμαιρα), Chimaera: monstrous offspring of Typhon & Echidna, part lion, part goat, & part serpent, killed by Bellerophontes: Apd. I| Hes. 320| *HH* 3g| Hyg. 57| Pal. 28| Paus. G| Ver. 6b.

Chiron: see Cheiron.

Chloris (Χλωρίς): daughter of Niobe & Amphion, married Neleus: Apd. M5| Hell. 125| Hyg. 9, 69.

Chrysaor (Χρυσάωρ): "Golden-Sword," born from the neck of Medousa alongside Pegasos, father of Geryones & Echidna: Apd. J1, K12| Hes. 282, 284, 288, 988| Hyg. 30.

Chryseis (Χρυσηίς): ***I*** Oceanid: Hes. 361| *HH* 2f| ***II*** daughter of Chryses *I*: Hyg. 106| Proc. A.

Chryses (Χρύσης): ***I*** priest of Apollo, Trojan ally whose daughter Chryseis was taken by Agamemnon: Hyg. 106, 120| Luc. *Sac.* 3| ***II*** son of Minos slain by Heracles: Apd. K11, L1.

Chrysippos (Χρύσιππος): son of Pelops & Axioche, abducted by Laios: Apd. M5| Hell. 157| Thu. 1.9.

Cilix (Κίλιξ): son of Agenor who founded Cilicia after searching for his sister Europa: Apd. L1.

Cinyras (Κινύρας): king of Cyprus who had incestuous relationship with his daughter Smyrna, producing Adonis: Bion| Ov. 4.97.

Circe (Κίρκη): daughter of Helios & Perseis, sorceress on the island of Aeaea who changed Odysseus' men into animals: Apd. G4| Herac. 70| Hes. 964, 1019| Par. 12| Proc. F.

cithara: musical instrument, a kind of lyre.

Cleio (Κλειώ): a Muse: Apd. B1, B3| Hes. 78.

Cleodoxa (Κλεόδοξα): daughter of Niobe & Amphion. Apd. M5| Hyg. 69.

Cleopatra (Κλεοπάτρα): wife of Meleagros: A.L. 2| Apd. F.

Clotho (Κλωθώ): one of the Moirai: Apd. B1| Hes. 218, 910| Pi. 27| Pl. *Rep.*10| Ap3 D.

Clymene (Κλυμένη): Oceanid, mother of Prometheus by Iapetos: Hes. 353, 510.

Clymenos (Κλύμενος): ***I*** son of Oineus & Althaia: A.L. 2| Apd. F| ***II*** king of the Minyans: Apd. K2| ***III*** son of Deipylos: Bac. 5.145| ***IV*** father who had incestuous union with his daughter Harpalyce: Par. 13.

Clytaimnestra (Κλυταιμνήστρα), Clytaemnestra: daughter of Tyndareos & Leda, slew her husband, Agamemnon, upon his return from Trojan War: A.L. 27| Hyg. 77, 78, 98, 117, 119| Paus. E| Proc. E.

Cocalos (Κώκαλος): Sicilian king who protected Daidalos when he was fleeing Minos: Apd. N6.

Cocytos (Κωκυτός): a river in the underworld: Bac. 5.64| Ver. 6c, *G*.

Coios (Κοῖος): a Titan: Apd. A1–2, B5| Diod. 5.66–67| Hes. 134, 406| *HH* 3b.

Cornucopia: see Amaltheia.

Coronis (Κορωνίς): daughter of Phlegyas, the mother of Asclepios by Apollo: *HH* 3e, 16| Paus. G.

Corybantes (Κορύβαντες): children of Thaleia & Apollo, the attendants of Cybele: Apd. B3.

Corynetes (Κορυνήτης): see Periphetes.

Cottos (Κόττος): see Hundred-Handers.

Couretes (Κουρῆτες): ***I*** companions of Zeus in childhood: Apd. A1, H| Diod. 5.66, 5.70| Lucr. 2.633| Stat. 1.831| ***II*** name of a people in Aetolia who fought against the Calydonians: A.L. 2| Apd. F| Bac. 5.126| ***III*** worshipers of Cybele, called Phrygian Curetes or Corybantes: Lucr. 2.629.

Cratos (Κράτος): the personification of Strength: Apd. A2| Hes. 386.

Creios (Κρεῖος): ***I*** a Titan: Apd. A1–2| Diod. 5.66| Hes. 134, 376| ***II*** the constellation Aries: Erat. 19, 21| ***III*** a man named "Ram": Pal. 30.

Creon (Κρέων): ***I*** king of Corinth, murdered by Medeia: Apd. G5| Ov. 12.54| ***II*** son of Menoiceus, king of Thebes, & uncle of Oidipous: A.L. 41| Apd. K2, M6, M8–9| Hyg. 31, 67, 72.

Creousa (Κρέουσα): ***I*** daughter of Erechtheus: Apd. E3| Con. 27| ***II*** daughter of Creon, king of Corinth, killed by Medeia: Ov. 12.53. See also Glauce II.

Cretan Bull: Heracles' Seventh Labor: Apd. K9| Hyg. 30.

Cretheus (Κρηθεύς): son of Aiolos, father of Aison & Pelias: Apd. E3, G1.

Creusa: see Creousa.

Crios: see Creios.

Cronides/Cronion: "Son of Cronos," see Zeus.

Cronos (Κρόνος), Saturn: a Titan, youngest son of Ouranos & Gaia, father of Zeus and his siblings. He castrated his father & was deposed by his own son Zeus: A.L. 36| Apd. A1–2| Call. 5| Diod. 5.66, 5.68–71| Hdr. 34| Hes. 19, 74, 138, 169, 175, 397, 413, 456, 463, 470, 476, 480, 489, 497, 630, 651, 858, W131, W195| *HH* 5a, 29, 32, 33| Hyg. 54| Luc. *Sac.* 5, 11| Lucr. 2.638| Ov. 4.132| Pi. 111| Pl. *Rep.*2| Sall.| Ap2 T.2| Ap3 D, F.

Curetes: see Couretes.

Cybele (Κυβέλη): the "Great Mother," a Near Eastern fertility & earth goddess: Lucr. 2.608–659 *passim*| Ov. 4.48.

Cyclopes (Κύκλωπες): name ("Round-eyes") given to three separate groups (explained in Hell. 88): ***I*** sons of Ouranos & Gaia, makers of Zeus' thunderbolts (Arges, Brontes, Steropes): Apd. A1–2| Hes. 140–145| Luc. *Sac.* 4| Ver. 6i| Ap2 F| ***II*** one-eyed giants, of whom Polyphemos is most famous (he is often called by the singular "Cyclops"): Herac. 70| Luc. *DSG* 2, *Sac.* 13| Theoc.| ***III*** the builders of Mycenae's massive walls: Apd. N2(?)| Pher. 12(?).

Cycnos (Κύκνος), Cygnus: ***I*** name of two different sons of Ares, killed by Heracles: Apd. K13, K20| Hyg. 31| ***II*** son of Poseidon, killed by Achilles at Troy: Proc. A.

Cyprian, Cypris: see Aphrodite.

Cytherea, Cythereia: see Aphrodite.

Cyzicos (Κύζικος): king of the Doliones, killed by Jason: Apd. G2.

Daidalos (Δαίδαλος): Athenian inventor, father of Icaros, built the Labyrinth for the Minotaur & wings to escape from imprisonment: Apd. K15, L2, N3, N5–6| Pal. 2, 21| Paus. M. See also Ap1 1.

Damastes (Δαμάστης): see Procrustes.

Damkina: wife of Ea: Ap4 *EoC* I.78, 84, V.81, 83.

Danae (Δανάη): daughter of Acrisios & mother of Perseus by Zeus, who came to her in the form of golden rain: Apd. J1–2| Con. 40| Pher. 10–12| Sim.

Danaos (Δαναός): son of Belos *I* who had fifty daughters, eponymous ancestor of the Danaans: Call. 5| Hor. 3.11.23.

Daphne (Δάφνη): nymph loved by Apollo, turned into a laurel tree: Luc. *DG* 16, *Sac.* 4| Par. 15.

Dardanos (Δάρδανος): son of Zeus & Electra, founder & first king of Troy, eponymous ancestor of the Dardanians: *HH* 5d| Ver. 6i.

Dawn: see Eos.

Death: see Thanatos.

Deianeira (Δηιάνειρα), Deianira: daughter

of Oineus, Heracles' second wife who led to his ultimate demise: A.L. 2| Apd. F, K19, K21| Bac. 5.173| Hyg. 31.

Deidameia (Δηιδάμεια), Deidamia: mother of Neoptolemos by Achilles: Proc. A| Stat. 1.823.

Deino (Δεινώ): one of the Graiai.

Deion (Δηΐων): ***I*** father of Cephalos: A.L. 41| ***II*** son of Aiolos: Apd. E3.

Deiphobos (Δηΐφοβος): ***I*** Trojan, son of Priam & Hecabe, married Helen after Paris: Con. 34| Proc. C, D| Hyg. 91, 110| Ver. 2f, 6g| ***II*** son of Hippolytos *II*: Apd. K15.

Deipyle (Δηιπύλη): wife of Tydeus, mother of Diomedes: Apd. M7| Hyg. 69.

Deipylos (Δηίπυλος): father of Clymenos III: Bac. 5.146.

Delia: see Artemis.

Demeter (Δημήτηρ), Ceres: daughter of Cronos and Rhea, goddess of fertility and grain. With Zeus she had Persephone. When her daughter was abducted by Hades, she searched for her, eventually coming to Eleusis. Mother and daughter are worshiped in the Eleusinian Mysteries held there annually. With Poseidon she had the horse Areion; with Iasion she had Ploutos: Apd. A1, C, D1, H, K14, M9| Call. 6| Diod. 5.68–69| Erat. 9| Hes. 458, 917, 976, W43| *HH* 2a–g, 13| Hyg. 83| Lucr. 2.656| Ov. 4.67| Paus. K| Ver. 6f| Ap2 M.

Demophon (Δημοφῶν): ***I*** son of Theseus, king of Athens after his father: Apd. N7| Proc. D| ***II*** son of Celeos & Metaneira, nearly made immortal by Demeter: Apd. C| *HH* 2c.

Deo: see Demeter.

Destiny: see Moirai.

Deucalion (Δευκαλίων): ***I*** son of Prometheus, he & his wife Pyrrha alone survived the great Bronze Age flood & repopulated the earth afterward by tossing stones behind them: Apd. E2–3| Con. 27| Hell. 125| Hyg. 153| Thu. 1.3| ***II*** son of Minos & Pasiphae: Apd. L1, N7.

Dexamenos (Δεξαμενός): saved by Heracles from having to marry his daughter to a Centaur: Apd. K7| Hyg. 31.

Diana: see Artemis.

Dictys (Δίκτυς): fisherman of Seriphos who rescued & protected Danae & Perseus: Apd. J1–2| Pher. 10–12.

Dike (Δίκη), Virgo: one of the Horai, the personification of Justice: Apd. B1| Bac. 17.25| Crit.| Diod. 5.72| Erat. 9| Hes. 907| Hyg. 130| Pl. *Prt.*| Ap2 T.38| Ap3 D.

Diomedes (Διομήδης): ***I*** son of Tydeus who took part in the Trojan War & was a member of the Epigonoi: Apd. B3, M10| Call. 5| Con. 34| Hdt. 2.113–20| Hyg. 69, 98, 102, 108| Proc. C, E| Ver. 2c| ***II*** a king of Thrace who fed all strangers to his mares, killed by Heracles: Apd. K10| Hyg. 30| Pal. 40.

Dione (Διώνη): ***I*** a Titaness, Nereid, or Oceanid, sometimes the mother of Aphrodite: Apd. A1–2, B1| Bion| Hes. 18, 355| *HH* 3b| ***II*** wife of Tantalos, mother of Pelops & Niobe: Hyg. 9, 82, 83.

Dionysos (Διόνυσος) or Bacchos or Bromios, Bacchus or Liber: god of wine, intoxication, & ecstasy, the son of Zeus by Semele. His mother was killed before his birth, but Zeus saved her child by sewing him into his thigh until he was ready to be born. While Linear B tablets show that he was a very old member of the Greek pantheon, he was portrayed in myth as an outsider whose worship was resisted with horrible consequences (see Pentheus & Lycourgos). His kindly side can be seen in his gift of viticulture & his ability to release people temporarily from their cares. He was portrayed as both young & old, accompanied by his worshipers, Satyrs & Mainads: A.L. 2, 10, 28| Apd. B2, D1, F, G1, M2, M4, N5| Arr.| Call. 6| Corn. 30| Diod. 4.25, 5.72| Erat. 11| Fulg. 2.12| Hdr. 34| Hes. 948, 954| *HH* 1, 7, 19, 26| Hor. 2.19 *passim*| Hyg. 2, 3, 130| Luc. *Sac.* 5| Lucr. 2.656| Ov. 10.48| Pal. 33| Paus. B| Sall.|

Eos (Ἠώς), Aurora: goddess of the dawn, mother of the Winds by Astraios, mother of Emathion & Memnon by Tithonos: A.L. 41| Apd. A2, B5, D1| Bac. 5.40, 17.43| Hes. 20, 373, 379, 382, 454, 992| *HH* 4e, 4g, 5d, 31| Ov. 4.95| Proc. B| Ver. 6g| Ap2 T.30.

Epaphos (Ἔπαφος): son of Io, king of Egypt: Apd. H, K13.

Epeios (Ἐπειός), Epeus: builder of the Trojan Horse: Hyg. 108| Pl. *Rep.*10| Proc. C| Verg. 2d.

Ephialtes (Ἐϊάλτης): ***I*** one of Aloeus' giant sons who attacked Olympos: Hyg. 28| Pl. *Symp.*| Ver. 6h| ***II*** a Giant: Apd. D1.

Epicaste: see Iocaste.

Epigonoi (Ἐπίγονοι): sons of the Seven against Thebes, they successfully sacked Thebes: Apd. M10.

Epimetheus (Ἐπιμηθεύς): son of Iapetos & Clymene, brother of Prometheus, husband of Pandora: Apd. A2, E2| Hes. 513, W104–109| Pl. Prt.

Epopeus (Ἐπωπεύς): king of Sicyon who protected Antiope: Apd. M5| Proc. A.

Erato (Ἐρατώ): ***I*** a Muse: Apd. B1| Hes. 79| ***II*** a Nereid: Apd. A2| Hes. 247.

Erebos (Ἔρεβος): son of Chaos & Night, the personification of Darkness: Hes. 123, 125, 517| *HH* 2e–f| Ver. 6a, 6e, 6i, *G*.

Erechtheus (Ἐρεχθεύς): son of Hephaistos, an early Athenian king: A.L. 41| Apd. E3| Con. 27.

Erginos (Ἐργῖνος): ***I*** son of Poseidon, an Argonaut: Apd. G1| ***II*** son of Clymenos, king of the Minyans: Apd. K2| ***III*** father of Trophonios & Agamedes: *HH* 3g.

Erichthonios (Ἐριχθόνιος): son of Hephaistos, an early Athenian king: Fulg. 2.11.

Erinyes (Ἐρινύες), Furies, Avengers: born of the blood that fell onto Gaia when Ouranos was castrated, avengers of crimes, particularly against blood kin, traditionally three (Alecto, Tisiphone, & Megaira). Also euphemistically called the Eumenides ("Kindly Ones") or "Unnamed Goddesses." The singular is Erinys: Aes. 193| Apd. A1, M6, M9| Eur. 660| Hes. 185, 477| Hor. 3.11.18| Hyg. 79, 119, 120| Ver. 2f, 6a–b, 6d, 6h, *G*| Ap1 1, 2, 5| Ap3 D, G.

Eriphyle (Ἐριφύλη): sister of Adrastos, wife of Amphiaraos, tricked her husband into taking part in the attack of the Seven against Thebes: Apd. M7, M10| Ver. 6f.

Eris (Ἔρις): daughter of Night, the personification of Strife or Discord: Hes. 225, 226, W21, W22, W28, W37, W43| Hyg. 92| Luc. *DSG* 7| Proc. A| Sall.| Ver. 6b.

Eros (Ἔρως), Amor or Cupid: personification of erotic Love, born either of Chaos or Aphrodite, later became used in the plural (Erotes, Cupids): Bion| Con. 24| Hes. 120, 201| Luc. *DG* 9, *Jud.*| Ov. 4.9–11| Paus. G| Ap2 F.

Errakal: a god of destruction: Ap4 *Atr.* II.vii.51| Ap4 *Gilg.* 104.

Erymanthian Boar: Heracles' Fourth Labor: Apd. K6| Hyg. 30.

Eteocles (Ἐτεοκλῆς): son of Oidipous & Iocaste, killed by Polyneices in the siege of the Seven against Thebes: Apd. M6–7, M9–10| Hyg. 67–69, 72.

Euadne (Εὐάδνη): Capaneus' wife, who threw herself onto her husband's funeral pyre: Apd. M9| Ver. 6f.

Eudora (Εὐδώρη, strictly Eudore): ***I*** Nereid: Apd. A2| Hes. 245| ***II*** Oceanid: Hes. 362.

Eueres (Εὐήρης): Teiresias' father: Apd. M8| Call. 5| Hyg. 68, 75.

Eumenides: see Erinyes.

Eumolpos (Εὔμολπος): son of Poseidon, king or leading figure of Eleusis: Apd. K14| *HH* 2b, 2g.

Euneos (Εὔνεως): one of Jason's sons by Hypsipyle: Apd. G2.

Eunomia (Εὐνομία): one of the Horai, the personification of Order: Apd. B1| Diod. 5.72| Hes. 907.

Eupalamos (Εὐπάλαμος): father of Daidalos: Apd. N3.

Euphrosyne (Εὐφροσύνη): one of the Charites: Apd. B1| Hes. 914.

Europa (Εὐρώπη, strictly Europe): ***I*** daughter of Agenor, sister of Cadmos, abducted by Zeus in the guise of a bull & taken to Crete, she gave birth to Minos, Rhadamanthys, & Sarpedon: Aes. 99| Apd. K9, L1, M1| Bac. 17.30| Con. 37| Erat. 14| Hdt. 1.1–5| Hyg. 106| Ov. 4.55| Pal. 15| ***II*** an Oceanid: Hes. 359.

Euryale (Εὐρυάλη): Gorgon, mother of Orion by Poseidon: Apd. B5, J1| Hes. 277.

Euryalos (Εὐρύαλος): ***I*** Mecisteus' son, an Argonaut & one of the Epigonoi: Apd. G1, M10| ***II*** Odysseus' son by Euippe: Par. 3.

Eurybia (Εὐρυβία): daughter of Pontos, wife of Coios, mother of Astraios & Pallas: Apd. A2| Hes. 239, 376.

Eurydice (Εὐρυδίκη): ***I*** Orpheus' wife: Apd. B2| Ver. *G*| ***II*** wife of Lycourgos, mother of Opheltes: Apd. M7| ***III*** wife of Acrisios, mother of Danae: Pher. 10, 12.

Euryganeia (Εὐρυγάνεια): possibly the mother of Oidipous' children: Apd. M6| Paus. N.

Eurynome (Εὐρυνόμη): ***I*** Oceanid, Apd. A2, B1| Hes. 360, 912| ***II*** daughter of Iphitos: Hyg. 69.

Eurypylos (Εὐρύπυλος): ***I*** king of Cos, killed by Heracles: Apd. K16| ***II*** son of Telephos, ally of Troy, killed by Neoptolemos: Proc. C| ***III*** Greek warrior at Troy: Ver. 2c.

Eurystheus (Εὐρυσθεύς): son of Sthenelos & grandson of Perseus, ruled Tiryns & Mycenae, imposed the Twelve Labors on Heracles: Apd. K2–14| Diod. 2.46| *HH* 15| Hyg. 30| Pal. 38, 39| Thu. 1.9.

Eurytion (Εὐρυτίων): ***I*** Centaur: Apd. K6–7| Hyg. 31| ***II*** herdsman of Geryones: Apd. K12| Hes. 294| ***III*** son of Actor: Apd. F.

Eurytos (Εὔρυτος): ***I*** Giant killed by Dionysos: Apd. D1| ***II*** king of Oichalia who refused to hand over his daughter, Iole, to Heracles as promised: Apd. K15, K21| Hyg. 31| ***III*** taught Heracles archery: Apd. K2| ***IV*** son of Hermes, an Argonaut: Apd. G1| ***V*** one of giant conjoined twins: Apd. K17| ***VI*** son of Melaneus: A.L. 4.

Euterpe (Εὐτέρπη): a Muse: Apd. B1, B3| Hes. 78.

Evadne: see Euadne.

Eve: ***I*** first woman: Ap4 *Gen.* 2–4| ***II*** unnamed, as generic "woman": Ap4 *Gen.* 1.

Fates: see Moirai.

Fury: see Erinyes.

Gaia (Γαῖα) or Ge, Tellus: Earth & the procreative force of nature. One of the four primordial beings in Hesiod, she produced by herself or with male partners many of the physical features of the world, as well as other children, including the Titans, Cyclopes, Hundred-Handers, Typhon, & the Giants: A.L. 6, 28| Apd. A1–2, B4, C, D1–2, K13| Diod. 5.66, 5.71| Hes. *passim*, W21, W31, W141, W161, W178, W190| *HH* 3b, 3g, 4h, 30, 31| Hyg. 31| Long. 3.23| Luc. *DSG* 9| Lucr. 2.589–660| Ver. 6a, 6h.

Galateia (Γαλάτεια): ***I*** Nereid, loved by the Cyclops Polyphemos: Apd. A2| Hes. 251| Theoc.| ***II*** daughter of Eurytios: A.L. 17.

Galene (Γαλήνη): Nereid, the personification of Calm Seas: Hes. 245| Luc. *DSG* 7.

Ganymedes (Γανυμήδης), Ganymede: handsome Trojan youth abducted by Zeus to serve as cupbearer of the gods: Apd. K11| Erat. 26| *HH* 5d| Luc. *DG* 9, *Jud.*| Pi. 44.

Ge: see Gaia.

Geryones (Γηρυόνης), Geryon: a triple-bodied giant killed by Heracles: A.L. 4| Apd. J1, K12| Hes. 288, 310, 990| Hyg. 30| Pal. 24, 39| Ver. 6b.

Giants (Γίγαντες): "Earth-Born" offspring of Gaia, defeated by the Olympian gods in the Gigantomachy: Apd. D1–D2, K16| Call. 5| Diod. 5.71| Erat. 11| Hes. 50, 186| Hor. 2.19.21.

Gilgamesh: Mesopotamian hero: Ap4 *Gilg. passim.*

Glauce (Γλαύκη): ***I*** a Nereid: Hes. 245| ***II*** daughter of Creon, killed by Medeia: Apd. G5| Paus. C. See also Creousa *II*.

Glaucos (Γλαῦκος): ***I*** son of Sisyphos, father of Bellerophontes: Apd. I| ***II*** Trojan ally killed by Ajax: Ver. 6f| ***III*** son of Minos: Apd. L1| Hyg. 136| ***IV*** person addressed by the poet Archilochus: Herac. 5| ***V*** Spartan who consulted Delphic oracle: Paus. E.

God (Judeo-Christian; sometimes as Yahweh, sometimes as Elohim): Ap4 *Gen. passim.*

Golden Fleece: the fleece of the ram that carried Phrixos to Colchis, retrieved by Jason & the Argonauts: Apd. G1, G3, G5| Hyg. 3| Ov. 12.108, 12.128, 12.200| Pal. 30.

Gorge (Γόργη): daughter of Oineus: A.L. 2| Apd. F.

Gorgons (Γοργόνες): the name ("The Grim Ones") for the three sisters Stheno, Euryale, & Medousa, the last of whom was mortal. They turned anyone who saw them into stone: Apd. A2, J1–2, K14, K17| Con. 40| Hes. 275| Pher. 11, 12| Ver. 6b| Ap3 C.

Graces: see Charites.

Graiai (Γραῖαι) or Phorcides, Graeae: daughters of Phorcos & Ceto who were born old & shared one eye & one tooth (Deino, Enyo, Pemphredo): Apd. J1| Hes. 271, 273| Pher. 11.

Great Mother: see Cybele.

Gyges (Γύγης) or Gyes: see Hundred-Handers.

Hades (Ἅιδης) or Aidoneus or Plouton, Dis or Orcus or Pluto: god of the underworld, son of Cronos & Rhea, he ruled the dead in the underworld, although he was also associated with the ability of the earth to produce wealth, especially under the name Plouton. His wife was Persephone: Apd. A1–2, B2, B5, C, D1, J1, K12, K14, K17, L1, M4| Bac. 5.61| Call. 5| Diod. 5.68–69| Herac. 70| Hes. 312, 459, 773, 780, 857, 918, W175| *HH* 2a, 2e–f, 4h, 5c| Hyg. 79| Luc. *DG* 9| Pal. 39| Pher. 11| Pl. *Rep.*10, *Symp.*| Soph. 941| Ver. 2g, 6b, 6e, 6g, *G*| Ap2 G, H| Ap3 E.

Haimon (Αἵμων), Haemon: son of Creon *II*: Apd. M6| Hyg. 72.

Ham: son of Noah: Ap4 *Gen.* 5–9.

Hanish: a god of destruction: Ap4 *Atr.* II.vii.50| Ap4 *Gilg.* 102.

Harmonia (Ἁρμονία): wife of Cadmos: Apd. M1, M4| Con. 37| Herac. 69| Hes. 942, 982| *HH* 3d| Hyg. 2| Pal. 4.

Harpalyce (Ἁρπαλύκη): daughter of Clymenos *IV*, seduced by father, killed son: Par. 13.

Harpies (Ἅρπυιαι): "Snatchers," winged monsters (Aello & Ocypete) who carry off persons & things. The daughters of Thaumas & Electra, they plagued Phineus & were driven away by the Argonauts: Apd. A2, G2| Hes. 268| Ver. 6b.

Heaven: see Ouranos.

Hebe (Ἥβη): daughter of Zeus & Hera, the personification of youth, cupbearer of the gods until supplanted by Ganymedes: Apd. B1, K21| Hes. 18, 927, 959| *HH* 3d.

Hecabe (Ἑκάβη), Hecuba: wife of King Priam of Troy: Hyg. 91, 93, 111| Luc. *Sac.* 2| Ver. 2h–i.

Hecate (Ἑκάτη): a powerful & mysterious goddess in early Greek myth (perhaps related to the underworld), closely associated with magic, darkness, & crossroads, often identified with Artemis & Selene: Apd. A2, D1| Hes. 413, 420, 443, 455| *HH* 2a, 2f| Ov. 12.168| Thph.| Ver. 6a, 6h| Ap2 G| Ap3 D.

Hector (Ἕκτωρ): son of Priam & Hecabe, the greatest Trojan warrior, killed by Achilles: Diod. 2.46| Hdt. 2.113–20| Hyg. 103, 106, 107, 111| Ov. 1.14–15, 1.36, 3.86, 3.126| Proc. A| Stat. 1.883| Ver. 2e, 2i. See also Ap1.7.

Hecuba: see Hecabe.

Helen (Ἑλένη): wife of Menelaos, her seduction/abduction by Paris sparked the Trojan War: A.L. 27| Acus. 39| Con. 34| Hdt. 1.1–5, 2.113–20| Hes. W187| Hyg. 77–79, 92, 98, 118| Luc. *Jud.*| Par. 4| Proc. A, C, D| Thu. 1.9| Ap3 A.

Helenos (Ἕλενος): son of Priam & Hecuba, a seer: Con. 34| Proc. A, C.

Helios (Ἥλιος): the Sun, son of Hyperion, later associated with Apollo: A.L. 41| Apd. A2, D1, G1, G4–5, K7, K12–13, L1| Bac. 17.50| Diod. 5.71| Herac. 70| Hes. 20, 372, 764, 963, 965, 1019| *HH* 2a, 3h, 4c, 4g, 31| Hyg. 3, 88| Ov. 10.91| Pal. 30| Sall.| Stat. 1.243| Ver. 6j| Ap3 D, F, G.

Helle (Ἕλλη): daughter of Athamas & Nephele who fell off the golden ram into the Hellespont ("Sea of Helle"): Erat. 19| Hyg. 2–3| Pal. 30.

Hellen (Ἕλλην): son of Deucalion & Pyrrha, father of Aiolos, & the eponymous ancestor of the Hellenes (an ancient name for "Greeks"): Apd. E3| Con. 27| Hell. 125| Pal. 30| Thu. 1.3.

Hephaistos (Ἥφαιστος), Vulcan or Mulciber: the god of metalworking & crafts, son of Hera alone, or of Zeus & Hera. He was either born lame or became so when cast out of heaven. He trapped his mother in a golden throne & would not release her until Dionysos reconciled them. He also used his skills to trap his wife Aphrodite in bed with Ares. In some authors he is married to one of the Charites. His attempt to have sex with Athena produced Erichthonios. His fabulous creations appear in numerous myths: Aes. 193| A.L. 28| Apd. B4–5, D1, E1, G1, G3–4, K2, K8, K12, M1, N4| Diod. 5.72| Erat. 11| Fulg. 2.11| Herac. 69| Hes. 573, 582, 872, 933, 952, W78, W89| *HH* 3g, 4d, 20| Hyg. 106| Luc. *DG* 5, *Sac.* 5–6, 8| Paus. B| Pl. *Prt.*, *Rep.*2, *Symp.*| Proc. B| Ver. 2f| Ap3 B.

Hera (Ἥρα), Juno: queen of the gods & goddess of marriage. She was the sister & wife of Zeus, with whom she had Ares, Hebe, & Eileithyia. She had Hephaistos alone or with Zeus. In myth she appears most often opposing the children Zeus had by mortal & divine lovers, such as Heracles, Dionysos, Apollo, & Artemis. When Paris slighted her in favor of Aphrodite, she became a major instigator of the Trojan War & sought every chance to destroy the city. She was a protector of cities & heroes. Her major religious centers were Argos & the island of Samos: Apd. A1, B1, B4–5, D1, G1–2, G4–5, H, K1–2, K11–13, K16, K21, M2, M4, M6, M8| Bac. 5.89| Call. 5| Corn. 3| Diod. 3.56, 5.68, 5.72–73| Erat. 11| Hdr. 34| Hes. 12, 316, 330, 458, 926, 932, 960| *HH* 1, 3b, 3g, 4a, 5a, 12, 18| Hyg. 2, 30, 52, 75, 92, 102| Luc. *DG* 9, *DSG* 7, 9, 11, *Jud.*, *Sac.* 6, 10| Ov. 4.35, 12.87| Pal. 42| Paus. B, D, M| Pl. *Rep.*2| Proc. A| Ap1 6| Ap2 I.

Heracleidai (Ἡρακλεῖδαι): descendants of Heracles & Deianeira who conquered the Peloponnese: Apd. L1| Hell. 125| Thu. 1.9, 1.12.

Heracles (Ἡρακλῆς), Hercules: greatest of the heroes, deified at the end of his life. The son of Zeus by Alcmene (his mortal father was Amphitryon), he performed deeds so numerous that they are nearly impossible to catalog, although the most famous were his Twelve Labors (see Apd. M & Hyg. 30). His life was also characterized by adversity, mostly caused by Hera. His Twelve Labors, for instance, were a way to purify himself from the murder of his children by his first wife, Megara, in a fit of madness induced by Hera. His second wife, Deianeira, unwittingly poisoned him. His horrific suffering from the poison ended only when he was burned alive on a pyre, at which point he was made a god & married Hebe: And.| A.L. 4, 26, 28| Apd. B2, B4, D1, E1, F, G1–2, K1–9, K10–21, K20–21, N7| Arr.| Bab. 20| Bac. 5.57, 5.79| Call. 5| Diod. 2.46, 5.72| Erat. 11, 12| Hdr. 13, 14, 30, 34| Hdt. 2.113–20| Hes. 290, 316, 333, 529, 532, 950, 957, 990| *HH* 15| Hyg. 30, 31, 54, 69, 72, 79, 89, 102| Pal. 24, 38–40, 45| Paus. J| Proc. A| Stat. 1.260| Ver. 6e| Xen.| Ap2 J| Ap3 B.

Hermes (Ἑρμῆς), Mercury: god of heralds, travelers, thieves, & shepherds, the son of Zeus by Maia. On the day of his birth, he showed himself to be a prodigious god, inventing the lyre and stealing Apollo's cattle. His descendants inherited his cleverness

(e.g., Autolycos & Odysseus). He was the god who both protected boundaries and helped to cross them. The messenger of the gods, he was also the escort of souls to the underworld (Hermes Pyschopompos). Often known as Argeiphontes, which the ancients took to mean 'Slayer of Argos': A.L. 10, 28| Apd. D1–2, E2, G1, H, J1–2, K2, K10, K14–15, M2, M5| Bab. 117| Diod. 5.67, 5.72| Hdr. 34| Hes. 446, 945, W86, W97, W104| *HH* 2e–f, 3d, 4a–h, 5c–d, 18, 19, 29| Hor. 1.10.1, 3.11.1| Hyg. 92, 103, 106, 164| Luc. *DG* 16, *DSG* 7, 11, *Jud.*, *Sac.* 8, 11, 14| Par. 29| Paus. G, I| Pher. 11| Pl. *Prt.*| Proc. A| Ap2 D, G| Ap3 G. See also Ap1 6.

Hesione (Ἡσιόνη): daughter of King Laomedon of Troy, rescued by Heracles from a sea monster. Later, she bore Teucros to Telamon: And.| Apd. K11, K16| Hyg. 31, 89.

Hesperides (Ἑσπερίδες): daughters of Night, dwelling in the far west where the sun set, guarded the golden apples of Hera: Apd. K13| Hes. 215, 276, 520| Hyg. 30, 31.

Hesperos (Ἕσπερος): the Evening Star, brother of the Hesperides: Bab. 68| Call. 6| Hdr. 14.

Hestia (Ἑστία), Vesta: daughter of Cronos & Rhea, goddess of the hearth, an eternal virgin with little role in mythology: Apd. A1| Call. 6| Diod. 5.68| Hes. 458| *HH* 5a, 24, 29| Ver. 2e.

Hippasos (Ἵππασος): ***I*** father of Actor *II*: Apd. G1| ***II*** son of Ceyx *I*: Apd. K21| ***III*** torn apart by mother Leucippe: A.L. 10.

Hippocoon (Ἱπποκόων): son of Oibalos, he seized power from Tyndareos in Sparta. He & his twelve sons were killed by Heracles, who restored Tyndareos to his throne: Apd. K17| Hyg. 31.

Hippodameia (Ἱπποδάμεια), Hippodamia: daughter of Oinomaos, wife of Pelops, mother of Atreus & Thyestes: Apd. J1| Hell. 157| Hyg. 84, 88| Pi. 71.

Hippolyte (Ἱππολύτη): daughter of Ares, queen of the Amazons, her war-belt was Heracles' Ninth Labor: A.L. 34| Apd. K11, N7| Diod. 2.46| Hyg. 30.

Hippolytos (Ἱππόλυτος): ***I*** son of Theseus & the Amazon Antiope, his stepmother, Phaidra, fell in love with him, eventually leading to his death: Apd. N7| Hyg. 47| Ov. 4.36, 4.164| Paus. G| ***II*** father of Deiphobos *II*: Apd. K15| ***III*** Giant: Apd. D1.

Hippomedon (Ἱππομέδων): one of the Seven against Thebes: Apd. M7, M9.

Hippomenes (Ἱππομένης): father of Megareus: Apd. N2.

Hipponoos (Ἱππόνοος): father of Capaneus: Apd. M7.

Hippothoe (Ἱπποθόη): a Nereid: Apd. A2| Hes. 252.

Horai (Ὧραι), Seasons: daughters of Zeus & Themis, goddesses personifying order, stability, & prosperity (Eunomia, Dike, & Eirene): Apd. B1| Diod. 5.72–73| Hes. 906, W94| *HH* 3d, 6| Luc. *Sac.* 8| Paus. D.

Hubris (Ὕβρις): personification of Insolence: Apd. B5| Bab. 70| Crit.

Hubur: epithet of Mummu-Tiamat: Ap4 *EoC* I.133, II.19.

Hundred-Handers (Ἑκατόγχειρες): enormous sons of Ouranos & Gaia with a hundred arms & fifty heads (Cottos, Briareos, & Gyges), instrumental in the Olympians' victory over the Titans: Apd. A1–2| Hes. 150, 622, 623, 658, 717, 739, 823| Ver. 6b.

Hyacinthos (Ὑάκινθος): ***I*** beautiful youth loved by Apollo, killed by a discus either by Apollo himself or Zephyros: Apd. B3| Luc. *DG* 16, *Sac.* 4| Ap3 B| ***II*** father of the Hyacinthids: Apd. N2.

Hyades (Ὑάδες): daughters of Atlas, changed into the constellation of the same name: Apd. M2| Erat. 14.

Hydra (Ὕδρα): "Water-Snake," the multi-headed offspring of Typhon & Echidna, Heracles' Second Labor: Apd. K4, K13, K21| Hes. 314, 315| Hyg. 30| Pal. 38| Ver. 6b, 6h.

Hylas (Ὕλας): Heracles' young attendant on the voyage of the *Argo*, abducted by Nymphs: A.L. 26| Apd. G2| Ap3 B.

Hymen (Ὑμήν): the god of the wedding procession, during which the ritual cry "Hymen, O Hymenaios!" was sung: Bion| Luc. *Jud.*| Lucr. 1.97| Ov. 12.137, 12.143.

Hyperboreans (Ὑπερβόρειοι): a mythical race residing in the extreme north: Apd. B5, K13| *HH* 7| Ver. *G.*

Hyperenor (Ὑπερήνωρ): one of the Spartoi: Apd. M1.

Hyperion (Ὑπερίων): a Titan, a god of the sun: Apd. A1–2| Diod. 5.66–67| Hes. 134, 375, 1019| *HH* 2a, 3g, 28, 31.

Hypermestra (Ὑπερμήστρα): ***I*** the only daughter of Danaos not to murder her husband: Hor. 3.11 [unnamed]| ***II*** a woman who can change her sex: A.L. 17.

Hypsipyle (Ὑψιπύλη): queen of the Lemnian women, mother to two of Jason's sons, saved her father during the slaughter of all males on Lemnos: Apd. G2, M7| Hyg. 120.

Hyrieus (Ὑριεύς): father of Orion: Par. 20.

Iambe (Ἰάμβη): servant of Celeos & Metaneira who cheered Demeter: Apd. C| *HH* 2c.

Iapetos (Ἰαπετός): a Titan, father of Atlas, Menoitios, Prometheus, & Epimetheus: Apd. A1–2| Diod. 5.66–67| Hes. 19, 134, 509.

Iasion (Ἰασίων) or Iasius, Iasus: ***I*** lover of Demeter, father of Ploutos: Hes. 977| ***II*** father of Atalante: Ael. 13.1.

Icarios (Ἰκάριος): ***I*** father of Penelope: Ov. 1.81| ***II*** father of Erigone, spreads viticulture: Hyg. 130.

Icaros (Ἴκαρος): son of Daidalos who plummeted to his death because he flew too close to the Sun: Apd. K15, N6.

Idas (Ἴδας): ***I*** son of Aphareus & brother of Lynceus, participated in Calydonian Boar hunt, an Argonaut, killed Castor: Apd. F, G1| Proc. A| ***II*** son of Clymenos *IV*: Par. 13.

Idyia (Ἰδυῖα): Oceanid, wife of Aietes: Hes. 354, 966.

Igigi-gods: lesser gods of the Mesopotamian pantheon: Ap4 *Atr.* I.6–181 *passim*, I.234, III.vi.6, III.viii.16| Ap4 *EoC* II.121, III.126, V.81, VI.27, 69.

Ilion or Ilios: another name for Troy.

Inachos (Ἴναχος): a river god, father of Io: Acus. 23| Apd. H, L1| Call. 5| Hdt. 1.1–5| Luc. *DSG* 11.

Ino (Ἰνώ): daughter of Cadmos, second wife of Athamas, after death she becomes the sea goddess Leucothea: Apd. M2| Fulg. 2.12| Hes. 983| Hyg. 2| Ap2 Q.

Io (Ἰώ): a priestess of Hera, loved by Zeus, transformed into a cow, mother of Epaphos: Apd. H| Erat. 14| Hdt. 1.1–5| Pal. 42.

Iobates (Ἰοβάτης): king of Lycia: Apd. I| Hyg. 57.

Iocaste (Ἰοκάστη), Jocasta: mother & wife of Oidipous, sometimes called Epicaste: Apd. M6| Hyg. 66, 67| Par. 13| Paus. N, O.

Iolaos (Ἰόλαος): nephew of Heracles & his companion in many of his exploits: Apd. K2, K4, K15| Hes. 319| Hyg. 103| Pal. 38, 45.

Iole (Ἰόλη): daughter of Eurytos *I*, won by Heracles in an archery contest: Apd. K15, K21| Hyg. 31.

Ion (Ἴων): son of Xouthos & ruler of the Athenians, his descendants were called Ionians: Apd. E3| Con. 27.

Iphianassa (Ἰϊάνασσα): see Iphigeneia.

Iphicles (Ἰϊκλῆς): son of Amphitryon & Alcmene, twin brother of Heracles: Apd. F, K1–2, K17| Hyg. 103| Pal. 38.

Iphiclos (Ἴϊκλος): ***I*** brother of Althaia who took part in the hunt for the Calydonian Boar: Apd. F| Bac. 5.128| ***II*** son of Thestios: Apd. G1.

Iphigeneia (Ἰϊγένεια): daughter of Agamemnon & Clytaimnestra, sacrificed by her fa-

Lapiths (Λαπίθαι): a Thessalian race known for fight with Centaurs: A.L. 17| Apd. K6, K20| Pal. 1| Paus. A| Ver. 6h.

Latinos (Λατῖνος): son of Circe by Odysseus or by Telegonos: Hes. 1021.

Latona: see Leto.

Learchos (Λέαρχος): son of Ino & Athamas, killed by his father: Apd. M2| Hyg. 2.

Leda (Λήδα): daughter of Thestios & wife of Tyndareos, seduced by Zeus in the form of a swan, mother of Castor, Polydeuces, Helen, & Clytaimnestra: Apd. F| *HH* 17, 33| Hyg. 77–79| Luc. *Jud.*

Lemnian Women: women on the island of Lemnos who murdered their husbands for having taken foreign concubines, welcomed the Argonauts (see also Hypsipyle): Apd. G2, M7.

Lernaian Hydra: see Hydra.

Leto (Λητώ): daughter of Coios & Phoibe, mother of Apollo & Artemis by Zeus: A.L. 17, 28| Apd. A2, B5, M5| Bac. 5.122| Diod. 5.67| Hes. 19, 408, 923| *HH* 3a–d, 3i, 4d–h, 5c, 27| Hyg. 9| Luc. *DSG* 9| Proc. B| Ap2 N.

Leucippe (Λευκίππη): ***I*** daughter of Minyas: A.L. 10| ***II*** a nymph companion of Persephone: *HH* 2f.

Leucippos (Λεύκιππος): ***I*** name of girl raised as a boy: A.L. 17| ***II*** Apollo's companion, mortal father of Phoibe, Hilaira, & Arsinoe: *HH* 3e| Paus. G| ***III*** son of Oinomaos, wooer of Daphne: Par. 15.

Leucothea (Λευκοθέα), Leucothoe or Mater Matuta: Ino after her deification: Apd. M2| Hyg. 2. See also Ino.

Liber: see Dionysos.

Lichas (Λίχας): delivered poisoned clothes to & was killed by Heracles: Apd. K21.

Licymnios (Λικύμνιος): uncle of Heracles, father of Argeios & Melas: And.| Apd. K17, K21.

Lotophagi (Λωτοφάγοι), the Lotus-Eaters: a people visited by Odysseus who ate the lotus, a plant that made men lose their memory: Herac. 70.

Love: see Eros.

Lycaon (Λυκάων): ***I*** Arcadian king, father of Callisto, turned into a wolf: Paus. J| ***II*** son of Priam, sold into slavery by Patroclos: Proc. A.

Lycomedes (Λυκομήδης): king of Scyros: Hyg. 96| Proc. A| Stat. 1.850 [unnamed].

Lycos (Λύκος): ***I*** king of Thebes, father or uncle of Antiope: Apd. M5| Proc. A, perhaps the same as| ***II*** king of Thebes who tried to kill Heracles' wife & children: Hyg. 31| ***III*** king of the Mariandynoi visited by Argonauts, Heracles: Apd. G2, K11.

Lycourgos (Λυκοῦργος), Lycurgus: ***I*** father of Ancaios & Cepheus: Apd. F, G1| ***II*** king of Thrace, opposed Dionysos: Apd. M4| Hor. 2.19.16| Paus. B| ***III*** king of Nemea whom Hypsipyle served: Apd. M7.

Lynceus (Λυγκεύς): son of Aphareus, brother of Idas, participated in Calydonian Boar hunt & expedition of Argonauts: Apd. F, G1| Proc. A.

Lysianassa (Λυσιάνασσα): ***I*** daughter of Epaphos, mother of Bousiris: Apd. K13| ***II*** a Nereid: Apd. A2| Hes. 259.

Machaon (Μαχάων): son of Asclepios, healer who fought in Trojan war: Hyg. 108| Paus. G| Proc. C| Ver. 2d.

Maia (Μαῖα): daughter of Atlas, mother of Hermes, sometimes included in the Pleiades: Hes. 944| *HH* 4a–d, 4f, 4h, 18, 29.

Mainads (Μαινάδες): "Maddened Women," female worshipers of Dionysos (see also Bacchai): Apd. B2| Corn. 30| *HH* 2e| Ap2 Q.

Mami (see also Nintu): Mesopotamian mother goddess: Ap4 *Atr.* I.193, I.235–247, 296, III.iii.33.

Marathonian Bull: one of Theseus' exploits: Apd. K9, N2, N4.

Marduk: chief god of Babylon: Ap4 *EoC* II.126–VI.120 *passim.*

Mares of Diomedes: Heracles' Eighth Labor: Apd. K10| Hyg. 30.

Mars: see Ares.

Marsyas (Μαρσύας): a Satyr who found the double-flute invented by Athena, lost to Apollo in musical contest & was flayed alive: Apd. B5.

Mater Matuta: see Leucothea.

Mavors: (= Mars) see Ares.

Medeia (Μήδεια), Medea: daughter of Aietes, wife of Jason, a sorceress. She helped Jason get the Golden Fleece and, according to some, killed her brother Apsyrtos. She convinced the daughters of Pelias to kill their father. Later when Jason abandoned her, she killed their two sons along with Jason's new wife & father-in-law: Ael. 5.21| Apd. G1, G3–5, N4| Hdt. 1.1–5| Hes. 968, 1000| Hyg. 3| Ov. 12 *passim*| Pal. 43| Paus. C.

Medeios (Μήδειος) or Medos: Medeia's son by Jason: Apd. G5| Hes. 1009| Paus. C.

Medon (Μέδων): ***I*** son of Codros: Hell. 125| ***II*** suitor in Odysseus' palace: Ovid 1.91| ***III*** fallen Trojan warrior: Ver. 6f.

Medos: see Medeios.

Medousa (Μέδουσα), Medusa: the mortal Gorgon, killed by Perseus, mother of Pegasos & Chrysaor: Apd. I–J2, K14| Hes. 277| Paus. G| Pher. 11.

Megaira (Μέγαιρα): one of the Erinyes: Apd. A1| Ap3 D.

Megara (Μέγαρα): ***I*** wife of Heracles, killed by him in a fit of madness: Apd. K2, K15| Hyg. 31, 72| ***II*** city captured by Minos: Apd. N2| Paus. L.

Megareus (Μεγαρεύς): son of Hippomenes, killed by Minos: Apd. N2.

Melanippe (Μελανίππη): ***I*** daughter of Aiolos, loved by Posedion: Eur. 660| ***II*** daughter of Oineus: A.L. 2| ***III*** an Amazon captured by Theseus: Apd. N7.

Melanippos (Μελάνιππος): ***I*** a Theban, fought against the Seven against Thebes: Apd. M9| ***II*** brother of Tydeus: Hyg. 69.

Melanthios (Μελάνθιος): goatherd of Odysseus, sided with suitors: Ov. 1.96.

Melas (Μέλας): ***I*** son of Licymnios, fought beside Heracles: Apd. K21| ***II*** Phrixos' son: Hyg. 3| ***III*** a place: Apd. G4.

Meleagros (Μελέαγρος), Meleager: son of Oineus or Ares by Althaia, he was the hero who killed the Calydonian Boar. Destined at his birth to live only as long as a log in the fire lasted, his mother eventually burned it in revenge for his killing her brothers, although his death is told differently in Homer's *Iliad*: A.L. 2| Apd. F, G1, K14| Bac. 5.77, 5.93, 5.171| Luc. *Sac.* 1| Ov. 3.92, 4.99| Ap3 C.

Melicertes (Μελικέρτης): younger son of Ino & Athamas, became sea god Palaimon: Apd. M2| Hyg. 2.

Melpomene (Μελπομένη): a Muse: Apd. B1, B3| Hes. 78.

Memnon (Μέμνων): son of Eos & Tithonos, Ethiopian ally of Troy, killed by Achilles: Hes. 992| Proc. B.

Menelaos (Μενέλαος): Atreus' son, Agamemnon's brother, Helen's husband: Hdt. 2.113–20| Hyg. 78, 88, 92, 95, 98, 107, 108, 116, 118| Luc. *Jud.*| Paus. D, H| Proc. A, C–E| Ver. 2c–d, 2g–h, 6g| Ap3 A.

Menoe-: see Menoi-

Menoiceus (Μενοικεύς): ***I*** father of Creon *II* & Iocaste: Apd. K2, M6| Hyg. 66, 67, 72| ***II*** son of Creon *II*: Apd. M8| Hyg. 68.

Menoites (Μενοίτης): ***I*** herdsman of Hades' cattle, killed by Heracles: Apd. K12| ***II*** challenged Heracles to wrestle in underworld: Apd. K14| ***III*** servant of Laios who exposed Oidipous: Hyg. 67.

Menoitios (Μενοίτιος): ***I*** son of Actor, father of Patroclos: Apd. G1| Hell. 145| Ov. 1.17, 3.23| ***II*** son of Iapetos: Apd. A2| Hes. 512, 516.

Mercury: see Hermes.

Mermeros (Μέρμερος): son of Jason & Medeia, killed by mother: Apd. G5| Paus. C.

Merope (Μερόπη): daughter of Oinopion: Apd. B5.

Metaneira (Μετάνειρα): wife of Celeos, mother of Demophon: Apd. C| *HH* 2b–c.

Metis (Μῆτις): daughter of Oceanos &

Tethys, personification of Intelligence and Resourcefulness, impregnated & then swallowed by Zeus; from this union Athena was born: Apd. A2, B4| Corn. 20| Hes. 360, 891, 899.

Minos (Μίνως): son of Zeus & Europa, king of Crete: Aes. 99| A.L. 41| Apd. G4, K9, K11, L1–2, N2–3, N5–7| Bac. 17.8, 17.50, 17.69, 17.121| Eur. 473| Hes. 955| Hyg. 47, 136| Ov. 4.61, 4.157, 10.91| Pal. 2| Paus. A| Thu. 1.4, 1.8| Ver. 6f.

Minotaur (Μινώταυρος): half-man, half-bull offspring of Pasiphae & the bull sent by Poseidon: Apd. L2, N2, N5| Ov. 4.58| Pal. 2.

Mnemosyne (Μνημοσύνη): a Titaness, the personification of Memory, by Zeus the mother of the Muses: Apd. A1, B1| Diod. 5.66–67| Hes. 54, 135, 920| *HH* 4h.

Moirai (Μοῖραι), Parcae, Fates: "Apportioners," the collective name for Clotho, Lachesis, & Atropos, the daughters of Zeus & Themis (although Hesiod also names Night as their begetter) who determined one's destiny at birth: A.L. 2| Apd. B1, D2, F| Bac. 17.24, 17.89| Bion| Call. 5| Eur. 660| Hes. 217, 909| *HH* 2c| Ov. 1.101| Paus. K| Pl. *Rep.*10| Stat. 1.255| Ver. 2a, *G*| Ap3 D.

Moon: see Selene.

Mother Goddess: see Cybele.

Mousaios (Μουσαῖος): ***I*** Cretan Giant who defected to the side of Zeus & received honors: Diod. 5.71, perhaps the same as| ***II*** famous singer/seer: Ver. 6i.

Mulciber: see Hephaistos.

Mummu: vizier of Apsu: Ap4 *EoC* I.30–78, 118.

Musaeus: see Mousaios.

Muses (Μοῦσαι, strictly Mousai): daughters of Mnemosyne & Zeus, goddesses of art & poetry: Apd. B1, B3, M6| Bac. 5.4, 5.193| Diod. 5.72| Erat. 28| Hes. 1, 26, 35, 37, 52, 76, 94, 96, 98, 101, 114, 921, 972, 1029, W1| *HH* 3d, 3i, 4a, 4h, 5a, 9, 14, 17, 19, 20, 25, 27, 32, 33| Long. 3.23| Luc. *DSG* 7, *Sac.* 5| Pi. 112| Proc. B| Theoc.

Mygdon (Μύγδων): ***I*** king of the Bebryces: Apd. K11| ***II*** father of Coroebus: Ver. 2f.

Myrtilos (Μυρτίλος): the charioteer of Oinomaos bribed by Pelops to rig his master's chariot to misfunction during race, later thrown into the sea by Pelops: Hyg. 84| Paus. E.

NAM.ḪE: see Teshub.

Namtar: Sumerian god of pestilence: Ap4 *Atr.* I.380–407.

Napšara: primeval Hittite god: Ap4 *SoE* 1, 10.

Nara: primeval Hittite god: Ap4 *SoE* 1, 10.

Nauplios (Ναύπλιος): ***I*** son of Poseidon by Amymone: Apd. K18| Pher. 10| ***II*** (not always distinguished from ***I***) father of Palamedes: Hyg. 116| Soph. 432.

Nausithoos (Ναυσίθοος): Odysseus' son either by Calypso or Circe: Hes. 1026.

Nebula: see Nephele.

Neleus (Νηλεύς): son of Poseidon & Tyro, twin brother of Pelias: Apd. G1, K15, K17, M5| Hell. 125| Hyg. 31 [called son of Hippocoon]| Par. 13.

Nemean Lion: Heracles' First Labor: Apd. K3| Hes. 329| Hyg. 30.

Nemesis (Νέμεσις): daughter of Night, personification of Retribution: Call. 6| Hes. 223, W233.

Neoptolemos (Νεοπτόλεμος): son of Achilles & Deidameia, fights at Troy after the death of his father, also called Pyrrhos because of his red hair: Hyg. 96, 108| Ov. 3.136| Proc. C–E| Ver. 2d, 2h, 2i.

Nephele (Νεφέλη): ***I*** first wife of Athamas, mother of Phrixos & Helle: Erat. 19| Hyg. 2–3 [called Nebula]| ***II*** mother of the Centaurs by Ixion: Pal. 1.

Nephilim: descendants of sons of God and the daughters of humans, heroes of old: Ap4 *Gen.* 6.

Neptune: see Poseidon.

Nereids (Νηρηΐδες): sea goddesses, daughters of Nereus & Doris. Names are given at Apd. A2| Hes. 240–265.

Nereus (Νηρεύς): shape-shifting sea god, offspring of Pontos & Gaia, father of Nereids by Doris: Apd. A2, K13, M4| Hes. 233, 240, 264, 1011| *HH* 3g| Ov. 3.74.

Nessos (Νέσσος): ***I*** Centaur who attempted to rape Heracles' wife Deianeira as he carried her across a river: Apd. K6, K19, K21| Hyg. 31| ***II*** a river: Hes. 343.

Nestor (Νέστωρ): youngest son of Neleus & Chloris, survived Heracles' sack of Pylos & took part in the Trojan War: Ov. 1.37, 1.63| Proc. A, E. See also Ap1 8, 9.

Nicothoe: see Aello.

Night (Greek Nyx, Νύξ): daughter of Chaos, mother of many abstract forces: Call. 5| Hes. 21, 108, 123, 124, 177, 211, 213, 223, 276, 731, 749, 753, 762, 763, W29| *HH* 4c| Ver. 6a| Ap3 D.

Nike (Νίκη): personification of Victory, the offspring of Pallas & Styx: Apd. A2| Bac. 5.33| Hes. 385| *HH* 8| Ov. 10.105.

Nintu: Mesopotamian goddess of birth, also called Mami and Belet-ili: Ap4 *Atr.* I.198, 210, 225, 278, 295, III.iii.28, III.iv.4, 14; III.v.39, III.vi.43, 46.

Ninurta: Mesopotamian god of hunting and war: Ap4 *Atr.* I.9, 126, 138, II.vii.52| Ap4 *Gilg.* 17, 105, 179.

Niobe (Νιόβη): ***I*** daughter of Tantalos, wife of Theban Amphion, whose children were killed by Apollo & Artemis because she offended Leto: Apd. M5| Hyg. 9| Paus. J| Pl. *Rep.*2| ***II*** daughter of Phoroneus, first mortal with whom Zeus slept: Acus. 23.

Nisos (Νῖσος): son of either Ares or Pandion (called Deion in Hyg.), ruler of Megara, betrayed by daughter Scylla: Apd. N2| Luc. *Sac.* 15.

Noah: survivor of flood in *Genesis*: Ap4 *Gen.* 5–9.

North Wind: see Boreas.

Notos (Νότος): the South Wind: Hes. 381, 876| Luc. *DSG* 11| Ov. 3.58, 10.30| Ver. 2g, 6c–d.

Nudimmud: see Ea.

Nusku: Enlil's vizier: Ap4 *Atr.* I.76, 78, 116, 120, 132, 153.

Nycteus (Νυκτεύς): king of Thebes, father of Antiope: Apd. M5.

Nymphs (Νύμφαι): female spirits of nature.

Ocean: see Oceanos.

Oceanids (Ὠκεανίδες): daughters of Oceanos & Tethys, minor sea or river goddesses. Their names are given at Apd. A2 & Hes. 351–363.

Oceanos (Ὠκεανός): the eldest Titan, the personification of the river that ran around the known world, father of rivers & Oceanids: Apd. A1–B1, C, G3, J1, K12| Call. 5| Diod. 3.56, 5.66| Hes. 21, 133, 216, 241, 266, 275, 283, 289, 293, 295, 339, 364, 366, 369, 384, 390, 509, 698, 782, 795, 797, 822, 848, 912, 967, 987, W192| *HH* 2a, 4c, 4e, 5d, 32| Pher. 11| Ver. 2d.

Ocypete (Ὠκυπέτη) or Ocypode or Ocythoe: a Harpy: Apd. A2, G2| Hes. 268.

Odysseus (Ὀδυσσεύς), Ulysses (Ulixes): son of Laertes, husband of Penelope, father of Telemachos (among others). Hero noted for his cleverness and eloquence, he wandered for ten years after the Trojan War: Apd. B3| Con. 34| Herac. 5, 70| Hes. 1020, 1025| Hyg. 78, 95–98, 102, 105, 107, 108, 111, 116| Luc. *DD* 23, *DSG* 2| Ov. 1 *passim*, 3.29, 3.129| Par. 2, 3, 12| Pl. *Rep.*10| Proc. A–F| Stat. 1.847, 1.866| Ver. 2a–d, 2h, 6g.

Oe-: see Oi-

Oiagros (Οἴαγρος): father of singers Orpheus, Linos, & (sometimes) Marsyas: Apd. B2, G1| Diod. 4.25.

Oibalos (Οἴβαλος): king of Sparta, father of Hyacinthos & Tyndareos: Hyg. 78| Luc. *DG* 16.

Oicles (Οἰκλῆς): father of Amphiaraos, accompanied Heracles against Troy: Apd. F, G1, K16, M7| Paus. J.

Oidipous (Οἰδίπους), Oedipus: son of Laios & Iocaste, exposed at birth, fated to kill his

father & marry his mother. After answering the riddle of the Sphinx, he became king of Thebes, marrying his mother & fathering sons, Eteocles & Polyneices, & daughters, Antigone & Ismene: Apd. M6, M9| Hes. W185| Hyg. 66–69| Pal. 4| Paus. N, O.

Oineus (Οἰνεύς), Oeneus: king of Calydon, mortal father of Meleagros & Deianeira by Althaia, father of Tydeus by Periboia. When he omitted Artemis in a sacrifice, she sent a giant boar to ravage Calydon: A.L. 2| Apd. F, G1, K19, M7| Bac. 5.98, 5.119, 5.166| Hyg. 69| Luc. *Sac.* 1| Ov. 3.92, 4.99| Soph. 1130.

Oinomaos (Οἰνόμαος), Oenomaus: king of Pisa, father of Hippodameia, lost a chariot race to Pelops: Apd. J1| Hell. 157| Hyg. 84| Par. 15| Pi. 77, 88.

Oinone (Οἰνώνη): Paris' lover before Helen: Luc. *Jud.*| Par. 4.

Oinopion (Οἰνοπίων): son of Dionysos & Ariadne whose daughter (either Leiro or Merope) was desired by Orion: Apd. B5, N5| Par. 20.

Olympos (Ὄλυμπος): highest mountain in Greece, traditionally home of the Olympian gods.

Omphale (Ὀμφάλη): queen of the Lydians whom Heracles served for three years after murdering Iphitos: Apd. G2, K15| Stat. 1.260 [unnamed].

Opheltes (Ὀφέλτης): son of Lycourgos, also called Archemoros, consumed by a serpent. The Nemean Games were held in his honor: Apd. M7.

Opis: see Rhea.

Orchomenos (Ὀρχομενός): *I* son of Themisto & Athamas, father of Minyas: A.L. 10| Apd. B5| *II* a place: Apd. K2.

Orcus: see Hades.

Oreithyia (Ὠρείθυια), Orithyia: *I* daughter of King Erechtheus of Athens, abducted by Boreas, mother of Zetes & Calais: Ver. *G*| *II* a nymph: A.L. 34.

Orestes (Ὀρέστης): *I* son of Agamemnon & Clytaimnestra, killed mother for her role in father's death: Hyg. 117, 119–120| Paus. D| Proc. E| *II* a descendant of Deucalion: Apd. E3.

Orion (Ὠρίων): giant son of Poseidon or Hyrieus, blinded by Oinopion, attempted to rape Artemis: Apd. B5| Erat. 7| Par. 20.

Orithyia: see Oreithyia.

Orpheus (Ὀρφεύς): son of Oiagros & the Muse Calliope, a magical singer, an Argonaut, tried to retrieve his wife Eurydice from the underworld: Apd. B2, G1, G4, K2| Diod. 4.25| Hor. 3.11.13| Pal. 33| Pl. *Rep.*10| Thph.| Ver. 6i, *G*.

Orthos (Ὄρθος): offspring of Echidna & Typhon, the two-headed dog of Geryones: Apd. K12| Hes. 294, 310, 328| Pal. 39.

Otos (Ὦτος): one of Aloeus' giant sons who attacked Olympos: Hyg. 28| Pl. *Symp.*| Ver. 6h.

Ourania (Οὐρανία): *I* a Muse: Apd. B1| Bac. 5.14| Hes. 79| *II* an Oceanid: Hes. 352| *HH* 2f.

Ouranos (Οὐρανός), Uranus: the personification of Sky, son & husband of Gaia, castrated & deposed by youngest son Cronos: Aes. 193| Apd. B1, D1| Diod. 3.56, 5.66, 5.71| Hell. 88| Hes. 46, 107, 126, 133, 148, 156, 159, 177, 207, 424, 467, 474, 489, 503, 621, 649, 706, 742, 847, 896| *HH* 3b, 3g, 30, 31| Luc. *Sac.* 5| Pl. *Rep.* 2.

Palaimon (Παλαίμων), Palaemon: *I* divine name of Melicertes: Apd. M2| Hyg. 2| *II* son of Hephaistos, an Argonaut: Apd. G1.

Palamedes (Παλαμήδης): son of Nauplios *II*, discovered Odysseus' ploy to escape Trojan War, later undone by Odysseus' plot: Hyg. 95, 105, 116, 117| Proc. A| Soph. 432| Ver. 2c.

Palladion (Παλλάδιον), Palladium: a statue of Pallas Athena that protected Troy: Con. 34| Proc. C| Ver. 2c.

Pallas (Παλλάς): *I* a title of Athena: Bac. 5.92| Call. 5| Hes. 579, W96| *HH* 2f, 11, 28| Hyg. 116| Stat. 1.824| *II* (Πάλλας)

Giant whom Athena slew & whose skin she stripped off & used to cover her own body: Apd. D1| ***III*** son of Creios, husband of Styx, father of Nike: Apd. A2| Hes. 377, 384| *HH* 4c [where father is called Megamedes]| ***IV*** son of Pandion, who with his fifty sons rebelled against Theseus: Apd. N5.

Pan (Πάν): Arcadian god of pastures & the countryside, son of Hermes & Dryops (or Zeus & Hubris): Apd. B5| *HH* 19| Long. 2.34, 3.23| Luc. *Sac.* 14| Ov. 4.171 [plural]| Paus. K.

Pandion (Πανδίων): ***I*** early king of Athens| ***II*** a later king of Athens, father of Aigeus, Nisos, & Procris, grandfather of Theseus: Apd. N2| Bac. 17.15| Pal. 2| ***III*** father of Lampros: A.L. 17.

Pandora (Πανδώρα): ***I*** first woman fashioned by Hephaistos out of clay, married to Epimetheus: Apd. E2| Hes. 574 [unnamed], W101| Luc. *DG* 5 [unnamed]| Pal. 34| ***II*** a mistake for Pandrosos, daughter of Cecrops: Fulg. 2.11.

Panope (Πανόπη), a Nereid: Apd. A2| Hes. 251| Luc. *DSG* 7.

Parcae: see Moirai.

Paris (Πάρις) or Alexander: son of Priam & Hecabe. Because his mother dreamed she gave birth to a torch, he was abandoned on Mount Ida and raised by shepherds. He later returned to Troy, where he regained his position as prince. He then seduced Helen, thus beginning the Trojan War, in which he killed Achilles & was subsequently killed by Philoctetes. He is known variously as Paris, Alexander, or Paris Alexander: Acus. 39| Call. 5| Con. 34| Hdt. 1.1–5| 2.113–120| Hyg. 91, 92, 98, 107, 110| Luc. *DSG* 7, *Jud.*| Par. 4| Proc. A–C| Sall.

Parthenopaios (Παρθενοπαῖος): son of Meleagros (or Melanion) & Atalante, one of the Seven against Thebes: Apd. M7, M9–10| Ver. 6f.

Pasiphae (Πασιφάη): daughter of Helios, wife of Minos who slept with a bull and gave birth to the Minotaur: A.L. 41| Apd. L1–2| Eur. 473| Hyg. 30, 136| Ov. 4.57| Pal. 2| Ver. 6f.

Patroclos (Πάτροκλος): son of Menoitios, accompanied Achilles in the Trojan War: Hell. 145| Hyg. 106| Ov. 1.17, 3.23| Proc. A.

Peace: see Eirene.

Pegasos (Πήγασος): winged horse, offspring of Medousa & Poseidon, captured by Bellerophontes: Apd. I–J1| Hes. 282, 285, 326| Hyg. 57| Pal. 28.

Peirithous (Πειρίθους): son of Zeus & Ixion's wife Dia, companion of Theseus: Apd. F, K14| Hyg. 79| Luc. *DG* 9| Ov. 4.110, 4.112| Ver. 6e, 6h.

Peitho (Πειθώ): ***I*** the personification of Persuasion: Aes. 161| Hes. W93| ***II*** an Oceanid: Hes. 351.

Peleus (Πηλεύς): son of Aiacos, father of Achilles by Thetis: Apd. F, G1| Hell. 145| Hes. 1014| Hyg. 54, 92, 96| Luc. *DSG* 7| Ov. 3.135| Proc. A, E| Stat. 1.823, 1.884| Ver. 2i| Ap3 B.

Pelias (Πελίας): son of Tyro by Poseidon, twin brother of Neleus, half-brother of Aison & thus uncle of Jason, killed by his daughters: Apd. G1, G3, G5| Hes. 1004| Ov. 12.129| Pal. 40, 43| Paus. C| Ver. 2h.

Pelopeia (Πελόπεια): ***I*** daughter of Thyestes, mother of Aigisthos by her own father: Hyg. 88| ***II*** mother of Cycnos by Ares: Apd. K20| ***III*** daughter of Niobe & Amphion: Apd. M5.

Pelops (Πέλοψ): son of Tantalos, who served him to the gods; gave his name to the Peloponnese ("Island of Pelops"), father of Atreus, Thyestes, & Chrysippos: Apd. K17, M5, N1, N4| Bac. 5.181| Hell. 157| Hyg. 82–84, 88| Luc. *Jud.*| Paus. E| Pi. 24, 95| Pl. *Rep.* 2| Thu. 1.9| Ver. 2c.

Pemphredo (Πεμφρηδώ) or Pephredo: one of the Graiai.

Penelope (Πηνελόπη): wife of Odysseus: Ov. 1.1, 1.84| Par. 3| Proc. F.

Penthesileia (Πενθεσίλεια): an Amazon,

daughter of Ares & Otrera, ally of the Trojans, killed by Achilles: Diod. 2.46| Proc. B.

Pentheus (Πενθεύς): son of Echion & Agaue, he rejected Dionysos & was torn apart by his mother: Apd. M4–5| Hor. 2.19.14| Paus. B| Stat. 1.839.

Periboia (Περίβοια), Periboea: ***I*** wife of Polybos *I*, adoptive mother of Oidipous: Apd. M6| Hyg. 66, 67| ***II*** mother of Tydeus by Oineus: Hyg. 69| ***III*** another name for Eriboia, the Athenian captive girl desired by Minos: Bac. 17.14| Paus. A.

Periclymenos (Περικλύμενος): ***I*** son of Neleus, an Argonaut, according to some accounts killed by Heracles: Apd. G1, K17| Hell. 125| ***II*** son of Poseidon & Chloris who killed Parthenopaios in the siege of the Seven against Thebes: Apd. M9.

Periphas (Περίφας): ***I*** brother of Meleagros: A.L. 2| ***II*** Greek fighting with Neoptolemos: Ver. 2h| ***III*** pious Athenian: A.L. 6.

Periphetes (Περιφήτης): also called Corynetes ("Clubber"), a brigand killed by Theseus: Apd. N4.

Persaios: See Perses *I*.

Perseis (Περσηίς): Oceanid wife of Helios, mother of Aietes, Circe, & Pasiphae: Apd. L1| Hes. 358, 964.

Persephone (Περσεφόνη) or Kore, Proserpina: daughter of Demeter & Zeus, abducted by Hades & became queen of the underworld: Apd. B1, C, K14| Bac. 5.59| Bion| Diod. 4.25, 5.68–69| Hes. 773, 780, 918| *HH* 2a, 2e–g, 13| Hyg. 79| Paus. F, K| Ver. 6a, 6e, *G*| Ap2 G| Ap3 D.

Perses (Πέρσης): ***I*** son of Creios & Eurybia, father of Hecate: Apd. A2| Hes. 378, 411| *HH* 2a [Persaios]| ***II*** brother of Aietes: Apd. G5| ***III*** son of Perseus, the eponymous ancestor of the Persians: Apd. J2| ***IV*** name of the poet Hesiod's brother: Hes. W19, W42.

Perseus (Περσεύς): son of Zeus by Danae, he slew the Gorgon Medousa. When Danae's father, Acrisios, learned that a grandson would kill him, he first locked Danae away in a chamber, but she was impregnated by Zeus in the form of golden rain. Acrisios then set Danae & her baby afloat in a chest, but they were rescued by Dictys on Seriphos. Polydectes sent Perseus to get Medousa's head, a task he accomplished with the assistance provided by Athena & Hermes. He rescued Andromeda. He eventually killed Acrisios accidentally: Apd. A2, J1–2| Con. 40| Hes. 281| Pal. 38| Paus. G| Pher. 10–12| Sim. 6| Thu. 1.9| Ap3 C.

Persuasion: see Peitho.

Phaedra: see Phaidra.

Phaethon (Φαέθων): either son of Eos & Cephalos, or of Helios & Clymene *II* (or Merope). He asked to drive the chariot of the Sun, to his undoing: Hes. 995.

Phaidra (Φαίδρα): daughter of Minos & Pasiphae, married to Theseus, attracted to her stepson Hippolytos: Apd. L1–2, N7| Hyg. 47| Ov. 4 *passim*| Ver. 6f.

Pheres (Φέρης): ***I*** father of Admetos: Apd. F–G1| ***II*** son of Jason: Apd. G5| Paus. C.

Philammon (Φιλάμμων): son of Apollo & Chione, father of Thamyris: Apd. B3.

Philoctetes (Φιλοκτήτης): son of Poias, keeper of Heracles' bow, one of Helen's suitors. He was left on the island of Lemnos after being bitten by a snake but was brought back to Troy when it was revealed that the bow was necessary to take the city: Hyg. 102| Par. 4| Proc. A, C| Thu. 1.10.

Philomela: see Procne.

Philyra (Φιλύρα): Oceanid, the mother of the Centaur Cheiron by Cronos, turned into a linden tree: Apd. A2.

Phineus (Φινεύς): ***I*** blind king of Thrace with the power of divination, plagued by the Harpies: Apd. G2| ***II*** brother of Cepheus *III*, fiancé of his niece Andromeda, turned to stone by Perseus: Apd. J2| Con. 40.

Phlegyas (Φλεγύας): son of Ares, father of Coronis: Apd. M5| *HH* 16| Paus. G| Ver. 6h.

Phoe-: see Phoi-

Phoibe (Φοίβη), Phoebe: a Titaness, mother of Leto: Apd. A1–2| Diod. 5.66–67| Hes. 136, 406.

Phoibos (Φοῖβος), Phoebus: epithet ("Shining") of Apollo or Helios.

Phoinix (Φοῖνιξ): ***I*** son of Agenor, brother (or father) of Europa, the eponymous ancestor of the Phoenicians: Apd. L1| Bac. 17.30| Con. 37, 40| Pal. 15| ***II*** advisor to Achilles: Ov. 3.27, 3.129| Proc. E.

Phorbas (Φόρβας): ***I*** father of Augeias: Apd. K7| ***II*** son of Triopas: *HH* 3e.

Phorcides: see Graiai.

Phorcos (Φόρκος) or Phorcys: son of Gaia & Pontos, had many children by Ceto, including the Graiai: Apd. A2, J1| Hdr. 30| Hes. 238, 271, 334, 338| Pher. 11.

Phoroneus (Φορωνεύς): son of the river god Inachos, the first mortal, father of Niobe *II*| Acis. 23.

Phrixos (Φρίξος): son of Athamas & Nephele, escaped from his stepmother's plot with his sister, Helle, on a golden ram & went to Colchis: Apd. G1–2| Erat. 14, 19| Hyg. 2–3| Ov. 12.8| Pal. 30.

Pirithous: see Peirithous.

Pittheus (Πιτθεύς): son of Pelops & Hippodameia, king of Troizen, father of Aithra: Apd. N1| Bac. 17.37| Hyg. 79| Ov. 4.105, 10.111| Plut.

Pityocamptes: see Sinis.

Pleiades (Πλειάδες): seven daughters of Atlas & Pleione who became the constellation by the same name: Erat. 14.

Plouto (Πλουτώ): ***I*** Oceanid, companion to Persephone: Hes. 357| *HH* 2f| ***II*** mother of Tantalos: A.L. 36| Hyg. 82.

Plouton: see Hades.

Ploutos (Πλοῦτος): son of Demeter & Iasion, the personification of Wealth: Hes. 976| *HH* 2g.

Pluto: see Hades.

Podarces (Ποδάρκης): see Priam.

Poias (Ποίας), Poeas: father of Philoctetes, an Argonaut: Apd. G1, G4, K21| Hyg. 102.

Pollux: = Polydeuces, see Dioscouroi.

Polybos (Πόλυβος): ***I*** king of Corinth who raised Oidipous: Apd. M6| Hyg. 66, 67| ***II*** a suitor of Penelope: Ov. 1.91.

Polydectes (Πολυδέκτης): king of Seriphos who wooed Danae & sent her son, Perseus, after Medousa: Apd. J1–2| Pher. 10–12.

Polydeuces (Πολυδεύκης), Pollux: see Dioscouroi.

Polydoros (Πολύδωρος): son or son-in-law of Cadmos, king of Thebes: Apd. M2, M5| Hes. 986.

Polymnia (Πολυμνία) or Polyhymnia: a Muse: Apd. B1| Hes. 79.

Polyneices (Πολυνείκης), Polynices: son of Oidipous, brother of Eteocles, his rivalry with his brother led to the Seven against Thebes: Apd. M6–7, M9–10| Proc. A| Hyg. 67–69, 72.

Polypemon: see Procrustes.

Polyphemos (Πολύφημος): ***I*** the Cyclops tricked by Odysseus (see Cyclopes *II*), loved Galateia: Hell. 88| Luc. *DSG* 2| Theoc.| ***II*** an Argonaut, sent to look for Hylas & left behind: A.L. 26| Apd. G1–G2.

Polyphontes (Πολυφόντης): herald of Laios: Apd. M6.

Polyxena (Πολυξένη, strictly Polyxene): daughter of Priam & Hecabe, sacrificed at Achilles' grave after Troy fell: Hyg. 110| Proc. D.

Polyxo (Πολυξώ): Actorion's mother: Call. 6.

Pontos (Πόντος): son of Gaia, personification of the Sea: Apd. A2| Hes. 108, 131, 233, 237.

Porthaon (Πορθάων) or Portheus: father of Oineus, grandfather of Meleagros: A.L. 2| Bac. 5.69.

Poseidon (Ποσειδῶν), Neptune: god of the sea, horses, & earthquakes, the son of Cronos & Rhea. Although he was married to Amphitrite, he had many other children, some quite violent, by women both mortal & divine. He was sometimes regarded as

the father of Theseus & was the ancestor of many other heroes such as Danaos & the kings of Thebes. In the Trojan War he vigorously opposed the Trojans & later greatly hindered Odysseus' return home. He competed with Athena to be the patron god of Athens but lost: A.L. 17| Apd. A1–2, B5, D1, G1–2, G5, I–J2, K2, K6–7, K9, K11–13, K16–18, L1–2, M9, N1, N4, N7| Bac. 17.35, 17.60, 17.78| Call. 6| Diod. 5.68–69| Erat. 19| Eur. 473| Hell. 125| Herac. 56, 69| Hdr. 34| Hes. 16, 279, 443, 460, 737, 824, 935| *HH* 3e, 5a, 7, 22| Hyg. 3, 28, 31, 47, 89, 135, 164| Luc. *DSG* 2, 7, 9, *Sac.* 4, 11| Lucr. 2.655| Ov. 3.151, 4.109| Paus. A, H, K| Pher. 10| Pi. 26, 76| Proc. A| Ver. 2d| Ap1 2, 3, 5, 6| Ap2 C.

Priam (Πρίαμος, strictly Priamos): youngest of Laomedon's sons, originally named Podarces; king of Troy during the Trojan War. With Hecabe he had Hector, Paris, Cassandra, & other children, along with many other children by other women: Acus. 39| Apd. K16| Con. 34| Hdt. 1.1–5, 2.113–120| Hor. 1.10.13| Hyg. 89, 91, 93, 105, 106, 108, 110–111| Luc. *DSG* 7, *Jud.*| Ov. 1.4, 1.34, 3.20| Par. 4| Paus. F| Proc. D| Ver. 2a–c, 2e–i, 6g.

Procne (Πρόκνη): daughter of Pandion, she was married to Tereus & after he raped her sister Philomela, served her son Itys to him as dinner. In some accounts the names of the sisters are switched: Soph. 583.

Procris (Πρόκρις): daughter of Erechtheus (or Pandion), wife of Cephalos: A.L. 41| Pal. 2| Ver. 6f.

Procrustes (Προκρούστης): also called Damastes or Polypemon, a bandit who fit all strangers to a bed; killed by Theseus: Apd. N4.

Proitos (Προῖτος), Proetus: king of Tiryns who hosted Bellerophontes: Apd. I, J1–2| Hyg. 57.

Prometheus (Προμηθεύς): son of Iapetos, humanity's benefactor & sometimes its creator: Apd. A2, B4, E1–2, K6, K13| Diod. 5.67| Hdr. 30| Hes. 512, 523, 530, 536, 538, 545, 548, 552, 561, 567, 618, W66, W69, W72, W106| Hyg. 31, 54| Luc. *DG* 5, *Sac.* 5–7| Pl. *Prt.*

Proserpina: see Persephone.

Protesilaos (Πρωτεσίλαος): son of Iphiclos & Diomedeia, originally named Iolaos, he earned his name ("First of the Army") when he was the first of the Greeks to disembark at Troy: Hyg. 103, 104| Proc. A.

Proteus (Πρωτεύς): ***I*** shape-shifting sea god, herdsman of Poseidon's flocks: Apd. K11| Luc. *Sac.* 5, perhaps the same as| ***II*** the king of Egypt at the time of the Trojan War: Apd. M4| Hdt. 2.113–120| Hyg. 118| Ver. *G.*

Protogeneia (Πρωτογένεια): lover of Zeus, mother of Aethlios: Apd. E3.

Psamathe (Ψαμάθη): Nereid & mother of Aiacos: Apd. A2| Hes. 261, 1012.

Pylades (Πυλάδης): close friend of Orestes: Hyg. 119, 120| Proc. E.

Pyrrha (Πύρρα): daughter of Epimetheus & Pandora, wife of Deucalion, mother of Hellen: Apd. E2–3| Hell. 125| Hyg. 153.

Pyrrhos: see Neoptolemos.

Pythia (Πυθία): prophetic priestess of Apollo at Delphi, or the oracle itself: Apd. B5, K2, K15, M1, M6| Arr.| Hyg. 2, 67, 88, 120| Paus. E, G, N, O| Pher. 10| Plut.| Ver. 2c.| Ap2 Q| Ap3 B.

Python (Πύθων): the serpent killed by Apollo either to gain control of Delphi (so that place is often called Pytho) or to protect his mother: Apd. B5| *HH* 3g.

Qingu: Tiamat's consort, god from whom humans are formed: Ap4 *EoC* I.148–161, II.36, 45, IV.66, 81, 119, V.69, VI.29.

Rhadamanthys (Ῥαδάμανθυς), Rhadamanthus: son of Zeus & Europa, became a judge in the underworld: Aes. 99| Apd. K2, L1| Ver. 6h.

Rhea (Ῥέα) or Rheia: a Titaness, married to Cronos, the mother of Zeus and his siblings, she conspired with her children

against their father: A.L. 36| Apd. A1, M4| Corn. 3| Diod. 5.66, 5.68–70| Hdr. 34| Hes. 135, 456, 472, 630, 639| *HH* 2a, 2f, 3b, 5a, 12| Luc. *Sac.* 5, 7, 10–11| Stat. 1.826| Ap2 T.19.

Rhesos (Ῥῆσος): ***I*** a Thracian ally of Troy, famed for his horses, killed by Odysseus & Diomedes in a night raid: Apd. B3| Ov. 1.39| Ver. *G*| ***II*** a river: Hes. 342.

Salmoneus (Σαλμωνεύς): son of Aiolos, king of Elis, he pretended to be Zeus: Apd. E3| Hell. 125| Ver. 6h.

Sarpedon (Σαρπηδών): ***I*** son of Zeus & Europa, ally of Troy, killed by Patroclos: Aes. 99| Apd. L1| Hyg. 106| Ov. 1.19| ***II*** son of Poseidon killed by Heracles: Apd. K11.

Saturn: see Cronos.

Satyrs (Σάτυροι): half-man, half-goat attendants of Dionysos; animal spirits of the woods: Apd. M4| Corn. 30| Erat. 11, 28| Ov. 4.171| Soph. 1130.

Sceiron (Σκείρων), Sciron: bandit who forced travelers to wash his feet & then kicked them over a cliff; killed by Theseus: Apd. N4.

Schoineus (Σχοινεύς), Schoeneus: Arcadian father of Atalante & Clymenos: Apd. F, G1| Eur. 1130.

Sciron: see Sceiron.

Scylla (Σκύλλη): ***I*** sea monster, living opposite Charybdis, with six heads & dogs growing from her loins: Apd. G4| Herac. 70| Ov. 12.123–124| Ver. 6b [plural]| ***II*** daughter of Nisos, king of Megara: Apd. N2.

Seasons: see Horai.

Seilenos (Σειληνός), Silenus: an old Satyr in general (so sometimes in plural) or, in particular, a companion of Dionysos who raised the god & acted as the leader of the Satyrs: Apd. K6| *HH* 5d.

Selene (Σελήνη), Luna: personification of the Moon, daughter of Hyperion (or Helios) & Theia (or Euryphaessa): Apd. A2, D1| Hes. 20, 372| Hyg. 30| *HH* 4c–d, 31, 32| Luc. *Sac.* 7| Ap3 D.

Semele (Σεμέλη): daughter of Cadmos & Harmonia, mother of Dionysos by Zeus, her divine name is Thyone: Apd. M2–3| Diod. 4.25| Fulg. 2.12| Hes. 946, 983| *HH* 1, 7, 26| Hyg. 9| Paus. L.

Šeri (bull): bull that pulls the stormgod's chariot: Ap4 *SoE* 11, 19, 21.

Seven against Thebes: team of generals assembled by Adrastos on behalf of Polyneices to retake Thebes from Eteocles. See also Epigonoi.

Shem: son of Noah: Ap4 *Gen.* 5–9.

Shullat: destructive god: Ap4 *Atr.* II.vii.50| Ap4 *Gilg.* 102.

Sibyl (Σιβύλλη, strictly Sibylle): woman who gained prophetic powers from Apollo, the name can also be used as a title: Plut.| Ver. 6 *passim.*

Silenus: see Seilenos.

Sinis (Σίνις): killed passersby by having them bend pine trees, so also called Pityocamptes ("Pine-bender"). He was killed by Theseus: Apd. N4.

Sinon (Σίνων): Greek who convinced the Trojans to take Trojan Horse inside the city: Hyg. 108| Proc. D| Ver. 2c–d, 2f.

Sirens (Σειρῆνες, strictly Seirenes): half-woman, half-bird sea monsters, daughters of Acheloos & the Muse Melpomene, they lured sailors to their deaths by singing: Apd. B3, G4| Herac. 70| Pl. *Rep.*10.

Sisyphos (Σίσυφος): son of Aiolos known for his cunning, founder of Corinth: A.L. 4| Apd. E3, I, M2| Crit.| Ov. 12.204.

Smyrna (Σμύρνα): ***I*** mother of Adonis by her own father: A.L. 34| ***II*** a city in Asia Minor: *HH* 9| Paus. G.

South Wind: see Notos.

Spartoi (Σπαρτοί), Sparti: "Sown Men" who sprang from the serpent's teeth Cadmos sowed in Thebes. Five survived & became the ancestors of Theban nobility: Echion, Oudaios, Chthonios, Hyperenor, Peloros: Apd. M1, M8| Con. 37| Hyg. 67, 68, 72.

Sphinx (Σφίγξ): monster with face of a wom-

an, body of a lion with wings, the offspring of Typhon & Echidna who vexed Thebes until Oidipous solved her riddle: Apd. M6| Hes. 327| Hyg. 67| Pal. 4| Paus. O.

Sterope (Στερόπη): ***I*** one of the Pleiades, mother of Oinomaos: Hyg. 84 [called Asterope]| ***II*** daughter of Cepheus *II*: Apd. K17.

Steropes (Στερόπης): see Cyclopes *I*.

Stheneboia (Σθενέβοια), Stheneboea: wife of Proitos who falsely accused Bellerophontes of trying to seduce her: Apd. I| Hyg. 57.

Sthenelos (Σθένελος): ***I*** son of Perseus, father of Eurystheus: Apd. J2| Pal. 38| ***II*** son of Androgeos: Apd. K11| ***III*** son of Capaneus who took part in the Trojan War: Apd. M10| Hyg. 108| Paus. F| Verg. 2d.

Stheno (Σθενώ): one of the Gorgons: Apd. J1| Hes. 277.

Strife: see Eris.

Stymphalian Birds: Heracles' Sixth Labor: Apd. K8| Hyg. 30.

Styx (Στύξ): an Oceanid, river in the underworld, the first to side with Zeus in the Titanomachy, for which she was honored as being the river upon which all gods swore their oaths: Apd. A2–B1| Hes. 363, 384, 390, 399, 782, 812| *HH* 2c, 2f, 3b, 4h| Ver. 6d, 6f, *G*.

Sun/Sun god: see Helios.

Sungod of Heaven: Hittite god: Ap4 *SoE* 14, 20.

Symplegades (Συμπληγάδες): the clashing (or wandering) rocks through which the *Argo* sailed: Apd. G2, G4| Ov. 12.121.

Talaos (Ταλαός): father of Adrastos: Apd. M7| Hyg. 69.

Talthybios (Ταλθύβιος): herald of Agamemnon in Trojan War: Ov. 3.9–10| Paus. G.

Tantalos (Τάνταλος): ***I*** son of Zeus & Plouto *II*, killed his son & fed him to the gods, for which he is punished in the underworld: A.L. 36| Apd. M5| Hyg. 9, 82–84| Luc. *Sac.* 9| Paus. E, J| Pi. 37, 55| ***II*** son of Amphion & Niobe, so grandson of *I*: Apd. M5| ***III*** son of Thyestes, so great-grandson of *I*: Hyg. 88.

Tartaros (Τάρταρος): deepest region of the world, placed below the underworld: Apd. A1–2, D2| Hes. 119, 685, 725, 728, 730, 741, 813, 828, 848, 858, 874| *HH* 3g, 4f–g| Pl. *Rep.* 10| Ver. 6e, 6g–h.

Tašmišu: Hittite god: Ap4 *SoE* 6, 17.

Teiresias (Τειρεσίας), Tiresias: son of Chariclo & Eueres; a blind Theban seer: A.L. 17| Apd. K1, M8, M10| Call. 5| Hyg. 67, 68, 75| Proc. E, F.

Telamon (Τελαμών): son of Aiacos & Periboia *III*, father of Ajax, an Argonaut & a member of the Calydonian Boar hunt: Apd. F, G1, K16| Hyg. 89, 107| OV. 3.27| Pl. *Rep.*10.

Telegonos (Τηλέγονος): ***I*** son of Odysseus by Circe (or by Calypso). Hes. 1022| Proc. F| ***II*** son of Proteus, killed by Heracles: Apd. K11| ***III*** king of Egypt, husband of Io: Apd. H.

Telemachos (Τηλέμαχος): son of Odysseus & Penelope: Hyg. 95| Ov. 1.98, 1.107| Proc. A, F.

Telephos (Τήλεφος): son of Heracles & Auge, guided the Greeks to Troy after being wounded & then cured by Achilles: Apd. K18| Luc. *Sac.* 5| Proc. A, C.

Terpsichore (Τερψιχόρη): a Muse: Apd. B1| Hes. 79.

Teshub (also KA.ZAL, NAM.ḪE, and Storm god): Hittite/Hurrian Stormgod: Ap4 *SoE* 6, 11, 12, 13, 14, 19, 21.

Tethys (Τηθύς): a Titaness, wife of Oceanos: Apd. A1–2| Diod. 3.56| Diod. 5.66| Hes. 136, 339, 364, 369.

Teucer: see Teucros.

Teucros (Τεῦκρος): ***I*** ancestor of Trojan kings, eponymous ancestor of the Teucrians: Hdt. 2.118| Ver. 6g, 6i| ***II*** son of Telamon & Hesione; half brother of Ajax *I*: Hyg. 89| Ov. 3.130.

Teuthras (Τεύθρας): king of Mysia or Teuthrania who took in Auge & her son, Telephos: Apd. K18.

Thaleia (Θάλεια), Thalia: ***I*** a Muse: Apd. B1, B3| Hes. 78| ***II*** one of the Charites: Apd. B1| Hes. 914.

Thamyris (Θάμυρις) or Thamyras: challenged Muses to musical contest & was blinded as a result: Apd. B3| Par. 29| Pl. *Rep.*10.

Thanatos (Θάνατος): personification of Death: Aes. 161| Hes. 212, 764| Ver. 6b, *G*.

Thaumas (Θαύμας): son of Pontos & Gaia, father of the Harpies & Iris: Apd. A2| Hes. 237, 266, 786.

Theia (Θεία): a Titaness: Apd. A1–2| Hes. 135, 372, 375.

Themis (Θέμις): a Titaness, the personification of Eternal Law, according to some the mother of Moirai & Prometheus: Apd. A1, B1, B5, K13| Diod. 5.66–67| Erat. 9| Hes. 17, 135, 906| *HH* 3b–c, 5c, 8, 23| Pl. *Rep.* 2| Proc. A| Ap3 G.

Themisto (Θεμιστώ): a Nereid: Hes. 262.

Therimachos (Θηρίμαχος): son of Heracles & Megara: Apd. K2| Hyg. 31, 72.

Thersandros (Θέρσανδρος), Thersander: son of Polyneices, one of the Epigonoi who also took part in the Trojan War: Apd. M10| Hyg. 69, 108| Proc. A| Ver. 2d.

Thersites (Θερσίτης): son of Agrios, the ugliest & most spineless of the Greek fighters at Troy, killed by Achilles: Pl. *Rep.*10| Proc. B.

Theseus (Θησεύς): son of Aigeus (or of Poseidon) by Aithra, who, like Heracles, performed many exceptional deeds. The greatest was the slaying of the Minotaur. After growing up in Troizen, Theseus went to join his father in Athens, killing various bandits along the way. Theseus was sent along with other young Athenians to Minos in Crete to be sacrificed to the Minotaur. He slew the Minotaur & escaped from the Labyrinth with the help of Minos' daughter Ariadne, whom he then abandoned on the island of Naxos. Aigeus killed himself because Theseus failed to change the color of his sails. As king of Athens, Theseus was given credit for uniting Attica: A.L. 27| Apd. F, G1, K14–15, L2, M6, M9, N4–7| Bac. 17.3, 17.74, 17.99| Hyg. 30, 47, 79| Luc. *Jud.*| Ov. 4.65, 4.111, 4.119, 10 *passim*| Pal. 2| Paus. A–C, G| Plut.| Proc. A| Ver. 6e, 6h. See also Ap1 7.

Thestios (Θέστιος): king of Pleuron in Aetolia, father of Althaia, Leda, & many sons: A.L. 2| Apd. F, G1| Bac. 5.136| Hyg. 77, 78.

Thetis (Θέτις): a Nereid, mother of Achilles by Peleus: Apd. A2, B4, G4| Hes. 245, 1014| *HH* 3g| Hyg. 54, 92, 96, 106| Luc. *DD* 23, *DG* 5, *DSG* 7, 12| Proc. A, B, E| Stat. 1.242–282.

Thoas (Θόας): ***I*** son of Dionysos & Ariadne, Lemnian king saved by his daughter, Hypsipyle: Apd. G2, M7, N5| ***II*** the king of Tauris when Iphigenia was priestess there: A.L. 27| Hyg. 120| ***III*** a Giant: Apd. D1| ***IV*** Greek general in Trojan War: Hyg. 108.

Thyestes (Θυέστης): son of Pelops & Hippodameia, feuded with his brother, Atreus: Hell. 157| Hyg. 84, 88, 117| Luc. *Sac.* 5| Paus. E.

Thymoites (Θυμοίτης), Thymoetes: ***I*** king of Athens: Hell. 125| ***II*** a Trojan: Ver. 2a.

Thyone (Θυώνη): the divine name for Dionysos' mother Semele: Apd. M4| Diod. 4.25| *HH* 1.

Tiamat: "Mother Ocean," primeval Babylonian goddess: Ap4 *EoC* I–IV *passim*, V.73, VI.24, 30.

Tigris (river god): Ap4 *SoE* 6, 17.

Tiphys (Τῖφυς): first helmsman of the *Argo*: Apd. G1–2.

Tisiphone (Τισιφόνη): one of the Erinyes: Apd. A1| Ver. 6h| Ap3 D.

Titanomachy: "Battle of the Titans"; see Zeus.

Titans (Τιτᾶνες): collective name for some of the children of Ouranos & Gaia, the youngest of whom, Cronos, overthrew his father, hence the name Titans, "Overreachers." They were defeated by Zeus in the

Titanomachy. The name is sometimes also applied to the Titans' own children (e.g., Prometheus or Helios): Aes. 193| A.L. 36| Apd. A1–2, D1| Diod. 5.66–67| Erat. 27| Hes. 208, 394, 426, 636, 637, 651, 653, 667, 672, 677, 679, 700, 721, 734, 820, 826, 858, 888| *HH* 3g| Stat. 1.243| Ver. 6h, 6j.

Tithonos (Τιθωνός): son of Laomedon, loved by Eos & by her produced two sons, Emathion & Memnon: Apd. K13| Hes. 992| *HH* 5d.

Tityos (Τιτυός): a giant son of Zeus & Elare, killed by Apollo & Artemis, punished in the underworld: Apd. B5| Hor. 3.11.21| Ver. 6h.

Tlepolemos (Τληπόλεμος): ***I*** son of Heracles & Astyoche, took part in the Trojan War: Apd. K19| Ov. 1.19–20| ***II*** an official at Delos: Ap2 N.

Toxeus (Τοξεύς): brother of Meleagros: A.L. 2| Apd. F.

Triopas (Τριόπας): ***I*** a descendant of Niobe: *HH* 3e| ***II*** father of Erysichthon: Call. 6.

Triptolemos (Τριπτόλεμος): either a nobleman of Eleusis or one of Metaneira's children who spread the cultivation of wheat over the world: Apd. C| Call. 6| Diod. 5.68| *HH* 2b, 2g.

Tritogeneia: see Athena.

Triton (Τρίτων): ***I*** a sea god, son of Poseidon & Amphitrite, sometimes used in the plural: Apd. B5| Hes. 936| Luc. *DSG* 9| Paus. J| ***II*** a river: Apd. B4| Diod. 5.70, 5.72.

Trophonios (Τροφώνιος): a mythical architect, paired often with Agamedes: *HH* 3g| Proc. F.

Tyche (Τύχη): ***I*** Oceanid: Hes. 362| *HH* 2f| ***II*** personification of Fortune: Erat. 9| Ov. 12.73| Ver. 2c, 2g| Ap2 O.I.

Tydeus (Τυδεύς): son of Oineus & Periboia II, father of Diomedes *I*, accompanied Polyneices in the Seven against Thebes: Apd. M7, M9–10| Hyg. 69| Stat. 1.819, 1.843| Ver. 6f.

Tyndareos (Τυνδάρεως): Spartan king, husband of Leda, mortal father of Castor & Polydeuces, Helen & Clytaimnestra: Apd. K17| Hyg. 77–79, 92, 117, 119| Paus. E| Proc. A| Thu. 1.9.

Tyndaridai: see Dioscouroi.

Typhon (Τυφών) or Typhaon or Typhoios: monstrous offspring of Gaia & Tartaros, defeated by Zeus: A.L. 28| Apd. D2, I, K3, K12–13, M6, N4| Diod. 5.71| Hdr. 30| Hes. 308, 829, 844, 875| *HH* 3g| Hyg. 30, 67| Sall.

Tyro (Τυρώ): mother of Neleus & Pelias: Hell. 125.

Unnamed Goddess: see Erinyes.

Uranus: see Ouranos.

Utanapishtim (see also Atrahasis): man who survives great flood: Ap4 *Gilg. passim.*

Venus: see Aphrodite.

Vesta: see Hestia.

Victory: see Nike.

Vulcan: see Hephaistos.

Wandering Rocks: see Symplegades.

War: see Ares.

West Wind: see Zephyros.

Xouthos (Ξοῦθος): son of Hellen & ruler of Athens, father of Achaios & Ion by Creousa *I*: Apd. E3| Con. 27| Hell. 125.

Yahweh: see God (Judeo-Christian).

Zephyros (Ζέφυρος): the West Wind, the son of Eos & Astraios: Hes. 380, 876| Luc. *DG* 16, *DSG* 11| Lucr. 1.11| Ver. 2g.

Zetes (Ζήτης): son of Boreas & Oreithyia: Apd. G1–2.

Zethos (Ζῆθος): son of Zeus & Antiope, twin brother of Amphion. Exposed at birth, the two eventually became corulers

of Thebes: Apd. M5| Hyg. 9| Pal. 41.

Zeus (Ζεύς), Jupiter: son of Ouranos & Rhea, sky god & king of the Olympian gods. He led his siblings in the revolt against his father & other Titans (Titanomachy) after obtaining essential help from members of his father's generation (e.g., Cyclopes, Hundred-Handers, Styx). He then became the king of the gods. He faced further challenges to his power from Typhon & the Giants, but none of his own children were ever in the position to overthrow him. While he was married to Hera & had children by her, he had an exceptionally long list of affairs with goddesses & mortal women, producing most of the younger gods (e.g., Apollo, Hermes, Dionysos) & many great mortals (e.g., Heracles, Helen, Minos). He has many roles in myth: storm god, protector of the city (Zeus Polieus), philanderer, & upholder of justice: Aes. 70, 99, 193| A.L. 6, 27, 28, 34, 36, 41| Apd. A1–B1, B4–G1, G4, H, J1, K1–3, K6, K9, K11, K13, K15–16, K21, L1, M1–5, M8–9, N2| Arch. 122, 177| Arr.| Bab. 68| Bac. 5.19, 5.178, 5.199, 17.20, 17.31, 17.53, 17.67, 17.76, 17.87| Call. 5| Cle.| Con. 27, 34, 37| Corn. 2, 20| Diod. 2.46, 5.68, 5.70–73| Erat. 7, 9, 10, 12, 14, 26, 27, 28| Eur. 660| Fulg. 2.11–12| Hell. 125| Herac. 5| Hdr. 14, 34| Hes. *passim*| *HH* 1, 2a–g, 3a–d, 3g–i, 4a–h, 5a–d, 7, 12, 14, 15, 17–19, 23–29, 31–33| Hor. 1.10.5| Hyg. 2, 9, 30–31, 52, 54, 68, 75, 77, 79, 91, 92, 94, 106, 153, 164| Luc. *DG* 5, 9, *DSG* 7, 9, 11, 12, *Jud.*, *Sac.* 2, 5–6, 8–11, 14| Lucr. 2.634| Ov. 3.73, 4.36, 4.55, 4.132, 4.163, 10.68| Pal. 15| Par. 15| Paus. D, F, J, K, M| Pher. 10| Pi. 10, 43, 45, 57| Pl. *Prt.*, *Rep.* 2, *Symp.*| Proc. A, B, D| Sall.| Sapph.| Sem. 72, 93, 96| Sim. 24| Soph. 941| Stat. 1.263| Theoc.| Ver. 2f, 6b, 6h| Ap1.1, 2, 3, 5, 6| Ap2 F, T| Ap3 D, F.

ANTHOLOGY OF CLASSICAL MYTH

Anthology of Classical Myth

Primary Sources in Translation

Second Edition

Edited and Featuring New Translations by

Stephen M. Trzaskoma, R. Scott Smith, and Stephen Brunet

with Additional Translations by Other Scholars and an Appendix on Linear B Sources by Thomas G. Palaima

Hackett Publishing Company, Inc.
Indianapolis/Cambridge

Printed in the United States of America

19 18 17 16 1 2 3 4 5 6

For further information, please address:
Hackett Publishing Company, Inc.
P.O. Box 44937
Indianapolis, IN 46244-0937
www.hackettpublishing.com

Cover design by Rick Todhunter
Text design by Jennifer Plumley

Wooden Horse of Troy: detail of a 7th-century BC Greek vase from Mykonos, Greece.

Library of Congress Cataloging-in-Publication Data
Names: Trzaskoma, Stephen, editor. | Smith, R. Scott, 1971- editor. | Brunet, Stephen, 1954– editor | Palaima, Thomas G., editor.
Title: Anthology of classical myth : primary sources in translation.
Description: Second edition / edited and translated by Stephen M. Trzaskoma, R. Scott Smith, and Stephen Brunet with an appendix on linear B sources by Thomas G. Palaima. | Indianapolis ; Cambridge : Hackett Publishing Company, Inc., 2016.
Identifiers: LCCN 2016002493| ISBN 9781624664977 (pbk.) | ISBN 9781624664984 (cloth)
Subjects: LCSH: Classical literature—Translations into English. | Mythology, Classical—Literary collections. | Mythology, Classical.
Classification: LCC PA3621 .A585 2016 | DDC 880/.08—dc23
LC record available at http://lccn.loc.gov/2016002493

The paper used in this publication meets the minimum requirements of American National Standard for Information Sciences—Permanence of Paper for Printed Library Materials, ANSI Z39.48-1984.